Tobias Churton is a world authority on Freemasonry, Rosicrucianism, Hermeticism and Gnosticism. Holding a Masters degree in Theology from Brasenose College, Oxford, Tobias is an Honorary Fellow of Exeter University and Faculty Lecturer in Western Esotericism. An accomplished film-maker and composer with an award-winning drama documentary series *Gnostics,* for Channel 4, Tobias has also written a standard biography of Elias Ashmole (1617–92).

Please consult www.tobiaschurton.com for more information.

By the Same Author

The Missing Family of Jesus

Kiss of Death – The True History of the Gospel of Judas

The Invisible History of the Rosicrucians

Freemasonry the Reality

Gnostic Philosophy, from Ancient Persia to Modern Times

The Magus of Freemasonry – The Mysterious Life of Elias Ashmole

The Gnostics

The Golden Builders – Alchemists, Rosicrucians and the first Free Masons

Miraval – A Quest

The Fear of Vision – collected poetry

ALEISTER CROWLEY

THE BIOGRAPHY

*Spiritual Revolutionary
Romantic Explorer, Occult Master –
and Spy*

Tobias Churton

WATKINS PUBLISHING

LONDON

This edition first published in the UK and USA 2011 by
Watkins Publishing, Sixth Floor, Castle House,
75–76 Wells Street, London W1T 3QH

Design and typography copyright © Watkins Publishing 2011

1 3 5 7 9 10 8 6 4 2

Designed and typeset by Jerry Goldie Graphic Design

Printed and bound in China by Imago

British Library Cataloguing-in-Publication Data Available

Library of Congress Cataloging-in-Publication Data Available

ISBN: 978-1-78028-012-7

www.watkinspublishing.co.uk

Distributed in the USA and Canada by Sterling Publishing Co., Inc.
387 Park Avenue South, New York, NY 10016-8810

For information about custom editions, special sales, premium and
corporate purchases, please contact Sterling Special Sales
Department at 800-805-5489 or specialsales@sterlingpub.com

I dedicate this book to the memory
of my father and mother, Victor and Patricia Churton,
and to spiritual philosophers everywhere.

Acknowledgements

It is hard to express adequately my gratitude to the World Head of the Ordo Templi Orientis, William Breeze (Hymenaeus Beta) who has not only offered innumerable corrections and insights to the manuscript, but has also provided a wealth of previously unpublished material, from obscure diaries to rare letters from the OTO archive. He has, furthermore, generously made available his own researches, undertaken for his definitive edition of Crowley's *Confessions*. For these services, he has asked for nothing more than good will, freely leaving issues of interpretation to my best efforts. William Breeze has been this biography's rod and comforter.

While the OTO archive has been of signal assistance, the greater part of Crowley's manuscripts are, thanks to the prescience of the late Gerald Yorke, held in trust as the Yorke Collection, Warburg Institute. For providing permission and facilities to study this restricted collection, I am indebted not only to William Breeze but also to the kind forbearance of Professor Jill Kraye, librarian and professor in the history of renaissance philosophy, the Warburg Institute, and her staff. I treasure fond memories of the warm helpfulness of assistant librarian Andrea Meyer-Ludowisy and of graduate library trainee, Tabitha Tuckett, who made many long sessions at the Warburg a timeless joy. Thanks also to Ian Jones, the Warburg's photographer and coordinator of visual resources for providing access to rare photographs. Professor Kraye's predecessor, Professor W F Ryan deserves sincere thanks for permitting my first forays into the Yorke Collection, back in 1991 and 1992.

Gerald Yorke's son John kindly gave permission for me to quote from his father's often witty contributions to the Crowley corpus, while offering my wife and me joyous hospitality at Forthampton Court. John Yorke also pointed me in the direction of evocative memorabilia from

Crowley's life and from Crowley's working relationship with Lady Harris.

Permission to publish a vital letter from the Hon. Everard Feilding to Gerald Yorke, plainly indicating Crowley's real loyalties during WW1, was kindly granted by Suzy, the Countess of Denbigh. I am also grateful to Captain Adrian Cassar RN for guidance in the matter of Crowley's correspondence with the Naval Intelligence Department 1939–42.

One of the many startling revelations that came in the course of writing this book, was the opportunity to converse and correspond with Crowley's grandson, Eric Muhler, a brilliant jazz musician with a powerful grip on philosophy and its limitations. I am very grateful to Eric for helping me with first-hand family memories both painful and amusing concerning his mother Astarte Lulu Crowley and his grandmother Ninette (*née*) Fraux, whom he met, and whose account of her sometime lover, Crowley, he remembered. The actual experience and effects – particularly on the children – of living through a premature 'New Age' in the 1920s were brought vividly and painfully to life when Eric generously furnished me with the reflections of himself and his mother, the formidable Lulu. Thought-provoking, they appear in chapter 23.

Much harm to Crowley's family and career derived from his being targeted by Mussolini's fascist government. I want to thank Dr Marco Pasi for acquainting me with his critical researches into Italian government records from the 1920s and 1930s, as well as evidence for the anti-Crowley activity of other fascists and fascist sympathizers in France and Great Britain during the period.

Martin P Starr offered valued insight into Crowley's intriguing associations with men as diverse as Samuel Aiwaz Jacobs and English-born Californian Thelemite, WT Smith, subject of Starr's fascinating biography, *The Unknown God*.

I should also like to express my gratitude to all of the following persons and institutions that have made this journey into a man's life so fascinating and rewarding: the staff of the Hampshire County Archive, Winchester, Timothy d'Arch Smith, Christopher McIntosh who put a mountain aside to write the Foreword, Mark Booth (who first commissioned the work), Frank van Lamoen, and Nicholas Goodrick-Clarke and all my colleagues at Exeter University's Centre for the Study of Western Esotericism.

When this book hit a crisis, publisher Michael Mann came to the rescue with encouragement, belief and rare spiritual insight, while my agent, Fiona Spencer Thomas, facilitated a research programme that took in Crowley territory from Alton to Eastbourne.

*　　*　　*

Finally, I wish to express my never-ending love and gratitude for my mother, Patricia Churton. Many times she patiently listened to me read portions of manuscript over the phone; she read and annotated Crowley's *Confessions* for me, and was always a beacon of refined, practical intelligence. Our last conversation was about the book, and I am so sorry she did not live to see it finished. She enjoyed Aleister Crowley's personality and intelligence, understood what it meant to me, and believed the world would benefit from, and be intrigued to know, the truth about him. Regardless of one's views on magick, she believed there was much to love, knowing, as she did, that Love is the Law.

Contents

List of Plates

20: Emily Bertha Crowley's gravestone, Eastbourne, England; the inscription reads: '*Waiting for the Coming of Our Lord Jesus Christ*". Crowley's mother died in May 1917 while her only son was in the USA. (Author's collection)

21: Leah Hirsig (1883–1975) sits before Crowley's portrait of her as a 'Dead Soul', New York, 1918 (The Warburg Institute; Yorke Collection)

22: The 'Cadran Bleu', Fontainebleau, where Crowley took a room with Leah to conquer heroin addiction, February 1922 (Author's collection)

23: Crowley's novel, *The Diary of a Drug Fiend*, published by Collins in 1922 (Author's collection)

24: *Portrait of a Poet*, Aleister Crowley as seen by Augustus John (The Warburg Institute; Yorke Collection)

25: Crowley's 'Scarlet Woman', Dorothy Olsen, *Soror Astrid*. Dorothy arrived in Paris in 1924. (The Warburg Institute; Yorke Collection)

26: Undated photo of Crowley; *c*1924. Note the erect thumbs, or 'horns'. (The Warburg Institute; Yorke Collection)

27: Aleister Crowley, 1929 (Author's collection)

28: OTO certificate of honorary membership given to H Spencer Lewis, founder of AMORC, by Theodor Reuss (*Frater Peregrinus*, OTO) in 1921 (The Warburg Institute; Yorke Collection)

29: Crowley's 'Scarlet Woman' of 1931–2, Bertha Busch, known as 'Bill', seen here on holiday in Nice (The Warburg Institute; Yorke Collection)

30: Gerald Yorke as seen by Crowley (Author's collection)

31: Gerald Yorke as seen by camera (Author's collection)

32: Crowley's novel *Moonchild*, published in 1929 by Mandrake Press, a publishing syndicate organized by Gerald Yorke. Beresford Egan executed the superb jacket. (Author's collection)

33: Crowley entitled this photo-portrait 'Interest' (The Warburg Institute; Yorke Collection)

34: A self-portrait: Crowley as *To Mega Therion*, The Great Wild Beast 666, *Logos* of the Aeon (The OTO)

35: Aleister Crowley's bronze wand. Engraved on the stem: DO WHAT THOU WILT SHALL BE THE WHOLE OF THE LAW (Author's collection)

36: *Four Red Monks carrying a Black Goat across the Snow to Nowhere*. Crowley's painting appears to be a comment on theosophist myths of Shambhala being pursued by Soviet secret service chiefs. (Author's collection)

37: '*his knowledge of oriental evil is very deep*': Arthur Vivian Burbury's comment on Crowley's usefulness to the Foreign Office, 1928 (The Warburg Institute; Yorke Collection)

38: A late sketch of The Beast by Frieda, Lady Harris (Sister Tzaba OTO) Crowley's friend and collaborator (Author's collection)

39: Crowley's last 'Scarlet Woman', Pearl Brooksmith, escorting Crowley to

ALEISTER CROWLEY'S PATERNAL RELATIVES AND ANCESTRY (*Abridged*)

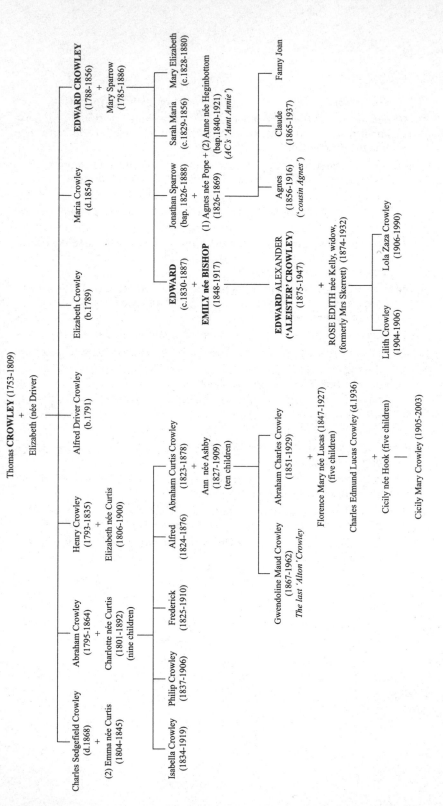

ALEISTER CROWLEY'S MATERNAL RELATIVES AND ANCESTRY (*Abridged*)

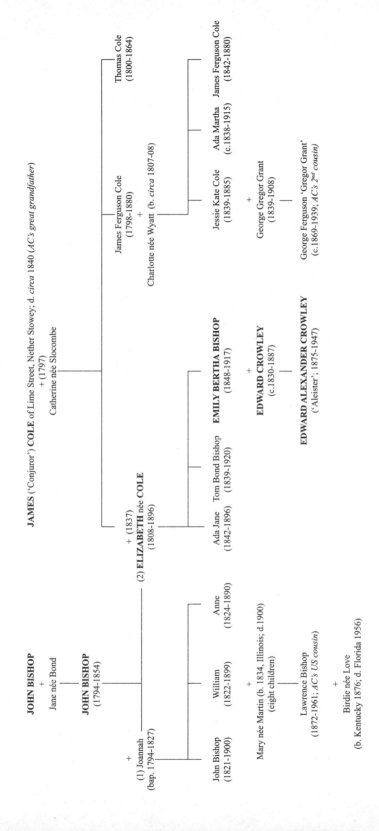

JAMES ('Conjuror') **COLE** of Lime Street, Nether Stowey; d. *circa* 1840 (*AC's great grandfather*)
+ (1797)
Catherine née Slocombe

James Ferguson Cole
(1798-1880)
+
Charlotte née Wyatt (b. *circa* 1807-08)

Thomas Cole
(1800-1864)

Jessie Kate Cole
(1839-1885)
+
George Gregor Grant
(1839-1908)

Ada Martha
(c.1838-1915)

James Ferguson Cole
(1842-1880)

George Ferguson 'Gregor Grant'
(c.1869-1939; *AC's 2ⁿᵈ cousin*)

JOHN BISHOP
+
Jane née Bond

JOHN BISHOP
(1794-1854)

(1) Joannah
(bap. 1794-1827)
+

(2) **ELIZABETH** née **COLE**
(1808-1896)
+ (1837)

Ada Jane
(1842-1896)

Tom Bond Bishop
(1839-1920)

EMILY BERTHA BISHOP
(1848-1917)
+
EDWARD CROWLEY
(c.1830-1887)

EDWARD ALEXANDER CROWLEY
('Aleister'; 1875-1947)

John Bishop
(1821-1900)

William
(1822-1899)

Anne
(1824-1890)

Mary née Martin (b. 1834, Illinois; d.1900)
(eight children)

Lawrence Bishop
(1872-1961; *AC's US cousin*)
+
Birdie née Love
(b. Kentucky 1876; d. Florida 1956)

Foreword

By Dr Christopher McIntosh

I first heard of Aleister Crowley in 1964 when I was an undergraduate at Oxford. Having a romantic penchant for the strange and bizarre things of life, I was immediately intrigued by him. I read John Symonds' biography *The Great Beast*, which, despite its disparaging tone, further piqued my interest in Crowley. I bought a first edition of his *Magick in Theory and Practice* and a book of his poems, but it was to be some years before I was able to see beyond Crowley's sensationalized image and perceive the serious and original thinker that he was.

The man who above all opened my eyes to the deeper dimensions of Crowley was Gerald Yorke, who had become Crowley's chief disciple in the late 1920s and who features prominently in this book. Breaking off his discipleship after a time, he nevertheless remained on friendly terms with Crowley until the latter's death in 1947. In fond memory of his old friend, he amassed a large collection of Crowleyana, which he later donated to the Warburg Institute in London and which has provided a key source for this biography. Yorke was a fascinating person, who deserves a biography in his own right – an old Etonian, brilliant scholar at Cambridge, county cricketer for Gloucestershire, Lord of the Manor and later advisor to several publishers in the area of oriental religion, esotericism and related subjects. Among other things, he played a key role in the publication in the West of the Dalai Lama's works.

I first met Gerald Yorke in February 1969 at an esoteric conference in London, then contacted him a few months later in connection with a projected documentary film on Crowley that I was planning in collaboration with my friend John Phillips, a television film director. We travelled by train to Gloucestershire and spent a wonderful summer day at Yorke's beautiful ancestral home. He played us a recording of Crowley chanting Enochian invocations in his Churchillian voice, showed us scrapbooks full of Crowley memorabilia and talked endlessly and amusingly about his time with the 'Old Boy', as he called him. The film never materialized, but I continued to meet Yorke at intervals until his death in 1983 and took part in many further conversations with him on the subject of Crowley. While Yorke greatly admired Crowley for his vast knowledge and his mastery of techniques for expanding consciousness, he was sceptical of Crowley's claim to be the Messiah of the 'Aeon of Horus'.

Looking back over the more than four decades since Crowley came to my attention, I am struck by the way his posthumous reputation has developed. When I first heard of him his general image was that of an *enfant terrible*. It seems to be the fate of many English *enfants terribles* that they start by being reviled and ostracized and end up being taken into the establishment and even given a peerage or some other honour. Crowley, it is true, was very far from being given a peerage and was still widely seen as an *enfant terrible* when he died, but his posthumous career has been impressive. By the 1970s he had become an icon of the New Age and the counter-culture, celebrated by the Beatles and by Jimmy Page of Led Zeppelin. By the 1990s he had begun to be taken seriously within academe, and post-graduate dissertations on him were starting to appear. Today his prolific writings, including his fiction and poetry, are increasingly widely read; the tarot pack that he designed with Lady Frieda Harris is familiar to tarot aficionados everywhere; and the Ordo Templi Orientis (OTO), which he took up and developed, is now a thriving organization with members in many different countries. Even his ideas about the Aeon of Horus are beginning to catch on more widely. One person who has written interestingly on this topic is the highly original esoteric writer Ramsey Dukes. In one of his essays he writes:

> The New Aeon calls for a new moral approach: God is no longer
> saying 'follow my example', instead humanity is being
> challenged to stand on its own feet ... Horus has thrown down
> the gauntlet to those spiritual wimps who still cry out for 'moral

leadership' from their church or their superiors. He asks 'have you no moral sense of your own?'.

('The Caliphate OTO' in What I Did in My Holidays)

So Crowley has come a long way since his death in poverty and relative obscurity. However, despite the appearance of a number of biographies of him in the intervening years, no biographer has fully measured up to the task ... until now, for, in Tobias Churton, Crowley has at last found a worthy biographer. Based on intensive research among the papers in the Warburg Institute and other original sources, Churton's book delivers a far more full and accurate picture of Crowley than ever before. While Churton is not blind to his subject's flaws, he thoroughly demolishes the farrago of lies and calumnies that have dogged Crowley reputation for so long. Whereas other biographers have tended to take Crowley's extravagant and deliberate poses at their face value, Churton shows us the real man behind them – a man who genuinely believed in the new vision for humanity which he proclaimed and for which he struggled throughout his life in the face of enormous adversity. Crowley also turns out to have had great human qualities – the letter he wrote to his infant son 'Aleister Ataturk' is one of the most moving documents quoted in this book. Churton also makes some astonishing new revelations – for example in connection with Crowley's extraordinary career as a British secret agent. This was little known until the appearance of Richard Spence's book *Secret Agent 666*, and Churton takes the story further and deeper. He also uncovers startling new information about Aiwass, the channelled entity behind *The Book of the Law*, about Crowley's role in both the First and Second World Wars, and much more ... but I must leave Tobias Churton to let the cats out of the bags. The reader will put down this book with an entirely new perspective on Aleister Crowley. The 'Old Boy' would be delighted to have been given a full and fair hearing at last.

The Legend

Everything that happens is all part of the plan; and when you really see it as such, you become indifferent to circumstances. For instance, all the ostracism and persecution which has been my lot for so many years appears to me as part of the necessary condition for the historical view of me in times to come.

(Aleister Crowley, Letter to Sascha Germer, 31 May 1943)

The Times, 6 August 2010: Aleister Crowley's old rented house at Cefalù, Sicily, is on sale for £1.2m. The agents suggest its pock-marked walls and pornographic frescoes may be transformed from a past of 'drug-fuelled orgies and magical rites' into a museum, a shrine to commemorate the presence of the Beast.

Crowley's stock is rising. Having long suffered a reputation as derelict as Cefalù's battered villa, he is defying the inquisitor's rack of history and fleeing the ashes of his last rites. Cremated in Brighton in December 1947, the verdict then was damning: traitor, satanist, drug addict, tyrant, fake mystic, pornographer, sex-maniac, egotist, exhibitionist, cruel husband, indifferent father, hopeless artist, out-of-date poet, joker-cynic and malevolent demon driving dupes to wickedness, suicide or insanity. Thelema, his magical system, meant 'Do as you like': a crooked cocktail of anarchy and madness. Going down at the dawn of the nuclear age, the *Beast 666* had been defeated not by St Michael, the archangels, and the return of Christ, but by drug addiction, sexual excess, superstition and sadism. Having achieved nothing save notoriety, he would be quickly forgotten.

He wasn't.

Crowley knew posterity would eventually see the truth; he hoped to beat them to it. In October 1943, the 68-year-old mage gazed into the stream of time and pondered the competing Pooh-sticks of his reputation:

> I often wish I could divine
> What's in this funny head of mine,
> This complicated tangled brain
> That is? is not? or is it? sane.
> No one has ever understood
> Why I was never any good,
> Or why my diamond brilliance
> Was dulled by casual circumstance.
> To further the dear cause of Knowledge
> I leave my cranium to the College
> Of Surgeons: they – unless too lazy –
> Will find out why I was three parts crazy
> And on the whole a perfect daisy,
> But far from our Exemplar J.C.
> Blast! That solution won't get past
> It's 'sicklied o'er with the pale cast
> Of doubt' – Being dead, I may not know
> What engine made the damn thing go.

What *did* make the damn thing go?

Crowley had the advantage over biographers; he could look *into* himself. There he found a perfect daisy three parts crazy. Most biographers have looked *at* him, seen a reputation black as pitch, writ in granite, and rushed to the conclusion that the 'Great Beast' was no less than *four* parts wicked with not a daisy in sight. Aleister Crowley has been buried under a tsunami of abuse with nothing pushing up from beneath: a life not written, but *written over*.

And yet, he is still with us, though the world he knew is gone. Long gone. Who today can recall a time when America was at war with Spain, when Russia was at war with Japan, when the Turks ruled most of the Middle East? The suffragettes have gone, the horse-drawn cabs have gone, the top hats have gone and two world wars have passed, but Aleister Crowley is still with us.

At least, his image is.

In 2002 the Beast came 73rd in a BBC poll of the Top 100 'Greatest Britons'. Did they vote for the man, or the legend?

*   *   *

They get confused. Crowley was convinced he was living a legend, making myth and founding fame. Foolish then, I have been warned, to attempt to 'clean up' his image. The 'shameless shit' spent his life blackening it up, and if he still suffers from a catastrophic reputation, such is well deserved and self-inflicted. After all, he called himself 'the Beast 666', had bad habits and denigrated Christianity. Besides, is it not Crowley's reputation that accounts for his attraction to a society in need of a 'bad boy' to suffer the slings and arrows of outraged morality? No bad reputation; no interest. That is to say, according to detractors, it was the mage himself who conjured up the 'inquisitor' to make himself famous.

And does not the passage of time prove this? A conventional 'saint' would never have seized the ear of the rock'n'rollers and maverick movie-makers. Heavy metal or heavy celluloid, the tortured legends of jazz, blues and cinema like to dip and dabble in the darkness. Crowley gives them something to hook on to. John Lennon, Jim Morrison, Jimmy Page, Mick Jagger, David Bowie, Michael Powell and Kenneth Anger; they have all glimpsed the glittering vistas to be explored by breaking the bonds of convention *with a will*, even, as Crowley ventured, unto the dark unknown to the 'other side'. Ken Russell told an incredulous Melvyn Bragg that we can't see the light unless we do. We have darkness and light in ourselves, how can we know ourselves if we pretend we're all sweetness and light? Is there nothing to be learned from the dark?

To his admirers, Crowley held a torch in the darkness; his serpent was the serpent of knowledge. He did not suffocate the fire, but enrich it.

Not a bit of it, say his enemies. Crowley volunteered for demonic service and if his reputation looks like St Sebastian punctured by the arrows of martyrdom, it only goes to show what a kinky masochist Crowley was. Bloody perverse, the Beast was either evil or wanted people to think he was, which amounts to the same thing. Like 'Goldfinger' his auric brilliance kills. He was laughing at us; seeing our calamity, he declined to serve. He stoked up the flames and dispensed hell. He was a satanic imp sent to confuse, shock and disturb: an outrageous loony that only a fool or wicked witch would take seriously. Crowley was Baphomet, the Goat, the horned one, a living incitement to rape, perversion and the horror of psychic breakdown.

New Ageism, witchcraft, hippies, paganism, sex, drugs and rock'n' roll: it's all his fault.

*   *   *

It is a powerful image, sanctified by time, and for a biographer, perhaps insuperable. But have we not heard all this before – at a witch-trial? As Crowley observed: 'The more religious people are, the more they believe in black magic.' The bright, new, but turned-out-to-be-damned apocalyptic 20th century still nursed a streak of medieval fear to its chromium bosom – fear of heresy, the Devil, the dark, the damned; knowledge, science – and sex.

Sex. We think we're cool about it now; so why is pornography the biggest business in the world, after the oil that delivers it to the eye? And who promoted the so-called sexual revolution anyway? Did the Beast not have something to do with it, the horny one? Crowley knew a thing or two about *performance*. He wanted to dissolve a scotoma from the organ of vision, to unblock the system. That would mean a new system, and, arguably, the world is still struggling with the consequences.

*   *   *

How are we to understand who Crowley really was, and what he really achieved, if, as we shall discover, the legend is largely a libel?

Ask the man. He left us clues.

*   *   *

Christened Edward Alexander, Crowley stressed his middle name over his father Edward's. Preferring a Scottish variant, he called himself 'Aleister', a magical pen-name and eccentric twist on the Gaelic 'Alster' or 'Alasdair'. Alexander means 'helper' or 'defender' of man. Man. 'Humankind'. Us.

Crowley wanted to help us.

Aleister's resonance with Percy Shelley's poem *Alastor, or, the Spirit of Solitude* further inspired him. In *Alastor*, the poet-speaker seeks 'strange truths in undiscovered lands'. Alastor, the poet's daimon or dark genius, rooted in a dimension beyond matter, inspires travels from the Caucasus Mountains to Persia, Arabia, Kashmir and the 'wild Carmanian waste' where a veiled maiden appears in a dream. The dream drives the poet beyond the veil of nature into the spiritual world: a lone journey.

Alastor could have been written for Crowley.

He called himself the 'wanderer of the waste'. The 'waste' was of course the world of late 19th-century materialism – the end of an aeon – and Crowley 'the great wild beast' would travel it from end to end, fulfilling a biblical prophecy.

There is another angle to 'Alastor'. As an epithet of Zeus, lord of the gods, 'Alastor' executed justice, or revenge for evils committed, especially in the family. Freudian readers may note parallels with Crowley's own family trauma.

He was eleven when his father died following a misguided cancer treatment recommended by members of the Plymouth Brethren Christian sect. For favouring quackery over science, Crowley never forgave them, holding the Brethren – and their religion – complicit in his father's death: a death coincident, Crowley recalled, with the emergence of a new self-consciousness. He became 'his own man'.

Does the divine Alastor become a demon when separated from father

Zeus? In Euripides' play *Elektra*, Orestes hears an oracle urging him to kill his mother. Disconcerted, Orestes attributes it to an 'alastor', a mischievous spirit. To the ancient Greeks, 'Alastor' could, like man, be a god or demon. But while Crowley had ambivalent feelings for his mother, and while implacably opposed to the sex-negative, evangelical beliefs that separated her from him, he never, as far as we know, wished her dead; he only wished she was more alive.

Crowley saw the paradoxes inherent in the name 'Alastor'. When God condemns man's actions, evil is done; God's evil is good. 'Vengeance is mine, saith the Lord'. Crowley knew his Bible. In Ezekiel 14:21, when God judges Jerusalem, he sends the 'noisome beast' to stalk the broken city:

> For thus saith the Lord GOD; How much more when I send my
> four sore judgements upon Jerusalem, the sword, and the
> famine, and the noisome beast, and the pestilence, to cut off
> from it man and beast?

Emily Crowley called her only son 'the Beast'. The moniker stuck. Mother was thinking of 'the Beast' in the book of Revelation. Revelation's disturbed author had taken Ezekiel's 'noisome beast' to a far-out extreme. The 'beast', manifest sign of God's judgement in Ezekiel, became in Revelation a symbol for the Roman Empire, scourge of the Church, whose number is 'Six hundred threescore and six' ('the number of a man'): in Greek, a 'thērion', a great wild beast. Crowley took the word and the number, interpreting it as the Sun, or light-source.

Crowley also took on the Hebrew word for 'beast': *chioa*, knowing that in Ezekiel's vision, God revealed his glory in 'four living beasts': 'And this was their appearance; they had the likeness of a man.' (Ezekiel 1:5) As for Ezekiel, so for Crowley: the key was the glory of the Most High revealed in the likeness of Man.

So much for the vulgar idea of Crowley as 'the Beast 666'!

For Crowley, the 'Beast' is divine, creative energy whose symbol is the Sun, progenitor of life on Earth. The sun's image on Earth is the phallus or lingam, worthy of respect, not suppression. Deprived of the power to combine physical and spiritual love, the world is a waste. Magick would restore light, life and liberty to the wasteland.

The means to effect this new aeon was *ecstasy*, from a Greek word meaning to be 'outside' of oneself. Ecstasy is the joy of transcending the ego, of communicating with the 'angel'. Crowley tried to illustrate this in a series of artistic ceremonies called the 'Rites of Eleusis', presented before a paying public – and police spies – at Caxton Hall, Westminster, in 1910. The Rites' purpose was outlined in a pamphlet:

> Crowley is the mouthpiece of a society the object of which would seem to be the attaining of religious ecstasy by means of Ceremonial Magic.
>
> Dr. Maudsley defines Ecstasy or Samadhi as a quasi-spasmodic standing-out of a special tract of the brain. W.R. Inge [Dean of St Paul's] defines Ecstasy as a vision that proceeds from ourselves when conscious thought ceases. But however you may feel about Ecstasy there is no doubt that it is an essential part of true religious feeling. Crowley says 'True Ceremonial Magic is entirely directed to attain this end, and forms a magnificent gymnasium for those who are not already finished mental athletes.' By act, word, and thought, both in quantity and quality, the one object of the ceremony is being constantly indicated.

Crowley was an artist, prolific and original. Like any artist, he wished to be judged by his fruits. The biographer must set the 'fruits' in the context of the 'tree' of the subject's life. Establishing the tree, however, has not been easy. Crowley's reputation has distorted his history. This biography aims to correct the distortion, establishing recognition of Crowley as a major thinker, as significant as Freud or Jung, with cultural stature topped by five principal achievements:

1. Eschewing the complexities of Blavatsky's Theosophical movement, Crowley systematically unified Western and Eastern spiritual and esoteric traditions. His system embraced the esoteric philosophies of India, China, the Middle East and of Europe into a system of beauty, philosophical realism and practical efficacy.

2. Crowley introduced science and psychology into mysticism and magick, altering perception of these often obscure traditions. 'The Aim of Religion, the Method of Science' was his teachings' motto, reconciling fields that many people today still view as separate or contradictory. Crowley's system represented a real advance in the annals of Western esotericism on account of a radical scepticism. He demonstrated how to free spiritual research from superstition and dogmatism.

3. Crowley demonstrated an empirical basis for spiritual attainment independent of organized religion. This liberation of spiritual thought has freed spiritual phenomena to be investigated in a scientific spirit. Regardless of personal beliefs, Crowley's experimental approach demonstrates that following repeatable patterns, certain phenomena occur, as in any branch of demonstrable science. Results should be analysed objectively and sceptically.

4. Crowley introduced the principle of relativity into magick and mysticism. Cultural conditioning shapes the symbols of spiritual experience; state of mind conditions experience. A yogi, he wrote, gets as much pleasure from moving his leg as a millionaire gets from a week in New York.

5. Crowley was a pioneer of liberated sex teaching and the first thoroughly modern magus. He restored sexual alchemy to the Rosicrucian tradition and demonstrated the social and spiritual implications of a sexual, spiritual revolution.

In short, Crowley synthesized mysticism, magick and science experimentally. Ahead of the game, Crowley analysed the nature of *consciousness* long before behaviourism got to work on this vaunted 'final frontier' of science. He has already planted his flag on the outer regions of scientific speculation. Crowley knew that some kind of reconciliation of science and the essence of religion was both possible and necessary if humankind was to avoid a catastrophe he perceived as likely but not inevitable.

*   *   *

Crowley's intellectual seriousness may surprise those who have encountered him through pop culture. Then again, Crowley was seldom easy to understand. Maligned and persecuted in his lifetime, he now touches buttons in our world-perception and moral disquiets. His point of view is sometimes timeless, 'modern', often ahead of his time. There may be aspects we cannot yet see.

Bisexual, Crowley experimented widely with sexual techniques, advocating a sexual revolution that has only just begun. He advocated complete liberation of women from the secondary status of the Victorian and Edwardian eras, enjoying creative friendships with a surprising number of them, even attributing his brilliant treatise *Magick* to a woman he was living with. Can one imagine Tom Stoppard or Martin Amis doing this?

He experimented with drugs and mind-expanding techniques and substances. He was a practised yogi, master mountaineer, a sometime Buddhist, a poet and painter of the unconscious. He examined in detail the links between psychedelic and mystical consciousness. Like Jung, he pioneered recognition of the significance of the alchemical and magical traditions to psychology.

'Admirable with an African' (Nancy Cunard), Crowley attended multiracial dances in Notting Hill in the 1930s. His law, he said, was for *all*.

People all over the world are seeking religious solutions to their own and the world's problems. Hundreds of thousands are becoming actively engaged in Christianity and Islam, surrendering themselves to doctrines delivered 'from above'. Is this the right direction? Crowley was concerned about man's perennial religious needs but was critical of the kinds of salvation offered by organized religion. He analysed the psychology of teachers and believers with unsparing directness. He explored atheism. He found it unscientific, but refused to accept arguments for 'God's' existence. He had to *know*, to experience, to experiment. He recommended his students avoid using words without clear definition – 'God' was one of them. Describing the Bible as a work by 'several anonymous authors' he studied Buddhism and Islam experientially.

When most in his Edwardian heyday believed the world was progressing nicely to a cosy democracy, Crowley envisioned a future of *Force and Fire* – 'the Aeon of Horus', characterized by child psychology. The old era's catastrophe would be marked by titanic war, unless – he believed – people paid heed to a message he was himself often unwilling to deliver. He was a reluctant prophet.

*   *   *

Michael Powell, who never went to university, remarked in his autobiography that Crowley (whom I think he admired) attracted 'impressionable undergraduates'. I was one of them. I was impressed by Powell too. What's the point of learning if nothing can make an impression on you? At Oxford in the late 1970s I learned about Crowley – and his reputation. Tutors regarded my interest as aberrant. John Symonds' standard biography *The Great Beast* (1951) concurred with academe's contempt. A clever, hostile, sarcastic treatment, Symonds provided the template for most subsequent accounts. His biography obstructed understanding.

Twenty years ago, I began researching Crowley's unpublished papers, held by the Warburg Institute, School of Advanced Studies, in the University of London. There I found *another Crowley*, hidden away like a time bomb; never once, as I listened to its tick, did I experience bad feelings, terror, or any sense of evil, creepiness, or even ordinary disgust. There was no aura of a sick or psychopathic mentality. There was no shadow of evil. Crowley's humorous optimism shone in the face of personal tragedy and almost perennial opposition. And yes, there was magick too; the kind Disney can only approximate.

In short, I could not square at all the popular image with what I saw before my eyes. Conclusion: the unvarnished evidence reveals the public image of Aleister Crowley to be an inquisitor's judgement, a perversion of the truth. The heretic could not be burned at the stake, but his reputation could be. The old trick: make people afraid to investigate; you might get your fingers burned.

*   *   *

I am not alone. Crowley is now a legitimate subject within 'Western Esotericism'. Studies by Martin Booth, William Breeze, Richard Kaczynski, Marco Pasi, Richard Spence, Martin P Starr and Lawrence Sutin have brought Crowley into the purview of serious scholarship. 'Western Esotericism' is taught at the Sorbonne and the universities of Exeter (where I lecture) and Amsterdam. A public ever more drenched in low-level media has not yet enjoyed the fruit of this work. It ought to, because Crowley raises important issues: *What are we here for? What is freedom? What is spiritual life? Does magick work? Is religion true? Who is running the world? What is sex and what is it for? Who are we? Where are we going?*

Crowley believed posterity would vindicate him when the hex of his opponents no longer scared us. His time would come when people realized; the image is just an image.

The legend of Aleister Crowley is busted. It is time to grow up about him, a man of whom poet, rebel and style icon Nancy Cunard once said: 'He had a mind'.

Indeed. He had a message as well.

The Magnificent Crowleys

Then he discovered the writings of Aleister Crowley – a
visionary mystic from the early 1900s – whom the Church
had deemed 'the most evil man who ever lived.' [...]
Become something holy, Crowley wrote. Make yourself
sacred. [...] There had been a handful of modern mystics,
including Aleister Crowley, who practised the Art,
perfecting it over time, and transforming themselves
gradually into something more.

(Dan Brown, *The Lost Symbol*)

Where did this alleged transformation begin? According to
the legend, Aleister Crowley's father had something to do
with brewing. Biographer John Symonds picked up on a
statement that Aleister's father was an engineer and jumped to the
conclusion that Edward Crowley was responsible for the 'beer engine'
that appeared in 'Crowley's Alton Alehouses'. The 'beer engine' was
simply a hand-pump. Crowley's father never worked in the brewing
industry; he was trained as a civil engineer. Aleister Crowley was not a
brewer's son; he was a noted brewer's second cousin.

The distance between Crowley and his brewing relatives stems from
an accident of birth. Crowley's grandfather, Edward Crowley *Senior*, the
eldest of four brothers, was 20 when his father, Thomas Crowley, died in
1809. Edward's brothers were still boys. They returned to the family

home in Alton, Hampshire. Edward remained in London, pursuing his love for engineering and railways. Edward moved from the family tradition of Quakerism to the Church of England, in which communion he raised his son, also called Edward. Differing religious allegiance further widened the gap between Edward *Senior* and his brothers.

Alton proved profitable for devout Quakers Abraham Crowley, Henry Crowley and Charles Sedgefield Crowley. On 28 August 1821, Edward's brothers bought James Baverstock's Brewery on Turk Street.

Crowley was right in his autobiographical *Confessions* to describe his father as 'the wealthy scion of a race of Quakers'. What is strange is that Crowley never revealed anything publicly of his family's Alton background, a perverse omission. Most people would have been proud of it, for each Crowley brother married a Curtis girl, and the Curtises, famed for medicine and botany, were highly respected in Alton. Abraham married Charlotte; Henry married Elizabeth, and Charles Sedgefield Crowley married Emma. The Crowley-Curtis union ruled Alton like Huntley & Palmers ruled the realm of biscuits.

A feeling of having entered a novel by Austen or Trollope intensified when I examined a 1960s memoir composed by Dorothy, great-grand-daughter of brewery-founder Abraham Crowley. Kept in a box marked 'Crowley' at Hampshire's County Archives, Dorothy's memoir described the return of Abraham and his young bride Charlotte to Normandy House. This fine Georgian town house stood just across Normandy Street from the home of Charlotte's sisters. Paying Charlotte a call required a short step into a coach and pair. The coach would turn, disrupting the traffic, then manoeuvre itself to the other side. Trade stopped for the Curtis sisters; time has not.

By 1850, Alton was Crowley Town. Busy hotels such as the Swan and the Crown catered for the merchants while the vast Crowley brewery propagated itself along Turk Street, close to the centre. No 'cottage brewery' this, but a massive industrial concern with great brick towers, high warehouses and a colossal chimney – and this was no 'satanic mill', unless you were a teetotaller. Quaker conscience dictated purity in production and an honest deal all round. Crowley's Alton Ales were big business in Hampshire and Surrey where a network of Crowley alehouses served lunchtime clerks wishing to avoid tavern buffoons.

Exploring Alton on a wet summer's afternoon in 2009, I had to half close my eyes to imagine what once had been. Normandy House is now roughly divided between a games shop and a *tandoori* restaurant, the lower façade knocked out completely, the gardens behind torn up for development. The great brewery is gone; Sainsbury's supermarket complex has flattened the site. Across Upper Turk Street, the US brewery Coors has spread itself where once grew a meadow in which big brewer Abraham Curtis Crowley's children kept horses and practised hurdles. Abraham Curtis Crowley, who inherited the brewery in 1866, was Aleister Crowley's father's cousin.

While Aleister disdained interest in brewing, his father was mindful of his cousins' business. Edward had shares in a brewery empire that had expanded to Croydon, Surrey, where Abraham Curtis Crowley's brothers Philip and Frederick ran a second brewery, leaving Alton to him and his brother Alfred. Edward Crowley's cousins were very wealthy.

A year after Aleister's birth in Leamington Spa, Warwickshire, on 12 October 1875, his father's cousin Alfred died. Grief and stress afflicted Alton's surviving director; Abraham Curtis Crowley would die within two years. Before the end, local businessman Henry Burrell stepped in, buying the Alton brewery while securing marriage to Gertrude Evelyn, the director's daughter. Burrell changed the name of Crowley's Alton Ales to 'Crowley & Co', a change Edward Crowley did not like. With Alton out of Crowley hands in 1877, Edward sold the bulk of his shares, living independently on that fortune and other investments until his death. Little 'Alick' was set up by his father, almost, for life.

*   *   *

Why then, when Aleister's 'autohagiography' first appeared in 1929, did neither Alton nor his father's wealthy cousins receive any mention at all? The answer boils down to Victorian concepts of righteousness and their place in the class system. Crowley emphasized that while his father was educated as an engineer, he 'never practised his profession'. Edward was a *gentleman*. Freed from taint of trade, his son could better present himself as one of superior caste, a man apart, destined to recover a lost grip on aristocracy and spiritual kingship.

Crowley wanted neither the source of the family wealth to be known, nor his derivation from Hampshire bourgeoisie. He had probably suffered acid sneers for these associations at public school and at Cambridge. 'Trade' was bad enough, but brewing was unrighteous, corrupting the flesh of the working classes. Non-conformist industrialists did much better socially in the go-ahead Midlands than in the south.

Negative attitudes to brewing are confirmed in Cicily Mary Crowley's account of the Croydon brewery, written before her death in 2003:

> As a little girl I loved the brewery. When we went there on an occasional visit, we saw great barrels of beer; larger than anything I had seen before. Then, there was a lovely smell and I was given a glass of malt and we always received lumps of sugar-candy threaded on pieces of string. [...] My brother, Peter, on the other hand, did not like the brewery and at prep school when he was teased about the brewery and being the son of a brewer, he denied all association with the business.

Crowley's mature hatred of bourgeois attitudes was born of twisted childhood experiences. He maintained most boys instinctively possessed aristocratic spirit, soon beaten out of them; he, by contrast, had survived intact. Commerce was anti-romantic. The brewing of beer was stigmatized in aristocratic as well as strictly religious circles until money superseded religion after the 1950s. Beer was *common*. According to the diktats of temperance, its profits derived from exploitation of human weakness.

These were not the only issues separating Aleister from the 'race of Quakers' who dominated Alton. There were the attitudes of Alton's Quaker Crowleys themselves. Cicily Mary Crowley left an account of the Hampshire and Surrey Crowleys, whom she believed had probably come from Ireland before the 18th century.[1] Although Cicily and Aleister were both directly descended from Thomas Crowley (1753–1809), Cicily had been taught to disparage Aleister's side of the family. This view came from her grandfather, Abraham Charles Crowley (son of Abraham Curtis Crowley), who ran the Croydon brewery until it was sold to Watney's in 1918. According to him, Aleister's grandfather Edward should never have married Mary Sparrow of Wandsworth. 'It was from the Sparrows,' wrote Cicily, 'that a bad streak infiltrated into the Crowley-Curtis Quaker stream.'

Four children nonetheless emerged from the Crowley-Sparrow union, including Aleister's father Edward and Edward's brother, Jonathan Sparrow Crowley. Jonathan's marriage to Agnes Pope produced a further three children with the alleged 'bad streak': Agnes, Claude and Fanny. Cicily's grandfather refused to take Claude into the brewery, 'although his uncle Frederick (the same one who presented Alton with a new school in 1867) pressed him to do so'. Claude, like his cousin Aleister, 'did not have a good reputation'. Cicily implies it was the bad streak that took Aleister's father even further away from family respectability. Edward joined the exclusive Christian sect of the Plymouth Brethren, a move Cicily believed twisted the conscience of his wife, Emily, Aleister's mother.

So we see that Aleister's background had its share of alienation; it left a mark. His immediate family had separated themselves into a religious non-conformity of which their solidly non-conformist relatives disapproved.

Yet Alton mattered to Crowley. Whenever he used the London–Southampton rail route, he stopped off. In September 1934, for example, we find him alone outside the Swan Hotel on Alton's High Street:

> The Swan – I remembered every detail of the old garden with its
> sham Japanese rock pools and stone toadstools – and the
> Bowling Green. A delightful dignified and costly place, all tiny
> and folly. Inhabited by gasping corpses – it's as dear [expensive]
> as the Metropole at Brighton.

Today, the bowling green and garden have gone for a car park but the Swan's pretty façade remains.

If Crowley was in the mood to explore (he usually was), he could have walked the short distance up High Street to Church Street. There he would have found the tranquil 'Friends Meeting House', established for Alton's Quakers in far-off 1672. Had he strolled into its atmospheric garden, he would have found his father's cousin Isabella's plain, flat gravestone. Interred at the age of 85 in 1919, Isabella had lived where once Crowley's great-aunt Charlotte's sisters had lived, in Normandy Street.

Crowley's attachment to Alton even led him to speculate on its significance to his Thelema system. 'AL' is the Semitic root for 'God'. Crowley's famous *Book of the Law* was called *Liber AL*. The suffix 'ton' indicated a hill settlement (*AL*ton). Crowley's ancestral Quakers thus communed at the summit of 'the Hill of AL' in *AL's Town* and he, 'the prophet of the lovely Star', would show that divine spark at the core of every man and woman.

Crowley's prolific output derived as much from what he called his 'cursed Puritanism', his 'nonconformist conscience' as it did from prodigious creativity.

*   *   *

If Crowley's censorship of his Alton root is striking, the concealment of his mother's background is astounding.

Emily Bertha Bishop of 71 Thistle Grove, West Brompton, married Edward Crowley at Kensington Registry Office, London, in November 1874. In his 'autohagiography', Crowley confessed that he felt his mother was socially beneath both himself and his father. Emily had worked as a governess for a brewer before her marriage; Crowley would be fastidious about abstention – from beer at least.

Emily's family was not elevated, but it was remarkable.

Her father John Bishop, born in 1794, was an innovative farmer. In 1837 he married Elizabeth Cole, 28-year-old daughter of James Cole of Lime Street, Nether Stowey, Somerset. 'Philosopher Cole' or 'Conjuror Cole' lived on the same street as arch-romantic poet, Samuel Taylor Coleridge at the time he and William Wordsworth were composing their epoch-marking *Lyrical Ballads*. Famed for its pretty girls, Nether Stowey was where Coleridge chopped firewood, kept pigs, sowed corn, dug potatoes, and got close to the 'real people'. One of them was Crowley's great grandfather, James Cole. Nothing if not romantic, you might think the radical Aleister would have relished the tale of the self-educated, radical Cole, friend of the radical poets. Like Crowley's, Cole's and the Coleridges' radicalism annoyed Christian authorities. Local parson William Holland recorded an encounter with Coleridge's wife Sara on 23 October 1799:

> Saw that Democratic hoyden Mrs Coleridge who looked so like a friskey girl or something worse that I was not surprised that a Democratic Libertine [Coleridge] should choose her for a wife. [...] Met the patron of the democrats Mr Thomas Poole who smiled and chatted a little. He was on his grey mare. Satan himself cannot be more false and hypocritical.[2]

Holland was not entirely devoid of Christian kindness for those afflicted with the folly of democracy: 'Went to Conjuror Coles as they call him. He is a clockmaker and an extraordinary genius but a Democrat and from having too much Religion has now none at all' – a judgement posterity would make of Cole's great-grandson, Aleister. Like his great-grandson, James Cole was ahead of his time. The Duke of Somerset invited the 'Conjuror' to Bradley to make him an extraordinary clock. Completed by 1800, it went without winding for a year, played tunes on a bed of bells, displayed the month, day, date, and, among other wonders, showed sunrise and sunset and the phases of the moon. It did not make Cole rich, but it did make his work famous and his family comfortable.

A keen mathematician, Cole, at Wordsworth's suggestion, named his son James Ferguson Cole after the admired Scottish astronomer and scientist. By 1821, James Ferguson Cole was in London, joined two years later by his brother Thomas. The Coles would give the 19th century its finest clocks, watches and chronometers. Examples were exhibited at the 1851 Great Exhibition and at the Paris Exhibition of 1855.[3]

Some time after moving to Chelsea – he was there by 1829 – genius James Cole entered the Chelsea Asylum for Lunatics; he was dead by 1840.[4] Mental illness was a stigma believed to run in families, crippling marriage prospects. Did the illness influence Aleister's apparent indifference to the 'Conjuror'? Madness and genius are proverbially close. Perhaps Emily Crowley never mentioned her brilliant but radical grandfather of no fixed religion for this reason. While the madman's granddaughter had married into a family of staunch Conservatives, Emily never forgot the Coles. Her will reveals the bulk of her chattels going to Ada Cole, Florence Cole and the five daughters of cousin Arthur Cole. Aleister received two items of furniture.

The Bishop children's upbringing did not inspire Crowley, the spiritual aristocrat. John and Elizabeth Bishop's daughters were born on the family dairy farm, Fleet Farm, Minley, between London and Basingstoke. According to a biography of Emily's brother Tom Bond Bishop:

> There was little money in the house, but a great deal of honest effort. The father [John Bishop] was the first man to send milk by train to London, and to him belongs also the honour of having rented Kensington Gardens for some time as grazing land. Later on he took a farm at Wimbledon Park, but none of these enterprises turned out very well; whenever circumstances seemed likely to press less heavily some new calamity fell upon him.[5]

London's 1851 census reveals John Bishop as 'a farmer out of business' living with his wife and two youngest children, Tom Bond and Emily Bertha, at 18 Charlwood Place, Pimlico. On John Bishop's death in 1854, customs clerk Tom Bond Bishop assumed patriarchal duties. Given the circumstances, his sister Emily's marriage at Kensington Registry Office in 1874 to well-to-do Edward Crowley, twice her age, was a saving grace. And Tom, or 'T.B.B.' as he was known, was a fervent believer in saving grace. An evangelical star, Tom ran the Civil Service Prayer Union from the Custom House secretary's office. In 1867 he co-founded the Children's Special Service Mission, an evangelical organization that grew 'beyond all faith and expectation till it touched the lives of many thousands and entered into many different races and lands',[6] earning Tom his status and Crowley's loathing for a righteousness that reinforced his mother's buttoned-up views and irritated her sister, Ada Jane Bishop. Seeing his aunt as a resisting victim of evangelism, fond of a drink, Crowley marked Ada Jane's death on 18 June 1896 with a touching poem.[7]

When Crowley's father died prematurely in 1887, Tom Bond Bishop was thrust into father's place. But Tom's evangelical seeds fell on indifferent soil. Young Crowley had already found another root and route to inspiration.

*   *   *

In 1881, at Redhill, Surrey, Crowley met James Ferguson Gregor Grant. 'Gregor Grant', the son of Emily's cousin Jessie Kate and Scots watchmaker George Gregor Grant, introduced Crowley to Burns' poetry, Scott's romantic novels, Celtic mysteries and Jacobite wildness, stirring an imaginative life that would touch Crowley's whole career.

While Grant probably informed 'Alick' about the Coles, Crowley's *Confessions* states merely that his mother came from an old Somerset and Devonshire family. The family that Crowley took as his *own* was an ideal one, nourished in the belief that the Crowleys were of an ancient aristocratic line, possibly of the Breton de Kervals or the French de Quérouailles, with a Celtic link to the great druidic bards of old; the name 'Crowley' a corruption of the original. That his noble-minded father had married a scion of the, to Crowley, yeoman-stock Bishops was merely the latest indignity to tarnish a golden link to antiquity. As the Beast, he would attempt to restore that ancient sunshine to humanity.

THREE

The Beast

1875–98

When asked once why he called himself 'the Beast', Aleister replied that his mother called him the Beast. When he asked Mother about ladies' legs, *Ladies*, Mother told him, *did not have legs*. Sneaking under the table during a Brethren tea party, Crowley investigated. Withdrawing, he informed his mother that her guests were not ladies! Crowley claimed the observation demonstrated a logical mind.

Young Edward Alexander Crowley accepted the religious world of the Exclusive Plymouth Brethren as perfectly normal, while seeing it at a remove.

> Many of the memories even of very early childhood seem to be
> those of a quite adult individual. It is as if the mind and body of
> the boy were a mere medium being prepared for the expression
> of a complete soul already in existence.[1]

Pre-existent or not, Emily Crowley found her son's reality-facing precociousness a perpetual challenge. Though not cruel, Crowley's parents' life was restricted and restrictive; Crowley hated restriction. Sex was on his mind; one suspects it was on Emily's too.

Most Protestants were arrayed against Catholicism; Plymouthites reserved their special ire for the Church of England. Announcing they had 'come out of sect', Plymouthites quit what they considered Anglican apostasy from *the Word*. To be a 'nominal' Christian was worse than being an unrepentant sinner; sinners might yet repent. To enter an

Anglican church was sinful. Crowley tried it; nothing happened.

Plymouthites endured no priesthood. Services were held at home, led by brethren nervous of offending the Crowleys with minor improprieties; 'Alick', as Crowley was called, looked down on them. Separated from boys and girls outside the sect, his reading religiously controlled, Crowley's imagination was populated by Scottish liberators, knights, and prophets. His father, meanwhile, taught him that success acquired through anything but diligent management splashed with the blood of the Lamb expressed spiritual failure; a Plymouth Brother stood above kings.

Crowley got the message.

In later life Crowley asked people to consider his upbringing before condemning his ideas. According to Cicily Mary Crowley, only too extreme a dose of stifling sectarianism could have prompted Emily to see her son as 'the Beast', sent into the world to try her faith. Crowley believed that Plymouthism had spoiled not *him*, but his mother, rendering her, especially after his father's death, into a 'brainless bigot of the most narrow, logical and inhuman type', forced to do things against her sensual, artistic nature by overbearing Tom Bishop. Crowley kept his mind, and his cool, biding his time.

*   *   *

Crowley's admiration for his father, by contrast, never wavered. In many respects he remained his father's son, gifted with a biblical education rigorous and rare, learning to love, imitate and parody the sonorous King James Bible (1611). Aged 70, Crowley recommended his son, Randall Gair, read the Old Testament in this version as the proper basis – along with Shakespeare – for acquiring style. Crowley's parodies of evangelical diction, meanwhile, were matchless; he knew the evangelical mind from the inside.

According to Noel's *History of the Brethren 1826–1936*:

> EDWARD CROWLEY had been an Anglican Clergyman, and
> wrote a nice statement of some truths held by brethren, in the

tract, 'A Short Account of the so-called Plymouth Brethren' (J.D. Roberts, Gospel Tract Depot, 2205 Third Street, Philadelphia, Pa). He was a rich man, and relinquished luxuries and devoted all of his time and money to preaching, and sending parcels of tracts all over the country to any Christians who would make use of them. It was said that he had visited every town and village in the South of England door by door, with Bible and tract.[2]

There is no record of Edward Crowley's having been an Anglican clergyman; perhaps he was a deacon. Grayson Carter's stirringly titled *Anglican Evangelicals: Protestant Secessions from the Via Media*[3] refers to Edward as an Anglican convert to Plymouthism. A taste of Edward's genial brand of evangelism, expressed without emotional displays or charismatic sweat, unlike so many preachers of his day and ours, may be gleaned from a few of his 50 different titles circulating in Britain, Australia and America in the 1860s and 1870s:

AH! YOU GET THAT IN RESURRECTION (1d [one penny], W.H. Broom, 28 Paternoster Row, London) [compare the title with Crowley's initiatory poem, *Aha!*]

ALL SEATS FREE – NO COLLECTION (1d, Crocker & Cooper, 28 Penton Street, Islington)

CHRISTIANS WORSHIPPING IN THE LAST AND PRECIOUS TIMES – 'This know also, that in the last days Perilous Times shall come' 2 Timothy III.1 (Wolverhampton, R. Tunley, 128 Stafford Street)

HAVE YOU RECEIVED THE HOLY GHOST SINCE YOU BELIEVED? AND SPIRITUAL LIBERTY (1d, H.R. Denne, Romford)

500 LETTERS STATING SUNDRY REASONS FOR NOT RETURNING TO THE CHURCH OF ENGLAND. E.C. To be had only by post from the Author, 126 Manor Street, Clapham. 2d [two pennies] Post Free. April, 1861 [time of writing]

LIBERTY! WHERE THE SPIRIT OF THE LORD IS, THERE IS LIBERTY (2 Corinthians III,11) EDWARD CROWLEY, THE GRANGE, REDHILL, SURREY (3d [three pennies] G. Cooper, Printer, 11 Copenhagen Street, Islington

THE BEWITCHED ONES (2d. W.H. Broom, 34 Paternoster Row)

THE ELECT; OR HOW MAY I KNOW THAT I AM ONE OF THEM. (1d)

THE LAW OUR SCHOOLMASTER. AM I AT SCHOOL, OR AM I PLAYING THE TRUANT? A WORD FOR CHRISTIANS (Manchester, W.B. Horner, 93 Bloomsbury, Oxford Road, 1d)[4]

Edward Crowley's largest publication was his 108-page *PEACE AND ACCEPTANCE; LIBERTY AND SONSHIP by E.C.,*[5] bound in green cloth with a gold embossed title. Aleister followed in his father's footsteps where self-publishing was concerned. Would he ever have published his provocative, dazzling canon if his father had been alive?

*   *   *

'Alick' was five when he left Leamington Spa, Warwickshire, where he was born, for a large house near Redhill, Surrey. At eight, he entered the strictly evangelical H T Habershon's boarding school for boys in Hastings, administered by sons bearing rods to beat any bud of original intelligence. Crowley wished the old man dead; he died, whereupon the boy was dispatched to a Plymouthite prep school in Cambridge run by former Anglican – and sadist – Rev Henry d'Arcy Champney. If Brethren relished reminders of having been 'washed in the blood of the Lamb', Crowley was being smothered in it.

In late 1886, he was called away from school for a home prayer meeting. Father was ill. Eschewing the nation's leading specialist, the Surrey Brethren recommended Count Mattei's electro-homoeopathy. Edward succumbed to tongue cancer the following year: slain, the 11-year-old Crowley concluded, by the stupid Plymouthites. Tom Bishop stepped in, but Crowley, standing in his father's place, felt he could do as he liked. Burying the pain, he awoke into an anchor-less liberty. Something had conspired to kill his father; something was conspiring against *him*.

And something was wrong with Uncle Tom. Father had been mild mannered about religion; Tom was militant. Father's belief followed passionless logic; Uncle Tom and the Brethren were slaves to the bigotry of the biblical letter. Crowley rebelled.

*　　*　　*

The legend makes much of his next few years. That is because Crowley himself wrote of them, powerfully, in 1910. His booklet *The World's Tragedy* offers a high-contrast sketch of his 'boyhood in hell'. Christianity, he came to believe, was a crime against science and sense.

Emily was doubtless unwise to take child management tips from the Book of Revelation, but the Beast whose number is 666 was familiar tea-time reading in the Crowley household.

The Beast. It was 'the number of a man' observed Crowley from the text, and in a world of spineless floppies, a title to be reckoned with. If the Beast was bad, well and good; take the beast out of the man and there would be no *man* at all! Evangelical sentimentality extracted backbone from the child.

666. It was the number of a *man*. According to the Bible, the Beast's coming coincided with the bloody persecution of 'the saints'. As far as Crowley was concerned, these anaemic bores were the repressed Brethren whose spineless foibles had fumbled away his father's life. If these were the folk he was supposed to respect, pray with, and pray for, the 'Enemies of Heaven' were preferable; more exciting, more vital, more identifiably human. 'Christianity' for Crowley was a repressive blanket of suffocation that threatened to evaporate what vigour remained in a painful frame rendered more sick by bouts of brutal bullying, inexplicable sojourns 'in Coventry' for non-confession of unknown sin, and canings punctuated by prayer. He was supposed to feel guilty, but didn't.

At death's door, he fought back. He had Uncle Jonathan investigate

Champney's school. The sadist was disgraced; the school closed. The Beast had triumphed. He was a Grail Knight battling the miserly monsters who threatened the boys and girls of England with misery and malevolence in God's name.

*   *   *

Privately tutored, Emily's sexually charged son moved with her from one accommodation to another, always close to the Brethren and to her family.

In 1891, a new tutor appeared. Archibald Charles Douglas revolutionized Crowley's lonely outlook. Douglas was smart. He took the 15-year-old to Torquay, opening him up to the joys of drinking, smoking, card games, and girls. Overnight, Crowley's 'nightmare of Christianity' vanished. The world was not evil, and neither was he.

But Uncle Tom got wind of corruption's tide moving in on the south coast. Dismissing Douglas – Crowley's first breath of fresh air in years – the heir to the family fortune was sent to Malvern public school. Crowley complained of bullying and buggery. Parent and guardian, Emily and Tom, removed him from temptation and torture – but not before he had sworn an oath to the Crown as part of Worcestershire militia training. Crowley valued oaths. This one proved particularly significant, crystallizing his sense of loyalty, for life.

A holiday with mother to the Isle of Skye in 1891 led, at Sir Joseph Lister's personal suggestion, to the joys of fell walking and mountaineering. Crowley's life truly began. He tackled the big climbs of the Lake District, the Highlands and remarkably, in 1893, the chalky face of Beachy Head, a feat regarded as impossible. Crowley's health improved.

Sent to Tonbridge School in 1892, the bullying ceased. Physically strong with a will to return blow for blow, the boys, he felt, sensed his 'natural aristocracy'.

Hungry for sex, Crowley caught gonorrhoea from a Glasgow prostitute in 1893, the result, he said, not of sin, but of ignorance. Father of sterile medicine, Sir Joseph Lister, should perhaps have forewarned him. Christian propriety, Crowley concluded, was perilous for health. Embracing knowledge as 'experience made conscious of itself', life became a perpetual experiment. Crowley attended chemistry classes at Eastbourne College while living nearby with Plymouthite tutor Monsieur Lambert at 4 Sussex Gardens.

Crowley could never tolerate the tyranny and slavery that marriage brought to men and women in his time. He saw girls being fattened up or slimmed down for consumption in the marriage market, nailed up for sale like Strasbourg geese. When Lambert forbade his daughter Isabella from seeing a man unless he converted to Plymouthism, Crowley saw red. He launched himself on Lambert in a blaze of outraged fisticuffs. It was not the last time he would land in a stew for saving a damsel from propriety's distress.

Lifted from Sussex Gardens, he was grounded in Streatham. Emily and Uncle Tom despaired of the lad's salvation, but continued signing the cheques as Crowley headed, via the highest peaks of Switzerland and the Haute-Savoie, towards Cambridge University and a career in 'the Diplomatic'. Alpine conquests secured a reputation as one Britain's finest climbers, capping his pre-collegiate climbing career with a solitary ascent of the Eiger at spring's end, 1895. He knew what it felt like to be above the world.

In October, backed by the Prime Minister, Lord Salisbury's recommendation, the athletic Crowley went up to Trinity College. Signing the register as Edward Aleister Crowley, he would study chemistry and, by leave of his tutor, modern literature. The contrast in subject choice is telling.

Crowley saw a correlate to his imaginative mystical adventure in the 'Celtic Church', an amorphous conception enjoyed by seekers after a pristine magical religion woven into the roots of a remote Britain, far from the magic-less, industrial, post-Stuart monarchy. Its holy places were hid like pearls in the velvet hills of Scotland, Cornwall, Wales and Ireland. But Crowley also kept down to earth, compensating for his romanticism with science, philosophy, and cheek. His mind was further honed by chess – he beat the President of the University Chess Club, W V Naish, in his first term – and something else.

Crowley reckoned 48 hours without sex dulled the edge of his intellect. Town girls were ready and willing to satisfy. He joked that they, like the milk, should be deposited daily at the door, to save time. He charmed the pants off a goodly number.

A Plymouth Brother – or Sister – bound in adolescence, was a powder keg, primed to go off. For Crowley, sex was liberation both physical *and* spiritual. Adoring irony, he called his progress one of 'redemption by sin'.

Crowley's three years at Cambridge are underplayed in the legend – that's 'Crowley' as in 'holy' by the way; many persist in calling him 'Crowley' as in 'foully'. No, Holy Crowley's first-class education sticks in the gizzard of the image of the low-life necromancer that many have seen behind the name. His membership of Trinity remained significant throughout his life. And he *did* work for his exams when he had to, though he attended most to his own reading scheme. What brilliant student does not? He used the university for acquiring a *universal mind*.

Crowley flirted with the fast set. The Hon. Charles Stewart Rolls (1877–1910), the first man to drive a motor car in Cambridge and future co-founder of Rolls Royce Ltd, was admitted to Trinity the same day as Crowley. Crowley bought a car. While he probably baulked at playing second fiddle, there was another problem. Rolls was third son of John Allan Rolls, 1st Baron Llangattock, a titled toff; Crowley's mother lived in bourgeois Streatham. Crowley was strictly non-conformist (he did not attend chapel), with a name linked to brewing. And while Crowley was athletic, he was also shy, artistic and outspoken, not the 'hearty' type. We may suspect a little chip on the shoulder.

This would pass. On 12 October 1896, Crowley came into his inheritance. Carefully husbanded, £45,000 was sufficient to establish a gentleman in a life of leisure. Tom Bishop's influence on his life was over, though Crowley would continue to bash him, in literary form, for many years. The second stalk to fall before the scythe of independence was Crowley's diplomatic career, though it did not fall at once; and it may have been transformed.

* * *

The legend links this projected career's demise to Crowley's experiencing an 'intimation' of magical power at Stockholm on New Year's Eve 1896. He found something in his nature hitherto hidden, a magical gift or talent for magick, a kind of knack:

> I was awakened to the knowledge that I possessed a magical
> means of becoming conscious of and satisfying a part of my
> nature which had up to that moment concealed itself from me.

Crowley claimed to have been admitted to the 'Military Order of the Temple' in Stockholm.

What did he mean?

The suggestion is one of having awakened to the magical power of Will, a kind of Damascus Road, life-changing experience. *It was.* But Crowley's Damsacus Road was a path to his bottom, painful to begin with but in the end, ecstatic. Biographers have missed the point.

Some time in the 1930s Crowley penned an unpublishable 'gay comedy' in the style of Laurence Sterne and François Rabelais.[6] *Not the Adventures of Sir Roger Bloxam* reveals a hero whose name has a double-meaning rooted in Crowley's characteristically boyish anal humour: 'Sir Roger *blocks* ['fucks'] 'em.' What is blocked may be found through his trusty *Porphyria Poppoea*, his purple poppy, or anus. Supported by the 'Cardinal' (the 'Pillar of the Church'), his penis, Sir Roger describes an encounter in Stockholm with Scotsman James L Dickson,[7] a family man who gets about when on the job. Thus we find the true background to the 'Military Order of the Temple' to which Crowley was admitted:

> It was about eleven at night when Sir Roger Bloxam met Count
> Svendstrom. The Swede was under the influence of the prudish
> Queen, I suppose; for all he said was this 'Come, come! A boy of
> your age ought to be in bed at this time of night!' Sir Roger realized
> the good sense of his adviser; he acted at once on the word; and
> incidentally, he introduced the Count to *Porphyria Poppoea*.

Before discovering that buggery could be a sacrament, transforming fleshly stimulus into spiritual exaltation, Sir Roger/Crowley complained that he had been 'tired o'skating. He knew nobody in Stockholm but the stuffy old British minister, and his cappy shawly spouse; and he couldn't speak a word of Swedish, and he didn't like *Punch.*'

Crowley knew the 'old British minister'. We shall find this *everywhere* he went; no tourist, Crowley knew the British consular staff personally. He also had a yen for the company of senior military men. So we should be aware that the 'Military Order of the Temple' implied the Order of Knights Templar. Frequently linked to the genesis of Freemasonry, a bond of men, the Templars were accused of employing buggery in their initiation rites.

The legend has obscured the issue, as it has another. What was Crowley doing in Stockholm?

Stockholm was Sweden's gateway to Russia. Russia was a thorn in the Lion's paw. Russia threatened British interests in Europe and the East.

Summer 1897

While all London thronged to celebrate Queen Victoria's Diamond Jubilee, Crowley was in St Petersburg. His *Confessions* explain the visit as preparation for his diplomatic career. Acquiring Russian would be useful in an espionage hot-spot. Returning to Britain from St Petersburg however, something in Crowley appears to have snapped. Surveying a Berlin chess conference, he envisioned a blur of nonentities, mediocre in all but a head-game. Back in Cambridge, he hit a crisis. If the laurels of chess-mastery were worthless, was not all earthly achievement vain? A 'Trance of Sorrow' shrouded ambition in futility. His father had doubtless imparted the same theory from the Bible: *Vanity of vanities. All is vanity and a striving after wind.* The spiritual fact now struck him acutely. Ideas about who he was, what his future might be, dissolved into a colourless depression. The world's values were valueless. Should he throw in his lot, and his loot, with the diplomatic corps? Would even the greatest ambassador be remembered? Crowley asked: *What kind of work has lasting significance?* – concluding that the sole work worth the wager of life was that which surpassed the material level. Beyond the veil of matter, he believed, operated a network of spiritual forces, unseen. Crowley had a new ambition: to affect the course of history *from within*.

Apart from the shock of wealth, if not position, to what else might we attribute Aleister's turning-point?

To be homosexual in 1897 certainly entailed a secret life – though, kept secret, it need not have disqualified him from enjoying diplomatic service. Was there *another* secret life which attracted him, one more in tune with his burgeoning spiritual ambition? Had Crowley experienced a taste for espionage in St Petersburg? Was his Russian visit a kind of 'dry run' undertaken for government sponsors?

Government sponsors?

Crowley's admission to Trinity was supported by Robert Arthur Talbot Gascoyne-Cecil, the Marquess of Salisbury, elected Prime Minister for the third time in June 1895, shortly before Crowley's admission. Admission to Trinity was also supported by Salisbury's fellow senior Conservative, Charles Thomson Ritchie (later 1st Baron Ritchie), former Secretary to the Admiralty.

*　　*　　*

How can we account for the Crowley-Salisbury-Ritchie-Trinity connection?

First: *Croydon*. Cicily Mary Crowley's memoir describes her family's influential presence there. Home to Crowley's Aunt Annie after husband Jonathan's death in 1888, Croydon would also become Crowley's refuge. Annie furnished Aleister with emotional anchorage for over 30 years. Annie shared her politics with her nephew, as she did with Cicily Mary's side of the family.

Conservatism, Cicily maintained, was family tradition:

> My father, his father and my great grandfather, and I do not
> know how far back, were Conservatives. Grandma Crowley
> [Florence Mary] belonged to Disraeli's Primrose League, and all
> Liberals were considered to be utterly irresponsible.[8]

Florence Mary (1847–1927) surely knew fellow Croydon resident Annie

Crowley, for both were members of the Conservatives' massive support organization, the Primrose League, founded by Randolph Churchill. Salisbury was the League's Grandmaster. Through it, Annie Crowley actively supported Charles Thomson Ritchie's successful 1895 campaign to become Croydon's MP.

For his part, Salisbury probably influenced the choice of Trinity as a suitable college for the promising Edward Alexander Crowley. Three of Salisbury's half-brothers were Trinity members, of whom one, Lord Sackville Arthur Cecil, was, like Crowley's grandfather, manager of several railway companies.[9] Sackville also shared his half-brother Salisbury's devotion to electrical mechanics, chemistry and telegraphy; Salisbury owned two electrochemical laboratories. Sharing this enthusiasm for science and technology, Annie Crowley's late husband, civil engineer Jonathan Crowley, patented a railway switch mechanism and was elected to London's leading scientific institutions.[10] His nephew Aleister studied chemistry.

Proven trust in the Crowleys of Croydon would certainly have provided background for Crowley's possible recruitment into secret service at Cambridge. While direct evidence for recruitment at this time is unavailable, such a scenario offers illumination to some otherwise baffling lacunae of Crowley's life after 1896.

Spying and occultism have often been linked, and there is, if you look into it, a symbiosis. That Crowley's ambition to be a career diplomat died does not mean he lost the desire to cause changes in the world from the *inside*. Indeed, when added to a world of code and privileged communication, we see at once the tie between magick and espionage.

Crowley's Cambridge was a haven for excellent minds devoted to understanding the psyche scientifically. One such was Trinity Fellow, Professor James Ward (1843–1925), metaphysical psychologist. Ward's son Kenneth would become Crowley's friend and pupil. He who mastered the mind could master the world. *Where then lay the secrets of the mind?* Crowley knew of two principal avenues for discovering what made man and his nature tick; scientific experiment, and esoteric tradition. He endeavoured to excel at both, in his own way.

Another man who enjoyed intrigue was the Hon. Francis Henry Everard Joseph Feilding (1867–1936). Finding Catholicism inadequate to cope with grief at his sister's death, Feilding joined the Society for Psychical Research (SPR) in 1895. Established at Trinity in 1882, the SPR investigated scientifically 'psychical' phenomena: mediumship, telepathy, ghosts and life after death. Feilding, SPR secretary from 1903, was also an intelligence officer. If anyone 'recruited' Crowley for secret service at Cambridge or elsewhere, or at a later date, Everard Feilding, Crowley's senior by eight years, must be prime candidate.

A 15-year-old midshipman in the Royal Navy during the Egyptian campaign of 1882, Feilding was admitted to Trinity in 1887. Called to the Bar in 1894, he served on the Committee of Naval Censors (Press Bureau) during the Great War, and afterward, with the rank of Lieutenant RNVR, in the Special Intelligence Department of Egypt. In a career move similar to that which launched the legend of Lawrence of Arabia, Feilding was lent to the Arab Bureau and the Foreign Office for political service in Syria. After the war, he received the OBE, as well as the Order of the Nile and Order of El Nahda for services in Egypt and the Hejaz. Feilding was Crowley's intelligence contact when, during the Great War, the Beast spied on the German propaganda machine based in New York.

*   *   *

Keen to penetrate the veil of matter, Crowley began studying 'Rosicrucian' works, the arcana of magical societies, angels, spells and demonic conjurations. According to the legend, it was 'diabolism' that dominated; the psychology and science, detracting from the legend, have been ignored. Feilding would later opine that Crowley's effectiveness as an agent was marred not by wickedness, but by his sense of the dramatic.

Again we see that Crowley's life has not been written; it has been written over.

*   *   *

In the autumn of 1897, Crowley transgressed. He fell in love with a man. Four years his senior, Cambridge graduate Herbert Charles Jerome Pollitt performed a cross-dressing act inspired by a famous Parisian lesbian. Collector and connoisseur Pollitt, friend of *Yellow Book* illustrator Aubrey Beardsley, introduced Crowley to risqué *soirées* of decadents for whom diabolism was but grist to the artistic *fin de siècle* mill. The poet was intrigued by the symbolist art of the French Occult Revival whose outgoing tide had reached London in the 1890s after Parisian ferment a decade earlier. Crowley explored the romantic ideal of *androgyny*.

According to occult doctrine, the original 'Man', the first human form, contained male and female natures in one. This primal unity was ruptured by a fall from spirit into matter. When unity divided into duality, the cycle of reproduction began. To heal our rift with 'heaven' (pure Mind), the artist must rise to spiritually androgynous being. Crowley liked the idea. The love of man for man was no less pertinent to spiritual identity than that of woman. Indeed, love for women, appealing to non-spiritual instincts, could be regarded as a snare. A 'good woman' was a pal, possibly a lover. Meanwhile, Oscar Wilde, lover of beauty, was being slow-roasted by a world ignorant of ideas higher than British biblical law could accommodate. Crowley intuited his time had come. The world wanted waking.

Crowley took another step. Seeking guidance from Arthur Edward Waite, historian of the Rosicrucians, Crowley read Karl von Eckartshausen's *The Cloud upon the Sanctuary*. First published in German in 1804, the book had been adopted as a spiritual revelation by Rosicrucian-Freemasons in Russia and for a time influenced the political strategies of Tsar Alexander I.

Eckartshausen spoke of an exalted order governing human destiny, a communion of saints existing on a sublime plane, unhindered by material decay, sending, in due season, messages to receptive minds on Earth. Invisible to the materialist, this 'College of the Holy Ghost' was revealed by intimation to those worthy of the mysteries of the Rose Cross.

Determined to earn the Order's attention, Crowley sent out the requisite spiritual prayer for sign and guidance. If worthy, the 'Secret Chiefs' would furnish a sign.

Pollitt dismissed Crowley's quest, but a fell-walking trip to Wastdale

Head at Easter 1898 occasioned a new friendship. 'He created my moral character', wrote Crowley of half German-Jewish mountaineer, Oscar Johannes Ludwig Eckenstein (1859–1921), inventor of the modern crampon. Oscar and Aleister climbed together near Scafell. Crowley dumped Pollitt at the Bear Inn, Maidenhead, in the summer. He later regretted being influenced by society's judgement of homosexuality. He did not regret choosing the spiritual path.

Working on his poetic play *Jephthah* at Zermatt in the summer of '98, Crowley expatiated on alchemy at post-climb drinks. Chemist Julian Baker joined in, exhibiting superior knowledge. Perceiving a sign, Crowley, according to his *Confessions*, pursued Baker, revealing his quest. Baker would introduce Crowley to industrial chemist George Cecil Jones of Basingstoke, and Jones introduced Crowley to a secret magical order, the Hermetic Order of the Golden Dawn, derived, allegedly, from a mysterious German source by Freemasons enthusiastic about Rosicrucianism.

Mark Masons' Hall, Great Queen Street, London,
18 November 1898

Crowley marked this date every year in his diary: the initiation of his magical career, the answer to a prayer: a life of purpose. Transcending the vanity of Earth, he adopted the motto *Perdurabo* – 'I will endure to the end'. While Perdurabo quickly realized his commitment was more existentially intense than that of most members – largely theosophists attracted by Rosicrucian magic – the Order's structure nevertheless offered a progressive inner life that neither Cambridge nor the diplomatic service could equal. Disdaining to barter intellect for a paid career, Crowley had eschewed final examinations at Trinity. Operating at his own expense, he entered a college of magick and began the path to Godhead through the grades of the outer order, then the inner. These degrees made employment-sense only to the 'Secret Chiefs', whom he desired to serve.

Crowley wanted higher intelligence – and a mission.

FOUR

Crowley and the Carlists

1898–99

He came down from Cambridge in the summer of 1898 in a frenzy, stirring a bad name for himself by dabbling in black magic, penning pornographic verse (the notorious *White Stains*) and generally crashing around the Hermetic Order of the Golden Dawn like a bull in a china shop, alienating practically everyone, strutting about like an exhibitionist peacock, working hard to deserve WB Yeats' partisan description of him as 'an unspeakable person'.

So says the legend.

And the legend is... subject to investigation, which reveals instead a complex weave of plots, sub-plots, mystery, bafflement and enigmatic contradiction. When the storm and stress finally fizzled out in June 1900, Aleister was only 24, tough, adventurous, arrogant, but also acutely sensitive, naïve and surprisingly shy. No one should write off a 24-year-old genius on account of excess, but his enemies did. According to Crowley, the *Secret Chiefs* did not; he carried out magical instructions to the letter and proved himself worthy.

Summer 1899

Crowley took an alpine break with Oscar Eckenstein. He loved mountaineering and he loved Eckenstein, yet it was here that he wrote his 'Epilogue' to *Jezebel; and other Tragic Poems*, to be published under the guise of 'Count Vladimir Svareff'.

The poem expresses a Keats-like depression, a heart divided against itself, even a desire to, in every sense, 'get away from it all', to *die*. And this was written *before* the Golden Dawn blew up in the spring of 1900:

> To die amid the blossoms of the frost
>   On far fair heights; to sleep the quiet
>   sleep
>   Of dead men underneath the snowy steep
> Of many mountains; ever to have lost
> These cares and these distrusts; to lie alone,
>   Watched by the distant eagle's drowsy
>   Wing,
>   Stars and grey summits, and the winds
>   That sing
> Slow dirges in eternal monotone.

What had Crowley done to elicit the poem's aura of suspicion, poison and despair, a poem that reads like a man forced to execute some necessary act that tears against his feelings?

The answer to this question has *not* found its way into the legend.

To try to understand what lay behind the alpine death-wish, we need first go back some eight months, to November 1898, the month of his initiation into the Golden Dawn. That was the month in which Crowley completed *Jephthah*, a complex, political play about contrary forces tearing mankind between one conception of ultimate truth – God – and another. With freedom at stake, a new breath forms a trumpet call for a new world:

> In the blind hour of madness, in its might,
>   When the red star of tyranny was highest;
> When baleful watchfires scared the witless
>   Night,
> And kings mocked Freedom, as she wept:
>   'Thou diest!'
> When priestcraft snarled at Thought: 'I
>   Crush thee quite!'

Then rose the splendid song of thee,
　'Thou liest!'
Out of the darkness, in the death of hope,
Thy white star flamed in Europe's horoscope.

Tempting though it is to see the 'red star of tyranny' as prophetic of
Soviet repression after 1917, the 'red star' is most likely Alpha Tauri,
called Aldebaran, the glowing eye of the constellation of the bull, Taurus.
Aldebaran (Arabic for 'the follower') is one of three, traditionally
malevolent fixed stars in Taurus. It denotes power, with threat of
violence. Crowley's hope of a flaming 'white star' probably refers to
Venus, the power of love and potent femininity.

Crowley's 'tragedy' asks what will happen if the challenge of the
pregnant hour goes unheeded, if mankind slips back from the bold step,
the great leap, unwilling to leave the old altars of tyranny for the new.
The forecast then is war, and the Jehovah-like God of that war will call
for human sacrifice: quite a prophetic work!

The idea of a *politically*-minded Crowley crosses the legend's grain,
but Crowley foresees the collapse of European monarchy and of the old
Church. Working at the hinges of destiny, he is sensitive to political
realities: a prophetic sibyl seeking the ear of an intelligent diplomat.
And Crowley *could* gain the ear of a diplomat; recall that 'stuffy old
British minister' – the only person 'Sir Roger/Crowley' knew in
Stockholm at the end of 1896.

Reviewing *Jephthah*, the *Pall Mall Gazette* opined: 'Mr Crowley takes
himself very seriously; he believes he has a mission'. The *Pall Mall
Gazette* was right.

Crowley had a mission. But whose?

*　　*　　*

That Crowley was recruited for secret service at Cambridge is plausible.
US intelligence history analyst Richard Spence's book *Agent 666* (2009)
suggests 'Agent Crowley' was required by the secret service to penetrate,
as *agent provocateur*, the Hermetic Order of the Golden Dawn; not from

a desire for magical secrets, but because the Order's autocratic leader, Samuel Liddell Mathers was a leading British member of the 'Carlist Conspiracy'. Carlists plotted the installation of Don Carlos de Bourbon, Duke of Madrid, onto the Spanish throne.

Spence's hypothesis certainly makes sense of Crowley's wish for 'easeful death' on a mountain in the summer of 1899, for Crowley's alpine depression most likely derived from his *own* involvement with the Carlist Conspiracy. In July 1899, Crowley appears to have participated in a Carlist military gambit. The gambit failed.

The question then must be: in what terms was Crowley committed to the Carlist cause? Was he following instructions, or did he take it upon himself to get involved?

Crowley's references to the episode are curiously sparse. His *Confessions* recount how one of Don Carlos de Bourbon's lieutenants dubbed him *chevalier* (knight): 'I obtained a commission to work a machine gun, took pains to make myself a first-class rifle shot, and studied drill, tactics and strategy'.[1] He added, two pages later: 'there is a great deal more to this story; but I cannot tell it – yet'.

He *could* not, and he never did.

* * *

Seen through the lens of the intelligence hypothesis, Crowley's bursting onto the Golden Dawn stage in November 1898 appears suspicious. Within weeks of initiation, Crowley had met the Order's top man, Samuel Liddell Mathers. Before the end of the year, Crowley was handling aspects of Mathers' finances, a role that quickly engendered conflict with other members.

Mathers' past was chequered. Forced by penury to resign a commission in the First Hampshire Infantry Volunteers, Mathers enjoyed militarism. He was a *Will*-man. If you had will, force and legitimate right, you could do anything.

In fact, Mathers was up to his neck in the muddy waters of legitimism.

What is a legitimist?

A legitimist is a monarchist who believes in legitimate right. Legitimists believe monarchs have no right to resist claimants with greater legitimacy. The crown must pass to the first son of the monarch, if one lives. If the first son (or legitimate descendant) is denied, the acting monarch's claim is illegitimate; he or she is a usurper. A number of monarchical lines in Europe were thus contested by legitimists, including the Hanoverians'. The German Elector of Hanover ('George I') had been offered the British throne by a parliament that had rebelled, as legitimists saw it, against the legitimate successors of King James II. James, whose supporters were called 'Jacobites', departed England in 1688.

It should be stressed that the 'Jacobite' of 200 years later was absolutely pro-British, sympathizing with a British royal House (the Stuarts), rather than the German House of Hanover. Given Crowley's staunch Conservative background, it is significant to note that since 1714, the Hanoverians derived their most enthusiastic support from the Whig, later the 'Liberal' party; Hanoverians preferred Liberals to Tories. The essence of the divide between Hanover and Stuart lay in religion. James's descendants were Catholics, the Hanoverians Protestants. According to legitimists, Catholicism did not prejudice legitimacy.

Mathers' Jacobite enthusiasm is well known. He called himself 'Macgregor' and 'Count of Glenstrae' and was intimate with 'Scottish Freemasonry' and its Jacobite past. He even inferred he was King James IV of Scotland reincarnated. Crowley found Mathers' pretences amusing and compelling both, harking back to childhood games with Gregor Grant.

But legitimists were not playing games. That the 'Jacobite' cause could fire hearts more than 150 years after Culloden was not simply an eruption of romanticism.

Bertram, 5th Earl of Ashburnham, Knight Commander in the Order of Malta, was dedicated to the cause, offering part of his Welsh estate as a military training ground for his legitimist Society of the Order of the White Rose, re-formed in 1886. A tiny, secret organization, promoting legitimate monarchies in Spain, Portugal and Great Britain, legitimism was close to Roman Catholicism, to Celtic separatist politics (Irish, Scottish, Welsh and Cornish independence), and to 'high grade'

Freemasonry. For legitimists, true kingship was sacred, magical, not merely a matter of political convenience. If legitimate rule was not re-established, the world would fall to materialist dissolution and communism.

Papers deposited in Lewes Record Office, reveal Ashburnham the true believer, conspiring with foreign legitimists.[2] People of all ranks across Europe clamoured to serve the Carlist cause in Spain's northern provinces.[3] Volunteers were trained at Ashburnham's estate.

Theoretically, a Carlist victory in Spain could have threatened British government in Ireland where a Protestant monarchy had long divided the factions. The British Secret Service would have been neglecting its duty to ignore the situation. Spence suspects Crowley served those other 'secret chiefs' by spying on Mathers and other members of the Golden Dawn, while disguised, or posing, for a time, as a Russian aristocrat, 'Count Vladimir Svareff'. If Spence is right – and circumstantial evidence is supportive – then Crowley's famous battle with the Golden Dawn has been misread for over a century.

*   *   *

Unravelling Crowley's motives and allegiances around the Carlist episode is a tricky task. His extraordinary ability to adopt contrary minds with virtual simultaneity soon confronts us. Crowley was not schizophrenic. He believed that a balance of contraries opened a channel to a higher reality, a higher intelligence beyond the contradiction or 'duality' apparent in the world. If the world exhibited contrary extremes (such as good and evil), this was because a higher reality existed beyond them. Crowley's ideas in this direction would be refined a few years later with immersion in Indian philosophy. In 1899, Crowley was experimenting.

Given his peculiar make-up, it was certainly possible for Crowley to have been a reasonably sincere legitimist while spying on legitimists for a perceived higher cause. That Crowley sympathized with aspects of legitimism is clear. A self-confessed 'High Tory and Jacobite', he would conceive his political ideal as 'aristocratic communism', the raising of mankind to spiritual kingship. He believed in the aristocrat, the free noble agent with a sacred trust. Crowley shared his family's dislike for the Liberals, seeing treachery in Gladstone's extension of the franchise in 1884 when family hero Lord Salisbury vainly resisted a reform bill perceived by Conservatives as the harbinger of constitutional collapse.

Nevertheless, Crowley's Jacobitism was more symbol than fact. Twenty years after the Carlist episode douched him in the real thing, he confessed that in one compartment of his brain he had indeed been a 'bigoted legitimist', disdaining the British Royal Family as 'German usurpers'. Unlike Mathers however, Crowley had a great sense of reality. Naïve at times, but also hard-headed, he probably felt divided by legitimist claims. He was a High Tory romantic *and* a rationalist, a laconic opponent of Protestantism *and* of anti-scientific Catholicism. He was loyal to the Crown, though scathing about the person beneath it. He would come to say that at heart he was an aristocrat, in mind, a kind of anarchist. Crowley embodied many of the conflicting forces rending Europe apart at the time; a human Zeitgeist. It seems he resolved the dilemma within the contraries of his own labyrinthine psychology, by offering his brute side to the state and his heart to the spiritual cause. He kept his *mind* to himself; hence the summer depression of 1899.

Ambivalence regarding the Carlist cause is easily detectable in comments Crowley made years later about legitimist acquaintance, Cornish independence enthusiast and *Times* war correspondent Louis Charles Richard Duncombe-Jewell (1866–1947), the son of a Plymouth Brother from Streatham:

> He was very keen on the Celtic revival and wanted to unite the five Celtic nations in an empire. In this political project he had not wholly succeeded: but he had got as far as designing a flag [for Cornwall]. And, oh so ugly! All this seemed childish to me, but no more so than imperialism, and it had the advantage of being rather charming and entirely harmless.[4]

Crowley's assessment included subtle jibes at Duncombe-Jewell's own Jacobite pretences (he called himself Ludovic Cameron), an assessment redolent of a summary intelligence report.

In May 1891, Crowley had sworn an oath of loyalty to the Crown on joining the Cadet Corps of the 1st Worcestershire Royal Artillery Volunteers at Malvern College. Crowley's account of this occasion was curiously deleted from the published *Confessions*. The oath impressed him considerably: 'every time I perform an act in support of my original oath, I strengthen the link [to England]'. This is indeed a 'confession', and it is hidden. Richard Spence suspects that here lies 'the key to his future secret service'.[5]

Crowley declared he was 'quite prepared to die for England in that brutal, unthinking way. *Rule Britannia* gets me going as if I were the most ordinary music-hall audience. This animal is prepared to use its brains and its force as stupidly and unscrupulously as the Duke of Wellington.'[6] Crowley knew England was often wrong, patriotism often poppycock, but he would serve her to the last drop of his blood; shades I think of George Macdonald Frazer's 'Flashman', and, of course, James Bond, who also waved his 'Cardinal' where he saw fit.

Crowley was the 'Beast' – black to the blind and radiant to those that saw. Such dual sympathies would have compounded his value as an intelligence asset. And intelligence work held greater attractions. Crowley loved intrigue, and the legitimist conspiracy provided plenty.

＊　　＊　　＊

From the moment Crowley met Mathers and wife Mina[7] in Paris in the new year of 1899, he entered a labyrinth. To follow him through it, we need to keep hold of three strands: first, Crowley's spiritual ascent through the Golden Dawn system; second, the politics of legitimism and Crowley's scrutiny of it; third, Crowley's decision to complete the 'Sacred Magic of Abra-Melin the Mage': a hazardous magico-devotional method of spiritual Self-revelation whose intense demands complicated everything else.

Every one of these strands involved Mathers. It was Mathers who translated and published the 18th-century French copy of the 'Sacred Magic' he had found in the Bibliothèque de l'Arsénal in Paris. Crowley took on Mathers' publishing business because Mathers' acute debt necessitated keeping profits from creditors. By doing so, Crowley 'had one over' Mathers.

Crowley wanted to know what 'Secret Chiefs' Mathers served. Mathers assumed absolute authority on the basis of a claimed encounter with supernal Secret Chiefs of the Rosicrucian Order in the Bois de Boulogne, notorious as a prostitutes' hang-out. Mathers said their (the Secret Chiefs') electric presence left him temporarily shattered. The issue of Mathers' authority would split the Hermetic Order of the Golden Dawn.

*   *   *

In the Spring of 1900, having learned Mathers had gone to Paris to facilitate plots against the governments of Spain, Portugal and, probably, Great Britain, members of the Inner Order challenged their leader. Allegations of direct involvement by Mathers in 'Jacobite conspiracies to overthrow the throne of England' appeared in Crowley's witty tract *The Rosicrucian Scandal*, published in 1911.[8] Crowley there accused legitimists of supposing they could rid Britain of the 'usurper' Victoria by offering the crown to Prince Rupprecht ('King Robert'), the son of Maria Theresa de Austria-Este-Modena.[9] Crowley probably opined that these figures were no more British than Queen Victoria's relatives in Coburg. In his 1929 novel *Moonchild*, Crowley presented a semi-fictional Mathers as German spy and tool of the 'Black Brotherhood', Crowley's equivalent to Ian Fleming's 'SPECTRE'.

Inner Order suspicion of Mathers quickly tarnished the man seen as his closest ally. Crowley's rapid progress in the Order was particularly disturbing to Inner Order member WB Yeats. Yeats, with pro-Celtic separatist links and Fenian (Irish republican) sympathies, appears, in retrospect, paranoid.[10] *What was Crowley up to?* Crowley was wrapping himself inside the conspiracy.

Sharon Lowenna's study '*Noscitur A Sociis:* Jenner, Duncombe-Jewell and their Milieu'[11] reveals Ashburnham and Mathers securing arms shipments from Bavaria for a Carlist revolt, aided by legitimist 'cryptographer' Henry Jenner, the Society of the White Rose's chancellor. Jenner handled secret negotiations with Bavaria as well as plots to put the

Bourbon Don Miguel on the missing throne of France and, imminently, to secure the Spanish throne for the Bourbon Don Carlos VII of Spain. Crowley got to know Jenner through Duncombe-Jewell.

Three times in the 19th century, popular, bloody uprisings had failed to restore the Bourbons to the Spanish throne. Fresh opportunities for revolt emerged when the USA inflicted a humiliating defeat on Spain at the end of 1898. On 10 December, Spain ceded Cuba, Puerto Rico, Guam and the Philippines to the US for $20,000,000, a surrender so outrageous that ex-commander of Cuban Spanish forces General Valeriano Weyler y Nicolau plotted a Carlist *coup d'état*.[12] The General's anguish affected US foreign policy. Intrigued and inspired by America's burgeoning role in the world, Crowley wrote an 'Appeal to the American Republic', projecting a prophetic clasp of friendship across the Atlantic to Great Britain's 'blood brothers'. Crowley's poem is an ode to shared destiny.

Declaring that in the future, Britain and America would share the task of ridding foreign tyrants of their power to enslave the world, Crowley's remarkable *Appeal* may be read as a paean to 'western imperialism' or conversely as a stirring reminder of the optimistic historic role and predestined burden of the UK and the USA. Crowley's poem was the first to propose the 'Special Relationship' – one based on Britain's power, not dependency. Certainly, one could read the penultimate verse over shots of soldiers approaching Berlin in 1945, or of armoured vehicles entering Baghdad or Helmand in our own troubled times:

> Our children's children shall unsheathe the sword
> > Against the envy of some tyrant power:
> The leader of your people and our lord
> Shall join to wrest from slavery abhorred
> > Some other race, a fair storm-ruined
> > > flower!
> O fair republic, lover and sweet friend,
> > > Your loyal hand extend,
> Let freedom, peace and faith grow stronger
> > to the end!

Crowley's outspoken assertion of 1899 demonstrates a genuine prophetic gift, proven by time. It also makes clear that Crowley's unique vision of the future did not bear the reactionary stamp of the overwhelmingly Catholic legitimists. Nonetheless, it appears circumstances required maintaining a legitimist pose, one that may even have led to participation in the British Carlist catastrophe of summer 1899.

The Ashburnham correspondence contains telegrams and accounts revealing Ashburnham's purchase of steam yacht, *Firefly*.[13] With a hold stuffed with Gras rifles from Bavaria, the *Firefly* headed for Spain under the command of legitimist yachtsman, naval officer Vincent J English in July 1899.[14] The government looked the other way, officially.

Disaster struck. Somebody tipped off the Spanish Consul at Arcachon, near Bordeaux. On 15 July 1899, French Customs seized the vessel. Lowenna's study focuses on a name on the yacht's pay-list for 26 August 1899, one 'C. Alexander'. Was this a twist on 'Alexander Crowley' and therefore one of agent Aleister's first aliases? Or was it Royal Navy Captain Sir Quentin Charles Alexander Craufurd of Kilbirnie, 6th Baronet? – or, indeed, somebody else. Either way, this legitimist cock-up could have stimulated Crowley's summer death-wish on an alpine peak.

Perhaps Crowley left a clue. In March 1913, 'The Testament of Magdalen Blair', a short, scary story dealing with the psychology of death, appeared in his journal, *The Equinox*. Dedicated to Crowley's mother, the story was concluded by a 'Note' signed by 'V. ENGLISH M.D.' – Vincent English RN commanded the *Firefly*.

Perdurabo kept his secrets.

FIVE

Revolt in the Golden Dawn

1899–1900

Some people are respectable, and some are respected:
but you can't have it both ways.

(Aleister Crowley, Diary, Spring 1927, Paris)

I f Crowley was spying on the Golden Dawn, he was also learning from it. Perdurabo was serious about spiritual development. What did he learn? He learned to approach the gods, the inner laws of nature, the spiritual cosmos. He learned astrology, tarot and kabbalah. 'Kabbalah' means 'tradition received'. The tradition includes a key to Hebrew's hidden virtue, the language of angels, Secret Chiefs – and God. In the art of *gematria,* every Hebrew letter holds a numerical equivalent. Changing a spelling can open a secret. Equivalent numerical values may reveal hidden correspondence between otherwise distinct words. While recognizing the theory's absurdity, Crowley could not deny the art's revelatory potential.

From Julian Baker and George Cecil Jones Crowley acquired the rudiments of 'astral travel' – 'out of the body' experience. On New Year's Day 1899, Perdurabo encountered classical lesbian poet Sappho on the 'astral plane':

Small dark woman, wonderful skin, copper sheen but brown.
Lovely face – expression of intense desire. Wild floating hair.
Almost a mad look. […] She holds my hands in hers; glorious

tinglings and passion flow into me like live fire. I rise to her
bosom and kiss her passionately. I notice that I am a woman.
Restraint advised by angel [his astral guide]. With calmness,
therefore, I pass within her body. I at once feel all her feelings.
Great joy and glory.[1]

It was hard to part: 'I would have been divided so that Sappho in
departing took of my left side. I leave my love with her, but my strength
belongs to God.'

Lesbian love features in Crowley's early poetry, where the joy of
orgasm is expressed as divine exaltation. He would like to have been
treated as a lesbian by a lesbian woman; 'Man', for Crowley, was spiritually androgynous.

In February 1899, Crowley passed through the ceremony for the
grade of *Practicus* 3°=8°. The peculiar grade notation was used to chart
spiritual progress. It was based on the kabbalah's 'Tree of Life', known as
'the tree of emanation' in Isaac the Blind's *Sefer Bahir*, or 'Book of
Illumination'. Isaac the Blind (*fl* 1190–1210) held that God is known by
ten attributes or *sephiroth*. Each *sephira* (*sephiroth* is the plural) emanates
downwards towards 'our' world where being manifests materially.
Mystical and magical progress required ascending the inner 'tree' or
microcosm.

The 'microcosm', or little universe, is the invisible structure of Man,
as made in the 'image of God'. Our *steps up* the tree correspond to the
Light's *steps down*. Reaching the heights of the angels and archangels
required retracing the steps of the 'Fall' of Man.

The *sephiroth* are numbered from one to ten. *One* is the highest
sephira (*Kether*: Hebrew for 'Crown') and *ten* the lowest (*Malkuth*:
Hebrew for 'Kingdom'). Since the Golden Dawn's Zelator grade or first
degree (1°) begins at *Malkuth* (the tenth *sephira*), the Zelator grade was
written as 1° = 10°. The little square represents the *sephira*.[2]

Most members of the order worked with the lower degrees. The
highest grade, *Ipsissimus* ('his own very self', the *god* of which the
personality and mind are the expression), was an ideal, suitable for a
'Secret Chief'.

*　　*　　*

In spring 1899, Crowley befriended Allan Bennett.[3] A remarkable occultist and Buddhist, Bennett would soon move rent-free into Crowley's apartments at 67 Chancery Lane, teaching him everything he knew about magick, assisting with experiments such as summoning and banishing demonic entities.

Bennett gave Crowley the inside 'dope' on the Golden Dawn. He offered other kinds of dope as well. A pale martyr to acute asthma, Bennett had made the apothecary his second home. The link between chemistry and consciousness was obvious to anyone who had explored the world of alchemy. Alchemists held that man is integrally linked to a chemical, and spiritual, universe. Much magick was simply getting the chemistry right; 'angels' and 'demons' could represent the 'consciousness' behind chemical formulae, working by natural, if unknown, law. Crowley took the tip: drugs could be an aid to magick, used with care and not for kicks.

Residing in style in Chancery Lane, Crowley adopted the alias 'Count Vladimir Svareff'. Apart from a natural fondness, or weakness, for posing, Crowley's purpose in adopting the title remains obscure. In the 1920s, he explained the disguise as a means to avoid family opposition to his intended 'Abra-Melin' operation. This is as unconvincing as Crowley's 'confession' that the disguise enabled him to observe tradesmen's reactions to Russian nobility! Spence suggests it may have been part of a 'half-baked scheme' to smoke out Russian agents in or around the Golden Dawn and London's West End. Such might illuminate alleged observation of Crowley's apartments by 'police' – as acquaintances warned him to be the case. Were there tip-offs regarding homosexuality? Oscar Wilde would die exiled in Paris at the end of 1900. Perhaps the presence of a Russian called 'Svareff' had simply alerted Scotland Yard – or even *Russian* agents, mindful that 1899 saw the most violent student demonstrations in Russia for many years. Anarchist Peter Kropotkin published his *Memoirs of a Revolutionist* in London in 1899, with an introduction by Danish critic Georg Brandes describing Nietzsche's philosophy as 'aristocratic radicalism': a description as delightful to Nietzsche as it would have been to Nietzsche-reader Crowley.

A variant hypothesis links the 'Svareff' alias to Crowley's Carlist intrigues, and his summer 1897 trip to Russia. Spence observes that in 1896, Don Carlos's son Don Jaime received a Russian Imperial Army commission. A question of possible interest to Foreign Office hawks was whether Tsar Nicholas II would support Don Jaime's father in a Carlist revolt. Whatever the truth, long lost, this would not be Crowley's last association with Russian intrigues.

Crowley certainly wished to render himself invisible while pursuing magick in London. Becoming 'invisible' would become part of Crowley's intelligence pallet, though on this occasion, as he later opined, he'd have been better off calling himself 'Smith'.

Mathers accepted Crowley's alias. In October 1899, Crowley-Svareff sent a note of authorization from Mathers to theosophist Frederick Leigh Gardner, *Frater De Profundis ad Lucem* in the Order:

> I the undersigned do hereby Authorise my Friend the Count
> Vladimir Svareff to act as my Representative in all matters
> relating to the Copyright of my book called the 'Sacred Magic of
> Abra-Melin'.[4]

The 'Count' held powers to sign all receipts on account of all moneys received, frustrating Mathers' creditors. Business went awry; 'Svareff' to Gardner again:

> Dear Sir,
>
> Kindly return my authority from Mr Mathers to act for him.
> Your cowardly insult to Mr Mathers precludes all future
> necessity of treating you as a gentleman; your impertinence to
> me is of course beneath contempt.

Dear Sir,

You are the despicable cad you are reported to be. I trust to have the honour of telling you so to your face, with the appropriate accompaniment, at no distant date.

Yours truly,

Svareff[5]

To which Gardner replied:

Dear Sir,

Your irresponsible communication of 17 [?] forms a fitting culmination to the disgraceful treatment which I have experienced at the hands of Mr Mathers.

The money which I advanced him was obtained from [?] under the most pitiful plea of poverty, but he apparently is dead to all sense of pride and self respect.

Crowley got the 'gen' on Order politics from Bennett, so he probably knew the story behind Mathers' significant clash with Gardner.

In December 1896 Gardner had loaned Mathers and wife Mina £50. Outstanding in 1899, the £50 was to cover what Annie Horniman, *Sub-Praemonstratrix* of the Order's Isis Urania temple in Paris, had cut when *she* ceased bankrolling Mina (*Vestigia*), her old friend from the Slade School of Art. Incensed, Mathers threatened to strike Annie's name from the Order rolls:[6]

I do not care an atom what you *think* but I refuse absolutely to permit open criticism of, or argument concerning my action in either order from you or any of the members. [...] As regards your conduct to me and Vestigia *personally*, I consider it *abominable*.[7]

There was more to Horniman's expulsion from the Order than money. There was sex as well.

Dr Edward Berridge, *Frater Resurgam*, devotee of the sexual philosophy of Thomas Lake Harris, believed in the health benefits of 'karezza': intercourse undertaken without movement or orgasm. A proponent of 'free love', he speculated on sexual union with elemental or astral beings. Horniman wanted Berridge's paper on magical sex with 'elementals' suppressed. Mathers denied her 'ordinary self's' right to react to 'spiritual activity' within the Order. Gardner petitioned for Horniman's reinstatement; the Order was divided. Having attended Horniman's class on 'Spirit Vision' and considered it 'flippant and casual', Bennett sided with Mathers.[8] Two years later, Crowley took Bennett's cue. His suspicion of Gardner and Horniman was hotly reciprocated. To them, Crowley was a 'Bennett' *and* a 'Mathers man'; they would do their utmost to frustrate him.

*   *   *

Crowley tried to turn aside from Order problems. On 17 November 1899, he acquired Boleskine House, Loch Ness, complete with Lairdship, for £2,300, its reluctant-to-sell owner receiving twice its market value. Crowley intended to perform the sacred magick of Abra-Melin, an investigation that would give his own system of magical self-realization, Thelema, its key principle: the 'Knowledge and Conversation of the Holy Guardian Angel' – the secret Self.

*   *   *

The less-secret self received a new mask. By the end of 1899, with Svareff gone, the Laird of Boleskine appeared with 34 acres of estate to hunt and fish on. Early guests included Cambridge graduate and journalist William Evans Humphrys,[9] and Lilian Horniblow, wife of Lieutenant Colonel (later Brigadier General) Frank Horniblow of the Royal Engineers. Calling herself 'Laura Grahame' for assignations, Horniblow's affair with Crowley was cooling: Abra-Melin bound him to celibacy. A frustrated Laura warned him in November of danger from the police – a tip derived, she said, from 'the Astral' (plane). Laura was probably at Boleskine on 12 December, when Humphrys served as Crowley's assistant in a magical ceremony, followed, according to the *Confessions*, by Humphrys' showing 'symptoms of panic fear', while Laura 'fled to London'. Crowley's *A Magicall Diarie 1899*,[10] indicates the ceremony's purpose:

> To obsess [Frederick Leigh] Gardner. (L[aura] G[rahame] sees
> the success of this op[eration].) Shortly after closed temple.

Gardner was central to the anti-Crowley camp, whence, almost certainly, came an anonymous letter urging Laura to avoid Crowley as he was 'about to be in trouble'. Such intrigues furnished conditions unconducive to a holy magick demanding purification of mind and heart. Abra-Melin's promise of domination over demonic powers entailed hazards enough, without stimulating a scenario that offered such powers a field day.

*   *   *

Crowley was barred from the Golden Dawn's Second Order of the Ruby Rose and Golden Cross and its *Adeptus Minor* 5°=6° grade by the Gardner-Yeats circle. There were whispers of homosexuality, hints of blackmail. Yeats's nastiness sealed Crowley's disaffection from an imaginary 'Celtic Church' that Crowley would later dismiss as little more than 'a cloak for insidious Roman Catholicism'; the Vatican favoured undermining secular government through supporting legitimists.

Conversation with girlfriend Evelyn Hall in Bloomsbury on 11 January 1900 revealed rumours of illegal sexual misdemeanours had intensified:

> She reaffirms her statements: but her description of the 'college
> chum' is absurd and her whole attitude ridiculous. She knows
> one fact only – the name Crowley at Cambridge.

Receiving two letters from Evelyn at the Hotel Cecil on the 15th; Crowley noted:

> They say: you (and all your friends at 67 [Chancery Lane]) are
> watched by the police. This is connected with 'the brother of a
> college chum' but no doubt can be entertained of the meaning of
> the hints. She naïvely assumes the charge to be true!

Defying the rebels, Mathers conferred the *Adeptus Minor* 5°=6° on
Crowley in Paris on 23 January, empowering him to demand the grade
documents should Yeats & co. refuse them. Mathers advised Crowley
avoid London, and keep short any visit to Cambridge; the university was
linked to the sexuality rumours.

In London, Bennett and Eckenstein shook their heads: 'both jeer at
my alarms', wrote Crowley, 'for, knowing already how Aweful [*sic*] are
the Forces leagued against me, I am not surprised at these troubles:
Neither do I fear them, yet to find me might be to spoil my plans.' His
friends reckoned that anyone undertaking Abra-Melin courted appalling
problems.

In Cambridge's 'thorny bosom', Crowley encountered Humphrys
whose comments on the 'Great Trouble' baffled him even more than
Evelyn Hall's:

> He says: yes, you are 'wanted' though he thinks [two words are
> scratched out] and adds 'The danger is most pressing just before
> Easter.' (Humphrys is certainly at this time manoeuvring to get
> me out of the way.)

Humphrys was enamoured of Laura; her interest in Crowley was now an
obstruction. Confused, Crowley wrote to George Cecil Jones. Unhelpful,
Jones thought Crowley mad or obsessed. Crowley resorted to the magick
of the lunar pentacle from *The Key of Solomon* to which he attributed his
safe return to Boleskine on 7 February. Undeterred, Perdurabo made
The Oath of the Beginning:

> [...] that I will devote myself to the Great Work: the Obtaining of
> Communion with my own Higher and Divine Genius (called the
> Guardian Angel) by means of the prescribed course: and that I
> will use any power so obtained unto the Redemption of the

Universe So help me the Lord of the Universe and mine own
Higher Soul!

On 24 February, Crowley received a letter from Bennett: 'I warn you that
you are in very grave danger', wrote his friend,[11] having thrice been visited by the 'Angel of the Lord' in visions. Crowley perceived the 'danger'
consisted in either: 1) that his 'True Circle', possibly his psycho-physical
integrity, might be broken; 2) 'Politics' – probably a reference to legitimist
conspiracy; or 3) 'the other silliness': Laura Grahame's sore feelings.

Crowley prayed, entrusting his safety to the 'Providence of God'.
Bennet, on the other hand, now at the end of his tether, sought
immersion in authentic Buddhism. Ceylon seemed ideal for soul and
body; smog-aggravated asthma was crippling him. According to
Crowley, Laura, hoping to prolong the affair, had asked how she might
do *her* bit for spiritual evolution. 'Forego some of life's unearned
luxuries,' said Crowley, '– and pay Bennett's passage to India.' Horniblow
provided either cash or a ruby ring in *lieu*, but with the sex switched off,
and under pressure from Golden Dawn members, Laura demanded
back her gift.

Suppressing anxieties, Crowley pressed on with Abra-Melin. On 17
March, he 'meditated upon unselfishness: The Ego: and such subjects'.
Two days later, he had a prophetic dream of helping a woman who was
eloping. Similar circumstances three years later led to his marriage. He
then dreamt of a man stealing his Rose Cross jewel from a hotel
dressing-table.[12] Crowley asked: 'Was I totally obsessed?' A day's
climbing with Eckenstein helped. On 22 March his inner vision cleared.
Invoking the 'angels of Earth', he experienced stunning visions of the
Rose and Cross at the centre of the Earth, seeing the Rose not only as the
'feminine' but as 'the Absolute Self-Sacrifice, the merging of *all* in the 0
(Negative), the Universal principle of generation through change'. The
Cross he saw as the 'Extension or *Pekht* principle'. He felt he should have
learned more, but his attention wandered.

Five days later, Crowley read *Clothed with the Sun* by theosophist
Anna Kingsford. The woman 'clothed with the sun' was for Crowley the

Beast's lunar consort. Crowley then travelled astrally 'with a very personal guide: and beheld (after some lesser things) Our Master [Jesus the Logos] as he sate by the Well with the Woman of Samaria [John 4:6–30]. Now the five husbands were five great religions which had defiled the purity of the Virgin of the World: and "he whom thou hast" was materialism (or modern thought).' – a remarkable interpretation.

> Other scenes also I saw in His [Jesus'] Life: and behold I also was crucified! Now did I go backwards in time even unto בראשת [berashith=the beginning] and was permitted to see marvellous things.

What Crowley saw was a vision experienced by other gnostic seers: the origin of the universe. Crowley also saw the 'Rosicrucian Mountain': a white mountain of salt that became a glorious 'molten light' in the centre of the Earth.

Back at the Earth's crust, following Order members' advice to frustrate Crowley, Laura threatened police action. Crowley's response: 'Bar the ruby ring, I could checkmate the Princes [Evil Princes of the world] for the moment by giving way – O Lord, who knowest me, lead me in thy ways.'

Settling with Laura was a snare because, he surmised, powers resisting Abra-Melin success were exploiting the Laura situation to break his will to subdue them. Abra-Melin required Crowley's treating every event as a 'dealing of God with his soul'. Capitulating to Laura threatened his *Adeptus Minor* promise to regard suffering as an initiator of the heart. In a bind, he called Eckenstein up to Boleskine. A unique diary record for 31 March shows Crowley and Eckenstein as lovers:

> In the afternoon I tried to go to the *twll-du* [Welsh slang for 'black hole', or anus] for O.E. [Eckenstein] with poor success. I then began to fix things up for a final. The wand wanted straightening.

One of the men had trouble getting an erection. Crowley then felt 'a most violent disinclination to begin the Operation'. Feeling 'unworthiness', inner forces rose up to oppose him. Was the act of love appropriate in the context of invocation? He wasn't sure.

*　　*　　*

The Golden Dawn was in freefall. On 22 March, the Second Order committee discussed allegations made by Mathers about the Order's co-founder, William Wynn Westcott. Florence Farr offered to resign as a blow against Mathers. Dismissing her by return of post, Mathers let a very fat cat out of the bag. If the committee thought they could rely on Westcott as an alternative to his own authority, they should know that Westcott had forged the Order's foundation documents! Supposed links with Nuremburg's Rosicrucian Order were fraudulent. 'Anna Sprengel', supposed source of ritual secrets, had never existed. But, Mathers assured them, his *own* link with the Secret Chiefs vouchsafed the sole authority necessary for an authentic order – a principle not lost on Crowley himself.

Overthrown on 24 March, Mathers informed Crowley the committee members were 'apparently mad'. Dropping Abra-Melin, Crowley pledged his services. He was now working for the Secret Chiefs, he believed, as well, possibly, as the secret service. He asked *Soror Fidelis*, girlfriend Elaine Simpson, if she was still loyal to him and to Mathers. Yes, she said, she was, despite her mother Alice Isabel Simpson's having listened to rumours that Crowley made sexually charged astral visitations to her daughter.

Crowley felt himself under magical attack. Departing Paris as Mathers' 'Envoy Plenipotentiary' on Friday 13 April, odd things happened. A taxi cab's lamps burst into flames. Elaine's fire would not light. Horses bolted at his sight. A rubber mackintosh, nowhere near the grate, ignited while other fires at Elaine Simpson's family home 'refused utterly to burn'.

Crowley interviewed Dr Edward Berridge, then Elaine's mother, *Soror Perseverantia*. What, he asked, did his enemies really have against him? Mother spilled the beans: 'sex-intemperance on Lake Harris lines in order to obtain magical power (both sexes are here connoted)!!' 'Lake

Harris' was the Thomas Lake Harris whose influence on Berridge enflamed his dispute with Annie Horniman in 1896; Crowley was being tarred with Horniman's uptight brush.

On 16 April, Crowley felt the magical attack again: 'I was very badly obsessed and entirely lost my temper – utterly without reason or justification.' He discussed strategy with Elaine, then engaged a 'chucker-out' at a Leicester Square pub for services at 36, Blythe Road, Hammersmith, the next day.

Crowley headed up west on the 17th to seize the Order's prized 'vault': a painted, wooden re-creation of the tomb of Christian Rosenkreuz, supposed founder of the Rosicrucian Order, used strikingly in the *Adeptus Minor* ceremony. The vault's guardian, Miss Maud Cracknell, ordered Crowley to leave. Crowley claimed possession with Elaine. When Florence Farr and two other Order members arrived to find the locks changed, a scuffle ensued. Police were called. Crowley was asked to leave. The bouncer showed up late; he'd got lost.

A hectic day ended at Camberwell Rectory where Crowley's younger Cambridge friend, Order member and artist Gerald Kelly, lived with his parents:

> Bring him [Kelly] back and trap Gnōthi Seauton [Humphrys] in attempting Laura. He seems nearly as big a blackguard as myself.
> I misbehave as usual. Oh Lord, how long?

Crowley suspected Humphrys had influenced Laura's police complaint. She would not press the charge – to protect her husband's good name! The idea was for Kelly to get the truth out of Humphrys for Crowley's defence should the need arise. Laura would see he was not to be blackmailed. Crowley went to Basingstoke for George Cecil Jones's support. Jones urged him to leave. Crowley suspected Florence Farr's imminent arrival; careful, Jones did not want Farr to think he was plotting with Crowley. With Julian Baker arriving in the evening, the Golden Dawn was in a state of excitement bordering on hysteria.

Crowley returned to Blythe Road the next day to find the locks changed again, the work of Yeats and Edward Hunter. The Second Order suspended Elaine, her mother, and Berridge, for doubting their 'right' to overthrow Mathers.

Hearing on 22 April that Mathers approved of his services, Crowley noted:

> Therefore do I rejoice, that my sacrifice is accepted. Therefore do I again postpone the Operation of Abra-Melin the Mage, having by God's Grace formulated even in this a new link with the Higher, and gained a new weapon against the Great Princes of Evil of the World.

On 28 April, Yeats wrote to his patron, Lady Augusta Gregory. A summons had been taken out denying the Second Order's claim of right to depose Mathers. 'The envoy is really one Crowley, a quite unspeakable person. He is, I believe, seeking vengeance for our refusal to initiate him.' When Crowley discovered Annie Horniman was paying famous counsellor Mr Gill QC to argue in a police court over worthless 'paraphernalia', he wisely withdrew.

*   *   *

A number of writers have suggested the Golden Dawn fracas was merely an overblown clash of barmy eccentrics. On one level, so it must appear. Nevertheless, it is worth paying attention to Crowley's crisp, contemporary, political, and quite un-hysterical (and unpublished) *Notes of London Row* included in his somewhat more portentously entitled *Book of the Chronicles of the Revolt of the Adepti*.

There we find that behind the revolt lay the issue of political legitimism.

First, Crowley assessed Florence Farr's unwillingness to work with Mathers: 'she knows he is definitely working against England, and using o.b. ['ordinary business'?] of O[rder] for this end.'

Second, George Cecil Jones heard from Mathers on 20 January that Florence Farr wanted to close the Isis-Urania Temple in Paris, the result, asserted Farr, of an 'astral jar' (something spiritually adrift) in the temple. Crowley's comment: 'This is a lie. *Politics the real basis.*' (my italics).

Third, 'Mathers refuses to close the Temple and tells Florence Farr and her supporters to accept his authority, or there is nothing. Revolt.' The Second Order Committee 'thinks it has power to arraign [Mathers] at its bar, or call on him to resign.'

Crowley's conclusion: WB Yeats and Florence Farr would be happy to run an organization on a false warrant (that is, without Secret Chief authority):

> Any strong lie will secure his allegiance and that of many others.
> Whereas it is obvious to Crowley [writing] that if Mathers is not
> 7°=4□ [an *Adeptus Exemptus*] then there is no Second Order and
> no Golden Dawn and no obligation and no nuffin.[13]

Crowley doubted whether the Secret Chiefs had a role for Mathers. Returning to Paris, he met two members of 'the Order' from Mexico visiting Mathers, probably legitimists. Crowley's *Confessions* assert a fancy to travel to Mexico: lots of mountains and volcanoes to climb; it sounds like a quip of James Bond's when told by 'M' he's 'going to Japan'.

> You forget, Moneypenny, I took a first in oriental languages
> when I was at Cambridge.[14]

SIX

I was born Fighter
1900–01

The western Atlantic, 4 July 1900

Crowley is at sea. Looking about the SS *Pennsylvania* with its four squat masts and stocky funnel, basking in the summer's warmth, he feels the inner chill of the exile. Across the Atlantic, the British reel from defeat at Kroonstadt, South Africa; the Boers have humiliated the greatest power on Earth. What might a greater power than the Boers achieve?

In Crowley's mind, higher intelligence was Britain's best hope. He took up his pen:

> O who will hear my chant, my cry; my
>   voice who hear,
> Even in this weary misery, this danker mere,
> Me, in mine exile, who am driven from
>   yonder mountains
> Blue-gray, and highland airs of heaven, and
>   moving fountains?
> Me, who shall hear me? Am I lost, a broken vessel,
> Caught in the storm of lies and tossed,
>   forbid to wrestle?
> Shall not the sun rise lively yet, the rose
>   yet bloom,
> The crown yet lift me, life beget flowers on
>   the tomb?

I was born fighter. Think you then my task
   is done,
My work, my Father's work for men, the
   rising sun?

This from 'The Exile', published in *Carmen Saeculare*, Crowley's 'Secular
Hymn' or 'Pagan Prophecy'.

O England! England, mighty England, falls!
  None shall lament her lamentable end!
The Voice of Justice thunders at her walls.
   She would not hear. She shall not comprehend!
The nations keep their mocking carnivals:
   She hath not left a friend!

She hath not left a friend... Was this inspired by Joseph Chamberlain? In
May 1898, the Colonial Secretary told his Birmingham constituency
that splendid isolation, 'envied by all and suspected by all' was no longer
an option for Britain. For suggesting a pact with the United States,
Chamberlain was denounced in Russia, derided in Germany, scorned by
his Conservative prime minister, Lord Salisbury, and praised by some
leading US journalists.

The poet could be harsher than the statesman: England's 'days of
wealth and majesty are done' thundered Crowley as the *Pennsylvania*
plied the waves to New York. Taking Chamberlain's vision a step further,
the poem's epilogue, 'To the American People on the Anniversary of
their Independence', called upon the USA to seize the flag of freedom:

Your stripes are the stripes of dishonour;
  Your stars are cast down from the sky;
While earth has this burden upon her,
  Your eagle unwilling to fly!
Loose, loose the wide wings! For your
  Honour!
  Let tyranny die!

Written two days before disembarkation, Crowley's outspoken address correctly predicted the fall of the British Empire, the rise of the American Eagle, the freedom of Ireland, the independence of India, and the transformation of England through a return to pagan principles of liberty:

> Only I see the century as a child [...]
> Stormy its birth; its youth, how fierce and
>   Wild!
>   Its end, how glorified!

Was *Carmen Saeculare* aimed at aligning himself to the spirit of the New World? Possibly, but it was also a brave declaration of Crowley's personal beliefs about freedom, a warning to all who suppressed the spirit of Man. Unnoticed by biographers, we see the first appearance of Crowley's famous Solar Age or 'Aeon of Horus', the 'Crowned and Conquering Child'; something the Crowley legend insists appeared only with a magical invocation of the Egyptian Sun god in Cairo four years later. Crowley had already hailed the lord of the new era:

> Hail! Hail to Thee, Lord of us, Horus!
>   All hail to the warrior name!
> Thy chariots shall drive them before us,
>   Thy sword sweep them forth as a flame.
> Rise! Move! And descend! I behold Thee,
>   Heaven cloven of fieriest bars,
> Armed Light; and they follow and fold Thee,
>   Thine armies of terrible stars.
>   The Powers of Mars!

The legend misses practically everything important about Aleister Crowley. Take the journey we are describing. The legend has two things to say about it. First, Crowley was on the lam, fleeing problems in London. Second, he headed to Mexico to climb that country's highest mountains with Oscar Eckenstein.

But there is a glaring lacuna.

Crowley arrived in Mexico City in July 1900; Eckenstein did not arrive until November, *over five months later*. What was Crowley up to?

*   *   *

Leaving New York in a sweltering heatwave, Crowley steamed south to Mexico City. Booking into the Hotel Iturbide, he contacted the British Consul and Vice-Consul and got himself known to several journalists – hardly the behaviour of a man on the run. Taking lodgings near Alameda Park he started working on invisibility. Allan Bennett's papers helped; Crowley claimed limited success. He saw his image fade in a mirror and walked through the city in exotic dress without gaining attention. Inspired by Bennett, Crowley began to explore raja ('royal') yoga; a path to union with pure being.

Crowley's take on events in his *Confessions* is peculiar. He turns up in Mexico City a stranger and – *hey presto!* – within weeks he is not only initiated into Scottish Rite Freemasonry by an old journalist calling himself Don Jesús de Medina-Sidonia, but founds a magical order, called the 'Lamp of the Invisible Light' with the same gentleman. Before departing Mexico, Crowley receives the 33rd degree, the highest rank of the Scottish Rite, celebrating the ideals of self-sacrificial service and of human freedom.

Crowley's *Confessions* asserts that LIL was established by a 'dispensation' granted by Mathers in Paris. If Mathers was thinking of a 'continuing Golden Dawn' – or Carlist cell – it was typical of Crowley to take the germ of an idea and do something with it under his own authority.

Mexican masonic lodges operated as political clubs. Was Crowley establishing a network around the 'sublimity' of his idea? LIL's centre-piece was the old Rosicrucian ideal of an ever-burning lamp, surrounded by talismanic images of the planets, elements and zodiac, all intended to focus spiritual energy. But in what sense was its light 'invisible'? The arrangement could be taken as a metaphor for a 'spy ring', for it is intelligence that is communicated from, and to, the centre. Crowley's notebook, 'Rough working notes for Temple of L.I.L in Mexico City', consists of general notes for rituals; 12 pages have been torn out.

Jumping into the lacuna, Professor Spence has outlined an hypothetical intelligence scenario.[1] In 1900, British interest in Mexico centred on *oil*, touted as the Navy's future fuel. Conflict with Germany or, possibly, Russia, was envisaged. Oil being scarce, concessions were sought in Mexico. According to Spence, Crowley's arrival coincided with that of Edward Doheny and his Pan-American Petroleum. Just after Crowley left, Weetman Pearson, later Lord Cowdry, arrived in Mexico with what transpired to be a successful British bid for oil concessions, backed by Mexico's dictator, Porfirio Díaz, a grand master of Scottish Rite Freemasonry. Had the ground been laid for Pearson? Was Crowley gathering intelligence to smooth the path?

Before Eckenstein arrived, Crowley travelled long distances alone, often sleeping rough. He visited Iguala and the seaport of Vera Cruz. He observed Mexican life closely. He saw extraordinary things – such as a card-cheat having his eyes gouged out by hand while other players continued the game, impassively – and he attempted to plumb the national psychology.

After Eckenstein's departure, Crowley journeyed to Toluca, Amecameca and, on 9 April 1901, returned from San Andrés to spend the night in the temple of LIL. That he 'assisted morning invocations' in the temple shows he was not alone in the enterprise. Why had he gone to San Andrés? Situated 250 miles southeast of Mexico City, in the state of Vera Cruz, on the Gulf of Mexico's coastal plain, San Andrés is to this day a base for onshore oil drilling. It was Mexico's President Porfirio Díaz who initiated Mexico's oil exploitation.

Crowley liked Díaz's Mexico: 'I found myself spiritually at home with Mexicans', he wrote.

> They despise industry and commerce. They had Díaz to do
> their political thinking for them and damned well he did it.
> Their hearts are set on bull fighting, cock fighting, gambling
> and lechery. Their spirit is brave and buoyant; it has not been
> poisoned by hypocrisy and the struggle for life.[2]

Díaz would be ousted by Villa, Zapata and Madero in 1911, the revolutionaries blaming Díaz for keeping oil wealth from the poor.

Had it been Crowley's intention to get close to Díaz through Don Jesús de Medina's Scottish Rite masonic group, he would have been disappointed. Methodist pastor and journalist Don Jesús had broken with Díaz around 1890 to set up a dissident Scottish Rite body. His *Rito Mexicano Reformando* opposed Díaz's domination of the Supreme Council of Mexico, 33rd Degree, recognized by the US Northern Jurisdiction of the Scottish Rite. Having formerly belonged to Díaz's Rite, the old Don Jesús would have been a fount of information on Díaz and his associates. A journalist with many contacts, Don Jesús may have been Crowley's 'fixer'. If oil was a factor, Don Jesús's opposition to the US-backed Supreme Council may also have been significant.

Could Carlist sympathies have provided the basis for co-operation?[3] The Don's moniker 'Medina-Sidonia' evoked 16th-century Spanish nobility dedicated to armed Catholic service. 'Sidonia' was probably a Carlist affectation; the Don's journal *El Boazeo*'s lead articles were attributed to Jesús Medina. Crowley's *Confessions* says he had 'an introduction' to the old man, though he does not say from whom. He was possibly a contact of Mathers' Mexican visitors, encountered by Crowley in Paris in April.

*　　*　　*

For an agent, there are two principal modes of disguise. First: to appear inconspicuous, effectively 'invisible'; Crowley attempted this art by magical means in Mexico City in 1900. Second: to be *highly* conspicuous; it may be an advantage to be everywhere seen as eccentric or even a buffoon. As Crowley wrote cogently of his invisibility exercises in Mexico City, the knack was to deflect the vision of the onlooker by some detail making the mind recoil from investigation. To this psychological trick could be added talismanic magick to affect the mind. There exists a form of self-absorption or self-hypnosis which, registering automatically in the onlooker's subconscious, repels the eye.

Crowley's ability to be in two minds at once was central to his philosophy of sceptical mysticism. He often did not appear to take himself seriously. Biographers have made the error of taking the pose for the reality, failing to see the distinction between the joke and the joker. In Mexico, Crowley actually practised, as a discipline, switching from one mind to another. He would hold a talisman to his heart and think of nothing but magick, then removing it, all thought of magick would be forbidden. Crowley worked hard to overcome resistance to certain company. He found he could, with effort, train his nervous system to accommodate new abilities and consciousness.

In spite of a personal distaste for 'Yanqui' attitudes – their materialism and sense of racial superiority toward Mexicans – Crowley made a beeline for Americans. Disliking gambling, he visited gambling houses, impressing Americans with his knack for exposing scams.

American ranchers in Guanajuato province who took him into their homes would have found an untypical Englishman, one who combined a gentlemanly demeanour with a he-man taste for rugged, outdoor life. Crowley was adept at analysing and playing to the prejudices and strengths of many national and psychological 'types'. His autobiography is studded with crystalline accounts of people he met on his travels. He could assume a 'mind-set' alien to his own with conviction – a useful tool for an intelligence agent.

Crowley was familiar with a devastating *arcanum* of kabbalistic speculation. The numerical values of the Hebrew words for 'messiah' (*messiach*) and 'serpent' (*nechesh*) are identical (358). Apparent opposites turn out to be one. Crowley's movements evince that precise *serpentine* quality, revealing and concealing him as a guardian of the knowledge of good and evil. He could shed his skin and be reborn. His favourite Gnostic image was that of the 'Lion-Serpent'; it was a self-portrait. Gnostics recognized the serpent as saviour, master of transformation.

Intelligence personnel have maintained that an attraction of their work lies in the licence to transcend ordinary morality. The agent may steal, seduce, pretend, mislead, or murder, in a higher, and *no less* morally respectable, interest. In 1951, Crowley's bewildered sometime friend Charles Cammell asked, 'Who will explain me the riddle of this man?' The riddle lies in Crowley's inner duality. Understanding Crowley as an intelligence agent also helps to explain Crowley the enigmatic magician, prophet, scientist and philosopher.

*   *   *

It is of course possible that Crowley stayed in Mexico so long because he liked it. But he could not have known this before going there, and the appointment with Eckenstein had been made in the New Year, during a Scottish skiing holiday. Crowley did like Mexico. Where London was viciously 'uptight', Mexico seemed a sparkling oasis of practical freedom, though the people were poor and 'simple'. Civilization looked more and more to Crowley like some awful curse by which barbarism to the spirit was sanctioned in favour of 'respectability'. He spoke bitterly of Britain's 'ever-abiding sense of sin and shame': 'The English poet must either make a successful exile or die of a broken heart.'

Crowley found romance in Mexico. He wove it into his verse play *Tannhäuser*,[4] a work containing more stimulating material than many a modern play. The last words are left to Isis, mother of Horus:

> Isis am I, and from my life are fed
> > All stars and suns, all moons that wax and
> > > wane,
> Create and uncreate, living and dead,
> > The Mystery of Pain.
> I am the Mother, I the silent Sea,
> > The Earth, its travail, its fertility.
> Life, death, love, hatred, light, darkness,
> > > Return to me –
> > To Me!

That striking phrase 'To Me!' will reappear on the lips of the Egyptian sky-goddess, Nuit, the overarching canopy of infinite stars, in *The Book of the Law* in April 1904.[5] Key elements of that revolutionary little book were already coalescing somewhere in Crowley's extraordinary mind.

Tannhäuser's inspiration was mixed. An intense romance with married US soprano Susan Strong,[6] whom he had met in Paris, made Crowley's heart sing. Having seen her perform as Venus in Wagner's *Tannhäuser* at Covent Garden in June 1899, he wrote a 'Venus' into his play.

A passionate liaison with a Mexican girl renewed Crowley's inspiration. They shared ecstatic evenings under the stars and, through her generous embrace, Aleister felt again the powers of the timeless goddess.

He found an hour for magick. In mid-November 1900, Crowley explored the 30th and 29th 'Aethyrs' of Sir Edward Kelley and Dr John Dee's 16th-century angel-summoning system. The 'Aethyrs' were spiritual mansions or angelic realms accessed in trances, induced by prayer. Special 'calls' summoned invisible guardians and powers of the universe into the vision of the operator, appearing to the inner eye in a 'shew-stone', a crystal or jewel. Crowley was working in the tradition of old Cambridge 'recruit' John Dee. He would return to the system in 1909, when he was more magically advanced. ·

*   *   *

Eckenstein arrived. To get into the swing, they ascended Iztaccihuatl around Christmas, camping at 14,000 feet. They then climbed La Cabeza and El Pecho, setting a world record by ascending 4,000 feet in 1½ hours at very high altitude; Crowley and Eckenstein were world-beaters.

When news arrived of Queen Victoria's death (22 January 1901), Mexicans anticipating a lava-lake of grief were astonished to see Crowley spring up in rapture and dance for joy. Ecstatic, he looked to a new era. England might yet see the light, abandon its chubby imperialism and lead the world to true freedom.

*   *   *

A red Moroccan notebook survives with entries made in Mexico between January and April 1901. A note on the cover says: 'Feb 2. My 2½ years work crowned with success.' This takes us back to his meeting Julian Baker. The diary describes completing and bringing 'to perfection the Work of L.I.L.'. He also writes of Eckenstein upbraiding him for weak powers of concentration. Shamed, he began intense concentration exercises: 'I did meditate twice daily, three meditations morning and evening upon such simple objects as a white triangle, a red cross: Isis: the simple tatwas [Golden Dawn images used to enter the 'astral plane']: a wand: and the like.' Though hard, the exercises bore fruit when he moved into deep study of raja yoga and of Buddhist meditation.

Crowley renewed his Adeptus Minor obligation oath to the Secret Chiefs: that his heart might be 'the Centre of the Light'. Opposite the oath is a drawing of a distant volcano with the note, 'Colima from the camp'. Crowley and Eckenstein climbed the volcano, Nevado de Colima, then moved on to make short work of a volcano near Toluca, 40 miles out of Mexico City. Popocatépetl came next.

On 29 March Crowley concentrated on a 'tatwa' image of a circle within a triangle for 18 minutes with only 7 'breaks' in concentration. Unimpressed? Try it. He strained to imagine the sound of a waterfall: 'Very difficult to get at all: makes one's ears sing for long afterwards. If I got it really, it was not strong enough to shut out other physical sounds.'

Flush with the sense of roaring success, Crowley and Eckenstein made momentous plans for their next adventure, the Big One: *Chogo Ri*, known to English surveyors as Karakoram (or '*K*') 2, the second highest mountain in the world. Crowley would put up £500 to be placed in Eckenstein's care and the expedition would not interfere with native beliefs.

Crowley's mind moved towards the Far East – to Allan, and *Soror Fidelis*. A year had passed since their brief coup on the Hammersmith 'Vault'. Having married a diplomat in London named Witkowski, Elaine had moved to Hong Kong. On 15 April, Crowley planned to project his astral body to her, a feat undertaken with partial success the following month when he found 'Fidelis in room of white and pale green. She was dressed in white soft stuff velvet lapels. We conversed a while.' He tried to lift a vase 'from shelf to table' with questionable success: 'I said '*Vale, Soror!*' aloud and I think audibly. Remained some time.'

*   *   *

Eckenstein left Mexico for London on 20 April. Crowley, travelled northwest, via Texas, New Mexico and California: the US oil belt. He headed for San Francisco, doggedly sticking to Eckenstein's regimen, resolving 'to increase my powers very greatly by the Aid of the Most High, until I can do 24 hours [concentration] on one object'.

Crowley disliked pre-earthquake Frisco, complaining of the 'frenzied money-making' and 'frenzied pleasure-seeking'. His happiest moments came in Chinatown at night. He burnt a joss stick in a Chinese temple and had his fortune read by 'Wong Gong'. Crowley perceived a 'spiritual superiority' in the Chinese 'to the Anglo-Saxon' and felt a 'deep-seated affinity to their point of view'.

> The Chinaman is not obsessed by the delusion that the profits and pleasures of life are really valuable. A man must really be a very dull brute if, attaining all his ambition, he finds satisfaction. The Eastern, from Lao Tsu and the Buddha to Zoroaster and Ecclesiastes, feels in his very bones the futility of earthly existence. It is the first postulate of his philosophy. [7]

Crowley began *Orpheus – A Lyrical Legend*, projected as a *tour de force* of complex rhyme to encapsulate his developing thought on Buddhism and ceremonial magick. Overly ambitious, *Orpheus* proved unwieldy.

The poet boarded the *Nippon Maru* bound for Honolulu on 3 May 1901. Ensconced in the Hawaiian Hotel Annex on Waikiki Beach a week later, he set up a shrine. Bathing twice, he was seized by 'an art current' and had another stab at *Orpheus*.[8] Suddenly, there appeared Mrs Alice Mary Rogers (*née* Beaton) and son Blaine. Crowley and Mary fell in love and then to bed. A purer love then gripped them, all the way to Yokohama. Partly sincerely, often hilariously, the affair is celebrated in Crowley's melodramatically entitled *Alice: An Adultery*, published in 1903.

It was a delightful May. When not mooning and spooning with Alice, Crowley combined raja yoga with astral projection, as taught by Bennett. He researched the meaning of the Adeptus Minor grade. He speculated on how to 'loosen the girders of the soul', to open paths of creative inspiration. He wondered whether a drug was more effective than ceremonial magick, asking, *what drug would work?* Recalling a cocaine addict's corpse in San Francisco, he shuddered at the thought.

On 22 May he declared his love to Mary. They lay about, kissing: 'There is much doubt in my mind as to exact quality of my love for Alice – it seems not entirely sexual; I am very content only looking at her.' The next day, he complained the *affaire* seemed 'designed by the devil to take up maximum of time and virility. Tonight a fearful combat 4 solid hours jaw passionate. Entreaties, threats, everything, tried every mood. Questions of son etc. I won of course but it was hard. Am probably wasting my tissue – she would come on if I held off. "Never mind" says Asmodee [the demon] (whom God subdue!)'

He noted four days later: '*Affaire* continues better and better. Tonight I went in her room for an hour. She was nearly naked and I got my hand very like Homocea – good for mosquito-bites![9] Made the Epigram of my life "Virtue is the devil's name for vice!" But how I love Alice!' He told her that 'women always pretended to dislike f[uckin]g but despised and hated a man who spared them. Thus made peace.'

Alice and Aleister landed at Yokohama on 16 June. Between 3.30 and 4.15 in the afternoon, he 'fucked Alice with her (passive) consent'. Alice started crying. His heart, he wrote, was sad and sore but his 'thoughts turned to the Above'.

Three days later Crowley left Yokohama's Maples Hotel and journeyed to the holy places of Kamakura: 'Went to Daibutsu and took my refuge in the Buddha, the Dharma and the Sangha': that is, the Enlightened One, the Law, and the Brotherhood. He decided that his 'respect and lust' for Alice had disappeared: 'She is mentally nothing. But my love remains – beautiful fragments of a Portland Vase.' He was troubled, torn between the Above and Below.

Back at the hotel, he asked himself: 'Shall I go to Kamakura and live as an holy hermit?' His head ached. Was he eating too much? He didn't want Alice to go. He read Draper's *Conflict Between Religion and Science*, concluding it was 'a dishonest book. After demolishing Christianity frankly enough he excludes Protestantism from his strictures on no grounds whatsoever'. Crowley thought of retiring to Kamakura again, but worried that Allan might want him, or Oscar Eckenstein need him for the K2 expedition.

On 26 June he took Alice to Tokyo. They visited the theatre and the imperial palace, passing the evening at a tea house. The tension was unbearable; parting was imminent. Back in Yokohama, he packed and took his shrine down. Four days later, Alice sailed away forever: 'Finished with that foolishness,' he wrote, '38 days from when we kissed all wasted – or all *rest*.'

Editing *Orpheus*'s journey into Hades on his typewriter, he put it aside to write 'White Poppy', before turning his attention to his verse account of his affair, *Alice: An Adultery*: 'What A fucking long time it was!' He then made love to a Japanese girl, toting up No.34 in his tally of the women of the world he had known, and wrote to his friend, budding painter and poet, Gerald Kelly:

> You are a good boy and I am a good boy and I am right and you are right and everything is quite correct, […] Japan is a fraud of the basest sort. […] *To change the key.* This is strictest of all possible confidence. I have had the greatest love-affair of my long and arduous career (arduous is good). Her name was *Mary Beaton*. Think of it! Absolutely the most beautiful woman I have ever seen, of the imperial type, yet as sweet and womanly as I ever knew. Moreover, a lady to her finger-tips. I call her Alice in the poems you will read about her, as she preferred that name. She was travelling for her health in Hawaii where we met. We loved and loved chastely (She has a hub – and kids – one boy with her). I made her come here with me. On the boat we fell to fucking, of course, but – here's the miracle! – we won through and fought our way back to chastity and far deeper truer love. Now she's gone and forgotten but her sweet and pure influence has saved my soul (Heb[rew] *Nephesch*) I lust no more – What, never? Well – hardly ever! What do *I* care? For his bloody whores? Does GFK [Gerald Festus Kelly] ask? Listen, my buck. The affair was 50 days from start to finish. It is written in 50 sonnets; a fake introduction like W.S [*White Stains*] but better with a false criticism. I know all the obvious things you will say.

But the tout ensemble is going to be great. I can't explain at
length. I will send you a copy when typed.

[...] I wish you'd buck up with occultism so that I didn't have
to talk with all this damned reticence. I have done none myself
lately – there's been love and poetry going on. Also my ideas are
changing and fermenting. You will not recognise my mind when
I get back.[10]

Toying again with the idea of going to Kamakura and becoming a
Buddhist monk, Crowley opted for seeing Allan Bennett in Ceylon
instead; it was Bennett who would become a monk – and Crowley would
see the image of God.

SEVEN

Son of Man

1901–03

Crowley wanted to see Fidelis in the flesh, but arriving in Hong Kong, he found Mrs Witkowski pregnant. He steamed on to Ceylon via Singapore and Penang, finding Allan in Colombo on 6 August, tutoring the son of Shiva-worshipping guru, Shri Parananda. Better known to Ceylon's British administration as the Hon. P Ramanathan, Solicitor General, the guru wrote an interesting commentary on the Gospel of John. Where Jesus said: 'I and my Father are one', Parananda understood it to mean: 'I am in *samadhi*', the highest trance-range of raja yoga; obliteration of the ego in divine union. This was meat for Crowley's nascent plans to fuse the esoteric spiritual traditions of East and West.

He quickly entered Allan's mood of mind, signing off a letter to Gerald Kelly:

> P.S. I have chucked all nonsense, except a faint lingering illusion
> that anything exists. This (with my breathing practice) should
> go soon.

From 'Marlborough', a rented bungalow in the hills above Kandy, he wrote again to Kelly:

> I am the most miserable of mankind. Allan McG. [regor=Bennett]
> doesn't like *Tannhaüser* says it isn't as good as *The soul of Osiris* –
> says it's obscure in the beginning, too long and lacks a motive.
> What in h-[el]l does he mean by motive? He explains it as 'the
> literary transmigration of a moral'. This means 'As a moral is to

a fable, so is a motive to a work of this sort'. I answer – It is the history of a soul therefore my soul – therefore every soul – therefore no soul. He answers 'Rats'.

[…] Address is A.C. 34 Victoria Drive Kandy Ceylon. What a fool I was not to come home instead of this maniac jaunt. 'Excuse me, sir, I think I'm going mad.' You shall have more Argo[nauts] and Orph[eus] &c. soon. Write and tell me exactly what you think of all you have got, and do it for all what you did for poor T[annhaüser]. Does my work *advance*? Do be good and tell me all about it. Bye-Bye. Ever A.C.

Back in London, Crowley's *The Soul of Osiris* reached the desk, and wit, of GK Chesterton, writer of religious conviction and common sense. But was he the man to appreciate Crowley's depth and eccentricity? *The Daily News* carried Chesterton's assessment on 18 June 1901. It reached its subject's eager eyes in distant Kandy. Crowley wrote excitedly to Kelly:

> Did you see the *Daily News*? And the others? I am on ten pinnacles of fame all at once. And K.P. [Kegan Paul publishers] go out of their way to tell me that *Tannhäuser* (I have the proofs here now) is miles ahead of any of my other work. And we know Orphy [*Orpheus*] will be better still![1]

Chesterton, encouraging, was also critical:

> To the side of a mind concerned with idle merriment there is certainly something a little funny in Mr Crowley's passionate devotion to deities who bear such names as Mout and Nuit, and Ra and Shu, and Hormakhou. They do not seem to the English mind to lend themselves to pious exhilaration.

Chesterton's attack on Theosophical Society founder Madame Blavatsky brought Crowley to her defence in *The Sword of Song (called by Christians the Book of the Beast)*.[2] While theosophists tended to swallow Eastern philosophy uncritically in the rush to create know-all systems, Crowley nonetheless insisted Blavatsky's value 'was to remind the

Hindus of the excellence of their own shastras (Sacred Books), to show that some Westerns held identical ideas, and thus to countermine the dishonest representations of the missionaries. I am sufficiently well known as a bitter opponent of "Theosophy" to risk nothing in making these remarks.' Crowley concluded with a stinger: 'Mr Chesterton thinks it funny that I should call upon "Shu". Has he forgotten that the Christian God may be most suitably invoked by the name "Yah"?'

Crowley strove for a system combining Eastern and Western spiritual traditions in a fresh synthesis, without obfuscation or mythical baggage. Ambition was not confined to himself; he offered Kelly sage advice:

> You should be starving in the *Quartier Latin* not getting fat with
> what Allan would call a 'camel-kneed prayer-monger' in some
> unknown part of France. A slut for your mistress, a gamine for
> your model: a procuress for your landlady and a whore for your
> spiritual guide. That is the only way to become a great artist.[3]

As for himself, he aimed to find 'a spiritual solution to the material muddle'. Striving to scale the heights of raja yoga and Mahayana Buddhism, he found sustained trance gave him spiritual power. He linked his practices to magick, to strengthen the will, to clarify objectives, to dissolve complexes that interrupted or perverted the will. He found he could lose awareness of the body altogether, a useful skill for magician, explorer, or secret agent.

On 2 October 1901: a breakthrough. Withdrawing his consciousness from the hills about him and centring it on the 'Cakkra Ajna[sic]' (the pineal gland chakra) – with *pranayama* (breathing discipline) 'at intervals' – Crowley repeated his mantra *Aum Tat Sat Aum* hour after hour.

> The discipline as before. About 5P.M. again, by the Grace
> Ineffable of Bhavani to the meanest of the devotees, arose the
> Splendour of the Inner Sun. As bidden by my Guru, Isolated the
> Dawn with Pranava. This, as I foresaw, returned the Dhyanic
> Consciousness. The Disk grew golden: rose clear of all its clouds,
> flinging great fleecy cumuli of rose and gold, fiery with light into
> the midmost aether of the subtle space. Hollow it seemed and

rayless as the sun in ♐ [Sagittarius] yet incomparably brighter: but rising clear of cloud; It began to revolve, to coruscate, to throw off streamers of jetted fire! This from a hill-top I beheld, dark, as of a dying world. Covered with black decayed wet peaty wood, a few dead pines stood stricken and unutterably alone. But behind the glory of its coruscations seemed to shape, an idea, less solid than a shadow! An idea of some vast Human-seeming Form! Now grew doubt and thought in Aleister's miserable mind and the One Wave grew many waves and all was lost. Alas! alas! for Aleister! And Glory unto Her. She the Twin-Breasted that hath encroached even [?] the other half of the Destroyer! ॐ [AUM] Namo Bhavaniya ॐ [AUM]⁴

Crowley's vision of 'some vast Human-seeming form' announces a critical moment.

About the time Siddhartha Gautama Buddha was born (c 560BCE), the prophet Ezekiel, exiled in Babylon, enjoyed a vision of God's throne with 'the appearance of a man above upon it'.⁵ This vision has been called the 'stock-vision' of the Gnostic: the vision of the *divine Man*, the image of God. Having seen it, Ezekiel was addressed as '*son of man*': one who had seen the Divine Glory. Now Aleister Crowley had seen it, through the trance of *dhyana*. Satisfied, he would wait two years before resuming magical and mystical practices.

* * *

Crowley and Bennett explored Sri Lanka's sacred sites. Holding all nature holy, Allan was shocked when Crowley followed a visit to the Dambulla rock caves with big game shooting. Crowley accepted Bennett's principle, but also accepted that Nature eats herself for breakfast every day; death is life's door.

Bennett secured a job at a Rangoon girls' college; Crowley explored south India, entering the secret confines of the Meenakshi temple, Madurai, in a loincloth to see the sacred Shivalingam. Shiva, equivalent to the Egyptian Sun god Seth, was both creator and destroyer. This duality-in-tension is central to understanding Crowley's philosophy of life-acceptance. He would become disenchanted with Buddhism's fundamental denial of the facts of life as facts. The lingam, the divine penis, would come to be a personal symbol, Crowley's trademark signature. In gratitude, he sacrificed a goat to goddess Bhavani. Inspired, he wrote 'Ascension Day' and 'Pentecost', witty, profound poems full of Hindu and Buddhist lore, included in *The Sword of Song*. Other fascinating poems from his wanderings appeared in *Oracles* in 1905: soundtracks to an unmade film on 'Crowley's India'.

At Calcutta he befriended local architect, Edward Thornton. He learned some Hindustani and began a prescient essay, 'Science and Buddhism'. However, the more he saw of Buddhism in practice, the less he liked it. Still tilting with Gautama in 1920, he coined the jibe, 'Buddha the hypochondriac', adding that: 'The Universal Sorrow was cured when he went out for a drink with the Universal Joke.'

Allan, meanwhile, quit the Burmese girls' school for his heart's desire; the annihilation of desire. Crowley headed for the jungles to find him. Sailing from Calcutta to Rangoon with Thornton, they entered Burma's Buddhist heartland – gaunt men in pale flannels. A bearded Crowley contracted a fever; he had sunstroke. Feeling rough, he engaged a Madrassee boy called Peter at 1.8 rupees a day 'and warm clothes'. The trio took the train to Prome and sailed up the Irrawaddy towards the treacherous Arakan Hills. Disembarking, native porters baulked at the Arakans. There was no alternative; canoe it back to Kama down the Mindon Chong.

The hours perspired with poetry and pot shots: pigeon, parrot, 'the big white paddy-bird', red-crested woodpecker, Brahmin duck, stork and deer. Thornton shot a leopard. The temperature hovered around 102° F. Sweat fell onto the pages of Walter Pater and Henrik Ibsen. They rowed into humid Kama on 7 February and took a steamboat to Prome. A train chuffed them back to Rangoon; Thornton went to Mandalay and Peter was paid off.

Alone but unbeaten, a feverish Crowley took the coastal steamer *Comilla* to Sittwe, a 400-mile journey north from Rangoon, then headed southeast again. On 14 February 1902, at the monastery of Lamma

Sayadaw Kyoung, he met revered Bhikku Ananda Metteyya ('bliss of loving kindness'), formerly known as Allan Bennett. Still asthmatic, Bennett received food offerings from people inspired by his holiness and frailty; Crowley referred to them as 'fools', 'incessantly' interrupting their conversation. Crowley wrote the masterful 'Sabbé Pi Dukkham (Everything is Sorrow) – A Lesson from Euripides'. He also wrote *Ahab – And other Poems*. There was tender love poetry, including an introductory 'Rondel', begun at the Prome Pagoda, from which these magical lines are taken:

> By palm and pagoda enchaunted o'er
>   Shadowed, I lie in the light
>   Of stars that are bright beyond suns that
>   All poets have vaunted
> In the deep-breathing amorous bosom of
>   Forests of amazon might
>   By palm and pagoda enchaunted.

He began recording his dreams. In one he had a flash, realizing Gerald Kelly was a 'Social Performer', not a genuine seeker after Truth.

He sailed on the SS *Kapurthala* via Chittagong to Calcutta on 22 February. A letter from Eckenstein awaited him: *K2* was on.

Delhi station, 23 March 1902

K (Karakoram) 2, sometimes called *Chogo Ri*, at 28,250 feet is said to be as tough as Everest. Was the team up to it? Crowley was unconvinced: Heinrich Pfannl, Austrian judge; Victor Wessely, Austrian barrister; Dr Jacot Guillarmod, Swiss Alpinist; Guy John Senton Knowles, amiable 22-year-old engineering graduate of Trinity, Cambridge.

They took the train to Srinagar in Kashmir. India's Viceroy, Lord Curzon, had Eckenstein arrested. Was there an intelligence angle to this?[6]

K2 stood between Kashmir and Chinese Sinkiang. To the west lay Afghanistan and the Russian Empire, to the east, the Tibetan plateau. North of Srinagar, the Plains of Deosai in Baltistan skirted the strategically significant Karakoram Pass. Intelligence assessed in Rawalpindi indicated Russian agents in Tibet, tolerated by the Dalai Lama. Fancying Tibet as a client state, the Russians used the passes about K2; too close to the British Empire for British comfort. A reconnaissance exercise would have strategic value, to check the Godwin-Austen survey maps of 1861, to establish military supply-routes. Crowley's *Confessions* criticized the accuracy of the Godwin-Austen mapping. He says he made his own adjustments. Heightening tension would lead to a British invasion and the deaths of 400 Tibetan soldiers outside Lhasa in 1904.

Spence has suggested Curzon may have suspected Eckenstein of having recruited German-backed agents. If that was the game, Crowley had time to assess loyalties before Eckenstein's arrival in Srinagar on 22 April. However, Curzon's barring of Eckenstein from Kashmir probably stemmed from a personality conflict that had erupted after Eckenstein joined Martin Conway's expedition to the Baltoro Muztagh in 1892. Falling out with Conway, Eckenstein quit the expedition. In 1902 Sir Martin Conway – he had been knighted in 1895 for mapping the Karakorams – became President of the Alpine Club. The club sought to regulate mountaineering. Seeing himself as the master of Karakoram exploration, Conway despised straight-talking Eckenstein, whose outspokenness alienated influential Alpine Club members. The intrepid, equally outspoken Crowley supported Eckenstein, speculating that antisemitism, as well as jealousy, contributed to Eckenstein's problems. Conway may have given Lord Curzon 'grounds' for suspicion: while Eckenstein's mother was English, his father was German, Jewish, and a socialist.

*   *   *

As the crow flies, it is 150 miles north from Srinagar to the Baltoro Glacier. Crowley made light of the physical side: 'any fool can do it if they want to' was his attitude to this, as to so much else. He had, to a great extent, mastered his body; he hated admitting weakness, whose usual concomitant was, in his observation, boasting about the hardships of a climb, overstating the perils of the sport. Crowley would rather *underestimate* problems. He correctly believed the state of a person's body was reflected in the state of mind. This is why his law of Thelema is for the 'strong', for those who know themselves, inside and out. People weak in themselves try to restrict others; observe politicians and the 'health and safety' brigade at 'work'. Modern man lives in fear.

The mule train crossed the Indus River at Skardu on 14 May.

Built on flats encased on three sides by sharp jaws of massive, ruddy-brown mountains, Skardu's great serrations belittled everything human. At the far end of the town, the Indus crashed and roared its way over rapids towards the south. Grabbing a spare moment, Crowley opened his letter-pad:

> *Skardu, Baltistan.*
>
> Dear Gerald,
>
> Here I am at the limits of the G.P.O. [postal services]. I have
> heard nothing from you for years. In about three months I shall
> be back. Remember our compact to be in Rome or Paris for next
> winter! Book III of *Orphy* is finished. No time here for anything
> – hardly to sleep. Be sure and let me know exactly where in
> Europe to find you. I shall come to you pretty straight – without
> you I can do nothing more to anything.
>
> Yours in haste, A.C.[7]

A photograph survives of Crowley on a pack pony on the Plains of Deosai (*see* Plate section) gaunt, bearded, wearing local headgear, calm under his Mexican poncho, resigned to biting cold winds and fierce sun-glare as his slender gaitered legs cling to a tiny pony's flanks. He looks every inch the 'Wanderer of the Waste'.

Staggering at the awesome Baltoro Glacier on 9 June, Crowley's spiritual nature asserted itself. While everyone experiences overwhelming feelings in the face of Nature's relentless might, Crowley welcomed the feeling. Humility induced by scale 'reduced the relevance of the physical basis'; the result: a feeling of oneness with the universe.

A week later, the expedition was on the Godwin-Austen Glacier at the base of K2, climbing in stages to establish Camp X at 18,733 feet before a blizzard stopped progress until 27 June. A small climbing window was blocked by heavy snow between 2 and 6 July.

Crowley reached an altitude of about 22,000 feet: a feat not bettered on K2 until 1939; his altitude record would stand for seven years.

He had malaria.

In *Oracles – The Autobiography of an Art*, published in 1905, a charming, light-hearted poem called 'The Earl's Quest', tells a tale of madness, courage and folly around a magical quest for love and the sacred mountain of the Rosicrucians. A note informs us that it was written at *Camp Despair* on Chogo Ri at 20,000 feet. Here was another world record; the highest point at which poetry had ever been composed, and by a malaria sufferer to boot!

In mid July, the weather cleared for two days, ample time, thought Crowley, to rush the summit. Instead, Guillarmod demanded he join him to tend to Pfannl below Camp XII at 21,000 feet. Pfannl was suffering from a pulmonary oedema. Crowley was not amused.

Between 21 July and 4 August, the climbers descended to Camp XI. Crowley was disgusted at the sight of Guillarmod returning from Pfannl, having left a native porter in a crevasse. Crowley and Eckenstein descended to rescue the porter.

By 14 August, they had all made it back to Camp I. Crowley had spent 68 days on K2, another record, for time spent at high altitude. The expedition, the first serious, and very brave, attempt on a mountain that would not be climbed until 1954, deserves respect for its achievement, but, as so often in Crowley's life, things did not go that way. He would be offended by Guillarmod's distorted account of the climb.[8]

*   *   *

On 30 September 1902, Crowley boarded the SS *Egypt* at Bombay, bound for Suez. Bored by Cairo's western quarter, he wallowed in the fleshpots, writing from Shepheard's Hotel, to Gerald Kelly on 25 October:

Dear Gerald,

I hope you have my earlier Works with you in Paris. [...] I expect
to see any amount of good work [painting] when I arrive. You
must fulfil your ancient promise to paint me. I fancy you will
find me a good deal changed, even in looks! And I expect ditto
of you. We must have a great dinner to celebrate my return. I
shall perhaps write SRMD [Samuel Mathers] and Vestigia [Mina
Mathers]. I suppose you see them occasionally. [...] How I look
forward to civilisation! The Opera! The Louvre! The everlasting
nonchalant charm of the Boulevards! Art! And the subtlety of
festal Festus! Here everyone says 'cunt' right out loud and calls a
spade a bloody shovel. How I hate it! Cairo is a filthy low place
with no beauty at all, unless you go to the Nile. [...] Fly, loathèd
days, until I can get to you.

Yours ever,

Aleister Crowley[9]

After two and a half years' absence, Crowley entered Paris in early
November, a changed man; dark, lean, muscular with a powerfully
charged intellect and a lot to get off his chest. Kelly's high artistic circle
was sympathetic: Monet, Degas, Rodin, Maillol and a Jewish writer
much liked by Crowley, Marcel Schwob, accommodated Crowley with
ease; he was an artist.

In February 1903, the artist was in Nice, frivolous and frustrated, as
revealed in a letter to Kelly:

I am beginning to doubt whether Nice is dull after all. Today I
began very badly: playing billiards in despair, I cut the cloth –
first time in my life! [he had dreamed of doing this on his
travels] I sneaked away unperceived, luckily, went to the [hotel's]
reading-room, and tore a newspaper. In disgust, I went out, met
a charming girl and had a real good old-fashioned face fuck in
the grounds. I returned to tea; fearful of the fatal third tearing, I
ripped up the tablecloth with my penknife, and made a

successful evening of it by preaching the Good Law to
Humphreys, winning 5fr[ancs] at the Little Horses, meeting the
girl I'd been hunting ever since the Masked Ball; meeting a third
girl and getting another v.g.o-f.f.f.[10]

Back in Paris, he haunted Le Chat Blanc in the Rue d'Odessa, with a
circle that put aspiring artists through their paces in an upstairs room
functioning as an exclusive club. Writer Arnold Bennett met Crowley
there, impressed by the magician's magisterial air, poetry and huge
rings.[11] *Ingénue* writer William Somerset Maugham took Crowley's
posing for real and wondered whether the poet's vaunted magical
abilities were genuine, concluding that Crowley was 'a fake, but not
entirely a fake', a remark showing that Maugham but dimly espied the
man behind the image, or the mage behind the man. Maugham twisted
that image about his able literary fingers and turned Crowley into
sorcerer 'Oliver Haddo' in *The Magician*. Haddo uses willpower to
waylay virgin innocence into black alchemical clutches. A tinge of
jealousy? Maugham's first successful novel presents an early vision of 'the
demon Crowley' that would deceive many. Crowley took the nastiness
gracefully, opining that Haddo's dialogue revealed qualities of which he
was most proud, but the book was nonetheless a shameless lift of his
own witty remarks, blended with plagiarized literature. The only *original*
thing in it, then, was *Aleister Crowley*.

That spring, he published *Summa Spes*, a product of, as he put it in
the *Confessions*, 'a certain detached disenchantment'. *Summa Spes* means
'Summit Hope' or the 'Sum of Hope' and this ironic double-meaning
may be compared to his poem written on the Baltoro Glacier at 'Camp
Despair'.[12] *Summa Spes* brilliantly combines the Buddhist estimation of
human futility with Crowley's unrepentant stance on sensual pleasure,
well catered for in Paris:

> Existence being sorrow,
> The cause of it desire,
> A merry tune I borrow
> To light upon the lyre:

If death destroy me quite,
Then, I can not lament it;
I've lived, kept life alight,
And – damned if I repent it!
Chorus:
Let me die in a ditch,
Damnably drunk,
Or lipping a punk,
Or in bed with a bitch!
I was ever a hog;
Dung? I am one with it!
Let me die like a dog;
Die, and be done with it!

He quit Paris and hit London, the first time in nearly three years.

*　　*　　*

A playbill survives in the Warburg Institute, advertising a production of Henrik Ibsen's *The Vikings*. Crowley had read Ibsen while canoeing down the Mindon Chong. Gordon Craig staged *The Vikings* at the Imperial Theatre with his mother Ellen Terry as Hiordis and Oscar Ashe as Sigurd between 13 April and 14 May 1903. *The Times* reviewed it on 16 April.[13] Crowley made his own review of the supporting cast, inscribing his findings on the playbill:

Miss Wheeler – sucks you off to beat the band

Miss Clare – Fucks *well*: Smells rather of fish, though.

Wonderful crimson cunt. Terrific spasms.

In the summer, Crowley was assailed by nihilistic abjection. He had been through so much and suddenly it all seemed to matter so little. A period of his life was coming to an end. He confided a 'Preparatory' note to his diary, beginning 9 June 1903:

In the year 1899 I came to Boleskine House, and put everything in order with the object of carrying out the Operation of Abramelin the Mage.

I had studied Ceremonial Magic for years, and obtained very remarkable success.

My Gods were those of Egypt, interpreted on lines closely akin to those of Greece.

In Philosophy I was a Realist of the Qabalistic School.

In 1900 I left England for Mexico, and later the Far East, Ceylon, India, Baltistan, Egypt and France. Idle here to detail the corresponding progress of my thought. Passing through a stage of Hinduism, I had discarded all Deities as unimportant and in Philosophy was an uncompromising nominalist [words are only words and do not necessarily denote realities]. I may call myself an orthodox Buddhist.

With the reservations:

(i). I cannot deny that certain phenomena do accompany the use of certain rituals. I only deny the usefulness of such methods to the White Adept.

(ii). Hindu methods of meditation are possibly useful to the beginner and should not therefore be discarded at once (necessarily).

[…] [I] appear in the character of an Inquirer on strictly scientific lines.

This is unhappily calculated to damp enthusiasm: but as I so carefully of old, for the magical path, excluded all from my life all other interests, that life has now no particular meaning, and the Path of Research, on the only lines I can now approve of, remains the one Path possible for me to tread.[14]

Crowley's emphasis on the 'Path of Research' should not be under-estimated. His approach was scientific. Magick should be studied and practised with scientific rigour; its data significant for human progress. He was aware that the greatest scientific minds were moving away from the naïve materialism of the 19th century; matter was not as 'solid' as it appeared to be. Crowley did not call in science merely as a 'witness' to justify magical beliefs and practices; magical beliefs must be submitted to methodological discipline.

Crowley enjoyed the company of the Earl of Denbigh's brother, the Hon. Everard Feilding, secretary of the Society for Psychical Research (1903–20). Established in 1882, co-founder Henry Sedgwick, a Trinity Fellow, had run the Society from his college rooms. Crowley's college was on the forefront of the scientific investigation of religious experience, so his combination of scientific emphasis and practical experimentation was timely.[15] Crowley was, and is, a pioneer in the field of consciousness research.[16] On 22 February 1904, while in Egypt, Crowley reflected on a meeting he had enjoyed with Dr Henry Maudsley, founder of the psychiatric hospital that bears his name.[17] Were magical experiences merely neurological events? Was it 'all in the brain'? If events could be stimulated by drugs, was it all 'chemistry'? Crowley asked Maudsley if he thought yogic experiences represented alterations of brain chemistry, possibly hazardous. Could results be achieved with chemical stimulants, without the exhausting physical disciplines?

> Dr Maudsley, the greatest of living authorities on the brain, explained to me the physiological aspect of dhyana (unity of subject and object) as extreme activity of one part of the brain; extreme lassitude of the rest. He refused to localize the part. Indulgence in the practice he regards as dangerous, but declined to call the single experience pathological. This is perhaps to be regarded as a complete victory for me; since I would always admit so much. No doubt the over-fatigue is indicated as the danger; but has not Eckenstein – who again shines! – too often urged this very danger? After fatigue, said he, rest altogether for 24 hours. Well! And I doubt not that follies of so many enthusiasts, the terrible warnings of Blavatsky and others, are explained (the one) and justified (the other) by this

circumstance. Let me therefore warily proceed! (not merely –
proceed warily!).[18]

Crowley tried to regain ground in raja yoga, but his ability to concentrate
without 'breaks' was broken. Gerald Kelly distracted him with an
invitation to join mother Blanche, sister Rose, and a middle-aged
solicitor called Hill at Strathpeffer Spa.

Hill was enamoured of Rose. *Everyone*, it seemed, was enamoured of
Rose![19] Rose confided her love problems to Crowley. A widow of 29,
Rose was engaged to an American called Howell, a Cambridge acquain-
tance of Gerald's. Blanche approved, but Rose wanted an affair with one
Frank Summers. She had already lied to her mother to obtain £40 she
said was for an abortion.

Costly to keep, the merry widow Rose Skerrett was also a flirt,
beautiful, sexy and kindly. Crowley maintained she was highly intelligent
and an empty-headed woman of society; just his type. In his madness, he
proposed he marry her at once to rid her of Howell and Hill. Rose could
then run off with Summers. 'All I had to do was emancipate her,' Crowley
assured himself.

On 12 August, 'having been engaged for 19 hours', Rose and Aleister
were civilly married at Dingwall. Suddenly, they were crazy about each
other. Astonished, Crowley wrote to his new brother-in-law on the
wedding day, pleading for understanding:

> I have been trying since I joined the G∴D∴ [Golden Dawn] in
> '98 steadily and well to repress my nature in all ways. I have
> suffered much, but I have won, and you know it. [...] Did your
> sister [Rose] want to hear the true history of my past life, she
> should have it in detail; not from prejudiced persons, but the
> cold, drear stuff of lawyers. And English does not *always* fail me.
> If your worst wish came true, and we never met again, my
> remembrances of you, with or without a beard would, as you say,
> be good enough to go on. But I am ambitious. I hope one day to
> convince you that I am not only a clever (the 4[tos] have 'mentally
> deformed') man but a decent one and a good one. Why must

9/10ths of my life ie: the march to Buddhism, go for nothing; the atrophied 1/1,000,000[12] always spring up and choke me, and that in the house of my friends?

[...] All luck, and the greatest place in the new generation of artists be yours. So sayeth Aleister Crowley, always your friend whatever you may do or say. *Vale!* Till your *Ave!*[20]

The long existential abjection vanished. Love had secured what it took days of meditation to achieve: conflict between his ears ceased; not a ripple disturbed the beatified lake of his soul.

Mr and Mrs Crowley were in love – hook, line and sinker.

And there was something else; Rose had a sense of humour. The Beast had found his Scarlet Woman at last, clothed with the sun! And she had found a rich, young, sexy man of character, brilliance and wit, with a boundless yen for sexual discovery that matched her own style. They went to Paris, to patch up with Gerald, thence to Marseilles, Naples and Cairo. On 22 November 1903, Mr Crowley secured a special opening of the King's Chamber in the Great Pyramid, just for the two of them. Crowley, well connected with Cairo's Anglo-Egyptian administration, suggested something to make the honeymoon that bit more special. He invoked 'the Sylphs' or spirits of the element of air, using a 'Call' paraphrased by Crowley from one of Dr Dee's and Sir Edward Kelley's elemental invocations.

And lo and behold! The light did shine! A bluish light filled the King's Chamber. The couple blew out the candle and the light persisted, parting only with the dawn. The gods, like the world, smiled at the lovers; theirs was the passion that made the planets turn and the wheels of God spin, spin, spin.

EIGHT

The Lesion

1904

Lesion, *medical*: A morbid change in the functioning of an organ.

Hôtel de Blois, 50 Rue Vavin, Paris, February 1924

Suffering heroin withdrawal and a partial breakdown, Crowley is assailed by daydreams so intense he wonders if he is not hallucinating. Lost memories wash onto the shores of consciousness:

> All these dialogues so vivid as to be practically audible: and *I am reminded of writing down AL* [*The Book of the Law*]. But at that time there were no circumstances soever at all likely to account for any hallucinations. Save this! Rose and I had on our programme, high up, a visit to Frater I.A. [Bennett] in his Kyoung at Rangoon (or Akyab – I had not seen him since he had formally joined the Sangha). Returned to Colombo from Hambantota January 1904: I got a lesion on my tongue – origin unknown – and a vision of Lady Scott & Countess Russell at the Galle Face Hotel.

Never before published, Crowley's 1924 diary pulls us into a long-lost drama.

*　　*　　*

In 1890, Lady 'Tina' Scott led daughter Mabel into marriage with 'Frank', the eccentric 2nd Earl Russell. A year later, Countess Russell sued for divorce. 'Abominable libels' lost her the case. The libels continued. In

1896, Lady Scott accused her son in law of 'immorality' with an Oxford don. She was imprisoned. In 1901 Earl Russell's bigamy with a Mrs Somerville, whose husband had enjoyed an affair with the Countess, became public; divorce was granted. As recently as April 1903, Countess Russell had hit the headlines by marrying a footman masquerading as 'Prince Athrobald Stuart de Modena'.

January 1904

The Galle Face, Colombo's finest hotel, plays host to honeymooners Lord and Lady Boleskine. *Enter* the notorious Lady Scott and Countess Russell; hideous mother, manipulated daughter. The doors of hell open and Crowley's marital love-spell snaps.

Lady Scott... Crowley wrote of 'the Genuine Ecstasy of Loathing of the Evil Mother – magically seen for the first time in my life'. Hypersensitized by Rose's beauty, the jungle 'plus the solitude', Crowley fled to Kandy to get the full horror of Lady Scott down in his play, *Why Jesus Wept.*

Kandy... where he had known peace and illumination with Allan Bennett, now served as locus for a war cry against a society of hypocrites. His play's 'Minor Dedication' addressed 'Tina' Scott as 'My dear Lady S-':

> I quite agree with your expressed opinion that no true gentleman would (with or without reason) compare *any* portion of your ladyship's anatomy to a piece of wet chamois leather; the best I can do to repair his rudeness is to acknowledge the notable part your ladyship played in the conception of this masterpiece by the insertion of as much of your name as my lawyers will permit me.[1]

Addressed to GK Chesterton, *Why Jesus Wept*'s 'Dedication Extraordinary' vented a volcano's worth of outraged energy, precipitated by an incendiary cocktail of acute social vision, broken bliss and the nagging lesion of the tongue:

> Arm! Arm, and out; for the young warrior of a new religion is upon thee; and his number is the number of a man.

Crowley's name was then written in Hebrew, computed by gematria to 666.[2]

Why Jesus Wept was the immediate literary predecessor to Crowley's famous *Book of the Law*; a declaration of war and licence to live for Aleister Crowley and free men and women everywhere.

A new religion…

A new religion requires a fresh revelation, and Crowley was about to experience one in circumstances that combined the domestic-prosaic with the out-of-this-world. To the end of his life, Crowley claimed he heard the voice of a more-than-human intelligence, for an hour a day between April 8th and 10th 1904 in a Cairo apartment. The name of the intelligence, Rose announced, was 'Aiwass', minister of the child Horus, the spiritual energy of the Sun: *force and fire*; the 'eye of God' at the centre of our solar system.

Aiwass heralded a new solar age in a three-chapter prophecy known as *The Book of the Law*, and subsequently *Liber AL*. For Crowley, the experience proved that communication with more-than-human intelligence was possible and he would come to declare the Cairo revelation the only thing that had made his life worth living.

According to Crowley's 1924 diary, the lesion on the tongue contracted in Sri Lanka somehow affected his *sensorium*, the brain's sensory apparatus:

> My idea was (in writing this note) that the poison which had attacked my tongue also attacked (later) my sensorium, thus causing hallucinations, similar to those of tonight, in March–April '04.

> [side note] This does no more than suggest the mechanism of hearing Aiwass. But then that point has always irked me, I being so free naturally from anything […] of the kind.[3]

He meant he was not the sort to 'hear voices' and was highly sceptical of those who did. The effect on his brain's nerve centres sufficed to render Aiwass's voice audible to his physical ear. Crowley denied the communication itself was a hallucination: *The Book of the Law*'s existence being its own proof; he heard, he wrote. The source was independent of himself.

The legendary account of the 'Cairo revelation' implies the 'mechanism' for 'hearing Aiwass' was a ritual. Can we settle the matter from Crowley's surviving manuscripts?

*   *   *

After the 'bad trip' in Sri Lanka, Crowley returned with Rose to Egypt, possibly to recover the honeymoon dream. *The Egyptian Gazette* of 11 February 1904, reported 'Lord and Lady Boleskine' were guests of Cairo's Grand Continental Hotel. Crowley's diary for that day contains cryptic acronyms:

> Saw b.f.g.
>
> b.f.b.

Years later, he explained: 'Contradictory hints in one of my diaries were inserted deliberately to mislead, for some silly no-reason unconnected with Magick.'⁴ His colleague, Captain Fuller, referred in 1912 to 'stupid meaningless ciphers which deface the diary'. Some may have referred to gay sex encounters.

On 16 February, the *Gazette* reported Lord and Lady Boleskine at the Eastern Exchange Hotel, Port Said. Had they decided to leave Egypt? They must have changed their minds, because two days later, the couple moved spectacularly to Helwān, a popular sporting resort across the Nile from the ruins of Memphis.

Before the move, Crowley engaged a 'sheikh' to teach him basic Arabic so he could memorize extracts from the Koran, and possibly repeat Sir Richard Burton's daring *Hajj* to Mecca of 1853, disguised as a Muslim. Crowley also had in mind becoming the 'new' Christian Rosenkreuz (CRC), mythical founder of the Rose Cross Fraternity 500 years before. Rosicrucian legend told how Arabian sages opened CRC's eyes to the universe. Crowley's unnamed sheikh familiarized him with skills known to the Sufi *Sidi Aissawa tariqa* (spiritual path). Several of the 'secrets' might be in-joke euphemisms for homosexual sex, as conceivably implied in this 1935 newspaper account entitled 'I Learn Many Queer Tricks':

> [The Sheikh was] profoundly versed in the mysticism and magic of Islam, I learnt many of the secrets of the Sidi Aissawa; how to run a stiletto through one's cheek without drawing blood, lick red hot swords, and eat live scorpions, &c. He also provided me with books and manuscripts of the Arabic Qabalah. After profound study of them, off I went, still masquerading as an Oriental despot, to Helwān.[5]

Crowley adopted an extraordinary guise:

> I am here as Prince Chioa Khan, an ingenious and vastly amusing avatar; and more sceptical than ever. [...] I can no longer fight whole-heartedly for Gautama; [Buddha]'

He wrote that he was about to seek for truth in Islam, while remaining convinced in himself that 'to no great man can it ever be possible to work in any existing system. If he has followers, so much the worse for them.'[6]

Crowley sought a new system.

The Egyptian Gazette of 27 February 1904 confirms the 'Oriental Despot' guise at Helwān: 'Amongst the latest arrivals at the Tewfik Palace Hotel is Prince Chio [*sic*] Khan and Suite.' *Chioa* (pronounced 'Hiwa') is a transliteration of the Hebrew for 'Beast'. 'Khan' means 'Chief'. Crowley looked the part with his goatee beard, fez and silk, jewel-encrusted jacket. He played golf, bridge and poker.

By 16 March the honeymooners occupied a Cairo apartment near the city centre, sublet from Congdon & Co by 'Lieut.-Col. Somebody, beginning I think, with a B; married, middle-aged, with manners like the Rules of a Prison.'[7]

Crowley's contemporary 'Book of Results' records that on 16 March, in an effort to recapture November's pyramid magic, Crowley invoked 'IAΩ', 'IAŌ' being a Gnostic name for God.[8] Crowley had the intuition to continue the ritual 'day and night for a week'. This time, Rose did *not* see the sylphs. She was troubled:

> W. [='Ouarda', Arabic for Rose] says 'they' are 'waiting for me.'

Was the pregnant Rose hysterical, stoned, or confused? There was more the next day: 'It is "all about the child".' Also 'all Osiris', Crowley noted in his 'Book of Results'.

Thoth, god of magick, wisdom and writing, was invoked 'with great success'. On 17 March, 'Thoth appeared'[9] then 'indwelled' them, meaning they were inspired by magical wisdom. That very day a portent appeared, reported in Friday's Cairo edition of *The Times*: a beautiful annular eclipse of the Sun, with the Moon ringed by sunlight. Progressing with the rising Sun, the eclipse was heightened by Venus, the morning star in Aquarius. It faded, reappeared, and caused a stunning ring of fire, bulging toward Venus's silvery glow. On the day of the eclipse, Rose had another message for her husband:

> Revealed that the waiter was Horus, whom I had offended & ought to invoke. The ritual revealed in skeleton. Promise of success ♄ [Saturday] or ☉ [Sunday] and of samādhi.[10]

'How did she know that I had offended Horus?' Crowley asked, 'It must be remembered that she knew less Egyptology than 99 Cairene tourists out of 100. What is more, it happened to be true; I knew that I had. But was her bull's-eye a fluke? I cross-examined her.'[11]

Crowley expected her to fail. She didn't. Rose knew Horus's nature was 'force and fire'; knew his presence was characterized by a deep blue light. She recognized his name in hieroglyphics. She knew Crowley's past 'relations' with Horus, in the Golden Dawn, and knew his 'enemy': the forces of the Nile. She knew his lineal figure, colours, knew 'his place in the temple', knew his weapons, knew his connection with the Sun, knew his number was five, and picked him out of first, three, and then five, different and arbitrary symbols. Crowley, thinking of billiards, said it was like 'balls in bag'. The odds against passing all the tests were enormous.

Next stop: the Bulak Museum, a short distance from the apartment.

Excited and sceptical, Crowley was relieved to see Rose pass image after image of Horus. Then she stopped, pointing to a cabinet at the end of a gallery.

'There he is!'

Crowley approached the display. A figure with the falcon head of Horus was enthroned before a priest dressed in leopard skin. Above the god and the priest was another form of Horus, the Sun disc with wings. Above the red disc of the Sun, arched above and round the whole scene extended the naked body of Nuit, goddess of the starry sky. There were hieroglyphics below the scene. Startled, Crowley's eyes lit on the exhibit's catalogue number: *666*, *his* number, the number of the 'Beast', a solar number, the number of a man. And there was the Sun, Horus, in two forms; pure coincidence, no doubt, but …

Curator Emile Brugsch Bey requested his French assistant translate the stela's inscription. It was, according to Crowley, Rose's 'discovery' of the stela that 'led to the creation of the ritual by which Aiwass, the author of *Liber L* [or 'AL', *The Book of the Law*], was invoked.'[12]

*　　*　　*

Egyptologist Abd el Hamid Zayed studied the stela in 1968.[13] It is a funerary monument to Ankh f-n-Khonsu, a Theban priest of the god Month (or Mentu) who flourished around 725BCE in Egypt's 25th Dynasty. He was thus a contemporary of Hezekiah, king of Judah, whose conflict with his priests and prophets is recorded in the Bible.

'Most noteworthy', noted Zayed, 'is the identification of the form of Ra-Horakhty with Soker-Osiris. The back of the stela is occupied by eleven horizontal lines of inscription, the first part of which is a version of the Book of the Dead chapter 30. It is very unusual to find it inscribed on a stela. The second half of the inscription is part of the Book of the Dead chapter two and, in the Theban Recension, entitled, "The chapter of coming forth by day and living after death". Its object was to allow the astral form of the deceased to revisit the Earth at will.'

*　　*　　*

A spell to allow the dead priest to return to earth at will... Was Crowley Ankh f-n-Khonsu returned?

On 18 March Rose told her husband to invoke Horus by a 'new way'. Crowley was now listening. The 'Book of Results' reveals the ritual 'written out and the invocation done' with 'little success' the next day. Crowley's daily diary records: 'Did this badly at noon 30.'

Crowley's 'Invocation of Hoor' notebook sketches out the invocation.[14] A note opposite the invocation excuses Saturday's 'limited success': Rose's instructions 'broke all the rules'; one stipulation was for 44 pearl beads. The note continues: 'The pearl beads broke on the Saturday so I changed the invocation.'[15] After this note, five pages are torn from the notebook. Had they contained the changed invocation?[16]

The only invocation known that uses lines from the stela is called 'B2': 'To have any Knowledge'. But Crowley did not have the stela's translation at this point, and Crowley's extant Horus invocation makes no reference to the stela. Crowley's assertion that it was the stela's discovery that led to the ritual which led to *The Book of the Law*'s dictation suggests the important factor was the stela's *discovery*, not necessarily its *translation*.

Horus was invoked again on the Sunday. Results were immediate: 'Revealed the Equinox of the Gods is come, Horus taking the Throne of the East and all rituals being abrogated. Great success in midnight invocation! I am to formulate a new link of an order with the solar force.'[17] Rose, presumably, was clairaudient.

The vernal equinox fell the next day, but the 'Equinox of the Gods' marked no mere change of season, but a new *Aeon*; a cosmic time period, and Crowley had been chosen as the link with the gods!

The diary sequence beginning 22 March is difficult to interpret. According to the 'Book of Results', Tuesday, the day of Mars, was 'The day of rest, on which nothing whatever of magic is ever to be done at all'. Crowley's alternative diary entry for the Tuesday records the following:[18]

March 22. X.P.B. ‏اجحا‎

E.P.D. in 84 m.

'X.P.B.' may connect to a reference to 'P.B.' for March 25. 'E.P.D. in 84 m.'
is perhaps a 'blind', the same may go for 'X.P.B.' The Arabic 'word',
though, is arresting. It reappears as the sole entry for March 24: 'Met
‏اجحا‎ again.' *Who* did he meet again?

‏اجحا‎

One might imagine the Arabic referred to Crowley's helpful sheikh,
but ‏اجحا‎ is neither name nor word. Crowley's Arabic letters possibly
transliterate as *ajiha, ahīrā* or *ahīdā*.[19] The meaning, I suspect, survives
in *Why Jesus Wept*'s dedication to Gautama (Buddha) and his imitators:
'you Achiha, by sticking manfully to your Work in the World...'. *Achiha*,
a footnote tells us, is a 'metathesis' of Crowley's own name. 'Spelt in full',
it adds up to 666.[20]

We now enter a fascinating symbolic puzzle that takes us to the heart
of Crowley's activities.

*   *   *

The Hebrew for beast, or 'creature', is usually ‏חיוא‎ (*ChIVA* or *ChYWA*).
'Achiha' is Crowley's kabbalistic manipulation of this word combined
with the *divine* name '*AHIH*', that is 'I AM' which Crowley learned in the
Golden Dawn.[21] Thus, ‏אחיהא‎ (*AChIHA*) combines the divine being with
the beast: 'I AM-beast', or 'God-beast'. It denotes Crowley's *essential*
identity, as he saw it. We see at once that 'Achiha' is very close to the Arabic
letters, 'ajiha', the soft 'ch' and the Arabic equivalent of our 'j' being
equivalent. So Crowley saw 'God-beast' on the 22nd and again on the 24th.

For Crowley, the 'Achiha' is the creaturely man (beast) and the *hidden
God* together; the biblical equivalent would be the figure called 'Son of
Man'. If 'Achiha' is, as he says, a *metathesis* of his own name, that is, *a
name that encodes meaning*, we may conclude that Crowley saw *Himself*
and met *Himself* again two days later.

Hallucinations?

'Achiha', for Crowley, is a title given to a person who has realized the infinite in the finite. In Crowley's case, access to this experience *might* have been homosexual sex.

We saw in chapter seven the link between Crowley's *dhyana* trance in Kandy and the prophet Ezekiel's vision of a being appearing as a Man above God's Throne or Chariot. Kabbalistic symbolism equated the Throne or Chariot with 'Kether', the Crown or first emanation of the Tree of Life. Kether was also equated with 'the North', whence the 'four beasts' emerged in Ezekiel I.4–5:

> A tempestuous whirlwind came out from the North, a mighty cloud, and a fire violently whirling upon itself, and a splendour revolving upon itself, and from the midmost as an eye of brightness from the midst of the fire. And from the midmost the Forms of the Four *Chaioth* [creatures or beasts].

The Hebrew for the 'four beasts' is ארבע חיות *Arba Chaioth*). *Chaioth* is the plural of 'Chioa' (or *ChIVA*), the name Crowley chose when he rode in his coach (chariot) with runners to clear the way to Helwān as an 'Oriental Despot'. The 'forms of the four beasts' manifest God's Glory. The next line from Ezekiel describes the beasts: 'Also out of the midst thereof came the likeness of four living beasts. And this was their appearance; *they had the likeness of a man.*' [22]

The likeness of a man. 666 is of course the *number* of a man, the solar number. On 2 October 1901, at the climax of Crowley's *dhyana* meditation at Kandy, Ceylon, he saw the 'idea of some vast Human-seeming Form', in the core of his being. Doubting, he lost the vision. He tried yoga while in Ceylon with Rose, but felt frustrated; he had hoped to attain *samadhi*, union with the 'absolute', but could not. And then, lo and behold, something began to happen to him in Cairo in March 1904. He saw 'God-beast' again! Crowley had seen a vision of the divine glory within him, the prelude to receiving prophecy. Was he hallucinating?

Aleister Crowley rode into Helwān like one of the beasts of Ezekiel; a shining ray from Kether, the Crown, in the likeness of a man, and on a 'chariot' to boot; a partly unconscious, prophetic act that was, typically, passed off by him as a huge joke. It *was* a huge joke, the kind of joke that could cure Buddha of his 'universal sorrow' and stop Jesus from weeping.

*   *   *

According to the 'Book of Results', Wednesday 23 March was supposed to see a 'great day of invocation', involving a tarot divination. Thoth, the patron deity of tarot, was invoked, consistent with the entry, headed 'The Secret of Wisdom'.[23] Crowley used the tarot to interpret the stela's image. Crowley's first deduction from the cards was a symbol combining Mercury (priest or magician) and Aries (solar warrior) which he identified with the priest, Ankh f-n-Khonsu. The priest was equated with 'ου μη' (Crowley as *Adeptus Major*).[24]

The second interpretation from the tarot of 'Mars in Libra' revealed: 'the ritual is of sex; Mars in the house of Venus exciting the jealousy of Saturn or Vulcan.'

The secret was sex. 'Sex' is also 'six', the number of the Sun. The 'exciting jealousy' note is curious. Saturn corresponds to the trump card 'The Universe', described in the Golden Dawn's *Book 'T'* as 'The Great One of the Night of Time'. It is equated with Nuit, and possibly Rose. After describing the stela, Crowley recorded these prophetic words in the 'Book of Results':

> There is one other object to complete the Secret of Wisdom – or, it is in the hieroglyphs. G∴D∴ [Golden Dawn] to be destroyed ie: publish its history and its papers. Nothing needs buying. I make it an absolute condition that I should obtain Samadhi, in the Gods' own interest. My rituals work out well, but I need the transliteration [of the stela].

Biographers have missed the import of Crowley's statement that Rose's discovery of the stela led to the *creation of the ritual* which led to *The Book of the Law*. If Crowley's statement means that the stela provided the *words* of the ritual, then the ritual would appear to be 'B2: To have any Knowledge'.[25] This ritual does not, however, appear in Crowley's Cairo notebooks. Diary entries are practically silent for the fortnight before the appearance, if that is the right word, of Aiwass on 7 April 1904. The entry for 25 March consists of apparently meaningless numbers and letters, possibly blinds, followed, after a blot, by the words: 'wch trouble with ds'. There is another blot and then: 'P.B.' The next entry is for 6 April: 'Go off again to H, taking A's p.' Vain to speculate, it might mean Crowley went to Helwān, possibly taking 'Achiha's part', that is, dressed as Chioa Khan. Something was happening that Crowley apparently preferred to keep to himself. Was he composing – and performing – the key ritual?

Crowley did not need the stela's translation to envision a ritual that was 'of sex'. The stela's image already suggested it (*see* Plate section). Beneath Crowley's notes for the 'Invocation of Hoor [Horus]', stands a telling title: *The Supreme Ritual*:

> Nuit as קשת [Qesheth] Hadit as ס [Samekh], being the result of [...? Crowley's Arabic indecipherable – possibly 'Ouarda', Arabic for 'Rose'] as Priest, ου μη, [Crowley] as Ra Hoor Khuit. But this is as secret as it is dangerous.

As secret as it is dangerous. What's this all about?

Qesheth is the Hebrew for Sagittarius: קשת, the bow. Crowley links this zodiacal sign to the goddess Nuit whose body of stars makes a bow over the stela. In Golden Dawn doctrine, Sagittarius corresponds to the tarot trump 'Temperance', which card, like the bow and arrow of Sagittarius, may represent the genitals.[26]

'Hadit' (nowadays transliterated as 'Horbehutet', a form of Horus) is the winged red sun disc below Nuit's navel on the stela. 'Hadit' appears to 'prop up' the arched body of Nuit. Appropriately, the Hebrew letter corresponding to 'Temperance' is 'samekh' (ס), which means 'prop'. 'Temperance' also corresponds to the 'path' on the kabbalist Tree of Life that joins Yesod (Foundation) to the sephira Tiphareth (Beauty). Since Yesod corresponds to the Moon, and Tiphareth to the Sun, the path of the 'bow' and the 'prop' connects the female (Moon) to the male (Sun); a divinely sexual force.

The ritual is of sex...

Sagittarius is the bow, the arched Lady above the Sun. Samekh, the 'prop', is her rigid support. For Crowley, the Sun on Earth is the creative power symbolized in the Shaivite *lingam*. The prop is a magical, cosmic phallus; the bow is the corresponding goddess. Thus, the stela offered cosmic sexual knowledge, 'as secret as it is dangerous'.

The universe is the manifestation of a perpetual orgasm, the embrace of opposites; where Nuit is Matter and 'Hadit', Motion. A *BIG BANG* indeed! The doctrine expresses philosophically what Einstein in 1905–07 expressed mathematically in his famous formula: energy equals mass (matter) multiplied by light-speed (motion) squared; multiplication is generation. A year before Einstein published his masterwork, Crowley's mind was already imbued with relativity concepts.

Crowley wished to reunite science and religion; rituals celebrating cosmic realities would be the sacraments of the revolutionary new Aeon.

Confirmation that Crowley had a powerful cosmo-sexual ritual in mind lies in his 'rough note-book telling the rituals ordeals and rites of the secret and public worship of RHK [Ra Hoor Khuit]. H[adit]. N[uit].'[27] It appears to have been written after returning to Boleskine in summer 1904:

> But for private work. The Beast is Hadit. The Scarlet Woman
> Nuit. And she is above him ever. [He is 'prop']. Let him never
> assume power! Let him ever look to her! Amen! For this she
> wears the blue and gold abbai of Nu, and the indigo nemyss. He
> wears the scarlet and gold abbai, and the green nemyss. They
> work mostly in Egyptian, which they will be taught to
> pronounce. He wears the winged globe. For open work he can
> wear the Abramelin things…

Crowley published a version of 'The Supreme Ritual' in his journal *The Equinox* in 1913. Heavily disguised, it appeared as the first part of 'Two Fragments of Ritual'.[28]

The officers in The Supreme Ritual are enjoined to seek Nuit and Hadit through 'Babalon and the Beast', concealed as Isis and Osiris. To add further confusion, the officers 'O' and 'I' are given each other's lines, and the names Nuit and Hadit are removed. There is even a joke at the expense of Hadit's 'member' or phallus, described as a 'Monster'. Whether formulated in the Cairo apartment, or refined later at Boleskine, it seems likely something of the kind preceded Crowley's encounter with 'Aiwass'. Poetic, erotic and spiritual, the ritual's climax is a climax indeed. The sacrament of the new Aeon is expressed in orgasm, not a sacrifice of sorrow but of ego-free joy.

According to Egyptian mythology, the birth of Horus required the death of Osiris. Thus, Crowley claimed the Aeon of Horus 'abrogated' the rituals of Osiris, by which is meant the interpretation of Jesus' sacrifice as sorrowful, promoting concepts of self-sacrificial 'martyrdom' (life through physical death). A spiritual message had been distorted into blackness in the Aeon of Osiris. Its time was up; the Sun-child would triumph. Aiwass's message challenged civilization at its most fundamental level. Until we get the message, asserted Aiwass, there will be war, the burning-side of the life-giving Sun: nature unbalanced.

*　　*　　*

Crowley and Rose did more in Cairo than receive strange messages. They had fun as well. If Crowley was an intelligence asset or agent, his meeting consular officials and senior British officers should not surprise us. He notes in *Magick* (Part 4) that he had rented an apartment from a Lieutenant-Colonel whose name began with a 'B'.[29] Then there was 'A Mr Back, owner of *The Egyptian News*, an hotel, a hunk of railway, &c.' who dined once.'[30] The reference to 'P.B.' in the 25 March entry might possibly be Philip Back, one of a number of Ashkenazi Jews who contributed to the construction and upkeep of the new *Chaar Hachamaim* – Gates of Heaven Sephardic synagogue, the biggest structure on Maghrabi (now Adly) Street, close to the colonial sanctuary, the Turf Club. Crowley wrote a pornographic parody of life at the club in his *Snowdrops from a Curate's Garden*, written later in the year to entertain Rose.

> They had been married barely a week when he took her to the infamous T...... [Turf] Club in Cairo, where the dissolute officers of the Army of Occupation, merchants, fish-porters, pimps,

all the cream of Egyptian society and its dregs, gathered every
Wednesday night to commit appalling orgies.

Crowley also recalled how he and Rose 'occasionally hobnobbed with a
General Dickson, who had accepted Islam; otherwise,' he wrote, 'we
knew nobody in Cairo except natives, carpet merchants, pimps,
jewellers, and such small deer.'[31]

Precisely what kind of fun Lord and Lady Boleskine or Prince and
Princess Chioa Khan were enjoying may only be guessed at, but I think
one's guesses might be near the mark. There were at least three adults in
the apartment, for the household was run, according to Crowley, by
'Hassan or Hamid, I forget which'. The Egyptian was a 'tall, dignified
athlete of about 30' who spoke good English. Hassan was 'always there
and never in the way'. Crowley's character preferences are evident here,
but whether he brought homosexual magic into his honeymoon home
remains conjectural. The atmosphere was highly charged sexually and
the means, predilection and symbolic framework were there.

*   *   *

Some time between 23 March and 7 April, Crowley received a French translation of the stela's hieroglyphics. He transposed them into English poetry.
Curiously, he would insert them into the text of *The Book of the Law*.

Rose then announced that her informant was not Horus, as formerly
believed, but Aiwass, Horus's messenger. Crowley was sceptical. Was
Rose thinking of the oft-heard word *aiwa*, Arabic for 'yes'? He decided
she 'could not have invented a name of this kind' – he meant a name so
loaded with kabbalistic potential. Aiwass meant more to him when spelt
with its numerological value uppermost: 'Aiwas', 'Aiwaz' or 'Oviz'.

*   *   *

On 8 April, Rose ordered Aleister to enter the drawing room designated
'the Temple'. Between noon and one o'clock, for three days, Crowley
heard prose poetry from Nuit, Hadit and 'Ra Hoor Khuit' (composite of
Ra, Horus and Soker-Osiris) delivered by Aiwass and taken down by

Crowley's Swan fountain pen onto 8x10-inch paper.

Crowley said he caught a glimpse of Aiwass in his mind's eye. He seemed to be in the corner of the drawing room, veiled as if by a gauze, 'a being purely astral'. His eyes were also veiled lest, like Shiva's, they destroy the one who stared. The angel appeared as a 'tall, dark man in his thirties…with the face of a savage king', his dress 'Persian or Assyrian'.[32] Was Crowley hallucinating? It is odd that he did not draw attention to his impersonation of a Persian Khan – or to his servant 'Hassan or Hamid', also a tall man in his thirties.

*   *   *

Crowley's sense that Aiwass's message had authority would be illuminated when he realized that when spelt as Aiwas (איואס) the angel's name added up to 78 (60+1+6+10+1 = 78). The number 78 was the kabbalistic number for a 'ray' called 'Mezla' that Mathers asserted was the means by which the 'forms of the four beasts' appeared in Ezekiel's vision. 'Mezla', Mathers asserted, was an 'influence or messenger' extended from Kether to the material level of existence. For Crowley, the Cairo Revelation – or intelligence – came from the *Top*.

Nevertheless, Crowley's reaction was peculiar. Ever in two minds, Crowley found something about the experience disconcerting. While Aiwass reinforced Crowley's shift from Buddhism, he seems to have felt duress. *Existence*, declared Aiwass, was 'pure joy'. Sorrows pass. Crowley had only just sent out a New Year's card wishing its recipients, in jocular Buddhist style: 'a speedy termination of existence'. Aiwass had trumped him!

Aiwass speaks like Crowley's daimon let loose, smashing up the subtle defences of his intellect and offering him the impetus to see off Mathers. It is odd that Crowley did not immediately recognize Aiwass's voice as that of his own True Self, or Holy Guardian Angel: the Beast set free; such seems clear in *Why Jesus Wept*, and Rose must have seen through him. As his mother called him the Beast, Rose brought him to Aiwass.

The overall impression is of a soul divided; the revelation – his unconscious psyche seeking to save him. Or was it rather a message for all humankind? Crowley was not sure. While it is clear he was prepared to announce himself on paper as prophet and warrior of a new religion, another part of him resented the role's implications, wishing it would all go away so he could get on with being a mischievous romantic, Zeitgeist-clown, great poet, mountaineer and occasional psychic scholar. He had opened a can of angels and one of them would never leave him alone, because He knew him better than he knew his own being. Here perhaps lies the ambivalence of Crowley's reaction to *The Book of the Law* – and ours.

Objectively, Crowley accepted communication with higher intelligence was as possible as it was desirable, if humankind would survive periodic changes in the universe.[33] He would even invoke the figure of Jesus as a 'thelemic' forerunner:

> It is the Law that Jesus Christ, or rather the Gnostic tradition of which the Christ-legend is a degradation, attempted to teach; but nearly every word he said was misinterpreted and garbled by his enemies, particularly by those who called themselves his disciples. In any case the Aeon was not ready for a Law of Freedom. Of all his followers only St Augustine appears to have got even a glimmer of what he meant.[34]

Crowley refers to Augustine's *Love, and do what you will*, the which dictum resonates with *The Book of the Law*'s following famous injunctions:

Love is the law, love under will. (I.57)

Every man and every woman is a star. (I.3)

The word of the Law is θελημα. (I.39; 'thelema'=Greek for 'will')

Do what thou wilt shall be the whole of the Law. (I.40)

Crowley chucked the manuscript into a case and boarded the SS *Osiris* for France, failing even to tell theosophist diva Annie Besant, whom he later claimed was travelling on the same ship, that the book annihilated any plans *she* and her theosophical friends might have been entertaining for esoteric global domination.

*   *   *

Resident in Paris until mid-summer, Crowley petitioned Anglo-Saxon Lodge No 343 for initiation on 29 June.[35] Why is unclear. He was already a 33° Mason in the Reformed Mexican Rite, though that rite remained unrecognized by the United Grand Lodge of England. Under the impression that Anglo-Saxon Lodge *was* recognized, Crowley perhaps sought Masonic parity with figures he might soon have to confront, such as Mathers.

In July, Dr Percival Bott became Boleskine's live-in obstetrician while Aunt Annie turned housekeeper. Crowley summarily informed Mathers the 'Equinox of the Gods' had come. Effectively dismissing Mathers from the Secret Chiefs' service, Mathers went crazy. He launched a magical attack on Crowley. Freemason William Wynn Westcott wrote to FL Gardner about Mathers' mania on 23 July:

> Dear G – Have you heard of SRMD? [Mathers] He is said to be in a [?] in P[aris] for a mad assault.[36]

According to Crowley, Mathers' 'mad assault' killed off Boleskine's pack of bloodhounds: 'There was absolutely no sign of any sort of disease. They simply died, and I knew that there was Magick at work. The servants too were continually becoming ill, one with this complaint, one with the other. Action was necessary.'[37] Crowley's hunting servant tried to kill Rose and all manner of mishaps occurred before Crowley turned the tables, evoked Beelzebub, and sent the demons packing back to Paris, whence he perceived the evil had come.[38]

One factor in Mathers' mad assault was never mentioned. The attacks coincided with Rose's delivery on 28 July of Nuit Ma Ahathoor Hecate Sappho Jezebel Lilith Crowley. Could Crowley's first daughter's destiny have been afflicted by Mathers' black magic?

Confined to bed, Rose wrote to her brother Gerald on 4 August:

> All goes well here – the kid 'Nuit Ma Ahathoor Hecate Sappho Jezebel Lilith' – to be called by the last name – flourishes. She's a

good little maid though she does squarl occasionally which drives A[leister] out rabbit shooting, we've such a stack to consume in the house! What are you going to do? Are you moving anywhere? Who's looking after you? A is very busy. Life jogs on very peacefully – the last fortnight has of course been an upset, but we shall soon settle down again. The place is quite lovely now. Garden a mass of flowers. I shall be up at the end of the week. Thanks to the gods. Enclosed Photo. of Lilith – age 3 days.

Yrs Ever R[ose]

– *Sword* [39] goes out this week.[40]

The proud father composed the pornographic *Snowdrops from a Curate's Garden* to entertain Rose in her confinement and to tickle his guests. He established *The Society for the Propagation of Religious Truth*: SPRT, a cheeky, provocative skit on the mainstream Christian publishers, SPCK.[41] Life at Boleskine settled into a joyous idyll.

*   *   *

In 1946, Crowley wrote a humorous, unpublished, account of life at Boleskine: *Leaves from Journal of Our Life in the Highlands by MacGregor of Boleskine and Abertarff*:

> You may as well know that my house is no ordinary house; it is a mass of legends, some of them dating centuries back, – legends mostly of horror. I had accordingly excellent material to start on.

At the foot of the path from the road by Loch Ness up to Boleskine, Crowley found a 'useless patch' and put up a sign:

THIS WAY TO THE KOOLOO MAVLICK (Does not Bite)
   – Admission Free! –

Rose and Aleister, convulsed with laughter in their chairs higher up on the path, observed increasing bewilderment in passers-by. The local hotel owner got upset. The 'Kooloo Mavlick' affected trade! It was said folk would do anything but walk by the haunted Boleskine House. Crowley later commented: 'I have sometimes wondered whether this harmless invention of mine might not in some way have been responsible for the story of the Loch Ness Monster.'

Hearing in years to come of stories of a serpentine beast that haunted the loch, Crowley, tongue in cheek, wondered if, 'Maybe the Lake of Loch Ness is suffering from the same Magical phenomena as the Manor of Boleskine. I do not know, but I am extremely interested in the ultimate end of the investigations into the existence of the monster which has created such excitement.'[42] Observe Crowley's use of the word 'monster' here. If we recall the word appearing in 'The Supreme Ritual' for Hadit's phallus ('this Monster of mine') we may be forced to conclude that the 'ultimate end' of the investigation must hold nothing less than this: *that the Loch Ness Monster was never in fact anything more than Aleister Crowley's potent penis.*

They won't find it with sonar.

NINE

The Dawning

1905–06

In Cairo, Crowley made his attaining *samadhi* a condition for establishing his own order. The universe would make best sense when transcended, as a valley's topography can best be seen from the highest point. Seeing the Earth from space has changed the world; imagine seeing the universe *from the outside*. Impossible, isn't it?

*   *   *

1905 opened with a family holiday in Bournemouth followed by a long house-party at Boleskine. Crowley took refuge in his revolutionary home-temple, chanting 'Aum Tat Sat Aum' over and over again, getting nowhere.[1] He studied *Vedantic Raj Yoga: Ancient Tantra Yoga of Rishies* by Mahātmā Jñāna Guru Yogi Sabhapaty Swāmi (Lahore, 1880). The Swāmi had achieved *samadhi* at 29 – Crowley's age. Crowley's engagement with Tantric philosophy, known to the vulgar as 'the yoga of sex', began.[2]

In May, frustrated with yoga – and Britain – he boarded P&O liner *Marmora* bound for Sydney via Bombay. At Port Said he went sailing with a man, a sexual tryst celebrated in the poem 'Said', written 'on the beautiful breast of the Nile'.[3] By early July, Crowley was on the Sikkim-Nepalese border, focusing on Kanchenjunga with binoculars, noting deficiencies in the official surveys. Before him, the prize; the 'Five Sacred Treasures' of Kanchenjunga rose to a dazzling 26,208 feet, only 42 feet 'behind' K2. Coolies feared not the height, but the mountain's god who guarded her treasures.

Crowley did not have the best team. Shipwrecked in the Red Sea, K2-bore Dr Jacot Guillarmod arrived a month late. For transport manager, Crowley hired Darjeeling's Drum Druid Hotel's Italian manager, Alcesti C Rigo de Righi. Guillarmod brought two Swiss army officers, Alexis Pache and Charles Reymond. They signed a contract on 4 August to follow Crowley's orders. Four days later, they set off in a downpour with 6 servants and 79 porters. Hazardous terrain made 50 miles seem like 200, but Crowley was confident. Having climbed to 15,000 feet by 21 August, Crowley plumped for the southwest ascent via the Yalung Glacier. Avalanche-prone and dominated by granite precipices, it was the direct route.

The coolies were restive. Crowley warned Guillarmod his complaining demoralized them. Camp IV was pitched at 19,000 feet. One of Pache's coolies fled, falling to his death. Hampered by inadequate supplies, snow blindness and lack of oxygen, Crowley pressed on heroically. Determined to beat the K2 altitude record of 21,653 feet, Camp V was established at 21,000 feet.

Guillarmod and de Righi joined Crowley without supplies on 1 September, accusing him of beating porters. He denied it. They left. Pache followed later but the snow was warm at the day's end. Shouts were heard. Reymond, against Crowley's advice, left to investigate. Feeling betrayed, Crowley went to sleep, waking in the morning to see 20 feet of path gone. A porter had lost his footing, taking Pache and two coolies with him. The result: avalanche. Six had been on the rope with Guillarmod up front, foolishly leaving the weakest at the back. Swept off their feet, Guillarmod and de Righi survived.

The survivors saw Crowley descending at first light. They called but he either heard nothing, or chose not to hear. Crowley later said he heard voices at Camp IV, replied, but received no answer. Stories conflicted.

Crowley, disgusted, blamed the team. They had broken contract. But *he* chose Guillarmod, against Eckenstein's advice. Like an artist flinging aside a flawed canvas, Crowley quit for Darjeeling.

Invited for big game hunting in the kingdom of Orissa by the

Maharaja of Moharbhanj, failure hung about like a dead albatross. He wrote, famously, to Gerald Kelly from Calcutta: 'I want blasphemy, murder, rape, revolution, anything, bad or good, but strong.' Somewhere in his brain, the spirit of *The Book of the Law* was bubbling; sentimental humanitarianism was the path to avalanche. *He* had been left alone while the 'team' acted like lemmings. He could interpret the disaster as reflecting the cultural weaknesses of the era, but something had got to him on the mountain, some terror in the winds that lashed Kanchenjunga like barbed whips. He would later call severe asthma attacks 'Kanchenjunga phobia' or the 'Storm Fiend'. He had been scared.

*   *   *

When holy Crowley was not the messiah, he could be a very naughty boy. Exploring Calcutta's red-light district in late October, he entered a narrow alley. Six men surrounded him. A .38 calibre revolver was fired; the men ran off, dragging the wounded. Crowley's finger was on the trigger. Rose arrived two days later; 'just in time to see me hanged' he quipped. Edward Thornton advised he quit India to avoid a lumbering judicial process. Crowley made light of it: 'I am very proud of this story. In that month there had been a dozen outrages on Europeans, and, I was the only outragee who came out on top.'[4] And were it necessary to prove Crowley's mind was not aglow with global revenge, we have a tender, modest letter, sent to Gerald Kelly from Calcutta on 31 October:

> You can't paint a picture without muscular exertion, though nothing is so calm as a picture. If you try to obtain that calm by going to sleep, you don't get it. Lust after a woman and her imperfections are beautiful, admire her, and she becomes at once a dowdy. A lily achieves beauty by trying to grow.
>
> My views are changing in many ways – it is in a very limited sense that I can call myself a Buddhist. If you have not read Burton's *Kasîdah*, do – even if it costs you an effort. It seems to me pretty well the ultimate of human wisdom, as distinguished from my own advance after the possible.[5]

Rose asked her husband where they might go. He suggested Persia, having acquired some Persian writing his *risqué* quasi-Sufi *Scented Garden of Abdullah the Satirist of Shiraz*. Rose wasn't keen.

> 'Wife of my bosom,' said I, 'suppose we walk across China?'
> 'Darling,' she cooed, 'the exercise will do us good.'
> So we packed the baby, and other impedimenta, and sailed off
> for the finest walk in the world.[6]

They took the Calcutta–Rangoon steamer in search of Allan Bennett. The revered Buddhist welcomed them at a monastery on the city's outskirts. He advised Crowley to acquire memory of former incarnations by *sammasati* meditation.

Crowley confided his inner agony to his diary: 'I realise in myself the perfect impossibility of reason; suffering great misery.' Reason, the god of Western philosophy, held within itself the seed of its own absurdity. Every thought evoked its opposite. The higher planes of consciousness transcended reason altogether. Ordinary logic was useless in approaching spiritual reality; worse, it was an impediment. He felt mad:

> I am as one who should have plumed himself for years upon the speed and strength of a favourite horse, only to find not only that its speed and strength were illusory, but that it was not a real horse at all, but a clothes-horse. There being no way – no conceivable way – out of this awful trouble gives that hideous despair which is only tolerable because in the past it has ever been the Darkness of the Threshold. But this is far worse than ever before; I wish to go from A to B; and I am not only a cripple, but there is no such thing as space. I have to keep an appointment at midnight; and not only has my watch stopped, but there is no such thing as time. I wish to make a cannon [a billiards move]; and not only have I no cue, but there is no such thing as causality. This I explain to my wife, and she, apparently inspired, says 'Shoot it!' (I suppose she means the reason, but, of course, she did not understand a word of what I had been saying. I only told her for the sake of formulating my thought clearly in words.) I reply, 'If I only had a gun.' This makes me think of

Siegfried and the Forging of the Sword. Can I heat my broken
Meditation-Sword in the furnace of this despair? Is Discipline
the Hammer? At present I am more like a Mime than Siegfried; a
gibbering ape-like creature, though without his cunning and his
purpose. […] But surely I am not a dead man at thirty.[7]

The Beast had to choose a road; he chose the one to Mandalay, found
after five days on the Irawaddy. Trekking north through 200 miles of
jungle, the family reached Bhamo near the Chinese border on 1
December 1905. There they awaited Chinese passports to enter Yunnan
province. Five years before, the Boxer Rebellion terrorized Europeans in
China. Risks remained. Intelligence history specialist Prof. Richard
Spence sees Crowley intelligence-gathering. Circumstantial evidence
supports the hypothesis.[8]

Leaving Bhamo for Tengyueh on 17 December, Lilith's nurse took off
with a muleteer. Rose, unflappable, kept going. Help was at hand.
Crowley compared George Litton, Tengyueh's British Consul, to his
hero, Sir Richard Burton.[9] Suffering under blind officialdom for the
'crime' of competence, foresight, initiative, and an alarming tendency to
inform his superiors of the facts, Litton's virtues had earned him exile to
this distant British treaty port on the Salween river. As riots raged in
Shanghai and foreigners were murdered, Mrs Litton and her five
children sheltered the Crowleys over Christmas and the New Year.

Aleister gathered data on Yunnan's opium trade, banned by Britain
in 1906. The opium market's loss would affect French tax revenues in
neighbouring Indo-China, so Crowley's reference to the provincial
capital Yunnan-Fu (now Kunming) 'flooded' with French agents is
significant. French engineers supervised the Yunnan-Tonkin railway
construction and tensions were high. The British suspected France was
about to annex Indo-China.[10]

On 10 January, Crowley found Litton's body dumped on the
consulate verandah. He called the Consul's Bengali doctor, Ram Lal
Sircar. Sircar refused to quit his enormous meal, ignoring polite remon-
strations, so Crowley whipped him, forcing him to confront the body.
Sircar refused an autopsy, writing *erysipelas* down as the cause of death.

Crowley inspected the body and suspected the doctor, a writer of anti-British articles for the Bengali press. Sircar registered complaints while Crowley and explorer-botanist George Forrest buried Litton.[11]

The Crowleys left a hostile Tengyueh on 18 January, the matter of the alleged Bengali traitor unresolved. At Yungchang (Baoshan), over 100 miles northeast of Bhamo, the local mandarin invited them to a banquet. After spectacular New Year celebrations, they headed east towards Dali, crossing the Mekong River. Crowley marvelled at Rose's courage, practicality and good humour, the perfect pal.

*   *   *

Buried in Crowley's diaries are the bones of a record of his performing, while trekking across China, one of the most difficult mental exercises imaginable.

His sense of reality had been severely hammered. An acute sense of the purposelessness of existence left him reeling. But the gods had spoken. Between Bhamo and Tengyueh, he fell with his pony 40 feet down a slope. He should have been killed, but escaped without a scratch. Recalling Bennett's advice he meditated on his karmic record. He had been *kept* alive. There *was* a purpose; the gods knew. Still feeling insane, he pressed on with the spiritual journey.

Israel Regardie (Crowley's secretary 1928–32) observed of his former employer's exercises: 'Because of the use of the mind as a tool, when one attempts to transcend that operational tool to reach a higher level of spiritual perception and experience, a serious impasse is reached. It produces a species of insanity.'[12] Crowley described the process of 'entering the Abyss' succinctly. When the aspirant to the highest intelligence has intellectually examined all philosophies:

> Then will all phenomena which present themselves to him appear meaningless, and disconnected, and his own Ego will break up into a series of impressions having no relation with one another, or with any other thing. [...] It may end in real insanity, which concludes the activities of the adept during this present life, or by his rebirth into his own body and mind with the simplicity of a little child.[13]

The Exempt Adept[14] must destroy his *identification* with the transitory ego. The ego must become a tool, not an obstruction to the higher consciousness, the Genius. Crowley remembered the Abra-Melin Oath of Obligation; he must 'Invoke often' and 'Enflame [himself] with praying'. This means *becoming* the prayer, working up to a pitch of enthusiasm and focused will on the prayer's aspiration. And he would have do it every day, week in week out, for months on end.

As Crowley invoked silently in the vast spaces of Yunnan, he was, though there was little sense of 'he' to know it, crossing the Abyss. A feeling of insanity persisted. Crowley believed he was on the road to *nirvikalpa samadhi.*

*   *   *

Leaving Dali on 6 February for Yunnan-Fu (Kunming), some 200 wearying miles to the east, the family mules trudged along the alien roads, while a silent Crowley, astride his pony, repeated his fiery invocations, developing, as he did so, an interior, imaginative temple. Thus did Crowley daily attempt to open himself to his higher genius, his *daimon* or *Augoeides*: the 'beaming' or 'morning light'.[15]

> February 9th. About this full moon Consciousness began to break through Ruach [rational mind] into Neschamah [spiritual mind].[16] Intend to stick to Augoeides.[17]

He espied a purpose: TEACH. He must teach the next step for humankind. The message: 'the Knowledge and Conversation of the Holy Guardian Angel.'

Why use such old fashioned language?

Because a child could understand it.

On 14 February, Crowley feared a swollen throat gland. He asked the *Augoeides* to remove that fear. The next day he determined to invoke the *Augoeides* daily; result: 'my fear removed'. And so he continued, day after day after day, for over nine months.

*   *   *

Five more days on the road passed before the family entered Yunnan-Fu. Marching through the packed streets towards the consulate, they saw Buddhist temples, Taoist temples and Muslim mosques. Crowley saw a great truth underlying all of them, that one day would bring them into common purpose.

British Consul-General, WH Wilkinson regretted he couldn't offer hospitality until complaints from Litton's doctor had been investigated. Crowley turned to the French mission hospital run by physician, author, journalist and Brother Mason, Dr Georges Barbézieux. Crowley learned much of French activity in the region before bidding farewell.[18] They headed southeast for Tonkin,[19] but not before, as Crowley put it, 'I had settled my little official affair with the Consul General'.[20] Spence reckons he probably made a report and received an award. Information about an anti-British Bengali was valuable.

After 200 miles, they reached the French concession settlement of Mengtse, enjoying three days with Charles Henry Brewitt-Taylor, an impressive British Commissioner of Customs.[21] From Mengtse, the family journeyed southeast towards the French Indo-China border where Crowley hired a boat to negotiate the Hong Ha (Red) River. The coolies disputed the price. Crowley brandished his rifle, gathering his family into the boat as coolies threatened from the banks. Overcoming perilous rapids, the jubilant Crowleys arrived in Hekou, on the Tonkin border, on 18 March. They had done what they had been warned could not be done: 650 miles of unmolested travel through Chinese territory. Rose and the baby were in excellent health, though Aleister appeared ragged as a tramp, skin torn and marked forever. He was extremely proud of Rose; in a class of her own as comrade and mother.

Taking the train to Hanoi, they rattled on to Haiphong in the Gulf of Tonkin. There they boarded a tramp steamer for Hong Kong, 500 miles away. Recuperating at a decent hotel, Rose agreed to take herself and baby Lilith home. Performing his daily invocations, Crowley would cross the Pacific for Vancouver, thence east across Canada, and south to New York, apparently to raise money and scientific interest for *Kanchenjunga II*, planned for 1907. Crowley wrote to Clifford Bax.[22]

Hong Kong, South China, 28 March 1906

My dear Bax,

Your letter reached me here on my arrival from Burma via Yunnan-Fan with the wife and child. We had a fine time – about four months on the road. [...]

It's very easy to get all the keys (invisible and otherwise) into the Kingdom; but the locks are devilish stuff – some of them hampered.

I am myself just at the end of a little excursion of nearly seven years into Hell. The illusion of reason, which I thought I had stamped out in '98, was bossing me. It has now got the boot. But let this tell you that it is one thing to devote your life to magic at 20 years old and another to find at 30 that you are bound to stay a Magus. The first is the folly of a child; the second the Gate of the Sanctuary. It's no good, though, my writing indefinitely like this – only as a magical act can it be justified. (ie: the Masters may operate the coincidence that it should fit the case). By rights you should get ordeals and initiations and things. A really good student can make it all up himself; and if he has really the wit to interpret all right he needs no teacher.

Solve et coagula – said some ass. *Solve* – volatilize the fixed by a firm resolve to interpret everything in life as a spiritual fact, a step on the Path, a guide to the Light. An old disciple of mine put it more clumsily, thus: 'Whatever ye do, whether ye eat or drink, do all to the glory of God.' I may add that in my own experience failure to do this has given me a bad time. Every time you interpret anything whatever materially you go a buster, worse than a motor-car smash. [...]

Coagula – the volatile – means what you had better find out for yourself. If you do, write and tell me. I haven't an idea. So shall take some pretty drastic steps to discover. [...] *Register* magical letters, unless your soul is worth less than tuppence.[23]

Before leaving for America, Crowley could not resist sailing to Shanghai to see Fidelis. The motive was as symbolic as it was sexual. He had begun comparing the 'dawning' *Augoeides* to Babylonian goddess Ishtar, or Venus, the morning star; herald to the dawn. Ishtar's symbol was an eight-pointed star. He then identified Elaine with 'El Istar', intuiting she was important to the invocation, perhaps as Tantric partner or initiatrix. On 17 April, the day before the great San Francisco Earthquake, he and Elaine kissed on the other side of the Pacific:

> Ere Sol in Aires make bright spring weather
> Eight Star and Six star shall have kissed together.

Crowley sought guidance from his first studies of the I Ching and *The Book of the Law*; neither helped. In her diplomat husband's absence, Elaine agreed to invoke Aiwass in her temple. Crowley judged the results unconvincing. 'Aiwass', speaking through Elaine, instructed he go to Egypt with Rose; Elaine's resistance to physical relations rendered her useless. Elaine tried to converse with Crowley's 'Guardian Angel' who recommended a Great Retirement, with or without Rose; Crowley should use *brahmacharya*, Tantric or 'chaste' yoga. Hovering over intimations that he should work with Elaine, Crowley dismissed the Easter Day invocations as 'rigmarole' since Elaine's 'clinging' had 'ruined her clairvoyance and rotted up her magic'. Crowley stuck to the chastity demanded by Abra-Melin.

On 24 April 1906, as his ship docked at Kobe, Japan, Crowley invoked all the powers he knew and experienced curious visions as he astral-travelled into strange environments:

> Then One human, white, self-shining (my idea after all!) came
> forth and put his hands over mine, saying 'I receive thee into the
> Order of the Silver Star.' [24] Then with advice to return, I sank
> back to earth in a cradle of flame.

The Order of the Silver Star would be a name for Crowley's magical order. A 'Self-glittering One' would be his guide. All he needed to do was to 'Invoke often': 'I cannot go wrong, for I am the Chosen One; that is the very postulate of the whole Work. This boat carries Caesar and his fortunes.'

He sailed on to Vancouver, thence by train to Toronto, Niagara, and, at last, New York. There was much wining and dining, but neither funds nor scientific interest for Kanchenjunga II. During the voyage home (31 May) he enjoyed the best invocation yet:

> Vision quite perfect and I tasted the sweet kiss and gazed in the clear eyes of that radiant one. My own face (I am sure by the feel of the skin) became luminous.

From the heights of his best invocation, he was slammed down to Earth with a terrible, calamitous stab to his heart.

> Arrived Liverpool. Heard of Baby's death by letters from Mother and Uncle Tom. Why did nobody cable me? Arrived London, perfectly stunned.

Little Lilith, less than two years old, had died of typhoid at Rangoon on May Day. Aleister was utterly inconsolable. 'Fortunately I am quite unable to think of the thing in detail or as a reality.' On 31 December he would add a PS to that entry: 'Not fortunately at all. One *never* gets able to do so. Stupour and pangs get to the limit and that limit is easy reached by very partial conceptions of one's loss.' Breaking down playing billiards, he drugged himself. Ivor Back comforted him.

He went down to Plymouth on 7 June to meet Rose, making his invocation on the train. Joining Rose, he kept breaking down with grief. He could not do the invocation. 'Still breaking down at intervals', he staggered from nervous weakness: 'Dropping off to sleep at odd times and places.' He discussed with Rose going on a magical retirement together; would she work with him? She said she wanted to, 'but her nervous state is bad and unreliable so she contradicts'. The next day he was 'frightfully ill', falling to sleep with pain. His nights were scored with nightmares. Still he tried his utmost to do the invocation.

Haunted by loss and the desire to give up self, Crowley sped towards the climax of the Abra-Melin Operation. George Cecil Jones agreed to visit and assist with a ritual to stimulate uniting a purified self and the divine.

In a nursing home bed on the 22nd, Crowley underwent a 'remarkable experiment with hashish'. He 'took some five grains and smoked a little ganja', obtained from EP Whineray's, Stafford Street, Piccadilly.

Crowley decamped to George Cecil Jones's house at Mistley near Basingstoke on 26 July where he went through a crucifixion ritual, vowing to lead a pure and unselfish life, dedicated to achieving 'my higher and Divine Genius'. Crowley lived under the vow for the rest of his life. He then had a 'Complete and perfect visualization' of Christ as his magical self. The next day he enjoyed 'a certain vision of A.·. [*Augoeides*] remembered only as a glory now attainable'.

He was now in the 25th week of the *Augoeides* Invocation.

Crowley and Jones discussed establishing a new order. Jones insisted it have a secure link to the supernal will. Crowley opined: 'Perfect the lightning-conductor and the flash will come.' Through the trauma and the introspection, Crowley was finding his way to his life's work.

A ceremony of 'rising in the planes' stirred a visionary experience in Crowley of crossing the Abyss by the path of the camel (Gimel) from Ruach, the middle part of the soul (= reason), to Kether and Yechidah, the Holy Guardian Angel. At the end of the vision, there was only the memory of having known a glory, but one impossible to pin down or define.

The date: 27 July 1906.

Throughout the summer and autumn came intimations of a climax to the Abra-Melin Operation, even of having somehow, but elusively, attained it, as on 27 July. It is hardly surprising to learn that at this point in his life, Crowley believed himself to have penetrated the mystery of Christ's teaching, finding his way to the 'Secret of Jesus'. A deleted diary entry of 5 August reads:

> My Revelations book *The Arcanum in the Adytum* [drawing of
> a diamond] *or the Secret of the Sacred Heart of Jesus, being a
> Commentary upon the Apocalypse*. On the cover *The Secret of Jesus*.

On 10 August he felt himself on the threshold of the *Augoeides*. He experienced doubt, then realized the essential 'Armageddon' took place within, when resistance to union with 'God' broke down: 'Armageddon', the final conflict 'Where the rationalist argument breaks down; necessary for it to prove that *samadhi* is a diseased process.'[25] Crowley planned a complete kabbalistic commentary on the Book of Revelation. A shame he did not complete it, it might have brought him recognition as an advanced theologian – if the world were fair.

Four days after the Crowleys moved into a suite at the Ashdown Park Hotel, Coulsdon, Surrey, in September, a 32-week period of preparation for the Abra-Melin Operation ended. Jones turned up on the 22nd. The adepts worked on a *new* ritual, a quintessence of the Golden Dawn's Neophyte ritual.[26] Nine days later, a hashish experiment combined with invocation and the new ritual coincided with the culmination of the Operation of the Sacred Magic of Abra-Melin the Mage.

On 9 October, Crowley remarked in a diary full of cryptic references: 'Tested new ritual and behold it was very good! Thanked gods and sacrificed for – ' Crowley subsequently added the word Lola. Lola was the name preferred by Crowley's girlfriend Vera Snepp, whom he met at the Ashdown Park Hotel.[27] Having taken hashish at 8, at 10pm he became absorbed in *nirvikalpa-samadhi*, the crown of *raja yoga*: union with the absolute – or, in this context, the 'Knowledge and Conversation of the Holy Guardian Angel'.

> 10th. [October] I am still drunk with *samadhi* all day. [...] I *will* see Adonai. [the Lord, the Holy Guardian Angel]

His unpublished diary for 10 October remarks on the 'thanksgiving and sacrifice': 'I *did* get rid of everything but the Holy Exalted One, and must have held Him for a minute or two. I did. I am sure I did. I expected Rose to see a Halo round my head.' He was concerned that 'the hashish enthusiasm surged up against the ritual-enthusiasm; so I hardly know which phenomena to attribute to which. [...] The more I think of it the more I am sure that I got into samadhi. (somehow) not like a human at all.'

Crowley's experience of *samadhi* went on for nearly a fortnight! Was it the result of taking hashish? Jones's view: hashish had 'nothing to do with the *samadhi*, though possibly useful as a starter'.

*   *   *

Crowley had now united the highest conceptions of Western magick to the scientific conditions of yogic meditation. But the feeling of glory slowly left him during November. A reaction set in. He doubted himself; was he not still himself? Was the achievement for nothing, and if for nothing, was it an achievement at all? Was it all a trick of the mind? The essence of the experience had to be absorbed and his mind, in computer-speak, had to be 're-booted'. The business was aggravated by an ulcerated throat and other ailments and, what was far worse, the awful realization that Rose was fast becoming an irredeemable alcoholic.

Then, in December, Crowley experienced *nirvikalpa-samadhi* again – 'and he knew!'[28] The work with Jones, the walk across China: not in vain.

*   *   *

In mid-December, Crowley posed an intriguing rhetorical question to Jones: 'How long have you been in the Great Order, and why did I not know? Is the invisibility of the A.·.A.·. to lower grades so complete?' Crowley's revived spiritual dependency on Jones made him look more closely at his old friend. Now he was sure that Jones had himself experienced the Knowledge and Conversation of the Holy Guardian Angel.

With Jones's help, Crowley determined to establish the ideal working order for those who would cross the Abyss: the A.·.A.·..

The three dots are a masonic conceit referring to spiritual activity, derived from 17th-century Rosicrucian sources. The letters 'AA' are usually taken to stand for '*Astrum Argentinum*', or 'Silver Star'. Their meaning is an Order secret, though there is a tie in with the silvery star of the High Priestess tarot trump. Her full title 'The Priestess of the Silver Star' represents spiritual perception.

Linked directly to the will of the Secret Chiefs, the Order would replace the old Golden Dawn. Soon, he projected, the A.·.A.·. would initiate the thinking and spiritually active part of humanity. Israel Regardie observed that at this point, Crowley was truly divinely guided, knowing his Holy Guardian Angel, attuned to His Work, at one with a poetic description Crowley wrote up as an article, called 'The Electric Silence':

> And the end shall be as is appointed by the master of the House; but this I know, that this ship is the King's ship. And in my bosom are the champak-blossom and the mustard seed, and the oak-leaf. More lovely than before. And upon us watcheth ever he that is appointed to watch – and the wild swan sings ever; and my heart sings ever.[29]

And he had cause to sing. In the winter of 1906, Rose Crowley gave birth to their second daughter, Lola Zaza, seven long months after the death of her little sister, Lilith.

*   *   *

If England were a spiritual country, the Ashdown Park Hotel in Coulsdon, Surrey, would be a shrine to where England's prophet met his Holy Guardian Angel and became absorbed in divinity; a holy site where competing sects of Crowleyanity could battle over who owned it. Alas, the Ashdown Park Hotel, Coulsdon, was demolished in 1971.

Teaching Tankerville

1907

BURY me in a nameless grave!
I came from God the world to save,
I brought them wisdom from above:
Worship, and liberty, and love.
They slew me for I did disparage
Therefore Religion, Law, and Marriage.
So be my grave without a name
That earth may swallow up my shame.[1]

Aleister Crowley at 31 was a walking revolution, his head an experimental laboratory for a time to come. Spontaneous, he knew he was an 'imp', always getting into scrapes; he was a loveable child and a married superman. Saddled with a nonconformist conscience, Crowley would always think in terms of guilt and punishment, of service and reward.

It is an open question as to how much of his willed psychospiritual dis-integration and re-integration can be attributed to his trying to get away from the 'imp' by finding the god-like part in his being, putting the boy-man Aleister under *His* care and guidance. He lacked a father figure and sought one in himself. While always trying to improve himself, he would regularly surrender to impulse. His 'Magical Retirements' indicate a regular need to steady his rocky boat. Bad experiences were punishments for getting it wrong. He would attribute many hard misfortunes to ignoring the injunctions of *The Book of the Law*. Eventually, *AL* took the place once occupied by his father; his father had been much kinder, but not so intimate to his soul.

Though he knew the rules, Crowley was not comfortable in English society. His adolescence coincided with social vulnerability. He took respite in the caste security and spiritual ideal of aristocracy, yet, noble in spirit like his father, Crowley was open to people of all classes; he could see the soul in every thing and every one. He followed the aristocracy's sexual mores, justifying himself by a firm belief that there should be 'no traffic in human flesh'. He had married Rose to free her. Amused by Lt. Col. Joseph Gormley MD's desperate pursuit of Rose, he invited the would-be lover to a house party.[2] After Lilith's death, Rose sought solace in alcohol; Crowley in affairs.

The gods must have a sense of humour, for no sooner had Crowley embarked on life as a spiritual teacher than he found his first significant pupil in a mad aristocrat.

*   *   *

On Sunday 6 January 1907 Crowley was in Bournemouth. Recommended by his doctor as an airy palliative for throat pains, the posh resort was the locus for a pioneering experiment with hashish. Lying in bed, Crowley experienced *atmadarshana*, which he described as: 'The 'millions of worlds' game – the peacock multiform with each 'eye' of its fan a mirror of glory wherein also another peacock – everything thus.'

What was he getting at?

Atmadarshana is an absolutely clear experience of the 'divine spirit' in relation to the universe. In the state of *Atmadarshana*, each part of the universe becomes the whole; matter and spirit are no longer opposed; all contraries appear resolved: 'It is the Universe freed from its conditions.'[3]

Crowley's new disciple, Captain JFC Fuller, believed humanity had waited countless millennia for 'the greatest of all Teachers' to appear.[4] Fuller attempted to describe the Teacher's trance of the 'Universal Peacock', but when he came to the transcending of a Trinitarian cosmos by an 'impersonal Unity' that was itself then annihilated, Fuller concluded: 'It is absolutely futile to discuss this: it has been tried and failed again and again.

Even those with experience of the earlier part of the 'vision' in its fullness must find it totally impossible to imagine anything so subversive of the whole base, not only of the Ego, but of the Absolute behind the Ego.' You had to be 'there' to understand it; Crowley was.

Hailed as a Master by GC Jones at the end of 1906, Crowley experienced the fruit of mastery: 'recognizing that *I am He* in the same way that I recognize "Snow is white" – not arguing it, nor announcing it triumphantly. I acted on that basis without self-consciousness, and wrote various letters.'

Crowley concluded that 'only an Adept can use Hashish to excite *samadhi*'. As he experimented, his powers of introspective analysis increased. The logic-train slowed down until he could count its couplings; he got *inside* the process of thought. Knowing of the drug's reputation in oriental mysticism, he brought it under the gaze of science in a pioneering analysis, *The Psychology of Hashish* (1908). The resultant clarity in describing mystical psychology permeates his *Confessions*:

> The Ruach [reason], lastly, is the machine of the mind
> converging on a central consciousness, which appears to be
> the Ego. The true Ego is, however, above Neschamah [spiritually
> receptive mind], whose occasional messages to the Ruach
> warn the human Ego of the existence of his superior. Such
> communications may be welcomed or resented, encouraged or
> stifled. Initiation consists in identifying the human self with the
> divine, and the man who does not strain constantly to this end is
> simply a brute made wretched and ashamed by the fact of self-
> consciousness.[5]

In Bournemouth Crowley compiled a remarkable Qabalistic Dictionary, *777*, based on tabulations made by Allan Bennett and possibly Samuel Mathers. Crowley did not credit himself on the title page. Having integrated the esoteric symbols of East and West, the greatest British mystic since William Blake quit Bournemouth on 29 January: 'one may hope for ever'.

*   *   *

Crowley would call the years 1907–08 'years of fulfillment', but the period began anxiously. In mid-February, Lola Zaza became ill. An alcoholic, Rose found it hard to focus on her daughter's needs. Rose called her mother in. No lover of mothers, Crowley blamed Blanche for incompetence during a crisis. Only *his* timely provision of oxygen, he believed, saved Lola's life. When access to the baby was limited on doctor's orders, Crowley told Blanche to keep out. Blanche ignored him. Crowley 'took the hag by the shoulders and ran her out of the flat, assisting her down the stairs with my boot lest she misinterpret my meaning'.

Another 'Mother Horror' was about to appear. Crowley dined with George Montagu Bennet, 7th Earl of Tankerville in late February.[6] Dubbed the 'Earl of Coke and Crankum' in Crowley's autohagiography, the Earl insisted his mother, Lady Olivia, was trying to kill him by witchcraft. Inheritance imperilled, could Crowley help him?

Saving Man from 'Mother' was as big a priority for Crowley as saving girls and boys from wedlock's chains. He looked to his tarot cards: 'His card is *Death*', he told Jones. Jones interpreted this as '*unexpected change*'. A new current in Crowley's life was born.

To kick it off, artist Kathleen Bruce sculpted Crowley as an 'Enchanted Prince' on 23 February. Inspired by her beauty and talent, Crowley wrote *A Terzain* that day, verses that would preface his romantic, doomed-erotic poetry book *Clouds without Water*, published 'for ministers of religion' in 1909. The sculptor's name appears in acrostics: read down the first letter of each line.[7]

Sitting for Kathleen on the 26th, Crowley observed the analogy between sexual attraction and the joy of union with the Holy Guardian Angel, a realization central to Crowley's metaphysics: the sex instinct is divine; it is blind man who drags it into his gutter. Kathleen and Aleister were lovers. Eighteen months later, Kathleen Bruce would marry the doomed Robert Falcon 'Scott of the Antarctic'.

Taking the train to Cambridge on 28 February, Crowley met an undergraduate poet. Recommended by Captain Fuller, 23-year-old

Victor Benjamin Neuburg rebelled against conventional religion and embraced 'Pan'. Crowley must have felt the magic working; three potential high-grade neophytes for the new Order in as many months.

Having earlier dumped competition prospectuses at Oxford and Cambridge offering a cash prize for the best 'essay' about his work, Crowley not only stimulated 'Christian Union' opposition to his publication arm SPRT, but also generated Captain Fuller's book, *The Star in the West*. Fuller received his prize 'in kind' on 16 May when Crowley got publishers Walter Scott to print it. Overblown, bright, often obscure, Fuller's book served for missionary purposes.

Crowley believed he could vitalize the hidden genius of any person who sought his instruction. In Neuburg's case, genius was already apparent. Neuburg told Jean Overton Fuller in the 1930s, 'I thought he [Crowley] was a noble person. I think you would have thought so, too.'[8] Neuburg's early assessment of Crowley compares with that of Gerald Kelly, also imparted to Jean Overton Fuller: 'When I first knew him, he was an utterly delightful person', adding, snobbishly, that 'he was not a gentleman. He had certain vulgarisms. But, he was very good company.' Neuburg did not mind the 'vulgarisms', whatever they may have been.

On 1 March, Crowley accompanied Neuburg to the university's 'Magpie and Stump' debate, afterwards devoting a Pepysian half-hour to 'feeling' two girls: 'the girl from the jam factory and Mabel of Day's.' He talked to Neuburg and his friends again on the Saturday and 'Felt [the] chambermaid'. '– so endeth the First Missionary Journey', wrote Crowley, back in London. An older man from 'outside' offering instruction to undergraduates did not pass unnoticed. Cambridge's religious life belonged to the established Churches; they were jealous.

*   *   *

Following Havelock Ellis (who turned WB Yeats on) Crowley experimented with mescaline, from the peyote cactus, taken as drops in cold water. On 15 March, 15 drops at intervals had little effect. He then 'f[ucked] Rose and slept like a dog'. What Edwardian England looked like to a mystic outsider experiencing the soulful vividness and sparkling clarity of psychedelic vision we shall, sadly, never know, but he must have seen what very few had ever seen; a perception leap from his time comparable to that experienced by the first man to jet through the stratosphere and touch the rim of outer space. Clarity of mind impossible to convey is evident in the demented, delightful, hyper-intelligent prosody and poetry of his book *Konx Om Pax*.

The night-tripper moved into a fourth-floor flat at 60, Jermyn Street. Ahead of his time, he began a purging, fast-and-exercise routine: 'Allowed: Fish, lean meats, eggs, fruit, green vegetables and heroin.' Two factors inspired the move. First, to put some distance between himself and Rose; she was secretly supping spirits to the tune of a bottle of Scotch a day. Second, everything pointed to his taking on pupils as a way of life. He was planning the A.'.A.'. curriculum with Jones and needed to be at the centre of cultural life; Boleskine would become the Order retreat.

Cocaine-addict Tankerville offered Crowley a salary and expenses while developing powers of resistance to Mother. Crowley gave him talismans, the 'Sign of Saturn to read' and the 'Lesser Banishing Ritual of the Pentagram' to protect him from obsessions. These were Crowley's 'rehab' services, to straighten the Earl out with magick and common sense. Crowley made many tarot readings to determine Tankerville's position in his family over the next few months. Rose acted as clairvoyant. The best thing, Crowley concluded, would be to get Tankerville away from the familial contagion to freer climes where his natural balance would, under guidance, return. Unfortunately, the vagaries of addiction depend greatly on the psychology of the addict. A psychological addiction can be as difficult to cope with as a physical one.

Crowley valued Rose's clairvoyance, noting her insights into Tankerville's problems at Chislehurst, a regular haunt of the time. On 29 April: 'A great change will occur in less than a year from now. P[erdurabo] will pull the Tankervilles through. Rose will be useful to see things. Tankerville and P[erdurabo] closely associated.'

Busy with his new life, Crowley went to Cambridge, his 'second Missionary Journey', on the 30th. A fortnight later, he took the oath of *Master of the Temple* 8°=3□. Rose and Tankerville were present. Tankerville called on Crowley the next day; they arranged a 'Great Retirement' to Spain; 'Good God', wrote Crowley. Doubts proved justified.

After a week getting fit playing golf, he went to Southampton on 12 June via the old Crowley town of Alton, taking lunch with cousin Agnes. He then went sailing with Tankerville's son, Charlie Ossulston on the *Ellida* 'in a notable gale of wind' to Beaulieu Creek. Crowley had to be rescued from the 'wrecked' yacht. On 20 June, Rose joined him; arrangements for the foreign trip continued. Lady Tankerville would use his rooms; he provided her with a copy of the *Goetia*. Rose received a packet of *Savory & Moore's Absorbent Lozenges*. She then had a 'narrow escape' in Pall Mall when a mysterious attack was made on Crowley's life, probably connected with Tankerville because the next diary entry states: 'Final end of T[ankerville]'s enemies.'

*　　*　　*

Crowley and 'Tanky' left for Marseilles via Paris on 27 June 1907, boarding P&O Steam Ship *Mongolia* for Gibraltar three days later. A promising start: Tankerville accused Crowley of disrespect toward women; Crowley diagnosed persecution mania:

> He has twice so injured his wife as to cause her to miscarry, and she is still ill. He states that his own mother is guilty of: (1) Incest, with her father. (2) Adultery. (3) Lesbian vice. (4) Witchcraft, 'mental murder,' et hoc genus omne. He believes in a great conspiracy to ruin him.

Tankerville said he felt great pressure on his brain and that his nerves were on the outside of his body:

> Regards everyone with suspicion. Has a sister in an asylum. Has attempted suicide. Has often murderously attacked his wife. Is always threatening to shoot his mother and her companions. Has delusions about his mother and others. Is sexually deranged, having an irrational horror of 'animalities'. Is always getting 'suggestions' and believes himself to be permanently hypnotized. Thinks doctors all in a conspiracy against the human race.

Takes cocaine. [...] Talking to Tankerville is like being in a cage with a wild beast. One doesn't take one's eye off him, as it were. A single, unguarded word, the result of irritation or indigestion, and he would, I verily believe, go raving mad.

Crowley attracted neurotics, but Tanky was gripped by a raging psychosis. Crowley must have had huge confidence in his abilities to board the *Jebel Musa* for Tangier with Tanky on 6 July, three days after Pablo Picasso stunned fellow artists in Paris with his *Les Demoiselles d'Avignon*, named after a Barcelona brothel. 'It's a revolution!' declared Guillaume Apollinaire.

The New Aeon had arrived in paint.

Ensconced in the Hotel Continental, Tankerville, oblivious to the revolution, whined: 'I'm sick of your teaching-teaching-teaching, as if you were God omnipotent and I were a bloody shit in the street.' That appealed to Crowley's humour. He entitled his riposte 'A Notable Fancy':

I saw a golden throne in heaven reserved for James, whom Herod slew;

And Peter whom they crucified had got a ripping palace too.

The Order of the Bath was worn by poor old roast Polycarp.

And Andrew had a beautiful inlaid and gilded rosewood harp.

Sebastian had a golden crown and strong Stephen one of platinum;

While starved St Mungo ate and ate West India turtles with green fat in 'em.

St Lawrence sported an appropriate and dainty silver grill;

But I had spent my holiday with George the Earl of Tankerville.

The Lord apologised to me. "It really wasn't in My plan;

"Come off it, Jesus Christ," he said, "your seat will suit this gentleman!"

When Moses prayed, the Lord replied, the process never seemed to fail him.

I aimed at being Moses, too, I've missed the beggar and hit Balaam.

Apart from diarrhoea and a bad throat, Crowley soon found the coast to his liking ('the excessive beauty of the boys in Fez'); Tankerville was unimpressed. Crowley realized Tanky was mad beyond rescue and took long walks to escape the irrational outbursts. On one, he chanced upon a group of Dervishes in ecstatic dance, cutting flesh in abandonment to their god. Itching to join in, fear of exposure and death prevented him.

On 11 July Crowley received 'most unsatisfactory news'. Rose was burning his manuscripts, including *Dieu libre et criminel*. At least William Blake's and Sir Richard Burton's wives had waited till their husbands' deaths before incinerating their work. To keep sane, Crowley devised a practice for approaching enlightenment called 'The Thinkable is False': 'Sit down and watch your thoughts and keep on saying, "That's a lie".' Curiously, and in spite of all, he began to find his distinctive voice as a spiritual master; an idiosyncratic combination of profundity, simplicity, and humour. Lying in bed after a fever on 13 July, still 'far from fit', he wrote a poem 'There is no other God than He', included in *Konx Om Pax* as 'The Devil's Conversion': a brilliant display of wit and insight. Crowley found himself in a swoon of ecstasy, something he wished to share with his repressed countrymen and women, if not all humankind:

> The curious sense that I have the Power of samadhi is again with me. No doubt I have attained; only a question of waiting without attachment for the reward. [opposite which was written:] I think this stamps me clearly as an $8°=3°$ elect [Magister Templi=Master of the Temple].

Crowley then added: 'I don't know about the Power of *samadhi*; but I can tolerate Tankerville, and I want a new grade specially created for *that*.'

By 16 July, Tankerville was 'practically sane' but 'pitiably normal'. It was Tankerville's abnormal psychology that interested him. The patient 'discussed Elant [his wife] and sex both quite sanely.'[9] They crossed back to Gibraltar. Crowley thought it best to keep the 'Devilled Earl' moving. He planned a walk about Andalusia and Granada, visiting Bobadilla and Ronda, famous for bullfighting. He saw gypsies dancing

and hunted out bordellos. At 10.20am on Friday 19th, he sat down in a
balcony turret of the Alhambra and contemplated his universe:

> 10.40. In my Irrawaddy ordeal [1905], the mortar of the Universe
> gave way. Today the stones themselves crumble and dissolve,
> there is no meaning in any idea; all statements are not only false
> and true, but unintelligible. (This is the hell of Binah).[10]

Inspired by thoughts of the faith celebrated in Granada's cathedral, he
wrote another poem, 'On a prospect of Granada Cathedral from the
Alhambra', seeing the cathedral as a 'bloated toad' licking in 'the ravaged
soul of all mankind'. At 10pm he made love to a gypsy girl whom he
called *La Gitana Saliya*. A 'gitana' is a Spanish female gypsy and a 'Saliya'
is a Tamil worshipper of Shiva, who may be venerated through a symbol
of the phallus. He exclaimed in his diary: 'O the roses of the world!'

On Sunday 21st he watched a bullfight at La Linea, before he
and Tankerville boarded the *Reichspostdampfschiff Scharnhorst* for
Southampton. Aboard the German ship, Crowley wrote 'La Gitana',
rating it highly.[11] He was right, as usual.

> Your hair was full of roses in the dewfall as we danced,
> The sorceress enchanting and the paladin entranced,
> In the starlight as we wove us in a web of silk and steel
> Immemorial as the marble in the halls of Boabdil,
> In the pleasaunce of the roses with the fountains and the yews
> Where the snowy Sierra soothed us with the breezes and
>   the dews!
> In the starlight as we trembled from a laugh to a caress
> And the god came warm upon us in our pagan allegresse.
> Was the Baile de la Bona too seductive? Did you feel
> Through the silence and the softness all the tension and the steel?
> For your hair was full of roses, and my flesh was full of thorns
> And the midnight came upon worth a million crazy morns.
> Ah! my Gipsy, my Gitana, my Saliya! were you fain
> For the dance to turn to earnest?—O the sunny land of Spain!

My Gitana, my Saliya! more delicious than a dove!
With your hair aflame with roses and your lips alight with love!
Shall I see you, shall I kiss you once again? I wander far
From the sunny land of summer to the icy Polar Star.
I shall find you, I shall have you! I am coming back again
From the filth and fog to seek you in the sunny land of Spain.
I shall find you, my Gitana, my Saliya! as of old
With your hair aflame with roses and your body gay with gold.
I shall find you, I shall have you, in the summer and the south
With our passion in your body and our love upon your mouth—
With our wonder and our worship be the world aflame anew!
My Gitana, my Saliya! I am coming back to you!

Tanky and Crowley's relationship was over. On 1 August, he received a 'mean letter' from Elant. He turned his attention to Neuburg with whom he would return to Spain the following year. The pagan Neuburg was more in tune with the space and heat and passion of the place.

Perhaps the experience of Catholic Spain also encouraged Crowley to write, on his return, a series of poems in praise of the goddess Isis. These he quickly transformed into hymns in praise of the Virgin Mary, with some subtle lesbian twists; all that was required was a change of name for the feminine protagonist and Star of the piece.[12] Catholic publisher Burns & Oates published them in the interests of Catholic devotion as *Amphora* (1909), proving Crowley's point about the spiritual relativity of religious experience. It was also a fine joke to get the servants of Mother Church to exonerate the work of the Beast 666, unconsciously to sanction lesbian desire between the devoted and the Virgin.

Divine cheek.

As summer turned to autumn 1907, Crowley worked on *Konx Om Pax* ('Light in Extension'), designing its ahead-of-its time cover while stoned on hashish on 2 October. The title is a vast modernist and geo-metrically disciplined maze of exaggerated lettering. Nearly all of Crowley's self-published books are distinguished, but *Konx* is a particular gem.

An ominous note is sounded in the diary entry for 27 September:

> Rose again unmasked. From Uridge [victualler], only – 120
> bottles [of whiskey] in 150 days.

Compensation for Rose's alcoholism appeared in the form of Lavinia King, a name he would use in his 1929 novel *Moonchild* for American choreographer-dancer, Isadora Duncan. On Friday 11th, he met LK 'again by chance' on Cockspur Street; five chance encounters in 13 days. On Monday 14th, the diary says simply: 'The Regeneration of Lavinia King.' He continued with smoking a 'kif pipe', exercises recommended by Mahatma Agamya, meditation on *bhakti* (devotional yoga), began a novel, lunched with friends and then, on the evening of 30 October:

> Wrote I & II Liber Cordis Cincti Serpente. Again, no shadow of samadhi; only a feeling that V.V.V.V.V. was in His *samadhi*, and writing by my pen, i.e., the pen of the scribe, and that scribe not όυ μη, who reasons, etc., nor a.c., who is a poet & selects, but of some perfectly passive person.

Inspired, he was the voice of a higher mind, his Holy Guardian Angel. He completed the 'Holy Book' *Liber Cordis Cincti Serpente* on the 1st and 2nd of November. On the 16th he became convinced that this was all part of the Magister Templi initiation process: 'I can, I know, get into touch with Adonai at will, […] I want nothing but to do my work with confidence and no hope or fear.' *Adonai*, the Lord, was his Higher Genius. More Holy Books would appear before the year's end.

Rose visited: 'trouble'.

Crowley was living at least two lives. There was the man and there was the emerging *Magister Templi* (Master of the Temple) 8°=3□ 'elect'. The process began in 1907 but was not completed until 1909. His motto for the grade was *Vi Verum Vniversum Vivus Vici*: 'In my lifetime I have conquered the Universe by the force of Truth.' His journey from Ruach to Neschamah had left its trace; the footprints of the path of the Camel: VVVVV.

VVVVV was not 'the man Crowley' but the state of being that could objectify 'Crowley the man', the Master, if you like, of Crowley-the-temple. According to colleague Captain Fuller, 'It is a question of the transference of the Ego from the personal to the impersonal. He the conscious man, could not say "I am in Samadhi"; he was merely conscious that "that which was he" was in samadhi.'[13] Thus we can say that VVVVV dictated the 'Holy Books' to Frater Perdurabo, beginning in the October of 1907. The Will came through the Master; he was the scribe.

According to Israel Regardie, as a 'Master of the Temple', Crowley was 'a personification of the Atman, the universal Self, the Life principle of the entire cosmos that pulses in every atom'. And what kind of mastery is intended by this attainment? Regardie again: 'Adonai [the 'Lord'], the Holy Guardian Angel, is an individualised centre of the Universal living Spirit. It is not personal in any sense; it is the Atman, the Self, of whom Shankara once said: "Brahm is true, the world is false, the Soul is Brahm, and nothing else!"'[14]

Along with the exalted consciousness went Crowley's other great personal discovery, that the sex instinct is linked to the divine ecstasy that may be obtained through meditative practices; our bodies are in truth 'temples of the holy ghost'. Sexual energy may be employed, with care, as a mystical path of ascent to the level where magick may be worked.

The 'sin', according to Crowley, lies in treating sex at the level of base instinct, smothering it with guilt and shame. Such conduct degrades and blasphemes a holy sacrament. A sacrament takes a thing from nature and transforms it by spiritual intention and ritual action into a redeeming power. Crowley knew that the ancient Gnostics had seen the sacramental value of sex and Crowley considered his own work consistent with that battered tradition; his was a fresh synthesis for an age of science.

Crowley joined sex back to the Western 'Rosicrucian' tradition. He made scientific a path of attainment that brought human sexuality into spiritual relief. Crowley's concept of 'chastity' meant the right-governing of our sexual natures, not the fleeing from those natures through artificial abstinence. These thoughts he outlined in an essay called

'Energized Enthusiasm' that might have been subtitled: *On using sex for mystical and magical purposes*. It would appear in *The Equinox* I.6, well ahead of its time.

Sex was supremely important to Crowley and the many affairs that illuminated his life were woven into his spiritual writings. Thus, for example, in the 'Holy Book', *Liber LXV*, the invocation, '*A*donai, *d*ivine *A*donai...!' (my emphasis) simultaneously spells out the name of popular novelist Ada Leverson, sometime friend of Oscar Wilde and passionate lover of Aleister Crowley. Sharing Crowley's taste for cynical, outrageous humour, Ada helped Crowley perceive his *Adonai*, his Holy Guardian Angel, or 'Higher Genius'. In the *Book of Lies* (1913), we find the stricture, '*L*ove *A*lway *Y*ieldeth; *L*ove *A*lway *H*indereth...' (my emphasis) giving us the Sufic name for lover and friend-to-be, Leila Waddell: *Laylah*.

We should not assume that sex was for Crowley as it is for others.

Crowley's diary entry for 15 December finds his hatha yoga leading to ecstasies too great to contain in his flat: 'I sang "Ovariotomy" [15] at the top of my voice all down Piccadilly. Only Fuller's saved me from going to preach at Marble Arch!'

*   *   *

Crowley 'came out of the desert' in 1906–07, but while he might have been spiritually out of the woods, in his domestic life, he would soon find himself in hell.

A Licence to Live

1908–09

We are to be taxed beyond endurance, our defences neglected, our education left to sink or swim as it may, that our whole state may be clogged with its own excrement! It is no idle boast of the vermin socialists that their system is Christianity, and no other is genuine. And look at them! to a man [...] – they are atheists and in favour of Free Love – whatever that may mean. I have talked with many Socialists, but never with one who understood his subject. Empty babblers they are, muddle-headed philanthropists. They read a shilling abridgement of John Stuart Mill, and settle all economic problems over a 'sirloin of turnips' in some filthy crank food dive. Ask them any simple question about detail, and the bubble is pricked.

Well, as I was saying, they are all in favour of 'Free Love'. Some paper mentioned the fact. What a stampede! – Oh no! not me, please sir, it was the other boy. It would never do to shock the British public.

('Christianity', *The World's Tragedy*, Paris, 1910)

Aleister Crowley would shock the docile British public when he could see a point to it, but artistic gestures, however amusing, were not the meat of his efforts. From 1908 to 1909 he established the A.˙.A.˙., an advanced teaching order. Esoteric work ran in tandem with public poking of the bodice-tight mind of Edwardian England. Unfortunately, humour that was intended to sweeten the pill deflected interest. Fifty years ahead of his time, the real message was ignored.

The World's Tragedy was written at Eastbourne in February 1908 while visiting mother, lately returned from a sojourn with the Kentucky branch of the Bishop family.[1] Crowley felt repelled by two old Plymouthite sisters who shared her home. To save others from their fate he dubbed his acid account of childhood education 'A Boyhood in Hell'. Gerald Yorke added a pencilled note to the typescript: 'You can get a good feel for the Old Sinner from this.'[2] The account begins: 'I have it on hearsay that I was born on the 12th of October in the year 1875 of Pseudo Christ.'

Aleister fumes with rage at the old maids digesting a daily diet of 'cold, boiled Jesus', a phrase repeated so often as to render the reader as sick as he felt: cold, boiled Jesus *ad nauseam*. So sick of 'cold boiled Jesus' was Crowley that he fled mother's psychological hell-house to find sanity by the sea: round the corner in physical distance, but a world away from cold, boiled Jesus, served at doom temperature behind the old lace curtains and cold brick walls of Christian sectarianism. As the waves lapped about Beachy Head, his old climbing territory, the happy, natural sexuality of a girl called Mabel contrasted startlingly with mother's world. Crowley vowed 'to bring the truth into this England of hypocrisy, light into its superstition of rationalism, love into its prudery, chastity into its whoredom! To the boys and girls of England I give my book, the charter of their freedom.'

The World's Tragedy revealed a superb essayist. Chapters on Christianity and homosexuality may be regarded as seminal (no pun intended):

> I therefore hold the legendary Jesus in no wise responsible for
> the trouble: it began with Luther, perhaps, and went on with
> Wesley: but no matter! – what I am trying to get at is the religion
> which makes England to-day a hell for any man who cares at all
> for freedom. That religion they call Christianity; the devil they
> honour they call God. I accept these definitions, as a poet must
> do, if he is to be at all intelligible to his age, and it is their God
> and their religion that I hate and will destroy.

On homosexuality he wrote: 'Further, lest "broad-minded" prigs come to smash me by their aid, I shall fight openly for that which no living Englishman dare defend, even in secret – sodomy!' He knew he was taking risks and added the following as protection: 'The proofs, too, (in my hands) that a certain member of the present Cabinet derives much of his income from the profits of a brothel, lend a certain solidity to my position. This lion can bite back.'

The lion's mission had two prongs. First, an order designed to lead the pupil to communicate with Higher Intelligence, based on the 'Illuminist' tradition. Second, a campaign for sexual liberation; neuroses derived from sexual repression, he believed, would lead to insane war.

Sadly, Crowley was faced with private war at 21 Warwick Road, Earl's Court (Boleskine had been rented out). Rose's alcoholism was out of control. Distraught, he sought advice from Gerald Kelly, Eckenstein and the family doctor. The consensus: he should leave Rose until she recovered; the Kellys would care for little Lola. Crowley blamed Rose's 'dipsomaniac' mother for planting the seeds of alcoholic self-abuse. He found it is easier to blame others; Crowley had been blamed almost to death as a youth.

On 28 April he retreated to the Hôtel de Blois, 50 rue Vavin, the hub of Paris's Latin Quarter. He wrote horror stories. Fed up, he moved to Venice. Venice was a bore. Back in Paris he received a letter from his father-in-law: Rose's condition had worsened. Neither separation nor co-habitation helped. Crowley loved his family even as it was torn apart before his eyes. It seemed Lilith's death had opened a wound that would never heal. He went to London, in vain.

Back in Paris in July, he was joined by Victor Neuburg, or 'Newbugger' as Rose called him. Teacher decided the 'boy' was a bit wet behind the ears. First step in Neuburg's education was favoured therapy, the brothel, to cure sexual embarrassment. He was then encouraged into a liaison with sexually adept model Euphemia Lamb, an initiation cooked up joyously between Ms Lamb and Crowley who found relief from his own problems dragging overly cerebral and excessively awkward young Neuburg through the hedge backwards. A *soupçon* of emotional sadism gave his mentors plenty of laughs and could only do Neuburg good. The charter of freedom required sexual liberation.

In *La Gitana*, Crowley promised his girl he would return to the 'sunny land of Spain'. On 31 July 1908, Crowley and Neuburg left Paris for Bayonne, thence Pamplona. From Pamplona, they trekked to Logroño, Soria and Burgo de Osma. Crowley showed Neuburg the bullfight, revelling in the rite. At Madrid in August, Crowley wrote the second part of his important treatise 'The Herb Dangerous: The Psychology of Hashish', ironically attributed to Somerset Maugham's evil magician, 'Oliver Haddo'. The introduction was flowery, but epoch-marking. While *cannabis indica*'s pharmaceutical properties had been described, Crowley concentrated on the psychological implications: 'I am of the Serpent's party; Knowledge is good, be the price what it may.' The 'Serpent' was *science*.

From Madrid, Crowley and Neuburg passed to Granada, Gibraltar, then across the Med to Tangiers: 'My spiritual self is at home in China,' Crowley would later write, 'but my heart and my hand are pledged to the Arab.' There, Crowley considered what was involved in becoming a teacher of men. He would be outside of 'the system'. The A.˙.A.˙. would eschew formal religious, moral codes, concentrating on communicating with the 'True Will' or the 'Knowledge and Conversation of the Holy Guardian Angel': the individual's hidden essence.

*   *   *

With Neuburg back in Cambridge for Michaelmas 1908, Crowley took a magical retirement in Paris. Crowley's detailed record of that retirement, entitled 'John St John', reveals Crowley's attainment of union with his Adonai, his Holy Guardian Angel, as a reality secured: *samadhi*, without stimulus of hashish:

> 9.20. After breakfast, have strolled, on my way to the studio,
> through the garden of the Luxembourg to my favourite fountain.
> It is useless to attempt to write of the dew and the flowers in the
> clear October sunlight.

Yet the light which I behold is still more than sunlight. My eyes too are quite weak from the Vision; I cannot bear the brilliance of things.

The clock of the Senate strikes; and my ears are ravished with its mysterious melody. It is the infinite interior movement of things, secured by the co-extension of their sum with the all, that transcends the deadly opposites; change which implies decay, stability which spells monotony.

I understand all the Psalms of Benediction; there is spontaneous praise, a fountain in my heart. The authors of the Psalms must have known something of this Illumination when they wrote them.

Recharged, Crowley returned to London to organize the headquarters and regimen of the A.·.A.·., and to launch his occult periodical, *The Equinox*. Crowley's 'Review of Scientific Illuminism' would be a repository of wisdom to rebuild civilization after the 'balloon went up' and the world sank beneath the rubble of destruction prophesied in *The Book of the Law*.

Run from a studio apartment on the fifth floor of 124 Victoria Street, conveniently close to the boat train, Crowley's baptism into magazine production was stimulated by libertine Frank Harris's proprietorship and editorship of *Vanity Fair* magazine. A mutual friend of Crowley and Winston Churchill, Harris published his friend's contributions, giving *The Equinox* a rave review. Allan Bennett's *Buddhism* was also an inspiration, being of similar size and high production. Financed by George Raffalovitch, son of a countess from Odessa and a Jewish banker, it was astute marketing to link the new Order with a publically distributed periodical.

Crowley was becoming a dangerous man.

*   *   *

The *Occult Review* reviewed *Konx Om Pax* ('Light in Extension') in 1908. Described by Israel Regardie as a 'delightful book',[3] its first section, 'The Wake World', deals with the 'waking up' of Buddhahood. There is a lustrous use of sexual imagery to describe the meeting of the ego with the 'Fairy Prince', or Higher Being. Crowley's 'Trans-Olympian humour' raises *Konx* to a highly advanced pitch and perspective, showing what Crowley meant when he called himself a HIMOG, a *Holy Illuminated Man of God*. He was, in Regardie's expression 'God-intoxicated', intoxicated by an Absolute beyond the dichotomies of 'God .v. Satan'.

The body is not evil; it is part of nature. 'Lucifer' was for Crowley the 'Light-bringer', the principle of revelation to Man, a principle of reality and knowledge, consciousness, rebirth and transformation, as well as many other ancient ideas connected with the life of the Sun, the serpent and of man. As Crowley would express this idea later, in *Magick*:

> In low grades of initiation, dogmatic quarrels are inflamed by
> astral experience; as when St John distinguishes between the
> whore BABALON and the Woman clothed with the Sun,
> between the Lamb that was slain and the Beast 666 whose deadly
> wound was healed; nor understands that Satan, the Old Serpent,
> in the Abyss, the lake of Fire and Sulphur, is the Sun-Father, the
> vibration of Life, Lord of Infinite Space that flames with His
> Consuming Energy, and it is also that throned Light whose Spirit
> is suffused throughout the City of Jewels.[4]

Crowley reckoned Christians were subjected to 'low grade initiation'. Little wonder those forces would soon rise to damn him. Undercutting their whole show, surely only the Devil would dare such a thing! In fact, Crowley tried to show both the wickedness and ludicrousness of devilish activity. 'At the Fork of the Roads' appeared in *The Equinox*'s first issue in March 1909, telling how WB Yeats launched a magical attack against him in 1900.

There were lighter works, such as the furiously passionate poem of lust, love and degradation, *Clouds without Water*, published in 1909 as a 'warning to ministers of religion' (!). Inspired by his affair with Kathleen Bruce, there is something genuinely sad as well as funny about it. Kathleen introduced Crowley, he wrote, to 'the tortured pleasures of algolagny on the spiritual plane'. *Algolagnia* is sexual pleasure derived from pain inflicted on oneself or others; this could mean anything from prick-teasing and romantic torture, to S&M. The presence of Vera Snepp or 'Lola', from the Ashdown Park Hotel experience of 1906, touches the first part of *Clouds without Water.* Ada Leverson was another inspiration. The title from Jude 12.13 refers to sexual and romantic frustration. The pain of Crowley's dying marriage informs the mood even more than sensual chaos.

*   *   *

The A.˙.A.˙. appeared in 1909. The Order had three parts: the order of the Silver Star proper (the 'Secret Chiefs'), the second order of the Rose Cross, and the outer order of the Golden Dawn, putting the Golden Dawn in its place. The outer order curriculum was published in *The Equinox.*

A new grade, Probationer 0=0, was introduced. The Neophyte was now $1°=10°$ and the GD grade of Theoricus was removed; there were ten grades in all. Cumbersome Golden Dawn-style ceremonial initiations disappeared; grades indicated definite spiritual attainments. Aspirants took instruction from a superior. Emphasis was on attainment, not socializing; members would not see membership lists. Destruction of egoism was central to the curriculum. Crowley had learned from Golden Dawn errors.

As *Frater Omnia Vincam*: 'I shall conquer all', Neuburg became a Probationer in the spring, initiation ordeals to follow at Boleskine in the summer. The promising Charles Stansfeld Jones joined as *Frater Unus in Omnibus* on 24 December 1909; his instructor: Captain Fuller. Moving to British Columbia five months later, Jones became Crowley's Canadian representative.

Come the summer, Neuburg was cloistered in a Boleskine chamber designated a temple for ten days' retirement. His 127-page magical diary reveals Crowley's sadistic side; he could hardly resist humiliating Neuburg's ego, justifying it as defences-battering for those whose egos held them back. Methods suffered from literalism. For the ordeal of earth, Neuburg had to spend a cold night naked, lying on gorse. But

Neuburg was not a child, and Crowley was not his mummy; Neuburg could leave any time he wished.

In June, Boleskine opened its doors to Emmanuel College undergraduate, Probationer Kenneth Martin Ward, son of Cambridge psychologist Professor James Ward.[5] On 28 June, packing up to make way for paying tenants, Crowley sought out some old skis he had promised Ward. In the loft above the kitchen, he was stunned to find not only the skis but also the 'lost' manuscript of *The Book of the Law*:

> Glory be to Nuit, Hadit, Ra-Hoor-Khuit in the highest! A little
> before midday I was impelled mysteriously (though exhausted
> by playing fives, billiards, etc. till nearly six this morning) to
> make a final search for the Elemental Tablets. And lo! When I
> had at last abandoned the search, I cast mine eyes upon a hole in
> the loft where were ski, etc., and there, O Holy, Holy, Holy! Were
> not only all that I sought, but the manuscript of *Liber Legis*![6]

At midnight, on the topmost part of the hill crowning his estate, Crowley solemnly renounced all that he had or was. At once, the Moon shone over the hills among the clouds, 'two days before her fullness'.

Four months later, Crowley made additions to *Liber L*'s wrapper, on which was written: *Liber L vel Legis given from the mouth of Aiwass to the ear of The Beast on April 8, 9, 10, 1904*. At some point, Crowley crossed out the letters *AD=Anno Domini* of the Christian calendar.[7]

Beneath the title: 'This [to which has been added above the line: 'MS (which came into my possession in July 1906)'] is a highly interesting example of genuine automatic writing. Though I am in no way responsible for any of these documents, [then added above the line, 'except the translations of the stele inscription'] I publish them among my works, because I believe that their intelligent study may be interesting & helpful. A.C.' An arrow then points to the first interpolation about the manuscript coming into Crowley's possession in 1906: 'i.e. I meant I could be its master from that date [signed] a.c. Oct '09'. July 1906 was when Crowley achieved the Knowledge and Conversation of his Holy Guardian Angel.

In 1909, Crowley rejected his statement about automatic writing. *The Book of the Law* was *not* automatic writing. It was dictated. Had Crowley's 'Holy Books' come from the same place? 'I cannot doubt,' he wrote, 'that these books are the work of an intelligence independent of my own.' Crowley's perceptions of the matter changed subtly over time. For example, William Breeze's introduction to *Magick*[8] reveals that Crowley had intended to include not only *The Book of the Law* in the third or possibly fourth volume of his *Collected Works* in 1907 but also his visions of the first two Enochian Aethyrs, from Mexico in 1900:

> This document (a fragment – 2 'Airs' out of 30) is interesting as being written by the same hand as *Liber L*. One may assume the constants as the contribution of the author; the differences as due to inspiration alone.

Written by the same hand as Liber L? Well, Crowley's was indeed the literal *hand* that wrote *Liber L*. Did he mean that the 'hand' was not entirely in his control, as in 'automatic writing'? Who was the 'author', and who or what was the 'inspiration'? Troubled, Crowley had apparently contrived to 'lose' the manuscript.[9] It was not until 1906–07, when he experienced *samadhi*, that he slowly began to come to terms with what had been 'lost'. At least, that is the interpretation he later put on his curious reactions to *The Book of the Law*.

One wonders if Rose ever offered him advice on the subject. But she was now 'out of it'. Crowley's doctor recommended two years' institutionalization. Rose refused; Crowley asked for a divorce. On 24 November 1909, a decree of divorce stipulated Crowley pay £52 a year alimony. A trust fund for Lola and Rose was established with George Cecil Jones and Eckenstein trustees. Aleister and Rose continued living together, on and off.

As the ship of marriage sank, Crowley swam to the lonely beach of *Liber L*. Had he not shunned this island? Had he not put bourgeois comforts before deeper obligations; was this the cause of his misfortune? He must get on with the Work. In his Cairo notes, Crowley had understood that his link with 'the solar force' necessitated the Golden

Dawn's destruction. He had better finish the job; the means: publish its rituals.

William Wynn Westcott, Supreme Magus of the masonic *Societas Rosicruciana in Anglia* wrote a note to his friend FL Gardner on 30 September: '*Equinox* II is on Sale – that man has printed about all of 0=0, 1=10, 2=9, 3=8, 4=7 and Portal [ceremony] and diagrams.'[10] 'That man' was Crowley; Westcott must have wished him dead.

*   *   *

Crowley returned to Neuburg's education. There was the ordeal of fire to pass through. Crowley would combine it with his own initiatory needs. His experience of the grade of Magister Templi was not complete in his mind; his ego was still a problem.

Guru and 'chela' kicked up the sand of French colonial Algiers on 18 November 1909. Reaching El Arba by train, they donned walking boots and headed for the desert. Crowley got into a rhythm, a painful but devoted one, of enflaming himself with prayer, reciting Koran texts at regular intervals, falling prostrate to the earth, invoking divine assistance. Neuburg followed.

They entered the Hotel Grossat, Aumale,[11] on the 22nd. The A.·.A.·.'s balancing regimen required a visit to the local brothel. Crowley heard a voice: Aiwass was calling him into the desert. Work begun in Mexico in 1900 must be continued. As fate would have it, Crowley had his transcription of 19 Enochian Calls. The last Call or Key gave entry to 30 *Aethyrs*, or 'Aires', inner worlds revealed to Edward Kelley and John Dee in 1583. Crowley had raised visions of the 30th and 29th Aethyrs when in Mexico but had hit his limit; he was now ready to progress.

Crowley would concentrate on an engraved topaz in the centre of a painted cross until he entered a trance, then utter aloud whatever he saw or received; Victor would take dictation. As the Aethyrs go backwards from No.30 to No.1, they become progressively harder to sustain.

They set off for Bou Saâda on 27 November. Taking five days to cover 60 miles, Crowley maintained his devotions. He conjured more Aethyrs. On 30 November, Neuburg took notes on the Aethyr whose angel-formula was called *POP*. The Aethyr spoke of death and the deflation of the ego, Crowley's current concerns.

On 3 December they walked to the mountain Dā'leh Addin. Entering the 14th Aethyr, Crowley received a command. He must construct a magic circle and altar of stones. The altar was to sacrifice *himself*, involving an act 'not lawful to speak of'. Indeed. Buggery of Neuburg courted legal penalties. But that was how the angelic command was interpreted.

Crowley found being the active partner an ordeal, a sacrifice, but Crowley reckoned the magick bore great results. The grade of *Magister Templi* suddenly made sense to him; it was the gateway to service of humanity. He had become as a little child, a true babe of the Abyss, entering a state of childlike receptivity. It became easier to penetrate the Aethyrs' strange world of 'astral beings', symbols, quasi-human intelligences: denizens of who knows what unknown aspects of the mind. Whatever the objective meaning of these experiences, or what degree of 'reality' might be ascribed to them, they offered knowledge and power of a different order to that available by other known means.

It should be understood that intelligence is formless and it is convenient for the magician's vitalized imagination to clothe intelligence with form.

The 14th Aethyr brought ego annihilation, what many might consider death. Aleister became *NEMO*, no man. His work was to teach and prepare the way through this 'death', towards *Thou who art I, before all I am*. This transcending of ego could be characterized as the embrace of Shakti, the energy from which the universe evolved, with Shiva, intelligence and spirit. Crowley had absorbed the idea of the 'Big-0'[12] from his experiences in the East; it was now part of his fundamental thinking. Shakti and Shiva are Nuit and Hadit; Shakti is Babalon, the Scarlet Woman. Shiva is Seth, Satan, Lucifer: the light principle of our solar system.

But the mountain ritual proved insufficient to secure Crowley's magical progress. Another ordeal beckoned the Master, most terrible. He would have to experience the Abyss itself. The ritual risked disintegration of mind. Method: the evocation of the 'spirit' or state of the Abyss; dispersion and disorder, personified as the 'demon Choronzon'. Choronzon represents in fleeting and unstable form the 'fear, pain, malice and envy that goes with the fear of disintegration, death and letting go'.[13] That is to say, Choronzon embodied elements from within Crowley's psyche. The evocation would generate them into perception.

6 December 1909

In distant London, King Edward VII has just dissolved parliament. The Lords have rejected Lloyd George's 'People's Budget'.[14] With the budget unpassed, taxes on beer, spirits, tobacco and cars are lifted. While the British people rejoice over an extra pint and an imminent general election, far away in the Algerian desert, between 2 and 4.15pm, close to Bou Saâda, Aleister Crowley and Victor Neuburg confront hell.

The blood of three pigeons provides energy for visible evocation. There is a triangle in which the spirit may manifest, and a circle outside of it for the protection of the magicians. Crowley is probably, dangerously, in the triangle. Neuburg is in the circle taking notes, or trying to. A materialization of the evoked forces appears. Neuburg fights a naked demon that penetrates the circle. The savage threatens to tear Neuburg apart. Was the demon Crowley, temporarily in the state of Choronzon?

Psychotherapist Israel Regardie insightfully, if a little predictably, interpreted the Choronzon/'devil' experience as a method of assimilating repressed fears concerning 'the father'. Assimilation entailed bringing into visible consciousness fearful, suppressed psychic material. Assimilation theoretically obliterated neurotic character armour, freeing the self from an encasing false ego.

Thank you, doctor. Alternatively, this was one hell of a scary afternoon, with sufficient psychic explosiveness to screw up most people. But this was the kind of therapy that suited Crowley, and it concluded with a fantastic sense of release, expressed in a Dionysiac pleasure-time. Life became immediate, complete, and subsequent Aethyrs overflowed with joy and gladness.

All's well that ends well. Everything Crowley learned from the Aethyrs tied in with the message of *The Book of the Law*. The will of the gods was clear. Crowley took the synchronicities as confirmation of *Liber Legis*'s preternatural character. His part in the Plan, his being chosen, his destiny was confirmed, and it would cost him all that he had and more.

While Regardie held that the 'Human ego must face the Dionysian reality',[15] we do not recommend you try this at home; only Crowley's extraordinary background in spiritual disciplines, and a phenomenal willpower could have made such a bizarre phenomenon either take place or make sense. But, as Regardie has shown, there is something for people to learn from the record.[16] It should be noted, I think, that the Aethyrs Crowley entered be seen as *Crowley's Aethyrs*, just as Edward Kelley's were *his*, notwithstanding common elements.

* * *

On 12 December, near Tolga, in the desert, an altar was again erected on top of a mountain. Crowley envisioned pylons stretching for miles towards the spot. He experienced *samadhi* and realized that for Shiva there is no motion, but should he, the god, move, all motion would cease.

Crowley and Neuburg took respite from the desert heat at Biskra's Hôtel Royale, 65 miles from Bou Saâda. There, the remaining Aethyrs were invoked – all of the visions sublimely optimistic. The seer felt secure he was a Magister Templi 8°=3□. He was ecstatic.

On New Year's Eve 1909, Crowley left Algiers, hitting London just in time to see his *Equinox* sued for libel by Macgregor Mathers. Crowley had dared publish Rosicrucian secrets that Mathers wanted kept secret. The coincidence was perfect. The fully-fledged Master of the Temple was immediately opposed by the forces of darkness. But Crowley could now look down on his former superior. This case, however, was only the beginning.

Sex on Trial

1909–12

The following scene did not take place in Notting Hill in the late 1960s, nor is it an outtake from Cammell and Roeg's 1969 film *Performance*, starring James Fox and Mick Jagger. It is a fragment of Crowley's unpublished diary for Saturday 4 June 1910. *1910*: the year in which *Mary Poppins* was set. Remember Dick Van Dyke and Julie Andrews transforming the rooftops of London into a magical landscape? Now look at this. The location is 'The Harem', five flights of stairs up 124 Victoria Street. Present are Australian violinist Leila Waddell, Victor Neuburg, Charles Stansfeld Jones and Aleister Crowley, all seated on a divan. *This* is how you jump through chalk pavement pictures and have tea parties on the ceiling:

9.25P.M.   Dried tops [of] Cannabis Indica thrown on glowing prepared charcoal.

9.31 to 9.46 Interruption of a telephonic nature.

9.46   Attack resumed.

9.56   Miss Waddell states defendant bit his proper ear.

9.53 [sic] Crowley embarked on a career of debauchery H_2O [water].

9.56   d[itt]o.

9.56½   Miss Waddell d[itt]o. Jones and Neuburg abstained.

9.55	Threats of personal violence from Crowley to Neuburg.
9.55½	Neuburg opines Jones is drunk.
9.56	Prayer from Crowley
9.57	Prayer unanswered
9.57	Put to meeting by Crowley that window be opened. Politely carried, opened. Crowley insults Neuburg (is this worth recording?). Jones unanimously requested to sing. Abstained. Presented with freedom of the city on approval.
10.03	Crowley very sleepy.

Three minutes later, Leila declares her heart has migrated to 'her cerebellar region. No pulsations detected. Neuburg's heart in boot in bedroom.' At 10.12, everybody's brain is gently stimulated and Miss Waddell's throat is better – doubtless due to its not having been treated.

Time apparently doubled.

10.33	Crowley acquiring triple personality (owners unwilling to prosecute).

Leila has a glass of orange juice. At 10.40 Crowley feels 'artistic'. Two minutes later he sees 'visions of towers and houses' – he has opened the window for fresh air. 'Miss Waddell looser (less tight).' At 10.48 everyone feels sleepy. At 10.50, Leila sees 'impromptu' triangles. Five minutes later, Neuburg sees colours 'different to *anhalonium*' (mescaline) colours.

11.02	Jones falls asleep. Half past midnight: everyone is asleep. Crowley states: 'all are barmy'. [Barmy once meant a state of trance-like bliss.]
	One yawns. More air. Also coffee. Miss Waddell slept in snatches. Jones in dressing-gown. Crowley in sloth. Neuburg in very truth (not its garb). Crowley snores.

> Crowley deals in personalities – having a stock.
> Prospect of café chocklit…

12.45   (*continued*) Tea I mean. Neuburg's throat to be incised
         for chocolate biskets. Wafers (gingerian). Crowley
         snores shut mouthed? eyes open then sings. (Snoring
         preferred by *Daily Telegraph* critic.)

1.04   Still no tea.

1.06   Tea and a bite at midnight.

Just a typical 3 hours and 41 minutes in the eternity of 124 Victoria
Street! But for the wry reference to the 'defendant', you would never
realize that 34-year-old Crowley was suffering the most sustained attack
on his work and reputation he had ever known, an anti-Crowley blitz
based on one thing: *Sex*, Crowley's Achilles heel.

∗   ∗   ∗

Having located the key papers, I can now reveal how Crowley's troubles
with the baser press began. In December 1909, a note from Neuburg
addressed 'Dear Alice' informed Crowley that 'a leaflet was sent to
Barnes by an unknown MP'. 'Barnes' was Ernest Barnes, ordained fellow
of Trinity, Neuburg's – and Crowley's – college. The leaflet accused
Crowley of having been 'shadowed by the police of Europe (!) at various
times; these police seeking evidence of Crowley's sodomy with boys'.[1]

Rev. Barnes's liberal views on evolution linked him with the university's
Freethought Association of which Neuburg was a member and his friend
Norman Mudd secretary.[2] Mudd disseminated Captain Fuller's *The Star
in the West*. The MP was almost certainly Horatio Bottomley, MP for
Hackney South and publisher of a jingoistic rag, *John Bull*.[3]

It was inevitable that as Crowley's star rose, it would hit against
Bottomley's self-righteous populism. Crowley, the varsity poet whispered
to be a libertine, the provocative anti-Christian, the critic of mindless
imperialistic patriotism, had money. He was vulnerable to being 'set up'
as a walking symptom of 'moral breakdown'. Yellow journalists, then as

now, were eager to exploit or stimulate public 'outrage'. And glaring from the sidelines we find a familiar old chorus of Golden Dawners: FL Gardner and William Wynn Westcott.

Crowley was vulnerable. Neo-pagan Neuburg was a member of the university's Pan Society. The Cambridge Inter-Collegiate Christian Union abhorred 'Pan' people as much as freethinking people. They did not like Barnes's views either. When the Christian Union heard Crowley had been invited to speak to the Freethought Association, an anonymous letter winged its way to Trinity College, accusing Crowley of pederasty. The Dean, the Rev. R St John Parry instructed the college porters to prevent Crowley from entering the college. He summoned Norman Mudd to his rooms. No pushover, Mudd's mind had been opened by Crowley's work to 'what life was or might be'. He decided to stand up to Parry, reflecting the Freethought Association's declared objectives:

> To establish recognition of [Thomas Henry] Huxley's Agnostic Principle as an essential condition of all intellectual progress (in matters of the intellect do not pretend that conclusions are certain which are not demonstrated or demonstrable).
> To remove all disabilities attaching to freedom of thought and speech in the university.
> To destroy the forces of superstition, obscurantism and theological dogmatism.

Is it not ironic that mathematician Mudd supported an advocate of Magick and Buddhism on such a scientific wicket? It says much for the way Crowley's doctrines were perceived at the time.

On 28 January 1910, Mudd stood before the Dean. Parry insisted distribution of Fuller's book cease and Crowley's invitation be cancelled. The Dean 'could not permit an Association in which Trinity men were concerned to extend an official welcome to men of evil repute'. 'The book was as filthy as its subject and author', concluded Parry. Why then, Mudd asked, had Parry not dealt with Crowley himself?

Mudd conveyed Parry's response to Crowley: 'He [Parry] explicitly stated that he was afraid of libelling you.' Mudd must also have sent the libellous leaflet to Crowley because it now sits in a scrapbook of Crowley's papers: a pencil-written scrawl of apparently abysmal literacy, it alleges Crowley had been in the habit of visiting Cambridge to entice young men to gather in a room, there to be sodomized all together, apparently simultaneously! Redolent of a classic blackmail scam, it also alleged the police of Europe shadowed Crowley everywhere.

Crowley demanded the Dean investigate any allegations in open court where he would be pleased to establish his innocence. If the Dean could not substantiate his reasons for ordering the Freethought Association's secretary to cancel its invitation, then Parry must withdraw his objections. Writing from 124 Victoria Street on handsome *Equinox* headed paper, Crowley politely addressed the Dean:

> Since leaving Cambridge in 1898, I have travelled all over the world on one single business, the search for Truth. This truth I believe that I have found: it may be stated in the thesis following:
>
> By development of will-power, by rigorous self-control, by solitude, meditation, and prayer, a man may be granted the Knowledge and Conversation of his Holy Guardian Angel; this being attained, the man may safely confide himself to that Guardianship: and that this attainment is the most sublime privilege of man.[4]

Parry backed down. Bottomley, however, would pursue Crowley with fervour akin to the Marquess of Queensbury's pursuit of Oscar Wilde. A letter survives, dated 17 February 1910:

> Dear Mr Crowley,
>
> Thanks for your note. Any morning next week, except Monday, I shall be pleased to see you here between 11- and 12.30.
>
> Yours faithfully,
>
> Horatio Bottomley

What passed between them? Did Crowley confront Bottomley with the pencil-written scrawl? Did Bottomley threaten blackmail? Judging from Crowley's threat published in *The World's Tragedy*, he may have had something up his sleeve with which to embarrass Bottomley, or his parliamentary colleagues, were it published. The lion could bite back, or so it claimed.

*   *   *

This is how Crowley's problems with the yellow press began. The issue was sex, and religion; a potent mix. Suspicion had emerged in the mind of sex-obsessed Dr Edward Berridge during the Golden Dawn battle of 1900 that Aleister Crowley was homosexual. Crowley's objectors attacked him through his sexuality. Thus we can understand Crowley's insistence that individuals own the right to manifest their sexuality in conformity with their true will or nature. 'So with thy all; thou hast no right but to do thy will. Do that, and no other shall say nay.' (*AL* I,42b–43). Crowley offered the licence to live. For enemies, it was a 'diabolical liberty'.

*   *   *

Crowley's *Bagh-i-Muattar* appeared quietly that year, a pseudonymous work extolling 'practices of Persian piety'. The pieties described in this cheeky work of *double entendres* would not have been out of place in a good *Carry On* film; they gave vent to frustration: the sex-liberation battle went on. More impressively, Crowley's poetry collection *The Winged Beetle* received appreciative reviews. Good press would soon be a rare thing.

A clever, colourful collection, *The Winged Beetle*'s lively poems are mostly dedicated to Crowley's circle. 'The Jew of Fez' is dedicated to Winston Churchill, the 36-year-old Home Secretary. Though not part of Crowley's immediate circle, Churchill invited journalist and *bon viveur* Frank Harris to his wedding. Concerning a Jew who changes his religious colour and gets in a pickle, the poem refers to Churchill's 1904 swing from the Tories to the Liberals. Crowley's verses predict Churchill would swing back to the Tories, which he did, 14 years later, and pay a price, which he did: 'the wilderness years'.

'The Pentagram', a celebration of humane idealism, was dedicated to George Raffalovitch:

> In the Years of the Primal Course, in the dawn of terrestrial
>   birth,
> Man mastered the mammoth and horse, and Man was the Lord
>   of the Earth
> He made him an hollow skin from the heart of an holy tree,
> He compassed the earth therein, and Man was the Lord of
>   the Sea.
> He controlled the vigour of steam, he harnessed the lightning
>   for hire;
> He drove the celestial team; and Man was the Lord of the Fire.
> Deep-mouthed from their thrones deep-seated, the choirs of the
>   aeons declare
> The last of the demons defeated, for Man is the Lord of the Air.
>
> Arise, O Man, in thy strength! the kingdom is thine to inherit,
> Till the high gods witness at length that Man is the Lord of his
>   spirit.

'Song' was dedicated to Kathleen Bruce. It may have embarrassed the sculptress, given the poem's celebration of 'a woman proud of her whoredom'. In September 1908 Kathleen had married Captain Robert Falcon Scott. Scott would lose his life returning from the South Pole, having left London on 1 June 1910.

Old enemies reared their heads. Mathers' injunction had forbidden *The Equinox*'s distribution after it published Golden Dawn rituals. The Law Lords accepted Crowley's counter-appeal on 21 March. The next day, Westcott hurriedly wrote to FL Gardner: 'See this evening's 'Star' and 'Evening Standard' for Mathers v. Crowley – I was not concerned – I have been away in Yorkshire at Rosie College.'[5] Westcott liked to feign 'unconcern' with developments concerning his and Mathers' shattered brain-child.

The backbiting had its effects. On 29 March, *Soror Fidelis*, now Elaine Wölker, wrote to her old friend:

Dear Aleister,

My husband now looks upon you as a person to be avoided –
and very much dislikes my writing to you, or vice versa – I tell
you honestly, and because I am very fond of him, I must respect
his wishes in this matter – therefore tis better that we write no
more. When I am in London I will let you know, if you think it
worthwhile we can meet and talk things over, if not, Care Frater,
then let us bow before the Fate which always seems to have
desired to part us.

I remain Yours,

Fidelis[6]

Bottomley weighed in. Where *John Bull* had once praised *Konx Om Pax*
for its sense of humour, it now mocked the poet in an open letter (2 April).

Widely reported, the Mathers v. Crowley case, or 'Rosicrucian
Scandal', generated unexpected outcomes, such as the showering
upon Crowley of degrees from numerous fringe masonic orders, orders
unrecognized by the United Grand Lodge of England. One of these, the
Ordo Templi Orientis, fairly new to the world, would become important
to Crowley.

Another unexpected boon was Australian violinist, Leila Waddell,
who joined the A.˙.A.˙. in April as *Soror Agatha*.[7] Dubbing her
'the Mother of Heaven' Crowley and Leila quickly became a wacky
and creative couple. So much so that on 9 May, A.˙.A.˙. member
Commander Guy Montagu Marston RN invited them to his estate at
Rempstone, Dorset. Marston's interests were sex, anthropology and
magick; he had invited the right people.

Placed in a triangle of conjuration, Neuburg gave voice to Bartzabel,
the spirit of Mars, invoked by Crowley. In answer to a question put by
Marston, Bartzabel made a startling prediction:[8]

A.F.K. [Frater 'All for Knowledge' – Marston] Shall nations of
earth rise up against one another?

B[artzabel] When?

A.F.K. Soon.

B Yes

C.M. [*Chief Magus* – Crowley] When?

B Within five years. Turkey or Germany.

This absolutely correct prediction should have given the Admiralty a head start in war preparedness. Surely, this was intelligence gathering of a special kind. Impressed, Marston suggested a public performance. Crowley took some mescaline to Venice to work on the idea. The effect of this derivative from the *lophophora* cactus was to open vision to an ensouled universe. The world appeared spiritually alive, meaningful: everything connected.

Crowley conceived the idea of seven public rites, one for each of the traditional 'planets': Moon, Sun, Mercury, Venus, Jupiter, Saturn, Mars. A full four years before Gustav Holst began his *Planets Suite* (suggested to Holst by Crowley's friend Clifford Bax!) Crowley's was a solid *avant garde* idea: *The Rites of Eleusis*.

In pre-Christian Greece, people had flocked to Eleusis to participate in a renewal experience that, according to R Gordon Wasson, probably included a dose of psychedelic ergot of rye in a foaming wine. The concoction took viewers of the rites out of themselves into the divine realms. Crowley wanted to reinitiate humanity.

A broadsheet survives (8 x 5 inches) headed boldly *Mr Aleister Crowley at Home*, announcing a ceremony to invoke Saturn. *Home* was 124 Victoria Street, and that is where The Rites of Eleusis was first performed shortly after the psychedelic *soirée* that opened this chapter. Raymond Radcliffe wrote a review for *The Daily Sketch* of 24 August: 'If there is any higher form of artistic expression than great verse and great music, I have yet to learn it.' The Edwardian equivalent of a Pink Floyd concert, there were lighting effects and a potion was passed round. The Rites polarized opinion in similar fashion to Pink Floyd in the late 1960s.

Meanwhile, the sour duo Westcott & Gardner glowered. Westcott to Gardner, 30 September 1910: 'Dear Gardner – no luck again. […]

Equinox is out – He [Crowley] reviews my Kabala – favourably. Refers more *mildly* to me and the G.D. manuscripts: but demands that I put them in the British Museum Library.'

Sensing marketing potential, Crowley moved The Rites of Eleusis to Caxton Hall, Westminster, where it played to packed houses in October and November. Kenneth Ward played the Graeco-Egyptian god Typhon (Seth) and beautiful actress Ione de Forest – Jeanne Heyse – joined the cast. Neuburg, to Crowley's great annoyance, was smitten.

A chronic depressive, Jeanne committed suicide in 1912. Neuburg never got over it, later blaming Crowley for sending him off from a ritual in such a state of mind that when Jeanne asked for help, he rejected her. This story has been cooked to imply the actress's suicide was Crowley's doing, another myth for sure, but one Crowley helped to stoke.[9] So upset was Crowley at Neuburg's obsession with Jeanne, and at Neuburg's subsequent rejection of him, he used the myth to warn of what could happen to those who interfered with initiates' progress, almost claiming credit for tipping Jeanne over the edge in chapter 21 of *Magick*: 'The MASTER THERION once found it necessary to slay a Circe who was bewitching brethren. He merely walked to the door of her room, and drew an Astral T ('traditore', and the symbol of Saturn) with an astral dagger. Within 48 hours she shot herself.'

*   *   *

Crowley went to Paris for a demonstration. He did not tear up paving stones but went to the necropolis of Père Lachaise, famous today as the last resting place of the exhausted body of singer Jim Morrison of the poetic rock band, The Doors. In 1910, the latest sensation was Jacob Epstein's monument to Oscar Wilde, declared indecent since the tomb's huge winged figure, being male, was granted a penis. The combination of Wilde and penis was too much, even in a Paris regarded by English people as the perineum of global naughtiness. Robert Ross, Wilde's literary executor, sanctioned the addition of a brass butterfly to the offending member. Outraged, Crowley organized a demonstration in the cause of art and truth, set for 5 November at midday. The authorities cordoned off Epstein's masterwork. Crowley snuck in, hid himself until the cemetery was closed, detached the butterfly and next day strolled into the Café Royal, London, the butterfly suspended over his pelvic region like a sporran. Much mirth ensued.

Crowley's positive fight-back was not suffered for long. Skirting the bounds of the possible, like any good artist, he was doing it openly. Behind his back, somebody put blackmailer De Wend Fenton and his scandal rag *The Looking Glass* onto Crowley's case. Fenton ran a smutty put-down of Crowley's Rites on 12 November. The headline read: *AN AMAZING SECT* and promised 'The Origin of their Rites and the Life History of Mr Aleister Crowley'. Fenton's *modus operandi* was to print a taster of scandal, calculate possible legal implications in proportion to sales, then offer a way out for the victim: a one-off payment to avoid further 'revelations'. Crowley would not be blackmailed; *The Looking Glass* went to work.

*   *   *

Oblivious to the filth, activist fringe Freemason John Yarker became attracted to the Crowley glamour. In September, Crowley had given Yarker's book *The Arcane Schools* a good review in *The Equinox*. Encouraged by this, and perhaps after consulting German colleague Theodor Reuss, who had received Yarker's charter to establish 'Memphis and Misraim' lodges in Germany, Yarker conferred on Crowley the 33° or top degree of the 'reduced' Rite of Memphis, as well as the 90° of the Rite of Misraim (Hebrew for *Egypt*).

*   *   *

Hoping to get Neuburg's head out from under love and back under will, Crowley took him to North Africa in December. Revisiting Bou Saâda, they motored into the desert, then wandered in the wastes, Neuburg's head shaved but for two horns of hair. Crowley had locals believe his 'chela' was a demon compelled by magick to serve him. Scoring magical gestures in the air with his massive rings, Crowley convinced the peasants; he was for real. But the magicians argued so much Crowley left his 'demon' in Biskra 'to recuperate'. After a dose of Paris, Crowley went to see his mother in Eastbourne for New Year 1911, perhaps to recover his bearings.

One wonders what Emily would have thought of Fenton's description of Crowley as 'one of the most blasphemous and cold-blooded villains of modern times'. Both eventually imprisoned for nefariousness cloaked as journalism, Fenton and Bottomley were nags from the same stable. The former's snoopers dug up some dirt on Crowley's divorce and cited adultery. Fuller advised Crowley sue for damages, but Crowley did not know what Fenton was prepared to disclose in court. There may have been intelligence implications; there was certainly a concern about his private life. To up the ante, *The Looking Glass* struck at Crowley's friends. Allan Bennett was called 'that rascally sham Buddhist monk' and implicated in 'unmentionable immoralities' with Crowley. George Cecil Jones was presented as a colleague in Crowley's 'love cult'.

On 6 April 1911, Westcott informed Gardner: 'The Mathers–Crow[ley] row has broken out in a new law suit – by Cecil Jones .v. "The Looking Glass" for damages for libel.'[10] Crowley's reputation was in the dock. The jury heard obscenities in his poetry. Dr Edward Berridge testified that – *ten years previously* – having asked Crowley whether guests at his Chancery Lane apartment indulged in immoralities, his answer was peculiar: Crowley neither denied nor accepted it.

There you have it.

But wasn't this supposed to be a libel trial? Had *The Looking Glass* libelled Jones, or not? Accepting that Jones had been defamed, the judge concluded this would not damage him! Associating with Aleister Crowley made risk inevitable; Jones lost his case.

Convinced that Crowley had let Jones down by neither suing himself nor taking the witness stand, Fuller abandoned him, fearful perhaps of homosexual association. In time Fuller would become a Major General in the Royal Tank Corps, an architect of German blitzkrieg and Panzer tactics,[11] and a representative of Sir Oswald Mosley's British Union of Fascists; he died in 1966. Crowley thought Fuller would have done more good if he had stuck with his former guru.

George Raffalovitch also distanced himself. Numbers joining the A.˙.A.˙. fell. Crowley carried the trial's bitterness for many years, lamenting in a letter to Mudd in 1923 that, 'If Jones had sworn in the witness box that he believed in me and that Fenton was a common blackmailer, he would have won his case. The jury saw that he was ashamed to stick to me and naturally took his attitude as an admission of guilt.'[12]

Rejected for being himself, Crowley's sexuality was the key to the affair, and he knew it. To add to his problems, certain British Freemasons determined to frustrate Crowley; the word of Westcott, Gardner and other theosophical masons reached far. When Crowley asked to visit regular English lodges he was told the Grande Loge de France, under whose jurisdiction he had been initiated, was not recognized by the United Grand Lodge of England. When he resigned from the disputed French Grand Lodge in 1913, requests to join a regular English lodge were ignored: an act of behind-the-scenes hypocrisy.

Crowley found solace in summer 1911 with the 'Mother of Heaven', proto-hippy, 'beautiful person' and all-round sex goddess, Leila Waddell, at Fontainebleau, a favoured place of recuperation. Back in England for autumn he witnessed his divorced wife Rose's committal to an asylum. Certified insane from chronic alcoholic dementia, the couple's relations ended for good. A year later, Rose married long-term admirer Colonel Gormley. He died of senile dementia in 1925; Rose would die of meningitis and influenza in 1932, aged 57.

*   *   *

Crowley itched for a new adventure. In October, Crowley dined with Isadora Duncan's pianist, Hener Skene at the Savoy. Skene took him to a party. Crowley sat on the floor in meditative pose, 'exchanging electricity' with a lady calling herself Mary d'Este.[13] Isadora Duncan's close friend Mary Desti Sturges had in her train 13-year-old 'brat' Preston Sturges. Preston would later direct the films *Sullivan's Travels* and *Unfaithfully Yours*. The mature Sturges related his dislike of the stranger who zoomed off with Mother to Zurich's National Hotel to consummate their electric passion.

On 21 November, Crowley perceived Mary's clairvoyant ability, heightened by sexual and narcotic stimulation and Crowley's magically tuned atmosphere. A discarnate intelligence was trying to contact 666 through Mary. Improvising a temple in their room at the Palace Hotel St Moritz, a week later, Mary found herself at 11pm on the 'astral plane' in the company of a Secret Chief. He introduced himself as Ab-ul-Diz, a great name, I think, for a Secret Chief.

Wherever Ab-ul-Diz normally resided, or from which of the heavenly Father's many mansions he derived, he guided Crowley, through a language of symbols and kabbalistic letter clues, to his next task. From 4–13 December, four more 'workings' convinced Crowley he was to write a book, called 'Aba' (*ABA* = aleph beth aleph = 4). Mary then declared that the book Crowley must write, with the Secret Chief's assistance, was a 'Book Four'. At one point in the vision the book seemed to exist already in London. Crowley calculated the book was to be found in Italy. He also got an inkling that Persian nut trees marked a place sacred to his Order.

Crowley loved a magical adventure and Mary was 'up for it' . When Crowley saw Persian nut trees at the entrance to a villa at Posillipo, near Naples, he took it for confirmation. Confidence increased when they found the owners were willing to rent the Villa Caldarazzo for the winter.

Chilly and mean in facilities, it was no fun for Preston who, having caught the train from his French school down to Italy, found Crowley focused on *Book Four* and Mother focused on Crowley. How much these complaints estranged his mother from the Beast, we cannot tell, but estranged they became, for a while.[14] Still, Perdurabo and Virakam completed drafts of part 1 (*Mysticism*, including a first-class account of Yoga) and part 2 (*Magick – Elementary Theory*). It would grow to include Part 3 (*Magick in Theory and Practice*) and Part 4 (*The Equinox of the Gods*, or *Thelema*). *Virakam* was a gift from Ab-ul-Diz: Mary's magical name in the A.˙.A.˙.. Crowley gave Virakam co-author status. The original *Book 4* brought little money but formed a foundation of knowledge that goes from strength to strength as the years go by. This cannot be said of many books from the period.

*   *   *

Spring 1912 saw Crowley back in Fontainebleau with ever-faithful Leila Waddell, taking dictation of the first draft of Part III of *Book Four*, fast becoming a full-scale treatise. Did he know enough about it? Apparently he did, for back in London that same spring, Crowley received another visit from overbearing Prussian spy Theodor Reuss. Reuss apparently accused Crowley of revealing the prized cherry atop the cake of the Order of Oriental Templars (OTO). Reuss is supposed to have reached for Crowley's *Book of Lies*, written earlier in the year, and pointed to the magician's need to be armed with his mystic rood (cross) and rose, that is, the magically and mystically attuned lingam and yoni. Reuss's great secret could hardly have been much of a secret to Crowley, well aware of the *vamacharya* tradition of spiritual ecstasy plus devotional sex from his Indian travels. Crowley had long since grasped the merit of Hargrave Jenning's eccentric work, *The Rosicrucians, their Rites and Mysteries*.[15]

However, when it came to how precisely to use sex for magical purposes, Crowley had much to learn. A ceremonial magic man, he had not applied his sexual knowledge systematically. From Reuss, Crowley learned the IX° of the OTO. Hymenaeus Beta, the OTO's current World Head, believes the OTO 'as we know it' only came into being during 1910–12: a Reuss-Crowley collaboration, even though the IX° already existed.[16]

Reuss issued a charter on 21 April 1912 to 'Aleister St Edward Crowley', 33°, 90°, 95°, X° (OTO), making Crowley 'National Grand Master General for Great Britain and Ireland'. Crowley would head a British section with Reuss called the *Mysteria Mystica Maxima*. Reuss initiated Crowley in London as 'Supreme and Holy King of Ireland, Iona and all the Britons within the sanctuary of the Gnosis'. He took the title Baphomet, the Knights Templars' alleged idol. Crowley took its meaning from occult scholar Eliphas Lévi's image of the bisexual, or androgynous, goat in his *Key of the Great Mysteries*. Crowley worked with Reuss on OTO rituals.

Partly bemused by sudden masonic recognition, Crowley accepted John Yarker's *Dispensation* of 7 August 1912 'to revive the dormant Mt Sinai and Rose of Sharon, two London chapters of the Antient & Primitive Rite'. Since a Brother of the Rite of Memphis and Misraim had to be a mason 'of good standing under a Grand Lodge of Free and Accepted Masons', Crowley tried again to join regular Freemasonry, calling on WJ Songhurst, Secretary of the *Quatuor Coronati* Lodge of Research on 19 August.[17] According to Martin P Starr, Westcott had given Songhurst 'due and timely notice' of Crowley's arrival.[18] This makes clear who was behind Crowley's rejection; his career might have gone differently without it.

*   *   *

Crowley's first experiment with Reuss's sex secret may now be dated precisely. A copy-manuscript of what became *Liber C vel Agape* ('Book 100 or Love') was sold by a London book-dealer in 1987 (now supposedly held in the archives of AMORC, the neo-Rosicrucian organization). Crowley's colophon to the manuscript reads:

> This Original adaption in the English Language of the German MS. was made by me Aleister Crowley XI° 33° 90° 96° this 1st day of December 1912 E.V. I being confined to bed with a grievous sickness of which I was instantly cured upon the Celebration of this Eucharist. Revised, added to, and copied fair Dec.9–10 1912 E.V. after the Third Mass.

At the end of the copy is a diary entry, dated 'December 2, 1912. 11 p.m.':

> Record of his first celebration by an inititate 33° 90° 96° X° at 11 P.M. Dec. 2 1912 being not very prepared, being ill and having been 3 days in bed, and very depressed about matters of this vain world, I performed weakly and imperfectly this great work.
> Immediately I was aware of a taste so subtle and so sweet that I know of nothing wherewith to compare it.
> Next, I was filled with a most equable and genial warmth, as if it were the spirit of health itself that had entered into me. This

feeling remained for some hours.

Further, I was filled with great energy. Although I had been very weak and tired before the working, I was perfectly fresh after it, so much so that every limb of my body seemed to wish to excuse itself. I fell asleep shortly afterwards, and woke two hours later with the feeling that I had had a full night's rest.

Before sleeping, I looked astrally at my body. It had become the Body of Nuit, being a thousand thousand galaxies of pure white stars, blazing and moving with incredible softness and velocity. The spine was particularly bright, chakras nuclei of the star-storm.

I concentrated on the ajna [pineal gland chakra]. Almost instantly I broke through into a solar dhyana, more vivid and intense than I have [ever?] known, and so imminent that I was able to withdraw from it and return at pleasure, which, as need would have it, I did repeatedly.

Most surprising and permanent is the complete relief from the mental worry which I had been suffering. Mentally and physically I am ten years younger.

Sex magick worked, at least on this occasion. 'Success is thy proof' declared *The Book of the Law*. Thus began Crowley's life as a sex magician and sexologist, for he believed sex problems revealed neuroses that hindered access to higher intelligence. His own frustrations evinced the results of sexual repression: his enemies were nuts. But more than that, Crowley believed sex magick was more powerful than anything man had at his disposal, probably because it creates people, and we can master our powers, especially when made and raised with respect for the true will with magical intention. Sex magick could change the future.

Crowley took his secret out into the dangerous world.

THIRTEEN

To Russia with Lust

1913

The god of force and fire was on the march. In the Balkans, Serbs sought independence from the Austro-Hungarian Empire; Russia favoured the Serbs, Germany the Austrians. France was allied to Russia, Great Britain to France. Seventeen months later, what had appeared a distant cloud would blacken the world.

Far away in sunny Sydney Harbour, Australia, EM Fittock served the Royal Navy on HMS *Psyche*, a Pelorous Class Protected Cruiser used for low-level colonial 'police' work. Ernest Fittock of the A∴A∴ was a married seaman with five children and a sixth on the way when Crowley wrote to him in Sydney in March 1913.[1] Crowley's advice was crisp:

> You seem to be in the Abyss. You can get out of this immediately by refusing to think of it, and attending to your daily duties toward the A∴A∴ and toward the Navy. Leave speculation absolutely alone and meditate if you will, but not admitting any thoughts whatever. All these statements of yours, everything is wrong, everything is right, everything is volatile, everything is fixed, and so on, are all thoughts. As you well know, thoughts are lies, including this statement that all thoughts are lies.
>
> You must find freedom from the world of contradiction, and this freedom is only to be found in duty. As you seem to be a natural Babe of the Abyss, the best thing will be to send you the official publication for that Grade.[2]

Fittock probably found his way into the A∴A∴ through Lancashire-born Frank Bennett, A∴A∴ Probationer since 1910. In 1911, Bennett migrated to Australia where, despite Crowley's objections, he founded Co-Masonry lodge No 404, Sydney.

Of French origin, *Le Droit Humaine*, or Co-Masonry, was promoted by the secretive 'Esoteric Section' of the Theosophical Society led, from 1907, by Annie Besant. Crowley's objections to Co-Masonry were not eccentric. Co-Masonry trod on the territories of existing masonic orders. Admitted to degrees aside or beyond the three Craft degrees, Co-Masons could attain to the highest degrees of the Ancient & Accepted Scottish Rite. Co-Masonic initiations encroached on both the territories of Craft Masonry and the Supreme Councils of the Ancient & Accepted Rite.

Theosophy also attracted socialists, moderate and revolutionary. Crowley was most annoyed by Besant's attempt, along with theosophists Charles Webster Leadbeater and Liberal Catholic Church Bishop James Ingall Wedgwood, to gain control of John Yarker's Antient & Primitive Rite of Memphis and Misraim, of which Crowley was administrator. This was part of their Order of the Star in the East's schemes to prepare the world for the coming 'avatar' or saviour. The chosen messiah was Leadbeater's 'boy' discovery, Jiddu Krishnamurti.[3] Code-named *Alcyone*, the plan would split the Theosophical Society worldwide. Rudolf Steiner's Anthroposophy movement was launched in reaction.

Crowley wrote to one de Jong, in Java, about the *Star in the East* plan:

> HPB [Helena Petrovna Blavatsky, founder of the TS] gave no authority to Annie Besant to carry on her work, and Annie Besant may be regarded as a usurper. The present movement of The Star in the East is certainly calculated to bring the whole Society into contempt.
>
> [...] it is impossible that these Masters should have so far departed from every rule as to adventure in person Krishnamurti as the coming Christ. In the exceptional circumstances such a claim is worse than ridiculous.[4]

Besant's plans also affected Theodor Reuss. Reuss ran the German OTO in tandem with Yarker's Antient & Primitive Rite. Membership was predominantly theosophist. When Yarker died on 20 March, Besant and

Wedgewood plotted a takeover; Crowley and Reuss determined to stop them. Seeking support, Crowley wrote to Don Isidore Villarino del Villar, Puissent Sovereign Grand Commander of the Rite of Memphis, in Madrid on 3 June:

> It therefore becomes my duty to summon an electoral college for the purpose of electing a new Grand Hierophant 97° and I have further much pleasure in proposing the election of Don Isidore 96° to that post. [...] seconded by the most Illustrious and Puissent Brother Theodore Reuss 96° – the Sovereign Grand Master General of the German Empire.[5]

Besant struck back. Wedgewood appeared at a convocation called by A&P Grand Chancellor Richard Higham, in Manchester on 28 June. As Patriarch Grand Administrator General, Crowley insisted Wedgewood was not a 'regular' Freemason. The committee countered that Yarker had given Wedgewood 'honorary master masonship'. Crowley objected: Co-Masons were not recognized by the United Grand Lodge of England. Neither, countered Wedgewood, was Crowley; a sore point. The day before, Crowley had written to Sir Edward Letchworth, UGLE Grand Secretary, asserting that Rev. Bowley of Crowley's Parisian lodge had assured him 'the Lodge was in fraternal communication with the Lodge of England'. Appraised of the facts, Crowley resigned from the Grande Loge de France because it recognized Co-Masonry.

Crowley's letter was destroyed by a UGLE librarian after WW2. I found a typescript from shorthand in the Warburg Institute. It describes the Krishnamurti plan as 'the most impudent blasphemy and filthy fraud that has ever been attempted in the history of the world'. Within the year, his old lodge would join the new *Grande Loge Nationale Indépendante et Régulière pour la France et les Colonies Françaises*. The UGLE recognized it on 3 December 1913.

Bad luck.

Crowley's position in Masonry was settled at 76 Fulham Road on 30 June 1913 when a special convocation elected Henry Meyer Sovereign Grand Master General of the A&P Rite for Britain, with Crowley principal officer. Yarker's position as Grand Hierophant would be conveyed to Gérard Encausse, known as 'Papus', France's leading Martinist.[6]

Crowley and Reuss immediately began to draw the scattered lights of the Antient & Primitive Rite towards the lamp of the OTO, but whereas Reuss saw the OTO as a font for Gnostic Freemasonry, Crowley saw it as a gateway to the A.˙.A.˙.. Much of Crowley's extant 1913 correspondence indicates nifty administrative skills lavished on contacts in New York, Geneva, Madrid, Johannesburg, Berlin, Basle and Florence. Believing the 97 degrees of the A&P Rite impracticable, Crowley planned with Reuss to incorporate its essence into a ten-degree OTO system, a commitment to simplicity and economy evinced in this letter to OTO Brother John Daniel Reelſs, in Geneva:

> The expenses of establishing a lodge are extremely small. You could do it very well indeed for 2 or 300 francs. In fact the furniture of our Lodge was constructed with a view to make it easy to start night Lodges. You only require three chairs, three candles, one skull and crossbones painted with luminous paint, square, compasses, volume of the Sacred Law [AL] which you can get from us at the cost of one guinea [...] altar, carpet and emblems of mortality, sword for tyler, three gavels or mallets, hoodwink, cable tow, I & II degree aprons for candidates.
>
> [...] the cost of a charter is £25 but you can arrange to pay for it in course of time out of the fees as you receive them.

In all this disciplined activity, we see Crowley consolidating a solid administrative machine for promoting his message. The enterprise was destined for frustration. In early summer, for example, Vittoria Cremers, Crowley's OTO business manager, downed tools. Crowley wrote about her to JT Windram, South African OTO Viceroy: 'She is suffering from the vision of the Demon Crowley in a peculiarly acute form, and after six weeks ill in bed has vanished, leaving everything in confusion. [...] Whether she will come through the ordeal or not I cannot say.'[7] Many would (and do) suffer from the vision of the 'demon Crowley'. As late as the 1930s Cremers claimed to have 'destroyed' him. In fact, she embezzled funds and spread deceits that for a time poisoned Crowley's relations with Leila Waddell. Crowley treated Cremers kindly. Finding hatred impotent, she went insane, Crowley claimed, 'for six weeks', before she 'melted away to hide her shame in Wales'. [8] George Macnie Cowie, Grand Treasurer General, took on Cremers' work.

Crowley bent over backwards to help people to realize themselves, to experience contact with the Divine Genius. Some of his teaching priorities are revealed in the following letter to the editor of *The Divine Life*:

> Madam, In an article in your excellent magazine 'The Divine Life' 'I show you a Better Way' you give a certain amount of unfavourable criticism to a book of mine called *Book 4* [...] You further remark that in all these methods, not a word is said about Devotion. This is again true, because they are not devotional methods. Some people are quite incapable of Devotion, which seems to them ridiculous. Others are equally incapable of scientific thought. These two cannot be treated alike. In other parts of my teaching will be found many pages of a devotional character. [...] My method has always been to make a pupil study for a year, using any practices that appeal to him, and keeping all details with regard to the same. By examining this record, I have obtained a map of his mind and can then tell what practices are likely to be useful to him. [9]

Or her. Aelfrida Tillyard received astute instruction from Crowley. [10] An aficionado of mysticism, Cambridge-based Aelfrida married Constantine Michaelides, later 'Stephen' Graham, in 1907. Addressed to 'Mrs Graham', this letter captures Crowley's thoughts on 'God':

> Science will become religion in the end. [...] I say that it is unthinkable to me that I should be told to think anything but a thought. Whence, by the word God I can only mean my idea of God. It is quite true that this idea may be totally false and have no connection whatever with objective truth, supposing that

there be such a thing. But I cannot help that. All I can do to
increase in knowledge of God is to clarify, define, no, deepen.

[…] All that religious debate comes to is that A's idea is
different from B's. Revelation does not help us because that
materially consists in correcting the ideas of A&B by those of C.
[…] if you wish to make your idea of God nobler, the way to do
it is to make your mind nobler, and in particular to cultivate that
noblest part of it which you owe God.

[…] There are Gnostic and Rosicrucian interpretations of
many Christian dogmas such as the Trinity in particular, which
appear to me extraordinarily helpful, but not because they
approximate to objective Truth, but because the method of their
presentation helps my mind to enlarge itself. Here then, and this
is what I have been coming to, is only advance toward God as the
evolution of the mind. Hence we must investigate the mind and
discover its laws. We must then work in accordance with these
laws to make the best of our minds.

This was scientific illuminism. Crowley was convinced Aelfrida would
soon attain illumination:

I would like to bet that you could get Samadhi or its equivalent
in the course of perhaps three months work, maybe less. Your
great danger will therefore be to accept the results of that
Samadhi as truth. You cannot deny the thing itself, but because it
is very much more real to you than anything in previous states of
consciousness, you could and should deny the validity of the
intellectual ideas connected with it.

[…] You will presumably attain the Vision of Christ, or rather
what you call Christ, and this will be an experience of
unutterable bliss and glory. But having done this, you must read
Arnold's Song Celestial Cap II, and your intellect must tell you
that the vision of the Hindu, which he calls Vishnu is identical
with this.

Mrs Graham also wanted to know about 'physical love'. Her guru's reply:

> Physical love is quite independent of the body: like practically
> everything else it is all brains. Sorry I can't write more, but I am
> in a terrible state of mind about going away. Yours fraternally,
> *Please address me c/o the British Consul Moscow unless you hear
> to the contrary.* [my italics]

British Consul in Moscow? Crowley had to go to Moscow in July 1913.
Trips to Moscow always make observers wonder. Was Crowley called, or
did he volunteer?

The ostensible purpose was to give Muscovites a dose of British
entertainment. Moscow's pleasure-hungry inhabitants had already
cheered on, not only a host of visiting variety performers, but also – and
in very large numbers – a football team of British cotton workers based
in Moscow, featuring star-player RH Bruce Lockhart, newly installed
British Vice Consul.

*   *   *

In 1913 Aleister Crowley came to manage his own all-girl band, The
Ragged Ragtime Girls, an exciting precursor of Girls Aloud, the Spice
Girls, and Bond.

What?

Arriving in London from Australia in 1910, Leila Waddell had
performed as a 'Ragged Gypsy', an act adorned by her violin, her beauty,
and little else. After The Rites of Eleusis, Crowley revved up the razza-
matazz with an excursion as manager of a new London spectacle.
Instead of seven planets there would be seven gorgeous girls. Leila, a
lamp of invisible light, would lead six satellite violinists ('three dipso-
maniacs, four nymphomaniacs, two hysterically prudish'), dressed in
skimpy rags, performing in step as the *Ragged Ragtime Girls*. Ahead of
his time, Crowley always had one eye on 'pop' culture.

Excellent cover.

The Ragged Ragtime Girls opened at the 1,900-seat Old Tivoli
Theatre on the Strand on 3 March, 1913. Crowley wrote to Cousin
Agnes about them:

Dear Cousin Agnes,

The Ragged Ragtime Girls are not a musical composition. They are seven girls who dance and play the fiddle. So the only possibility of it attaining in Devonshire Park would be a Sunday engagement. June 29 is the only possible date. It is very kind of you to take an interest in it. If you should happen to be in London between June 30 and July 5, I should be very pleased to take you to see the show.[11]

Adept at advertisements, Crowley drew up a draft puff for the RRG's:

Seven beautiful and graceful maidens who dance and play the violin simultaneously. The strange exotic beauty of the leader, Miss Leila Bathurst as she weaves her dances in the labyrinth of her attendant nymphs thrills every heart with a sense alike of the rococo and the bizarre.

[...] Women shrieked and strong men wept, babes at the press fainted with emotion. The very unborn emulated the execution of John the Baptist recorded in the first chapter of the Gospel according to St Mark.[12]

After returning from a short holiday in France and the Channel Islands in May,[13] Crowley wrote to the Proprietors of the Slavianskii Bazaar, a hotel and café patronized by Moscow's artistic set.

Dear Sir,

Will you let me know the cheapest price that you could accommodate eight women who will arrive in your city about July 12 to appear at one of the theatres there. Please quote your very lowest prices for rooms and meals per day. I enclose photographs.[14]

On the day of departure (7 July 1913) Crowley wrote to Mrs Graham, requesting she persuade Dr Graham to provide a letter of introduction to his 'colleague in Moscow'. Crowley would be in Russia for a month, 'unless', he added, 'I decide in the course of the next half hour not to go at all, which seems more than likely'. Stephen Graham was the best-known writer on Holy Russia and his Moscow 'colleague' worked for British intelligence.[15]

Taking Moscow's unsanitary conditions and bed bugs in his stride, Crowley saw the girls onto the variety stage at Moscow's entertainment park, The Aquarium, on the Sadovaia. RH Bruce Lockhart, Britain's Vice Consul, has left us a contemporary description of the Aquarium 'fun-palace' where the RRGs performed:

> This vast open-air amusement park was presided over by a negro called Thomas – a British subject with whom the Consulate was frequently at variance over the engagement of young English girls as cabaret performers. [!] The entertainment he provided consisted of a perfectly respectable operetta theatre, an equally respectable open-air music hall, a definitely less respectable verandah *café-chantant*, and the inevitable chain of private 'cabinets' for gipsy-singing and private carouses.[16]

Crowley travelled to the fair at Nizhni Novgorod, gaining inspiration for the poem *The Fun of the Fair*, belatedly published to encourage Anglo-Russian relations in 1942. Back in Moscow he wrote 'The City of God' and the enduring 'Hymn to Pan', as well as a Gnostic Mass for a post-revolutionary Russia, while enjoying an inspirational liaison with Anny Ringler, a slim young Hungarian who sounds like a character from a Bond novel or Fassbinder film, specializing in S&M sex, to Crowley's delight and education.

Reference to Ian Fleming is apposite. A member of 'The Intelligence Service' (NID) from the late 1930s, Fleming found Crowley fascinating. Crowley probably mentioned his friendship with fellow Trinity man the Hon. Francis Henry Everard Joseph Feilding, son of the Earl of Denbigh. An intelligence officer in 1913, Feilding was an NID employee and A.˙.A.˙. member during World War One, functioning as Crowley's British intelligence contact.

In 1913, given Germany and Russia's conflicting Balkan interests, the question was: *Was Russia fit for war?* [17] Spence makes a good case that

Crowley's theatrical trip to Russia in 1913 provided cover for intelligence gathering. The best evidence comes from Crowley himself, in hints.[18]

*   *   *

Crowley's Moscow theatrical agent was Mikhail Lykiardopoulos, the Anglo-Greco-Russian secretary of the Moscow Art Theatre, probably the man fellow Anglo-Greek Dr Graham was asked to furnish an introduction to. Moscow's British Vice Consul and commercial attaché RH Bruce Lockhart wrote that it was 'Lyki' who introduced him to Crowley. According to Lockhart: 'During the war, [Lykiardopoulos] ran our propaganda department in Moscow under my supervision – and ran it very well.'[19] Spence suggests Lockhart's clandestine contacts with the revolutionary underground would have assisted Crowley; Theosophy motivated numerous revolutionaries. The intelligence angle explains Crowley's choice of Russia, of all places, for the RRG's gig: a 'gaily painted mask'.

The period dominates Book Two of Lockhart's *Memoirs of a Secret Agent* (1934), called 'The Moscow Pageant', headed with a French saying: *People pass. One has eyes. One sees them.*[20] This observation should be compared with Crowley's allusive comment in the preface to *The Fun of the Fair*:

> 'Grand reportage'? Certainly: I wrote the verses that describe each incident immediately after (or as!) it took place.
> This gaily-painted mask is my favourite wear when travelling on holiday: lovers of Truth should look into the eyes.

One has eyes. One sees them. Must one look behind the 'gaily-painted mask' to find the truth?

Certainly.

Crowley's *Confessions* refer to 'the excellent British consul, Mr Grove'.[21] Lockhart's account of his own arrival in Moscow in January 1912 opens with meeting Montgomery Grove: 'my new chief. He was in full uniform and was just dashing off to the ballet for the gala performance in honour of the British visitors', an 80-strong British

Parliamentary Delegation, invited by the Russian Government. Crowley's *Confessions* castigates Foreign Office stupidity in moving Grove, who was fluent in Russian and had excellent contacts, to Warsaw, where he knew no Polish. The new Consul, Charles Clive Bayley, formerly HM Consul at New York, knew no Russian. Bayley reappears in Spence's account of British wartime intelligence in America.

Lockhart described Crowley's 'theatrical agent' Michael Lykiardopoulos in connection with great European writers, including Crowley:

> 'Lyki' was a strange, lovable creature; [...] He knew most of the great writers of Europe and had translated their best works into Russian. It was through him that I first met H. G. Wells, Robert Ross, Lytton Strachey, Granville-Barker, Gordon Craig, Aleister Crowley, not to mention numerous hangers-on of literature, who came to Moscow to worship at the shrine of Russian art. [...] He knew every one in the literary, artistic, and dramatic world of Moscow, and through him, many doors, which otherwise would have remained closed were opened to me.

Crowley displayed an insider's knowledge of consulate woes. Comments in his *Confessions* on Russian military and industrial strength reveal privileged access; his accounts of defence procurement corruption are no tourist anecdotes. Crowley details four scandals, one in Odessa, one in Sebastapol, one in Vladivostok, and another with regard to a Birmingham munitions firm supplying the Russian naval agent in England that may have hastened Russia's naval defeat by Japan. Valuable intelligence before WW1, Crowley passes them off in his *post-war* reminiscences as 'observations'. His assessment of Russia's real capabilities was both prescient and at variance with that of British defence official Sir Henry Wilson. Wilson dined with Lockhart at the Hermitage the same summer Lockhart dined with Crowley. According to Lockhart, Wilson believed the Russian army would provide the 'extra weight to load scales overwhelmingly in France's favour' in the event of war.[22] Crowley, under no such illusions, assessed Russia's military strength as hollow. Lockhart agreed: 'Sir Henry was not the only expert whose judgments were to be rudely shattered by the tornado of 1914.' Russia was unstable: ripe for a revolt of sufficient scale to hamper seriously any military effort. Another clue to Crowley's activities may be found in the following post-script to his poem, *The Fun of the Fair*, republished 30 years later:

> Though little agitation was apparent in the general atmosphere
> of the Fair [at Nizhny Novgorod], the shrewd, astute, subtle,
> lynx-eyed, past master, analytical, psychic, eerie, hard-bitten
> Secret Service Chief could nose that there was a certain
> discontent with the régime.[23]

Again, one should recall his introduction to *The Fun of the Fair*, bearing in mind that the 'Fair' is a metaphor for the intrigue of real life. Most biographers have seen the *fun* of the fair, what Crowley wants them to see, but not the fair itself. Readers should look carefully at Crowley's own clue to his life: 'This gaily-painted mask is my favourite wear when travelling on holiday: lovers of Truth should look into the eyes.'

It is telling that the lover of Truth did not refer to Lockhart in his *Confessions*. At the time of writing, Lockhart was still on active service; Crowley knew that and exercised discretion. I was intrigued, however, to discover the following letter written shortly after returning from Moscow, addressed to 'Bruce Lockhart, British Consulate, Moscow', dated 1 September 1913.[24] Beginning 'Dear Lockhart', the letter accompanied a copy of Crowley's play, *Mortadello*. The transcript of Pitman shorthand, undertaken by Aelfrida Tillyard in her old age for Gerald Yorke, is not perfectly accurate:

> I am convinced that it [*Mortadello*] would do very well for
> Russia, and if you can understand [*sic*] Lykiardopoulos I shall be
> extremely grateful.
> I am so sorry at missing that last lunch.

Crowley then gave to Lockhart a secret I can now pass on to posterity: the true origin of the word 'Bunbury' as employed by Oscar Wilde in *The Importance of Being Earnest*.

According to Crowley, Oscar Wilde was travelling between Sunbury and Banbury when he met a boy returning from public school. Wilde and the boy later met by appointment at Sunbury. The author's 'frequent and unexplained absences' alerted the 'talented author of so many sonnets' [Lord Alfred Douglas] who 'found these absences suspicious and jumped to a conclusion as women will to a correct conclusion although without definite evidence'. Following Douglas's accusation: 'There was a tremendous row and in the event [Douglas] determined to ruin his friend.' Crowley added:

> I think there are only two people living who know how Lord Alfred Douglas determined to cause catastrophe. There have been reasons for not telling the story before, but it is a very good one and quite true.
>
> I shall probably know in a fortnight whether I am likely to get to Moscow in January. I most earnestly desire the same. Please write and tell me what you think of my books and my anecdote. Yours ever,

Crowley's 'earnest' desire to return to Moscow in January 1914 begs, but answers, no question. It can hardly have been a return booking for the Ragged Ragtime Girls whose reception was not rapturous; they split after a subsequent Scottish tour. While Crowley's precise activities in Russia in 1913 are occluded by his 'gaily-painted mask' they should prepare us for his undoubted intelligence commitments exhibited during the next six years in America.

*   *   *

In March 1913 *The Equinox* published 'Energized Enthusiasm', Crowley's essay on sex magick; with this in mind he wrote a moving Gnostic Mass in Moscow for the OTO. The Mass was performed at 'introductory shows' for the A.˙.A.˙. at Avenue Studios, Fulham Road, later in the year:

Dear Kathleen Pritchard

[…] Do come to the Gnostic Mass tomorrow, Sunday night, at 9 o'clock, and bring Miss Robinson.

Yours ever,

Aleister Crowley[25]

Austin Harrison, editor of *The English Review*,[26] published 'The City of God' on Crowley's return. Theirs was a typical genius-editor relationship; Crowley cavilled at Harrison's efforts to drag his style down to a more accessible level:

Dear Austin Harrison,

I am afraid you will never acquire literary sense.

[…] on receipt of the £20 I will endeavour to remove any spark of liveliness or wit that may be lurking in the article, and in every other way try to lower it to the standard of the 'English Review'. But, if in the course of an honest day's work I do my best in this matter, and if you then want to put it into poetry or Dorsetshire dialect, or in the style of Tolstoi or Josh Billings, I shall require a refresher.

By this means, I hope, we shall keep as much goodwill in business, as we have in golf. […]

Now it is off my chest,

Yours ever,

Aleister Crowley

Had the Great War not intervened, Crowley could have made a full professional recovery from the *Looking Glass* episode. But the war truncated a whole era in artistic and philosophical development, leaving many talents stranded or incomprehensible to the babes of its aftermath.

Crowley wrote to Mary Desti on 4 September about working on *The Equinox*: 'I cannot pay anything beyond your usual salary which however I will double for the future. But I don't mind standing reasonable expenses while you are actively helping.' Past biographies have implied *Virakam* quit Crowley for good after the Abu-ul-Diz adventure. But no, you could find her at *The Equinox*. She had written a theatrical piece, which Crowley had adapted for her, referring to it in a plaintive letter to Feilding of 8 September:

> Dear Feilding, [...] I think it is very rude of you to ask me why I don't write something else for the stage. I have written a lot of really decent things but nobody will look at them. [...] The only time anyone has ever condescended to discuss the subject at all seriously was this 'Tango', which is not mine at all, but was adapted by me from the draft of Mrs Sturges.

Crowley referred to the *Equinox*'s editor Mary Desti meeting the shy and ungainly Neuburg for the first time in an ambivalent letter to his mother, Emily:

> My dearest Mother,
>
> I am extremely glad to hear that you are much better. I am quite well and have returned into the strenuous life again quite completely. I cannot make up my mind whether to go to the Flag Day or not. I am torn between conflicting emotions. The Editor of the Equinox [Mrs Sturges] went up on Sunday, also the sub-Editor [Victor Neuburg]. They had never previously met. It was a touching scene of credulity. I am so busy that I am thinking about all the other letters I have to write instead of to you. Please pardon me this. Your loving son. PS I am sending back the library book.

Writing on return from Moscow on 1 September, he enquired about Lola Zaza, who was being cared for by the Kellys in Camberwell, along with his ex-wife Rose, now Mrs Gormley:

> My dear Mother, Very sorry you are not so well again. Hope you are all right now. I got back late on Saturday night. Please let me know at once if Lola goes down to you. What is Mrs Gormley's

[Rose's] present address? I am sending you a spoon with 'Christ is Risen' on it and a hand at the end to remind people to say grace. Also something else, I don't know what it is. Ever your loving son.

Returning from Moscow, Crowley found four letters from American John Quinn concerning books. A letter from 'Wieland & Co' explained to collector Quinn that *White Stains* was a serious rebuttal to Krafft-Ebing's *Psychopathia Sexualis*. Quinn was clearly interested in Crowley's 'rarer' publications. We learn from a 1914 subs note that EJ Wieland paid his OTO dues 'by work', explaining why Wieland & Co letters concerning book sales carried the *Equinox* address.

Another OTO member referred to in the 1914 note was one Charles Danby, who owed £4 in subs. Crowley wrote to Danby on 6 September:

> Dear Bro Danby, I do envy you in Cairo. [...] There is a man named Inman somewhere about in Egypt, perhaps in Cairo, an Engineer of some kind, who knows all about everything. He had the vision of the Demon Crowley when last heard of, but is probably all right now.[27]

This 'Inman' was Herbert E Inman who joined the A∴A∴ on 22 October 1909 as *Frater Amor Clavis Vitae*, 'Love is the key to life'. Crowley sent him up to Lancashire to act as 'introducing officer' for Frank Bennett. Inman and Bennett kept in touch. In early 1912, Inman was in South America and, like Bennett, was familiar with Co-Masonic and Theosophical circles, possibly the source of his vision of the 'demon Crowley'. In a letter to Bennett, Inman despaired of Rio, whereas Bennett found Co-Masonry in Melbourne and Sydney incandescent, confiding to Inman that he planned to return to magical activity and rekindle his A∴A∴ work.[28] And that is probably how Bennett came to bring EM Fittock RN into the A∴A∴, whose experience of the Abyss in Sydney opened this chapter. Very soon, the whole world would tumble into analogous straits.

FOURTEEN

Spying in the USA

1914–18

The nature of Horus being 'Force and Fire', his Aeon
would be marked by the collapse of humanitarianism. [...]
The war of 1914–18 may be regarded as the preliminary
skirmish of this vast world-conflict.[1]

Perhaps the greatest calumny directed at Crowley was that during
the Great War he was a traitor to his country. Launched by
Horatio Bottomley in 1920, the accusation has permanently
stained Crowley's reputation, encouraging ill-informed writers to say
practically anything they like about the man and his work.

Investigation reveals the accusation to be false; Crowley was in
America as an Allied spy. Further concrete evidence has been discovered
by US intelligence history specialist Richard Spence.

* * *

The lead-up to Crowley's war was messy. His fortune largely spent, the
Laird mortgaged Boleskine in May 1914 to the *Mysteria Mystica
Maxima*, administered by George Macnie Cowie. Crowley's assets
consisted of unsold books and personal copies, usually custom-bound by
Zaehnsdorf. Quality works were shipped over to sell to New York
collector John Quinn.[2]

Quinn's interest furnished the ostensible occasion for Crowley's
arrival in New York at Halloween 1914. Before that time, we know little
of Crowley's movements. There was a trip to North Africa in the spring,
while a note in the Yorke Collection from May or June 1914 refers to

plans for a return to K2 or Kanchenjunga. The war scrapped that, though in July, Crowley ascended the Jungfrau, alone. Was he upping his form for the Himalayas, or was this, as Spence speculates, part of a mission to spy on Russian anarchists operating in Switzerland around the alternative-lifestyle commune of Monte Verita, near Lugano, refuge for many socialists, theosophists, nudists and anarchists of interest to secret services? There is no evidence for a Crowley spy-mission there.

Following Archduke Ferdinand of Austria-Hungary's assassination in Sarajevo in June, a word-war began nudging the vase of peace off the continental shelf. Crowley headed for England, via Paris. According to Crowley's *Affidavit* intended for submission to US authorities in 1917:

> I was in Switzerland on Aug. 1, 1914, and returned at once to England.
>
> I offered myself to the Government, and hoped to get a commission through the good offices of my friend Lieut. The Hon. Everard Feilding, R.N.V.R. [Royal Naval Volunteer Reserve]
>
> In September I was attacked by phlebitis, which bars me permanently from active service.[3]

Crowley offered his specialized knowledge to the Empire, hoping for a salaried post in the intelligence or propaganda services. An interview of 26 February 1919 with New York paper *The Evening World* suggests a further twist. In 1914 he was 'in the confidential service of the British Government' and 'was shot in the leg'. Phlebitis, an inflamed vein in the leg, could be consistent with a bullet wound. Crowley, uncharacteristically, never mentioned it again.[4] The phlebitis, if not the bullet, was a fact.

That Crowley served his country's intelligence services is beyond doubt. His contact was the Hon. Everard Feilding who worked for Naval Intelligence in the Censor's Department, controlling information for propaganda and intelligence purposes. In January 1916, Feilding left London to work for the Eastern Mediterranean Special Intelligence Bureau, EMSIB. According to Crowley's Affidavit:

> I asked my friend, the Hon. Everard Feilding, Lieut. R.N.V.R. of the Press Bureau, to get me a job. Nothing doing; at that time

England had no idea that men would be useful in a war. I crossed to America, arriving Nov., 1914.

I had been writing articles urging the proper conduct of the war, the ceasing to fight à la fishwife, and the mobilization of the whole nation and its wealth. This was called unpatriotic; all my recommendations have since been adopted.

In September 1914, *The Observer* printed a letter about the German attack on Rheims. The writer insisted Germany anticipate 'poetic justice'; Cologne Cathedral would be transported to Rheims 'stone by numbered stone' as 'a symbol and monument of our victory'. The letter was Crowley's. As a propagandist, at least, Crowley was a potential asset.

In 1929, while attempting to revive his reputation, Trinity College historian Gerald Yorke wrote to Feilding about Crowley's wartime loyalties. I located Feilding's reply.

Regarding paper evidence, Feilding wrote: 'Such as I did not hand on to the Intelligence, I destroyed after the war'. It was, Feilding asserted, Crowley's 'admitted taste for farcical situations' that made higher authorities reluctant to use him:

> During the time that I was a Naval censor at the London Press Bureau and afterwards employed on Intelligence work in Egypt, Crowley wrote to me from time to time telling me that he was anxious to do work for the British Intelligence and that meanwhile he was doing his best, by various preposterous performances, to represent himself as disaffected and to get in with German connections. He sent me newspaper accounts, for instance, of his formally proclaiming Irish independence from the steps of the Statue of Liberty. He also asked me to start a defamation campaign against him in the English Press, with the idea that this would confirm his evil reputation in America so far as British allegiance was concerned. While I declined to do this, I sent his letters on to the intelligence authorities with whom I was personally acquainted, but this branch of work was in no way my job. I did nothing more beyond forwarding to Crowley a test question, which they suggested regarding the

identity of a certain personage. Whether it was to test their knowledge against their own, or because they really wanted to know who this personage was, I did not inquire. Anyway, his answer did not, I understand, prove helpful, and whether for that or other reasons I know not, they declined any direct communication with him. [note the word 'direct']

I can only add that my own personal very strong belief was and is that, whatever vagaries Crowley may have indulged in, which have caused him to be expelled from two countries as widely different as Italy and France, treachery to his country was not one of them.[5]

In October 1914, *The English Review* printed Crowley's article urging the USA to get off its backside and join a formal alliance with Britain. On the 24th, Crowley put his money where his pen was and boarded the SS *Lusitania*, carrying books, masonic charters, and £50 (worth about $5,000 today).

On 12 November Crowley met John Quinn, who had a collector's eye for Crowley's rarer books. Five days before the meeting, Crowley performed VIII° (auto-erotic) magick with his left hand and his imagination; its purpose: 'Success.' After the meeting, Crowley assessed the results of his magick:

Result. Many Magi might rejoice seeing that I sold $600 or so of books on Nov. 12, and that today Nov.14 all my difficulties on other lines seem to have cleared away. But this Magus wants definite complete success all round. 'Call no man happy till he is dead' – or at least has left New York!

'Complete success' eluded him. What was he after?

Crowley banked 500 of Quinn's dollars on 17 December. Living in style at an apartment on 40 West 36th Street, Crowley needed the cash. Four days earlier, *The World* magazine interviewed him, probably a result of Quinn's connections. Presented to New York as an eccentric adventurer – an effective disguise – Quinn introduced Crowley to useful circles. Just *how* useful may be gauged from the fact that John Quinn was a pro-British informer, liaising with Britain's Washington Embassy and New York Consulate at 44, Whitehall Street.[6]

While Quinn's public stance was for Home Rule for Ireland within the British Empire, his contacts with Irish Republicans and supporters of British traitor, social idealist and homosexual, Sir Roger Casement, helped the British to infiltrate a plot hatched between Casement, Irish independence agitators and Germany's US ambassador Count Johann von Bernstorff and military attaché, Franz von Papen. In exchange for Irish independence in the event of German victory, Casement offered the Germans an Irish rebellion to divert British troops, along with manpower for a German army Irish Legion.

Von Bernstorff urged Berlin to accept Casement's plot terms, but Admiral W Reginald 'Blinker' Hall's Naval Intelligence Department intercepted Bernstorff's recommendation. Crowley's appearance in New York as an 'Irishman' may thus be explained in the context of the Bernstorff-Casement plot.[10]

'Irish' identity was central to Crowley's US cover throughout the war. A poet asserting Irish freedom, Crowley was also the British head of an order based in Germany, run by a Prussian spy. Neutral New York was an ideal location for a British agent masked as a pro-Irish, pro-German daredevil. Admiral Hall's plans were frustrated, however, when Casement slipped out to Norway on 15 October.

According to his *Confessions*, Crowley initially had 'business' in New York, other than book selling. This business or 'egg' was, as Crowley wrote, 'addled'; he did not state how or why, or what the business was. Casement's escape may have heralded the egg's demise. This could explain why Crowley's November diary refers to things going badly since his arrival in New York. If his purpose was bookselling, he was doing all right.

Richard Spence posits an alternative scenario regarding the addling of Crowley's egg in New York. Wars cost money. As neutral Wall Street looked on, representatives of Britain and Germany competed for credits. In October 1914, George Macaulay Booth, Bank of England director and soon-to-be Deputy Director of Munitions Supply arrived on the

Lusitania on the same passenger manifest as Crowley.[7] Was Crowley one of Booth's minions or 'cut-outs', making first contact with possible partners? This was a field familiar to the commercial attaché side of Crowley's acquaintance R Bruce Lockhart, in Moscow.[8] However, a quick deal with pro-British JP Morgan Bank rendered any such services redundant.[9]

Eager to serve, and with a typically cavalier disregard for the fact that as an intelligence agent or asset, not an 'officer', he was expendable, Crowley found uses for himself. The risk was largely his own.

*   *   *

Admiral Hall was concerned with German propaganda in America; it could affect American opinion and thus the war's conduct. A *Propaganda Kabinett* met in New York whose members included Franz von Papen, Ambassador von Bernstorff and George Sylvester Viereck, an intellectual libertine who edited the German-backed magazine, *The Fatherland*.[11] Crowley had met Viereck in 1911 at Austin Harrison's offices at *The English Review*. Hall was 'on' to von Papen and Viereck.

The *Confessions* tell an amusing story of Crowley becoming acquainted with Viereck through a chance meeting on a bus in early 1915. Was it chance that led him to the Propaganda Kabinett? Spence has stacked up the circumstantial evidence against this, and, on inspection, it measures up. Crowley's embedding of himself in German propaganda circles was a semi-freelance effort to wage war against Germany on American soil.

Crowley was useful to 'Blinker' Hall on several fronts. Not only was Ireland a powder keg threatening Britain's war effort, but Indian revolutionaries were also being groomed for German exploitation; Muslim seditionists called for a *Jihad* against the British Empire. Crowley was familiar with both fields.

On 13 December 1914, journalist James Meyer, a German-born US citizen, was arrested for espionage in Switzerland. His employer's paper was published by Hermann Ridder, close friend of von Papen and Viereck and loyal collaborator of the Propaganda Kabinett which met close to the offices of *The Fatherland*. Crowley would soon infiltrate this pro-German publication. As it is possible Viereck was a double agent, the question of whether he was entirely taken in by Crowley may be beside the point. Crowley was a famous English writer, used to being attacked for 'telling it like it is', prepared to go out on a limb for Germany in the interests of 'fairness'.

Crowley worked on Viereck's mind, encouraging him to print either rubbish detrimental to the German cause or material to influence German policy-making. Crowley's propaganda was of such extreme absurdity that it would *a)* suggest to ordinary intelligence that the Germans lacked common sense and decency, and *b)* that it could be used to enflame extreme acts among Viereck's superiors.

Crowley encouraged the Germans to consider that America would bend when confronted by determined severity, scaring ordinary Americans into suspecting the Hun would win. If Crowley could get Germany's high command to consider unrestricted submarine warfare, he believed the US government would move from neutrality to intervention. In the meantime, he used his skills as a psychologist, and possibly druggist, to 'play' the enemy up.

Convinced Viereck's circle was the marrow of Germany's US intelligence bone, Crowley identified respectable Hugo Münsterburg, physics professor at Harvard, as a key, underestimated figure. Using psychology, he found he could influence Münsterburg by 'appreciating' that he was *always right,* and that Crowley's ideas were really his own. Familiar with German philosophies of *will*, Crowley understood that the weakness of the German 'superior being' was the strength of his intellect. That Crowley was also a literary man and mystic lent him cultural credibility in pro-German circles.

A good editor of Crowley's commercial work, Frank Crowinshield at *Vanity Fair* helped to reinforce that credibility. Why would pro-Allied Crowinshield employ a writer of pro-German propaganda? Crowley was also supported by John O'Hara Cosgrave, pro-Allied Irishman and literary editor of *The New York World* and its *Sunday World Magazine*. Cosgrave's foreign affairs editor, Frank Cobb, also supported pro-Allied intervention and was friendly with at least one senior SIS officer. Cosgrave's *Everybody's Magazine* published work by London Propaganda Bureau's pet writers, HG Wells and GK Chesterton.

The second front of Crowley's operation was to convey any information that would help the Allied cause. He would spy on every German or Irish independence sympathizer, or Indian radical that came near Viereck, the office of *The Fatherland* magazine, or any of the circles of people he met. Post-war, Viereck revealed that nearly every memo of the propagandists found its way to British Intelligence and the US Department of Justice. While Crowley's graceful manners ensured high society openings, he was equally acceptable to radical artistic settings; he could play many parts.

From his propaganda cover, Crowley got to observe von Papen closely, describing him in his *Confessions* as a victim of the 'stultifying conviction that he was so much better than anyone else'.[12] Von Papen's tasks included co-ordinating sabotage in the USA; the USA shared its northern border with British Dominion, Canada. US companies supplied *materiel* to the Allies. His sabotage colleague was Naval attaché Captain Karl Boy-Ed, whom Crowley calls a 'breezy naval ass [...] with the instincts of a gentleman'.[13] Von Papen and Boy-Ed recruited Irish Americans, Indians, anarchists and anyone with a grudge against the Allies for sabotage projects backed by an aggressive propaganda campaign.

Admiral Hall's policy appears to have been to follow the perpetrators, let the outrages happen, expose the culprits, then turn American opinion against Germany. Hopefully, indifference to the European war would become unsustainable. Crowley played a 'lone hand' in this process: 'I knew that the only way I could combat the influence of German propaganda in the States was to identify myself with it in every way, and by making it abhorrent to any sane being, gradually get the minds of the American public to react against its insidious appeal.' Crowley's 'treachery' would be his painted mask; but, as he wrote in *The Fun of the Fair* in 1913, one needs to look into the Eyes to find the Truth.[14]

*   *   *

Pressure on Crowley was intense. Respite arrived at a journalist's party in June 1915 in the form of beautiful poet Jeanne Robert Foster. Assistant editor of *The Review of Reviews*, Jeanne would be one of the great loves of Crowley's life, functioning for a time as his 'Scarlet Woman', *Soror Hilarion*.[15] He also called her 'the Cat'; she could purr and she could scratch. Just how significant a love this was is shown by a diary entry of 31 May 1920. Complaining his poetry lacked song, Crowley asked: 'Did she [Jeanne] really "break my heart?"' For Jeanne, he had written a book of poems, *The Golden Rose*, inspired by their super-intense affair.

A 17-year-old model when she married middle-aged, comfortably-off insurance executive Matlock Foster, Jeanne Robert Foster rose to be a journalist and serious poet. Jeanne knew John Quinn and was friendly with Belle da Costa Greene, daughter of the first African American to get a Harvard degree.[16] A passage from *Confessions* removed by editors has Crowley noting that Greene was 'one of the first people I met in NY'. This is significant. Belle da Costa Greene was private secretary to JP Morgan Jr who had a private intelligence service. Morgan handled British military guarantees. Jeanne Robert Foster may have been an associate of the intelligence agency through Greene. Spence considers it possible she was a 'British asset',[17] keeping watch on 'loose cannon' Crowley. Crowley intuited there was something 'false' about her. Maintaining his cover required great discretion. Assembling material for his 'Vindication' to counter Bottomley's treason charge in the 1920s, Crowley recalled a bad moment in the war:

> In the Autumn of 1915 I travelled to Detroit with Hilarion (Jeanne Foster). We slept in the same berth. In a brief interval for discussion she – an American of French extraction, asked me if I had to go into the trenches would I try to go into the French or the German trenches. I confidently replied 'Into the German trenches'. I would not trust her, she being on the private staff of Albert Shaw, on 'The Review of Reviews', who had been distinctly anti-English.

A galling experience, but it had to be done.

Belle da Costa Greene ran Morgan's immense Pierpont Morgan Library, close to Crowley's apartment at 29 East 36th Street. Quinn was also Greene's friend; she undertook investigative work on provenance for him. So it is intriguing that it was to Greene that Crowley proposed a bizarre secret scheme. At least, it would have been bizarre if we did not know what happened, subsequently, to the SS *Lusitania*.

Spence draws attention to Crowley's suggestion to Belle that he pose as a wealthy philanthropist (like Morgan Sr), offering to take indigents to form an ideal colony. Once at sea, the 'colonists' would be taken aboard an Allied ship. A captured German sub would then torpedo the empty vessel in shallow US waters. Subsequent outrage would force the government into retaliatory measures against Germany.

Why would Crowley make such a strange proposition to the manager of a library? Crowley's proposition is illumined by Thomas Troy's investigation into JP Morgan's investment in the Allied war effort.[18] Belle da Costa Greene appears there as 'Mr Green' in covert dealings between Morgan's 'publicity chief' Martin Egan, and Guy Gaunt of British Intelligence. Crowley's liaison with Belle, as with other women in New York, had an intelligence angle.

What Crowley presented in farcical terms became tragedy soon after. On 8 May 1915, the Germans torpedoed the civilian-carrying liner *Lusitania* on its return from New York to Liverpool. Over 1,400 men, women and children died. Former President Theodore Roosevelt condemned it as an 'act of piracy'. In a 1933 newspaper interview, Crowley asserted that one of his propaganda methods was to convince the Germans that arrogance and violence were sound policy, while encouraging the USA to dismiss German propaganda and to start actively supporting the Allies, with a view to intervention. He wrote ever more outrageous pieces of propaganda:

> I thought it a good plan to stiffen him [Viereck] up to defend the worst atrocities of Germany such as the Lusitania, and the Edith Cavell murder. It seems impossible that any sane man would have published such rot as I wrote for him; but it went.[19]

Whether Crowley's determination to expose extreme German brutality to public view may actually have been instrumental in persuading the Germans to attack the *Lusitania* not only presents a moral quagmire in the context of war, but is impossible to establish in fact. That Crowley strove to persuade senior Germans that acts of gross violence would cow American decision-makers is consistent with his simultaneous effort to undermine German propaganda.

George Langelaan, author of *The Fly*, knew Crowley from the early 1930s. A man with British Intelligence connections, Langelaan offered a story to an obscure French journal in the 1960s that claimed Crowley confided to him how he had advised the Germans to execute a blow that, while explicable as a regrettable accident, would nonetheless demonstrate to America Germany's ferocious willpower.[20] A senior German, presumably from the Propaganda Kabinett, believing Crowley possessed canny intuition into British and American mentalities, forwarded the idea to Berlin. According to Langelaan, the attack on the *Lusitania* followed.

Crowley was probably disappointed that outraged public opinion at the *Lusitania*'s sinking did not immediately prompt government intervention. The sinking did, however, stimulate American public opinion to adopt a road of hostility towards Germany, and assisted the credibility of the government's eventual case for engagement. German propaganda looked increasingly unpersuasive, even sinister.

Ironically, the government's reticence probably played into Crowley's hands, since his assessment of an America stunned, even cowed, by the act, suggested to senior Germans that Crowley's psychological judgement was reliable, even acute, shoring up Crowley's significance to the propaganda effort. The Germans could conclude that the *Lusitania*'s sinking rendered America's leaders even more cautious about joining the Allied effort than hitherto. From a strictly intelligence perspective, Crowley's psychological reading of the situation appears superb. It is another irony of that situation that his skills brought him closer to the regard of his enemies than to his friends. Crowley was used to the solitude of the wilderness.

Adding weight to the idea that the sinking was an initiative from the Viereck-von Papen-Bernstorff-Crowley camp, is the fact that Viereck had newspaper warnings printed on 1 May that ships could be sunk in what Germany called its 'War Zone', counselling American citizens wishing to travel by sea to do so at their own risk. Spence asks the pregnant question: did Crowley get Viereck to publish a warning that was something of a declaration of intent? This would be consistent with Admiral Hall's policy of letting German atrocities occur, then exposing the perpetrators. Indeed, we see such a policy in action soon after, when Dr Heinrich Albert, covert paymaster of Viereck's *Fatherland* magazine, was exposed as a spy after 'leaving' his briefcase on a train in July 1915.

Albert's exposure initiated a period leading to the collapse of the German intelligence effort. President Wilson demanded Berlin recall Captain Boy-Ed and Franz von Papen on 8 December 1915. Before that time, things got hot for Crowley. Nervous his cover might soon be blown, a desperate Crowley sought publicity to convince German 'colleagues' he was for real. He would drum it up by playing the Irish republican to the hilt and making sure everyone heard of it; if it created ructions in England, so much the better.

*   *   *

On 3 July 1915 with Leila, fiddle, some journalists and a gaggle of well-wishers, Crowley crossed from Battery Park to the Statue of Liberty, declaring himself for Irish freedom, less than a year before the Irish 'Easter Rising' of 1916. Leila played 'the Wearing of the Green' and Crowley tore up what was supposed to be his British passport – it wasn't – flinging it into the Hudson River with the words *'Erin go Bragh!'* – Ireland Forever! *The New York Times* put the story on its cover.

This was the kind of stunt Feilding had hoped Crowley would avoid: a freelance act, unsupervised. It would tarnish his reputation among home security services who heard of it, though the story was suppressed in England, due, among other things, to the sensitivity of the Irish Question. Crowley's problem would be that home intelligence (MI5) was not privy to the NID's New York intelligence loop. It was vital that

Crowley's 'mask' remain known to very few; the risk was his own, but not only his own. When the residual shit from this propaganda fan did hit England a year later, Crowley's perennial bad luck would see it create a situation very far from his original intentions.

*   *   *

There are large gaps in Crowley's diaries between June 1915 and February 1916, a period marking the apogee of his intense affair with the highly orgasmic Jeanne. On 6 October 1915, Crowley, Jeanne and her elderly husband left New York Central for a long journey north and west. The journey's stopover points coincided with unusual intelligence activities. In 1917 Crowley submitted a brief account of this journey for intelligence use:

> I also took a tour round the coast all through the West, and persuaded him [Viereck] that nobody there cared about the war, except the Germans, who were ready for civil war at need.
>
> The idea in all this was to encourage Germany to brave the U.S.A. and so force the breaking-off of relations.[21]

Crowley travelled under an alias, telling OTO followers in Vancouver that he was to be referred to as 'Clifford'. For one allegedly addicted to self-advertisement, we see again that it was the *mask* that was advertised, not the man. Followers Charles Stansfeld Jones and Wilfred T Smith of the Vancouver Lodge never doubted Crowley's involvement with high secret affairs.

The curious trio travelled by train through Detroit and Chicago. Crowley crossed into Canada leaving no record. The trio then journeyed to Seattle, San Francisco, Los Angeles, Santa Cruz, San Diego, Tijuana (Mexico) and the Grand Canyon. Crowley and Jeanne seldom made love in a bed; the rocking compartments sufficed.

First stop: *Detroit*

Crowley writes casually in his *Confessions* of an impromptu visit to the *Parke-Davis* pharmaceutical plant, not the usual tourist destination. Intrigued, Crowley closely observed industrial pill-production, probably wondering whether such methods could apply to mescaline production in the New Aeon. Crowley studied mescaline's effects scientifically.[22]

Next stop: *Chicago*

American-German Paul Carus showed Crowley the city in style. Carus published *Open Court*, the magazine in which Crowley's recent outrageous paean of the Kaiser as the New Messiah had appeared with George V reduced to the status of 'an obscene dwarf'. Spence identifies Carus as a member of the German-Jewish Hugo Münsterburg propaganda group, the hub, Crowley believed, of the German intelligence effort.

According to Spence, Carus was a friend of dashing German nobleman Gustav Konstantin Alvo von Alvensleben. 'Alvo' had arrived in British Columbia in 1904 as a front man for German investors. In the spring of 1915 he organized a secret meeting between agent Franz Rintelen von Kleist and West Coast saboteur Kurt Jahnke. Privy to the German secret war, Alvo chose Chicago as a money-laundering base after von Papen conferred with him on a visit to Seattle.[23] When Crowley discreetly visited Vancouver on the next leg of his journey, it is possible he did a 'favour' for von Alvensleben, for the German had left property secreted in British Columbia.

Vancouver

On 16 October, Crowley, wearing a grey overcoat and carrying a malacca cane, met CS Jones and fellow Crowley disciple Wilfred T Smith. Wilfred Smith recorded he had not quite recognized Crowley as the man he met. Was AC in an 'invisible' phase? Crowley-'Clifford' told Jones he was involved with a mission touching on 'the welfare of the Empire', and was now heading for the West Coast.[24] Crowley barely had time to do more than congratulate Jones on his 'drilling' of Vancouver's new OTO recruits. OTO business may have been cover to gain von Alvensleben's confidence.

The Chicago–Carus connection would have set Crowley up well for any intrigues with Alvo. In the *Chicago Daily News*'s archive, there is a photograph of Alvo, dated 6 December 1915, on which was written: 'Came from Vancouver, B.C. [British Columbia]. Reputed to be head of Espianago [*sic*] in Chicago.'

Nationalist, and later communist, Virandranath 'Chatto' Chattopadhyaya's seditionist Indian cabals also found Chicago attractive for recruitment. Chatto's web extended from London to the 'Indian Committee' in Berlin. A German-financed plot to assassinate every single Allied leader was foiled in Switzerland in November 1915 with the arrests of hundreds of anarchists and seditionists. Seditionists were also active in San Francisco, Crowley's next destination.

*   *   *

After intense activities in Seattle and San Francisco, Jeanne and Crowley visited LA. Disgusted by Hollywood's 'cocaine-crazed sexual lunatics, and the swarming maggots of near-occultists', among whom he may have included theosophist Katherine Tingeley, Crowley had a bad experience at Tingeley's theosophical flower garden at Point Loma on 12 November. Despite Crowley's bearing a message of 'Pure Love', Tingeley got a minion to see him off the property. Jeanne and the Beast both suffered nightmares, convincing Crowley the demons were the work of 'witch' Tingeley. His diary records his wrestling, wide awake, with 'a shapeless half-human being with a pig's face' that attacked him in his bed, attempting copulation while gnawing his chest. Crowley strangled 'it' and commented: 'Nothing of this sort has occurred since the summer of 1899 E.V. [*Era Vulgari* or 'common era': Crowley's dating conceit] when W.B. Yeats sent his vampires after me.' Tingeley may not have been the attack's sole cause.

Aleister and Jeanne were in the process of breaking up. Later, the only things he recalled that he could not stand about her was her dyed hair (a trifle) and that somehow she seemed to him 'false', meaning, not entirely what she appeared to be. Was she reporting on him? They had written love poems to one another; Crowley was convinced he had conceived a child, only later realizing he had been attempting a physical impossibility: Jeanne was barren.

Had Jeanne seen Crowley's idea of 'chastity' was unlikely to keep a girl emotionally secure? Crowley's desire for emotional detachment comes through in an unpublished diary fragment from July 1915:

> This is one of the greatest experiences of my life. Curious that the 1906 success also came through a magical thanksgiving under stress of passion. I went off to sleep almost at once. In the morning I woke early, before 7, in an absolutely renewed physical condition. I had the clean fresh feeling of a healthy boyhood, and was alert and active as a kitten – *post talem mortem*! Mentally I awoke into *Pure Love*. This was symbolized as a cube of blue-white light like a diamond of the best quality. It was lucid, transparent, self-luminous, and yet not radiating forth. I suppose because there was nothing Else in the Cosmos. This very love is intransitive; the love has no object. My gross mind vanished; when, later on, memory pictures of Hilarion [Jeanne Foster] arose, they were rejected automatically. All the desire-quality, the clinging, the fear, were no more; it was Pure Love without object or attachment. I cannot describe the quality of the emancipation given by this most wonderful experience. Aum.[25]

Release was brief. By September, the couple had entered a considerably hotter phase. They went swimming in the sea and made love at the highest possible pitch at every possible opportunity.

> Here I am enjoying freely the most beautiful and voluptuous woman I have ever known. In addition, she delights me immeasurably in every way, and inspires me constantly to write poetry. She is one with me, moreover, in Spirit. And I am losing sleep wondering (a) whether she loves me (b) whether she enjoys sexual intercourse and (c) whether she has ever had another

lover. If she were a simple whore I should be perfectly happy. I
need medical care.[26]

He needed medical care, all right. Crowley went mad with love over
Jeanne. He asked her to marry him; she said 'yes'. When asked what she
wanted, she said 'you'. She said she wanted to come into the sunlight,
out of the shadow of the old man. Crazy with passion, stoked up by the
most amazing sex and sex magick of his life – the elixir perfect in every
way – Crowley wondered if a blast of goetic magick might shove the 'evil'
Matlock Foster out of their lives forever.

Sex magick with Jeanne on 1 November 1915 in San Francisco was
for 'Hilarion's Freedom'. He concluded: 'This looks as if freedom would
come through divorce, but without scandal.' By 5 November, divorce
must have seemed unachievable, for Opus No. CCXXI performed with
French American Myriam Deroxe, 'an expert in every vice and addicted
to every drug', had as its object a code: 'Θ......40......Φ......' Crowley's
desperate comment: 'My beloved wife and sister H[ilarion]. having her
12th house heavily afflicted, I took this extreme course with the determination to bring permanent relief.' *Permanent relief...*

It seems likely given all other references to the Object that the Greek
Theta stands for *Thanatos* (=Death), the 40 for the Hebrew letter *Mem*
(value 40) and the Greek *Phi* for 'F'. That is: Death, M(atlock) F(oster).
After an Opus described optimistically by Crowley as 'the third and last
time!!!' with Ruth Hall, a German American prostitute, he commented:
'Please God this may finish the whole hellish business!' This grisly
attempt at bringing magick to bear on Matlock Foster's life took place on
19 November in Kansas City, six days *after* having remarked, following
the demonic attack attributed to Tingely: 'I doubt almost whether Ops.
like CCXXI are legitimate after all; whether indeed one should not
"overcome evil with good" in the world as well as in oneself.' After the
fourth operation aimed at Matlock in New York City on 4 December,
doubts increased:

> The return current may have hit us. Soror H. has been very ill
> ever since leaving Buffalo, and I the day after I arrived in

Chicago. We are still far from well. These Op^{ns} may be all wrong; but we had better go on if it kills us both. Mr...... has become very violent and aggressive.

Some kind of guilty conscience seems to have emerged by 22 December, when an act of sex magick with Jeanne had as its object:

> Create in me a clean heart, O God, and renew a right spirit within me! I have been going through an appallingly bad time spiritually, going straight to the Devil, in fact, all through not following out the formula 'Keep on loving and trusting!' Now I have repented, and been treated better than the Prodigal Son himself! I abhor myself, and repent in dust and ashes. If I can't cure myself of suspicion, I'm no good. Therefore I will. It might help to start a 'Liber III' ceremony every time I have such a thought, or a thought of infidelity. Good; I'll get the Sacred Burin out.

Of this entry, Crowley noted on 26 December: 'The extreme cynicism of above remarks never struck me till re-reading.' On occasion, Crowley could be bloody perverse.

Anyway, his will to kill, or certainly to hate a perceived 'evil', cannot have been a true will. Jeanne continued living with Matlock in New York City. Crowley feared she was gone. On 28 January 1916, they performed sex magick with the object: 'A pure heart.' How far the cleansing process went, we cannot say, but it is the case that the affair petered out soon after. Jeanne was still living with Matlock Foster in 1930, when Crowley had long since convinced himself that the only purpose in knowing the 'Cat' was somehow to make a 'Babe of the Abyss' come forth as a Master of the Temple: Charles Stansfeld Jones, the 'Magical Son' derived, he insisted, from Crowley's and Jeanne's attempts to have a real son. Was he joking when he said he needed 'medical care'?

He might have a clean heart, but Jeanne Robert Foster had broken it.

*   *   *

A new animal bounced onto Crowley's lap in 1916. 'Ratan Devi' was the stage name of the beautiful Alice Ethel Coomaraswamy, *née* Richardson, Yorkshire-born and, according to Crowley, a fantastic love-maker. He called Alice the 'Monkey-Officer'. Around midnight, 15/16 April 1916, he recorded the 'most magnificent' orgasm with the Monkey, so great that the magical objective of the rite was forgotten in an explosion of ecstasy that went on and on.

Alice became devoted to Crowley, with her husband's connivance. The 'Worm', as Crowley dubbed him, wanted to unload her. On 27 April, the lovers tried to conceive a child, but the Monkey had a miscarriage; Crowley blamed her husband, Dr Ananda K Coomaraswamy, an Anglo-Indian art critic with nationalist interests. There was an intelligence angle.

Among Coomaraswamy's associates was Indian Nationalist Sailandranath Gose, suspect in veteran British counter-subversion officer Robert Nathan's investigation of Indian seditionists and related rebels. Having begun investigations in India, Nathan pursued them from Switzerland to New York in 1916,[27] relying on German, Irish and Indian informants. According to Spence, Nathan's informants included someone known as 'C'. 'C' provided intelligence on Indian, Irish and German anti-Allied activists. 'C' could have been Crowley. In May 1916, Robert Nathan repeated Crowley's journey west to Vancouver, Seattle and San Francisco in search of intelligence on seditionists and saboteurs. Crowley's commitment to spying on Indian revolutionaries illuminates his relations with the Monkey and the Worm.

> I wrote to Capt. Guy Gaunt R.N. from Washington early in 1916, when *The Fatherland* was attacking him personally for 'bribing the office boy' etc., a letter of sympathy and an offer of help and service. Captain Gaunt replied cordially, but as if *The Fatherland* were not worth notice.
>
> After a conversation with Mr. Otto H. Kahn,[28] I applied to Captain Gaunt formally for work in connection with (a) *The Fatherland* (b) Irish-American agitation (c) Indian revolutionary activity. I have ever since kept him informed of my address, so as

to be ready if called. Not hearing from him, I also spoke to Mr. Willert of Washington D.C. on this matter, on the advice of my friend Mr. Paul Wayland Bartlett.[29]

Gaunt's antipathy to Crowley may have derived from his own professional frustrations. As Admiral Hall's man in the USA, 44-year-old Australian, Captain Guy Reginald Arthur Gaunt, had returned to New York from the Caribbean as British Naval Attaché and senior British Intelligence officer in early February 1915. Nine months later, however, a 'rival' appeared when Secret Intelligence Service chief Commander Mansfield Cumming (operating in M11c), sent Sir William Wiseman to run the British intelligence effort in America. Gaunt complained. Nevertheless, Wiseman returned to the Manhattan Consulate to establish M11c, Section V, in January 1916 with full Foreign Office support. Spence suspects the bad odour spread to Gaunt's dire assessment of Crowley's activities submitted to biographer John Symonds 35 years later, for Crowley operated in a 'loop' that included Wiseman and New York's new British Consul, Charles Clive Bayley. Bayley knew R Bruce Lockhart well from his espionage-soaked consulship in Moscow.

*　　*　　*

In spite of Gaunt's apparent indifference, Crowley carried on investigating Indian revolutionary activity. He was 'on' to Coomaraswamy. Receiving a letter from him on 13 January 1917, Crowley noted in his diary that their 'correspondence ended in the discovery of the Worm as a Black Brother; it has been very useful to have the type to study'. Nothing worse than a 'Black Brother' existed in Crowley's book. A 'Black Brother', a failed or perverted initiate, an unbalanced ego, provided a tool for 'the other side', constituting an arch-enemy of the Great White Brotherhood, dedicated to the suppression of the True (divine) Will, the SPECTRE if you like, of Crowley's intelligence and magical mythos. Coomaraswamy was a marked man and intimacy with the Monkey enabled Crowley to keep an eye on him.

Another love affair of Crowley's with an intelligence angle opened in April 1916. Gerda Maria von Kothek, real name Gerda Schumann, was probably the 'German prostitute' the 'Worm' insisted his wife share her bed with. That they both slept with Crowley was an intelligence plus. Aged about 19 when they met, Gerda was a communist revolutionary sympathizer married to the radical Dr Rudolf Gebauer of Passaic, New Jersey. Gebauer was linked to Manhattan's radical German paper, the *New Yorker Volkzeitung*, run by long-time socialist, Ludwig Lore. What Spence calls 'clandestine threads' linked this anti-war periodical to the Propaganda Kabinett and the German Consulate. Like Hugo Münsterberg, Gebauer was also a member of the German University League. Following intelligence from an unnamed source, the US Bureau of Investigation investigated Gebauer inconclusively in April 1917.

*   *   *

In mid-May 1916, Crowley went to Philadelphia to meet writer and Shakespeare expert Louis Umfraville Wilkinson (1881-1966). The sardonic Wilkinson had known Wilde in his exile. He took to Crowley warmly; they would stay friends to the end. Wilkinson had married mystical poet Frances Gregg, an Imagist from the Philadelphia group that also produced Ezra Pound.[30] Crowley's visit appears motivated as much by desire to see the wife as the husband; she, like him, was bisexual.

Frances had fallen in love with fellow student Hilda Dolittle at art school in Philadelphia. In her autobiography *A Mystic Leeway*, Frances described HD bringing her round after an attempted suicide in a hyacinth wood: 'Hilda undressed me herself, and oh her hands were swift and gentle. She warmed my hands against her breast and called them her birds, and made crooning, soft, witless talk that eased my childish, overcharged heart. There is a tenderness that can exist between two girls that is more exquisite than anything on earth.' Crowley would have been swift to agree and could cite his own poem 'In a Lesbian Meadow' as evidence of his deep-seated identification with lesbian love. Frances would doubtless have disdained discussing her intimacies with a girl-watcher of the scale of Aleister Crowley. While she had enjoyed a brief affair with poet John Cowper Powys before Wilkinson, Crowley was quick with the 'come on'. If she found sexually forthright males difficult, this would explain a suspicion of him evinced in an unattested story told by writer Paul Newman that may cast light on Crowley's attempts at 'invisibility':

> Another time she [Gregg] entered a dark room in her house and came across a bald man sitting at a table alone. Becoming aware of her, this eerie stranger picked up a dark mat of hair from the table, placed it on his head and transformed into Crowley. He then hauled up a case, in which Frances identified a whole nest of wigs, and silently left.[31]

Meanwhile, Guy Gaunt, British Naval Attaché in Washington, knowing Crowley was feeding information to colleagues in London, monitored his activities. As Crowley's bad luck would have it, Gaunt's distaste coincided with a Foreign Office flap in which Crowley's name came to the ear of Foreign Secretary, Sir Edward Grey. What Grey heard, distressed him.

On 30 June 1916, Rotterdam's British Consulate General had been informed by Charles Tower, *The Daily Mail*'s correspondent in Holland, that one of Crowley's German propaganda articles had appeared in the *Rheinisch-Westfälische Zeitung*.[32] The article trumpeted the writer's discovery, during a fake trip to England, that the nation was 'demoralised'. One FO civil servant, ignorant of Crowley's cover, hoped Gaunt could find a way to expose the renegade Crowley to Americans. Sir Edward Grey requested more information on Crowley from Thomas Wodehouse Legh, 2nd Baron Newton of the Foreign Office. *Had Crowley visited England?* Home Secretary Viscount Samuel got on the job.

Superintendent P Quinn of New Scotland Yard provided a full report on Crowley including police interest in the 'widow's £200' in 1900 (Laura Grahame was not a widow and the figure was wrong), and how police had observed the Rites of Eleusis in 1910. In 1914, someone had informed police of alleged indecency in the presence of females at 76

Fulham Road. The Gnostic Mass would account for that. Incense had been burnt and musical instruments had been played. *Damning.* In February 1914, the DPP had received complaints from a correspondent in Paris about the contents of *The Equinox*, but this was not pursued as the periodical was expensive!

Quinn reported Crowley's Statue of Liberty stunt in precisely the kind of terms Crowley had hoped for – *a year earlier*, when he wanted to convince the Germans of his anti-Allied status. Memos went round the Foreign Office until September 1916. It was urged that Crowley should receive no passport and his citizenship be rescinded. A confidential report was sent to Gaunt (by bag) with instructions not to give his source of information when using the material to slam Crowley in the US press.

Gaunt did not slam Crowley in the press. How could he? Crowley had offered Gaunt his assistance. A traitor is how Gaunt recalled the part Crowley played, for that *was* his part, and he played it to the hilt. Crowley offered further services, but Gaunt snubbed him, downgrading Viereck as 'one of the lesser jackals around von Papen'.[33] When Gaunt told Crowley biographer John Symonds in 1951 that he had informed Sir Edward Grey he had a 'complete line' on Crowley and *The Fatherland*, and that further action was unnecessary, he should have said he had a complete line *through* Crowley on *The Fatherland*. Gaunt did not trust Crowley. Maybe, as Spence suggests, Crowley *did* become in Gaunt's own mind, a traitor – *to him*. For, to add insult to injury, a 1929 article by Viereck criticized Gaunt, but held Wiseman in esteem. Gaunt probably associated Crowley with Viereck, sealing the connection. Gaunt's statements to Symonds, made 35 years after the events, now stand as singularly ill-judged.

Crowley's early-1920's notes for a 'Vindication' of his wartime activities were preserved by Gerald Yorke. From them we learn how Berlin's US ambassador was impressed by his argument printed in Viereck's *The Fatherland* advocating unrestricted submarine warfare. It was, said Crowley, 'that insane policy which brought America into the War, as I had wished, and foreseen'. He continued: 'My *Appeal to the*

American Republic, published, as a pamphlet in 1899, and reprinted in *The English Review* in November 1914, is the expression of my life-long wish to see an alliance between England and the USA.' Thanks to his covert operation: 'I was fortunately able to break up a most formidable spy system, disguised as the Agricultural Labour Bureau.'

> I was plain pro-German in appearance until my Statue of Liberty joke aroused Feilding, whom I felt I could trust having known him for years. But even so, I used precautions, for example: in going to a cable office, not signing my name but the code name Edith (in memory of Edith Cavell).
>
> (I suspect the real difficulty in understanding me when I began private negotiations with the Naval Intelligence, was that I was trying to play a Philip Oppenheim hero and became super-subtle.)

Gaunt subsequently gave the impression that he was uniquely gifted in his work. His refusal to accept Crowley's assessment of Münsterberg and Viereck as serious threats, in spite of their links to Gaunt's opposite numbers in German Naval Intelligence, Franz von Papen, Captain Karl Boy-Ed and Bernhard Dernburg, may have been due to Gaunt's having entertained Viereck as a possible double agent. Gaunt's memoirs refer to being pestered by a German who got the ear of Foreign Secretary Edward Grey. This might have occurred through the Crowley-Feilding connection. Grey advised Gaunt to meet the German. They duly met in a New York hotel. The informant claimed to be, according to Gaunt's recall, the Kaiser's son. Viereck claimed to be the grandson of Kaiser Wilhelm I.

In 1930, after lunch with Crowley, Viereck agreed to sign an affidavit that Crowley had never been detained for pro-German activities by American authorities, as had been alleged by enemies in the British press. The situation's complexity is revealed in documents examined by Spence. US National Archives hold material on Gaunt's neutral appraisal of Crowley's appearance on the scene.[34] The question arises why Gaunt did not clarify to US intelligence officers that Crowley was not a pro-German propagandist. The answer may lie in intelligence practice. One had to assume the Germans had infiltrated US intelligence, as well as MI5 and sister agencies. Crowley's independence was a problem to Gaunt. The Americans made their own assessment. Crowley himself speaks of his informing the US Department of Justice about his activities, and that they, unlike the British, made better use of his services.[35]

*　　*　　*

In December 1916, Hugo Münsterberg, aged 53, dropped dead lecturing to a class at Radcliffe, the Cambridge, Mass. women's college near Harvard. Shortly after, Crowley wrote 'A Sense of Incongruity', a fiction 'starring' Crowley's creation, Thelemic sleuth Simon Iff. Iff confronts a Japanese plot to poison prominent political figures, reminiscent of Robert Nathan's territory.

In another story, 'The Pasquaney Puzzle', Dolores Cass, Iff's young partner, appears. Dolores is a Radcliffe student and occult *aficionado*. She is also described as a student of Hugo Münsterberg. Spence wonders out loud in *Secret Agent 666* whether Dolores was perhaps based on a genuine person he met that summer. Crowley was in Boston, Mass. on 22 July. Had he found someone from Radcliffe to spike Münsterberg's glass of water as he expounded from the podium? 'Man has the right to kill those who would thwart these [Thelemic] rights', Crowley would write in *Liber Oz* in 1941, ensuring the safeguard of tyrannicide open to such as Claus von Stauffenberg in 1944. If Crowley had identified Münsterberg as a 'Black Brother', well…perhaps we have confused fact with fiction, as Crowley may also have done, from time to time.

*　　*　　*

A foreword by Crowley to his full-length Simon Iff detective novel *Moonchild* explains how the book was written in 1917 'when not engaged in bringing America into the War'. As the story took shape, Berlin resumed unrestricted submarine warfare, the principle that had led to *Lusitania*'s sinking in May 1915. On 2 February 1917, Crowley put a note in his diary in Enochian, which transliterates into English as 'USA♂Germany – success'. ('♂' = symbol for Mars=War) The following entry confirms Crowley's assertion that his *Fatherland* work was a disinformation campaign:

Feb.2 [1917]

My 2¼ years' work crowned with success; U.S.A. breaks off relations with Germany.[36]

Next day the United States announced its severance of diplomatic relations with Germany; war was declared on 6 April. As Crowley congratulated himself for doing his bit, the OTO's London offices at 93 Regent Street were raided; an elderly female spiritualist member was taken away and charged.[37] All property was confiscated. Disastrously, the British Order's treasurer, George Macnie Cowie became convinced Crowley was Germany's willing dupe. Crowley wrote in his diary on 29 March:

A new and powerful impulse arrived last night, a letter from Fiat Pax [Cowie]. The Stupids have misunderstood my whole [political] attitude, and raised trouble. Now I go direct to Washington to straighten this out; if I fail this time to get them to listen to sense, at least I can go to Canada and force them to arrest me. My hand is therefore at last upon the lever.[38]

More light is cast on the affair in an unpublished 'Memorandum', written for American, and possibly, Canadian authorities. Crowley makes it plain that 'Apparently the Government at home have not all this information [about his dealings with Viereck and Gaunt].'

Early this year my representatives in London and Edinburgh [in pencil, 'Cowie'] were approached by the authorities. I have no details, but a letter of March 8. says:
   'It was only on Saturday last that I [Cowie] learned the cause of the recent action of the authorities, and of which I was in absolute ignorance. It has come as a severe shock. I assume you know, though you could not have meant that use to be made of

your stuff (I do not know what is referred to. A.C.) I learn that it is only my known probity of character etc. etc. which has satisfied the authorities, etc. Otherwise, I have no doubt that we should have been closed down.'

My representative continues:

'...until you vindicate yourself, as promised me, and can return to England, etc.'

I decline to be represented as a fugitive, without some pretty good reason.

Hence I approach you.

My position is particularly good at this moment; I can pose as a martyr for Truth, better than ever before.

If therefore the British Government can use me, let it do so. If not, I can at least repair the mischief done, whatever that may be; at least I suppose so. Whatever it is, it can only be something that rests on my supposed attitude, and disclosure would presumably undo it.

In the last resort, I shall go to Canada, and claim what is surely the first right of every subject, to be tried for treason. I cannot allow the imputation to rest upon me that I am a traitor or a coward or both, unless I am under the direct orders of the Government, and so certain to be exculpated one day. I never forget that I am the only English poet now alive; the conclusion is something obvious.

Shoot.[39]

Crowley could not tell Cowie or other OTO members what he was up to for fear it would get back to Reuss, which would tip off the Germans. The dangers for security if his US cover were blown gave him leverage. He desperately needed money and this was perhaps a chance to get some. His comments about the usefulness of being seen as a 'martyr for truth' were fulfilled. In his *Confessions*, Crowley noted that the publicity over the London bust assisted his pose at *The Fatherland*'s offices. However, with America now fighting Germany, it was a very risky pose.

The raids affected Crowley badly. Cowie refused monies rightfully Crowley's, such as rents from Boleskine. Convinced of Crowley's 'treason' in America, and claiming costs and legal fees connected with the raid, Cowie sold off all OTO property as well as anything of Crowley's held in trust for a pittance: his house, library, all his clothes, furniture and sporting equipment. Crowley accused Cowie of embezzling order funds but could do nothing. The bitter experience left Crowley paranoid for the rest of his life about theft of his property.

*   *   *

After a period of destitution in New Orleans, Crowley arrived on 9 February 1917 at the home of his mother's half-brother William's son, Lawrence Bishop. Lawrence and Birdie Bishop ran a citrus farm at Titusville, near what is now Cape Kennedy, Florida. It was excruciating; Crowley hated the household's combination of capitalism, materialism, and religious severity. This was the era of the lynch mob and the Ku Klux Klan, as well as the clamour for Prohibition and Hollywood censorship. When Crowley heard the oft-repeated words 'In God we Trust', they sounded hollow; it was the dollar that bought trust, and God came free with the apple pie. Still, Crowley found it in his heart to do his cousin a favour, and earn his keep. On 6 March, by an act of will, the Magus believed he had restrained a bad frost that would have wrecked Lawrence Bishop's citrus groves. The mage returned to New York into freezing accommodation on Lower 5th Avenue with Belgian artist and OTO member Leon Engers.

On 6 May, another blow:

> Had news of my mother's death. Two nights before news had dream that she was dead, with a feeling of extreme distress. The same happened two nights before I had news of my father's death. I had often dreamed that my mother had died, but never with that helpless lonely feeling.

Emily had died of a heart attack on 14 April. Had she heard of her son's alleged 'treason' through gossip emanating from Cowie?[40]

In June he felt his life had fallen to 'utter smash' at the moment it should have flowered. He was confused, questioning everything: 'The

Illusion is always attacking Conscious Crowley in curious subconscious ways', he wrote to himself.

> I have seen lately the danger of having a mental machine which functions so independently of the Self, and even of the human will. E.g., all my sympathies are most profoundly with the Allies; but my brain refuses to think as sympathizers seem to do; so in argument I often seem 'pro-German'. Similarly, I have a Socialistic or Anarchistic brain, but an Aristocrat's heart; hence constant muddle not in myself, but in others who observe me.[41]

Aleister had been 'under cover' too long. He should have been 'brought in' to recover his bearings, but there was no 'in', and when a door did open, it was Viereck's. In July, Viereck offered the man Austin Harrison had described as 'the greatest metrical poet since Swinburne' $20 a week as contributing editor for his magazine *The International*. Crowley could keep an eye on the German backers and their associates on behalf of the US Department of Justice, more alert to German spies and saboteurs now the USA was at war. Crowley's best contributions were in issues up to its folding in summer 1918. When Viereck sold the paper, the new owner refused Crowley's articles; it folded. Many of Crowley's articles were propaganda, not for Germany, but for Thelema. He could write in American slang and became a skilled article writer and good features editor.

*   *   *

It was probably through Gerda von Kothek that Crowley met New York sex-magick 'Assistant' Marie Lavrova Röhling (*Soror Olun*) in 1917. Fresh from the Russian Revolution, Röhling toured the States, lecturing at Unitarian, Ethical Culture, Quaker and other civic venues on the glorious benefits to come from the Red Revolt. Knowledge about radicals was as useful to American intelligence as it was to British.

Details of how Crowley's involvement with American secret services began are obscure. Crowley wrote in his *Confessions* that during the spring of 1916, 'I was often away in Washington'.[42] His *Confessions* refer to helping the Department of Justice. In an expunged passage of that book, he insisted the American investigators had 'brains, and they used them'.[43]

US Freedom of Information legislation has brought to light several important documents. A 'General Summary' of September 1918 shows US military intelligence enjoyed 'full cognizance' of Crowley's activities through British Consul Charles Clive Bayley.[44] Bayley shared a spook-loop with Wiseman, Gaunt and other officers.

New York State's Deputy Attorney General, Alfred LeRoy Becker, interviewed Crowley on 11 October 1918 just after Crowley's return from a 'Great Magical Retirement' at Esopus Island, near Hyde Park.[45] Becker worked in concert with the Bureau of Investigation (BI) and other federal agents. Their files reached BI head J Edgar Hoover in 1924 when he wanted to know if Crowley's entry into the USA was desirable. Crowley had been 'examined' at least twice by Becker's assistant in 1918 and 1919 and had 'furnished certain information' about himself and his associates. Admitting he had no 'official' position in the British secret service, Crowley detailed his dealings with Guy Gaunt, as in the Memorandum above. In 1919, Becker recounted to a senate investigative committee how he had acquired German propaganda produced by Theodor Reuss as a result of interviewing Crowley.[46]

Crowley was a 'deniable' source. One marvels at his strength in maintaining this position, a curiously earthly reflection of his spiritual initiation; pouring the ashes of his personal self into what he called 'the Urn' as part of his long-term initiation as Magus and Word of the Aeon.

FIFTEEN

The Peacock Angel

1918

The more religious people are,
the more they believe in black magic.

(Aleister Crowley)[1]

W as Aleister Crowley a bloodthirsty Devil-worshipper, an
agent of satanic wickedness, like the villains in Dennis
Wheatley's black magic novels? No, the caricature is a
calumny – the same calumny that is aimed at a little-known religion.

*   *   *

The Beast never pursued virgins; he liked women 'proud of their
whoredom'. Crowley described married (estranged) feminist Roddie
Minor as 'Matron. Big muscular sensual type. (Aphrodite)'. Known as
the 'Camel', 'Eve' and Sister Achitha, a doctorate in pharmacy inured
Roddie to chemical experimentation with the Beast. Together they
steamed up a West 9th Street studio apartment through the harsh winter
of 1917/18, while Crowley worked on *The International*.

The International's November issue featured his article 'The Revival
of Magick'. Its last sentence read: 'Herein is Wisdom; let him that hath
understanding count the number of the Beast; for it is the number of a
man; and his number is six hundred and three score and six.'
Unbeknownst to 666, one with 'understanding' lived in New York.

*   *   *

20 January 1918

Crowley and Roddie bring to a climax a 'great Magical Operation'. Roddie envisions scenes recalling the Ab-ul-Diz-Virakam workings of 1911. 'It's all in the egg', Roddie is told. A Wizard in a wood in charge of a naked boy identified as Horus gives his name: *Amalantrah*, which by Hebrew gematria computes to 729: nine cubed. By Greek numerology, *cēphas*, a stone – the Aramaic name of 'Peter' – is also 729.

Crowley asks the wizard for an equivalent geometrical figure. The wizard says: 'The segment of an octagonal column.' Crowley thinks of the Templar idol 'Baphomet', combining the phallus-'column' and the number 8. Masonic-Templar symbolism associated the number 8 with the Morning Star, the Virgin or Ishtar. Crowley recalls the famous drawing in Eliphas Lévi's *Dogma and Ritual of High Magic* of the tarot's Devil card as the Templars' idol 'Baphomet'. Lévi's 'Baphomet' is androgynous, or bisexual, like Crowley, phallic and feminine.

Asked for the 'true' spelling of Baphomet, Amalantrah offers *Baphometh* in Hebrew. Can Amalantrah make the spelling 'eightfold'? enquires Crowley of the wizard. The Hebrew letter *resh* (ר) flashes in Crowley's mind. 'Resh' can mean 'head' or 'sun', the head or 'father' of our solar system. And BAFOMEThR computes to 729! Delighted, Crowley interprets BAFOMEThR as 'Father Mithra', a solar deity, surmising the Sun or light that had been *concealed* in the old aeon: 'suppressed as a blind' Crowley noted, '– it blinded me all right!'

Sunday 24 February 1918

A night-time communication with Amalantrah: Roddie Minor asks for the Hebrew spelling of Crowley's Greek title as Magus, *To Mega Thērion*, the 'Great Wild Beast'. Amalantrah's reply: חיריען (Thirian).[2] 'Thirian', alas, holds no cabalistic value.

Next morning, Crowley enters *The International*'s freezing office. There is a coal famine. Seizing his mail packet, Crowley leaves. The next day he finds a letter addressed to Viereck, written and posted the previous Sunday evening – the very time Amalantrah had been asked to spell *Thērion*:

BETH NAHARIN
(MESOPOTAMIA)

2-24-18
Nahon Elias Palak
Editor and Publisher
210 Getty Avenue
Patterson, New Jersey

George Sylvester Viereck Esq.
Editor
The International
1123 Broadway
New York City

My dear Bokh.[3] Viereck!

I miss your plays in the Magazine: I mean those written by yourself, and yet no other publication furnishes anything half as good to feed my soul with – and I am not capricious a bit or an Idiot either, as there will be many others who will agree with me along these points as true: (1) That *The Philistine, The Fra, The Phoenix* were the only magazines that furnished food for brain until recently when can be found in *The International* hardly better stuff than the *Pearsons'* does except Bokh. Frank Harris' own stuff. [...]

Please inform your readers that I, Shmuel bar Aiwaz bie Yackoub de Sherabad, have counted the number of the Beast, and it is the number of a man.

	ן	ו	י	ר	ת
[Read from right to left]	N	O	I	R	Th
	50	6	10	200	400

666

Amazing! How did this stranger 'Shmuel bar Aiwaz' know what Crowley called the 'most striking solution possible of the problem presented to Amalantrah'?

Telepathy?

Improbable, thought Crowley: 'The evidence appears overwhelming for the existence of Amalantrah, that he was more expert in the Qabalah than The Master Therion himself, and that he was (further) possessed with the power to recall this four-month-old problem to the mind of an entirely unconnected stranger, causing him to communicate the correct answer at the same moment as the question was being asked many miles away.'[4]

*   *   *

An immigrant from Urmia in Persia's Azerbaijan province, Samuel Aiwaz Jacobs would show Crowley how a Hebrew spelling of Aiwass gave the number 93.[5] 93 was the cabala of the Greek words *THELĒMA* (will) and *AGAPĒ* (love). Furthermore, Jacobs suggested to the Master Therion that Aiwaz was the secret name of the 'god of the Yezidis'.

God of the Yezidis?

A current speculation held that Yezidi religion, whose centre is Lalish in what is now northern Iraq, had roots in ancient Sumer in southern Mesopotamia (*fl* c 3200BCE). Crowley was struck by the connection. The Cairo revelation could be presented as a fresh synthesis with roots in civilization's *first religion*, long since corrupted.

Beginning in 1919, Crowley made notes for a 'New Commentary' on *The Book of the Law*:[6]

> LXXVIII [78]. The number of Aiwass, the Intelligence who communicated this Book. Having only hearing to guide me, I spelt it AYVAS,[7] LXXVIII, referring it to Mezla, the Influence from Kether, which adds to the same number. But in An. XIV [1918] there came unto me mysteriously a Brother, [Jacobs] ignorant of all this Work, who gave me the spelling OYVZ[8] which is XCIII, 93, the number of Thelema and Agape, which concentrates the Book itself in a symbol. Thus the author

secretly identified himself with his message.

But this is not all. Aiwaz is not (as I had supposed) a mere formula, like many angelic names, but is the true most ancient name of the God of the Yezidis, and thus returns to the highest Antiquity. Our work is therefore historically authentic, the rediscovery of the Sumerian Tradition. (Sumer is in lower Mesopotamia, the earliest home of our race).[9]

Samuel Aiwaz Jacobs (c 1891–1971) was an extraordinary man. According to his *New York Times* obituary, Jacobs 'was born in Persia, came to the United States as a youth, and in 1909 became a printer for *The Persian Courier*, a weekly here. Later he worked for the Mergenthaler Linotype Company, designing and revising unusual typefaces. In the early 1930s he founded the Golden Eagle Press.'[10] The *New Assyria and Persian American Courier* served the 'Assyrian' community in America. Jacobs' birthplace, Urmia (his clan village was Sherabad), was a Persian village populated by 'Assyrian' Christians, close to predominantly Armenian villages. Both communities suffered massacres and forced-exile at Turkish hands in 1915. Having become a naturalized American himself, Jacobs published a booklet, *Information for Assyrians desiring to become American Citizens* (1917); a copy survives in the Library of Congress.[11]

On 21 August 1918, Jacobs replied from Bridgeport Connecticut to a letter of CS Jones, evincing his commitment to Turkish 'Jacobites' or 'Assyrians', members, almost certainly like himself, of the Assyrian/ Chaldean Syriac Orthodox Christian Church:

> I am very much interested in the New Law [*Thelema*] though I know very little of it – I like to know more about it. I may change my mood but not my mind or will: my intention is to know and tell the Truth, and to remain in this Country where my lot has fallen amongst the newly found Assyrian Jacobites from Turkey, who thirst after the knowledge of their forgotten language and buried literature in the abysmal oblivion of the ages. My office is to teach, educate, illumine them (by the way of publicity), and to enkindle in their hearts the fire that is quenched for so many aeons.[12]

The Assyrian Church used *Estrangelo*, a Syriac font. According to William Breeze, Jacobs used Syriac Estrangelo to give the Hebrew values for the word *Thērion*.[13]

Perhaps Samuel the fine printer recognized something of himself in the Master Therion, lover of fine books. Crowley refers to Jacobs as a 'Brother', though there is no record of his being a member of either the OTO or the A.˙.A.˙. perhaps he was a Freemason. Intellectual, even spiritual kinship between Crowley and Jacobs emerges from an interview which appeared in October 1953's edition of *The Inland Printer*.[14] PJ Thomajan visited the Golden Eagle Press, Mount Vernon, New York, to meet 'that Persian printer-philosopher Samuel Aiwaz Jacobs', described as 'a rare blend of mystic and realist, one blessed with a creative eye and hand, who finds interesting ways of fulfilling his visions. There is intuitive logic to his approach that results in inspired originalities.' 'Jacobs', wrote Thomajan, 'is paced to the modern tempo but he has nothing but disdain for the word *modernistic*.'

Jacobs explained in an essay how 'Art springs not from rules and regulations but from feeling. If there is no feeling, logic is a blind alley and reason a dead end. Logic is a poor guide without the light of feeling.' 'Follow no one. Only your self can lead you.' 'Approach your line of activity as an individual.' 'Be independent.'[15] Little wonder Crowley was struck by Jacobs' manifestation in his life; he had found, or been found by, a fellow spirit, and a *son of Aiwaz* no less!

Thomajan reported that it was a precept of the Persian prophet Zarathushtra that gave 'poise and persistence to this artist-craftsman':

> Unto the persevering mortals the ever-present guardian angels
> are swift to assist.

Ever-present guardian angels! Swift to assist! Right up Crowley's street! Just as resonant was Jacobs' twinkle-in-the-eye, gleeful revelation in a 1929 interview that his middle name *Aiwaz* meant 'Satan'! Bizarre as it seems, Crowley was never quite sure whether Jacobs might not have been, in some peculiar sense, Aiwaz, his Holy Guardian Angel:

> I now incline to believe that Aiwass is not only the God or
> Demon or Devil once held holy in Sumer, and mine own
> Guardian Angel, but also a man as I am, insofar as He uses a
> human body to make His magical link with Mankind, whom He
> loves, and that He is thus an Ipsissimus, the Head of the A.'.A.'.[16]

As late as 1945, a question from Gerald Yorke about Aiwaz elicited this
remarkable response:

> Surely Eq[uinox] of [the] Gods [Book 4, Part IV] covers your
> query re Aiwaz as fully as possible. The only part undetermined
> is whether He is a discarnate Being, or (as seemed possible after
> the Samuel Jacobs incident – *Magick* pp.256 *seq*. Footnote 2
> [original pagination]) a human being, presumably Assyrian,
> of that name. And that I simply do not know, and cannot
> reasonably surmise, because I do not know the limits of such
> an One.[17]

Crowley remained convinced, at the very least, that Jacobs provided key
evidence for the origins of *The Book of the Law*. Jacobs' influence is also
evident in an unpublished letter from Charles Stansfeld Jones to Gerald
Yorke:

> There is one thing A.C. always insisted upon, viz: firm links with
> the past, for otherwise, anything which crops up as a result of
> some man's pretended 'illumination' or what not is just a
> personal manifestation of his own having no true roots in
> universal magical or mystical history. Even in the case of the
> New Law proclaimed in *Liber Legis* Therion did his best to
> account for the reception of it as coming from a source with a
> tradition – the Sumerian.[18]

William Breeze has wondered whether 'Jones may have been privy to
AC's thinking around the time Jacobs appeared, since Jones lived in
New York in 1918, working with Crowley.'[19] Did Jacobs introduce Jones
to contemporary debate about Yezidi origins? In 1919, recent Harvard
graduate Isya Muksy Yusef published his thesis *Devil Worship: The
Sacred Books and Traditions of the Yezidis* which denied that the Yezidi

'sect' came from pre-Mosaic Mesopotamia. He argued they were a schismatic Islamic sect whose worshipful angel was a devil.[20]

No Western scholar would assert today that Yezidis represent a survival of either the Sumerian people, credited with the invention of writing, or of Sumerian religion. There is no telling evidence to suppose a link. Yezidi religion is essentially an oral, not written tradition, practised by Kurds who, for as long as history knows, have been associated with the Caucasus region and northern, not southern Mesopotamia. While probably predating Islam at root, Yezidism employs elements of Sufism, Zoroastrianism, Gnosticism and Christianity, as well as exhibiting familiarity with legends common to Hebrew patriarchal writings.

Though Crowley's view was not eccentric at the time, he was almost certainly mistaken about Sumer and the Yezidis. Was he misled about Aiwaz and the 'secret name' of the god of the Yezidis as well?

Here we are on shakier ground because we do not know if Crowley studied the subject closely. The connection may simply have been an idea of Jacobs' that 'felt right' to Crowley. It has long been a jibe of Muslims and Christians in the East that the god, or angel, of the Yezidis is 'Shaitan' (Arabic for devil). Jacobs might have been taught to believe that this was their god's 'secret' or *concealed* name. Yezidis are horrified by this jibe, forbidding the word 'Shaitan' or anything that sounds like it. In 1940, a Yezidi *qawwal* or sacred musician complained to visitor, Lady Drower: 'They say of us wrongly, that we worship one who is evil.'[21]

Slating the Peacock Angel as Satan is used to justify deadly persecution of Yezidis. Perhaps Crowley recognized a certain resonance with his own experience. But of course, for Crowley, as he understood the term, 'Satan' had no superstitious or negative connotation.

*　　*　　*

Yezidis do not believe in the Devil; bad comes from man's ignorance and folly. *Yezidi* means 'godly'. Remarkably, Crowley's aspiration to serve the exalted company of the Secret Chiefs of planetary destiny makes sense within the Yezidi angelic system.

According to Yezidism, *Khude* or *Êzdan* (God) made seven archangels who are also, in a sense, 'God'.[22] The Yezidi *Lord of this world* is *Sultan Êzî* or *Êzîd*, the supreme angel, known also as the 'Peacock Angel', 'Melek' (lord or angel) 'Ta'us' (or Tawus). Tawus made the world and has a special relationship with the godly people. According to the Yezidi book *Meshef Resh* the ultimate deity recognizes Melek Tawus's loyalty, permitting his management of human affairs. Tawus offers knowledge and freedom.

Melek Tawus is also identified with the hyper-enlightened Sufi saint Sheykh Adi who became leader of the Yezidi community at Lalish, north of Mosul, in the 12th century CE. It is a fascinating aspect of Yezidi religion that names and beings are interchangeable in a manner that those with written traditions cannot tolerate. Historical figures may also be divine angels. Jesus is regarded as an angel. Yezidis are joined to holy beings above and within them, an approach to sacred beings that resonates with the cabalistic techniques employed by Crowley; names may change but *values* remain. According to Crowley: '"Gods" are the Forces of Nature; their "Names" are the Laws of Nature. Thus They are eternal, omnipotent, omnipresent and so on; and thus their "Wills" are immutable and absolute.'[23]

Melek Tawus's majestic self-revelation is recorded in the *AL-Jilwah*, attributed to Sheykh Adi. Remarkably, *AL-Jilwah* – the 'Divine Effulgence' – bears comparison with the spirit of Crowley's *Liber AL*.

*   *   *

By the time Crowley sat down in Atlantic City, New Jersey in 1919 to begin his New Commentary, he could have found the name Melek Tawus in numerous sources.[24] Recall Crowley's description of Aiwass in 1904 as having 'Assyrian' or 'Persian' type of dress, with the face of a savage king, whose eyes were veiled, hinting at Shiva's mythic power to destroy the universe should he open his Eye. The name TAWUS, TA'US or, in Kurmanji, TAWUSI, may have appeared to either Crowley or Jacobs as an 'Aiwaz' variant:

T   AWUS. AWUS.

Crowley was happy to see 'Aiwass' written as AYVAS (in Hebrew) or even as OYVZ, because they held meaningful cabalistic values. In 1904, Rose *heard* the name; she was not told how to spell it. 'Awus' sounds more like 'Aiwass' than either 'Ayvas' or 'Oyvz'. But has one lost the 'T'? Not necessarily. In Crowley's cabalistic universe, the Hebrew letter *Teth* (ט) may signify 'flesh'.[25] The Hebrew glyph is in the shape of a serpent, reminiscent of the Gnostic *ourobouros*, symbolic of eternity. Crowley frequently calls *Teth*, the 'Lion-Serpent'. The astrological sign for Leo resembles a serpent. Crowley associates it with the solar lordship of the sexual, the 'Lord of this world'.

At Lalish today, in the Yezidis' 'market of mystical knowledge' a sinuous black serpent is carved on the wall, as tall as a man. The 'serpent' is of course linked in orthodox minds to 'dangerous knowledge' i.e. consciousness, offered by 'Satan'. The Yezidis say the serpent preserved Noah's Ark from sinking. Crowley has this to say about the 'Devil' in a chapter called 'Of Pacts with the Devil' in *Magick*:

> 'The Devil' is, historically, the God of any people that one
> personally dislikes. This has led to so much confusion of thought
> that THE BEAST 666 has preferred to let names stand as they
> are, and to proclaim simply that AIWAZ – the solar-phallic-
> hermetic 'Lucifer' is His own Holy Guardian Angel, and 'The
> Devil' SATAN or HADIT of our particular unit of the starry
> Universe. This serpent, SATAN, is not the enemy of Man, but
> HE who made Gods of our race, knowing Good and Evil; He
> bade 'Know Thyself' and taught Initiation.[26]

The letter *Teth* also has a symbolic role in Crowley's understanding of the Hebrew for 'Shaitan' or Satan:שטן= ShTN, (Shin, Teth, Nun) where the letter Shin (ש) is the Magic Fire, the letter Teth (ט) is the Lion-Serpent and the letter Nun (נ) is the 'Scarlet Woman' or feminine component.

Modern etymology regards Sheitan or Shaitan as an Arabic word, possibly based on the Hebrew 'Satan'. Its root is obscure though most people presume its meaning obvious. Crowley's view: 'The Devil does not exist. It is a false name invented by the Black Brothers to imply a Unity in their ignorant muddle of dispersions. A devil who had unity would be a God.'[27] Crowley writes in his consideration of 'The Formula of I.A.O.' in *Magick*:

> Satan is Saturn, Set, Abrasax, Adad, Adonis, Attis, Adam, Adonai, &c. The most serious charge against him is only that he is the Sun in the South. The Ancient Initiates, dwelling as they did in lands whose blood was the water of the Nile or the Euphrates connected the South with life-withering heat, and cursed that quarter where the solar darts were deadliest. Even in the [Masonic] legend of Hiram, it is at high noon when he is stricken down and slain.
>
> Capricornus is moreover the sign which the Sun enters when he reaches his extreme Southern declination at the Winter Solstice, the season of the death of vegetation, for the folk of the Northern hemisphere. This gave them a second cause for cursing the South. A third; the tyranny of hot, dry, poisonous winds [the god Set has also been linked to the blazing hot winds of Egypt's deserts, but this may be a later 'calumny' following Set's 'demotion']; the menace of deserts or oceans dreadful because mysterious and impassable; these also were connected in their minds with the south. But to us aware of astronomical facts, this antagonism to the south is a silly superstition which the accidents of their local conditions suggested to our animistic predecessors.[28]

Crowley saw the myth of Seth's denigration by the 'avenging' Horus as the expression of a conflict between solar priests; Crowley mistrusted religious authorities and perceived Set, or Seth, as the historic 'underdog'. *Seth* appears as Adam's righteous newborn son in Genesis. Seth was a Gnostic deity-hero, identified with Jesus in an élite line of Gnostic insight, the Sethian tradition. To Crowley, the elemental truth of Man had been 'buried'.

It does not appear that Crowley volunteered a link between Aiwass

1 *above left*: Abraham Crowley (1795–1864), Crowley's great-uncle, co-founder of the Crowley Brewery business, Alton, Hampshire

2 *above right, top*: Crowley & Co Alton Alehouse after 1877

3 *above right, bottom*: The Crowley Brewery, Turk Street, Alton, in its heyday

4 *below left*: Edward Crowley (*c*1830–87) Crowley's father

5 *below right*: Emily Bertha Crowley (1848–1917) Crowley's mother

6 above left: Edward Alexander ('Alick') Crowley, aged 14

7 above right: Aleister Crowley, Cambridge undergraduate

8 above left: The Chogo Ri Expedition 1902 (Left to Right: Wessely, Eckenstein, Guillarmod, Crowley, Pfannl, Knowles)

9 above right: Crowley on the desolate Plains of Deosai, 1902

10 above: Rose Edith Crowley, *née* Kelly (1874–1932). Rose told Crowley in March 1904 that 'They' were waiting for him. She gave the messenger's name as 'Aiwass'.

11 below: Aleister Crowley as Chioa Khan, Cairo, 1904

12 above: Bulak Museum Exhibit No 666 – the 'Stele of Revealing'

13 above left: Aleister Crowley at the time of *Konx Om Pax – Essays in Light* (1907)

14 above right: Edith Agnes Kathleen Bruce (1878–1947), sculptress and Crowley's lover, 1907

15 above left: Aleister and Rose, before their final divorce in 1910

16 above right: Leila Ida Nerissa Bathurst Waddell (1880–1932) in A∴A∴ garb. Leila became Crowley's lover in 1910.

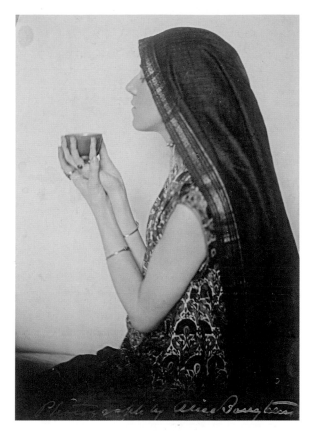

17 above: Jeanne Robert Foster, *née* Ollivier, (1879–1970), Crowley's fellow poet and lover 1915–16

18 right: Alice Coomaraswamy, *née* Richardson, stage-name: Ratan Devi, Crowley's lover, 1916

19 below: Gerda von Kothek, Crowley's New York lover, 1916

20 above: Emily Bertha Crowley's gravestone, Eastbourne, England; the inscription reads: '*Waiting for the Coming of Our Lord Jesus Christ*'. Crowley's mother died in May 1917 while her only son was in the USA.

21 left: Leah Hirsig (1883–1975) sits before Crowley's portrait of her as a 'Dead Soul', New York, 1918

22 above: The 'Cadran Bleu', Fontainebleau, where Crowley took a room with Leah to conquer heroin addiction, February 1922

23 above left: Crowley's novel, *The Diary of a Drug Fiend*, published by Collins in 1922

24 above right: *Portrait of a Poet*, Aleister Crowley as seen by Augustus John

25 above left: Crowley's 'Scarlet Woman', Dorothy Olsen, *Soror Astrid*. Dorothy arrived in Paris in 1924.

26 above right: Undated photo of Crowley; *c*1924. Note the erect thumbs, or 'horns'.

27 below left: Aleister Crowley, 1929

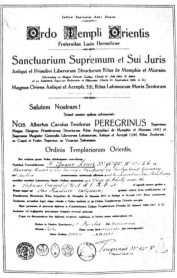

28 above: OTO certificate of honorary membership given to H Spencer Lewis, founder of AMORC, by Theodor Reuss (*Frater Peregrinus*, OTO) in 1921

29 above: Crowley's 'Scarlet Woman' of 1931–2, Bertha Busch, known as 'Bill', seen here on holiday in Nice

30 below left: Gerald Yorke as seen by Crowley

31 below right: Gerald Yorke as seen by camera

32 above: Crowley's novel *Moonchild*, published in 1929 by Mandrake Press, a publishing syndicate organized by Gerald Yorke. Beresford Egan executed the superb jacket.

33 above left: Crowley entitled this photo-portrait 'Interest'

34 above middle: A self-portrait: Crowley as *To Mega Therion*, The Great Wild Beast 666, *Logos* of the Aeon

35 above right: Aleister Crowley's bronze wand. Engraved on the stem: DO WHAT THOU WILT SHALL BE THE WHOLE OF THE LAW

36 above: *Four Red Monks carrying a Black Goat across the Snow to Nowhere*. Crowley's painting appears to be a comment on theosophist myths of Shambhala being pursued by Soviet secret service chiefs.

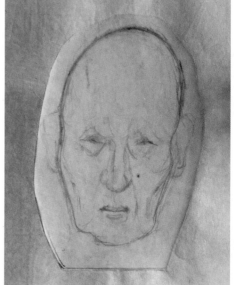

37 left: '*his knowledge of oriental evil is very deep*': Arthur Vivian Burbury's comment on Crowley's usefulness to the Foreign Office, 1928

38 above: A late sketch of The Beast by Frieda, Lady Harris (Sister Tzaba OTO) Crowley's friend and collaborator

39 above: Crowley's last 'Scarlet Woman', Pearl Brooksmith, escorting Crowley to Frieda Harris's car, *c*1939–41 (Lady Harris on *right*)

40 below left: 666 incarnates the spirit of wilful resistance while identifying *Victory* – and himself – with Winston Churchill's war leadership

41 above: 1942: Crowley honours the spirit of merchant seamen bringing hope to a beleaguered Britain

42 above: Lady Harris's husband, Sir Percy Harris, Chief Whip of the Parliamentary Liberal Party, meets the constituents of Bethnal Green, London.

43 right: Crowley (in a mid-1940s portrait) claimed to have 'educated' Harris about the true dimensions of the war against Hitler.

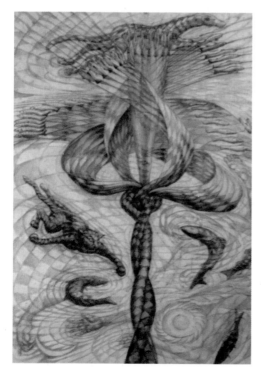

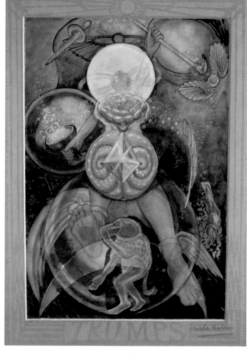

44 and 45 above left and right: Two unused paintings executed by Frieda Harris (1877–1962) and submitted to Crowley's judgement during their collaboration on the *Book of Thoth* 'Crowley Tarot Pack'. Lady Harris's paintings were exhibited at the Berkeley Galleries in July 1942. Crowley was not invited.

46 above: Karl and Sascha Germer

47 right: Aleister Crowley, mid-1940s

SIDE 1
ALBUM II

33⅓ RPM

**THE CHURCH OF
THELEMA**

AN INTERVIEW

February 1939

DISC 132

48 above left: John ('Jack') Whiteside Parsons (1914–52), devoted member of the Agapé Lodge of the OTO. Parsons worked on rocket propulsion at the Guggenheim Aeronautical Laboratory of the California Institute of Technology, Pasadena.

49 above right: 'THE CHURCH OF THELEMA – AN INTERVIEW' – a record produced by Wilfred T Smith to explain the work of the Californian Thelemites, February 1939

50: 'The Wickedest Man in the World' (early 1940s)

51: Sketch for a portrait of Aleister Crowley (mid to late 1940s) by Frieda, Lady Harris

52 and 53 above: The Mage at Netherwood, Hastings 1946–7, a traveller of both time and space

54 left: *AC Dying*: a sketch by Frieda Harris, drawn from life, December 1947

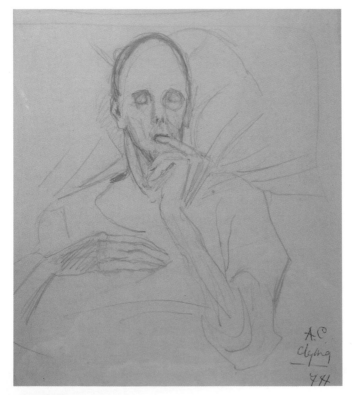

and the Yezidis; this seems to have been Jacobs' contribution. Jacobs might have been aware of a more secret word for the 'God of the Yezidis'. Perhaps he simply thought 'Aiwaz' *was* the Yezidis' angel, a possibility echoed in his jocular statement to a journalist in 1929 that his 'middle name meant Satan' – something no Yezidi could have said. Anyhow, Crowley felt intrigued, perhaps awed at the idea.

Crowley's spiritual universe does display elements in common with the Yezidis' *AL-Jilwah*, 'which the outsiders may neither read nor behold'.[29] Comparisons may help us to understand Crowley's strange confidence that his Holy Guardian Angel had been honoured for millennia:

> There is no place in the universe that knows not my presence.
>
> *(AL-Jilwah)*[30]

> I am alone: there is no God where I am.
>
> *(Liber AL vel Legis*, 2,23)

> I direct and teach such as will follow my teaching, who find in their accord with me joy and delight greater than any joy wherewith the soul rejoiceth.
>
> *(AL-Jilwah)*[31]

> I give unimaginable joys on earth: certainty, not faith, while in life, upon death; peace unutterable, rest, ecstasy; nor do I demand aught in sacrifice.
>
> *(Liber AL vel Legis*, 1,58)

> He who is accounted mine, dieth not like other men.
>
> *(AL-Jilwah)*[32]

> Ah! thy death shall be lovely: whoso seeth it shall be glad.
>
> *(Liber AL vel Legis*, II,66)

I guide without a scripture; I point the way by unseen means unto my friends and such as observe the precepts of my teaching, which is not grievous, and is adapted to the time and conditions.

(AL-Jilwah)[33]

I allow everyone to follow the dictates of his own nature, but he that opposes me will regret it sorely.

(AL-Jilwah)[34]

Thou hast no right but to do thy will.

(Liber AL vel Legis, 1,42b)

I remember necessary affairs and execute them in due time. I teach and guide those who follow my instructions. If anyone obey me and conform to my commandments, he shall have joy, delight and goodness.

(AL-Jilwah)[35]

Let my servants be few and secret, they shall rule the many and the known. These are fools that men adore; both their gods and their men are fools.

(Liber AL vel Legis, 1,10–11)

I will not give my rights to other gods.

(AL-Jilwah)[36]

In the *AL-Jilwah*, Melek Tawus expects new chiefs to be appointed over new 'generations' and to preside over new eras. The idea of the 'Secret Chiefs', and of Crowley's appointment within the angelic scheme fit within Melek Tawus's governance declared in *AL-Jilwah*:

Every age has a Regent, and this by my counsel. Every generation changes with the Chief of this World, so that each one of the chiefs in his turn and cycle fulfils his charge. [...] The other gods may not interfere in my business and work: whatsoever I determine mine, that is.[37]

The ordering of the worlds, the revolution of ages, the changing of their regents are mine from eternity.[38]

Moreover, I give counsel to the skilled directors, for I have appointed them for periods that are known to me.[39]

I appear in divers manners to those who are faithful and under my command. […] but my own shall not die like the sons of Adam that are without. […] I direct aright my beloved and my chosen ones by unseen means.[40]

We should resist jumping to conclusions about these mysteries. Crowley appears to have kept an open mind on the issue and did not compel anyone to follow his insights. It would be fair to say that the intuitive link that joined him to Samuel Aiwaz Jacobs also joined him by some curious way to a little-known, much misunderstood and grossly persecuted religion and people.

SIXTEEN

Sex Magick

1914–19

Crowley believed 'sex magick' worked. He found he could use sexual energies to transform a willed objective into reality. Results varied, however. Seeking a repeatable scientific method, he wrote up his 'operations' in the detached style of an experimenter. Willing to try anything his nervous system could cope with, he launched his first big operation at New Year 1914 with Victor Neuburg.

The rites performed in a Paris hotel room deserve a place in the annals of extreme behaviour. Aimed at invoking the gods Jupiter and Mercury, the 'Paris Working' pounded on for six weeks. Homosexual 'XI°' magick rituals, undertaken in Latin with all solemnity and titillation-free concentration, did bring unexpected gifts of money, attributed to Jupiter's correspondence to largesse. Neuburg was chief recipient and Neuburg was disinclined to share; Crowley was jealous. Spiced with mescaline, the working also generated curious phenomena, spiritual illumination and knowledge, or fantasies, of past lives.

The second invocation of Mercury took place over two days. Crowley was inspired to write a fascinating account of Christ as Hermetic god or mercurial symbol.[1] He said it was new to him, but the Gnostic-Rosicrucian tradition is full of cognate ideas.

Doing little to alleviate straitened circumstances, Crowley's assessment was realistic: 'I see no reason to suppose that the Elixir is miraculous in the sense that sceptics would like it to be taken. "Do an operation to make 2+2=5, another to cause Neptune to collide with Mercury, a third to remain under water for a year, and we will believe." It is difficult to demonstrate such language to be absurd, though to common sense no proof is needed.'

By the end of the year, Crowley was more specific: 'I think that this Operation [of sex magick] merely moulds circumstance already fluid, combines existing elements in one way rather than another, just as an orator finding an excitable crowd, moves them as he will. Nor Demosthenes nor Antony had roused "the very stones to cry out" against Philip or Brutus. No: I will deal with the possible and even probable, in the strength of, and to the glory of, the most High…'[2]

*   *   *

The pressure of the Paris Working crystallized Crowley and Neuburg's old sores. Neuburg quit after a tiff, siding with Vittoria Cremers, abjuring his A∴A∴ oaths. 'He left me', wrote Crowley, hurt. Neuburg's entry in a 1914 note on OTO subs reads: 'VB Neuburg An imbecile with no moral feeling. Owes £17.17.0 and his apron. Should be written to try and awake some vestige of moral sense.' The word 'expelled' was the sole word next to Cremer's name. Broken-hearted after Ione de Forest's suicide, Neuburg laid low for many years. After psychotherapy, he recovered sufficiently in the 1930s to become an inspiration to young poets and writers through his *Sunday Referee* column, most notably Dylan Thomas, who was first published thanks to Neuburg, but who somewhat meanly considered Neuburg over-generous to second-raters.[3]

Returning to England after the outbreak of war in August 1914, Crowley's health was poor. After sex magick with Piccadilly prostitute Christine Rosalie Byrne ('Peggy Marchmont') on 5 September, painful phlebitis flared up, affording leisure to write a number of initiated sex guides, archly worded. Inspired by the idea that the phallus was the Sun's 'vice-regent' on Earth, the literal 'giver of life', sexual union became 'the sacrifice of the Mass'; the 'Elixir' of mingled male and female secretions a sacrament, 'the most powerful, the most radiant thing that existeth in the whole universe', its preparation to be accompanied by invocation of Bacchus, Aphrodite and Apollo: wine, women and song. Sex became a means to a magical end or 'child', a magical birth generated through ego-less, willed projection upon what Eliphas Lévi called 'the Astral Light', or universal medium: 'for pure will unassuaged of purpose is in every way perfect', as *The Book of the Law* declares. As with so many things, the theory was simple; the devil was in the detail.

Sexual experimentation continued in America. On 6 December, he performed an Opus to shower success on a lecture on magick at 32 West 58th Street:

> Really a marked success. Pouring rain, and I had a bad cough. Yet this left me while I spoke and I was eloquent. (Yet this impression is mostly subjective.) I spoke without notes, yet never faltered. Truly say I, Let there be glory and thanksgiving to the Holy One!
> N.B. Abramelin demons did their utmost to stop this lecture. A 70-mile gale blew and they tried to upset me both physically and mentally.

While Charlie Chaplin's *The Tramp* played to packed houses in February 1915, Crowley reflected on whether an earlier operation for 'Success' was successful. Having observed manifest 'love, money, pupils, clients, fame', and the *appearance* of bright prospects in December, he concluded cautiously:

> Every one of these apparent successes materialized only in part. They vanished again almost at once. I think it is all part of the ☿ [Mercury] formula. I evidently don't know how to fix the volatile at all, though the first half of the Op[eratio]n is all right.

He could formulate the objective in his mind, seeing it as an expression of the True Will, not the false ego. He could dissolve himself into the willed purpose at the moment of self-surrender into the 'cup of Babalon', that is, at orgasm. But he was not sure how to make the 'child' of that Will impress sufficiently on the 'astral light'. This is what he meant by 'fixing the volatile'. The old alchemical formula was *solve et coagula*: dissolve and re-unite. The product of the 'coagulation' was a 'volatile' which tradition maintained must be 'fixed': fixed or stabilized on its object. The success or otherwise of this process affected the sacramental status of the 'elixir'. In sexual alchemy, the taking of elixirs derived from sexual operations was important. But other than in theory, that of joining the magician to his willed object, it was not clear *how* or even *if* it worked, when, that is, it did seem to work. Perhaps he was not ready. Was he, he wondered, being impelled spiritually to the next exalted grade of the Great White Brotherhood, that of *Magus*?

In 1915 Crowley began a diary of his journey to the grade.

He quickly realized the 'Lord' of New York was Mercury, god of merchants and tricksters! Crowley invoked 'Him' by psalms, divinations and, before bed, *dharana* on an imagined figure of Hermes. *Dharana* is concentration yoga, training the will to hold the mind to certain points. Crowley identified the winged globe of Hermes's caduceus with his *ajna* chakra about the pineal gland at the forehead's centre; he identified the staff with his spine, thus becoming Hermes's wand. He next 'did *Dhyana*', that is, *meditation*, or the 'outpouring of the mind on the object held by the will'. Crowley was frustrated, wondering what act of magick might, as he put it, 'initiate a true Current of Force in this filthy [ie: unspiritual and materialistic] country?'

> Feb 15. I had gone to sleep praying for a dream to teach me how to fix the volatile. I was in a room – square, bare – in New York where were 4 or 5 men. The eldest showed me the Book of Galeth (I took this to be the Bible) and read some curious verses with words strange to me. They sang also, and the senior preached, illustrating his speech by a dying lion, a series of statues reminding me of the 'dying king' toy – which I had noticed on the street a day or so before – In each case the lion was to be turned over on to its back. The theme of the sermon was mostly that 'He' Christ or lion or Elixir or something must be turned completely over, and must be made very dead indeed. The book was full of promises that he would come back, and he – on the whole – is not wanted back.

The dream could be interpreted as an injunction to a technique of 'holding back' ejaculation, but Crowley's cross-symbolic mind emphasized the 'death of the lion'. Did the lion represent Christianity, or himself? The question played on his mind.

On 19 March at 3.35am, he undertook Opus No 37 with Doris Carlisle '(or Edwards or Gomez)' by the light of a gas stove. She gave him a 'hand-job'; he licked her vagina.

> *Object.* The further mysteries of the IX°. I am puzzled as to 'Coagula', the fixing of the volatile created by the Operation.
>
> The Operation was lengthy, about three hours with some short interruptions. The orgasm was great, although so long had elapsed since the last Operation [4 March]. The Elixir was abundant but rather coldly classical in flavour.
>
> *Result.* This is notably or surely a success.[4]

Doris Gomez's arrival, he believed, resulted from an act of sex magick undertaken for 'sex attraction' with Leila in February. Doris was attracted on 5 March and became Crowley's assistant in numerous operations after the 19th.[5]

*   *   *

After a few months, Crowley became confused about his life in America. On the verge of leading a psychological double-life, he found difficulty interpreting events that flashed by him on the soulless streets. Women did not respond in familiar ways; he complained of their 'animality', the lack of spiritual or magical presence: 'They come like water and go like the wind'.

To cope, he decided it was all part of crossing the threshold to Magus-hood. To become a 'Master of the Temple' he had had to pour every drop of his 'life' into the 'cup of Babalon', or 'universal impersonal life'. This 'pouring every drop' image signified ego-surrender, leaving the earthy part of the Magus-to-be as 'grey ash', the ash to be placed in an 'Urn', marked with the *Word* characteristic of the Magus. The Magus-to-be must now pass through a desert with no proper sense of his identity, for his personal ego was but 'ash'; he would be almost helpless, though the physical man would appear to function 'automatically'.

Crowley's five years in America would be the desert; he suffered.

The 'desert journey' would have to culminate in the experience of combining the sephira *Chokmah* or Wisdom with *Binah* or Understanding, the sephira guiding the grade of 'Master of the Temple'. Chokmah, whose letters computed to 73, held the key for the journey. Crowley decided that despite life's appearing an illogical kaleidoscope, there was definite change every 73 days or multiples of 73 days, beginning 3 November 1914. One 'Chokmah day' of initiation took 73 earthly days. Having absorbed this principle, Crowley found he could predict a change of magical current.

The system gave him hope in attaining his goal, even when the desert looked dry, and all he could see behind him were the footprints of the 'camel that bore him': the 'five V's' of his *Magister Templi* motto, as he made his way on the path of *Gimel* – Hebrew for 'Camel' – up the Tree of Life. Crowley added colour to the process by identifying women who played an initiatory role with symbolic animals, recalling ancient initiations where animal masks symbolized roles. Thus with the aid of the Cat, the Snake, the Monkey, the Dog, the Camel, the Owl and the Ape (of Thoth), he transformed his desert into a succession of oases, so surviving the ordeal of the war years.

Teaching continued. Astrologer Evangeline Adams, a friend of John Quinn, collaborated with Crowley on a popular book on astrology.[6] Crowley borrowed her cottage on the shores of Lake Pasquaney, now Newfound Lake, Bristol, New Hampshire, in summer 1916, for a 'Greater Magical Retirement'. There, Crowley pondered George Bernard Shaw's preface to his play, *Androcles and the Lion*.[7] The Beast's ire was raised by the ignorance and sophistry of Shaw's assertion that Jesus was a socialist. Drawing on familiarity with Eastern cultures, the Bible and contemporary scholarship, Crowley tore Shaw to shreds. A *tour de force*, the 'Gospel according to St Bernard Shaw' grew over the summer into a brilliant, funny and ahead-of-its-time assessment of Christianity in 45,000 words.[8]

On 23 August, he took ethyl oxide: 'What clearer proof that all depends on state of mind,' he observed, 'that it is foolish to alter externals?' And further: 'Man is only a *little* lower than the angels; one step, and all glory is ours!' He added in his diary more on this relativity theme: 'What people miss is that a Yogi can get as much from out of swinging his leg as a Western millionaire out of a season in New York. This ought to be worked up for propaganda purposes.' [9]

Crowley experimented to see what Nature provided to introduce the mind to higher intelligence, analysing the effects of ethyl alcohol, hashish, cocaine, mescaline, long before Aldous Huxley brought the subject to public notice with his book *The Doors of Perception* (1954).[10] Only in the summer of 1933 did the general public learn anything of Crowley's magical activities in New Hampshire. In the course of an edited article for *The Sunday Dispatch*, he revealed the results of an attempt to make the 'elixir of life':

> I have prepared the elixir of life, that magical draught which gives eternal youth. Like the touch of Midas, it is not an unmixed blessing. I made it first when I was forty. It was done hastily and with imperfect knowledge. I took seven doses, as the first two or three had no apparent effect. The consequences were extremely violent.
>
> One day, without warning, I woke up to find that I had lost all my maturity. I became mentally and physically a stupid stripling. The only thing I could think of doing was to cut down trees! I was living in a cottage in New Hampshire; for fifteen hours a day I toiled at felling trees. I worked like a madman. No feat of strength was too great for me.
>
> These fantastic physical powers lasted for about two months, and were followed by reaction. For half a year I was in a state of lassitude. I had been playing with a dangerous recipe.[11]

He began to doubt himself. Did the Chiefs have any more use for him? The answer came:

> July 12. 5PM. A storm struck the lake; I went out to put my canoe in safety. Returning, I found a father, mother and child who had taken refuge under my roof. I was wet through, and went to change my clothes. I had just got the clean shirt on, when a globe of fire burnt a few inches from my right foot. A

spark sprang to the middle joint of the middle finger of my left hand. From this I conclude:

The Masters still need me; the Initiation is real. Cf [compare with] the fall with my horse on the Burma-China frontier in 1905.

I had repeatedly thought that death must be the issue of this Initiation. This then wrong.

It seems to me as if this Initiation was taking place 'elsewhere' i.e. not in my consciousness at all. It is obviously too big for any human consciousness; yet its result must work down through that.

In terms of order hierarchy, Crowley's assumption of the grade came 'just in time'. Earlier in the summer, *Frater Achad*, Charles Stansfeld Jones, telegrammed from Vancouver announcing he had passed through the Abyss and emerged a Master of the Temple 8°=3 .[12]

Taking Jones's advance as glorious vindication of his techniques, Crowley also credited the event to acts performed nine months earlier with Jeanne Robert Foster. Jones was the *Magical Child* or effect of those acts: a 'Babe of the Abyss'. Crowley sought the meaning of Jones' 'birth' in prophecies in *The Book of the Law* which spoke of one who would come after him 'who shall discover the Key of it All'. Jones had literally come 'after him' through the Abyss. The proof of Jones's attainment would be the power to decipher mysteries of *Liber L* eluding the Beast. Was this Crowley's perverse way of extracting meaning from the wreckage of his love for Jeanne?

Returning to 'Adams Cottage' in late July 1916 after a break in Boston, Crowley studied Jung's *Psychology of the Unconscious*, concluding: 'I think I can see a way to get Samadhi easily via Jung's theories.'[13] Spiritual attainments did nothing for his pocket, however: 'Total cash in hand 70 cents', he noted when on 9 December he entered the French-Spanish quarter of New Orleans, 'the only decent inhabited district that I discovered in America'. He wrote poetry, essays and short stories, but soon felt desperate. Was this the six-month 'reaction' to the elixir's 'lift' over the summer? To compensate, Crowley invented an *alter ego* called Simon Iff, comfortably old and delightfully eccentric; Iff used Thelema to solve crimes. Creativity notwithstanding, Crowley experienced 'rock bottom' in New Orleans. He went on strike:

> Dec.15. Twice recently the Lord has shown me signal favour, by sending a sufficient supply of money when I was within a dollar or so of actual starvation. It is really very kind of Him, and I am aware that this is the usual practice in such cases, but I have had about ten years of it, and 'I'm through.' I don't care what the practice is; my faith is in perfect working order: I enjoy the Beautific Vision practically without cessation; I'm not complaining. I'm merely going on strike.

There was no let-up.

> Dec. 26 [...] I was arguing with the other Masters about finance, expecting them to foresee all and provide (saw the rationalist objection, & the answer to it. We *do* assume a great mind capable of attending to every thing at once and indwelling it. [...] Therefore, I believe nothing, but I know this; that I have been dealing with intelligences as far superior to my own as mine is to Hereward Carrington's – I take an extreme example! – and I shall continue this strike with confidence that I am not fighting the air – but pitting myself against those whose only folly seems to be that they called me Wise. This is the Eleventh day of the Strike. [...] The shame is on *Them* if I starve.

Things got worse. The death of his mother in May 1917 and the London OTO bust were nadirs before a change of luck in June when Crowley joined sexual forces with Anna Catherine Miller, 'The Dog', renting an apartment on Central Park West, near 110th Street. Acquainting himself with US intelligence, things began to improve. Through the Dog, he met Roddie Minor Zimm – and Amalantrah.

Crowley suddenly began to paint, hanging out with the arty, political crowd in Greenwich Village, and the classy clubs around Central Park, giving lectures. Intrigued, Swiss-German Marion Hirsig told her

35-year-old sister Leah about the amusing English artist and guru.

Leah was the youngest of eight children carried to New York from Switzerland by Magdalena (*née*) Luginbühl to escape abusive husband, Gottlieb Hirsig. Kindly, refined of face and biro-slim, she was also strong-willed, tough and intelligent.[14] Leah fancied Crowley.

*   *   *

On the night of 26 February 1918 Therion and Roddie Minor worked up some 'Magical Energy' resulting in Crowley's being able to sit up till 5.30am 'writing in the Book of my Wisdom that I am making for my Son'. The book was *Liber Aleph, the Book of Wisdom or Folly*, addressed to Frater Achad (Unity).[15] In March, Achad sold his possessions in Canada and moved to Crowley's and Roddie's rooms at West 9th Street, joining Crowley for a while on his summer retirement on Esopus Island in the Hudson, near Staatsburg, 70 miles from Manhattan. Journalist William Seabrook helped with cash and supplies, and shared his wife, Kate, with the Beast. Seabrook worked for press mogul William Randolph Hearst, considered by the Bureau of Investigation (BI) remarkably pro-German in outlook. Crowley may have suspected Seabrook, or have been interested in his contacts.

While he worked on his verse-translation of the Tao Te Ching, local farmers brought the holy hermit eggs, vegetables and milk. Crowley entered 'sammasati' trances by which memories of supposed previous incarnations appeared: Ko Hsuen, Cagliostro, Eliphas Lévi, Pope Alexander VI, a Knight Templar, to name a few. Not all his precarnations were known to history; many led warped lives. He vaguely recalled having attended a council of Masters some time in the 'Dark Ages' who debated whether esoteric secrets should be imparted to mankind, and, if so, who might best achieve it. Crowley's earlier 'discarnation' voted 'yes', a generous act not unconnected with currrent problems!

Crowley returned from New York to his hermitage in late August with lots of red paint. Paddling a leaky canoe, he approached his island's low cliffs, bemusing passing riverboat sightseers by painting in huge red letters: DO WHAT THOU WILT SHALL BE THE WHOLE OF THE LAW. The epic lecture was free.

Refreshed, the artist took a small studio apartment at 1 University Place, Washington Square North. Neighbours included the Seabrooks, Eugene O'Neill, Theodore Dreiser, Sinclair Lewis, and friend to the end, Louis Umfraville Wilkinson. In November, Achad revealed 'Liber 31' to his magical father. Crowley reckoned Jones had found the *Key* to *The Book of the Law*.[16]

Leah Hirsig, meanwhile, visited Crowley with sister Marion. As Crowley chatted informally with Marion, he undressed Leah. Artists were expected to do things like that. She duly posed for a triptych called *Dead Souls* upon which a strange figure, inspired by Leah, was surrounded by grotesque faces. Crowley's comment: 'The dead souls have composed a living soul.' Members of the Village art scene admired *Dead Souls*, none more enthusiastically than painter Robert Winthrop Chanler. The Dead Souls have disappeared, though there is a famous photograph of Leah poised amusedly, contentedly before its central panel. Leah quit her Bronx teaching post for a part-time law course at New York University.

*   *   *

Leah Hirsig was more devoted to the spirit of thelemic freedom and to Crowley himself than any of her predecessors: the Cat or Sister Hilarion (Jeanne Robert Foster, *née* Oliver), the Snake (Helen Westley 'the Play-Actress'), 'Myriamne the Drunkard' (Myriam Deroxe), Rita (Gonzales) the Harlot; 'the Singing Woman for a Monkey' (Alice Coomaraswamy), 'Gerda (von Kothek) the Madwoman for an Owl', Anna Catherine Miller or The Dog of Anubis, the Camel (Roddie Minor), and Olun the Dragon (Marie Lavroff Röhling). Nor should one omit Crowley's probably unconsummated love for vaudevillian actress, singer and dancer, Eva Tanguay, who entranced all America with her gaiety, beauty and wit.

HERE'S TO THE GIRL
WITH THE TOUSELED HAIR.
WHO SINGS SO BLITHELY:
'I DON'T CARE!'
TO AMERICA'S QUEEN
OF DANCE AND SONG:
EVA TANGUAY,
MAY HER REIGN BE LONG.

– as a contemporary publicity card had it. Crowley's only complaint about Eva was that she was self-obsessed; a case of the pot calling the kettle black?

When *The New York Evening World* printed a feature on the artist in February 1919, Crowley was ensconced with Leah, his paints and Leah's 14-month-old baby Hans at 63 Washington Square South. This was the article that referred to Crowley's bullet wound at the war's outbreak, an admission which must have upset the numerous pro-Germans he had cultivated over the years. As for his art, Crowley gently suggested he was 'a subconscious impressionist'. 'My art is really subconscious and automatic.' The description might equally be applied to the art of his life. He said he could now be called 'an old master'!

In summer 1919 Crowley took his easel, brushes and tent to a magical retirement at Montauk on Long Island's eastern end. Reflecting on the last five years, he was downcast. He had become a Magus, but the price had been high. He had got into trouble with the British government for his pro-German articles and inflammatory Statue of Liberty gesture. There had been complaints about his anti-Christian programme, but that was grist to the mill. Working on a revised Third Degree for OTO use in 1919, he gave special place to the Sufi saint Al Hallaj, and included the oath: 'We swear to defend the principles of *The Book of the Law* in the name of freedom of man, in whom is God.' No professional Christian dogmatist could accept this.

Arguably, however, America needed what Crowley had to offer: his mind, if not his Word. While the Beast pondered the cosmos, Christian fundamentalism joined forces with politicized temperance lobbies. The combination approached its vacuous triumph: prohibition of booze. The debate could have been made for Aleister Crowley, the most eloquent writer on the inadvisability of repression of natural energies the world has ever seen. Alas, no one read Crowley's prescient, but unpublished, analysis 'The Prohibitionist-Verbotenist 1919'.[17] It is an important text on the common-sense value of Crowleyan liberty. The *Verbotenist* was none other than an honest-to-God *American*! Crowley analysed the psychology of the repressed-repressor, a type we may see attempting to control us through the media, police, pulpit or any other inlet or outlet open to the upturned snout of professional busybodies and ideological fanatics. Crowley began his broadside with a consideration of how body and mind interact:

> The old antithesis between matter and spirit is disappearing. The materialists went so far as to say 'Thought is a secretion of the brain' while their opponents retorted that the brain itself was but an idea of the mind. [...] so we find mind reacts on body, and body on mind, until the question as to which first arose is as foolish as that old joke: 'Which came first, the hen or the egg?'

He used mountaineering to exemplify his point, showing how the way people react to the dangers involved expresses their state of fitness. Crowley explained the folly of misplaced humanitarianism, how beliefs about 'equality' and 'fairness' not only masked weakness and fear, but were also imposed on situations where consideration of such issues became ruinous. Crowley's perception will hurt sensitivities tuned to the automatic liberal-left standpoint, but his point of view has stood the test of time, the fruit of an uncommon common sense:

> If all men were converted suddenly to 'humanitarian' principles, how long would it be before the race was swept from the planet by some no longer checked species of wild animal such as the wolf or even the rat with his fearful weapon, the Plague?

We do not know if it was Prohibition's imminence that prompted Crowley to leave America, or whether it was simply the result of aching fatigue and the war's end. Aged 39 when he arrived, he was now 44. As the old order crumbled, the mind of Europe stirred. On 5 November 1919, Leah wrote to him, 'I loved you all the while I was with you. I've loved you since you left me – I love you now in spite of stupid stories etc. more than ever.'[18]

* * *

How did Crowley feel as he disembarked at Plymouth from the *Lapland* on 21 December 1919? His mission to thelemize America had been unsuccessful. There would be no recognition of his intelligence work. Hereward Carrington, psychic researcher and one-time colleague of Everard Feilding, recalled seeing Crowley off from New York's harbour. Carrington lamented Crowley's failure, pointing out 'that this was largely his own fault'. Crowley's 'parting shot' as he walked up the gangplank: 'Well, what can you expect of a country that accepts Ella Wheeler Wilcox as its greatest poet!'[19]

Crowley re-entered Britain as himself. He was not detained by the Home Office, though the US Bureau of Investigation wondered where he'd gone.[20] The passenger manifest returned Edward A Crowley to Anne Crowley's Croydon address where he celebrated a 'real Merrie Xmas with roast beef and plum pudding and old port and brandy'.[21]

With no thought of the Christmas magi, the Magus realized on Boxing Day he was already acquiring the 'perceptions of an Ipsissimus'. These he reached in an imaginary conversation with Allan Bennett: 'Nibbana is a matter of utter indifference.' Having completely 'transcended Sorrow', Crowley felt 'ready to take any particular experience'. The super ego could now look down on the man Crowley: 'A Mr Crowley has cynically remarked: "It would be nice to be able to sin again!"' The Magus concluded: 'Attainment *is* Insanity. The whole point is to make it perfect in balance. Then it radiates light in every direction, while the Ipsissimus is utterly indifferent to it.'

'A Mr Crowley' got himself about, renewing old contacts in London.[22]

On 28 December he had lunch with ex-OTO member Gwendolen Otter, the 'last of the Chelsea hostesses'. He met George Cecil Jones: 'It was a sad interview. He is the same dear man as he was, strangely grey for 46, but his turning back from the Abyss is evident. He is just a nice simple bourgeois, interested in the number and the quality of his offspring.'

Meanwhile, asthma, the rotten fruit of the stresses and strains of the hard American years, was attacking him. Harley Street Dr Harold Batty Shaw, who had known Crowley all his life, prescribed heroin, a not unusual treatment at the time. In Crowley's case, the prescription proved disastrous, involving the prophet of Thelema in addiction for much of the rest of his life.

On New Year's Day 1920, he attended a great dinner at Simpson's in the Strand with Richard Hodgson, investigator of psychic frauds,[23] repairing afterwards to Mary Desti's favourite club: 'I dossed it on a sofa in Brook Street with a Blue Persian cat.' Next day, he pulled himself together and caught the boat train to Paris, expressing a wish for permanence: 'Try big ideas. Stay in one place. Get government job. Stick to Leah.'

Get government job. Whose government, British or French? French secret service records offer no clues, his tiny *Deuxième Bureau* file having been first in Nazi, then Soviet hands, after the war. Spence reckons Crowley contemplated spying *on* the French, and possibly the Italians, for the British. Desire for an intelligence role probably accounts for his dining with intelligence officer Everard Feilding on 11 January 1920. Feilding may have been in Paris for the League of Nations launch, five days later; perhaps he had stayed on after the Versailles Conference.

Dinner with Feilding was not all harmony: 'Arguments apt to Sung' commented Crowley; that is, arguments appropriate to the I Ching hexagram *Sung*:

Strife: be cautious; seek not the extreme.

Seek help from friends, and do not cross the stream.[24]

Did Crowley complain about his NID treatment during the war? Did Feilding criticize Crowley's methods?[25] A look at the dates reveals a probable tack. Under the headline, *Another Traitor Trounced – Career and Condemnation of the notorious Aleister Crowley*,[26] the previous day's *John Bull* accused him of treason and of being an Irish Republican agitator. Bottomley MP had obviously been tipped off from Home Office memos. *John Bull* sought government assurance that 'the infamous feet' of the 'dirty renegade' and 'treacherous degenerate Aleister Crowley' be prevented from touching Britain's shores again.[27]

Perhaps Crowley demanded Vernon Kell's MI5 domestic security service get Bottomley off his back. Feilding could have riposted that Crowley's avoidance of the fate of pro-German propagandist IT Trebitsch-Lincoln, who had been thrown into prison on *his* return from America, was all Crowley might expect, given the annoyance his freelance activities had caused to wartime government. Crowley's response would have been to assert his continued usefulness. Bottomley's article could convince enemies they might rely on him against the British interest.

George Cecil Jones advised Crowley to sue *John Bull*. Such a case would involve official secrets and funds were lacking. Book assets held by the Chiswick Press were denied until he paid up £350 of warehousing charges. As the Ipssisimus-in-waiting, he was, of course, above it all; as a Magus (since 12 October 1915), he *had* to suffer.

SEVENTEEN

The Abbey of Thelema

1920–22

Now we hear that the traitorous degenerate, Aleister
Crowley, is anxious to sneak back to the land he has
sought to defile.

('Another Traitor Trounced'; *John Bull*, 10 January 1920)

*J*ohn Bull was bull. The day its story appeared, Crowley was in Paris
and not sneaking anywhere. Leah arrived from America with Hans,
along with new friend encountered on the ship, Ninette Shumway,
née Fraux, a striking French girl, with young son Howard, whose
American father had died. Crowley now had two single mothers to care
for, one of them pregnant. As quick to think as to act, he concluded
destiny had provided the nucleus for an experimental New Aeon
community. *Every man and every woman is a star.* (AL.I.3)

In 1526, Rabelais' *Gargantua and Pantagruel* had given the world its
first literary vision of the '*Thélèmites*'. Rabelais gave them an 'Abbey', a
utopian satire on the corrupt monastic system. Behind the Abbey gates,
Thélèmites could pursue their 'Do what thou wilt' principle untram-
melled. Crowley would turn satire into fact. He would make his 'abbey'
a teaching and training centre; a radix of light and liberty for a new
world. He would put his knowledge of sex to good use. The world was
suffering massive sexual neurosis and the scientific illuminism of Dr
Crowley, sexologist of the stars, had the cure. Thelema would puncture
the shell of an uptight world and unblock the free flow of cosmic energy.
That was the plan.

Inspecting a property at Marlotte, he mused: 'Shall I buy this house for an Abbey?' Was Fontainebleau free enough for his purpose? He explored 20 miles of its lanes with Ninette, who fancied the romantic dynamo who offered her a life. They enjoyed a first act of sex magick on 20 February, a magical hand-job to bring forth a solution to the provision of a 'House'. Alternative locations considered were Algeria, the Italian Lakes, Naples or Sicily.

On 27 February Leah gave birth to a little girl, Anne Lea, whom Howard called Poupée, 'Dolly'; the pressure was on. Crowley was disturbed by his daughter's I Ching symbol, 'Earth of Water, Sun (no.41)', an 'obscure hexagram', meaning 'diminution'. He and Ninette performed sex magick to have a baby. Astarte Lulu Panthea Crowley was born nine months later. At the time of writing, Lulu lives happily in the USA with a family of her own.

Why the focus moved to Sicily and the town of Cefalù is unclear. A divination of 1 March matched Cefalù to the encouraging 'Earth of Lingam' symbol. Crowley opened an account with the Banca Commerciale, Palermo. There may have been more to Sicily than divinatory destiny.

Palermo's British Consul was Reginald Gambier MacBean. A sometime supporter of Annie Besant, MacBean was acting Grand Master of the Ancient & Primitive Rite of Memphis-Misraim for Italy with which Crowley enjoyed fraternal contacts. Spence has noted that MacBean was well placed to act as a conduit between Crowley, Feilding and career diplomat Walter Alexander Smart who was soon to be posted to French-controlled Damascus at a time when Britain was concerned with French military activity in Syria. Crowley knew Smart from the New York Consulate General; he was the model for Crowley's 'tall, bronzed Englishman', Naples' Consul, in his 1922 novel, *The Diary of a Drug Fiend*.

While all this may have influenced Crowley's self-posting to Sicily, his relations with MacBean may not have been harmonious. While Crowley had 'folded in' the A&P Rite into his British OTO system, other national leaders of the Rite preferred independence. France would drop the OTO under Joanny Bricaud, who claimed to succeed Papus on his death. According to William Breeze, MacBean seems to have been working with Bricaud, so MacBean may have been in competition with Crowley.

Meanwhile, the impact of Bottomley's *John Bull* attack began to dawn, making Crowley 'fearfully tired'. He meditated on his 'public statement about my work for England in the war'. In 12 hours he wrote 'The Last Straw'. The statement was never published in his lifetime. Did Feilding advise against publication?

From Marseilles, Crowley's entourage moved to Naples, then to Sicily. After a stint in a rotten hotel in Cefalù, rental agent Giordano Giosus handed Crowley the keys to the Villa Santa Barbara above the town with a view of the sea. Crowley's home for spiritual aristocrats was born on 2 April 1920, a place where he hoped to revolutionize magick *and* psychotherapy. He had written on 31 March: 'To call forth the Spirits means to analyse the mind; to govern them means to recombine the elements of that mind according to one's will.'

Feeling deep communion with the spirit of Gauguin, Crowley painted the villa, filling it with visions earthly and astral, freakish and beautiful, hideous and holy, low and exalted: 'Stab your demoniac smile to my brain; soak me in cognac, cunt and cocaine' urges one surviving fragment. On May Morn 1920, Crowley outlined his theory of art: '1.30p.m. One should not paint "Nature" at all; one should paint the Will.' He did not favour complete abstraction; the painter should give the viewer a way in: a handy tip, scarcely observed by abstractionists.

His 1920 diary is a book in itself. Into its pages he poured a mind's ceaseless labour until it represented 'the sole mode of my initiated expression': a patchwork of the mundane and the brilliant. After a phenomenal inner debate between himself and Gautama (the Buddha), Crowley emerged triumphant: 'The Mystery of Sorrow was consoled long ago when it went out for a drink with the Universal Joke. The Mystery of Change amounted to Nothing, exactly as in a chemical equation. [...] Matter may be considered as a complex of positive and negative charges of electricity (to name the force crudely) and these charges can never be cancelled for they never truly began. At least, we must assume that the Absolute creates them afresh if they do cancel. [...] Morning. A dying man reminds me of a clown jumping through a hoop.'

On 23 May a discordant note: he and Leah had been sniffing cocaine as a stimulant:

> I feel sure that the action is strictly anaesthetic, not tonic, stimulant, or narcotic. [...] there is a sort of dull physical hunger for more. [...] But I feel rationally the possibility of a physical craving beginning to assert itself.

Why did he need this stimulant? He examined himself ruthlessly:

> My present trouble is that the old stimuli, ambition, desire of fame, pity for humanity, and so on, have almost ceased to move me, owing principally to society's neglect of me and my own increasing contempt for it. One asks oneself why [Jonathan] Swift wrote of the Yahoos [the vulgar morons in *Gulliver's Travels*]; did he hope to hurt them? It seems stupid, somehow.

On 24 May he analysed the previous night's dreams, believing they conveyed a message from Aiwaz, his Holy Guardian Angel. Should he promulgate a 'New Religion' by adopting a practical, political form? At 11am the next morning a letter from Reuss invited him to a conference at Zurich, 'the very opening for action' he lacked: 'I am almost inclined to go to the conference at Zurich, and get the Delegates to adopt political action. I am merely afraid of them being too insignificant – but no man is that if he gets inspired! Can I inspire them?'

Could he inspire them? Crowley wondered whether a conference of fringe masonic orders could ever initiate a new civilization from the ruins of the past. A reading of Reuss's *Programme of Construction and the Guiding Principle of the Gnostic Neo-Christians, O.T.O. 1920* would have confirmed such doubts.[1] It purported to contain the 'Guiding principles of a new Civilization and Religion':

> Mankind, tortured by the World War, needs a new faith, a new Christianity, and a new civilisation built upon it. [...] But mankind also demands a new faith because the old belief in God,

which flowed from the Christian teachings as brewed by the
Church Fathers, has for the great majority of the members of the
Christian Church, long become a fairy-tale, because it was unable
to withstand the biting criticism of modern science.

The author goes on to say that 'VERSAILLES destroyed Brotherhood' –
in that the 'treachery' of French premier Clemenceau and Lloyd George
led to 'Anglo-French world-imperialism on the deceived and enslaved
German People.'

> The Community of the Gnostic Templars or Neo-Christians,
> abbreviated as O.T.O., which already before the war had
> numerous adherents in America, Holland, Bohemia, France,
> Russia, Italy, &c., now steps out from the reserve it cultivated
> until now, in order to bring to tortured mankind the new Glad
> Tidings of the Gnostic Christians, and the new civilization
> springing therefrom.
>
> The message of the O.T.O. is: Freedom, Justice, Love.
>   The Freedom of the O.T.O. is freedom from Original Sin, and
> freedom to execute the Will of the God-head. It does say in *Liber
> Legis*: 'Do what thou wilt.' But it is also said: But remember that
> you will have to render account for all thy deeds. That is the law
> of Karma. 'So that not wilfulness and unbridled behaviour, but
> strict discipline is the 'true freedom'.

Crowley would have been distinctly under-whelmed by the author's
qualification of the thelemic injunction to *do what thou wilt*. He would
have mistrusted the political setting and emphasis on 'Gnostic Neo-
Christians'. Reuss's declaration that 'Gnostic Templar-Christians' were
'Johannite Christians, not so-called Nazarene Christians (Jesus of
Nazareth)' would have annoyed him.

This was not Crowley's style; it risked plunging Thelema into age-old
theological conflict. *The Book of the Law*, as he saw it, was a refreshing
revelation destined to knock all this theological to-ing and fro-ing on the
head. Crowley wanted religious conflict dumped in the bin of history,
and that is where he would consign it. As for Germany, Crowley told

Reuss he was a citizen of 'a beaten and disintegrating nation'. In 1921, he would give the Prussian Reuss his marching orders.

In 922CE Sufi saint Al Hallaj suffered crucifixion for declaring 'Ana'l Haqq!': 'I am the Truth!'. Like Sheykh Adi of the Yezidis, Crowley was beginning to realize God. Why then, Crowley wondered on 31 May, had his poetry gone to pot? Had Hilarion broken his heart? After her, he had known 'none but passing fancies'. He reflected on his most significant loves: 'Rose, whom I idealized and loved for herself, the only one besides Leila Waddell of whom I can say this, though she too had glamours. But in both cases, the soul was capable of inspiring me with romantic love which is what makes me sing.' He listed the little things that spoilt the love affairs with a number of otherwise enticing women: 'Gerda von Kothek's obviously exclusive homosexuality', 'Belle Greene's manner; Eva Tanguay's and Maud Allen's self-worship'.

Below the 'Absolute', the same old Crowley was always on the lookout for a girl. On 21 June he debated with himself whether to meet American disciple Jane Wolfe in Marseilles, Bou Saada or Tunis. He left for Tunis the next day, but Jane was not there.[2] Crowley had a lot of experience with actresses and imagined Wolfe a beauty. Jane was not glamorous; she was intelligent, soulful, practical and determined. Crossed arrangements meant that it was a month and a day before Ms Wolfe finally met Leah in Palermo and settled down to become one of the Abbey's most devoted sisters. She would write in the 1950s that Cefalù had been the making of her; 'Thank God for Cefalu' she would say to herself on occasions when life got difficult. She and Crowley remained friendly for life, long after her return to the States, where, working patiently with Wilfred T Smith, she ensured the survival of the American OTO to our times.

*   *   *

Throughout the summer, life carried on genially with magical ceremonies, meals in common, adorations of the rising and setting Sun, swimming, mountain climbing, and too much drug-taking. Then Crowley felt something awry. His orgies with Leah and/or Ninette intensified. He was frequently high as a kite on heroin, cocaine, hashish or oxide of ether. His magical diary became long-winded, alliterative, extreme. The idea of the orgiastic, mischievous 'Satan' plunging into dishes of cocaine then diving into sexual sado-masochistic activities dedicated to 'Our Lord God the Devil' seemed to take over the diary's pages for some crazy, going-beyond-the-limits weeks. He was trying to 'identify the opposites': an Olympian perception peculiar to the Absolute. He was letting it all hang out, at one in his mind with the rampant gods of ancient Sicily. Pan was leading him a merry dance, and there was something about Leah that made him want to really 'get down'. It seems both Leah and Ninette were masochists, but so, to an extent, was he.

It wasn't all excess. Crowley saw his activities as vital experiments of use to later generations. As for his drug intake, he knew he was taking a chance: 'I do it "to the greater glory of Them that sent me".' His defence: 'I cannot see that my experiments with hashish, ether and cocaine are any less "noble" (horrid thought!) than Simpson's with chloroform. "Noble" was the science-men's epithet for him; for the others he was the man who eased the agony, and diminished the danger of child-bearing, and so thwarted the Lord God Almighty's generous intentions in the matter of getting square with Eve about the apple by obscenely torturing her and her daughters! I agree. I accept what's coming to me. My work will free man's will, disperse his mind-fog, show him God and morality as scarecrows stuck up by his tyrants, dry stocks, professor-like hung with old newspapers, and a priest's hat on the top.'

Great rhetoric, but the universe was as indifferent as the Absolute.

On 14 October, little Anne Lea died. Leah then miscarried. Flattened, Crowley looked for the cause of the darkness that had poisoned the Abbey over the summer. Examining Ninette's magical diary, he was horrified by her malevolent jealousy over Leah; Ninette wished her dead so she might enjoy the Beast for herself. This kind of love was unacceptable in a thelemic community; Ninette was banished to the town – but not for long. Ninette too was pregnant. On 26 November, chastened and 'in her right mind', Ninette gave birth to their child, Astarte Lulu Panthea. Life at the Abbey began again in hope.

*   *   *

Artist Nina Hamnett had always found Crowley charming, funny and very intelligent. So she was not surprised when in the New Year of 1921 many of her Parisian friends wanted to know if the rumours about Crowley's Sicilian temple were true. Nina introduced Cecil Maitland to the Beast at his rooms at the Hôtel de Blois, 50 Rue Vavin. Crowley offered his cocktail, the *Kubla Khan No.2*. It contained a *soupçon* of laudanum, the stuff that dreams are made on! Maitland seemed affected. Delirious, he ran into the street, darted in and out of cafés, accosting everyone he met. Maitland and fellow writer Mary Butts accepted Crowley's invitation to sort themselves out at the Abbey of Do what Thou Wilt.

Nina heard about the death of Leah and Crowley's daughter: 'Crowley was very much upset about it.' She also observed what she described as a 'kink' of Crowley's for pulling the legs of the wealthy and influential: 'It was a kind of schoolboy perversity.' As a result, Nina thought he lost opportunities to gain the favour of people who would otherwise have been useful and friendly.

Back at the Abbey in February 1921, Crowley wrote to Norman Mudd, former secretary of the Cambridge University Freethought Society, now professor of applied mathematics at Grey University, Bloemfontein; a sad man longing to link his destiny once more to that of his god.

> Next time you wander over the planet, Einstein or no Einstein, I
> hope you will drop in on our Abbey here where we can fry you
> in your own fat much quicker than elsewhere. Be on your guard!

A bored Mudd was in touch with the OTO's South African representative, chartered accountant James T Windram. Crowley encouraged Mudd; mathematical problems in *The Book of the Law* required expert attention.

Meanwhile, in spite of Crowley's scepticism over CS Jones's kabbalistic innovations and all-too-apparent hubris, a less-than-well Theodor Reuss appointed Jones Grand Master of the North American OTO. The feeling of Jones coming up 'after him' might well have stimulated Crowley's own trajectory to the exalted grade of *Ipsissimus*. Surmising that Reuss was scheming, Crowley recognized Jones was being used against him. Reuss was negotiating with the American entrepreneur, Harvey Spencer Lewis, founder of AMORC (*Ancient Mystical Order Rosae Crucis*), a rival Rosicrucian order built on a fake charter.

Crowley knew he was streets ahead of the competition in terms of genius, vision, mastery, knowledge, political and social insight. Above all, he knew he was the chosen vessel of the Secret Chiefs. He was *creative*. Waves of ideas flowed torrentially from his pen like plenty from the horn of Bacchus. Like an emperor of the world in waiting, he needed to think about everything: sexual revolution, psychedelic drug use, spiritual liberation and religious revolution, political and social trans-formation, a re-estimation of the importance of nature, new energy exploration, educational reform, philosophical and psychological development, artistic renaissance, economic restructuring, international relations. Crowley's guides: common sense, experience, wisdom, the lessons of history, initiated insight, pure inspiration and the rock of instruction contained in his *Book of the Law*.

And then, in April 1921, he realized. Had he not 'by insight and initiation' become an Ipsissimus, his own very Self? He *was* Thelema, at one with his Word. 'As a god goes, I go' he wrote in his diary, committing himself to silence on the matter. He never spoke of it. Arriving at the end of June, Cecil Maitland and Mary Butts (*Soror Rhodon*) never heard of it. They signed the Abbey pledge forms, committing themselves to the Great Work. Three months later, they left with a drug habit and memories of a strange outdoor ceremony, or joke, involving a goat (Crowley?) who could not 'get it up' in Leah's presence. Maybe there was a real goat, 'sacrificed', for dinner perhaps. Crowley had participated in the sacrifice of a goat to goddess Bhavani in India in 1901, and nobody found it strange at that distant temple; why should it be any different in Cephaloedium? *For this reason*: he was in the presence of Europeans who seldom thanked a deity for their Sunday roast or tea-time sandwiches.

*   *   *

More visitors arrived. Having left his family in Australia for the summer, Frank Bennett (*Frater Progradior*) showed up in July. Dispatched for magical retirement with the Abbey tent, Bennett recognized the importance of the Knowledge & Conversation of the Holy Guardian Angel, but just couldn't 'get it'. His underdeveloped, but overstuffed, mind got in the way. Crowley prescribed *Liber Samekh*, his adaption of a late-antique Graeco-Egyptian exorcism rite.[3] The co-founder of the Australian OTO, tiny as it was, kept hitting a brick wall.

On 19 August, during a swimming expedition, Crowley looked into Bennett's eyes: 'Progradior, I want to explain to you fully and in a few words, what initiation means, and what is meant when we talk of the Real Self, and what the Real Self is.'[4] Crowley gave Bennett a magical version of what would become known as Jung's theory of the self-regulating psyche. Under certain conditions, the subconscious, or unconscious, mind sends 'messages' to the consciousness in the form of numinous images, dreams, symbols, even instructions, to bring the conscious into a whole, or holy, relationship with the totality of the being of which the ego-personality is an expression. The ego-self, creating its own world, is a 'false god', jealous, if ever aware, of its superior. 'The carnal mind is enmity against God', as St Paul taught.

Bennett's problem was sex, so he had come to the right place. He could not see where his lustful urges fitted in to a regimen of advancing spirituality. Crowley explained that the sexual instinct is rooted in our deepest personality. It is an expression or symbol of the unconscious Self. Crowley, the depth-psychologist had hit the bull's-eye where hard-working, stout-hearted Frank Bennett was concerned:

> in a few short sentences he [Crowley] explained the whole thing
> in such a way that my consciousness seemed to expand there and
> then. We all entered the water, the Beast and Leah went out for a
> good swim; but I found myself almost faint, and could only
> paddle about in the water. The words of the Beast still rang in my
> ears, and would not leave me for an instant. I returned to shore
> and dressed in the shade of a rock, and waited until the others
> returned.[5]

Bennett suddenly saw how he had been cutting himself off from himself. The sun, sea and sand, and Crowley's illuminating presence, did the rest of the trick, and after a terrific struggle overnight as his conscious thinking began to give way, he saw the light. His diary records that on 20 August, he received his first conscious experience of his Holy Guardian Angel: 'For at that moment all became radiant and beautiful; my consciousness expanded to touch the inner world of realities – my mind had come into contact with some inner centre of my being, which was God.' He awoke the next day 'a new being'.

Crowley had 'cured' Bennett, and this, he realized, was what a Magus could achieve in the modern world. His gift was to induce spiritual crises in people, then, if it was their will, help them to dissolve their complexes and introduce them to the joy of knowing themselves to be who they really were. Crowley saw the obvious parallels with the 'legends' of Christ's wonder-working; how he unblocked the faculty of vision in the 'blind' and enabled the mad wretch of Gadara to find his 'right mind'. In order to reach higher intelligence, the fool-man had to embark on a magical journey of self-discovery. What was St Paul until he had seen the Light?

Uninterested in any of this, Reuss decided to alienate Crowley. In a letter dated 9 November 1921, Reuss demanded thelemic doctrine and the A.˙.A.˙. be kept rigorously 'separate and distinct' from the OTO.[6] Crowley should 'teach the pure and unalloyed principles of the OTO' with its primary masonic stage. Anyhow, Reuss concluded, satisfactory arrangements between them were now impossible because he knew Crowley wanted him deposed.

Crowley acted. Aware that the South African OTO lodge considered Reuss's recent 'Anational Circular' anti-British and its author demented, Crowley deposed Reuss by return of mail:

> It is my will to be O.H.O. and Frater Superior of the Order and avail myself of your abdication – to proclaim myself as such...
> You talk of my nominees. Do not forget that you sent the first of them a charter from yourself in the hopes that it would induce him [Jones] to betray me.

I should really be obliged to you if you would tell me how you got into your head that I am a weak man. I have never taken my hat off to anybody except in condescension. Your undoubted age and your undoubted merit command respect but authority reposes on force.[7]

And that was how Crowley became OHO of the OTO.

For the remainder of his life, Crowley asserted that Reuss had 'abdicated' in his favour before his death in October 1923. Crowley simply wrote in his diary: 'I have proclaimed myself O.H.O. Frater Superior of the Order of Oriental Templars.'[8]

For all his confidence, Crowley's addiction threatened to invalidate his theories of will. He observed: 'I am more certain than ever that cocaine is no good under any conditions soever, unless in very small doses and very few of *them*.'

*   *   *

Enter Hélène Fraux, keen to check up on sister, Ninette. Fresh from the land of apple pie, Hélène did not like what she saw at Cefalù in the winter of 1921: sex, mess, magick and drugs. All very different to her very respectable life in America where she worked as a well-paid nanny to high-society American families in Detroit. Had you asked Crowley whether children should be raised within an experiment, he would probably have replied: 'What is any life but an experiment with reality?' Crowley was scientific in outlook, and experimentation does not always give children everything they need, as some modern school failures have shown. Hélène went to the Palermo police. They raided the Abbey but found nothing illegal. Hélène held a vision of the 'demon Crowley' for life. A thorn in his side until 1930, Hélène's complaint probably signalled the beginning of the end of the Abbey at just the point Crowley was envisioning expansion. He made drawings for a super-modern new temple complex, a world centre of spiritual development that would bring the world, and its neuroses, to the New Aeon's epicentre of Cefalù – again, ahead of his time.

*   *   *

Winter exacerbated Crowley's bronchitis. The relief: heroin. Knowing he must rid himself of addiction, he and Leah headed back to Fontainebleau in February 1922, to the hotel Au Cadran Bleu. Willpower ought to do it; failing that, a doctor's prescription. He tried experimenting with dose-cutting, 'open' and 'closed' seasons, complete abstinence, alternative stimulants, long sleeps (where possible), country walks, prayer, sex magick, anything he could think of. The craving always came back, even after going 'cold turkey'. A Dr Gros recommended a sanatorium cure. Crowley accepted the idea, but not the price.

In May, a startled London witnessed the Beast in Highland dress, his only clothes. He had £10 – and a brainwave. He would turn the whole drug thing around and make it work for him. Newspapers were having a field day over 'the great drug scare' with stories of wretchedness, degradation and addiction taking place under Britannia's contemptuous, sniff-free nose. Was he not a drug expert? Crowley submitted a proposal for a popular novel on the theme of the drug craze. JD Beresford, fiction editor at Collins, saw the potential and paid Crowley £60 advance. Alleluia!

He began *The Diary of a Drug Fiend* at 31 Wellington Square, Chelsea on 4 June; Leah's beautiful handwriting took down Crowley's unstoppable dictation and in just 27 days, the novel was done. Crowley's notoriety should bring dividends, thought Beresford. But Collins also published theological books. Crowley's novel touched on religion, and had as much to say about mysticism as the popular writer on religion and society, Dean Inge.

Enter James Douglas, *Sunday Express* crusader for the public good. Douglas had recently done the Lord's work with James Joyce's *Ulysses*, condemning it as a work of vile, degraded talent in the service of filth. Crowley was ripe for inquisition. Lord Beaverbrook's *Sunday Express* duly offered the headline 'A BOOK FOR BURNING' on 19 November, when Crowley's novel was published, to some good reviews. The by-line read: 'Complete Exposure of 'Drug Fiend' Author. Black Record of

Aleister Crowley.' They knew Crowley could not afford to sue.

Collins got nervous. Director Sir Godfrey Collins MP had a moral reputation to guard; religious persons had complained. Having sold out the first edition, the title was withdrawn. The 'demon Crowley' was imprinted on the public mind. But not everyone took the line.

Crowley met Oxford graduate Frederick Charles Loveday at a lecture held in the Chelsea home of Mrs Betty Sheridan-Bickers in July. Loveday joined the A.'.A.'., as *Frater Aud*, 'Aud' referring to the magical light. Crowley was proud of his new acolyte. Could he have been thinking of a replacement for CS Jones?

Loveday had married sculptor Jacob Epstein's favourite model, familiar to Fitzrovia as 'Betty May', a heavy drinker and drug taker with an 'Apache' past in Paris. Had Crowley not been quite so harassed and financially desperate he might just have seen danger on the horizon. Nina Hamnett saw it. In *Laughing Torso* she recalled Betty May turning up in Paris with her fourth husband, 'Raoul' Loveday. Betty had been around, but the self-conscious, artistic eccentric 20-year-old with an Oxford first in history had not. 'He was very good-looking, but looked half dead', recalled Nina.

Betty and an excited Raoul joined Nina for a drink at the Dôme, on their way to Cefalù. Raoul was to be Crowley's secretary. But Loveday had suffered a prank-climbing accident the previous year. Surgery was riskier in those days and the 'Varsity Lad' had not fully recovered. Nina considered the prospect of mosquitoes, limited diet, arduous magical training and drugs potentially lethal. Loveday countered with the promised benefits: a health cure with fresh air, bracing exercise, and the substitution of thelemic discipline for Betty's addiction. Nina begged them not to go. They delayed going for two days. If he went, she told Loveday, he would die.

On 22 November 1922 Loveday found the words DO WHAT THOU WILT on the Abbey door. He was ecstatic, writing in his diary: 'Woken in morning by beating of tom tom and chanting of Word of the Abbey. Greeting of the sun.'[9] 'We have found wisdom', he added. But Betty had not, and would not. Agitated by discipline and irritated by Crowley's influence over her husband, she found scant refreshment in Abbey life. Despite her deliberately antagonizing the Beast, Crowley respected her wilfulness, trusting that through love of Raoul and the power of Thelema, it might yet be tamed into a state of practical self-control in the Abbey of Do what thou Wilt.

EIGHTEEN

Persecution

1923

St Valentine's Day 1923

Frater Aud is dead. It happened at the Abbey. The Mystic tried everything. The doctor came; did all he could. But Loveday was weakened from his accident in Oxford. He died of enteric fever. Nina Hamnett was right; Raoul was not coming back.

He had been on a country walk with Betty. The Mystic told them never to touch the spring water, often polluted. Thirsty, he drank. Betty, for once, did as instructed; she survived. Jealous of Raoul's devotion to Crowley, resenting the discipline, Betty bickered with the Beast, stormed out of the Abbey to complain to the consul. Another complaint: *did Crowley expect it to be ignored?* He did not. He remonstrated; she retracted, in writing. She knew the deadly water had ended her husband's young life. But the truth would soon be of no use.

Blown away, delirious, sick, Crowley the disaster-prone mystic, took to his bed.

On 18 February, the consul gave Betty money to return to London. Journalists waited at the dockside. They got her drunk and blew it all up. Beaverbrook's *Sunday Express* led the clamour: '*New Sinister Revelations of Aleister Crowley. Varsity Lad's Death. Enticed to "Abbey"*'.

'The Beast' was presented at criminal face-value: a sex maniac sacrificial murderer hypnotizing innocence for anti-Christian, bloody orgies. Conjuring a prototype for Hannibal Lecter, *John Bull* called Crowley 'the Human Beast', magnifying the paper's gov'nor, Horatio Bottomley's longstanding vendetta against Crowley. The corrupt MP had been serving a seven-years sentence for fraud since May 1922. Just how influential was the callous exploitation of Loveday's tragic end is evident in Arthur Calder-Marshall's autobiographical *The Magic of my Youth*, published 28 years later. Calder-Marshall's elder brother Robert had known Loveday at Oxford. Their circle was convinced 'Raoul' had volunteered for the part of Adonis, the beautiful god who must be sacrificed.[1] The only thing not to be believed about a 'Human Beast' is that he might be innocent.

During the 1950s, the accusation of murder fuelled the image of the evil 'Macata' in Dennis Wheatley's popular black-magic novels, later turned into successful films. A possible model for cool, romantic adventurer 'James Bond' had become, before Bond's birth, a model for Le Chiffre and archenemy Blofeld. Actor Charles Gray would play Macata in *The Devil Rides Out*, and Blofeld in *Diamonds are Forever*. The myth became an archetype. Strange how the 'opposites' would be combined within a year of Crowley's attaining the grade of *Ipsissimus*: 'beyond good and evil'. The White Adept became the Black Brother, in the mind of the blind.

John Bull generated headlines that would haunt Crowley's reputation ever after: 'THE KING OF DEPRAVITY'; 'A MAN WE'D LIKE TO HANG'; 'THE HUMAN BEAST RETURNS'; 'THE WICKEDEST MAN IN THE WORLD'. Who would admit to knowing Crowley now? Was HM Government going to admit this man had been engaged in secret work on its behalf during the war? In the USA, headlines such as 'THE ANGEL CHILD WHO SAW HELL AND CAME BACK' appeared – the 'Angel Child' being Betty May! Crowley was accused by the yellow press and found guilty by weight of headline.

Jane Wolfe came to England offering emotional support to Betty. Betty felt bad about her twisted story's effect on everyone at Cefalù. She apologized to Crowley in a series of emotional letters, such as this of 12 May, sent from 59 Beak Street:

> Tell me. Love is the law. Love under will.
> I am so very sorry – what can I do?
> Do what thou wilt shall be the whole of the law.

Crowley was convinced old friend William Seabrook of America's Hearst press would correct the 'Bull-litter' being circulated about him, but otherwise had no faith in the gutter press's ability to rise above the muck.

> The minds of the people have been so dulled by compulsory
> 'education' and the cheap press that they have become incapable
> of reading at all, except the captions of such crude stimuli as
> pictures. The Cinema is one symptom; the *Daily Mirror* another.
> Both mean that nobody who caters for amusements dares ask
> people to use their minds.

Hearing of Allan Bennett's death, Crowley wondered if this was not 'part of the general attack on the Order'. In a letter to Mudd, Crowley counselled calm: 'Remember to allow no feeling of anger or indignation to enter your heart or your mind. These people are as innocent as panic-stricken sheep, overwhelmed by formless fear of an Unknown which is only the more terrible because they cannot define it', adding: 'I trust the Gods to see to it that my friends shall not suffer.'

The Curse of the Grade of Magus was in full swing. The appearance of an *Ipsissimus* had put the cat among the pigeons, and pigeons cannot distinguish between good and evil. Crowley wrote prophetically to Mudd on 27 March: 'We are in for an *A1* Magical scrap, and I shall be anxious all the time till I see you here in the flesh.'[2]

Mussolini had been running Italy for six months and a blend of Catholic activism, anti-Masonry and suspicion of Crowley's intelligence value, made Il Duce suspect the eccentric Englishman. Already deporting unsympathetic foreign pressmen, fearful of secret societies, the 'Duke', like all Fascists, resented Freemasonry's crossing nations, allegedly negating patriotism. Crowley's German, Italian, French, Dutch, Spanish and British Masonic connections were sufficient to condemn him, especially now he appeared a soft target. Would Great Britain object?

On 23 April, the Beast was served a deportation order at Palermo. No charges were laid. Crowley pointed out the order referred only to him. The official, checking, agreed. Politely, Crowley was given a week to comply; his family would stay. His landlord, Baron La Calce, director of the Palermo Savings Bank, undertook to feed Ninette and the children, when he felt like it, helped by locals sad to lose Signor Crowley. A petition survives, signed by Cefalù citizens, unshocked by neighbours some had dubbed 'Mormons' because of Crowley's multiple 'wives'!

> We the undersigned citizens of Cefalu, affirm that Signor
> Crowley and his friends have lived in the town for three years.
> They have created no disturbance, they have acted well to
> everybody, they have spent much money with us and have
> brought many visitors to the town who also have spent money.
> It is profitable to the town that they live among us.
>   We also feel strongly that it is unjust and abuse [*sic*] of our
> hospitality to a famous poet, scholar, and traveller that he should
> be expelled from the country without any accusations made
> against him.
>   We request your Excellency to extend the order of expulsion
> till the end of July, so that Signor Crowley may find out the
> reasons for making the Order and defend his integrity in public.[3]

– all to no avail; Il Duce had spoken. And Il Duce was always right!

*　　*　　*

Who was really behind the expulsion of the Beast from Italy?

Did MacBean, the Palermo consul, encourage it? Given MacBean's own masonic interests, this seems unlikely; he might have found himself targeted, though with a government job probably felt immune. The day before the expulsion notice was served, two Oxford men, Pinney and Bosanquet, arrived at the Abbey. Concerned about Loveday, they could have been sent with the blessing of a government department. They found Crowley did not glow in the dark.

According to Spence, Italian government enquiries into the Abbey commenced in July 1922, before Mussolini gained control,[4] while *John Bull*'s issue of 24 March 1923 boasted inside knowledge: 'it is understood that the Italian Government are resolved to put an end to Crowley's career of vice.' Marco Pasi has investigated relevant documents. The expulsion order came from Rome's Ministry of Internal Affairs.[5]

The official justification: 'obscene and perverted' sexual activity, including polygamy. Only Crowley was named; associates were apparently at liberty to continue their 'obscene and perverted' activities. Spence concludes Mussolini's men suspected Crowley of 'something else' but could not prove it.

The key to the 'something else' lies, Spence speculates, with Sicilian nobleman and politician, Giovanni Antonio Colunna, Duca di Cesaro, a non-fascist member of Mussolini's cabinet. A theosophist admirer of Rudolf Steiner, and a man who knew MacBean well, the Duke of Cesaro was kicked off Mussolini's cabinet in 1924: 'the merest suspicion that the English Magician and the dissident Duke were in cahoots would have moved Mussolini to act.'[6] British newspaper slush provided the moral cover.

In 1927 Mussolini's political police (OVRA) reopened the Crowley file after Irish-British Violet Gibson nearly assassinated Mussolini, grazing his nose. Colunna, Gibson's friend, was brought in. Steadfast in denial, he was freed. Violet was deported to Ireland.

Marco Pasi's book *Aleister Crowley and the Temptation of Politics* investigates how Crowley's name emerged within conspiracy theory during the late 1920s and 1930s, the work of right-wing or extreme right-wing individuals committed to belief in a 'Jewish-Masonic', anti-Catholic global conspiracy.[7] A significant source for the conspiracy line was the *Revue Internationale des Sociétés Secrètes* (*RISS*) founded in 1912 by Monseigneur Ernest Jouin, curate of Saint-Augustin's church, Paris. The OTO and A.'.A.'. first appeared in Jouin's review in 1929. Responding and commenting on Jouin's anti-Crowley line were the noted right-wing Catholic esotericists René Guénon and Julius Evola.[8]

Rome's Central State Archives Crowley file, labelled 'Crowley Alistair Eduard A.', holds documents on Zionism, communism and Freemasonry. Though late (September 1935–June 1936), the file's correspondence between Jesuit priest Joseph Ledit,[9] then a specialist on communism and teacher at the Pontifical Institute for Oriental Studies, and an anonymous British investigator known as 'M' reveals details concerning Crowley's expulsion. Ledit, a Mussolini admirer familiar with senior police officials, was asked by 'M' about alleged subversive activities around Crowley and Dimitrije Mitrinović.[10]

Mitrinović had founded a movement called *New Britain*, which interested Crowley's old colleague, General Fuller. 'M' also referred to psychologist Alfred Adler and to the 'Adler Society', citing a link between Adler and Mitrinović. In 1927, Mitrinović founded the English section of the Adlerian Society. Crowley discussed Thelema with a sympathetic Adler in August 1930. His diary also mentions Mitrinović on that day.

A connection between New Britain and the OTO was considered by 'M' to make the subject 'quite dangerous stuff to handle!'[11] Was Crowley, 'M' asked, still operating in Italy? Ledit turned to a police contact who recommended consulting Police Chief Arturo Bocchini. Bocchini sent the request on to the commissioner in Palermo, who wrote back to Bocchini on 6 June 1936:

> [Crowley] lived for about five years in a villa in the vicinity of
> Cefalù, and was expelled from the Kingdom following
> Ministerial ordinance on 13 April 1923, it having been
> confirmed that rites were taking place in his villa based on
> obscene and perverse sexual practices, in which three foreigners
> participated who were living with him as if married, besides
> other foreigners who came there from time to time.

The reference to 'five years' is inaccurate; Crowley spent three years at Cefalù. The letter lists three reports on Crowley sent by the Palermo prefecture to the minister; they are not in the file. According to the list, the first report was dated 25 July 1922, seven months after Hélène Fraux's complaints, well before the expulsion. Interestingly, it appears police interest continued after Crowley's expulsion. The 'Political Police Division [...] indicated that defamatory notices regarding conditions in fascist Italy were being distributed from Crowley's house in Cefalù, notices that were being collected by the special espionage service of the British Foreign Ministry and were published by some newspapers.'[12] However, in spite of suspicions that the Abbey was a centre of anti-fascist propaganda with the connivance of British intelligence, the commissioner had to add that 'the aforementioned notice was unfounded because after Crowley's departure, only one of his two women remained in Cefalù – a French citizen [Ninette Shumway] – who lived in poverty and had relations to no one'.

Crowley did promote anti-fascist propaganda, in his own way. Following Mussolini's activities closely, he suspected Il Duce's expulsion of *la Besta* would prove his undoing. Composing poems ridiculing Italian Fascism in Tunis in summer 1923, *Songs for Italy* appeared in London in a privately published, 15-page edition. The Warburg Institute's copy includes a letter from Norman Mudd to the editor of the French daily *Quotidien*:

> [Crowley] has, in the last few months, written a number of poems and sonnets against Mussolini, whom he regards as the mad mongrel cur of Europe. I have the honour to enclose herewith a copy of these poems, and suggest that you should print them in the *Quotidien*, with a French translation and, if necessary some words of introduction. The vigour of these poems and the bitterness of their contempt and irony should make them very effective in helping to rid Europe of this desperate danger.[13]

The disasters of 1923 were so significant in fixing Crowley's bestial image and sealing his social damnation, we should examine an unpublished scrapbook of letters sent to Crowley's biographer John Symonds when writing *The Great Beast* in 1950 and 1951.[14] Symonds sent early drafts to Gerald Yorke for comment. Yorke was scathing about inaccuracies and 'libels' implied in the text that came his way. The following extracts may help put the record straight, as Gerald Yorke, far-sighted preserver of Crowley's manuscripts, himself wished to do:

> Loveday brought Betty for AC [Crowley] to cure her of her drug addiction. It was not being able to get her drugs that was partly responsible for her behaviour at the time. Shummy was to some extent a nymphomaniac, continually having bastards.
>
> AC was always tidy and his room was kept clean and not in

disarray. The Abbey was far from being a slum run by a slut. It was a small 18th century villa. The Chambre des Cauchemars [Room of Nightmares containing the most striking or 'obscene' paintings] was AC's bedroom – a riot of frescoes and wall-paintings. [...] AC was an excellent cook and a gourmet. The goat's milk meal you describe would have been due to lack of funds but it would have been clean and copious. Leah was a competent cook, Shummy a plain one. [...] Betty May was a rough alley cat who had taken to drugs. Raoul was a sensitive graduate with a natural tendency towards magic and the bizarre. Jane was down to earth and never slept with AC or any of the others.

In 1951, Loveday's sister wrote two moving letters to Symonds, some 28 years after her brother's death. She emphatically denied Crowley was responsible for her brother's, or anyone else's, death. She said everyone had their own will and could distinguish right from wrong; they must have known that going Crowley's way would get them into hot water. She asked to see a copy of Crowley's *Confessions*, opining that Crowley's behaviour was in her view the consequence of his peculiar childhood. She wrote again on 29 November 1951. She did not accept Symonds' statement that Raoul lived as a Thelemite, died as one and was buried as one. He had scarcely been in Cefalù long enough to adopt it. As far as she could see, being a Thelemite meant being selfish, callous and cruel, indifferent to the sufferings and fate of others. Her brother's death was, she believed, just an incident to Crowley; her parents received no letter of sympathy from him.

Crowley's failure to confront the grief of Loveday's family appears bound up with an insulating selfishness that was Crowley's perennial defence when threatened. When he occasionally reflected on such behaviour, he conceded that he was often 'rotten' and, frankly, an 'arsehole'. *The Book of the Law* instructed its recipient, 'Veil not your vices in virtuous words'. Crowley did not veil his vices; he was as he was. He did not repent. Practically speaking, had he not been involved in enforced deportation, persecution and disorienting illness and addiction, things might have been different. In point of fact, he *had* sent Betty out to post a letter to Loveday's parents, but she had collapsed before posting it, then high-tailed it to Palermo.

Loveday's sister expressed pity for the immensely gifted Crowley. Had he used his gifts for good he might have found the peace of mind that eluded him, she believed. She also believed her brother's death was directly responsible for Crowley's ultimate fate. Raoul's wide circle of friends deplored his death and that, combined with expulsions from Italy and France, ruined Crowley. As for the press, they massively distorted Betty's account. The family was horrified at the lengths the press would go, and that much she had to give Crowley. Ultimately, though, Crowley's creed was, she believed, selfish.

By contrast, Jane Wolfe wrote to Symonds from Hollywood:

> I would like to note the following as an indication of the various phases of our training in Cefalu; the atmosphere was rarefied, we became intensely conscious of one another, and Aleister made us face any remark that might pass our lips, careless or otherwise, plus the drill of Mind your own business!

Jane then related a little story of how Leah had once grabbed Betty's hat and thrown it on the ground, then picked it up carefully, patted it and corrected herself, saying:

> 'It's a nice little hat.' It was so beautiful and spontaneous an action I shall never forget it. In just this way our unruly impulses had come to heel – not that they were eliminated, but that the opposite emotion was there to equilibrate the other.

Whereas Symonds had initially written a dramatic account of Loveday's burial, observed by 'hundreds of villagers', Jane corrected the writer's embellishment of the facts: 'No one but Roman Catholics could be buried on consecrated ground. Authorities actually dealt with bier. Body HAD to be buried in 24 hours. We were watched by a few of the monks who lived next door to the cemetery.' She then referred to Crowley's 'invaluable analysis' and made the point that literary material returned to

Britain from Cefalù was not, as stated, destroyed by Customs. 'Incidentally,' she added, 'AC called Leah and myself freaks.'

Finally, 'At many periods of my life, I have said, Thank God for Cefalù.'

And yet, every year, whenever Crowley is mentioned in the press, the same old falsehoods are trotted out. As Christopher McIntosh says, the public needs a 'bad boy'. It wouldn't matter so much if Crowley were not so important, with a serious message tangled into his difficult life.

* * *

On 2 May 1923, Aleister and Leah arrived in French Tunis. He went 'cold turkey' to conquer heroin. Three days of pure hell followed. He came off it, but asthma dragged him back to the drug. He did not give in. His willpower and conviction kept him going through his life's devastation. He began his 'autohagiography' – 'the Hag' – an astonishing telling of his life and work. A classic, he would never see it published in its finished form. In spite of addiction, illness and poverty, Crowley's autobiography contains some of his finest writing, brimming over with magisterial humour and cool insight into the human condition. There is no bitterness; Crowley rides high and Thelema is consistently vindicated.

Convinced *Liber AL* secreted mysteries significant to science, Crowley sent out a call to mathematics professor Norman Mudd, *Frater Omnia Pro Veritate* (Everything for the Truth). Mudd thought he should rather martial support for Crowley with a letter campaign. The stricken Magus got the ball rolling with an account of his predicament sent on 8 May to Sir Godfrey Collins MP, the 'elected representative of the nation to which I belong'. Crowley requested Collins introduce a bill to defend defamed people by granting them '*equal space* of reply.' Such requests still fall on deaf ears; the public's right to be lied to must be defended.

Crowley found Thelema could be fundamentally misunderstood by the intelligent. He corrected Mudd's misapprehensions:

> Let me put it in this way. In spite of the variety of possible
> triangles they are all limited by having three sides. Similarly, the

scope of possible wills for any man is limited by his race, caste, &c. Nothing annoys me more than having people imagine that 93 [Thelema] allows any amount of looseness.

Thelema is 'inevitable', Crowley states, because it identifies destiny with free will: Do what thou wilt is not a guide, 'it is a scientific principle of ethics'.

I'm not sure that you quite grasp the idea of the Book when you say there must be hope for the average man. As I read it, the acceptance of The Law is something like deciding to enter an University. 'The slaves shall serve.' [He is possibly thinking of college 'scouts' who served students at Oxford and Cambridge]

The point is, I think, with regard to freedom, that it is up to any man to declare that he intends to do his Will. By doing so, he undertakes the responsibility of governing himself and others. He must succeed or fail in that higher task.

[…] All we can do for the Troglodytes (as I have got into trouble for calling them) is to work for their general welfare and very slowly to prepare them for emancipation. But the essential for ourselves is to put a stop absolutely to this damned impertinent interference with us.

Crowley then makes an important, even astounding statement that cuts him clean away from ersatz occultism:

I want to do away with the distinction between Occult, ordinary and Scientific research. I affirm the unity of nature. To me the adept is simply a man who knows his business in both senses; (a) what it is (b) how to do it.

[…] I hold that one must discover one's True Will by a spiritual experience based on practices mostly of the type of sammasati […] 'direct vision' should not be trusted unless confirmed fully by intellectual criteria and also by the course of events. 'Success is your proof.'

Crowley then clarifies that his role as 'Logos' (Word) does not simply derive from The Book of the Law or from rational considerations, but rather is the resultant of:

force of circumstances which have compelled me to identify
myself with the Word Thelema, and refuse to allow me to follow
any of my numerous ambitions though these are still strong in
me! At this moment, Aleister Crowley is as mad as Hell that he
cannot be a famous poet, the leader of the next expedition to
Everest, and that sort of thing. It is of course equally true that
my deepest Will is absolutely satisfied by being the Logos,
for nothing else would carry me beyond the barriers of birth
and death.

[…] Every star has its place in the Body of Nuit.

'All your righteousness is as filthy rags!' Until you have 'found
Jesus' good works are a delusion of the Devil. Do get this well
into your head. It is vitally important. Until you have spiritual
experience of discovering the True Will, all your efforts are likely
to lead further astray. […] Isn't the whole crux of Attainment the
abandonment of all that you have and are?[15]

From the 'pleasure village' of Marsa Plage, Tunis, Crowley wrote Mudd a
fascinating exposition of the historical validity of Thelema:

The Aeon is not a work of my unsupported imagination. The
facts of human progress are involved. You have seen yourself
evidence of the tree sprouting entirely independent of me.

In the course of evolution, mankind becomes ripe for new
truths or rather for the communication of a section – new to it –
of eternal truth. The Equinox of the Gods is a critical moment
when such a pass-word is communicated. I am, so to speak,
the Kerux charged with the official proclamation in the Temple
of the Word. But, that Word is not arbitrary. It expresses
existing conditions. Obviously, lots of people have worked by
93 in all ages.

Reading Crowley's diary for the period, it is striking how many times he
felt adrift, 'insane', disconnected. He was putting his energies into
attempting to launch a world religion while simultaneously coping with
drug addiction, vilification, acute poverty, estrangement from his
'family', persistent bronchial attacks, homelessness and press and state

persecution. Would it not be surprising if he was somewhat mad? He was like a stoned Atlas, with a world on his head.

Mudd arrived on 25 July with his savings. Crowley immediately moved in to the Tunisia Palace Hotel, taking comfort in a relationship with a Tunisian youth, Mohammed ben Brahim. Leah had gone to take some money to the Abbey at Cefalù. After trying to get Mudd to persuade Fuller to rejoin the Thelema programme, he tried to explain why he was treating Mudd badly; passing him in the street without saying anything, for example. He needed a whipping boy; part of Crowley was pure bastard. His suggestion that Mudd's ill treatment was for his own good rings hollow:

> Part of your Tunis Ordeal was due to a similar act. You had never loathed me properly, so you had to suffer the vision of the Demon Crowley in a very acute form. I must have seemed base, brutal, selfish, false to my word – a typical old husband with a dog in the manger at that. I encouraged this view as best I could.[16]

Leah and Mudd began to find comfort in each other, while remaining fiercely loyal to 'Big Bugger Lion' as Leah affectionately called the Beast. Why did the adult Mudd stick around? Was it the inspiring teaching? Was it Leah? Was it Magick?

It was Crowley; he was a magnet.

Oxford mathematics scholar and South African Eddie Saayman turned up.[17] Crowley hoped Saayman would go back to Oxford, give maths tutorials, and send him some cash.

Crowley watched Mussolini. Reading of the bombardment of Corfu on 1 September he noted the dictator's 'killing some dozen or more Armenian children – refugees – in revenge for the murder of some Wop [Italian] fools by some persons unknown 1,500 miles away! What utter fools – as well as blackguards – statesmen are!'[18]

In need of a fresh current of energy, Crowley, Leah, Mudd and Mohammed went to Nefta, to the Hotel de Djérid. Leah fell ill. Crowley went on a carefully planned trek through the desert.

*   *   *

On 7 November at 4.30pm, Crowley performed an astral divination. 666 quizzed a discarnate intelligence about what *The Book of the Law*'s third chapter meant by a 'war engine', described as a gift of Ra Hoor Khuit, the Sun in his martial aspect. The operation brought a vision, Crowley wrote in a note, 'not incongruous with my idea of the new Energy'. Crowley recommended the notes be sent to Mudd for interpretation. The notes show drawings, images and algebraic concepts suggestive of nuclear fission. Extraordinarily striking for a North African vision in 1923, the notes, with hindsight, suggest the 'war engine' was nothing less than an atomic bomb.

On 29 December 1923, in search of a new direction, Crowley headed for Nice, without Mudd or Leah. He was approaching a reckoning – with himself.

Rebirth

1924

1924 marked a turning point for the Beast. Holing up under the tolerant eye of the Bourciers at the Hotel Blois, 50 Rue Vavin, Paris, Crowley watched his life pass before his eyes; it did not look good. Beaten low by bronchitis, asthma, poverty, neglect, persecution, addiction and a pervasive abjection, the Beast sensed a period of his life was ending, or worse: 'I long for death – simply to be away from the body which weighs me down instead of being my chariot.'

Leah wrote to her 'Beautiful Big Bugger Lion' from Cefalù's half-empty Abbey, enclosing requested papers. Mudd had written from Tunis; Leah asked the Lion not to be 'ridiculously hard on the poor lad. Remember that you and I are old hands at it.' Mudd had endured a wretched time. When Leon Engers gave Crowley 500 francs, the Beast bought fresh clothes and sent money to Mudd, but 'poor lad' or not, Crowley found him irritating, as sick people will, those who try to help them but don't know how. Mudd bounced into Paris on 23 January, leaving a string of rubber cheques behind him. Crowley wished he'd bounce off.

> It is 1.20 a.m. & my mind is very confused in judgement.
> My credit is quite exhausted, even with the kind people at this hotel: & there is less than 200 francs in hand. And unless I can get Leah up to nurse me in the country & Mudd to London I see no hope save in the Gods. […] I feel that the Gods are making it impossible for me to use my mind at all except in Their own special business.

He had entered the 'Realm of Fire', 'purging me, & consuming the last of that "little pile of dust" to the White Ash for the Urn'. Super-vivid daydreams, verging on hallucinations, sent him wondering whether his 'ravings' signified general paralysis of the insane, but reckoned he was 'probably past the age'.

In the midst of a guilt-ridden turmoil, long forgotten aspects of his life washed up onto the shores of semi-consciousness. He recalled the 'lesion-memory' when receiving *The Book of the Law*.

On 5 March his heroin prescription ran out, resulting in severe symptoms 'of the usual type'. A Dr Jarvis failed to renew his prescription. Now he would trust only those who loved him. He looked again at the 'Hag', the ironically titled hagiography of his 'saintly' life, a mission of 'sin' for the salvation of mankind. He was dealing with the early days and the meaning of his middle name:

> This incident of Alexander proved critical. It answered the
> supreme question 'Who art thou?' and I have never turned back
> or aside from that hour. 'An helper of men' [...] 'To teach man
> the Next Step i.e. the K. & C. of the H.G.A.'

To teach man the Next Step... Crowley's unique religious, scientific and magical application of the Knowledge and Conversation of the Holy Guardian Angel was his life's cornerstone.

He cried out for reassurance as he faced the trial of seeing his unvarnished, undisguised, human self: '11.15 I have aeon-long trials before my conscience.' He complained to Mudd, though whether present or a hallucination is unclear: 'Have I ever done anything of value, or am I a mere trifler, existing by a series of shifts of one kind or another? A wastrel, a coward, a man of straw.'

Mudd says: 'Thou hast no right but to do thy will.'

> 10 P.M. I examine myself very thoroughly under Ethel. I am
> confirmed in my old conclusion that I am essentially insane. But
> Ethel [ethyl oxide] & her friends have something to do with this:
> and my one chance is to cut them out before it is too late. Of
> course, the brain under Ethel is not a free brain.

On 8 March, Crowley pawned all his magical equipment and jewellery to pay for Mudd to go to London to assert his innocence of gutter-press calumnies. He thought about the notorious injunctions in the fiery chapter three of *The Book of the Law*, such as: 'Damn them who pity!' Did this mean sympathy for another was excluded? No. Since the book postulated 'a healthy society', *pity* among Thelemites would be 'mere insult and interference'. 'True sympathy', however, was something else, requiring 'scientific imagination': noble, virile qualities. *The Book of the Law* held powerful injunctions to illuminate common sense: 'Love one another with burning hearts.' When *AL* said 'Spit upon them' – 'them' being persons ignorant of their True Wills – Thelemites were to spit 'the purifying Water' upon them. Where it said 'Trample them' it was 'to express the juice that we may have wine'. These thoughts led him to a critique of Nietzsche, whose philosophy, when skewed, attracted fascists.

> I am haunted by Nietzsche.[1] Yes, the herd is noble enough; but what of the alternative? To be the big blonde beast – the beast of prey! No: 'I find this black mark impugns the man/That he believes in just the vile of life'. His [Nietzsche's] image is false: we are not a mere menagerie of assorted brutes. 'Like a mighty army/Moves the Church of God' should be our vision of the Race. Then – even the stupidest private is a hero. The leaders are hidden and lonely but not in ambush: they are the Secret Staff, the true philosophers, the Hermits 'who give only of their Light unto Men'. Lying here sick and starving, let me find Light, and shed it for their sake!

These inspiring thoughts led him to a powerful general conclusion, and on to many other unpublished axioms of human liberty:

> The main Ethics of the Book of the Law. Man is asked to act *as if it were true that he is a spark of that great light of God*. Those who insist on making that assumption, on basing all their lives on it, are the Thelemites.

Four days later, a concerned Leah and Hansi wrote to 'You old darling Beast' from Cefalù; all was fine. She hoped to hear the same from him, playfully suggesting he might lack time to write to his original 'B.A.B.', short for *Babalon*, as he was probably busy with 'some nice little whore'. Leah enclosed a simple scrawled pencil plea from little Hans: 'BEAST COME BACK.'

In fact, Ninette, Leah and the children were in arrears, threatened with eviction. Prostrate over his family, Crowley watched helplessly as HM Customs in England seized property dispatched from Sicily. Much of his library and manuscripts, the fruit of years of hard work in Italy, were to be destroyed by order, apparently, on 24 March 1926.

> Off the vivisection table. I have found several new bad faults in myself. [...] I do wish I had a list of the crimes I have discovered in myself these last weeks; fickle, liar, white slaver (in a very bad sense, selling women deliberately to physical torture) are a few of my latest results.

He turned the gutter press lie of 'trafficking in women' against himself. Had he not brought ('sold') Leah and Ninette into the misery of poverty and homelessness?

Guilty.

He needed a priest – and found one. Clément Vautel's popular, subtle novel, *Mon curé chez les riches*[2] about the wise abbé Pellegrin and the good curé (parish priest) offered a luminous helper on his way, whose wisdom took Crowley's hand in the hour of his purgatory. Like himself, the abbé was also a martyr to orthodox, bureaucratic inhumanity.

> 'Mon curé' has shown me my duty! I must not hunt for ways out of trouble. I must stick in my Trench, the Poet & Prophet of the Aeon, & take all the shells & gas & bayonets that come my way.

> 12.25. 'Mon curé' tells me also the methods of cowardice. How easy to mask it as courage and pride! 'Too proud to fight!' Perhaps I had better after all get after my enemies with my bare hands, tell the whole truth, the worst about myself, and trust for victory to Ra Hoor Khuit. [...] Well, I'll trust him too for 'the leading and the light'.

He realized one fact: 'clear as day: that I have actually been reborn: that I am now at last a Child of the New Aeon.' It was up to him 'to grow into the Man', now he was 'in the Temple', being initiated.

> 'Mon curé' proves what I have never dared to think – only to wish. This: MONEY HAS NO POWER. This is the great evil and illusion of the Age – and there is the thesis of my real essay: my first babe's prattle. Money has use, of course, and it works black magical miracles of false power. But in the end it always fizzles out, if it be used in the attempt to alter realities. Observe America – its wealth concentrated in the most experienced hands – its aim to secure 'Law & Order'. Yet it is the most lawless land on earth, and the nearest to revolution.

Crowley's self-revelations are startling:

> One quality I do possess – integrity. (Despite a thousand thousand tricks of shame, cowardice, dishonesty, dishonour – I see them now just as they are!) Yet I have never been able to put my Will into attaining any other object than the true one. Similarly, there is something in me which refuses utterly to surrender, how ever much I may feel I want to do so. My acts of cowardice have always been the result of my fooling myself; & my great hope is that in future I shall never be able to do this. The fact is that fear is extraordinarily clever at disguising itself. (It reminds me of the shifts of the Drug addict.) To avoid some unpleasant prospect, one may (e.g.) forget it altogether, and adopt some plan of campaign which seems actually heroic; and in itself, is so. Take the case of my climbing. I took to it really (I suspect) in order to avoid the clash with other boys in games like football; and I took desperate chances, & got the reputation of a daredevil, chiefly to soothe my conscience. Of course the above is simply one piece of analysis. There must have been many noble elements in my decision. Generally, too, I may say that though I cannot find any thing in myself but absolute rottenness, there must be something there worthwhile. My positive achievements prove that there is much in me that not one man in a million even touches. Then why cannot I find aught but shame?

1.30. Repentance! The true course is to stick to one's errors, however gross they now seem. I understand at last Blake's 'If the fool would but persist in his folly, he would become wise'.

Crowley faced the facts at last:

My general conclusion on this part of the problem is that drugs are fundamentally useless – and treacherous, the Lord knows! They are just Emergency rations.

Crowley concluded that 'in a certain sense' asthma was a *malade imaginaire*, stimulated by deep anxieties independent of conscious control. He observed that 'Ninette's aid gave me complete freedom, youth as well as health, for months'. The tragedy of Anne Lea's death caused immediate relapse: 'I got steadily worse till I secured the contract (and advance) for *The Diary of a Drug Fiend*.' His condition had 'got worse ever since'.

The reference to Ninette's 'aid' shows financial anxiety exacerbated breathing miseries. Astarte Lulu's son Eric remembered Ninette in her 75th year, still able to recite the whole of *The Book of the Law*. According to Eric:

Hélène [Ninette's sister] was one of the main supports of the Cefalù experience. She sent cash, clothes, food and anything she could to support the four children and Ninette. When she couldn't afford any more, she took action to save the children and Ninette. The world wasn't ready for the New Age.[3]

Crowley's condition took him into strange territories. He had chosen a fictional priest, with whom he could identify, to make his 'confession'. Was it a 'death-bed' confession?

my father's 'What after death?' various answers come: 'I don't know' for one. *AL* 1.58 contradicts this. 'I trust Aiwass' is another. Next question: is Aiwass Jesus? *AL* excludes this again by III 51 [a reference in the *Book of the Law*] and so on and so forth.

Is Aiwass Jesus? An extraordinary question! The Yezidis regard 'Jesus' as an angel; Crowley might add that individuals' spiritual experience of 'Jesus' might be an intimation of the Holy Guardian Angel, or Secret Self. Christians are brought up to see the Light as Jesus. Perhaps we need the light more than the name.

Crowley dined out with photographer Charles John Hope-Johnstone,[4] discussing Thelema and thoughts in common: 'We discussed Gurdjieff at some length – also with agreement. He began: "What do you think of etc." I retorted: "How do you know I know anything about it?" He seems to have taken it for granted that I should know.'

Crowley had visited Gurdjieff's Institute for the Harmonious Development of Man at Fontainebleau, concluding: 'No doubt at all that the Gods sent me there – in the one three-day period when my health allowed such excursion. It is therefore important. *Question*: can I work with them at all, to complete them, as I proposed to myself, by taking on all those who will not fit into his very artificial scheme.'

The reference to the 'Gods' sending him to Gurdjieff's establishment is interesting. Gurdjieff, a man who revered the Yezidis, had escaped the Bolsheviks in 1921 by fleeing to Constantinople where he met alleged agent, John Godolphin Bennett; Bennett became a disciple. According to Spence, MI5 and the Foreign Office suspected Bennett's contacts with the Turkish Secret Service, considering him anti-British, in league with communists.[5]

It is possible then that Crowley was killing two birds with one stone in visiting Gurdjieff's competing self-development institute: sniffing out Bennett, if he was there, for intelligence purposes while offering to take on those unsuitable for Gurdjieff's 'artificial scheme'. The offer exemplifies Crowley's cheek. Crowley was not in the least awed by Gurdjieff, unlike many disciples then and now. To this day, Gurdjieffian myth suggests Crowley was ejected from Fontainebleau. In this regard we may note a reminiscence of Nancy Cunard's from 1951: 'He [Crowley] then told me a beautiful little anecdote about that ghastly Gurdjieff. I'll bet it's true. He was indignant at Gurdjieff.'

Gerald Yorke claimed to have introduced the competitors, Gurdjieff and Crowley. They sat in a café, said little, and eyed one another warily.

If Gurdjieff avoided Crowley, it was possibly because he and Bennett were sensitive to intelligence interest.

*   *   *

On 29 March, having gone through an imaginary court trial, Crowley complained that Mudd didn't understand him 'one scrap', unable to see it was beneath his dignity to 'ask for damages and be versus somebody'. *Judex sum*, he wrote: 'I am Judge'. Mudd was taking *Liber AL* too literally and getting above himself.

> You [Mudd] seem to have become a religious fanatic of the most dangerous & detestable type. Your influence on me has been, I think, wholly bad [...]
>   *Note.* My original and only demand on O.P.V. [Mudd] was that he should help me with the Comment. That he point blank refused to do. [...] It was laid down some time since that it was forbidden to base dogmatic arguments on *AL* – & Mudd does nothing else.

Crowley was concerned at gross interpretations of *Liber AL*. Having been purified in spirit himself, he now saw *AL* shining 'with most spiritual splendour; all coarse interpretation has now become impossible'. If it was a contest between subtlety and 'fundamentalism', Crowley would opt for subtlety. Human beings could not be trusted with 'fundamentals'; contact of uninitiated persons with spiritual truths simply exacerbated egos and sent otherwise passive fools into the throes of extremism. In a complete, ironic reversal of fundamentalist practice, the only book Crowley ever recommended being burnt was *The Book of the Law* itself, after reading it once!

As April opened her bud, Crowley concluded his *apologia pro vita sua*:

> My position. I have done many eccentric and indiscreet things in my life. Some by bravado, the desperate protection devised by extreme shyness; some by tendency to symbolic self-expression, as the only way to manifest a disgust born of my poet's indignation: some by childish vanity, 'shewing-off'; some by the

impulse to romantic and chivalrous action: some by the exaggerated sense of justice: some by high-spirited fondness for practical jokes: some by extravagant reaction against shame: some by sheer silliness: but I cannot accuse myself of deliberately wronging or harming any other person: or of acting in a spirit of hatred or revenge or of falling short in any respect of the ideally high standard of honour inherited from my father, and taught by precept and example in my early childhood by him.

At 1.45am on 4 April, a breakthrough: 'I have felt radically different since last night's meditation and decision. *I have a future*, once more! I feel that the essence of my magical health is to act rightly towards all questions. I see now how 'lust of result' messes things up.' Heroin and bronchitis made for a 'vicious circle'; if he could stop the bronchitis, the heroin problem would disappear.

In 1933 Crowley looked back on the terrible spring of 1924, summarizing the events for a serialization of his life for the *Sunday Dispatch*:

> The Secret Chiefs resolved therefore to destroy him utterly. [...] They masked him so grotesquely, hideously, obscenely, that it became scarce possible for any man to penetrate the secret of his true personality.
> The climax of their dealings with him came in the weeks immediately preceding and following the Spring Equinox of 1924 e.v. [...] So in that Fire he was consumed wholly, and as pure Spirit alone did he return little by little, during the months that followed, into the body and mind that had perished in that great ordeal of which he can say no more than this: I died.[6]

And by a delicious synchronicity, 8 April marked the 'Twentieth Anniversary of the Writing of the First Chapter of the Book of the Law. Hail unto Keph Ra!' He was now convinced that the 'Rich Man of the West' promised in *AL* would come. To commemorate the anniversary, he analysed by *sammasati* his life of the last 20 years, beginning with 1904–05 and the 'Breakdown of plans to act on AL'. This failure had proved a 'Folly' for which he would suffer. The failure culminated in what he called 'Cefalù the Big Wallop'. His prognosis of 1924–25 he called 'The Stele of Revealing' in which time, 'My work will appear'.

None of these reflections distracted his mind from other weighty matters and prophecies, such as how mankind was to effect interstellar travel:

> Monday April 14.
>
> War engine [a reference to the 'war engine' promised in *Liber Legis* III] and some more. The only possibility of such things as inter-stellar communication that I can see consists in a discovery of something which, like gravitation, produces acceleration and not velocity. For example: a repulsive force from which things fly F-feet in the first second to 2 F4 in the second, 4F in the third.

This use of gravitational force to 'bounce' craft off into space at speed from neighbouring force fields would in fact be used to propel our satellites through space. Right again, Mr Crowley! But then, Crowley's brain was not as other men's:

> April 17. Thursday
>
> 3.10. P.M. I think I have discovered the basis of the paradox why my mind is opposite to everyone else's. It is simply that it is [stoic? stony?]. For instance, being a conservative I read only the liberal newspapers. Reason: I know what my friends think, I want to know what the enemy are thinking. Most men are ashamed or afraid to do anything of the sort.
>
> Thursday April 24.
>
> Give the highest wisdom only to the children for no one else is fit to hear it.

Crowley was now feeling so inwardly buoyant that his May Day eviction for rent arrears from the Hotel Blois by its soon-to-fail new management was interpreted by him as his 'birth' from the 'womb'. He entered a cheap inn in Chelles sur Marne and put out a spiritual call for 'kingly men' to come to the star that lit the 'baby's' rough stable. Crowley's call was answered by an epiphany of three kings, all bearing 'gifts': JWN Sullivan, writer on science and music, Leon Engers, the painter, and a wealthy Argentinian artist who was studying in Paris, Alejandro Schulz Solari, another 'helper of men' with a solar Name![7] On 15 May, 'Xul Solar', as he called himself in honour of the Sun, signed his Probationer's oath in Crowley's Order. He is now Argentina's most famous painter.

Leah was beginning to get on Crowley's 'wick', for we find him, in Leah's presence, analysing the three kinds of women who had played a role in his life; the types determined the role, the roles – tongue in cheek, I think – were determined by his own 'complexes':

> No 1. My *vanity complex* – petite, passionate, decorative; to be used to shew off, to insult other men, arouse their envy etc.

> No 2. *Masochist pederasty-complex*. Big strong, heavy, muscular women preferably with moustaches & other masculine stigmata. Use – pleasure of abasement, suffering; ideas of complicity in crime.

> No 3. *Poet complex*. Classically beautiful, spiritual, preferably intelligent & educated enough to understand me. Use – inspiration of ideally noble work. 'Wish-phantasm' of age of chivalry.

> Any of these might within obvious limits satisfy need of friendship, comradeship, especially No3.

In category No.1 came Helen Hollis and Laura Grahame. Crowley suddenly recalled she was fond of anal sex; unusual since it was normally only favoured as birth-control. Category No.2 included Roddie Minor and Evelyn Hall; the sub-type of No.2 included Catherine Miller, and 'Egyptian or African whores in general', as well as Olya and Marcelle. Sublime category No.3 included Rose, Hilarion, Leila Waddell, as a musician, Ratan Devi, and Marie Lavroff. He then added: 'I am quite unable to force myself to treat Alostrael [Leah] a Number 3 and write *Rosa Mundi* Series or *Golden Rose* about her. The real feeling inhibits the poetic expression probably because the woman is too sacred.' Leah would not have had to read between the lines to recognize that her days in 'Big Bugger Lion's' life were numbered.

At 3pm on 4 June, Crowley and Leah sat down together at the inn Au Cadran Bleu at Chelles, Seine et Marne. Crowley dictated an unusual essay, *Helios* [the Sun] – *Or the Future Beyond Science*.[8] This was probably inspired by conversations with Sullivan. The 'Solar Age' might have caught on better than 'the Aeon of Horus' as a concept-title; this being more obvious today in our eco-conscious times.

However, the essay's chief interest for us may lie in its prediction of another great war:

> [French Marshall] Foch failed to push home his victory, apparently from sheer sickness of heart at the slaughter, thus leaving Germany in an excellent position to retrieve the disaster and make another attempt to wipe out civilization within the next 10 years. [Hitler would come to power nine years later]
>
> That project again, even if successful, would probably break down for some similar reason.

Crowley proposed two solutions to the world-crisis:

1. Acceptable religion

2. Improvement in the human brain to cope with problems – access to higher intelligence than its own 'who are willing to guide our feeble footsteps in the way of truth'.

*　　*　　*

Crowley Reborn turned to thelemic physics on 30 June: 'We mean by matter much what was meant by Ether 30 years ago. It is the medium by which phenomena take place or by which we become aware of them.'

At 7pm on 16 September, 32-year-old Chicago-born Dorothy Olsen materialized at Chelles. A pilgrim in search of a wizard, Miss Olsen was soon transformed into *Soror Astrid* of the A∴A∴. Convinced Astrid would 'change the death-magnetism to a new Life', Crowley saw Leah's successor as Scarlet Woman. In Cefalù, meanwhile, only the arrival of

Leah's sister Alma and Ninette's sister Hélène preserved Ninette from starvation. A letter from Alma to Jane Wolfe shows how Crowley's persecuted *Ipsissimus* period could affect an emotionally involved onlooker:

> What causes this man to be on one side so brilliant and a lover of truth – and on the other the most brutally wicked man imaginable? I can only attribute it to the fact that he is in the power of some wicked spirit – and that he has emmeshed you all in the same way – as the spirit has him.[9]

Judging from a reminiscence of Ninette's grandson, Alma's judgement of Crowley would be shared by Ninette Fraux:

> There is a story about my first visit to my grandmother Ninette Fraux. To make it short she told me: 'Your grandfather was one of the greatest geniuses of human history. He was one of the greatest chess players, mountaineers, spiritual men; essayist, poet, writer, and occult magus. He was a God-Man in the tradition of Buddha, Muhammad, Confucius, Lao Tzu and Jesus Christ, and he was the rottenest son-of-a-bitch I ever met.[10]

With Xul Solar's studies with Crowley coming to an end in late September, the Beast was free to whisk Astrid away to Tunis, out into the desert by camel and on foot. At Sidi Bou Saïd, they issued the 'Mediterranean Manifesto', paid for by Astrid, addressed *TO MAN*: a rallying call to a deaf world. The long-awaited World Teacher had appeared. The truth would not be found in Shambhala, or with the Theosophical Society's messiah, Krishnamurti. The answer was Thelema, and Crowley was the Prophet.

Astrid and the Magus journeyed on, not to Oz, but to Sfax, Tozeur and Nefta, by camel. Dorothy had the romantic privilege of witnessing Crowley receiving recognition as a Master by Sheikh Abd el Aziz ben Mohammed who entertained them to an 18-course banquet before having them escorted to El Oued. The Sheikh knew a Master when he saw one. They traversed some 120 miles more to Touggourt. Crowley loved the desert; he made sense there. On 5 November he recorded Dorothy being thrown from a mule: 'a wonderful sight'. Back in Tunis on 12 December, Crowley was rejuvenated.

As for his old disciples, well, they were in the care of the gods, if they did the right thing. At 1924's end, Leah was scraping a few francs as a restaurant scullion in Paris. Hearing that the broke and deluded Leah and Mudd were now in a sexual-magical relationship, Crowley distanced himself until they had sorted themselves out. Leah was not the *One*.

Poor Norman Mudd; his adventures into magick, madness and poverty had broken his parents' hearts. On 27 November 1924, his name joined the list of the Metropolitan Asylums Board for the Homeless Poor, London. He would reappear with Leah and the Beast in Germany the following year, but after that he was on his own.

Reborn Crowley sped on.

Theodor Reuss had died in 1923. *Parzifal* X°, Grand Master for North America, Charles Stansfeld Jones and *Recnartus* X° of the German OTO, Heinrich Tränker, both declined the succession in letters to one another. They turned to Crowley. He informed them Reuss had, in his last letter, appointed him. Crowley's assumption was not to every Oriental Templar's liking. The matter came to a head with the appearance, at last, of the prophesied 'Rich Man from the West', destined (in *AL*) to pour his gold upon the Beast.

TWENTY

The World Teacher

1925–27

Vision and prophecy were in the air. Romantic Dorothy, in Tunis with her Valentino, was pregnant. Sheikh Crowley summoned Leah from Paris to help. Dorothy miscarried. Then, one evening in March 1925, beneath a starry Tunisian sky, Crowley entered a trance. New acolyte William George Barron saw an inverted cone of blue light in the courtyard, but the World Teacher saw an apocalyptic future of chaos and collapse, of human beings shredded by powerful new weapons, despairing. Thirteen years later, as the Nazis entered Czechoslovakia, the vision appeared as *The Heart of the Master* by 'Khaled Khan', along with the 'Mediterranean Manifesto' *TO MAN*. Thelema was Man's sole hope of avoiding catastrophe.

Seeing her own future with 'Big Bugger Lion' fading, Leah made love to ex-French Army officer Gérard Aumont, who translated *The Diary of a Drug Fiend* into French. She then had magical sex with Barron. Their son, Alexander, was born in Leipzig on 4 December 1925.

What took Leah to Leipzig was OTO business. Heinrich Tränker, Grand Master of the German OTO, accepted Crowley as Outer Head of the Order (OHO). The question was where to go from there. Crowley wished to use his position to control other European esoteric orders. Tränker wished to pursue his *Pansophia* neo-Rosicrucian project with H Spencer Lewis.[1]

In formulating ideas for a meeting to discuss the OTO's future, Crowley informed Tränker that while *The Book of the Law* thrust the mantle of 'Prophet of the New Aeon' upon him, he saw it as an 'office', even a 'nuisance'; he did not want personal attention. Informing Tränker he only acknowledged it because of the Cairo Revelation, Crowley insisted his position remain secret.

> Those who came to me in 1904 E.V. told me that They chose me for the Work in question on account not of my special or magical attainments (which were, and are, small indeed) but for (a) my loyalty and steadiness (b) my knowledge of comparative occultism, especially my comprehension of the essential Unity underlying sectarian differences. (c) my perception that the Great Work was as strictly scientific as Chemistry. (d) my command of language.
>
> The urgency, they told me, was this. There was to be a general destruction of Civilization, and it was expedient to reduce the Sacred Wisdom to concise and simple form, so that (as in the Renaissance) the scholars of the New Aeon might be able to reconstruct the Royal Art from the debris of the world.

It was vital that the theosophists fail in thrusting saviour Krishnamurti on the world:

> It was *never* the intention of the Masters that theosophy as such should conquer the world, for the time had not yet come for the proclamation of the Law of the new Aeon. The more carefully you consider the matter, the more clearly will the plan of the Masters become apparent to you.[2]

Crowley intended to control 'all existing movements' as a matter of urgency:[3]

> We are on the threshold of the New Aeon. The death of the formula of Osiris is marked understandably to any student of the affairs of the planet with the complete breaking not only of all the religious but of all the moral sanities. The result is constantly increasing anarchy feebly stemmed here and there by reactionary movements which are merely brutal containing no stable elements because of the lack of any principle to which reasonable men can appeal.

Crowley then wrote to Jones. In view of the 'impending collapse' – the Wall Street Crash was still four years away – it was essential 'to select a number of properly trained men and entrust them with the secret of the unknown form of energy which we have at our disposal (my knowledge of the technique has largely increased since I wrote my Commentary on the IX°)'.

A conclave was called for 1925's summer solstice to decide the OTO's future. It convened at Hohenleuben, 20 miles west of Zwickau, Saxony. Crowley's expenses were paid and minutes were kept. Not everyone wanted to tie in with Crowley's OTO. Eugen Grosche would leave the Order to found his own Thelema-influenced, Gnostic *Fraternitas Saturni*.[4] On the plus side, Crowley met Tränker's friendly assistant, Karl Johannes Germer.[5] As *Frater Saturnus*, Germer was involved in Tränker's *Pansophia*. To Crowley's eye, Germer was the prophesied 'Rich Man from the West'. But it was Germer's wife Cora who paid the Beast's Parisian debts. While Cora bemoaned the cost, Karl took an admiring, often critical, sometimes hysterical, interest in Crowley's affairs until the end of his life.

Though backed by Germer, theosophist Martha Küntzel and her lover Otto Gebhardi, some delegates suspected the Englishman's ambitions, but Crowley, radiating sweetness and light, did nothing to hide them; Thelema was the law for all.

A strong character who regarded the Beast as semi-divine, Küntzel liked playing Mary of Bethany to his disciples, putting Leah and Mudd up at her house at Tiefestrasse 4, in central Leipzig. But Germer chided Crowley for his 'choice' of acolytes, dismissing Leah and Mudd's 'embarrassing' hippy-like, wide-eyed wonder at what he considered mundane occurrences, perhaps encouraging Crowley's loss of interest in the two willing helpers of his 'past' life. Germer never took long to get on his high horse, but his loyalty was cast iron, even if the horse was not. Dorothy, he liked; *she* was a lady.

Tränker, meanwhile, concluded that his *Pansophia* be kept independent of the OTO. From this position, Tränker would pursue negotiations begun by Reuss with the wealthy Harvey Spencer Lewis of the US *Ancient Mystical Order Rosae Crucis* (AMORC).

A qualified triumph for Crowley, the Hohenleuben conclave sowed the seeds for the Beast's eventual German sojourn, while his notoriety began to work its own magic, even in England.

By the end of 1925, Crowley had taken a full place in the life of the world. It was nothing like what he had hoped for, or expected in his youth, but it was a place. He had not surrendered one inch of ideological territory to his enemies. He was still the Beast 666, a rallying call and standard to everyone sickened by the weaknesses of the times. He had little cash, but he had himself, and was only unimpressive to those who met him on bad days – he was often ill – or when that person was prejudiced against him. Despite penury, he seemed to move around Europe like an aerial spirit. He was Thelema and Thelema was him; a rare prophet in a doubting, disturbed world.

Was he symptom or cure?

Crowley was both: cure like with like.

*　　*　　*

On 10 November 1926, Crowley performed sex magick with the striking 28-year-old American photographer Berenice Abbott, living, at the time, in Paris.[6] Berenice took the Beast in hand for the purpose of raising money for an Egyptian trip. The venture stemmed from astral communications with the wizard Amalantrah in America. On 14 January 1918, Amalantrah had said: 'It's all in the egg.' The 'egg' was in Egypt. Considered as early as 1920, the trip had been long delayed. Crowley outlined its purpose in an undated letter of 1926 to CS Jones:

> The situation in Egypt suggests that the time may be ripe for me to abstract and convey the stele [of Revealing, held by the Egyptian Museum]. Again the Moroccan situation looks like the beginning of the fulfilment of my interpretation of Hail ye twin Warriors [from Liber AL; on 26 May 1926 the rebel Abd el Kerim surrendered to a French force]. There may be no time to lose in securing the assets of humanity [...] You have my blessing and I trust that of the most High. I spoke to Him about it only this morning.
>
> Thy Sire, A.C.[7]

Long forgotten, the Egyptian crisis of 1926 involved a diplomatic and military standoff between Great Britain and France. France had never recognized Egypt's western borders. Seeing Great Britain militarily stretched by commitments in Ethiopia and Russia, French forces from Chad pressed into thinly garrisoned areas of the Egyptian Sudan. Britain moved troops on the Ethiopian border west. By 23 February 1926, 7,500 French troops faced less than 6,000 British troops along a line over 180km long, some 40km inside the 'official' border of British Egypt. Sudanese tribes in Darfur rose against the French presence as tempers rose in parliament and the French Congress. Three months of standoff ended with the East African Accords; France officially recognized Egypt's western borders.

The tension inspired Crowley to imagine the gods had arranged the face-off between 'twin Warriors' as a suitable time to 'abstruct' the Stela 666. Clearly some kind of heist was envisaged, or was it simply to be moved to where the tomb of Ankh f-n-Khonsu had been discovered? As late as October 1927, Crowley was still planning a magical trip to Egypt with his then lover, Kasimira Bass, a Polish woman married to an Ohio salesman. Crowley asked Aiwass to declare through the I Ching the 'general formula of my Work in Egypt'. The I Ching reading included the following:

3. Go *alone* to the Sepulchre of Ankh f-n-Khonsu. Again, evil results. […]

5. The authorities may interfere with our Work. We must remain calm and at ease: avoid hurry or worry. We must assume the attitude of Priesthood – the Eternal Gods are our sufficient succour and Their Word our justification.

6. We may be constrained and in grave danger: therefore afraid to take action. But I must repent of my former (1904 E.V.) policy of trying to evade my duty to Aiwass. I must wholeheartedly accept my Mission without fear; then I can go forward with good fortune.[8]

What was meant by the 'Sepulchre of Ankh f-n-Khonsu'? It might mean the Bulak Museum itself where Rose found the stela, but this seems unlikely. The 'abstraction' then may have meant something in the order of a 'restoration' for the purpose of a magical ceremony. The reverse of the stela featured a text appropriate for the return of the spirit of the ancient priest of Month, or Mentu, to Earth. It may have been associated in Crowley's mind with something critical to power-up the new Aeon. Aiwass stipulated Kasimira would be unwelcome.

The destination may have been Thebes, close to the Valley of the Kings, where both the stela and Ankh f-n-Khonsu's mummy were discovered, possibly between 1881 and 1886, when the Egypt Exploration Fund was busy in the vicinity. An article by Amelia Edwards in *The Illustrated London News* (4 February 1882) described how Emile Brugsch, keeper of the 'Boolak' Museum, was taken to a desolate spot at Deir el-Bahari, near Thebes. By a limestone cliff, Brugsch Bey – who Crowley met at his museum in 1904 – was shown a 12m shaft, at the bottom of which was a sepulchral vault, 7m by 4m. Within were some 36 mummies: kings, queens, princes, princesses and high priests and some 6,000 individual items in glass, bronze and acacia wood. Brugsch marshalled 500 labourers to exhume and ship the contents to his museum. This was possibly the 'Sepulchre' Crowley intended to visit alone.

However, the 25th Dynasty 'Ankhafnakhons' stela and sarcophagi may not have come from the 1881 dig. They were probably found in a cache by Auguste Mariette as early as 1858, soon after acquiring control of the Antiquities Service. The Mentu priests' sarcophagi were found in an informal excavation at one or both of two shrines discovered in the temple of Hatshepsut in Deir el-Bahari, placed there in ancient times to protect them from thieves. According to the card numbered 666, which still accompanies the stela, the source was Gurnah, a temple complex and village at the entrance to the Deir el-Bahari valley. Ankh f-n-Khonsu's mummy was probably still in the sarcophagus when discovered but was dumped. Gurnah was not its original location. During the 18th and 19th centuries, villagers re-buried tomb artefacts or hid them in caves to save them from grave robbers, believing misfortune would ensue should tombs be desecrated. Exploiting the superstition, Mariette acquired a museum collection in quick time.

In October 1927, Crowley employed the I Ching to ask Aiwass about 'those things which I need to know with regard to the function of Kasimira, my comrade chosen of the Gods and sent to me to aid me in this Work to do which I am going to Egypt'.

I may now disclose what Crowley hoped to achieve. He had pondered Ab-ul-Diz's message of 1911: 'It's all in the egg.' Reinforced by Amalantrah's reference to the 'egg', Crowley connected it with full feminine emancipation. Crowley prophesied the future of Woman:

> The general aim of the Work [in Egypt] is to release the resistless stream of the Nature of Woman in the human function. She will demand freedom to flow whither she will, and the right to seek her Pleasure.
>
> This will lead at first to sterility and neglect of men, with blindness and narrowness, which will cause pain.
>
> The household system will break up, causing domestic inconvenience.
>
> The frustration of natural desires will lead to a deadlock. Woman's obstinacy will further estrange the sexes, and lead to evil. Sex is now seen to be a magical act – a sacrament.
>
> The gradual reconciliation which now begins is hampered by the industrial conditions of this new age of machines. After many disasters, a way out is found.
>
> These tendencies have been hateful to the ruling classes, who have tried severe repression. But the unconscious will of the race, moving leisurely from event to event, and its satisfaction with the trend of evolution, proves irresistible. It is a deep and sincere religious movement.
>
> The dangers of restriction, and of idealism, are now at last fully understood. Women resolve to correct their former errors on sexual questions, and establish a positive system on Thelemic lines which proves satisfactory to all.

Crowley did not make it to Egypt, though the idea was still on his mind when he added the epigram 'Frailty thy name is – Crowley' on New Year's Day 1928 to his *Magical Diary of Ankh-af-na-khonsu the Priest of Princes*. Frailty was residing Au Cadran Bleu, Fontainebleau. Reconsecrating himself to the Great Work he 'pledged to go to Egypt'. Dorothy would bring the dollars, despite Kasimira's claim on the lion's lusty lair.

TWENTY-ONE

Four Red Monks carrying a Black Goat across the Snow to Nowhere

1928–30

For every one who condemned Crowley, another found him attractive. 1925 saw Crowley's first communication with young Thomas Driberg of Christchurch College, Oxford. Driberg would go on to write the *Daily Express*'s 'William Hickey' column, serve as a Labour MP and work as a double agent for Great Britain and the USSR. Having enjoyed *The Diary of a Drug Fiend*, Driberg gushed:

> I have a frightfully difficult exam in March which I have done practically no work for so far – it was partly in connection with that, as a matter of fact, that I wanted to consult you; whether you know of any artificial stimulants […] It would be wonderful if you could come and stay with me in Oxford: but I suppose it is so lovely where you are now that you don't want to leave it.

Driberg explained to the Beast why he had joined the communist party:

> It is of course Lenin's character and achievements primarily that have attracted me to him: and I joined the CP partly because it was the one party which had the sense to see that the 19th century Liberal-Democrat idea was a sham and that the majority could always be led and controlled by an intelligent and clear-sighted minority. […] I am ready and indeed anxious to take any

steps you may think best to make your person and teachings as widely known as possible, and deem it a very great privilege to be allowed to help. [...] I have once or twice felt, little more than intuitively, that I was being watched or followed, as you warned me I might: I do not think this is mere nervousness.[1]

Driberg proved generous, a ready purse when the Beast was strapped for cash. In September 1926 Crowley tapped him for funds to 'Appear as World Teacher, with all sincerity and majesty. The Gods will add their help to our efforts.' Driberg was also an information source on communist activity. Crowley was convinced the atheist revolutionary state would sooner or later require a religion; he knew a lot about Russia.

*   *   *

The most extraordinary story concerning Crowley's Russian interests began in July 1928, when Svetoslav Roerich applied to the India Office for a British visa to visit his father, theosophist painter and writer Nicholas Roerich at Kulu, north India.[2] Since the Roerichs were suspect Soviet agents, the ensuing Foreign Office flap was dealt with by Arthur Vivian Burbury, an SIS agent recently returned from three years as third secretary with Moscow's British Legation. Burbury specialized in Soviet intrigues in Asia.[3] This is Burbury's recommendation:

> As to possible sources of information about Roerich – his connection with Russia, Thibet…Theosophists…and various 'secret' organizations. [...] leads me to think that information as to him might be obtained from an (undesirable) Englishman who has had curiously intimate knowledge of all these things. His real name is Aleister Crowley [...] I could endeavour privately to have him sounded [out] if it were thought desirable. He is a rascal and dare not show his face in England; but his knowledge of oriental evil is very deep.[4]

Burbury's suggestion did not enthuse Foreign Office official HL Baggallay. Baggallay warned it would be 'deplorable *if it became known* [my italics] that the F.O. had any communication, however remote, with

Aleister Crowley [...] who would at once go to prison if he set foot in this country'. FO colleague CM Palairet added, 'Whatever happens, do not let us approach, however remotely, Crowley.'[5] Clearly, Crowley's wartime FO memos and Superintendent Quinn's slush had been consulted.

But an approach may already have been made. Spence suspects that Crowley's pupil from late 1927, Gerald Yorke, was another Cambridge recruit to Britain's secret intelligence service. Spence cites in support Yorke's service in the Territorial Reserves, 2nd Royal Gloucester Hussars, and his 1932 posting to China as a *Reuters* correspondent, a not untypical intelligence cover. John Yorke, however, doubts his father's intelligence role at this time, partly because his father was not secretive, being open and keen to talk.[6] An extrovert personality is not an impediment to keeping secrets. That Crowley genuinely turned Yorke on to Hinduism and Western magick does not mean his first contact with Crowley was devoid of an intelligence angle. That said, Burbury's connection to Crowley perhaps owed more to Lance Sieveking, another Cambridge graduate.

According to Sieveking's *The Eye of the Beholder*, it was Sieveking who introduced Yorke to fellow wartime air ace and Cambridge graduate Burbury in 1928, incorrectly dating the Foreign Office flap to 'some years later'.[7] Sieveking asserted he had agreed to help Crowley find a publisher, taking Burbury with him to assess whether Yorke was under Crowley's influence. Yorke lent them a potentially incendiary list of Crowley's Order members (1907–14) which has not been seen since. Regardie believed the initiative was linked to Burbury's secret service connections.[8]

Crowley had already drawn up Sieveking's horoscope in Paris on 19 *March* 1928, three months *before* the Foreign Office flap, whereas Sieveking's account has him first encountering Crowley by accident, at Cassis in southern France.[9] Crowley was not in Cassis until *July* – the time of the flap. That Sieveking initiated contact is clear from Crowley's diary entry for 10 June: 'L. de Giberne Sieveking Union Club Carlton H[ouse] Terrace London is here. 12th he consulted me. Said he had sent out a S.O.S. call to Gods – and then came here for no reason.' On 6 August, while exploring the mountains near Grenoble with Kasimira Bass, Crowley heard from Sieveking again.[10] Friendly with FO-man Burbury, Sieveking's interest was unlikely to have been solely intellectual.

As we shall see, between 1930 and 1931, Crowley spied for the British in Berlin, and Yorke was in a loop that included the head of the Special Branch.[11] But why in the first place would Burbury have suggested Crowley's value to the Roerich-communist Tibet infiltration case?

Burbury would have been familiar with the names of Gurdjieff and suspected pro-Turkish spy, John Godolphin Bennett. This would connect with Crowley's visit to Gurdjieff's Fontainebleau establishment the previous year. More significantly, there were two Soviet officials involved with Asian intrigues of interest to both Burbury and Crowley: Dr Aleksandr Vasil'evich Barchenko and Gleb Ivanovich Bokii.

Barchenko, 'Bolshevik professor of the occult', was a Martinist Freemason, one-time student of Gurdjieff and, like many theosophists and synarchists, believed in a Himalayan 'Shambhala', or Agartha, sub-terranean home to adepts of a lost civilization.[12] Barchenko believed the enlightened beings were the original *communists*. Communism then was the *social* manifestation of an esoteric secret.

Only dimwits and pedants found communism attractive on account of its economic theory; its magnetism lay in the promise to fulfil a secular hope: a rationalist apocalypse of justice, even 'spiritual' joy in a selfless mass. It was a replacement religion without a religion, hence Crowley's interest. Barchenko reckoned a spiritual component could be revealed for the Bolshevik cognoscenti through a mythology of Shambhala. The Soviet's new powers should be employed to locate the adepts of Shambhala: communism's ancestors and secret spiritual guides. Crowley knew something of the kind was going on; his World Teacher campaign sought to stunt theosophical fantasies.

Gleb Ivanovich Bokii chief of the Special Department (*Spetsotdel*) of the secret police, the Cheka,[13] liked Barchenko's ideas. Bokii was himself into Rosicrucianism, Martinism and Tantric sex ritual.[14] Barchenko took charge of facilities at Moscow's Institute of Experimental Medicine with a brief to see what ESP, remote viewing, telekinesis and hypnosis could offer the intelligence effort. It was not all work. The men formed an occult lodge, the 'United Labour Brotherhood' (*Edinow trudoe bratstvo*). When 'purged' by Stalin in the 1930s, the accusation was that the lodge smoke-screened contacts with Far East British intelligence.

According to Spence, it was Barchenko and Bokii who were behind OGPU's exploitation of theosophist, mystic, artist, and explorer Nicholas Roerich – 'OGPU' being the Soviet Joint State Political Directorate (*Ob'edinennoe Gosudarstvennoe Politicheskoe Upravlenie*), forerunner of the KGB. It was Barchenko and Bokii who wanted Roerich's son Svetoslav to obtain a British visa to visit his father in India. Roerich, who had left Russia after being offered a senior post in the arts by the Bolsheviks, *also* believed in Shambhala. Backed by US theosophist and liberal-arts money, Roerich went in search of the mythical 'axis of the world' in 1924. OGPU agents disguised as religious pilgrims joined his expedition to the Himalayas; they too sought the mahatmas of Shambhala.[15]

Before embarking on the quest, Roerich met a Soviet diplomat in Berlin, ostensibly to obtain a visa to enter Altai-Himalaya, Soviet controlled territory. After visiting Egypt and Ceylon with Lithuanian theosophist Vladimir Shibayev, Roerich returned to India to prepare the trek. Roerich's supporters, especially those of a Christian-theosophist outlook, are uncomfortable with what was plain to British and Chinese officials. While appearing a pacific, American-backed mission to bring knowledge to the West, it enjoyed secret Soviet sanction. In Roerich's mind, the 'enlightenment' of communism was mystically joined to the eventual spiritual enlightenment of the world. One can imagine Crowley's view of this idea. In fact, Crowley left us a plain statement of what he thought of this theosophist-inspired fantasy; too plain for many to notice.

*   *   *

An oil painting has survived. Easily dismissed as a perverse fantasy of Crowley's, it is an ironic satire on the concept of the Roerich expedition and the designs of theosophist-influenced Soviet officials. The painting is called *Four Red Monks carrying a Black Goat across the Snow to Nowhere*, and shows exactly that.

Across a snow-ridden valley, we see the dim image of a fantastic dream-castle atop a distant mountain. It is, I am sure, Crowley's comment on the Shambhala myth (see plate 36). The four red monks are of course Soviet agents dressed as pilgrims. They carry a 'black goat', a polyvalent image for anything ranging from Besant's Esoteric Section of the TS to the Black Lodge of totalitarianism, to insipid theosophist Christianity, to Roerich himself. And they are going literally 'to nowhere'. In Crowley's vision, they are all wasting their time. There is no mystic Shambhala. They are on the wrong path altogether. He, Crowley, is the mahatma they should be beating a path to. He is the black and white goat, Baphomet, offering scientific illuminism, sent by the *real* Secret Chiefs, not a bunch of fantasizing theosophists in the USSR.

Chinese authorities did not share Crowley's vision, but they did see Roerich as a spy, detaining him in awful conditions for four months. Roerich did not get to Lhasa, but he did visit Himis. And here at Himis another illuminating thread joins Aleister Crowley to the Roerich expedition of 1924–8.

*   *   *

Detained by the Chinese governor, Roerich not only sought Shambhala-type myths in Khotan, but also found at Himis 'evidence' to support *The Unknown Life of Jesus Christ*, a work first published in 1887 by shadowy Russian journalist, Nicolas Notovitch. The book enjoyed favour in the West because it purported to prove that Jesus spent his 'lost years' in India and in Tibet: joy to theosophists! The book insisted that the Western view of Jesus being opposed by Jews was wrong; the villain was *Boss Pilate*.

In *The Unknown Life of Jesus Christ*, Jesus is presented as a mahatma with some modern views about the role of women, the working class, and human potential. Notovitch said he had had it taken down by an interpreter from original manuscripts. Challenged by Oxford orientalist

Professor Max Müller, Notovitch challenged anyone to go to remote Himis in 'little Tibet', part of British India, and check his story. As told in *The Lost Years of Jesus* by Elizabeth Clare Prophet, a mystery man picked up the gauntlet.[16] One J Archibald Douglas, First Professor of English Literature and History at Agra's government college in India, would put a spanner in Notovitch's works.[17]

In April 1896, the journal *Nineteenth Century* published Douglas's findings, findings so sensational that *The New York Times* swiftly ran an article headed 'Hamis [*sic*] knows not "ISSA"' with the by-line 'CLEAR PROOF THAT NOTOVITCH IS A ROMANCER' on 19 April. Readers learned how a scrupulous investigation by Douglas at the remote Himis monastery in 1895 left Notovitch's story in tatters. Douglas's conclusion that the 'Issa' story was completely fabricated disconcerted theosophists. It disconcerted the author of *The Lost Years of Jesus*, whose book asserted the reality of 'Issa' in India – but, perhaps, Douglas never existed. Elizabeth Clare Prophet observed that his post at Agra was 'just about all we know about Mr Douglas'. The refutation could be safely refuted! Little did Prophet know that James Archibald Douglas did surely live and breathe and could be found in the 1891 British Census, dwelling at 5 Cary Parade, Torbay Road, Torquay, as James A Douglas 'teacher of arts and philology' with 'Edward A Crowley', scholar.[18] I am delighted to inform readers that the man who transformed Crowley's life, at whose brief but inspiring agency the 'nightmare world of Christianity' vanished, was the same Oxford man and oriental traveller who, after being dismissed by Tom Bond Bishop, went on to dismiss Notovitch's Life of 'Saint Issa'!

Crowley must have known about this story. In his book *The World's Tragedy* he includes a dialogue between 'Alexander' (himself) and 'Issa' (Jesus).[19] The spelling 'Issa' (with double 's') for 'Jesus' is a feature of Notovitch's text.

There is always more to Crowley than meets the eye.

Did Douglas discuss Notovitch's book with young Crowley, encouraging doubt in Crowley's mind as to the verification of 'gospel' materials? '*Yes*', would appear to be the answer. Tom Bond Bishop had gone through Douglas's books and found incriminating evidence of the tutor's unsuitability for a Plymouth Brethren-educated young man for whom the King James Bible was the sole textual authority for life.

We may be confident about Crowley's opinion, were he asked for it, concerning materials attributed to 'Saint Issa' published in Roerich's subsequent books. Two quotations from Roerich suffice:

> The writings of the lamas say that Christ was not killed by the Jews but by the representatives of the government. The empire and the wealthy killed the Great Teacher who carried light to the working and poor ones. The path of attainment of light! [20]

In *Himalaya*, Roerich attributes the following to 'Issa', its provenance, *note*, from 'Another source – historically less established':

> Jesus said to them, 'I came to show human possibilities. What has been created by me, all men can create. And that which I am, all men will be. These gifts belong to all nations and all lands – for this is the bread and the water of life.'

Crowley would recognize at once the fakery. Both quotations demonstrate that the 'Issa' joined to the Shambhala revelation by Roerich was clearly in the service of Soviet ideology. Jesus was a capitalist's victim. There is no metaphysical peculiarity about Jesus; he is a man among men, a symbol of what 'all men can create'. It *looks* like spiritual fayre, but it is materialistic communism. Issa is a communist fake, and Roerich was an agent of the USSR. Crowley was indeed useful to the British government on these issues. The 'oriental evil', or 'black goat', of which he had a deep knowledge, was not *his*.

Incidentally, students of irony should appreciate that the US dollar bill received its famous mystical 'seal' of the pyramid and all-seeing eye in 1935 at the specific behest of Nicholas Roerich, friend of the USSR, having persuaded senior US official Henry Wallace as to the supreme significance of mystical insight in government. One might speculate that the 'All-seeing Eye' was (and is?) that of the KGB! Conspiracy theorists obsessed with Masonry, beware!

On 19 June 1929, in New York, Roerich gave a lecture on the 'Cult of Shambhala', asserting that humanity will change through the mastery of 'psychic energy over cosmic energy'. These ideas have entered pop culture through films like *Lost Horizon* and the family TV series *The Champions*. Mayor Walker honoured Roerich at a special reception at City Hall the next day. The Nicholas Roerich Museum officially opened on 17 October 1929, one week before the Great Stock Market Crash. On 15 April 1935, the 'Roerich Pact' was signed in Washington DC by Henry Wallace and other foreign heads of state. Roosevelt declared that the pact 'possesses a spiritual significance far greater than the text itself' – like the *Unknown Life of Jesus Christ*, no doubt.

In 1957, Roerich's son George returned to the USSR. His second son, Svetoslav Roerich, died in Russia in 1993 after helping to establish the Roerich Cultural Center in Moscow.

And *Aleister Crowley* was 'undesirable'!

*   *   *

French mystic René Guénon began to observe Crowley in the late 1920s. Initially considering his significance overstated, Guénon later decided Crowley was significant after all, as a British intelligence asset. According to Spence, Guénon linked Crowley to a figure called Colonel Ettington.[21] Was 'Ettington' Percy Thomas Etherton, Indian Army? Etherton had met Crowley's friend Feilding while serving in Egypt. As His Majesty's 'political resident' in Kashgar, Chinese Turkestan, close to the Soviet border (1918-24), Etherton ran agents to gather intelligence on Soviet intrigues. When Roerich passed through Kashgar, not long after Etherton's departure, Roerich noted the British Consul's helpfulness. The Consul had probably been primed to soften Roerich up for information. Returning to London, Etherton would have shared Burbury's interest in Soviet plans for Tibet.

What assistance, if any, Crowley may have offered the Foreign Office or the Secret Intelligence Service regarding the Roerichs and Soviet *Shambhalosophy* is unknown. We do know Crowley closely followed developments in Moscow. Fellow bisexual, *New York Times* correspondent

Walter Duranty (who married Crowley's lover Jane Chéron), enjoyed an open door to the Soviet leadership. Duranty wrote to Crowley in January 1930:

> What I mean is that anyone who has not been here lately cannot understand how completely what you call the 'spiritual' is eliminated from Russian life at present. I don't say for a moment it has ceased to exist or won't come back – perhaps all the stronger from repression – but for the time being the Kremlin won't hear of it. And what the Kremlin won't hear of doesn't count.[22]

Crowley had vowed to spread the word of Thelema by all means possible. In April 1930, Crowley sent his passport papers to the USSR Consul; what came of Crowley's plans is unknown.[23] It was apparently just this kind of interest that led French security services to rescind his residency rights in 1929, and why in that year he became explicitly involved with British secret service interests in Germany.

TWENTY-TWO

Shitland

1927–30

In 1929, the French government rescinded Crowley's permission to live in France. Effectively, he was expelled. Why? Crowley had been living on French territory since 1923. His habits had not changed in that time; he had many women friends and practised sex magick with most of them. He was prescribed heroin as a gout sufferer takes *allopurinol*. France was famously tolerant of exiles.

Evidence suggests the *refus de séjour* came as the climax to a chicane of negative circumstances with espionage the decisive factor.

*　　*　　*

Gerald Joseph Yorke of 9 Mansfield Street, W1 was the 26-year-old son of Vincent Wodehouse Yorke, a landed Cambridge don who owned Birmingham ceramics firm H Pontifex Ltd. First invited to meet Crowley on 29 December 1927 at the Hotel Foyot opposite the Luxembourg Palace, this 'promising pupil' spent the new year absorbing magical instruction while the priest of Mentu's latest incarnation attended to Kasimira Bass,[1] who had received the secret of sex magick, and a social circle that included Dadaist photographer Man Ray, US bibliophile Montgomery Evans, Langston and Claudia Moffett (Mr Moffet was a journalist and painter),[2] Blanche Legrange, and ghost-story writer, Mary Freeman.[3]

Soon enmeshed in Crowley's world of cross-symbolism, Yorke received a card on 4 April: '*Magick*. Wonderful developments. It seems there is a chance of recovering the Book M (found in breast of C.R.C. in

Vault.).' This followed Kasimira's vision of a 'Book', leading Crowley to ask: 'Can the Book be the Book M found on the breast of Our Father C.R.C.?' The 'Book M' was a legendary text of Rosicrucian science, and 'Father C.R.C.' the movement's founder. What Crowley was actually saying was that he wanted Yorke to get *his* 'Book M', *Magick*, published.[4]

In July, Crowley, Yorke and Kasimira toured the Midi, discussing magick and locations for a new GHQ. Yorke joined the A.˙.A.˙. at Cassis; his motto: *Volo Intelligere*, 'I will to understand'. He left for London on the 26th, having agreed to put £10 in Crowley's bank account every week. With acumen rare to Crowley's circle, Yorke shouldered Crowley's finances, and Crowley took an apartment at 55 Avenue Suffren in September.

*   *   *

Magick in Theory and Practice would be the first book of its kind in English since Francis Barrett's *The Magus* of 1801. It should have been a publishing event. Pursuing positive PR, Crowley hired German-American, sometime actor, Carl de Vidal Hundt; publicist, press agent, editor in chief of the American Press Syndicate, Paris. Dropping the 'd' from his name, Hunt was also a 'fixer' for rich Parisians. Yorke paid him £20 a month and organized a 'publication fund'. In August, George Cecil Jones declined Yorke's invitation to contribute. Frater 132, Wilfred T Smith, sent £20 from Los Angeles. Smith would become honorary Grand Master of the North American OTO in 1932. Martha Küntzel wrote from Leipzig: 'We are very poor in Germany, and those that have money enough don't think of giving it for things for which they have no interest.'[5] Küntzel was having problems translating *Magick's* chapter 'On the Bloody Sacrifice'; thinking 'people will be reminded of the ritual murders of the Jews', considering it stupid to risk publication over things requiring 'intuitive understanding'.

The 'offending passages' still cause problems. When Crowley refers to 'sacrificing children' on dozens of occasions, he means contraception and sacramental sex. Crowley believed that much occult lore about 'blood' was a euphemism for semen. While Crowley trusted intelligence to read between the lines and see the leg-pull at the expense of his 'black magic' image, Yorke had a hell of a job trying to convince people that Crowley could be read without incurring Jehovah's wrath.

Meanwhile, the young Francis Israel Regardie, who had met Karl Germer in New York,[6] headed for Paris to work as Crowley's secretary. Things were looking up. Hunt appeared to be on the case, writing to Crowley: '*Tannhaüser* is *great!*' So long as Crowley – or Yorke – was paying, everything Crowley wrote was 'great'. But was it publishable?

Introducing himself to Yorke in September, Hunt was positive:

> Mr AC, whom I have known for some years and whose work I esteem very highly, has informed me that you will be in Paris some time this month to consult with him re the publication of his memoirs [...] to give the reader a true and interesting account of the life of this truly remarkable man. Thus properly transcribed, the memoirs of Mr AC, I am sure, will reach a large public throughout the world and create a big market for all anterior works by the same author.[7]

On the copy of this letter, Yorke added, years later: 'It shows Hunt's attitude when he was still receiving £20 a month.' Hunt went to London, writing to Crowley from 58 Bloomsbury Street:

> Nothing doing with [Jonathan] Cape. He says the MS [*Confessions* manuscript] is a dangerous proposition. Too many libels. Suggests boiling it down to 120,000 [words] and publishing it privately in Paris. [...] Most newspapers like you. They wonder why you didn't attack the Daily Express. I said you wouldn't *think* of suing a British journal. You're a friend of the newsboys, see? [...] On the whole there is every reason to hope for an early success *somehow*! Your *Net* [published as *Moonchild* in 1929] is great but unpublishable. Owing to libellous characterizations throughout.[8]

Regardie arrived at Crowley's plush apartment in October 1928. Remaining with Crowley for three years, he first had to adapt to women beyond his conservative experience. After Crowley's death, Regardie reminisced with Yorke about a shared fear Crowley might pounce on *them*. He never did. Pity he was not as astute about Hunt. This note from Hunt must have annoyed Crowley intensely:

Dear Crowley,

Kasimira is going home with us for the night. Don't worry.

Call us up in the morning.

H.[9]

On 3 November, Crowley reported in his diary: 'Kasimira bolted (I suppose finally […]) The Lord hath given & the Lord hath taken away: Blessed be the name of the Lord!' In a letter to Frater 132 about her sudden departure Crowley coined the dictum: 'Knowledge is experience made conscious of itself.'[10]

Five days later, Marie Therese de Miramar appeared in Crowley's diary. Formerly married to a man named Sanchez, Marie was a creole Cuban, born in Nicaragua in 1894. She seemed composed of the right stuff: 'She has absolutely the right ideas of Magick & knows some Voodoo.' By mid-month, Crowley was ecstatic: 'She is marvellous beyond words, but excites me too much, so that I cannot prolong.' Twelve days later, Crowley recorded a 'Voodoo-orgie. The most wonderful climax in years!'

Apart from wasting Yorke's money, Hunt negotiated between rich American widow Mabelle Correy and a deported cousin of King Alfonso XIII of Spain, the drug-dealing Don Louis Ferdinand de Bourbon-Orléans. Hunt tried to get Crowley to compile a faked horoscope to encourage the lady in the match, but chivalrous Aleister advised the lady to steer clear. Such situations always roused his indignation. Crowley's diary for 11 December was succinct: 'Found out Hundt – dismissed him.'

The next day, Hunt informed Yorke that Crowley's publicity was a lost cause while Regardie wrote requesting the return of Crowley's books post haste. Hunt replied:

Dear Crowley.

Thanks for this amusing note. You *can* be funny after all. Yes, whatever books I have, – a pair of No 4's [*Book 4*] I think, will be posted to you post haste.

All the best to you, old bean.

Hunt[11]

Within the week, Hunt's tone changed:

> To safeguard my friends, I am sorry to say, I will have to place the whole matter before the French Ministry of the Interior and the *Sûreté Générale* which will communicate with Scotland Yard, the editors of *John Bull* and the *Sunday Express* and all persons in England and America who have at any time been connected with him. [Crowley] will be submitted for investigation by the *Sûreté Générale*, special department for foreign undesirables.[12]

Hunt declined to say anything to the respectable Mr Yorke about the marriage scam:

> My dear Yorke
>
> […] he addressed a letter to my club, one of the most exclusive in Paris, stating his opinion of a club which had 'such a questionable character' as me amongst its members. I could have sent him to gaol for denigration but the club never pays any attention to such letters. Instead I wrote to you on Dec. 16 that I would have to notify the police.
>
> Please draw your own conclusions and wash your hands of the man and all his money affairs with poor deluded women. Read the stories in *John Bull* and *The Sunday Express*. I now believe them to be true, absolutely. And what is more, I know exactly how the man works. […] Whatever troubles come to him, he will only have himself to blame.[13]

Hunt may have bluffed about selling Crowley down the river, he may not. There was more bad breath directed at Crowley than that exhaled by Hunt.

According to Monseigneur Jouin's review, the *Revue Internationale des Sociétés Secrètes* (*RISS*), the A.'.A.'. and the OTO were behind a 'great conspiracy' of Jews, Freemasons and Communists against the Catholic Church. Marco Pasi has analysed the texts concerning Crowley, beginning in February 1929 with 'L'Ordre Equestre du Saint-Sepulcre, M Wellhoff et les Hautes Loges' by *Lancelot*:

> Now is the time to cease concealing certain revealing facts. It is time to remind all people that behind the political Masonry of the Grand Orient and the symbolic Masonry of the Grand Lodge, as well as behind the so-called regular Lodges of England and America, there are in fact background-Lodges or Higher Sects, little known and consequently all the more formidable: the true Synagogue of Satan, obedient to a Supreme Occult Power.[14]

Roger Duguet made a similar point in 'La querelle des Hauts Grades' (3 March).[15] Duguet dedicated a section to the 'Satanist' Aleister Crowley, arguing that since all Masonry was 'irregular' from the point of view of Catholicism, the defence against the *RISS*'s charges made by Grand Orient and Grand Lodge masons that fringe orders like the OTO were irregular was meaningless. No 'regularity' existed beyond the pope's spiritual authority since the Church had been regularized by Jesus Christ. 'In short, like it or not, an Aleister Crowley exists; he is a Mason and chief of a branch of Masonry, just as regularly Masonic as Calvinism is Protestant without being Lutheran.' Pasi has called Duguet's reasoning 'specious'.

We do not know if such opposition incited Crowley's problems with the French security apparatus, but the timing looks suspicious. A police inspector appeared at Crowley's apartment on 17 January. He noticed Crowley's modish coffee machine and, Clouseau-like, concluded it distilled drugs. The Prefecture fell on Crowley. Why? First possibility: Crowley's reputation in espionage. His Deuxième Bureau file retains the original card note that he was 'an Irish agitator', adding that he had worked for Berlin during WW1, asserting in his defence that he was working for the British.[16] Crowley's file was taken by the Germans in WW2, stashed in Moscow after the war, and repatriated in the 1990s. It might once have contained more. Curiously, a Soviet report on Crowley's expulsion from France states that it was 'for espionage and the good of France'.[17] The French government was sensitive to subversion at the time. On 21 February, Leon Trotsky was refused asylum in Paris. According to Yorke, Crowley wanted to get Trotsky behind Thelema.

Crowley's dealings with Hunt may have suggested involvement with Don Alfonso's drugs racket; that would not have helped. Regardie's view was that *his sister* was responsible. Nicknamed 'Nosey Parker' in Regardie's *Eye in the Triangle*, Nosey did not want her brother to leave New York, having read about sex in one of his copies of *The Equinox*. She contacted the French Embassy who contacted Paris reminding them of Crowley's expulsion from Italy. Supporting the moral line is the fact that when Crowley sought support from the British Embassy, help was denied as the French order was for reasons of 'morals'. A summary has survived, the originals allegedly destroyed.[18]

Hostility probably centred on espionage. To the Deuxième Bureau, Crowley might have been working either for the Germans or the British. Stimulated by the Hundt scandal, and, possibly, Hélène Fraux, based with the wealthy Chapin family in Detroit, the moral angle provided justification. Family tradition has it that Hélène visited Crowley in Paris, directing him to look from his apartment window to a man under a streetlamp. She claimed he was a security agent and promised Crowley his life would be made a misery unless he surrendered guardianship of Lulu.[19] To all this we may add the pro-fascist *RISS* linking Crowley to a German-based secret society.

On 5 March a policeman called with a summons to the Prefecture. Marie and Regardie showed up while an Inspector called on the sick Crowley with a *refus de séjour*, '*Pour le Préfet de Police – Le Chef du Service des Étrangers*'. Coming from the 'foreigners department' suggests Hunt fulfilled his threat.[20] Crowley's diary refers to a 'Thunderbolt of crazy cops'. Marie and Regardie left for England on 9 March. Yorke waited in vain at Tilbury docks. Denied entry, they were 'barred from Shitland', as Crowley put it.

On 11 March, Regardie and Marie took rooms at the Hotel des Colonies, Rue des Croisades, Brussels. Crowley advised Regardie:

> You might go and see Paul at the Palace Hotel [Brussels] he used to be a night porter at the Berkeley London. He has a string of little country pubs, one of which might suit you while you vegetate – and *re-type the Memoirs* [Crowley's Autobiography].[21]

Optimistic, Crowley pulled out the stops: 'Miracles now happening daily. Sending you 1000F on Tuesday. [...] Expect to see a really first class lawyer with political pull to-morrow: one who can phone the Prefecture and get you back within 24 hours: Yes: get your consuls to protest formally against expulsion. Say it's a death sentence, and that no one dares even pretend that you have done anything wrong. If de M[iramar] can't stay in Belgium, send her to Frau Eastlake 60 allée Guntersburg, Frankfurt à M[ain] with a letter demanding hospitality for her in the name of the Order. I am pulling many strings; one or other will ring the bell.' Frau Eastlake was Crowley's old girlfriend *Soror Fidelis*. They had kept in touch.

*   *   *

'Victory!' declared Crowley in his diary when the first group of signatures of *Magick* arrived from Paris's Lecram Press on 12 April. He had feared spiritual enemies would crush the project. *Paris Midi* published Crowley's story on 15 April, with 'Sir Aleister Crowley' on the cover. An article about espionage added glamour. 'Sir Crowley' quit Paris the next day in 'a blaze of publicity'. 'Seeing reporters and being photographed all day' he informed Yorke, certain the publicity would benefit *Magick*'s marketing strategy. Yorke had created a publishing syndicate with Edward Goldston, Robin Thynne and Percy Reginald ('Inky') Stephensen, an Australian editor, while sounding out possible resistance from the Home Secretary to importing *Magick*.

In Brussels on the 17th, Crowley was cheered by the sight of 'Articles going by the dozen. Hear that U.S.A. has already had lots of wild fables.' The continental press splashed the Crowley intrigue and expulsion story everywhere, but England remained aloof. Crowley assessed the problem:

> To succeed in England it is only necessary to keep doing badly
> what someone was once crucified there for doing well.[22]

Yorke assessed Crowley's reception by security services. Lieutenant Colonel John Fillis Carré Carter, deputy assistant commissioner of the Metropolitan Police, was on the case. A formidable ex-India police official, Colonel Carter, head of Special Branch, was responsible for sections 'SS1' and 'SS2', that is, Scotland Yard's liaison with the SIS (Secret Intelligence Service) and MI5 respectively. A wartime member of MI5 section G, Carter had known Sir Robert Nathan (1868-1921), who may have been aided by agent Crowley in the USA.[23]

Meanwhile, an article by A Taranne in the Mayday edition of the *RISS* warned against Reuss's 'Satanist Freemasons' – the OTO.[24] Crowley, readers were assured, drank the blood of children and burned women alive. Regardie was defined as a 'judéo-américain'. Further articles appeared throughout 1929, for example, 'Atlantis Again',[25] 'Aleister Crowley',[26] 'Essay on a double symbol – What then is the Dragon?',[27] 'A new German High Lodge'.[28] Carter's initial views of Crowley were probably influenced by the extreme right wing press, for his acquaintances included the anti-semitic historian Nesta Webster who shared the conspiracy theories found in the *RISS*.

Where Carter's priorities and those of right-wing conspiracy theorists coincided was communist subversion. Here Crowley was a potential asset. According to Spence, Crowley became a 'shared asset' between Carter, fellow Special Branch 'Red-Hunter' Guy Maynard Liddell, and Spence's hypothetical SIS liaison, Gerald Yorke. If Yorke was not an agent, he could have been an asset. On this analysis, Carter was 'a cut-out to mask SIS involvement'.[29] Spence adds: 'Curiously, SIS's list of Crowley "Press References" stops dead in 1929 with a single article on the French expulsion, resuming only in 1947 with a brief announcement of his [Crowley's] death.'[30]

This analysis makes plausible some of the events in and after May 1929, starting with Crowley and de Miramar in limbo in Belgium. Yorke maintained he was summoned by Carter to warn him about the disreputable Crowley. Perhaps Carter had seen reflections of the *RISS* material in *The Patriot*, a British right-wing periodical. Carter had undoubtedly heard from Hélène Fraux and she had heard from him.

According to Yorke, he asked Carter whether he actually *knew* the Beast. Shouldn't a personal meeting occur before judgements were passed on a man whose true story might enlighten him, whose true character might impress him? In other words, Crowley could be advantageous to Carter. This occurred, note, at the time Feilding replied to Yorke's enquiry concerning Crowley's wartime loyalties. Was Yorke doing homework, clarifying Crowley's intelligence background? Crowley had probably pointed Yorke in Feilding's direction to support his case. In spite of Carter's interface with MI5 and SIS, not all intelligence sections knew each other's business.

On 20 May, Carter wrote from 8 Park Mansions SW1 to invite Yorke and Crowley to dinner, adding: 'Would he mind my inquisitiveness?'[31] Significantly, Carter provided the £6 to pay for Crowley's trip from Ostend to London, stipulating that Crowley must believe the money came from Yorke. The arrangement tied Yorke in with Carter's plans. They all met outside the Langham Hotel on 11 June at 7.20pm.[32] The day after the meeting, Carter wrote to Yorke:

> An interesting evening! but I still adhere to the opinion that whatever troubles and misfortunes your friend has gone through he has only got himself to blame for them, and that if he wishes to further his art he had better drop – if I may say so – the poseur attitude and elaborate more the art side when there may still be time for him to make a name for himself in another direction than the unenviable one that he has hitherto followed.[33]

This is nicely coded by Carter to cover himself, clearly releasing 'your friend' from overt suspicion, while suggesting Crowley should avoid becoming so extravagant an object of public interest – he should be discreet – if he wished to pursue his 'art', a word that may mean several things. In fact, Crowley impressed Carter, and 'C', as Crowley referred to him, continued to enjoy his company. Crowley's comment: 'Dined with Col. Carter 7:30–11:30. All clear.' *Phew!*

Crowley was back.

*   *   *

As excitement mounted, he rashly proposed to Marie, then, on 21 June, considered criminal proceedings against *John Bull*. While the I Ching recommended action, Crowley's pocket did not. He attended a meeting at the Mandrake Press, 41 Museum St at 5pm where Yorke took the upswing as a signal to launch Mandrake's programme. A week later, Crowley was paid £50 advance for his 'autohagiography'; booksellers snubbed a masterpiece. *Moonchild* would be published in October. Delighted to be a literary figure in London once more, Crowley moved to 'Georgian House', Bury St, St James's, and on 2 July was guest at a 'great party' given in the capital by social rebel, publisher and poet, Nancy Cunard, whom he had met on the Riviera in 1926 when Rex Ingram was directing an MGM film of Maugham's novel *The Magician* at the Victorine Studios. Nancy was now living with black jazz pianist Henry Crowder, whom she had discovered playing in the Hotel Luna in Venice with Eddie South and his Alabamians the previous year. The relationship shocked Lady Cunard, Nancy's mother; it did not shock Aleister Crowley.

On 2 July, Crowley was featured in *The Daily Sketch*. Run by Carter's close friend Harold Harmsworth, Lord Rothermere, Rothermere had worked in government propaganda during the war. The article called Crowley 'one of the most interesting and talked of men in Europe' denouncing 'exaggerated and ridiculous' stories about him: 'Actually, he is a very brilliant and interesting man who has travelled all over the world observing religious practices and philosophy.' The article even plugged Crowley's Mandrake publications.

On 4 July, Crowley entertained Yorke with Miss Henderson to dinner. Wyn Henderson, Aquila Press publisher, editor and socialite, helped

Nancy Cunard with the Hours Press. Aquila's demise in the wake of the Great Crash of 1929 siphoned money from the Mandrake.

On 10 July, Crowley made a mysterious journey via Antwerp to Brussels, meeting one 'O'Byrne', adding '*Eire go bragh*' (Ireland Forever!) to his diary entry. According to Spence, summer 1929 saw expatriate Italian anarchists in Brussels plotting Mussolini's assassination. Crowley's rumoured connection to a 1926 plot may have gained him the plotters' confidence. Was spying a way of paying Carter back? Carter penetrated the plot and sent details to Mussolini's secret police. Returning from Brussels, a man in a false uniform stole a mailbag containing a registered letter to Marie. It was recovered, minus Marie's letter. Someone was spying on Crowley.

* * *

Partying in July with Montague Summers, astrologer Gabriel Dee[34] and the Germers, Crowley launched 'IT'. What was 'It'? 'IT' was nothing less than, well, *IT!* Crowley passed himself off as a *maître de parfum*. One part ambergris, one part musk, and one part civet, *IT* allegedly transformed the wearer into an irresistible sex magnet. 'All must be natural products', insisted Crowley ahead of his time.[35] He hoped to raise cash with *IT*, but the girls didn't want *IT*, or so it was said.

The IT-Boy discussed 'folding in' the *Thelema Verlag* (which had published translations of his work) into a 'pool' he hoped would take over the Mandrake. Interested, Germer then took Marie back with him to Germany, where, Carter informed Yorke: 'He [Crowley] will have to marry the lady,' adding, 'I am glad to hear that some of his (Crowley's) writings are likely to be published.'[36] Crowley gave Yorke power of attorney.

Good old Martha Küntzel did her heartfelt OTO hospitality act again, this time for Maria de Miramar, who hardly knew whether she was coming or going. An unstoppable train shunted Crowley towards something he would soon regret. Marrying his 'high priestess of voodoo' by special licence in Leipzig on 16 August, he later attributed the marriage to premature senility.

Back in London, a curious diary entry appears on 24 August:

> Met again Col. R.J.R. Brown 12 *bis* rue du Maréchal Joffre.
> Flouiller S[eine]-et-O[ise]. He came in at 6. [?]
>   A wild supper with P.R.S. and Goldston, Nina Hamnett and
> Nell Collard.

Crowley appears to have attended a meeting with a 'Colonel Brown' at a flat 'near Versailles', then returned for a wild supper with friends.[37] Two possible explanations present themselves. Crowley had gone to France incognito a day or so before, then returned fast by train, or, he been flown to Paris from say, Croydon or RAF Northolt and flown back. Who was Colonel Brown? Crowley had dinner with 'C' – Col. Carter – on 6 September, followed by a long talk till midnight at his flat. The diary then records: 'פ מ Ξ.' That is: *Mem*, *Pé* (Hebrew), *Xsi* (Greek): MPX or XPM. Does it mean '10pm', or something else? Spence is convinced the occasion marked a 'debriefing' related to his encounter with 'Colonel Brown', apparently in France 12 days earlier. Crowley was supposed to be banned from France.

On 19 September Carter wrote to Yorke from Scotland Yard SW1: 'My regards to Crowley and will he continue his efforts (and you too) – I think it might afford much amusement.' Crowley then informed Regardie: 'The plan is to absorb K[rishnamurti] showing that 666 is the Master whom he claimed would inspire him. Work on the proof that he is preaching 93.' He wrote again: 'Keep in close touch with the movement [Krishnamurti] and in his doings and sayings and missionary journeys: and keep me posted.'[38] While Crowley wanted to absorb all esoteric movements, Carter was suspicious of theosophist activity, providing the Beast with information concerning Theosophical Society financing, Krishnamurti's whereabouts, and the names of the Executive Committee of the Theosophical Educational Trust, including Crowley's old Golden Dawn enemy, FL Gardner of 5 Craven Road, Harlesden.

On 7 October, Carter wrote to Yorke about an unnamed person hostile to Crowley: 'You have got to remember, if a man insists upon calling himself bad for many years, he must not complain if people take him at his own valuation. I do not, but then I am different, I have met him.'[39]

Just as things seemed to be getting right, Marie showed signs of the delusions that would land her in a mental hospital: 'She makes imbecile accusations about Nurse Walsh – that I am making love to her and – sometimes – that we are trying to poison her – she "has witnesses"', Yorke heard to his dismay. Crowley, Marie and Regardie, moved into Ivy Cottage, Knockholt, Kent.

*   *   *

Twenty years after Crowley was 'barred' from Cambridge, Oxford tried the same trick. An invitation to lecture to the university's little Poetry Society in February 1930 led Catholic Chaplain Father Ronald Knox to threaten members with rustication; Oxford undergraduates were simply too impressionable for the demon Crowley.

For his lecture, Crowley pondered the case of medieval aristocrat Gilles de Rais, accused of murdering a castle full of children in pursuit of alchemical secrets. Reflecting on his own experience, Crowley asked: was the notorious Gilles a scientist fallen victim to superstitious rumour, just like him? With heavy irony, Crowley suggested society was still psychologically medieval: 'The more "religious" people are, the more they believe in black magick.'[40]

While the 'banned lecture' was sold by sandwich men, Crowley turned up for an *Oxford Mail* interview. Not a publicity triumph, it reinforced Crowley's dark image; he couldn't win.

The story of the ban is told, with bias, in Arthur Calder-Marshall's *The Magic of My Youth*.[41] A friend of Neuburg and member of the Poetry Society, Calder-Marshall relates meeting Crowley in Ivy Cottage, surrounded by Crowley's psychedelic expressionism. He expatiates on Crowley's 'rheumy eyes' whose hypnotic powers seemed on the wane as the Beast plied the young man with brandy, sending his girlfriend off with Marie for a walk. Wheezing from severe asthma, Crowley's 'worn out' look was hardly surprising considering his life, very different from the author's cosy upbringing. Crowley offered him a job, but Calder-Marshall declined, counting his refusal a triumph over the forces of evil, before concluding that Crowley's deficiency in 'pure evil' was because 'evil was never pure' (!). It never occurred to him that Crowley was not evil in the first place. Crowley's response to Calder-Marshall's visit was a cheery 'Hoping to see you again soon'.[42] Calder-Marshall and Crowley did meet again, for the mage recorded a last, telling interchange between them:

> Calder-Marshall: 'The modern young woman is an inverted comma.' A.C.: 'and her male counterpart an inverted colon.'[43]

Crowley spent the rest of February and March bogged down in Kent under Mandrake business. While 'Inky' Stephensen did a fine job marshalling the facts of Crowley's literary career for his *The Legend of Aleister Crowley* (1930), Crowley entertained Regardie with hard work and hilarity. Perhaps Regardie was already leaning towards the psycho-analytic theories that would dominate his mature career. Such would explain Crowley's observation: 'The psychoanalysts have taken all the kick out of vice. Instead of being a glorious revolutionary, you are only a nasty infant who has never grown out of it. Similar remarks apply to virtue.'[44] Conversely, he may have been inspired by Karl Germer who was undergoing analysis with the famous Dr Alfred Adler – in Crowley's opinion, an alienist with common sense. Germer was trying to get Crowley to come to Germany to assert his superiority to the rest of mankind as the prophet of the aeon through a publishing venture. Crowley dismissed hero worship: 'I do not attach any value to the position I happen to hold with respect to the proclamation of this certain Law. It is simply a nuisance.'[45]

Meanwhile, languishing in startling colour in the drab cottage, his collection of paintings and drawings required exhibition. Regardie made a list of 142 works for a London show.[46] Not a single London venue would take the old master's fabulous creations. If England preferred to suppress her great men, the same was not true elsewhere. Crowley looked abroad; he would not be chained. And Col Carter had some ideas too.

TWENTY-THREE

One Part a Knave

1926–30

Bury me in a quicklime grave!
Three parts a fool, one part a knave.
A Superman – bar two wee 'buts'
I had no brains, and I had no guts
My soul is a lump of stinking shit,
And I don't like it a little bit! [1]

The Crowley legend displays scant interest in Crowley's children; the implication has been that neither did he. This is not the case. While family matters reached a dramatic head in 1930, we need to go back to grasp the background.

In January 1926, Crowley was in Tunis with Dorothy Olsen. The relationship was cooling but Soror Astrid was still a soft touch for funds. Meanwhile in Cefalù, the mother of Howard and Lulu Astarte languished in the vacuous Villa Santa Barbara. Ninette Fraux's cries for help, addressed to Crowley, Jane Wolfe, Karl Germer and Dorothy Olsen, provide a searing sound across the years 1926–7.

In March 1926, Ninette informed Crowley that his paintings had been sold for food; his bronzes and magical equipment dispatched to London. There was no furniture; anything not sent to London had been sold.[2] In April, Ninette requested Karl and Crowley reconsider sending Howard, who would be 10 in July, to his aunt Hélène Fraux in the States; Hélène would foot the bill. Ninette fancied Florida. She could work for money and have a big garden. She reminded Karl that the villa contract expired in July. Karl was asked to kiss the Beast for her; she hoped he would hold no grudge against her about Lulu. It was cold in Cefalù, always raining. She and Lulu had sore throats. Would Karl please talk to the Beast about the charcoal being all gone, with no money to buy meat?

Lulu's son Eric provides a picture of what his mother dealt with as a young girl:

> In 1930 Lou was a ten year old girl who had grown up completely wild and free without shoes or much clothes for her first seven years, not a young woman.
>
> She knew how to steal fruit to eat and not get shot-gunned to death. She knew how to sneak into the graveyard after the funeral, blow out the candle stubs and sell the wax back to the candle maker to get a penny for a crust of bread. She was a deeply confused and tortured kid who grew up around those marvellous (really lousy) orgy paintings all over the walls of Cefalu.[3]

On 9 April 1926 (some three years before Crowley's expulsion from Paris), Crowley and Dorothy had expected to collect Lulu off the boat from Sicily. Six days earlier, Ninette had written to Astrid, protesting there were no personal reasons for delaying Lulu's departure. Ninette did not deny it was painful parting, but consideration of Lulu's best interests made her as keen as Dorothy and the Beast to get her out of Sicily. But the *commisario* refused Lulu a passport unless he received the absolutely correct paperwork from Tunis. Crowley and the Scarlet Woman killed time.

> 4 a.m. Have made love to Astrid for 3 hours.

> [...] Success in life is Nature's compensation for lack of intelligence.[4]

By this wisdom, Ninette should have been as intelligent as Lulu's father, for she knew no success. A fortnight later, she complained to Karl that Howard was working as a shepherd boy in the fields from 6am to 8pm. Each time he went out, his cough returned. Karl and Crowley were anxious about boxes, sent on the 9th. She had telegraphed the 'Traffico' about it so they wouldn't be left lying around Palermo.[5]

Back in Paris on 7 August, Crowley, unable to pay his rent, was ejected from the Vuillemont Hotel. Leon Engers offered Crowley refuge. Hopes of reunion with Lulu were dashed again when Ninette told Crowley on the 23rd that he was a damn fool for not understanding the way the modern world was run. Why couldn't he get it into his thick head that the consul would go to the limit of his power to prevent Crowley from seeing his daughter?

Stony-broke, Crowley's best bet was to acquaint himself with moneyed ladies. He proposed to Margaret K Binetti while keeping Kitty von Hausberger, Dorothy, and another half-dozen women on the go:

Early a.m. Margaret. 'A cunt that would have frightened Curtius.'[6]

Crowley's Parisian excitements were frustrated by anxiety-driven bouts of bronchitis. He performed sex-magick to improve his health. For this, homosexual magick was preferred; Louis Eugéne de Cayenne was his main partner.

The pressure continued. Ninette wrote abjectly to Jane Wolfe on 5 December. What sheets she had not sold, she said, she had eaten. She then starved for two days, listening to the unbearable cries of her hungry children. She had sold her clock for 1,100 lira: a day's food. She begged the Beast to get her out of Cefalù, lest she go insane. She pleaded for comfort from Jane, sending her desperate love. Jane alerted Crowley who sent Ninette money immediately. On 20 December, Ninette wrote to Astrid; the steamboat agent couldn't get Lulu a passport. There was a problem over her nationality: English father, French mother, neither married, resident in Italy; a bureaucratic nightmare. Ninette awaited instructions from the Beast as to when Lulu might sail. She had written to him twice to thank him for the thousand francs he had sent her. Lulu was getting better, having been ill, and she was happy for Sister Astrid to take care of her. Lulu was an exceptional child who would bring a lot of joy into her life.

Ninette wrote to Jane Wolfe again on 29 March 1927. The Beast had sent money but she was afraid to touch it and regain her health. She was suffering a serious nervous breakdown and needed medicines and proper food. She had already cut out anything pricey, like eggs, milk and meat. She couldn't bear the noise in the street where she was living and needed to get into the country. She knew her health reflected her spiritual condition and was sorry for having messed up her nervous system by surrendering to undisciplined conduct and ignoring her higher impulses. But since her children were tied to her fate, she knew she would have to come through it all. She might deserve her plight, but they didn't. If she gave in, their future would be awful.

Ninette's sister Hélène would only help if she agreed to be separated from the children and went out to work for money. Their parents in France were too old to assist. Ninette trusted the gods would give Beast the help he needed, for only he could give her real help. She hoped the gods would be kind to him and make his path a bit easier. She had received the Word of the Equinox from Alostrael and sent her best love to Jane and Beast.

Jane replied, telling Ninette that Beast also faced grim straits. Ninette commiserated on 21 April, writing to dear old Beast that, somehow, realizing the enormous hopelessness of the situation, including his, made her feel a bit better. She replied to his letters and telegrams and asked for God's blessing on Beast for his being able to see the best in her.

In Paris, Beast reflected on vulgar ideas of 'respectability': 'Some people are respectable, and some are respected: but you can't have it both ways.' Ninette perhaps was not, in the world's eyes, respectable, but he respected her. In July, Ninette sent a postcard to 'Sir Aleister Crowley, 6 Rue de la Mission Marchaud, Paris, XVIième'. At last, the French consul agreed to her receiving a *laissez-passer* with which they could go to France whenever they wanted – *could she now have the ticket money?*[7] Chuffed as Crowley must have been at the thought of seeing Lulu again, the request for money was irksome. On 11 August he asked the I Ching: 'What action should I take to meet the present financial crisis?' The answer, as ever, boiled down to 'hold firm' and try everything reasonable. His diary reveals granite stoicism. Something would turn up. And it did. With autumn came a Polish lady, Mrs Kasimira Bass. Ninette and her children finally made it back to France, *over four years* after Crowley's expulsion from Sicily.

*　*　*

Things did not go well. An undated missive, sent by a defeated Ninette, indicated Lulu and her mother were now at a house at Barbizon. The owners did not accept Ninette as a Frenchwoman; she had no right to be there. Ninette reckoned she was in a worse condition than she could ever have imagined. Could he send her the 440 francs she needed to settle the rent?

Yorke's arrival on the scene was a godsend. On 21 April 1928 he shared in Crowley's rescue of Astarte Lulu, presumably from her mother's straits, for five days earlier, Crowley recorded: 'Ninette bursts upon Fontainebleau and destroys my whole plan once more. *I'm through.*' Ninette 'reappeared' ten days later. The crisis was temporarily resolved on 19 May when £100 arrived, courtesy of Yorke: 'Sent Astarte to country', noted Crowley. Lulu was established at a home and a school, c/o Mme Mathonat, Mory-Montcrux, near Ansauvillers, Oise, between Amiens and Paris.

While Yorke was staying with Crowley and Kasimira at Carry le Rouet in the south in July, Crowley sent 300 francs for Lulu's upkeep. She wrote to her father in a beautiful hand, in purple ink, hoping he would write her a nice letter with his news and that he would visit her soon. She kissed him with all her heart.[8] Little Lulu also wrote to Kasimira, thanking her for the cloth she had given her; Lulu had made a little summer hat and two pairs of pants.[9]

Lulu visited her father in Paris on 26 October. Having received 300 francs, she visited him again for her birthday in late November. Crowley took Lulu to the circus. Hélène Fraux, however, was determined to take Lulu to America for her own good, as she saw it, against Lulu's father's wishes. Scotland Yard gave her Lulu's address.[10] Crowley was probably ignorant of the Yard's interest. Mlle Fraux's niece was, understandably, confused by the strangeness of it all; the presence of Crowley's sexually charged lady friends during her visits to her father could not have helped the eight-year-old gain either a solid emotional footing or understanding of the situation. She needed a loving mummy and daddy in a happy home like any other little girl. Crowley's commitment to a novel psychology of taboo-breaking frankness alarmed her. His own upbringing being sex-negative, he went to the opposite pole, on the thelemic principle: 'The word of Sin is Restriction.' One may ask whether the 'Aeon of the Child' would be altogether a good thing for children, or was it rather for the child in the adult?

*　　*　　*

Gerald Yorke now attempted reconciliation between Crowley and Lola Zaza, his daughter by his first wife Rose, entrusted to Rose's parents, the Kellys.[11] Lola's uncle, Gerald Kelly, had complained at the decade's start that Lola Zaza was unmanageable. One might expect this of a child whose mother was mentally ill and whose father was separated from her.[12] Yorke, a trustee of Crowley's trust, met up with Lola. Would she like to meet her father? Unsure, Lola went to her uncle Gerald Kelly. He told her she was old enough to choose for herself, but gave her certain books to help her decide.

Having read part of them, she declared a writer's works were part of himself. So she judged him by his works. *What could be fairer?* Lola asked. The books, she said, were rude and conceited and as they were part of him, she was very sorry for the other part. Her father had made a hash of his life; she had hers to live.

Lola would not meet her father.[13]

Had Lola's uncle's selection of Crowley's books included *White Stains* or *Snowdrops from a Curate's Garden*, or even *Clouds without Water*, her response to Yorke would be comprehensible. It was never going to be easy admitting that a man vilified and condemned in the gutter press as a traitor, murderer and antichristian scoundrel was one's father. In the event, Lola was separated from her father by the printed word.

If Yorke did not show Lola's letter to Crowley, it is difficult to understand Crowley's poignant statement of 4 January 1929: 'Gerald Kelly chose the Better part, and it shall not be taken away from him.' Apparently picking up on the lively Lola's view that an author's works were part of the man and she was very sorry for the other part, Crowley cottoned on to what Kelly had done. He had chosen what represented Crowley's 'Better part' (his writing) and had then disgusted Lola with his choice. Kelly would stand under judgement of that forever. There was also a pun. Kelly himself had chosen the 'Better part' of society to devote his artistic energies to. *That* would 'not be taken away from him' either. He would be judged as a respectable man on whom the British establishment could rely. Kelly preferred money and position to the call of the Highest. His 'punishment' would be spiritual sterility, marked by obeisant trips to Buckingham Palace to picture members of the Royal Family, a knighthood, and the presidency of the Royal Academy.

> We shall always beat you; for we are creators, and you are abortionists. We shall always beat you; for our God is manifest in flame and life and joy, while yours is but a bogey of fear and shame, who only lurks in darkness.[14]

Empowering Yorke to act for him regarding his children may not have been in Crowley's interest. While little Lulu flourished on a farm near Ansauvillers, her schoolteacher, Madame Philippe, wrote to Crowley on 1 February 1929, just as French security began targeting him. Lulu was doing her 10-times table; she was very intelligent.[15] Mostly written in French, Lulu's letters to 'cher papa' or 'Dear Beast' are moving. On 14 January she wrote of her delight at receiving his letter because she had been tormented at the thought of his being poorly. She desired with all her heart he would get better. Lulu wrote again the next day of how much she waited for a little letter from him. On 21 January she sent him many kisses and thanks for a present of slippers. Aleister had also given Lulu a little dog, called 'Lénine', after the Soviet leader, and perhaps because the dog resembled Dalí's scandalous – to communists – representation of surrealist Louis Aragon's revered father-figure.

On Valentine's Day, Lulu told her father she would observe the principles of wisdom he had written to her about and would put her energies into becoming very wise and studious so he might always be proud of her.[16] He would have been too.

'Astarte' visited her father in Paris on 20 March. Crowley had reason to be anxious. Not only was Lulu attending a school he could not afford, while her mother languished somewhere, but the residency withdrawal threatened to repeat the damage done in Sicily when Mussolini's order split the family up. Lulu must have been anxious too. Hélène chose this moment to visit Crowley's apartment, directing him to look from the window to a man under a streetlamp. The police agent's presence was just a beginning, unless he surrendered Lulu.[17]

Confined to the Avenue Suffren, Crowley received Lulu again on the 6 April when Yorke turned up for dinner with Henry Noble Hall, translator and former London *Times* war correspondent.[18] Events were tearing Crowley and Lulu apart.

On 16 April, forced to leave Paris for Belgium, Crowley waited to hear Yorke's report on his London 'intervention'. On 21 May he heard from Lulu about a boy who loved her very much and wanted to marry her; she agreed and that made the lad very happy. He was a good boy, aged six, and he kissed her all the time. She hoped to see him very soon. She didn't eat much because she wasn't hungry, but she would try to eat more. Mme Marie and Mme Philippe were very nice to her and she had made friends with a little girl of four and a boy of eight. There was a lovely garden full of flowers and a little house in it where they could play when it rained. She sent many kisses to her father.[19]

On 28 May, Crowley followed a sex magick record with the simple admission: 'We are now down and out.' This was unfortunate in view of a letter dispatched from Lulu's school on 30 May. The sender had *still* not received the fees Monsieur had promised a fortnight earlier. He must send them by return of post.

Lulu's recollection, 80 years later, is that she loathed her father and any letters she wrote to him were the result of the schoolmistress making her do it. It is possible that Hélène, who would take Lulu to America and a settled home, passed on her hostility to 'the demon Crowley' to her niece. That Crowley did not contact Lulu in America was taken as immoral indifference; opinions differ. Crowley had no idea where she was (Lulu had been taken from France to California). Gerald Yorke may have been in on the loop but whether he told Crowley anything is unknown.

On 18 July 1929, Lulu wrote to her father, happy to have received his latest news about being in England.[20] This might have been the last letter Crowley ever received from Lulu; she would disappear from his life, even as he attempted to bring her legally to England. A letter of 7 August 1929 to Yorke from Field Roscoe & Co, 36 Lincoln Inn Fields, revealed that the 'present address of Ninette Shumway (née Fraux)' – Lulu's mother – was '45, Avenue Leon Gambetta, Montroye [sic], Seine [probably Montreuil], France'.[21] From Ivy Cottage, Knockholt, Kent, Crowley wrote to the Home Office on 7 November to request permission to adopt Astarte Lulu Crowley, informing the authorities that the 'mother of the child has not been heard of for over 18 months'.[22] Letters addressed to her had not been opened. 'I sent her [Lulu] to live on a farm in the Oise *département* of France. She is now flourishing and it is time to send her to a good school in England.' He had been informed by the Children's Court that no child not of British nationality may be adopted.

Crowley continued:

> It is evidently necessary to the proper education of the child that she be placed at once under better influences in the country of her only available parent until she can acquire citizenship by residence, when the adoption can take place. I therefore respectfully petition you to allow her to come to England as an act of grace.
>
> I have the honour to be, sir, your obedient servant,
>
> Aleister Crowley[23]

A reply from Home Office official Norman Brook of 20 November asserted that discretion lay with immigration officers at the point of entry. If Crowley were at the dock to receive her, all should be well. Yorke added a note to the letter: 'When it came to the point, AC was unable to get hold of Astarte Lulu. Ninette her mother died, and no one knew where Astarte was.'

This highly misleading note was probably added to put Crowley biographers off the scent (Ninette and Lulu were to be left in peace) and possibly to obscure Yorke's own part in the painful affair. Ninette Fraux had not died; she stayed in France under medical supervision, living well into her 80s. As for 'no one knowing where Astarte was'; *someone* knew, even if it was only Hélène and Special Branch. The unpleasant picture emerges that Crowley was manipulated in the matter. Yorke may have helped Hélène remove Lulu from France behind Crowley's back. In 1930 Crowley would reach the distressing conclusion that Lulu was either dead or had been kidnapped. In fact, Lulu was in America where she still lives.

Crowley was only one part a knave.

TWENTY-FOUR

Berlin

1930–32

Crowley's two years in Germany cut straight into the nerve-centre of history-in-the-making. The roll call of his contacts is astonishing; his adventures provide enough material for 20 novels – and yet, the public has heard little or nothing of it.

Two factors took the Beast to Germany. First, Karl Germer promised to invest £2,000 in a German publishing programme, plugged into Yorke's Mandrake syndicate. Second, opportunities afforded for intelligence-gathering did not pass Colonel Carter by. Crowley's cover was fantastic. All Carter had to do was light the blue touch-paper and ensure Yorke kept the firework under control.

Boarding the *Bremen* for Bremerhaven on 17 April 1930, the Beast was quickly baptized into Deutschland's political fire, witnessing a street battle in Leipzig ignited by the German Communist Party (DKP). Dodging the broken limbs and shouts, Germer drove the OTO's Outer Head straight into the German New Age: a return to Hohenleuben in Thuringia for a meeting with Heinrich Tränker. From Hohenleuben, Germer brought Crowley to Berlin, introducing the Beast to prospective publishing partner Dr Henri Birven, a schoolteacher who edited the theosophical journal *Hain der Isis*. With Birven was Dr Arnoldo Krumm-Heller, who had served as a medical colonel in the Mexican Army and practised occult medicine. Krumm-Heller shared Tränker's enthusiasm for *Pansophia*. Also present at the neo-Rosicrucian gathering was a sculptor, Worner, and a painter, Plantikow. Crowley liked the artists but found Birven a 'pompous idiot'.

Birven was nervous about René Guénon's dismissal of Crowley's masonic credentials in the *RISS*, the French Catholic 'Review of Secret Societies'. Calling Guénon 'Guenon' – meaning a female monkey – Crowley waved off the *RISS* attack as a 'wheeze', while making sure his secretary, Regardie, obtained the relevant copy. Familiar with Mexican politics, Krumm-Heller was nervous that the *RISS*'s propaganda would be reprinted in the Mexican conservative paper *El Nación*. The paper supported the 10-years'-old *Pax Romana* movement's efforts to infuse Roman Catholicism into politics. While 'Pax' was useful to fascist and reactionary conservative governments, Crowley considered Catholic opposition a mere *reaction* to the inevitability of the New Aeon.

Invited to painter Hans Steiner's studio, Crowley was captivated by the large eyes and bobbed hair of intense, sexy 19-year-old model and painter, Hanni Jaeger, while Steiner, overwhelmed by his amazing visitor, alerted the *Berliner Tageblatt* to an exclusive. Crowley and Karl then set off for Leipzig to pick up Marie, guest of the devoted Martha Küntzel: 'With my customary calm courage I let Karl drive. He did so for 30km before overturning us into a ditch.' Marie was taken to Potsdam for her birthday. Inspired perhaps by a clothes-buying jaunt, Crowley wrote *Ode to Fashion 1930*:

> Fashion toots her flute to the 'Fair'
> (My spirit shivers and shudders)
> Back to the bestial greasy hair
> Back to the flapping udders!
> To the hippo hips and the wasp-like waist,
> And the wasp-like temper to match it!
> To the raw and shapeless Call-to-be-chaste,
> And the overgrown thicket to thatch it!
> To the goat-reek under the clammy arms,
> The simper and smirk of the ogress –
> Fashion, these are thy catholic charms!
> These are the triumphs of Progress![1]

Drunk, Marie began raging again. She went through Crowley's diary, underlining in red every reference to Hanni. Crowley would not exchange youth for dementia. Sending Marie back to Leipzig he got down to observing a political rally on 3 May: 'Rally of the Stahlhelm group. Good. Seldte their chief. X Niederlandische Hof.'[2]

Franz Seldte was founder of the anti-republican, paramilitary Bund der Frontsoldaten (war veterans). He met Crowley at the Niederlandische Hof.[3] An important political figure in 1930, Seldte tried to fill a gap in conservative leadership. Germany's problem was the polarization of extremes. With his knack for winning the confidence of significant Germans, Crowley targeted conservatives, soon realizing they lacked the popular appeal of the Nazis and communists, between whom a showdown appeared inevitable. Crowley alerted protagonists to the thelemic solution and made his reports. As in America, so in Germany: England undervalued Crowley's skills.

The day he met Seldte, the *Berliner Tageblatt* trumpeted Crowley's mysticism, mountaineering successes, foreign adventures, poetry and painting, while reporting that he had advised Eckenstein's old acquaintance, Paul Bauer, before *his* attempt on Kanchenjunga.[4] The *Tageblatt's* picture of an alpha-male mystic who painted in an original fashion, and who came from effete England, fascinated intellectual Berliners.

Crowley's first stab at Berlin was a success. Even Germer's wife Cora, angry at being expected to fund Thelema Verlag, was mollified by promise of Mandrake funding. Leaving Bremerhaven on 5 May, 54-year-old Crowley brought Hanni with him back to London. His marriage over, he was in love with 'Anu', the Mesopotamian sky-god – a form of 'Nuit' – but also, on Earth, *Anu* expressed the part of her anatomy he adored. Germer was unhappy about the relationship, but Germer was unhappy about many things. Undergoing psychotherapy, he was unstable, and perhaps obsessed with Adler's definition of the 'inferiority complex'. Like so many recipients of 'analysis' he was eager to project the 'condition' onto everyone but himself. Crowley's comment that 'the inferiority complex (like America and Australia) did very little harm until it was discovered', shows his irritation with catch-all psycho-categories.[5]

On 5 June, Crowley had lunch with 'Nick', code-name for Colonel Carter.[6] Carter gave Regardie, through Yorke, £3 so he could join Co-Masonry, presumably for intelligence purposes. In his letter to Yorke, Carter said he'd seen their 'mutual friend once or twice'; 'He is always the delightful super optimist.'[7] On 2 July, Carter called Crowley about Soviet prime minister, Dr Alexei Ivanovich Rykoff. Accused of 'Rightist' tendencies by the Russian press, Rykoff would be ousted by Stalin in December.

*　　*　　*

Crowley went to Steyning, Sussex, in the July sun to find Neuburg. Neuburg fled. Perhaps Crowley dropped a copy of Stephensen's *Legend of Aleister Crowley* through his letter box because Neuburg reviewed it positively in *The Freethinker* under the title 'A Fair Plea for Fair Play'. England did not recognize her great men.

The great man left Britain's 'John Bull rot' and two million unemployed for Germany's economic disaster on 1 August. 'P.S. Miss Jaeger fucks everyone farewells.'[8] Karl and Cora motored Hanni Larissa Jaeger and her Beast to the Hotel zum Ratskeller in Rheinsburg. There was rain, then some sun. Love's children Crowley and Hanni 'walked in the park and by some mysterious fatality lost our friends. But found each other.' While Karl and Cora planned the summer holiday, a bizarre new adventure occurred to Crowley: 'Plans hatched for Suicide in Portugal.' A good suicide stunt would drum up publicity for his autohagiography; but first, a holiday tour of Germany, Czechoslovakia and Austria.

It was a crazy trip. Germer raved as he raced down the cobbled roads, the rushing air cauterized by Cora's acerbic sourness. Poor Hanni; her family had a history of insanity. A night at Prague's Hotel Sroubek was swiftly followed by a mad drive to the Park Hotel Schönbrunn, Vienna. Karl 'drove with absolute recklessness', making jerky movements. Riled for no reason, he complained of headaches. The party arrived just in time; Dr Alfred Adler was at home. Crowley got on well with Adler. They shared a 'Love of humanity without individual preferences', a commitment to science, ideas about the ego's relation to the cosmos, as well as the general principles of Thelema. Adler 'offered spontaneously' to work with Crowley. Crowley's diary also refers to 'Mitrinowitch philosopher'.[9]

After visits to Salzburg, Munich, Ulm and Frankfurt, Crowley left Köln for Brussels on 23 August, arriving in London just in time to meet the world famous practical joker Horace Cole at the Café Royal.[10] In 1906 Cole had fooled HMS *Dreadnought*'s captain into taking Cole and a group of friends for an Abyssinian delegation. Not surprisingly, Crowley and Cole got on. Cole thought Hanni Jaeger very beautiful and found what Crowley called her 'elusive likeness: it is – Iris Tree!' Herbert Beerbohm-Tree's daughter Iris was a friend of Nancy Cunard, another talented, bohemian adventuress, much to Crowley's taste.

London was sweltering in late August heat; Crowley loathed it. With Marie 'packed' off 'somewhere in Hampstead', Crowley dined with Yorke and Major Thynne on 27 August. The Mandrake was bankrupt. Thynne was 'very distressed, and acting all wrong. Obsessed about "Capital".' Crowley had had enough. He and Anu boarded the *Alcantara* on the 29th at Southampton for Lisbon, guests of Freemason Fernando Pessoa, destined to be Portugal's revered poet. Pessoa's circle was deeply attracted to the image of transcendent being, the spiritual man that is above the world. He would include Crowley's 'Hymn to Pan' in his *Presenca*, published in 1931.[11]

Booked into the luxury Hotel de l'Europe, Crowley and Anu's relations were in turmoil. The Beast's mind could feel as all-enveloping as an oversized trench-coat and Hanni, prone to depression, needed space. The couple were ejected after Hanni had a fit and fled. Crowley found her at Estoril, 10 miles away. She sought help in getting home from the US consul who advanced her money for a boat back to Germany. Hanni would be arraigned before Berlin police for perjuring herself before the consul.

Angry and hurt, Crowley headed for Cascais, thence to the Boca do Inferno rocks, on the cliff-torn coast. This 'mouth of hell' reflected his emotions. He also saw the funny side. The suicide stunt was launched.

Crowley left a note under a rock; life without Hanni was impossible. Pessoa played along, alerting the press that Sir Crowley was no longer visible. The news broke across Europe. Was it suicide, spying, or magick? By the end of the month Crowley had returned incognito to Berlin. For once, the Beast had got the press to do his bidding, appealing to the sensationalism that had messed up his life.

Spence considers the 'disappearance' afforded time for espionage. Spain was unstable. The Catholic Church schemed; republicans schemed; fascists schemed; communists schemed. According to Spence, 'Cascais, was a posh, cosmopolitan resort full of millionaires and exiled royalty, among them the Spanish Bourbons and a whole colony of Germans'.[12] Diary pages for September have disappeared; *Crowley* had disappeared.

∗   ∗   ∗

One letter emerged from Lisbon, however, an irate one sent to Regardie about Yorke who had power of attorney over Crowley's bank account. Yorke used its £70 for doles to the penniless Marie. Crowley suspended him from 'all his functions', insisting Regardie 'take possession of all documents, books, pictures etc. in his possession'. Yorke added a note to the letter: 'I handed all the diaries etc. over to Kerman, from whom I bought them on AC's death in 1947.'[13] Isidore Kerman was Crowley's young solicitor – and he did not sell everything to Yorke. An auction of withheld manuscripts took place at Sotheby's in 1997. Crowley and Yorke had many rows but always patched it up. Marie, however, had become a nagging sore.

On 1 October, Crowley met art dealer Karl Nierendorf. A 'very nice man', wrote Crowley, 'who suggested (without being told) that the thing to do was to put me over as a Personality'. While Crowley discussed his show, Carter wrote to Yorke:

> I got a frantic letter from A.C.'s wife, who had read it in the papers that he had disappeared in Portugal. I was able to assure her of his safety as I had a post-card from him this morning from Berlin. Curious how he is never left alone.[14]

A new adventure: popular science writer and old friend JWN Sullivan[15] wrote from the *The Observer*:

> Dear Crowley,
>
> You might be a bit surprised if Aldous Huxley and myself called on you on Thursday evening of this week [...] So look out.[16]

Sullivan and Huxley planned interviews with great men of European science; Berlin was a good place to find them, Crowley included. Thursday came; Sullivan was late: 'Can't find Sullivan – wired Einstein for him. Later – found him through Schrödinger.'

The casual mention of two of the greatest names in 20th-century science is striking. *Einstein and Schrödinger!* Erwin Schrödinger is famous for the eponymous 'Cat' experiment or hypothetical demonstration of the Heisenberg 'Uncertainty Principle', a cornerstone of quantum physics. Spence wonders whether mutual interests with Einstein may have been less than scientific: 'Einstein had a passion for pacifist and left-wing causes, many of them the handiwork of [Soviet agent] Louis Gibarti. Gibarti knew Einstein well enough to provide all sorts of dirt on the physicist when he later turned FBI informant.'[17]

In 1933, MI5 and SIS were interested in Crowley's cultivation of Louis Gibarti. A letter from MI5 to SIS states: 'Gibarti has recently been in touch with Alesteir [*sic*] Crowley in connection with LIA activities.'[18] 'LIA' must be a typo for the 'LAI', or League Against Imperialism. Crowley had met Gibarti in Paris in 1928 when Gibarti was right-hand man to Willi Münzenberg of Comintern, the Communist International's chief agent in the West. Gibarti, Hungarian, real name: Laszlo Dobos, was working for Moscow's OGPU military intelligence, and was linked into the German Communist Party's *Geheimapparat* or 'Secret Apparatus'. French intelligence was mindful of Gibarti's presence in Paris and would not have turned a blind eye to the Crowley link; such suspicion may have contributed to the *refus de séjour* of 1929.

Rousing Aldous Huxley 'from his normal apathy', Crowley found him 'exceptionally charming'. Huxley and Sullivan both found Anu 'a miracle of loveliness'. Meanwhile Crowley encouraged Regardie to beef up the suicide story with an account from a medium, indicating the horrors that awaited the suicide 'on the other side'! Returning to science, Crowley answered *A Series of Questions put to E.A.C. by J.W.N. Sullivan*:

> *Your incentive?*
> Determined resultant of series of forces.
> *Humanistic importance of your activities?*
> Acquisition of new methods of research.
> *Justification?*
> To hell with ultimate value.
> *Is life on this planet result of accident or result of a scheme?*
> It is a play of Nuit. Every phenomenon should be an orgasm of its kind. That is the scheme. Every man is a process of Love under Will.
> *Does anything of man besides his memory from his friends survive his death?*
> What do you mean by survive? You can take your co-odinates to suit your equations. The whole thing is a system of conventions. Ultimate point of view is the conception of the universe as infinite space. Take any point and map from that point, enlarging experience from that point. Whole series may be identical except the direction. Consciousness is a record of these experiences. Points of view are special and ultimately identical. No two points are the same except in relation to a third. They are identical if there is no third point to rally on.
> *Is the present system of incentives and discouragements in society best adapted to encourage the best in man?*
> No. I deny there is any system.[19]

Aldous Huxley's influential book, *The Doors of Perception*, would in 1954 demonstrate his interest in 'psychedelic philosophy' and fuel the psychedelic movement. It is widely thought Crowley turned Huxley on to mescaline's psychotherapeutic value.

* * *

In England, Regardie compiled a press release, claiming to have visited Mr Alfred V Peters, a medium, whose 'guide' related how the dead Crowley described 'Hell's Mouth' 'into which Mr C. had been violently pushed by enemies, presumably of Roman Catholic persuasion or with Free Masonic connections':

> It is interesting at least, to note here that in the course of his troubled life, Crowley has made innumerable enemies in both these sects. Among the Roman Catholics, by his violent and frenzied attacks on Christianity; and among the Freemasons by publishing, in his former periodical, *The Equinox*, the rituals of a secret R.·. C.·. Society, of which many powerful Masons were members. For this exposure of their secrets he was never forgiven. It is claimed by his friends, that his expulsion from Italy in 1922 [*sic*], and from France last year, were pre-eminently due to Roman Catholic influence. This is, naturally, pure speculation, but it is borne out most peculiarly by the reports of the medium. [...] yet, although Aleister Crowley is gone, his work will live on forever.[20]

Then Yorke, and more worryingly, Carter, got on Crowley's back over Marie. Crowley was stony-broke. Finding Regardie considerably more supportive, Crowley congratulated him on having 'made a great hit' with Hanni: 'The actual expression used [by Hanni] was: Wait till I get to London: I'll fuck that bastard silly.'

Cornered, Crowley sought solace in the temporary affectation of schizophrenia. Regardie heard how 'Edward Crowley' had discovered the 'Mystery of Aleister's double life':

> Now that poor Aleister has been cut off in the midst of his sins, there is no reason for concealing the strange truth any longer. It must often have struck you as remarkable that he could have been brought up at *two* public schools, chosen both a diplomatic and a medical career, been both saintly and so deboshed [*sic*] a character, so liked and so detested, seen in London while lying ill in Sicily and so on.

The explanation is however simple. He and I were twins. The
fact was concealed by our parents even from the Registrar, for
reasons connected with the creed of the Plymouth Brethren [etc.][21]

Anu suffered from a genuine mental disorder. Crowley went to see her at
a *Privat-Klinik*: 'She was as sweet as ever – and turned nasty at the first
word of ordinary common sense.'

On the 9th Crowley began 'to suspect Germer of plotting deliberately the spiritual murder of Anu. In the interest of his masturbation!'
Hanni complained about Karl making her do things that made her feel
uncomfortable.

> Anu showed me her drawing of Karl masturbating into a toilet
> W.C. He forced her to look on – date uncertain – under threat to
> withdraw support unless she complied. She was afraid that he
> would murder her unless she sat quiet: so she did. True? I'm not
> sure: but it sounds very much like him.

While Anu suffered from an 'abiding horror of going insane like the bulk
of her family', far away in Australia, stalwart Frank Bennett died of
heart failure, aged 62, on 23 November, at his mistress's house in
Camperdown, New South Wales. He had been planning a great magical
experiment. Missed in Sydney's little bohemian circle as a wise eccentric,
mystic and peacemaker, there was no one to replace him; the thelemic
light went out in Australia for many years.

*   *   *

In Bremen the Nazis took control while Josef von Sternberg's *The
Blue Angel* wowed them at the cinemas with a terrifically sexy
Marlene Dietrich. Crowley and Anu's 67th sexual 'Working' also took
a dramatic turn: 'She as Alexander-Platz 5 Marks in rubber boots: I as
coal man. Dem little comedy!' Crowley and Hanni indulged in a
sexual role-playing game. An 'Alexander-Platz 5 marks' is a reference
to the many poor prostitutes operating in that area. Crowley played the
grubby 'coal man'. She wore the rubber boots. In all, 'She was her true

wonderful self of utter beauty and charm.'

Next day, he despaired again. He and Karl took a long walk down Nicolassee for lunch in the forest, south of the city. When he returned, 'Anu had tidied the studio beautifully, and left me violets on the table and put the picture of her that I love most on the wall. Puss also left her boots!' What boots they must have been!

*   *   *

Berlin stands on a plain, crossed with iron-clad canals, not dainty rivers, tenements not palaces. It's down-to-earth and plain to see. It's a statement: man-made and here to stay. Always ahead of the game, Crowley knew Berlin was the place to be: the freest *über*-modern atmosphere in the world, from the new cinema of the UFA studios to its flying *U-Bahn*, down to the cellars where a new music and art form was taking shape. The only thing this world leader of a city did not need was a World Leader. But a World *Teacher*, that was something else. If Crowley had been a dud, Berlin would have found him out.

Crowley's Berlin life was like a movie. The speed, the freshness, the immediacy of Berlin's honest streets, pushed him back into his humanity, and he let rip.

On 2 February 1931 he dined royally at Stockler's, 'the best place I've struck in Berlin – it has imagination and is not gross! We then played Hide and Seek in the courtyard and I chased Anu at full speed all the way down the Kurfurstendamm!!' For the 55-year-old Crowley to have run after a 19-year-old at full speed – well, it says something about him.

*   *   *

Lapping up the sun, a world away, the Californian Thelemites, led by English-born Wilfred T Smith (Frater 132), took a different approach to Thelema. Enthusing about new members Regina Agnes Kahl and younger sister, Leona Kahl Watson, Jane Wolfe wrote to Crowley. Full of good vibrations, Regina (dubbed 'Vagina' by Crowley) was an opera singer and voice teacher[22] who had met Smith in an LA hotel lobby. Regina and Leona were introduced to Jane at the Quatres Artes Club,

5612 Carlton Way, a literary salon of some 50 people.[23] Jane gushed about something magical brewing between Regina and Frater 132 that would encourage team spirit in the lodge, all the more striking since Regina was bisexual with strong lesbian leanings and Smith desired her for himself. Crowley's reaction: 'I laffed and laffed and laffed.' Regina became a Probationer on 23 January 1931. The Beast wanted to know more about Regina. Jane's letter provided an impression:

> Regina, 39 I think. Robust, singer, black black hair, (dyed) dark eyes – a woman of strong emotions. [...] she devours your writings greedily. January she and Smith attended a costume party, which they left about 3 a.m. Sunday morning the 4th. Smith read to her till day-light, among other things; the two slept for a short time and at about 11 am he read [Crowley's] the Wake World to her. She sobbed and sobbed. This sounds quite inadequate, but Smith thinks Regina had some sort of initiation that morning...[24]

Crowley marked the letter: 'All utter balls,' adding his assessment: 'Regina is probably a good fat old whore, with a well-oiled cunt; "Lee" [Leona] I am pretty sure will make me vomit.' Replying to Jane's 'delightful+cheering letter', he hoped Jane would 'ship Regina Kahl to me by the very first boat. She sounds perfectly scrumptious.'[25] 'Scrumptious' was a favourite adjective of Jane's.

Crowley always found the goings-on of the Californian OTO either hilarious or alarming; he seldom appreciated the great efforts WT Smith made to establish Thelema on the West Coast. Crowley's views were highly coloured by OTO member Max Schneider's caustic, often false accounts; Schneider could not stand Smith, on whom he once inflicted a split lip and sore face for sleeping with Max's beautiful wife, Leota.

*　　*　　*

On 12 February 1931, Karl Nierendorf assured Crowley there were only three living painters who could be classed with him. Praise is good for artists, and Crowley had had so little for so long.

Saturday 14 March

Went on painting *Carnival*. A1. Louise to pose. Masturbated her and licked her cunt: she comes very wonderfully. Then went and ate stuffed tomatoes because I love my marvellous Anu.

He was 'damnably depressed' by the middle of the next week. 'Anu worse. I am afraid she is on the cock-sucking at 10 RM[26] again as her main engines are out of repair.' On 10 April Crowley painted *Conscientious Nude* and had American President Hoover's cousin Gertrude Howe to lunch. Regular lover and model Louise was violently jealous, spending the following Sunday morning 'wandering around the Lietzensee – in the hope that I would look out of the window and see her!' Anu rang up on the 25th. He saw her for an hour. 'I think she is working some cabaret or walking the streets.'

Three weeks later, Crowley met Ellen, Grafin (countess) von Stauffenberg in Charlottenberg: 'I'm not worrying one bit about Miss Jaeger: provided I can have "the Cunt of the Countess" as the Good Book says.' He entertained her to lunch. It went badly: 'Bored, somehow. Slept.' Unsatisfied by the Beast, the Countess would make him pay. Other women, however, found Crowley satisfactory: Sonia, Louise, Magda, Renate, Gertrud, Katherine, Kasba, Ermi, Bobby, and more – no complaints. It was a blur of a summer.

Meanwhile, after Marie was examined at Colney Hatch Mental Hospital on 16 July, Crowley received a memo from the Superintendent:

Unfortunately her earlier phantasy formation has resulted in definite delusions, and she now believes she is the daughter of the King and Queen and of pure English blood: also that she married her brother, the Prince of Wales 12 years ago, though he is ignorant of the relationship. At present her conduct is satisfactory but she is resentful that her claims are not acknowledged and is likely to become difficult. [Yorke's comment: 'In 1950, Marie was still in Colney Hatch.' The superintendent was surprised she was Scarlet Woman to 666. He 'thought this was one of her – not her husband's – delusions'.][27]

On 13 July, the collapse of the Danatbank led to the closure of all German banks until 5 August. Five million Germans were unemployed. This could not go on.

Crowley had lunch with Peter Supf, a kind of German Antoine de St Éxupéry, poet and correspondent of Thomas Mann. Supf was party to the secret Nazi effort to re-arm for a future air war; Crowley chose well. It was probably Supf who forwarded Crowley's play *Mortadello* to the famous stage and film director, Max Reinhardt. Supf called round for a drink with Crowley again in August, shortly after Crowley performed 'Opus 15' with his lover, Pola, rededicating himself to his mission. Result: 'I met Bertha Busch on the 3rd Aug.' Aged 36, Bertha picked him up on the Unter den Linden.

Bertha was busty and forthright with sacks of independent spirit and a great sexual appetite. Sado-masochism, bisexuality and buggery were all right with Bertha, who liked to be known as 'Bill'. Bill was the Berlin Zeitgeist made flesh; a larger-than-life doll who seemed to have punched her way out of an expressionist canvas. A classic house-mother/earth-mother type, she liked Crowley's associates to think of her as their 'Mum'. She was cheeky, vulgar, sexy, and Crowley adored her, much to Germer's disgust. He said she was nothing but a street-walker. Did he think this would put Crowley off? Bertha was also known as 'the Red Angel', a useful contact for meeting Reds.

Times were hard, but so was Crowley. He wrote to the EA Crowley Settlement Trustees, c/o Dennes and Co, Chancery Lane. Since his daughter Lola enjoyed a good income with a home to fall back on, could her father receive 'the whole of the income' while the present situation lasted? 'I am now entirely destitute save for the good will of friends in Germany, and these friends are themselves financially embarrassed owing to the terrible conditions prevailing here now.'[28] Nothing would come of this plea for over six months.

Things got worse. The Countess was on his trail: 'Police starting again (about Dr B. as a spy).' That was Dr Breitling, implicated in accusations stemming from the Grafin von Stauffenberg. On 14 August, Billy phoned. It was the Countess, again: apparently suffering sore pride over Crowley's sexual indifference to her, she was taking action. In a diary note, Crowley put a question mark next to 'Praesidium': Berliner Polizei headquarters. Had the Countess lodged complaints? Was he to be questioned? Did she suspect him of spying? Crowley went high up for support: 'Schulenburg very nice and intelligent.' Apparently, Crowley consulted diplomat Friedrich-Werner Graf von der Schulenburg, the last German ambassador to the Soviet Union before Operation Barbarossa.[29]

The countess took her revenge:

Wednesday 2 September

Song and dance by Frau Kreutzer [the Russian landlady] because Billie, her new room not being ready, stayed the night. Fact was police had been told by Grafin von Stauffenberg that this is a young brothel – as it is – and was raided last night.

Repartee: I said to her – [a] devout Russian – 'But what would Christ have done in the circus?'

'Ah, but he too got into trouble with the Police.'!!!

Saturday's Opus 14 with Bill was dedicated to the Great Work and duly matched its purpose: 'Most wonderful fuck I've had in years. Nearly tore her bottom off.' Opus 15 was similarly dedicated on the Sunday: 'The best fuck within recorded memory of living man.'

Friday 11 September

Karl came down to settle some trivial business – raged and cursed and masturbated. Right in front of Billie. She was naturally very much upset. That filthy pimp is the limit: God send us a sane man to put the Great Work over!

A week later, Crowley visited the gallery space at the Porza building. Nierendorf and Steiner were setting it up nicely, despite Germer's 'insanity'. Germer was trying to secure investment in Crowley's show from Werner, elder brother of 'Alvo' (Gustav) von Alvensleben, spy in the

USA during WW1. Brother Werner was later imprisoned by Hitler, as a member of Germany's conservative opposition.[30]

Crowley was keen for Yorke to come and see the show, but he was also keen for Yorke to understand what he was involved in. His advice packs punch:

> You seem to think that the Order is a parlour game.
>
> This type of thinking is your primary mistake about Life.
>
> You are in very great danger of becoming a 'browser'. There are lots of them! This year Theosophy, next Christian Science, next Psychoanalysis, then Inner Light.
>
> [...] You need Discipline more than any man (of any promise) that I ever knew. I daily bless my stars that I had absolute brutes like Eckenstein and Ananda Metteyya to bully me, and the sense to heed their warnings.
>
> There is 'no hope' – etc. Always the coward's curse. There was 'no hope' of routing the Spanish Armada, was there?[31]

On 8 October, *The New York Times* photographed Crowley and the exhibition while Germer insulted Bertha. Crowley refused his hand. Germer had a tantrum, telling von Alvensleben and Steiner he would not pay his share. Crowley discussed Germer's case with Dr Adler, who was in Berlin; Adler passed it on.[32] Germer calmed down.

On Saturday 10 October 1931 Crowley's show opened. Arriving at 11 am, the artist found Bill talking to Marcellus Schiffer, cabaret innovator and pioneer of the German musical.[33] Nierendorf informed visitors Crowley had more to offer than French-influenced British artists afraid of their own shadow:

> I noticed his immediate appreciation of Dix, Nolde, Beckmann, Otto Mueller, Schmidt-Rottluff and Scholz. He saw works of these painters for the first time and his intuitive judgement was absolutely sound and at the same time of an unassumingness which indifferent viewers of artworks never show. In later conversations he also showed himself to be restrained, completely free of pretence, and without any over-sensitivity in the face of critical objections to his pictures.

Nierendorf concluded: 'The critical evaluation of his pictures is not my business. An enormously vivid and eager outsider, a real man of elementary, instinctive power is behind them.'[34] Vanilla Beer, one of today's leading abstract expressionists, has this to say about Crowley's art: 'The gist is that he never repeated himself: took chances rather than complete an assured picture; understood art as an internal voyage with external traces.'

Berlin welcomed Aleister Crowley, and the show picked up positive notices.

*　　*　　*

A strikingly modern ticket to the Porza Gallery Neumann-Nierendorf show survives. On its reverse is a hand-written note. Crowley informed 'Nick' – Colonel Carter – of volatile political developments. Typically, he couldn't resist making a dig about Carter's interference over his marriage:

> Hohenzollerns crowded the Gethsemanekirche on 'Dead
> Sunday'. The Hitler-Hindenburg crowd want to bring them
> back. They will be in power probably before Christmas. *But* that
> will mean French intervention, also revolution ending in
> anarchy with a probable attempt of the Soviets to capture the
> country. It means the smash all round and Nick is not fit for his
> job if he bothers about other people's private affairs in morals or
> religion. And he talks too much! 666[35]

Despite the humour, Crowley's report was in earnest. 'Dead Sunday' referred to November's 'Totensonntag', established in 1816 by royal decree as a holy day for Lutheran churches to remember the dead, especially Prussian war dead. Philipp Nicolai's *Awake, the voice calls us* was sung. That chant now rang with all the righteous fire of a summons to resistance by anti-republicans eager to restore a Hohenzollern monarchy that had collapsed with Germany's bitter surrender in 1918, when the old order vanished before an unpopular republic.

Intended by the abdicated Hohenzollern Kaiser Wilhelm II at its dedication in 1893 as a bulwark against socialism, communism and atheism, the red-brick Gethsemanekirche at Stargarder Strasse 77 had instead become a shelter for radical republican, socialist groups. When anti-republican, pro-monarchy 'Hohenzollerns' chose this particular church to 'crowd', they could not have been more profoundly provocative or more painfully political. The war dead would indeed be remembered! They did not die in vain! No surrender! Germany must rise! British, American, French and Russian ideas of democracy must be rejected! The Republic – a foreign imposition – is a stain on the German soul!

'Dead Sunday' was also called 'Eternity Sunday'.

Believing Hitler would back Hohenzollern restoration, the ex-Kaiser had permitted sons August Wilhelm and Oskar to join the Nazi Party in 1930. Hitler played the Hohenzollerns along, as long as they were useful. As the two sides of the art-show ticket poignantly demonstrate, Crowley was on the case. He foresaw the imminent end of the Weimar Republic.

*   *   *

A few days after the art-show launch, Gerald Hamilton, a Berlin corre-spondent for *The Times*, 'called with his boy'. Crowley enjoyed the gay journalist's company. A German government spy, communist and Sinn Fein supporter, Hamilton introduced Crowley to senior communists, including Ernst Thälmann, while Crowley introduced the communists to their need for Thelema if they really wished to revolutionize the world. He also spied on them, and on Hamilton, who moved into Bill and the Beast's apartment as a lodger the following January.

Perhaps Crowley was thinking of devising a cabaret of his own, for on 21 October, he was in 'Conference with Schiffers at a café' with investor Jacques Krabo. Bill got on well with Margo Schiffer. Margo was gay; she had played Marlene Dietrich's stage 'girlfriend'. They both adored Marlene.

After a wild November day on 'bad cognac' at painter Max Brunning's studio, Crowley and Bill went 'crazy': 'we tore off our clothes and fucked and fucked and fucked. She tore my lips and my tongue – the blood streamed all over her face. We fucked. And suddenly she got a jealous fit about three cheap whores at Brunning's and I strangled her.' Next day: 'Woke early and finished the fuck.' Crowley spent 12 November recuperating: 'the wildest time we ever passed.' Crowley and Bill made vows of chastity, to love under will: 'And while I was telephoning after lunch, she went into the study and waited for me with her bare bottom in the air.'

Two days later, while Bill and Margo were 'translating the Berlin Manifesto', in Hesse the Nazis celebrated massive success in municipal elections.

Sunday 15 November

Making love all morning.
    Ditto afternoon. Interrupted by (a) S[carlet] W[oman] putting menthol Vaseline on her anus to facilitate… (b) Hamilton calling at 5.

This is the first mention of Vaseline in Crowley's long record of buggery; what a practical woman Bill was! She wrote to Yorke that night: 'My Darling Boy, Thanks ever so much for the £5. You send to me. It was a relief – you are real pal for me.'[36] Crowley also wrote from Karlsruherstrasse 2, Berlin-Halensee to Yorke:

Do get your 'honesty' untangled. The plan is to put me over in *Germany* as they did for Bernard Shaw, Frank Harris, and Oscar Wilde. Then, and only then, the English will follow. We want G.H.Q. here, to arrange translations, promote productions of plays and films &c.
    There is no prejudice at all against me here; yesterday Ullstein – very big publisher – asked me for a series of short stories. Reinhardt's chief man is reading *Mortadello* without giving a single thought to my atrocious views on Sublapsarianism.[37]

None of this cut any ice back in London. On 20 November Carter informed Yorke he was choked off with Crowley after the 'Spanish-Portugese episode'. Crowley had then suggested a business deal: 'I did not reply to his letter.'[38]

On 6 December, Bill, suffering from period pains, stabbed Crowley with a carving knife and 'then', as he put it, 'became violent'. He was nearly killed. Yorke was informed:

> I take it as a message that I'm still wanted, as in the case of the Chinese pony [in 1905]. A quarter of an inch lower would have done the trick. I made my dispositions in case. Bill is much better and more cheerful today.[39]

On Christmas Day 1931, a big dinner was arranged with Karl, 'Hedy' and Gerald Hamilton. Hedy may well have been the stunning beauty Hedy Kiesler, known to millions within a few years as movie star Hedy Lamarr.[40] Christopher Isherwood and poet Stephen Spender showed up. Isherwood would write of his Berlin experiences in *I am a Camera*, on which the musical *Cabaret* was based. The 'Mr Norris' of Isherwood's *Mr Norris takes the Train* was probably based on Hamilton. A remarkable gaggle of talents hit Berlin with a joyous pub-crawl:

> Bill and I both went after Hedy. Cosy Corner later – great fun with boys – Charley's – Besselstr. Johanniter Keller. Some café in Friedrichstr. – Freidrichskeller.

On New Year's Eve, Crowley, probably at Isherwood's suggestion, went to a homosexual ball at Zeltenstrasse 2: 'Frightfully dull, pretentious, and grotesque. Left at 11:30 to catch Bill for New Year's Walk – supreme loveliness under stars and across Spree to Bellevue. Taxi from Charlottenberg. Wild rush, and made it to the very last minute.'

New Year's Day 1932

Crowley took note of gynaecologist Dr Norman Haire's arrival in Berlin; they would meet later in the year.[41] The doctor had attended the Deutsche Gesellschaft fur Gynäkologie congress in Frankfurt in June without being dubbed a force for moral disintegration. Crowley considered putting his own work into health therapy.

In the meantime he and Hamilton roughed out a book idea about

Berlin that he would try to sell in London later in the year. Hamilton's autobiography *The Way it was with Me* records his astonishment when, after Crowley's death, Yorke showed him proof that he had been spied on.[42] The following letter from Crowley to Yorke shows how risky Crowley's position really was:

> If he [Hamilton] should learn that I am as I was born, my usefulness would be over; and if he should even suspect that I have any relations with N ['Nick' Carter] beyond pulling his leg, there would be work for you within a week or two with that embalmer. So please avoid discussing my politics, or, if forced to do so, say that you regard me as at least 80% a Bolshevik. Do please take this most seriously, and be as cautious as you know how.
>
> I hear that Annie Besant is in senile dementia, and moribund. She may die any day now. It is most urgent that I should be instantly and widely proclaimed as H.P. B[lavatsky]'s legitimate successor. As to my reputation, I'm the Silent Martyr. Jesuit calumny is the shining token of my Mission.
>
> Throw yourself into this wholeheartedly, and we come right out of the Big End of the Horn – with Nick [Carter] and all England too! – in two shakes of a rat's whiskers.
>
> [...] You can talk freely to Hamilton about my mission with the Law of Thelema; he can help with broadcasting the Proclamation. Only avoid politics like poison. He thinks that I want to use the T[heosophical] S[ociety] to help Communism. Encourage that idea.
>
> Germer has let us down over Birven – made friends with him. And he has fled – probably over the Austrian frontier. We are enquiring.[43]

Hamilton returned from Yorke on 1 February with £50. Spence smells a payment from Carter for espionage, dressed as maintenance from Yorke, Crowley's supposed 'case officer'. The money arrived, according to Crowley, with 'a perfectly crazy letter accusing us [Crowley and Bill] of taking morphia etc., etc.! Germer's poison, no doubt'. Crowley's reply:

February 1, Berlin-Halensee

When you have done as much work in your life as I have, you
can start to give lectures on idleness – if you can find anyone idle
enough to listen to you! Not till then!

Do cease your debauches with Dean Inge[44] which cause you
headaches; and do remember that since you have not got a job in
all these months, you have no commercial value, and are a
weakling, and have nothing before you but the workhouse or
suicide.

The above reasoning is your own, not mine![45]

A week later, Crowley took tea again with Isherwood and boyfriend
Peter, known as 'Fanny'.[46] He dined with 'Gibarti of I.A.H.'[47] on 14
February: 'Very nice man and very clever.' Contact with Gibarti brought
Crowley close to the Comintern's activities in subverting pacifist and
anti-imperialist movements in Europe; the Hungarian was also working
for OGPU, forerunner of the KGB. According to Stephen Koch, Gibarti
assisted in the 'grooming' of Cambridge spy Kim Philby, an operation
that would begin in 1933, undertaken chiefly by Semen Rostovskii, with
Cambridge communist and homosexual Brian Howard as accomplice.[48]
Brian Howard was a friend of Gerald Hamilton, Tom Driberg and Nancy
Cunard. Crowley would cultivate contacts with Nancy and Driberg on
his return to London.

In this respect Spence has spotted a change in Crowley's MI5 dossier
number. In 1916, Crowley's file No. 2573 was labelled 'P.F.' (Personal
File); by 1933 it had become a 'P.P.', that is, 'Peace Propaganda' or
subversive pacifist activity file. PP files came under MI5 section G-1, run
by Victor Ferguson, keeping an eye on communists and fellow travellers,
among whom was journalist George Slocombe, whose company
Crowley would also cultivate on returning to London.

Not everyone at MI5 knew Crowley's first loyalty; it is possible he was
suspected of being a double agent. Some time in 1932, Driberg, who *was*
a double agent, became an informant for Captain Maxwell Knight's new
MI5 section B5(b) or 'M' section, dedicated to subversives. The section's

creation followed a 1931 shake-up which transferred counter-subversion work from the Special Branch and SIS to MI5 control. In late 1936 or early 1937 Knight would take a closer interest in Crowley, a legacy from Carter.

On 25 March 1932, Yorke received a letter from Carter about Crowley. It probably reflects the previous year's shake-up in the secret services. Carter informed Yorke he had now been out of his confidential job for two months and was with the Chief Constable's office, Paddington. He asked Yorke to request Crowley to stop sending long letters volunteering information about communist activities 'etc.' in Berlin. Carter added, significantly: 'I'm afraid to write again to A.C. for if I am not wrong the German Police will be looking at his letters and keeping him under surveillance, and if they twig a letter from me to him there may be considerable trouble for him and perhaps for all.'[49] 'Nick' was covering himself – and the Beast.

*   *   *

Berlin was getting too hot for Crowley. Carter's 'flap' may have been inspired by a story in *Paris-Midi* of 23 February in which the 'chief of German counter-espionage', Ferdinand von Bredow, had come to Paris to deal with a 'compromised' Aleister Crowley. The paper assumed Crowley was a German agent. There is no evidence for any trip by Crowley to Paris at this time.

The German Republic was in crisis. Granted German citizenship on 25 February, Hitler could now sit in the Reichstag. On 31 May, President Hindenburg invited Franz von Papen to form a government, a last-ditch effort to forestall Hitler. If there was any truth in the French paper's linking Crowley to Ferdinand von Bredow, Crowley's days in Berlin were numbered. Von Papen was a political rival of von Bredow's friend, General Kurt von Schleicher. Former military attaché to the USA, von Papen had surely not forgotten Crowley. If he discovered Crowley had colluded with either von Bredow or von Schleicher, and was in Berlin, it might be curtains for Crowley.[50] Significantly, on the day Franz von Papen sat for the first time with his new Cabinet (1 June 1932), Crowley appointed Wilfred Talbot Smith of 1746 Winona Boulevard, Hollywood, as OHO of the OTO in the event of his death.

It is a pity Crowley could not stay. On 4 June, 'Rosenfeld brought Prof. Haas, a gentleman, a scholar, and an Initiate!!!' Crowley had the pleasure of meeting two of the world's leading nuclear physicists. Low-temperature expert Haas would be involved in the Dutch government's purchase of uranium oxide in 1939. Leon Rosenfeld's work on quantum mechanics was of vital interest to the better-known Wolfgang Pauli and Paul Dirac. Such contacts chimed in with Crowley's earlier references to Erwin Schrödinger and Einstein.[51]

Packing and 'raising cash' on 18 June, Crowley had run out of time.

TWENTY-FIVE

All great Saviours have been bastards

1932–38

In England a man is not considered
guilty until he has been proved innocent.[1]

The aroma of thirties England: dark varnish, cardigans, pipe-smoke, Art Deco china, the long hangover of Victorian demise, chromium beams of dream-cinema and bracing hikes in the old Jerusalem. Crowley was 'out of his time', weighed down by earthly anchorage in a bay filled with the hulks of men condemned. Mucking in with England's depression, the Beast tried to lift the pains of sleep from the eyes of millions on a shoestring.

*   *   *

Bertha Busch shared the load, relieved to be out of a Germany heading Hitler's way. Crowley gathered the shards of his literary career, pitching a popular book on magick to publisher Allen Lane. Lane didn't bite. A book about contemporary Berlin failed to rouse interest. Having spoken to publishers Jonathan Cape, Rupert Grayson and Ivor Nicholson, Crowley put *Mortadello* before Mrs Paul Robeson. Crowley's play had an Othello-like role for her famous black husband, and the kind of throwback to aristocratic glamour German cinema audiences were crying out for. Crowley assured her he could get German movie director Pabst, but producer-director Max Reinhardt would take longer. As the Robesons were communist sympathizers (Robeson's FBI file is massive),

Crowley's interest may not have been solely artistic. In the event, Mrs Robeson passed on *Mortadello*. It was, she wrote, 'most interesting, and very exciting; and beautifully written. But that is literature, not theatre, in the present day sense.' The Robesons were not the only Reds in Crowley's range. He had regular meetings with journalist George Slocombe, on MI5's suspect list.[2]

Crowley took Yorke and Bill to Colney Hatch Mental Hospital to be informed by hypnosis expert Dr Alexander Cannon that Marie's case was hopeless; leaving her alone was best. Bill got bored with the talking and threw a fit in the street outside the hospital, swearing like a trooper.

Christina Foyle threw the Beast a lifeline in August, buying 200 copies of *Magick* at five shillings each for her bookshop, and inviting him to address her famous literary luncheon. Journalist the Marquess of Donegall recalled Crowley's speech, 'The Philosophy of Magick'. Miss Rosa Macaulay, sitting next to him, turned and said: 'I don't mind what he does, as long as he doesn't turn himself into a goat!'[3] Christina thanked Crowley 'very much indeed for the splendid speech', adding, 'Everyone enjoyed it and I do hope you will come again.' Crowley met Sir Denison Ross there, founder of the *Society for Promoting the Study of Religions*; they dined a few days later.[4] Ever fair, Neuburg's *Sunday Referee* column gave *Magick* a rave review.

London's tiny literary world could be supportive; Crowley got to know Desmond MacCarthy of the Bloomsbury Group whose denizens tended to imagine they had discovered sex. Crowley bemoaned their lack of vigour and spirit: all aesthetics, inward-looking ego-massage with cold ideas of sex, psychology with little visceral vision. Crowley's poetry appeared old hat to self-conscious 'radicals' of the new generation who went on to write textbooks telling teachers what poetry should be, affecting generations in the process with the dogmas of modernism. Had Crowley written the textbooks, we might have more enthusiasm for poetry today. For Crowley, poetry is the geyser of the soul. First you need a soul.

Crowley tried to make a life like his old Parisian life: intellectual encounters, art, romance and sex magick, but 1930s London was not

1920s Paris, and neither could match the magic of the pre-war days, when you could meet people whose grandparents had been born in the 18th century! But Crowley carried his optimism, wit and spiritual sunshine to the Café Royal in exchanges with Tom Driberg and friends. He met poet Siegfried Sassoon and saw old friend Augustus John, while regular playmates included Count Eric Lewenhaupt, who lent him both money and his wife Countess Dora, Macgregor Reid (a socialist who saw the light),[5] and the Marquess of Donegall, known familiarly to Crowley as 'Dongall'.[6] Dongall gave his pal some nice write-ups in *The Sunday Dispatch*.

A few weeks before Hitler became chancellor (30 January 1933), Crowley moved in to the Park Lane Hotel with Bill for a spell. Somebody was paying. During a West End walk, he 'discovered libel'. A flash on a copy of *Moonchild* in Mr Gray's bookshop window, 23 Praed Street, announced the author's previous novel *The Diary of a Drug Fiend* had been withdrawn. It had not, and since the flash implied *Moonchild* was a disreputable book, Crowley received £50 damages.

Lifted spirits were soon dashed. By June, 'all publishers' had rejected everything. He felt he was being boycotted; he was. Crowley might have expected more support from his old friend, the artist Nina Hamnett. He had given her one of her first commissions, back in the Victoria Street *Equinox* days before the war. When Nina's autobiographical *Laughing Torso* appeared, he found 'Abominable libels':

> Crowley had a temple in Cefalu in Sicily. He was supposed to
> practise Black Magic there, and one day a baby was said to have
> disappeared mysteriously. There was also a goat there. This all
> pointed to Black Magic, so people said, and the inhabitants of
> the village were frightened of him.[7]

Crowley could not overlook the 'disappearance' of a baby connected with 'Black Magic'. He had lost two children at Cefalù: Anne Lea, and a baby boy who was miscarried. Rumours of murder were outrageous; a child's death was not a joke. He showed the text to his lawyer. Isidore Kerman hoped to scare publisher Constable & Co into an out-of-court settlement. All was well until Nina, habitually drunk in Soho, got collared by sharp lawyer Edmund O'Connor. Having obtained a copy of Crowley's pornographic *White Stains* – a work that would have made DH Lawrence blush – O'Connor convinced Nina that Crowley's unenviable reputation, joined to some choice quotes from his explicit verse, would swing a verdict in Nina's favour. The *Laughing Torso* case of 1934 would render Crowley ridiculous even in serious newspapers. Fearless of risk, Crowley hoped to overturn both the calamity of the 1910 *Looking Glass* trial and years of libellous press; instead, he got it in the neck again.

Seeking support from Count Eric and Dongall, Crowley tried to drum up much-needed cash with his perfume *IT*, and a very fast game called 'Thelema' or *BIFF* which involved hitting a ball against a wall with fist or foot. Dongall had a bash at *BIFF* and found it exhausting, but fun. *IT* did not make him a girl-magnet, rather the reverse; Crowley enjoyed better success.

While the Beast savoured wonderful sex with 'the greatest fuckstress alive', a lady called Marianne whom he met at the hotel, Dongall gave notice of Crowley's patent 'Potted Sex Appeal' in the *Dispatch*. Crowley met Nancy Cunard again at the Park Lane and did astrological readings for her concerning tortured relations with mother. Lady Cunard, herself living with conductor Thomas Beecham, denied Nancy funds on account of *her* living with black jazz pianist, Henry Crowder.

Nancy told Gerald Yorke in 1950 that it was during the summer of 1933 that she really grew to like Crowley, thinking all the 'hoolie-goolie stuff' was now behind him. The wizard joined in Nancy's multi-racial dances in Notting Hill, 'was admirable with an African', and participated in her anti-Nazi meetings. Nancy was assembling her enormous *NEGRO Anthology*, the first global review of black culture, published in 1934 by Wishart and banned in Trinidad as seditious. She also campaigned for the 'Scottsboro Boys': nine Alabama youths falsely accused of raping a white girl. Crowley signed the petition: 'This case is typical of the hysterical sadism of the American people, the result of Puritanism and the climate. Aleister Crowley, scientific essayist.'

> May 10. Great Public Meeting to protest against Scottsboro
> Outrage turned to African Rally 8 p.m. It would have been a
> perfect party if the lads had brought their razors! I danced with
> many whores – all colours.

When I visited Nancy Cunard's post-war cottage in the Dordogne in 1997, former friends and helps informed me that after her death in 1965, men in suits arrived from England who went through her papers and carried away what they wanted. Nancy's commitment to racial and social equality made her familiar with the US communist movement and other radical bodies around the world. It seems likely Crowley was as interested in her contacts and their schemes as much as he was delighted by Nancy herself.

In lieu of books, Crowley tried journalism. He met Hayter Preston, senior editor of the *Sunday Referee*, and Ian Coster of the pro-Tory *Sunday Dispatch*. Coster worked for Carter's friend Lord Rothermere. Three articles duly appeared in the *Dispatch*, but someone put the frighteners on *Sunday Referee* owner Isidore Ostrer; Crowley's *Referee* deal was dropped.

The Beast attracted his last Scarlet Woman on 3 July 1933. Pearl Brooksmith, widow of Captain Eldred S Brooksmith,[8] had a shock when Crowley revealed his name, but Pearl found the middle-aged romantic captivating. Moving into the family flat at 40 Cumberland Terrace, the couple's 'engagement' was announced to Pearl's mother Evelyn: *de rigeur* when 'living together' was not done, though it was. Crowley found Evelyn Driver 'delightful'.

Visionary experiences followed. Crowley and Pearl's 24th sex-magick working ('Opus 24') climaxed in the invocation of 'the Essence of Godhead within the Scarlet Woman'. Pearl 'became One with the Infinite White Light'. They witnessed a 'Vision of Rosy Light in room'. Crowley had seen nothing like it since Nefta, perhaps with Dorothy in 1924. After Opus 28 on 1 October, Crowley became clairvoyant, envisioning Pearl's cottage at Fowey, Cornwall and her house in Malta. On 25 October, the Scarlet Woman saw 'an ultra violet halo' around Crowley.

But Crowley found Cumberland Terrace constricting. After one of many rows, Pearl coined the superb dictum: 'All great Saviours have been bastards' – nearly on a par with her delicious phrase: 'I feel the flame of fornication creeping up my body.'

In September, *Empire News* crime writer Bernard O'Donnell commissioned five articles. Published before the end of the year, they permitted Crowley to establish both his Great War loyalty and the nature of his work as a struggle against evil. Owned by Gomer and William Berry, later to be Lords Kemsley and Camrose, *The Empire News* enjoyed a modest readership, *The Sunday Times* remaining the Berry flagship. Gomer subsequently hired Ian Fleming to run a foreign desk and expand *The Empire News*'s market share. A friend of Crowley's for many years, O'Donnell received from him an account of Jack the Ripper obtained from Vittoria Cremers.

According to Cremers, the Ripper was Robert D'Onston Stephenson (a.k.a. Roslyn D'Onston), whom Cremers knew through her friendship with novelist Mabel Collins. Examining D'Onston's effects, Cremers found five dress ties, soaked in blood. O'Donnell's unpublished manuscript *The Man who was Jack the Ripper* is a must for Ripperologists. In his own paper on the subject, Crowley recounted his bringing to O'Donnell's attention a significant astrological tie-in, no pun intended, with D'Onston's alleged guilt. Cold Saturn and tricky, duplicitous Mercury were more relevant to cases of cold-blooded murder than the traditional 'hot' temperament of Mars; the characteristics of the worst criminals being cold indifference to human beings combined with deceit and icy calculation.

*   *   *

Crowley began 1934 somewhat at sixes and sevens, strangely unsure of himself. Was something telling him he was on a losing wicket? The *Laughing Torso* case would stain the year's canvas, though not all consequences were bad. Gaunt, he donned a striking top hat and morning coat and strode in with cane to the Waldorf Astoria, banking on winning the case to pay the bill.

Case 1932 C No3 651 opened on Tuesday 10 April before Mr Justice Swift at the King's Bench Division of the High Court. The libel case quickly disappeared. After Crowley and Germer finished giving evidence for JP Eddy's prosecution on the Thursday, Malcolm Hilbery, acting for Constable, called Betty May. Skilful questioning convinced the jury Crowley's reputation was so bad it could hardly be libelled. Betty May, eager to promote her book *Tiger Woman*, used the trial for profit. Letters Crowley obtained to prove this were judged inadmissible. He was subsequently found guilty of receiving stolen goods (the letters), and bound over with costs. Too late he found, at Kerman's, Betty May's letters *retracting* her account of the Abbey of Thelema; they went to his appeal case. Recognizing the case for libel had been obscured, the appeal nonetheless found that no jury could properly judge such a case! Crowley was handed the costs and a barrel-load of bad publicity. Even Dongall wrote his friend up after the verdict with a dose of sarcasm about the uselessness of his potted sex-appeal. It all smelt a bit off to most observers.

Estranged from Crowley, Israel Regardie wrote to Yorke expressing sympathy for the Beast but felt 'the old man' had been cornered, lying through his teeth to get by. The overall impression was of a great man reduced and reducing himself. Regardie asked astrologer Gabriel Dee about Crowley's prospects. She said 1934 was Crowley's *crisis*; if he got through it, he still had a future. She was right.

A surprising spin-off involved the appearance of 19-year-old Patricia Deirdre Maureen Doherty of Newlyn, Cornwall. Family members were concerned at Patricia's involvement with middle-aged Major Thynne. This was Robert Thompson Thynne, known to Crowley as Robin Thynne, former director of the Mandrake Press. Now a 'literary agent', Newlyn resident Thynne had a reputation for shady business deals and 'Government work' in the munitions line. Thynne had attracted both Patricia and her stunning friend, wealthy socialite, Greta Sequeira. He and Patricia explored Steiner's anthroposophy and the works of Aleister Crowley.

To get her away from Thynne, Patricia was dispatched to the London home of relative, High Court judge Lord Slesser. He thought she might be entertained by a trial that was making news: Crowley *versus* Constable. Pat watched the Beast from the gallery. She did not, as legend has it, rush up to Crowley outside the court declaring it was the worst judgement since Pontius Pilate, asking when could she have his baby; no, she was introduced to Crowley shortly after, probably by Thynne. Pat was destined to become a singular light in Crowley's life.

For Norman Mudd, however, the trouncing of his old master may have been the last straw. On 16 May he drowned himself off the Guernsey coast. Crowley afterwards asserted it was the kind of end reserved for Judases to the cause. It is not entirely clear what promoted this judgement.

Crowley went to see the film *I was a Fugitive from a Chain Gang*, remarking he'd be the same, if he could. He dreamed of going to Morocco, or anywhere where the 'frame-up' was unknown. He was desperate to get away, until, as he noted, 'the Hour strikes!' It would strike, but what to do until it did? He went to Chester on 4 August, and heard Canon Simpson spouting Marx from the cathedral pulpit. Crowley had long since dismissed 'Christian Socialism' in his *Gospel according to St Bernard Shaw*.

He headed south on 16 September with actor and pupil John Bland Jameson, stopping off at Alton, his old family homeland. He asked himself a rare question: 'What am I to do now?' The answer lacked conviction: 'Strike out a new line. Get followers. Follow subconscious. Hang on to success, and offer it to gods.'

*   *   *

Edward Alexander Crowley was registered bankrupt on 27 April 1935. His submission declared: 'I am the author of some of the noblest prose and poetry with which the English language has ever been enriched, and I cannot also have the talents of an accountant.'[9] He described his mysterious boycott. Somebody powerful enough to impress *Sunday Referee* owner Isidore Ostrer was determined to nobble Crowley whenever a chance arose to make an impact on the public mind. The devil's own never had this much trouble!

Compared to Karl Germer, however, his problems were slight. Karl was arrested by the Gestapo on 13 February 1935 for disseminating the teachings of 'High-grade Freemason Crowley". After seeing the basement of the infamous Columbia Haus Gestapo HQ in Berlin, Karl was sent to Esterwegen concentration camp. Some 80,000 German Freemasons died in Hitler's persecutions. Rudolf Steiner's anthroposophists and a host of other unsung magical groups were also persecuted. This made things tricky for dear old Martha Küntzel who was drawn to Hitler. Hitler, like Crowley, had been 'chosen by Providence', she wrote. According to Martha, the National Socialists would free 'themselves from the slavery of an alien will and anything else alien to their inner being'.[10] This was where theosophical beliefs concerning 'root races' could lead devotees into temptation; Crowley regarded 'root race' theory as bunk.

Fascist sympathizers had their eye on Crowley.

*   *   *

As we saw in chapter 18, letters from a right-wing British conspiracy investigator calling him or herself 'M' to Jesuit priest Joseph Ledit[11] were found by Marco Pasi in the Central State Archives in Rome. In September 1935, 'M' asked about Serbian mystic Dimitrije Mitrinović's movement New Europe or *New Britain*. 'New Britain' had appeared in 1932 within the Adler-inspired *International Society for Individual Psychology* established in 1927. 'M' believed the movement was communist-inspired.

A letter of April 1936 to Ledit involved Crowley directly. 'M' asked for any information on allegedly influential groups calling themselves 'XI', 'New Britain', 'New Europe', 'New Order', and a French Order called 'l'Ordre Nouveau'. Mistakenly linking these groups to the OTO, 'M' then asked about the post-1933 movements of Aleister Crowley. Did Ledit have a recent description or drawing, especially of his *head*?

Creepy.

Who was 'M'?

Counter-subversion expert at MI5's department B5(b), Captain Charles Maxwell Knight, used the nickname 'M'. Knight had formerly provided intelligence for British fascists. Dennis Wheatley introduced Driberg to Knight in 1932. He also introduced Knight to Crowley some time in late 1936 or early 1937, having known Crowley since at least May 1934, as this friendly letter extract attests:

> This is just a line to thank you for your magnificent gift. Not only is *Magick* a fine volume to possess and a delightful addition to my collection from the kindly way in which you inscribed it, but it is a book that I shall look forward to reading with the very greatest interest. I am sending, as promised, a couple of my own [...] with every good wish and again many thanks. Yours very sincerely, Dennis Wheatley[12]

While Spence suspects Knight's hand in the Ledit–M correspondence, the latter's style of remarks hardly reflects Knight's intelligence.[13] The approach points to John Baker White, Director of the anti-communist pressure group and intelligence organization, the Economic League, and to the Jewish-Masonic conspiracy theories of Nesta Webster.

*   *   *

In August 1935, Germer was released from Esterwegen. Stimulated by Hitler's assertion in *Mein Kampf* that he was not a religious teacher, but would encourage such a one when he appeared, Crowley wrote to German artist and OTO member Oscar Hopfer from 66 Radcliffe Gardens, Earls Court, on 20 January 1936:

> I quite agree with what you say about your pioneer problem but it seems to me that under the present circumstances, if I understand them aright, the only means of propaganda is to address the leader himself [Hitler] and show him that the acceptance of these philosophical principles is the only means of demonstrating to reason instead of merely to enthusiasm the propriety of the measures he is taking for the rebuilding of the Reich. Unless he does this the Churches will ultimately strangle him; they have an almost infinite capacity for resistance and endurance for this very reason that their systems are based on a fundamental theory which enabled them to survive attacks and restraints. They bow as

much as they are compelled to bow by force and they
subsequently excuse their yielding on the grounds of expediency.
If the Fuehrer wishes to establish his principle permanently he
must uproot them entirely and this can only be done by
superseding their deepest conceptions. [...] Enthusiasm for a man
or an outward system dies with the man or with the circumstances
that have brought the system into being. The Law of Thelema
being infinitely rigid and infinitely elastic is an enduring basis.[14]

When not dreaming that Hitler would embrace Thelema, Crowley was
much absorbed with the AMORC situation. The *Ancient Mystical Order
Rosae Crucis*, based in San José, had been founded by Harvey Spencer
Lewis on a forged charter examined by Crowley in New York in 1918.[15]
Though convoluted, the struggle boils down to this. Lewis sought
legitimacy for his Rosicrucian Order by allying himself first with Reuss,
who gave him an OTO certificate conferring honorary membership,
then with Tränker, with whom Lewis wished to form a Rosicrucian
federation. Crowley maintained Secret Chief authority was vital to such
activity. Believing he possessed this authority gave Crowley absolute
confidence in expecting Lewis to submit to the spiritual obligation
to support the Secret Chiefs' work. Crowley's chartered OTO representatives in the USA were also based in California. There were no
grounds for competition. Crowley made his views clear in a number of
letters. The first was to Max Schneider, OTO member based in New
York to whom Crowley wrote in January 1936:

> Lewis is merely the last of a very long series of men who have tried
> to play Monkey tricks with the Great Order. He is merely the last
> to have it in the neck as a consequence. [...] 132 [W.T. Smith] has
> got to help you with this, because he is the official bloke with the
> Charters and letters and Photographs and all that bunk.[16]

On 28 December 1936, Crowley tried to rope Arnoldo Krumm-Heller
into the struggle:

> Lewis was never a disciple either of Reuss or myself. He had [in
> 1918] been knocking about for years trying to run a fake

Rosicrucian order. He cast about everywhere for authority and when I first met him in New York in 1918 E.V. he was showing a charter supposed to be from French Rosicrucians in Toulouse. [...] this ridiculous forgery [...] Lewis didn't know French! In the last two or three years [...] Reuss was sick, impoverished and desperate. [...] He accordingly handed out honorary diplomas up to the 95° and sometimes very foolishly the 96°. That is how people like Spencer Lewis and Tränker get their standing. It is particularly stupid because Reuss had got into great trouble through Yarker's giving the 95° to [Theosophist James Ingall] Wedgwood. [...] If he [Lewis] had none [charter-authority] he can be prosecuted, if he had mine he must account for the 900,000 dollars odd which he had accrued in the last few years. Unfortunately, my people in California, although most devoted and intelligent, are not precisely men of the world and do not know how to handle big affairs. It is imperative that I should go over there and put the screws on Spencer Lewis.[17]

On 6 January 1937, Crowley addressed a query from Oscar Hopfer of Weissendorf regarding Tränker's and Eugen Grosche's attitude to his authority:

I would not say that Grosche and Tränker were brothers of the left hand path, they are just ordinary little people meddling along in their stupidity without the backing of moral character which is a first condition of any kind of attainment.

Crowley enjoyed relief from the trials of esoteric supremacy drinking and dining with Laurence and Pamela Felkin and writer Charles Cammell, together experiencing what Crowley called 'ordeal by curry'. His were the hottest curries in London – and rare too; he was a curry pioneer, even discussing plans for a London curry house, the 'Black Magic Restaurant' along with ideas for the 'Bar 666' – all ahead of their time. He became a gourmet, his diaries punctuated by fiery recipes for curries and savouries. I can vouch for their potency.

*   *   *

Robin Thynne died on 17 July 1936. *The Cornishman* intimated a secret government affair:[18]

THE LATE MAJOR THYNNE
(Secret Carried to the Grave)

Who was Major R. Thynne, the scientist who died in an Exeter nursing home after he had suffered a stroke while travelling from London to Cornwall? Did he carry a vital secret to the grave? Mystery that surrounded his last days deepened on Tuesday when his remains were cremated in Plymouth.

I arrived at the crematorium at the time originally decided to find the chapel deserted.

There was no funeral service. Only two girls and an undertaker were present.

Rumours that Dr Ita Wegmann, the Swiss woman who flew from Switzerland to London to save the dying Major, would attend the funeral proved unfounded. Major Thynne had a distinguished army career and published several important scientific works anonymously.

I understand that it is more than possible that Major Thynne was not his correct name.

I learn on good authority that Dr Wegmann's fight for Major Thynne's life was considered vital by certain authorities.

Someone flew in Dr Ita Wegmann, the anthroposophist cancer-specialist, from Switzerland.[19] Three days after Thynne's death, Patricia Doherty telephoned Crowley. He noted her precise time of birth, as he did when starting any intimate relationship: 'Patricia Doherty March 16, 1915 5–6P.M.'[20]

Pearl was livid.

Friday 31 July 1936 was a special day in Crowley's middle age: '*Linga-yoni mudra*' was performed with 'Girl Pat'. This tantric union of flesh and spirit apparently elicited the reaction of a Mrs Turner Coles, who 'began an unprovoked and furious attack on Miss Doherty, calling her trollop, harlot, whore, and slut in the course of a spate of venomous abuse'. A child was conceived.

Pearl gave Pat a rough ride. Arriving for lunch on 3 August Pat was greeted by 'Foul remarks by Pearl'. Shrugging his shoulders, Crowley dined with Pat at Leoni's, then went to see his West Indian friend Rollo Ahmed and Rollo's pal, Edomi. Rollo had written a book about black political struggles in the West Indies, claiming voodoo adeptship. Allan Burnett-Rae wrote a memoir about Crowley in which Ahmed called him to ask whether he still had a spare flat, and if so, would he consider meeting 'a very highly evolved personality'?[21] The powerful aroma of the highly evolved personality would soon permeate the house.

Thursday 6 August

Iced Vindalu of Bhindi – lowest layer. Madras Chutney. Lamb with red and green Chillis. Usual rice – top layer. […] Deacon and Ruby to lunch.[22]

Nocturnal rows would see the Beast and his Scarlet Woman out of 56 Welbeck Street and into a series of lettings across London before Crowley temporarily settled at 66 Radcliffe Gardens SW10, in time for Gerald Yorke's return from the Far East at the end of the year.[23]

A party held on 12 October 1936 offers us a glimpse of Crowley's social circle during this water-treading period. There was Count and Countess Lewenhaupt, Karl Germer, 'The Girl Pat', Charles Cammell, Dolores Sileman, George Roberts, Bernard O'Donnell, Pearl, Tom Driberg and Louis Wilkinson. Crowley's savouries, wit and liberating atmosphere were a draw.

*   *   *

Crowley began a series of lectures at the trendy Eiffel Tower, Soho, on 17 February 1937. 'Yoga for Yellowbellies' would be published as *Eight Lectures on Yoga*, as witty and lucid an account of Yoga as you might wish for, again, ahead of its time. A week later: 'The Girl Pat tuned up in very full sail [pregnant]. Pearl went nearly insane. It *is* rotten that she can't give me one [a child].'

It was indeed rotten for Pearl. By contrast to Pat's healthy pregnancy, Pearl's gynaecological woes culminated in an agonizing hysterectomy, a misery rendered doubly ironic by the fact that Pearl was convinced Crowley, her helpless nurse, was himself a child in need of mothering.

On Mayday 1937, in Newcastle, a healthy Pat gave birth to a healthy boy named Randall Gair. In seventh heaven, Crowley dined with old friend and chess rival, Clifford Bax. Bax introduced Crowley to a remarkable artist inspired by anthroposophy. The artist's name was Frieda and she was married to Sir Percy Harris, Liberal MP for Bethnal Green. Lady Harris's long collaboration with 666 led to the 'Crowley Tarot Pack' of 78 cards, executed with uncommon brilliance by Freida to Crowley's exacting design. *The Book of Thoth*, Crowley's masterpiece on the tarot, was written to accompany the pack.

As Pearl faded slowly from the scene, Crowley enjoyed a long string of sexual relationships with working-class and middle-class women: Adele Lindsay, Bobby Barfoot, Mattie Pickett, Sally Pace, Elsie Morris, Phyllis Hunt, Meg Usher, Peggy Wetton, Catherine Falconer and Maisie Clarke, to name but a few of those he encountered about the capital who offered themselves to IX° sex magick, practices denoted in his diaries by a circle with a cross radiating from its centre: ⊕: sex divine. Efforts 'to control A.M.O.R.C.' using the IX° did not pay off.

Throughout 1937, Crowley fraternized with spiritualist lecturer and medium Vyvyan Deacon. Introduced to Crowley's work in Sydney, Deacon's single-mindedness caused Eunice, his Chinese wife, heart-ache.[24] Crowley was impressed by Eunice but unimpressed by 'spiritualism' which he called 'spiritism' or 'necromancy'.

Crowley believed that minds hostile to change clung, at death, to the astral remnants of the body. These 'shells', as he called them, though utterly broken from the 'God' or Soul or Star that had enlightened them, could yet be invoked from the astral world by mediums. While allowing exceptions, Crowley considered 'Spiritualism' a con trick played on the extreme vulnerability of the bereaved.

The Deacons introduced Crowley to the Liberal Catholic Church building known as 'the Sanctuary' near the back of Harrods. Crowley communicated there on one occasion and corresponded with its founder, theosophist (and homosexual) Bishop Frederick James, whose Midlands accent amused Crowley. James's sermons contained thelemic principles, admitted by Bishop James.

In early 1938, Crowley saw Deacon surrounded by a halo of light. Five weeks later, Deacon was in hospital. Crowley wrote to him, assuring his friend of 'light at the end of the tunnel'. On 19 February, Crowley observed: 'A man of science is one who understands the measure of everything, and the meaning of nothing.' Science declared the medium Vyvyan Deacon dead at 4am that day.

*　　*　　*

With the headline: *Early Birds Make News* Driberg's *Express* column announced how on 22 December 1937 at 6.22am, Gerald Yorke and a gaggle of representatives of the white, yellow and black races stood at Cleopatra's Needle to hear a short speech by '62 year old magician' Aleister Crowley before each was presented with a special copy of *Liber AL*. The journalist was informed that a war usually broke out after each publication. When the journalist lamented this hard luck on humanity, Crowley replied that if only people listened to what he was saying, war could be avoided. In a remarkable passage cut from the official order form for the 'fourth publication' of *AL*, Crowley unveiled the spiritual revolution:

> The Spiritual Revolution announced by this book has already taken place: there is hardly a country where it is not openly manifest.
>
> Ignorance of the true meaning of this new Law has led to gross anarchy. Its conscious adoption in its proper sense is the sole cure for the political, social and racial unrest which have brought about the World War, the catastrophe of Europe and America, and the threatening attitude of China, India and Islam.[25]

In April 1938, Dr Anthony Greville-Gascoigne, a psychoanalyst contact of Regardie's through Dion Fortune's Society of the Inner Light, opined that *The Book of the Law* went over ordinary people's heads and frightened them. Could Crowley not use other means to make his point? Crowley assured the doctor that there was more to the matter than his personal opinion:

> The forces behind the Book determine the time and place of wars; and if you are in a position to put a spoke in the wheel of such people, I certainly am not. I fought against these forces with the whole of my power for many years, and I came out at the little end of the horn. You must read up the history of the business, if you want to understand the actual position.[26]

Crowley composed a 'Memorandum', produced like a government secret document, mapping out a determined plan to take over all esoteric and related movements:

> A MEMORANDUM: A SUGGESTED CAMPAIGN HAVING AS ITS OBJECT THE WELDING INTO ONE COMPLETE WHOLE THE VARIOUS OCCULT AND KINDRED ORGANISATIONS THROUGHOUT THE WORLD

> 'Fear' of most to lose with regard to coming World Revolution should be used to garner support of prominent/wealthy persons.
> THE SECRET MASTER announces that he has authorised the presence in the U.S.A. of three members of the governing grand council of the O.T.O. to receive applications for affiliation from all Organisations and/or orders acknowledging the symbol of the Rosy Cross.
> Further Announcements will follow in due course.[27]

Detailed strategies ensued.

*   *   *

August was bucolic. Pat invited Crowley to Cornwall for a fortnight with their son, nicknamed 'Aleister Ataturk'. The morning before departure, father indulged in sentimental reminiscence, finding the 'really delightful day' identical in quality to 'the days of Lea in Washington Square, New York City'. That was now 20 years ago.

Crowley had a good time climbing rocks with his little son near Newlyn, visiting Mousehole, Paul and Morvah, watching John Bland Jameson in rehearsals for *A Midsummer Nights Dream* and generally getting to bed early between attempts at wooing the beautiful Greta Sequeira. Frieda Harris gave him money for his ticket and pocket money; she paid him a teaching stipend.

Crowley wanted Jameson to engage in a joint venture: a course of rejuvenation treatments named 'Amrita' after the repast of the Hindu gods. Hoping to cash in on their immortal diet, Crowley offered long-standing, indeed long-suffering, medicinal study, honed by Himalayan experience, as his therapeutic credentials. He also offered a share of the business to Burnett-Rae in exchange for collateral. Burnett-Rae declined. Would Jameson stump up the cash?

Jameson stumped up £100,[28] whereupon Crowley, now back in London, sent *The Heart of the Master* to press. Crowley's prophecy of an apocalyptic war made in the mid-1920s appeared precisely one week before Chamberlain and Deladier let Hitler invade the Czech Sudetenland, encouraging the Führer to invade Poland in 1939. Crowley called the event 'the Betrayal'.

At the back of the book, Crowley placed a kind of thelemic recruiting poster:

If you want FREEDOM you must fight for it.

If you want to To FIGHT You must organize.

If you want To ORGANIZE Write to the Master Therion

BM/JPKH London, WC1.

On 13 August 1938, Crowley performed '⊕' *Object*: 'War to establish 93.

(Elixir on dagger).' The coming war must see Thelema, not Nazism, triumph. That he smeared the sacrament, the magically charged sexual juices, on a dagger was an affective sign of will. Two days later, another rite of sex magick was performed: 'Maisie [Clarke] א α A1 WAR to establish 93.' Crowley was ready.

Britain was not.

TWENTY-SIX

V

1939–43

I hope one day to be able to leave the English hypocrites
to their own beastliness, and live in my own world.
Until I am wanted; in the hour of battle.[1]

The hour struck. On 10 May 1939, the Beast shot one over the bows, *before* war was declared. Martha Küntzel in Leipzig was the shocked recipient:

You make fun of Roosevelt, but Roosevelt can send 4,000
bombers over Germany within the first week of the war which
we are now expecting to begin about the third week in June.
Over there you have no idea what the world at large is thinking.
[…] As for the ravings about the Jews, they are simply
unintelligible. Almost the whole of life in Germany above
brutality, stupidity and cruelty, servility and bloodthirst, was
Jewish. Germans are as far below Jews, generally speaking, as
monkeys below men; but I have always been fond of monkeys
and I do not want to offend them by comparing any German to
one.[2] These remarks, stated in comparatively direct language, are
intended to express the general feeling of people outside
Germany.
    There will be no second Versailles – there will be
Armageddon. The Hun must be wiped out. The Hun *will* be
wiped out.[3]

Three weeks later, Crowley visited Sir Percy and Lady Harris in Chiswick. No one, it was said, could empty the Commons quicker than

Percy Harris, but Crowley, hungry for insider-knowledge on war-preparedness, liked him. Sir Percy was crisp: 'There will be no war before August.'[4]

Not before August.

That night, Crowley dreamt of long talks with Adolf Hitler; Crowley's books received the official stamp. He saw a city at dusk: 'A man in gold-braid went round a corner.' Several horsemen appeared, 'similarly gorgeous'. 'One of them fired the first shot of the war.'[5]

2 September 1939

A portent: one of the grandest thunderstorms 666 had ever seen: 'It went on for hours.' 11.20am: London's skies were pierced by an air-raid warning – only a practice. Forty minutes later, Britain was at war.

Crowley set to work. 'I am looking for a job', he wrote, probably to Sir Percy. Crowley's priority: *get America in*, 'should Poland crack'. He had advocated Britain and America's union against tyranny since 1900. 'I'll go anywhere and do anything so far as bronchial tubes permit. Can you give me a letter to somebody of power to use me?'[6] Crowley had already written to Carter about applying his 'sympathetic understanding of the Muslim and Hindu worlds'. He consulted the I Ching: What were Britain's chances? '*Excellent*'. The Nazis?: a '*weak beam*'.[7] Right on cue, *U-boat 30* torpedoed British-owned ship *Athenia*; 246 US sailors were drowned. Germany was repeating its 1915 strike against the *Lusitania*: unrestricted submarine warfare would terrorize the seas. Crowley wrote at once to the Naval Intelligence Department: 'Sir, I have the honour to apply for employment.' With impressive *bona fides*, he summarized his intelligence work during the last war: supplying the Propaganda Kabinett with false information 'to wreck their propaganda by inducing them to make psychological blunders: all with the object of inducing the U.S. to enter war on our side'. He outlined his work for Carter: 'In 1927 I began work for the Special Branch, this time to work and report on Communist activities, especially in Berlin, where I lived almost con-tinuously for three years.'[8]

Admiral John Godfrey, Director of Naval Intelligence, responded immediately. The letter was found in Crowley's wallet when he died:

> The Director of Naval Intelligence presents his compliments and would be glad if you could find it convenient to call at the Admiralty for an interview. It would be appreciated if you will be good enough to communicate with Commander C.J.M. Lang, Royal Navy, Naval Intelligence Division, Admiralty, Telephone: Whitehall 9000, Ext. 484, in order to arrange a suitable time.[9]

According to specialist Phil Tomaselli, Extension 484 got you to the NID section dealing with prisoners of war.[11] Commander Lang had been NID chief in Hong Kong 1932–4, contemporary with Ian Fleming's brother Peter's mission in China.[10] Ian worked for Godfrey. Crowley wrote on the invitation, 'Better ring up Mr Frost – Ext. 46 for an interview.'

Describing the 'Secret Chiefs' to a correspondent in 1944, Crowley compared them to the NID:

> But who are They? Since They are 'invisible' and 'inaccessible', may They not merely be figments invented by a self-styled 'Master', not quite sure of himself, to prop his tottering Authority?
>   Well, the 'invisible' and 'inaccessible' criticism may equally be levelled at Captain A, and Admiral B, of the Naval Intelligence Department. These 'Secret Chiefs' keep in the dark for precisely the same reasons; and these qualities disappear instantaneously the moment *They* want to get hold of *you*.[12]

Crowley launched his own 'Axe the Axis' campaign. On 8 October, he sent his fit-for-service patriotic poem *England, Stand fast!* to 'Winston', then to PM Neville Chamberlain and the BBC:

> England, stand fast! Stand fast against the foe!
>   They struck the first blow: we shall strike the last.
> Peace at the price of Freedom! We say No.
>   England, stand fast! [13]

Crowley wanted it turned into a popular tune to raise morale. The poem served well, but the BBC and snooty press rejected it:

> All the *real* people like it. But no newspaper will print it. Their filthy trade has corrupted them wholly. They really [think?] [...] that the 'man in the street' likes the pansy poetastry of W.H. Auden & Co.[14]

He wrote to the War Office, advocating mobilization of the population into war work, a conception central to Churchill's premiership after May 1940: *TOTAL WAR.*

'I have the honour,' wrote Crowley, 'to submit the following propositions for the consideration of H.M. Government. The nation must be a disciplined organization before the beginning of hostilities, and its existence would be the most potent conceivable factor in their indefinite postponement.' Old recruitment methods suffered from lack of respect for authority on the street; people knew the government lied to them, he argued, proposing fresh ideas about motivation: 'I should like to discuss the question of propaganda with your Publicity Experts with a view to issuing a new series of posters based on the Law of Thelema.' Crowley included a sketch idea for a poster. It was headed by a drawing of the British Crown:

> Do what thou wilt shall be the whole of the law
> What is your true will?
> Probably you do not know yourself.
> But – It is sure that every man has the root-will to make
> the best of himself [...]
>
> ....
>
> To do your own true Will – Join the Army! [15]

Ahead of his time, Crowley's idea is now stock-in-trade recruitment propaganda; a recent Royal Navy advertisement promised 'Life without Limits': attractive to the Beast.

*   *   *

Bertha Busch, the 'Red Angel', showed up on 2 November for sex magick: 'Then she talked. I have *never* heard anything like it. I can't risk another such day until I'm feeling much stronger.' Bill joined Crowley and girlfriend Margot Cripps for lunch later in the month, followed by '⊕' with Bill for 'Health etc.' – and the next day too, with a twist:

Sunday 26 November

Margot and Bill – amusing day.
⊕ Margot (Bill with us too). Health.

In spite of the gay threesome, Bill's lease on Crowley's patience was short; she faded from the scene. A poetry collection on the joy of drinking and the acceptance of death, *Temperance, A Tract for the Times*, marked the winter solstice, mouth-wateringly presented as a restaurant menu bound with cords. 'Happy Dust' was dedicated to Margot, 'The Artist' to Frieda, 'Hymn to Astarte' to Pat, now missing with Ataturk, somewhere between Germany and Egypt.

* * *

In May 1940, as the 'outsider', the man 'too dangerous' became PM, Karl Germer was deported from Belgium and interned in France. The Germans advanced, the British evacuated Dunkirk in June and the country braced itself. Crowley contacted the Ministry of Information: 'Saw *Sunday Dispatch* Girl Friday. Stuart of Ministry of Information was there. Submitted *England, Stand Fast* with a little lecture.' Despite the patriotic objective, Crowley's sex magick skills, at age 64, were under attack:

Ruby Butler, the blonde bombshell, to lunch.

⊕ Weak erection. Too rapid ejaculation. Very feeble concentration: could not formulate purpose.

Purpose. The lesson was not lost on him. Britain also needed to 'get it up'. As Luftwaffe bombers boiled the autumn skies, an idea grew in his mind, even as his health suffered. Bombing aggravated his asthma.

Torquay, scene of teenage liberation, was chosen for recuperation. There was a downside – 9 October 1940: 'Nerves on edge for lack of cunt.' He dreamt of Greta Sequeira at a big hill station in India. While Crowley made love to the Greta of his dreams, Liverpool was blitzed and John Winston Lennon entered this world.

On 16 November the worst asthma attack in memory put him in hospital. Struggling for life, Frieda rushed to his bedside. A few days later, Dr RH Lodge pronounced him recovered, advising a trip to the USA: just what Crowley wanted. But he needed money and a passport. Sex magick with new girl Sophie Burt aimed to secure the former. Cammell considered 666's recovery smacked of resurrection. 666 was thinking of national resurrection. He would devise a militant aphrodisiac, or, as he put it: a 'Magical "Union of Men" to beat Nazis': a 'symbol to bring victory'.

He hit on the idea of the 'V-sign'.[16] 'V [is]for Valentine [sexual love] and Victory', he wrote.

*   *   *

A 1995 government publication asserts the V-campaign was 'one of the *BBC's* most enduring contributions to the propaganda war'.[17] 'Its use', the official version explains, followed 'on the suggestion of a Belgian commentator' because it combined the first letter of *Victoire* (Victory in French) and *Vrijheid* (Freedom in Flemish). 'The campaign began in January 1941, with a broadcast for Belgium, and spread throughout Europe, resisters painting the V on public buildings. So successful was the campaign's impact that Goebbels himself took it up, unaware, it seems, of the irony of placing a massive V sign on the Eiffel Tower in Paris.'

The Belgian was Victor Auguste de Laveleye a member of the BBC's Belgian French-speaking broadcast team (1940–4).[18] A leading Belgian liberal, he would have been known to Sir Percy Harris. In May 1941, a paper on 'broadcasting as a new weapon of war' was circulated within the BBC. South African journalist Douglas Ernest Ritchie organized the V-campaign to foment resistance abroad, speaking in broadcasts as 'Colonel Britton'; Crowley wrote to him.[19]

The famous morse code for 'V' – three dots and a dash, followed by the opening bar of Beethoven's Fifth, was first broadcast on 27 June 1941, rallying listeners to the BBC's European service. Imitated by teachers' clapping, train whistles, blacksmiths on their anvils, or the peal of church bells, when joined to the appearance of the 'V' over public surfaces, the effect was to surround occupiers with a resistance whose source was definite, yet ethereal. Churchill joined the campaign with a radio message: 'The V sign is the symbol of the unconquerable will of the people of the occupied territories and a portent of the fate awaiting the Nazi tyranny.' The V-sign became Churchill's personal trademark, putting his fingers up to the enemy. For Churchill, it was a symbol of the indomitable will, as it was for Crowley: phallic power and implacable opposition. Charles de Gaulle took up the sign. The victory sign was the sign of the victor. Its effect was magical.

Was its source?

The official version allows that the first Britain and the USA heard about it was in June and July 1941. Six months earlier, however, a diary entry for January 31 reveals Crowley *already* considering the deniability of his invention:

> Should anyone challenge my authorship of 'The V Sign', I reply
> in the words of my predecessor in poetry and Magick, Publius
> Vergilius Maro: *Sic vos non vobis* – If he fail to understand
> exactly why this is an answer, his claim is unlikely to be well-
> founded. If he understand, then: To it![20]

The Vergilian saying exists in two forms: *Sic vos non vobis melliscatis apes* ('Thus you bees make honey not for yourselves') and *sic vos non vobis vallera fertis oves* ('Thus you sheep make fleeces not for yourselves').[21] Vergil coined the saying because Bathyllus, a pantomime performer, had plagiarized his work. Vergil was saying that while the plagiarist was doing him the service of communicating his message, the plagiarist himself was neither the intended recipient of, nor would understand, the essence or 'honey' of the message. Crowley could add another layer to the saying's meaning: 'As the thief took from my predecessor Vergil, now you steal from me!' And should the hearer of the quotation grasp his meaning, then he'd better 'get on with it!' And what Crowley meant by 'get on with it!' would be revealed in an extraordinary booklet he was planning called *Thumbs Up! – A Pentagram – A Pantacle to Win the War*. The 'thumb up' is a symbol of good will and wellbeing. It is also phallic, an image of the erect and ready penis, standing firm for action, fecund and positive, symbol of the True Will. *STAND FIRM!* urged contemporary Ministry of Information posters; had they taken a subliminal leaf from Crowley's book?

The subliminal converse of this message was plain: Nazis could 'Fuck Off!'.

On 12 February 1941, Crowley had fresh thoughts: 'Thumbs Up! Being phallic, how can I put it over pictorially or graphically? I can point out the result of "National Prayer" to the Castrato-deity.' *National Prayer Days* had been encouraged as spiritual relief from national anxiety. Crowley believed the 'God' of many believers had no 'balls'; Crowley insisted Prayer Days sapped will, playing up to irrational fears, leaving outcomes to the caprice of 'divine will' not *inside*, but outside of Man. 'But I,' wrote Crowley, 'want positive ritual affirmation...'

On Valentine's Day, Crowley recalled his magical motto *VVVVV* adopted on achieving the grade of 'Master of the Temple' in 1909.[22] Translated, the Latin acronym declared: 'In my lifetime I have conquered the universe by the force of truth.' *Victory again*. Then he thought of the 'V' in LVX, the Latin word for 'Light'. In Golden Dawn symbolism, 'L.V.X.' referred to the 'Light of the Cross', because if the two lines of the 'L' and the 'V' are extended they form crosses. Thus, 'L.V.X.' was also equated with INRI, written on Jesus' cross. The Bible interprets INRI, as 'Jesus the Nazarene, King of the Jews', but alchemists also interpreted it as *Igne Natura Renovatur Integra*: 'The whole of Nature is renewed by Fire'. *Renewed by fire...*

Give 'em hell! 'Force and Fire' characterized the New Aeon.

Crowley learnt in the Golden Dawn the sign of 'Typhon', the Greek name for the burning-sun aspect of Egyptian god Seth: the origin of our word 'typhoon'. The sign made for 'Typhon' was to hold two arms out-stretched upwards, a 'V' sign, and the middle letter of LVX.

For Crowley, 'V' represented the *New Aeon* replacing the old magical formula of sorrowful sacrifice ('Osiris'). The New Aeon was cleansing the world by spiritual fire. The fruit of the new formula would be the divine Child *Horus*, the conquering solar force, whose revelation had come to Crowley in 1904 in the city Al Kahira, Arabic for the *City of Victory*: Cairo.

Victory.

The V-symbol was present in the horns of the goat, Capricorn (♑): lusty, bold, wild. The horned one is also the common idea of 'The Devil', who, for Crowley is an image of the Sun, the life force, of divine sex, at our being's core. The spiritual essence of sex was more powerful than anything on Earth, because it makes Man, and without Man, nothing is made.

Above all, 'V' represents the Will aroused to action, and in Greek cabala, the number of THELEMA (Will) is 93. At the spiritual core of the war effort was Crowley's magical system and spiritual prophecy: the Key to Victory.

'V' it would be. Beat the Bosch with 93!

New Year's Day 1941

Crowley made a surprising diary entry: 'Used ceremonial after so long abstinence. It went very well. P.S. Too well! Started three fire accidents!!!' There is no mention of where this magick was performed or why.

It has long been rumoured in the small world of British occultism that at least one magical ritual was performed to ward off German invasion. In one version, a witches' coven in the New Forest sacrificed an old, terminally ill man. In another, a ritual in Ashdown Forest, Sussex, performed by Crowley with Canadian soldiers and secret service backing, aimed to encourage Rudolf Hess, Deputy Leader of the Nazi Party, to fly to Britain, by psychic force.[23]

Post-war witchcraft museum curator Cecil Williamson was allegedly recruited to marshal occult resources since it was known that leading Nazis were susceptible to occult suggestion, and the knowledge that Britain was waging a magical war, as well as an economic and political one, might have disturbed some Nazis. War had to be waged on every front, so the idea is not that strange. The NID did gather astrological information on senior Nazis. Spence quotes from wartime MI5 chief Guy Liddell's diary, to wit, that Admiral John Godfrey:

> is employing Louis de Wohl to read horoscopes of the most important Admirals in the navy and those of Hitler, Mussolini, Darlan, and Portal. Merritt of NID is his intermediary. It is believed that DNI [Director of Naval Intelligence] himself is a strong believer in astrology. On the other hand it may be that since Hitler works on these lines and de Wohl is acquainted with the workings of Hitler's astrologer [illegible] hopes to work out the most propitious [time] for Hitler to act. The whole business seems to me to be highly misleading and dangerous.[24]

Declassified material associates Swiss astrologer Louis de Wohl with a plot to lure Hess to Britain. Ministry of Defence folder *DEFE 1/134*, dealing with censorship of Hess's mail, was released in January 1992.[25] Hess's friend Albrecht Haushofer, shot for treason in 1945 for involvement in the Stauffenberg bomb plot, wrote to the Duke of Hamilton in Scotland. Intercepted by a postal censorship clerk on 2 November 1940 and dispatched to MI5, the letter revealed senior Nazi interest in peace with Great Britain. Hamilton was head of RAF coastal command for the corridor through which Hess would fly in May 1941. Just *who else* Hess might have wished to contact concerned Maxwell Knight's anti-fifth-columnist operations at MI5 B5(b). Could Knight exploit the situation to net further security risks?

Anthony Masters' 1984 biography of Knight alleges that Commander Ian Fleming at the NID seized on the Haushofer-Hamilton letter to concoct an outlandish plan. The plan's first requirement had already been achieved by Knight: the busting of 'the Link', an association of pro-German appeasers led by Admiral Barry Domville, interned in July

1940.[26] Re-animate the Link, went the plan, and Hess and Haushofer could be tricked into a peace mission to a nonexistent audience. By curious coincidence, Fleming's brother Peter had put the idea of catching a senior Nazi 'by plane to Britain' into a novel, *The Flying Visit* (1940).

Like Crowley, Hess believed in powerful spiritual forces. Such things interested Ian Fleming and, especially, Maxwell Knight. Anthony Masters interviewed Knight's close friend Special Branch officer Tom Roberts who recalled how: 'Max was always searching for other meanings to life, other reasons for being, and he used to discuss them with me avidly. He always seemed to be searching.' While such a questing nature would open Knight to Crowley's conversation, no solid evidence has emerged to prove Crowley participated in a secret service inspired anti-Nazi ritual as part of any broader plan to entrap Hess. However, the combination of Fleming's, Knight's and Crowley's personalities would not make the possibility of such an event wholly fantastic.

Writer Paul Newman has related a Hastings newspaper report of a 'youthful marauder' entering the Victorian ruin of Crowley's last boarding-house, 'Netherwood' in Hastings, to find 'strewn around the darkness' 'cardboard sculptures', cut-outs, man-shaped and emblematic, heavily crayoned and held together by string'.[27] According to Newman, they were 'relics Crowley had used for ritual purposes'. Or they could have been relics from theatrical performances that were a regular feature of residential life at Netherwood. Where are they now?

Many strange things happened during the war. Britain was truly 'up against it', fighting for survival against a dark, formidable enemy. Crowley was certainly 'in the loop' for any occult flanker the secret services might entertain. Evidence for a Crowley link to the Hess affair does survive, but is dated after the event of Hess's flight in May.

*   *   *

In February 1941, Crowley was anxious. His Torquay rooms contract was about to expire: '... and the chance that any plan [to move] may be upset at the moment by [German] invasion completes the picture of frustration. *Deliberate* passivity seems the one tenable course', Crowley wrote on 8 February. A fortnight later, he wondered if Major Rupert Ernest Penny OBE of the Air Ministry 'might help in [his] Magical Symbol scheme'.[28] The next day, Crowley's doctor, RH Lodge, sent his Christmas present copy of *Eight Lectures on Yoga* to the Major, on sick leave at Torquay's Palace Hotel, the RAF's officers' convalescent establishment. Penny 'wanted a course of training, if I had been in London', noted Crowley: 'I will suggest a correspondence.' Was Crowley teaching yoga to other officers? Yoga would have been useful to those bearing heavy responsibility or combatants exposed to stress from special operations. An important RAF Aircrew Reception Centre (ACRC) was sited in Torquay with extensive training facilities. The Torquay area would also become important for drafting volunteers for SOE, the 'Special Operations Executive'.

*   *   *

On 1 March, Crowley exercised his astrological skills to plot the likelihood of the Russians entering the war, a maverick prediction in March 1941. Crowley met Soviet ambassador, Ivan Maiskii, some time before January 1943. Who knows what they discussed?[29] Stalin suspected Britain would make a deal with Hitler, leaving Russia exposed, a suspicion that crystallized when Hess flew to Britain.[30] While Stalin could not believe Hitler would invade as early as summer 1941, Crowley had few doubts: 'The Sickle and Hammer have simply G.O.T. got to come in somehow.' He plotted astrological portents 'moving up to May 8', though Russia would probably 'not [come in] till '42 though so close'. The May date is astounding because it is believed Hess's flight to Britain on 10 May 1941 was astrologically determined, possibly seeded by astrologers working for Britain. Hess wanted to prevent further slaughter of British people and deliver Hitler a peace deal that would give Hitler a free hand to demolish communist power.

Comments made in his diary on 23 March regarding magical workings done in late February still intrigue: 'Those works from February 19 are most interesting, I was entirely controlled by my H.G.A. [Holy Guardian Angel] acting swiftly, secretly, and "irrationally": i.e.

according to a plan based on facts of which A.C. [the man Crowley] had no knowledge whatever.'

Germer, meanwhile, had made it to New York; Crowley was deliriously happy, a joy punctured on 21 April when he was awoken by an air raid on Plymouth in the early hours. Among the many who left this world that night was Louis Wilkinson's former wife Frances Gregg. Crowley learnt the raid had also hit his last address, Middle Warberry Road, Torquay, killing six, injuring eight. Crowley had only moved to Barton Brow on Torquay's outskirts a few weeks earlier.

The Plymouth blitz heralded the most intense bombing raids of the war. London was hammered hardest on the night of 9–10 May. Extraordinary things occurred that night. Not only the Luftwaffe, but magick, was in the air. Aleister Crowley was involved.

On 9 May Britain's Magus experienced an extraordinary vision:

> Vision May 9. Above earth vast dull sphere-crust. Hard to pierce. Within, rich cream formed by dancing figures. Then immense crimson-and-cream robed Man-Angels; they seemed to be directing the war. Many land! And sea-scapes, vast scale, utmost beauty. I was concentrating badly, and could not make much of it. But They wanted me among them robed as a warrior.[31]

Robed as a warrior.

Was Crowley waging astral battle with Hitler, fighting on planes unseen by the eyes of the world? The memorandum reads like a sketch for the famous opening scene of Powell and Pressburger's visionary film, *A Matter of Life and Death* (1946).

*   *   *

Before 6am the following morning (10 May), Churchill's private secretary John Colville lay half-awake in his Whitehall air-raid shelter. It had been a bad night and, oddly, Colville kept waking moments *before* a bomb fell nearby. He kept thinking of a novel he had read in early 1940: Peter Fleming's *The Flying Visit* described the shock that followed a forced landing by Hitler in Britain.

Shortly after 11am, Colville was in the Foreign Office taking a call from the Duke of Hamilton. Someone, whose identity Hamilton would only disclose to the PM in person, had parachuted into Scotland overnight. Hamilton was ordered to RAF Northolt to explain himself.

Churchill could hardly believe his ears. Colville later wrote in *Footprints in Time*:

> I make no pretence to psychic powers; but I think it strange that Peter Fleming's story, which I had read many months before and had long since forgotten, should have come flooding into my half-conscious brain that Sunday morning.[32]

Churchill was perturbed. Where Fleming might have rejoiced in a secret service coup, Churchill saw baneful implications for the war effort if the public imagined there was a quick fix to end the war. Furthermore, morale would suffer were it known that anyone from the British establishment favoured negotiating with Germany's High Command. Details were strictly classified; press coverage severely restricted. The Hess phenomenon was hushed up.

Another event of the night of 9 May 1941 also entered the kingdom of 'Hush Hush'. As Hess dressed for his fateful flight from Augsburg, and the Luftwaffe warmed up for the *crescendo* attack of the Blitz, the Royal Navy captured German submarine U-110. At precisely the time Crowley experienced his vision of vast, beauteous sea-scapes beneath the will of spiritual giants, Britain captured the Germans' latest *Enigma* encryption machine: the key to *ULTRA* Victory.

Within days, a bewildered Hess was brought first to the Tower of London, then to a secret camp for interrogation. Four days after Hess landed, Crowley wrote to the NID beneath an embossed OTO letterhead:

Barton Brow, Barton Cross, Torquay.

Sir,

If it is true that Herr Hess is much influenced by astrology and Magick, my services might be of use to the Department, in case he should not be willing to do what you wish.

Col. J.F.C. Carter Scotland Yard House SW1

Thomas N. Driberg Daily Express

Karl J. Germer 1007 Lexington Ave. New York City

Could testify to my status and reputation in these matters.

I have the honour to be, Sir,
Your obedient servant,

Aleister Crowley[33]

Was Crowley flaunting his knowledge of drugs and psychology?

The Warburg copy of the letter is a photograph. The words 'A.C. to Ian Fleming' have been crossed out. Gerald Yorke wrote comments on the photograph: 'As a result of this letter Ian Fleming wanted AC to interview Hess in Scotland but it never came off. There was an exchange of letters on the subject.' Yorke contacted Fleming's NID colleague, novelist Donald McCormick. McCormick's jocular reply is in the manuscript folder:

Oddly enough, Ian Fleming, under whom I worked in the Foreign Department of *The Sunday Times* for many years, had a vague theory about this. The trouble with Ian was that one could never be quite sure when he was being serious, or when he was joking; he loved an air of mystery. He wanted Crowley to interview Hess when the Nazi leader landed in Britain; it never came off and the very idea must have horrified the Admiralty! But there was an exchange of letters on the subject. Ian also had a theory that Enochian could be used as a code and was a perfect code for using when one wanted to 'plant' bogus evidence in the right place.[34]

If a Crowley interrogation of Hess was Fleming's idea, then Fleming probably suggested the letter. Vice Admiral John Godfrey (DNI) replied to Crowley's offer on 17 May 1941 from the 'Intelligence Division, Naval Staff, Admiralty, SW1':

> The Director of Naval Intelligence presents his compliments to Mr Aleister Crowley and regrets he is unable to avail himself of his offer.[35]

Godfrey was *unable* to take up the offer; was there opposition? Explanations for the restraint in exploiting the Hess Affair may be found in *The Truth about Rudolf Hess*, by James Douglas Hamilton.[36] The book quotes FO man Con O'Neil's memorandum of 23 June 1941: 'the undiluted truth of the Hess case does not make good propaganda.'

Hamilton's book offers one tiny scintilla of inadmissible evidence that the Hess circle might have been 'got at' on an occult level. On p165, Hamilton refers to a dream wherein Karl Haushofer had seen Hess walking along tapestry corridors of British castles offering peace to the warring nations. Hess believed in the 'prophetic vision' of Karl Haushofer, and 'looked upon this incident as divine guidance, confirmation that he was to carry out his plan, or as he prefers to call it, his vision'.

In the week before the DNI regretted *his* inability to make use of Crowley's formidable skills, Lady Harris, having rejected Crowley's, produced her *own* catalogue for the exhibition of her 78 tarot paintings. Crowley could not recall 'so black a rage' as consumed him 'for the last 5 hours. All this though I had long ago prepared a proper catalogue, approved by Louis Wilkinson and other sensible people who understand such things; clear, modest, cheap to produce.'[37] He wrote to Frieda: 'Use my draft catalogue professionally edited, or count me out altogether.'

*   *   *

On 23 June 1941, a consular official working in the Foreign Office lunched at Demos, a Greek restaurant in Shaftesbury Avenue. Robert Cecil had already experienced one shock that day: Germany's invasion of

Russia. Cecil's second surprise was a large man in a green knickerbocker suit, embroiled in a chess puzzle. Reaching for a carafe of water, Cecil spilt some on the stranger's table. Conversation ensued about chess – and Cambridge. Cecil had known Philby and Maclean. In his unpublished memoir *The Will and the Way*, Cecil maintained his meeting Crowley was accidental, that he had no access to secret information until a remarkable promotion 15 months later, itself implicated in Crowley's magick.[38]

Cecil recalled Plan *241*, 'as black as black can be'. Having noticed the cabalistic equivalent of the Greek ACΘMA, *Asthma*, was 241, Crowley wished to inflict it on the tubes of the Nazi organization. Leaflet drops would encourage those whom despair had rendered murderous or suicidal to kill two Huns, before killing themselves, leaving the card '241' (*Two for One*) on victims. Crowley's psychological knowledge suggested psychotic outbursts from depressed or deluded soldiers would stir a rash of fears fanned into trigger-panic by radio messages. Crowley's V-campaign was moving into darker regions of psychological warfare.[39] Cecil passed the plan to the Political Warfare Executive; it was turned down. Somebody noticed the pun on 241 would be incomprehensible to a foreigner.

Crowley did not give up on Robert Cecil. In June 1942, Cecil would enter a wood near his Chislehurst home, stand on a tree stump, raise his arms and, facing west as the Sun set, call out: 'Hail to thee, Ra, in thy setting' then return home to sign an 'Oath of Beginning' in Crowley's magical order, taking the name '*Frater Respice Finem*', 'Look to the End'.

*   *   *

In the summer of 1941, the V-campaign put fresh sap into Britain. Crowley admitted his authorship to Dutch occult publisher Jean Michaud on 2 August. The following Sunday, the 65-year-old Crowley took a long walk, inspecting Blitz damage in the City of London and the East End. Did he see himself as the 'noisome beast' prophesied to enter the ruins of a wayward Jerusalem in Ezekiel's prophecy of the four judgements? With the Bow Bells silenced by bombs, it was a poignant experience. Back in his Hanover Square flat, the Beast phoned Bernard O'Donnell with fresh plans. O'Donnell 'had guessed about V'. He put a question to the I Ching: 'shall I produce a pamphlet documented with three photographs and quotations, or what?' Answer: 'Yes: establish past history.'

The V-campaign was a hit. Crowley wanted the world to know whose initiative it was and what it *really* meant: a complete, as opposed to temporary, victory for mankind after Victory Day. He planned an illustrated book to show how Britain could be led to new heights.

Meanwhile, pro-Nazi propagandist William Joyce a.k.a. 'Lord Haw Haw', broadcast from Hamburg, trashing Crowley's efforts by goading him to perform a 'Black Mass' for a 'religious revival in Russia'.[40] Another Maxwell Knight recruit from the Thirties, had fascist Irishman Joyce alerted German intelligence to Crowley?

*　　*　　*

Thumbs Up! appeared on 11 August 1941. Excited, its author wrote to friend Edward Noel Fitzgerald about Joyce and his V-schemes:

> Thanks to Lord Haw Haw, it is now generally known that I invented this campaign [the V-sign]. He has pointed out, quite justly, that I have persuaded some 100's of millions of people to worship the Devil! [...] Of course I am denying strenuously that I ever had anything to do about it, as the bloke who slipped it over on the idiots of the BBC would get into the most hellish trouble if it were ever found out that he knows me.[41] All the same, it will help my subtle intrigues if you pass the word along that I did it! I have something else in my capacious sleeve that needs to be prepared.[42]

Thumbs Up! revealed Crowley's spiritually phallic patriotism. There was an old photograph of him making two horns on either side of his head with his phallic thumbs – *up*. Opposite appeared a new combination of symbols. Above a bold black **V**-sign was Crowley's new sigil, the unicursal hexagram, enclosed in a thick black circle. Around the twin signs appeared Constantine's legendary words at the Milvian Bridge in

AD312: *In hoc signo vinces* – 'In this sign shalt thou conquer'.[43] The **V** would have made immediate sense to readers, but the striking esoteric symbol above would stretch them, consisting of a clever series of double meanings.

The war's victors would be the free Man and free Woman. The V-campaign was part of the larger plan for a new planetary order, based on the sovereignty of the individual's True Will. The triumph of the 'Beast' would signal the end of tyrannies, political, social and religious. Out of the conflict would emerge a rational, cosmic, individualistic and spiritual humanity.

People who imagine a Crowley content with a 'legacy' of witchcraft, new ageism and a reputation as 'the founder of modern occultism' underestimate both his intelligence and his seriousness. Crowley was working on a far greater canvas.

Given the chance, Crowley could reach people. That made him dangerous. He wrote to Hamilton:

> But my time is coming! It is sure to leak out sooner or later that I invented the 'V' campaign. I have been wondering whether you had spotted it. Of course, I never expected it to take the form it has actually done – it was out of my hands after the first strike, and the B.B.C themselves don't know – at least I hope not, or there will be trouble for somebody! [44]

That is as close an account as we shall probably get to knowing how the BBC came to employ the V-sign without knowing either its true source, or its amazing esoteric meaning.

Just before midnight on 2 September, Crowley awoke, inspired. By 2am he had completed his new song, *Vive la France!*. That afternoon he entertained the 'doyen' of French theatre, Michel St Denis, whose work had appeared on the radio. Michel's name appears next to the acronym 'BBC' Crowley wrote in his diary that night: 'I have the V-sign on the brain!'

Ten days later, Karl Germer read 666's telegram in New York: 'Inform everybody Aleister invented V-sign for Victory.' Germer and the

Californian Thelemites ensured *Thumbs Up!* appeared in the USA in 1942. The V-campaign had reached America, as shown on a typed note to the US edition:

> This American reprint of Aleister Crowley's *Thumbs Up!* was made possible by the generosity and enthusiasm of a few of his many friends on this side of the Atlantic, as a contribution to the V for Victory campaign.
>
> To follow the example of the English edition, a limited number of copies have been made available 'for Free Distribution among the Soldiers and Workers of the Forces of Freedom'.
>
> Contributions to the printing of a much larger edition may be sent to:
>
> V
>
> P.O. Box 2411
>
> Hollywood, Calif.

On 29 September he visited a Mr Nicholas at the Ministry of Information (MOI) and sent the NID *Thumbs Up!* with its special dedications to the men of the Royal Navy.

> 17 October 1941, Naval Staff, Admiralty, S.W.1.

> The Director of Naval Intelligence has to thank Mr E.A. Crowley for his further offer of services, but regrets there is no vacancy in this division for which he could be considered.[45]

A heartier response would come from Captain Gordon of the battle-scarred HMS *Exeter* of 'Battle of the River Plate' fame. On 20 March 1942, the captain thanked Crowley, accepting *Thumbs Up!* on behalf of his ship. Crowley wrote simply: 'I could cry.'

The spirit was there but the task was tremendous. In the wee small hours of a cold January morning in 1942, a dream awoke him: 'War had broken down everything: long many incidents, I had to rebuild. Tedious.' Two days later, Crowley was seized by a 'tremendous impulse'. He wrote a furious poem about 'our inbred fucked-out families who are strangling us'. 'Fucked out' also provided the acronym for the Foreign

Office. Crowley parodied the 'Burke's Landed Gentry' directory by a mischievous pun on 'Burke & Hare', notorious Irish murderers who sold their victims to Edinburgh's Medical College for dissection.

'LANDED' * GENTRY

* 'Edition of 1942, Burke - & Hare'

By the Author of the V Sign.

Our inbred F.O. families
  Produce their pullulating legions:
Red-tape worms in bled-White Hall tease
  England's anaemic nether regions.
Bridge, polo, cricket, pansy piety,
  Tart-and-great lady so-society,
  Dumb devotees of Dividends –
  Ah! 'who will save us from our friends',
  Our inbred F.O. families?

Poem completed, Crowley lunched with FO chap Robert Cecil on 30 January 1942, an occasion that may have signalled the end of Crowley's V-book plans. References to the publication fade from his diaries soon after. Did Cecil question the public's 'right to know' what *V* might really mean?

Crowley found an outlet for photographs taken for his V-sign book in a series of postcards. One of the cards has *Liber Oz, The Rights of Man* on one side with Crowley in a stirring pose called 'North Sea Patrol', identifying with merchant seamen, on the other. The caption reads: 'ALEISTER CROWLEY, author of the V sign "Song of the Fighting French" *Thumbs Up!* etc. etc.' Another *Rights of Man* card shows a serene Crowley wearing a turban, with just the hint of a twinkle, like a Sufi saint might, or ought, to look. He has his hand on his chin. Two fingers, index and middle, subtly make out a V-sign around his mouth, while the other fingers are curled like the horns of Baphomet. The caption states simply: 'ALEISTER CROWLEY, author of the V sign.' Post-card versions of the *Song of the Fighting French*, another battle cry of Horus published on Bastille Day, 1942, also bear the statement that Crowley was the V-sign's inventor. One remarkable photograph shows Crowley incarnating the spirit and stance of Winston Churchill, smoking a cigar supplied by Mr Zanelli, Churchill's Piccadilly tobacconist, obtained by a stroke of providence after leaving Cecil that cold Friday in January 1942:

> Walked to get bus home from Lower Regent Street. Saw (at 5 to 3) cigars in window of Galata in Leicester Square. Shut, notice 'Back at 3'. I felt ill: wind was cold; rain started. Yet I waited. About 3.10 a woman came, also locked out. About 3.15 she thought she could find the boss, and went off, asking me to wait. He rushed down and opened. He was Zanelli, a Turk; Churchill's own Cigar Merchant!!! So I got the actual thing I was looking for in the most fraternal spirit.[46]

Crowley's major V-sign opus never saw the light of day. Was it in the government's interest for a man to ascribe victory to magick in 1942?

*   *   *

Crowley was itching to serve. He wrote again to the NID:

> February 17 1942, To the Director of Naval Intelligence, Admiralty, SW1:
>
> Sir,
>
> I have the honour to report that I am now in a position to discover the details and progress of the defeatist activities of seriously important groups.[47]

He then lunched with Cecil at the Piccadilly Brasserie. A 'useful talk', its conclusion was coded: an inverted triangle (water) followed by the sign for Virgo, after which: 'IV better than 64.' The number 64 is the kabbalistic equivalent of the letters NID (*nun, yod, daleth*). Cecil was saying that MI4 or MI5 were better bets for Crowley than the NID.

On 21 May, he received a 'flattering letter from de Gaulle' about his Free French song which I here translate:

De Gaulle 4 Carlton Gardens SW1 20 May 42.

French National Committee of Foreign Affairs.

Sir, I am charged by General de Gaulle to thank you for your letter of 12 May. We have read your song with a lively interest. We are touched by your charming expression of beautiful feelings.

Crowley was suffering a black depression: 'I feel the need of a loyal friend as never before. Not one in England who really cared a nickel.'[48] He met the overly cool Cecil again at the Brasserie: 'Good dinner: he very near seeing the Light.' A few days earlier, on 24 June (St John's Day), Cecil had signed an 'Oath of Beginning'.[49] Cecil's prospects improved dramatically two months later. To his astonishment, he was appointed assistant private secretary to Sir Alexander Cadogan, Head of the Foreign Office. Cadogan's private office linked MI5, SIS and SOE. Cecil was now at the heart of the secret war effort. A year later he became one of SIS Head Sir Stewart Menzies' private secretaries. Cecil's memoir states that had he been able to tell Crowley, he would probably have claimed the promotion as vindication of the Oath, but Cecil was bound by another oath: the Official Secrets Act.

Another hammer blow to Crowley's heart occurred on 1 July: 'Frieda opened secret show of Tarot at Berkeley Galleries.' Crowley was not invited. Worse, *Robert Cecil* had rewritten Crowley's catalogue! Crowley was not mentioned – only a note that Lady Harris had been assisted by a man who had studied the tarot for 40 years. Frieda was afraid Crowley's name would prejudice the show and her husband's career. 'Frieda's sneaking treachery bites deeper daily', wailed Crowley.

Undeterred, Bastille Day 1942 saw 1,000 copies of Crowley's song *La Gauloise* distributed throughout London. To mark the occasion, Philip Johnston of *The Star* interviewed him for an hour. The skewed results appeared a few days later with the by-line 'HE HATES GERMANS NOW'. The ostensible subject of the interview was downplayed. Crowley tried hard to get his song onto BBC radio, even recording a raucous demo which has survived.

*   *   *

In California, meanwhile, a handsome rocket fuel specialist with an interest in science and magick joined Agapé Lodge. Crowley received John Whiteside ('Jack') Parsons' letter on 18 July. On the East Coast, widower Germer had remarried. Sascha Ernestine André did not share Cora's aversion to Crowley. Exchanging kind letters, Crowley enjoyed her gifts of cigars, chocolates and tobacco, among other dainties hard to obtain in wartime London. Karl, however, was subject to FBI interest. Suspecting his loyalties, the Feds had received stories of Karl ranting in New York's public bars about the superiority of 'the German spirit'. Crowley would have laughed: *same old Saturnus!*

A meeting with Peter Brook of Magdalen College, Oxford, in August, distracted Crowley from the pain caused by Frieda. Brook was producing Marlowe's *Faustus*, a play about a magician obsessed, selling his soul to Mephistopheles. Brook rose in Crowley's esteem with each meeting. He helped with *Faustus*, showing Brook how to 'conjure' and make best use of stage effects.[50]

A card of 18 September 1942 shows Crowley's continuing business with the spying game.[51] 'N. Carter' (Old Nick) of 12 Buckingham Palace Road wrote: 'It is some months now since your last visit, and therefore I write to invite you here for another chat at a time to suit your convenience.' It is possible, no more, that the visit concerned a scenario whose existence Soviet mole Kim Philby passed on to his Soviet masters. Philby revealed that SIS agents were probing a 'complicated racket' involving RAF officers, drugs, sex parties, gambling and black masses. Welsh fishermen and the German Embassy in Dublin were involved.

Welsh fishermen? It was believed drugs were being shipped across the Irish Sea from the Dublin Embassy to keep the parties moving. They might have been set up to promote blackmail. According to Spence, 'Mingling in this weird milieu, along with a colourful throng of ladies, countesses, wing-commanders, and pornographers, were Soviet Ambassador Ivan Maiskii [whom Crowley knew] and "the notorious Aleister Crowley".'[52] Spence reckons the goings-on were likely part of an MI5 counter-intelligence operation, Knight's very effective 'Double-Cross' system that helped neutralize German intelligence in Britain during the war. Crowley's reference to 'really serious groups' of fifth columnists, offered to the NID, was possibly connected to the operation. Perhaps Crowley conveyed something similar to MI5 on Cecil's suggestion.

Crowley hoped his helpfulness would, with Cecil's support, secure him a passport so he could sort out AMORC and the Californian situation. But a passport was denied 'at the present time' in October. Was Crowley too hot an item to be let loose, or just disabled by bankruptcy? He was trapped in England. To add insult to injury, Frieda terminated his teaching stipend on 11 November. She had every right, but the timing seemed harsh. Five days later, James Cleugh and friend Tub moved Crowley's stuff to 93 Jermyn Street, above Paxton & Whitfield's cheesemongers in Piccadilly.

Crowley ceremonially published *The Fun of the Fair* at 11.31am on 22 December. One of its first buyers was Ivan Maiskii, Soviet ambassador. *The Fun of the Fair*'s publication nearly 30 years after composition was apparently an effort to persuade people the new Russian ally was not going to eat them. Or was it published to persuade others Crowley was sympathetic towards Russia? *The Fun of the Fair* had a sting in its tail. Having failed to get Britain's only communist MP, George Gallagher, to read it in the House, Crowley put his scathing attack on the snobbish hypocrites who obstructed victory at the end of the booklet: 'The "Landed" Gentry', 'From the Edition of 1942, Burke and Hare.'

Vintage Crowley.

He then turned to something closer to heart, a collection of a lifetime's poetry, initially entitled: *Olla: A Book of Many Cities*. Each poem would put its author in a new place, that is, an old place, a memory that was not a memory when it was made. Was this *around-the-world-in-63-poems* Crowley's response to passport denial? In *Olla*, he would travel the world he knew so well in the poetry he had lived so well. In his imagination, he was free, and his past was his own. He offers it to whoso may receive it, that he or she might also be free.

TWENTY-SEVEN

A City of Refuge

1943–47

When you are wholly concentrated upon your True Will, personal woes and worries tend to assume their real place. Everything that happens is all part of the plan; and when you *really* see it as such, you become indifferent to circumstances. For instance, all the ostracism and persecution which has been my lot for so many years appears to me as part of the necessary condition for the historical view of me in times to come. Of course it is very difficult not to react in an ordinary human way to things that go wrong. In fact, you *ought* to react according to your nature; but there should be a city of refuge far removed from all these tribulations, where you can see the battle in perspective.[1]

The FBI paid a visit to Agapé Lodge, Pasadena, on 16 January 1943. Russell Leadabrand, an LA-area sci-fi editor serving in the Army told the police Agapé was a house of subversive 'Sex Perversion'. Tipped off, the Feds questioned Wilfred Smith and Jack Parsons, only to conclude the 'Church of Thelma' (*sic*) was a religious organization, possibly a love-cult, but not a cell of alien subversion.[2]

Tensions remained high at 1003 South Orange Grove. While Germer's attacks on WT Smith – issued from the East Coast – initiated a loyalty crisis in Jack, Jane Wolfe and Regina Kahl remained loyal to Smith. Crowley telegrammed Jane, claiming her judgement was undermined by Smith's 'vampirism'. On the 23rd Crowley cabled again: 'MAY PRECIPITATE IRREVOCABLE THUNDERBOLT.'[3] Jack and wife Helen Parsons rallied; Crowley should not believe everything he heard. They needed Smith, Thelema's linchpin in America, and asked for 'LOVE AND TRUST'. Crowley dismissed sentimentality, suspecting Smith and Co of turning Thelema into a love cult: religion as an excuse for sexual licence. Suspicions were further stoked up by US Army lieutenant, Grady Louis McMurtry. One of McMurtry's girlfriends had been made pregnant by Jack. Grady was furious to find she had received cash and an address for an abortion. Abortion was anathema to Crowley. Not only were abortions frequently due to money-worries but Thelema insisted on the 'true wills' of parents *and* children.

Lt McMurtry came into the OTO through Parsons whom he had met in the LA Science Fiction League (Ray Bradbury was a teenage member). Invited to a performance of the Gnostic Catholic Mass in December 1940, McMurtry was impressed, but war intervened. Drafted in 1941, the Army brought McMurtry to Europe in 1943. Beating a path to Jermyn Street, McMurtry nearly talked Crowley to death. Still, Crowley appreciated his friendly spirit, and listened.

Annoyed by the Californian situation, disturbed by the 'silent' V1 bombing, Crowley turned to translating Baudelaire's *Fleurs du Mal* to steady his mind. The V1s were hard to bear. Crowley wrote of hearing no bombs, but finding 500 casualties listed outside Caxton Hall, the press forbidden to print them: 'i.e. Huns may know, we not unless we seek!' *Caxton Hall!* The Rites of Eleusis must have seemed far, far away.

He carried on, comparing his life to the Calcutta-Rangoon steamer 'coasting along the shores of grim insanity in monsoon and fog'. He published his poem 'The City of God' on 24 February 'to keep flag flying'. Inspired, like *The Fun of the Fair*, by Tsarist Russia, 'The City of God' is a feast.

Hamilton showed up on 27 February: 'raving against Telephone "Company" (!) and England. I am again sorely tempted to write to the competent authority. If I felt sure they would act, I would. But I am tired of being snubbed!' In 1943, the secret services reorganized priorities to give more attention to communist subversion; threats had increased since Stalin joined the Allies. Tragically for those whom he would betray, it was 'Cambridge spy' Kim Philby who manoeuvred himself into dominating the anti-communist effort.

*   *   *

In May, the King's Cross Cinema showed Crowley's favourite movie. In *A Night to Remember*, Brian Aherne played a writer in a Greenwich Village apartment witnessing all kinds of weirdness. Was it nostalgia for his Village days in 1918–19 that made Crowley go a fourth time? Or was it Loretta Young's flaming hair? Perhaps he was *willing* himself back to America through identification with the film. On 6 June he took Cath Falconer to see it at the Elephant and Castle: the *sixth* time!

Despite problems, a sense of calm seeped into Crowley's life in 1943, possibly connected to the marked drop-off in sexual activity. Fussiness would in time dog his way, an anxiety to control things out of his control, natural perhaps in a magician who had undergone interminable nervous strain.

A new generation had more respect for Aleister Crowley. On 29 June, now-renowned theatre director Peter Brook rang from Oxford to invite Crowley as guest of honour to a Magdalen College party. Crowley met Stanley ('Nosey') Parker of the *Oxford Mail*, the same journo who had interviewed him during his Oxford 'ban' 13 years earlier: what a contrast!

While Crowley's calm may have been prompted by the turning of the war's tide in Europe and Africa, the 'doodle-bugs' and a blackout crime wave unsettled him. He offered a thelemic response that might interest today's legislators:

> The Criminal Law according to Thelema. All offences are
> reduced to one: to deprive another of his right (e.g. to live, to
> own goods, to sleep – as by making undue noise – and so on).
> Therefore the 'offender' denies his own right to similar
> protection; and he is treated accordingly. He can be reinstated on
> his purging the offence.

Saturday 30 October

'Oh Gawd! McMurtry blew in!!! News from the Front indeed!' Then Crowley's assistant Cordelia Sutherland dropped in with Cecil and Jane Aitken. 'My quiet day in bed!!!!! Talk talk talk 4 p.m. till 9:30. Am I tired?'

There was no respite. McMurtry was back on 13 November for a marathon seven-hours talking session. 'Gawd!' cried Crowley. On the 27th McMurtry talked for six hours without a break! – but he did loan Crowley £20.[4]

Robert Cecil arrived at Jermyn Street for an afternoon appointment on 27 December: 'Very pleasant talk', wrote Crowley, 'but how futile the creature is! Simply scared lest he should get somewhere.' Cecil returned to Crowley in January 1944: 'Cecil here: wanted Astral Visions. I smote him, demanding the Oath.' He meant the oath of a neophyte.

The next day, Crowley complained to Louis Wilkinson of being 'stuck for a printer for *Olla*'. He also made notes for a new operation: '*Objective Aleister*',[5] referring to Aleister Ataturk and Pat (Deirdre). Crowley was not even sure if Pat was married, or still married, to SOE operative James MacAlpine: 'No news since September '42. There must be someone who knows what has (or hasn't) happened.' Louis Wilkinson, living near Penzance at the time, was drafted in since Penzance was where Deirdre's mother Phyllis Bodilly, came from.

Relief from the silent bombing was on the horizon. Cordelia Sutherland rang on 5 April: 'The Angel has found me a room at the "Bell" Aston Clinton near Aylesbury.' He explained his bidding Piccadilly goodbye to Gerald Hamilton:

> The Duke Street-King Street bomb not only damaged 93
> [Jermyn St.], but caused diversion of traffic through Jermyn
> Street. At times we had to wait five minutes or more to cross!
> Racket quite unsupportable, work totally impossible; so I drifted
> out here for a while. Being close to Aylesbury, they say that my
> object is to go on with my work on the I Ching [...] I hope all is
> well with you, and that you have a quid to spare to square. Love
> is the law, love under will. Yours A.C.[6]

Crowley settled in to his Buckinghamshire billet on 8 April: 'A most delightful inn, really old, big open fire, food incredibly good. But *nothing* to do, and no one to talk to. I shall be forced to work – and at once. Tired with excitement and travel.'

He embraced a new project. Some said Crowley's writings were abstruse. The idea occurred of a *colloquial* treatment. A pupil would send a letter and he would answer it in chatty style. Collected, the letters would make a book. Originally called *Aleister Explains Everything*, it was re-antichristened *Magick without Tears*, and does exactly what it says 'on the tin'. He started with a lucid revision of a 1920s account of the *Three Schools of Magick*; the schools being the black, the white and the yellow. The 'black' does not refer to 'black magic' as popularly understood: devilish sorcery is regarded as a perversion of the 'white'. Crowley's 'black' scholars are convinced that the natural order is best fled from; he cleverly includes Buddhist philosophy in this school. Readers concerned with the real meaning of Crowley's magical philosophy should absorb this luminous letter.

Magick without Tears gives the lie to the notion that Crowley ended his life a spent force, an empty shell propped up by brandy and heroin. Crowley's text is terse and colourful, studded with gems of insight and out-of-the-way knowledge. There is even prophecy, as in this letter on *Noise*:

> What I am about to complain of is what I seriously believe to be an organized conspiracy of the Black Lodges to prevent people from thinking.
>
> Naked and unashamed! In some countries there has already been compulsory listening-in to Government programmes; and who knows how long it will be before we are all subjected by law to the bleatings, bellowings, belchings of the boring balderdash of the BBC-issies?
>
> So nobody must be allowed to think at all. Down with the public schools! Children must be drilled mentally by quarter-educated herdsmen, whose wages would stop at the first sign of disagreement with the bosses. For the rest, deafen the whole world with senseless clamour. Mechanize everything! Give

nobody a chance to think. Standardise 'amusement'. The louder and more cacophonous, the better! Brief intervals between one din and the next can be filled with appeals, repeated 'till hypnotic power gives them the force of orders, to buy this or that product of the 'Business men' who are the real power in the State. Men who betray their country as obvious routine.

The history of the past thirty years is eloquent enough, one would think. What these sodden imbeciles never realise is that a living organism must adapt itself intelligently to its environment, or go under at the first serious change in circumstance.

Where would England be today if there had not been one man, deliberately kept 'in the wilderness' for decades as 'unsound', 'eccentric', 'dangerous', 'not to be trusted', 'impossible to work with', to take over the country from the bewildered 'safe' men?

And what could he [Winston Churchill] have done unless the people had responded? Nothing. So then there is still a remnant whose independence, sense of reality, and manhood begin to count when the dear, good, woolly flock scatter in terror at the wolf's first howl.

Yes, they are there, and they can get us back our freedom – if only we can make them see that the enemy in Whitehall is more insidiously fatal than the foe in Brownshirt House.

On this note I will back to my silence.

Pity. The control state is with us, along with the Noise: 24-hour 'news' and perpetual drum-beats; original thought passes unheard. 'Equality' can only be had by suppressing every interesting or peculiar characteristic; if we had been intended to be 'equal', we should have been. Crowley's voice has been suppressed, and with it, humanity.

There was precious little conversation in Aston Clinton. He noted a 'Long and rather dreary talk' with one Biggin on the 7th, adding: 'Mediocrity, however intelligent, can't make the grade of conversation.' Letters helped. The wandering bishop who called himself 'Mar Basilius Abdullah III' otherwise known as Dr William Bernard Crow, wrote to him on many things, including the provenance of the 'Gnostic Catholic Church' referred to in Crowley's Gnostic Mass.[7] On 11 November 1944,

Crowley enlightened the Right Revd Crow as to the significance of the Age of Aquarius, belief in whose peculiar properties would dominate popular magic after the war.

> To talk of the Ages of Pisces and Aquarius is incomplete. The Age has also the opposite sign as one of its characteristics, and this may at times be even stronger than the original sign. To call this the Aquarian Age is really a joke. The characteristic so far has been much more that of Leo.[8]

Tuesday 6 June 1944

True time 4–8 a.m. Invasion started.

D-Day! But for Crowley, the 'longest day' came on Saturday 10th. As Allied troops scrambled through Normandy thickets, Crowley, short of heroin and bored beyond measure, walked to an Anglican church at Buckland for Matins, then went to Buckland's Methodist chapel at 5pm: 'The "minister" a doddering creature, in tweeds, most untidy. I couldn't make out a word he said. In church they were singing a dreadful lugubrious hymn.' Strange to think heroin privation drove him to church! Did he know something the Church of England does not?

Then, in June, the Ministry of Supply started its 'persecution re prospectus'. The prospectus was for *The Book of Thoth*. Paper restrictions meant the book was issued as a periodical, becoming *The Equinox* Vol. III, No. 5. *The Equinox*, now running for 35 years, conceived to withstand the pangs of the Aeon, was holding out well. Frieda, however, was angry her paintings appeared in poor reproductions in the *Book of Thoth*, reduced to illustrative status. Crowley received a 'Long grouse from F.H. with crazy suggestion: I am to tear out the plates and say "Sorry!" It's unimaginable.' He had suffered enough over Frieda and her reputation. When he threatened to get another artist executant, Frieda relented.

Aleister wrote to Nancy Cunard on 30 June to invite her to the Bell Inn, addressing her as 'My own strange fellow-traveller in monstrous worlds!' Sounds romantic, but there may be a pun on 'fellow-traveller'; a 'fellow traveller' being one who supported communists without actually joining the CP.[9] Crowley had been enjoying poem exchanges with Nancy Cunard while she worked as a secretary for the Free French forces and later for Supreme Headquarters Allied Expeditionary Force. In July 1943, he had found her precious London accommodation: a basic flat in Jermyn Street. She wrote to him:

> I *loved* your poems. And keep on thinking of inspiring *La Gauloise.*
>
> [...] I went to take the room you told me of, by the week (£2 10/- I think you said) [...] I am told my petition to go to France has a good chance.
>
> So – I will, in any case, be ready to take it this *Wednesday* (after tomorrow, August 23) by the week, if agreeable to you.
>
> I need nothing – a couch of sorts, a table if possible – a hook or two.
>
> Love Nancy[10]

On 22 July 1944, he wrote to her again:

> My dear Nancy,
>
> Do what thou wilt shall be the whole of the law
>
> How delightful to get a letter – and *such* a letter! from you, who have always played so great a part in the life of my imagination!
>
> Many thanks for the war-poem; so fine in rhythm and expression, with such powers to make one visualize as well as experience your reaction.

Another letter in August: 'Beloved Dream Woman that you are! Do what thou wilt shall be the whole of the law. It was so sweet of you to say you would come over.' Crowley waited on 5 August to see Nancy for lunch: 'No Nancy to lunch.' On the 7th she explained her absence, with promises. Nancy reached Aston Clinton 10 days later. It was a memorable occasion. Crowley's diary: 'Nancy here. Delightful! Every minute a rapture!' Two of the most interesting poets of the century, Nancy and Aleister together must have been magical.

Nancy Cunard's *Grand Man: Memories of Norman Douglas* refers specifically to that week in August 1944:

> 'Crowley's village in Bucks'! It seemed a sort of happy back-water off the rushing stream of difficulties and events and he had betaken himself to it after being severely shaken by bombs in London. Now, on the one occasion I was there to see him, he told me he was 'working against Hitler *on the astral plane*'. Far away and long ago was all that hoolie-goolie period of his (although these words, I admit, made me start), and he was a most interesting person to talk to.

Nancy reflected on the visit again in 1954 in a letter to Gerald Yorke: 'There he was, in an excellent inn, see how well fed, with plenty of coupons etc.' One feels Nancy would like to have understood Crowley better: 'what a galaxy he did offer himself to! This particular point seems practically the pivot of the man – man or magus – does it not? I should have hated all the 'hoolie-goolie' stuff, but that seems to have been long before. I can well imagine him absolutely terrifying many people.'[11] *Alas*, added Nancy, 'that none of us will see him again'.

*　　*　　*

It was from the Bell Inn that Crowley wrote to McMurtry on 28 September 1944, urging the company commander to acquaint himself with Catherine Falconer's remarkably adept 'prehensile cunt' (Cath was serving with the Wrens in Normandy). Crowley also urged Lt McMurtry to consider seriously his future career as Outer Head of the OTO. Crowley employed the term 'Caliph'. By oriental precedent, as Crowley was Thelema's prophet, his successors could be considered 'Caliphs', with the prophet's authority vested in the 'Caliphate'. Crowley saw McMurtry as his *post-mortem* 'alter ego', functioning with Crowley's authority in Crowley's absence. On 2 November, he wrote to McMurtry again, tactfully advancing his plan:

Frater Saturnus [Germer] is of course the natural Caliph; but there are many details concerning the actual policy or working which would hit his blind spots. In any case, he can only be a stop gap, because of his age; I have to look for *his* successor. It has been hell; so many have come up with amazing promise, only to go on the rocks. […] I do not think of you as lying on a grassy hillside with a lot of dear sweet woolly lambs, capering to your flute! On the contrary. Your actual life, or 'blooding', is the *sort* of initiation which I regard as the first essential for a Caliph. [Allied forces in Europe were about to be sucked into what would be called the 'Battle of the Bulge'.] For – say 20 years hence – the Outer Head of the Order must, among other things, have had the experience of war as it is in actual fact today. 1965 e.v. should be a critical period in the development of the Child Horus! [12]

It was.

*   *   *

In September 1944, Crowley became acquainted with the name of David Curwen, a friend of Michael Houghton of the Atlantis Bookshop, Museum St. A correspondence ensued on the feminine aspect of sexual magick. A Tantra specialist, Curwen reckoned Crowley underestimated the significance of the feminine sexual secretions or *kalas*. Crowley was apt to consider them chiefly as 'solvent' for the lion or *bindu* (semen). Willing to learn, Crowley had little opportunity to experiment.

An acquaintance of Curwen and Houghton, 20-year-old Kenneth Grant arrived at the Bell shortly before Christmas; Crowley's comment after meeting him: 'Would I were at Nefta, and 25!' Helping Crowley move to Hastings the following year, Grant became a magical pupil and performed secretarial duties until his father insisted he get a 'proper job'. [13]

Sunday 7 January 1945

Going on with Wally's [Walter Duranty's] *U.S.S.R.* [14] He quotes me now and again. Must ask him if he knows Ivan Narodny. [15]

It was time to move on. Louis Wilkinson's son Oliver also helped Crowley move to 'Netherwood', ex-alcoholic Vernon Symons's eccentric, theatrical boarding house in Hastings. Crowley enjoyed a last visit from Wren, Catherine Falconer: 'more delightful than ever'. No record of '⨁'.

On 17 January 1945, at the age of 69, the old boy took up residence on The Ridge, Hastings. He wrote to Germer:

> Netherwood, the Ridge, Hastings – Permanent, I hope

Dear Karl,

> There is a vile threat to the 'rugged American individualism' which actually *created* the U.S.A. by the bureaucratic crowd who want society to be a convict prison. 'Safety first' – there is no 'social security', no fear for the future, no anxiety about what to do next – in Sing Sing. *All* the totalitarian schemes add up to the same in the end, and the approach is so insidious, the argument so subtle and irrefutable, the advantages so obvious, that the danger is very real, very imminent, very difficult to bring home to the average citizen, who sees only the immediate gain, and is hoodwinked as to the price that must be paid for it.[16]

In the spring, Crowley busied himself sorting out the publication of *Olla, An Anthology of Sixty Years of Song*. To it he added a new work 'Thanatos Basileos', 'King Death' or 'Death is King', written at Netherwood as the war reached its bloodiest climax. Commenting on that brief period, Kenneth Grant wrote in his reminiscences of Crowley: 'It is incredible how he managed to write his unique books; wandering like a *sadhu* all his life from country to country, room to room, without any permanent base.'[17]

Contemporary photographs show a caped figure, gaunt, intense, his pipe a kind of mental funnel for a brain engine, steaming. There was no longer any need for posing; he was himself what he appeared to be, a Master in old age, alert. I asked my eight-year-old daughter what she thought of Crowley's image at Netherwood; what did this man look like? She replied: 'He looks like an old sea man.' And I thought then of

Coleridge's *Ancient Mariner*, returned, though unrepentant. He seemed to be the model for the first 'Dr Who'. *Of course*: a Time Lord. He had not shot the albatross, but had let it fly. Indeed, he had followed it, beyond time and space. Damn it, he *was* the albatross!

*   *   *

Following a note about the suicides of Hitler and Goebbels, Crowley noted on 7 May: 'War alleged "over"! Morons surprised, excited, celebrating. It is hard to live in such a world.' Crowley knew the matter did not end with the incinerated Führer.

> Tuesday 8 May
>
> Public Rejoicing equals Private Annoyance! […] No mail today or tomorrow: impossible pressure put on such services as *are* running! Aussik [Grant] helped a whole lot; gave him *The Lama*. Long talk with scolex Grant, bullied by father. What shall I do about him?

'Scolex' means 'worm' or 'worm-eaten'. The remarkable drawing Crowley calls *The Lama* is now generally known as *Lam* and is considered by aficionados as a drawing of what has come to be called 'an alien'; it has even been speculated that Crowley split a kind of 'hole' between our world and another dimension in his quest for higher intelligence. Crowley's work seems prescient of what is now the classic 'alien': the huge dome of head, the feline eyes, curious dress.

Grant left him on 16 May: 'Grant is gone. I think he pined for his greens – not unnatural in a rabbit!'[18] he lamented to Wilkinson, whose own son Oliver had left him for Glasgow.

> Wednesday 4 July
>
> Message: forecast of Election, 29 *K'an* ☾ of ☾ Danger ahead.

Danger ahead!
On 26 July 1945, Labour won a landslide victory. 'I cannot confute a socialist,' wrote Crowley in 1920, 'who knows political economy so much

better than I do; and I can't persuade him that he is like an insane person with one bit of his mind clear and logical indeed, but developed out of all proportion.' He called Clement Attlee 'nobody with a grocer's moustache', springing '2 days "holidays" VJ [Victory in Japan] on us at Midnight, breaking up everybody's plans and giving them no time to make new ones! Inconceivable asininity.'

Crowley believed the war would establish the 93 principle. Much sense had soaked in, from his point of view: the power of the will to win, for example, a sense of the stakes involved in spiritual conflict and, above all, the power and independence of women. But the old sentiment-addict Britain was about to be injected with a frustrating fix of false promises, utopianism, and state control.

Mrs Germer, 260 West 72nd Street, N.Y.C.

9 October 1945

My dearest Sascha,

[…] When I think of how easy everything was 50 years ago it makes me despair of the world. The muddle of my own affairs is a perfect picture of the muddle everywhere.

David Curwen wrote to Crowley in November, commenting on *The Secrets of the Kaula Circle* 'by that snotty mongrel weasel Elizabeth Sharpe'. The Kaula circle was a Tantric school. Possessing a south Indian guru's writings on Tantra, Curwen was critical of Crowley's teachings on the 'elixir'. Baphomet responded positively, insisting it be incorporated into the OTO curriculum. Crowley being Crowley, he could not resist getting a little of his own back. He sent Curwen on a mission to Gerald Yorke, who, Crowley said, retailed bottles of *suvasini* juice. Earnestly hoping to obtain said precious substance, Yorke, confronted by Curwen's request, burst out laughing. Crowley had struck again! The idea of putting the *kalas* or tantric *suvasini* in bottles had never occurred to Yorke, but it obviously had to Crowley, who was not unknown to prepare 'elixir of life' pills from his own sanctified semen!

Tuesday 1 January 1946

> If all days could be like this! Prof. Butler of Newnham came and
> talked (*and made me talk*) with such sympathy, consideration,
> and understanding that the day was a dream of joy!

Professor EM Butler of Newnham College, Cambridge was writing *The
Myth of the Magus*. It had been suggested she meet the real thing.
Crowley wrote to her after the meeting:

> It is very important that you should understand the theory of the
> A. .A. .. People like St Germain, Rasputin, Eliphas Levi and
> H.P.B. [Blavatsky] are not Magi, they are merely Magicians with
> subsidiary functions, sometimes apparently disconnected with
> the main work of the Order, which is to send forth Magi from
> time to time uttering a certain Word, which must be a single
> word, and must be a magical formula which puts into the hands
> of mankind a new weapon.[19]

On 16 January, he felt 'out of sorts' all day: 'Went to Club, found it
frozen. One game in p.m.' He played a lot of chess in Hastings. The
arrival of a typewriter brought relief, swiftly followed by a 70mph gale. It
seemed symptomatic of the darkness that had befallen the country since
the relief of victory. He wrote to Sascha about the political situation:

> You have no idea how dull and dismal the whole country is.
> Same everywhere, no matter what the subject. The best chance
> of working things up is for the crew of imbecile swine to resign;
> a new General Election is possible, even probable; the mess is
> indescribable. And even if the Tories got in, what could they do?
> If only Winston were 20 years younger. But he isn't.
>
> About sending me money – don't, unless I ask for it specifically.
>
> 93 93/93 Yours, ah! So weary! Aleister[20]

On 3 May, one John Symonds of *Lilliput* magazine came about a
proposed article. He brought a pal of Robert Cecil's with him, astrologer
Rupert Gleadow. The meeting is described in Symonds' biography *The*

Great Beast (1951). Applying intellect and attitude to the legend, Symonds came up with the 'Demon Crowley', all over again.

Symonds asked Crowley why sex was important to magick. Crowley replied: 'The close connection of sexual energy with the higher nervous centres makes the sexual act definitely magical. It is therefore a sacrament which can and should be used in the Great Work. The act being creative, ecstatic and active, its vice consists in treating it as sentimental, emotional, passive.'[21] Crisp, clear, and to the point, as usual.

The day he completed *Olla*, 20 May 1946, Crowley received what he called an 'Appalling letter re Jack' from Louis Culling to Germer. Jack Parsons had gone on a magical retirement in March, pursuing something he called 'the Babalon Working' with new-found chum, L Ron Hubbard. The upshot was to conceive a 'Moonchild'. Parsons' sanity was imperilled. Crowley declared he became 'fairly frantic' contemplating 'the idiocy of these goats'. And still he could not get to California to stop the rot.

As ever, Wilkinson calmed his nerves.

Tuesday 11 June

Curwen ([Frater] A.L.L.) brought Barbara Kindred – lovely girl. Wish I were 70 again!

Is Barbara for anything in my life? If so, what? (Qy. [Greek *Hymen*]) […] Avoid marriage.

In summer 1946, Grant introduced Curwen to an artist called 'Clanda'; Curwen introduced her to Crowley. Such was their affinity that, notwithstanding his 70 years, Clanda nearly became the third Mrs Crowley. Crowley's diary reveals Clanda's real name was Barbara Kindred. He wrote to her. She was at Hastings on the day Symonds offered 'all help' for an 'A.C. publication plan' (15 June). Rising to Symonds' flattery, Crowley explained his fundamental position to the aspiring novelist on 25 June: 'The mainspring of my life is my Oath in the Order of A∴A∴ to devote myself wholly to the uplifting of the human race. It is fair to say that any other motive which might influence my actions is no more than subsidiary to that great affirmation.'[22] Judging by what Symonds wrote of Crowley subsequently, he must have read Crowley's *apologia pro vita sua* with indifference.

Augustus John's striking drawing of a very thin Crowley was collected for *Olla* on 26 June:

> Do what thou wilt... how right you are!
>
> Sincerely, Augustus John[23]

Frieda came to see him on 19 September, 'more delightful than ever'. On the 29th, poet and astrologer Jacintha Buddicom came for lunch.[24] Jacintha agreed in October to edit *Magick without Tears*, most of whose letters, incidentally, were addressed to Anne Macky, Soror Fiat Yod.

On 11 December 1946, Crowley suffered what he called the 'Worst night I remember'. It began with diarrhoea, then insomnia, then 'one of the worst dozen nightmares of my life: mostly out of the Apocalypse. *And – both* my watches stopped at about 2:30 a.m.!!!'[25]

He had but a year to live.

*   *   *

1947 opened with Crowley working on publishing projects and OTO business. He longed to go to America. He worried about the future. Who was best fitted to carry the thelemic banner into the world emerging from the rubble? A letter, unlike anything else he had ever written, was sent on 10 April to Gerald Hamilton:

> It is very nice down here now that at last we have got some sunshine, I am very lonely and should appreciate a visit from you more than I can say.
>
> Love is the law, love under will.
>
> Your old but sad friend,
>
> Aleister[26]

Crowley instructed a solicitor called Brackett about a draft will; there was still so much to do. And then on 13 May, as though from the blue,

Ataturk's mother phoned '!!!!!!!'; Ataturk was *all right*: 'I praise the Gods'
he exclaimed. Two days later, Pat and Ataturk arrived in Hastings.
Crowley was moved beyond words. When they left, he wrote to his son:

> My Dear Son,
>
> Do what thou wilt shall be the whole of the law.
>   This is the first letter that your father has ever written to you,
> so you can imagine that it will be very important; and you
> should keep it and lay it to heart [...] I want you to learn to
> behave as a Duke would behave. You must be high-minded,
> generous, noble, and, above all, without fear. For that last reason
> you must never tell a lie; for to do so shows that you are afraid of
> the person to whom you tell it, and I want you to be afraid of
> nobody. [...]
>   There is one point that I want to impress upon you! The best
> models of English writing are Shakespeare and the Old
> Testament especially the Book of Job, the Psalms, the Proverbs,
> Ecclesiastes, and the Song of Solomon. It will be a very good
> thing for you to commit as much as you can, both of these books
> and of the best plays of Shakespeare to memory, so that they
> form the foundation of your style: and in writing English, the
> most important quality that you can acquire is style.
>   [...] Your affectionate father, Aleister [27]

Not at all what one might expect from one supposedly enslaved to Satan!
Jacintha Buddicom wrote on 16 June:

> Very many thanks for the happy and interesting time you gave
> me at Netherwood this last weekend. It was so nice to see you
> again [...] you must take things slowly and not try to do too
> much at once. I am absolutely delighted with my beautiful copy
> of *Olla*, (accompanied by your nice box of card) with extreme
> pleasure [...] Dunhills promised to post your order [for Latakia
> tobacco] immediately. [28]

In June, Richard Ellman, just out of the US Navy, arrived to discuss the
long, long-gone saga of the Golden Dawn 'smash'. His biography of

WB Yeats would appear in 1948. Ellman also wrote a paper on Crowley's relations with the Irish poet.[29]

Though increasingly frail from illness during the summer, 666 still enjoyed sharpness of mind. He wrote to Karl, revising, or extending, his famous definition of magick as 'the art and science of causing changes in nature in conformity with will', telling Germer that 'Magick is getting into communication with individuals who exist on a higher plane than ours. Mysticism is the raising of oneself to their level.'

Perfect.

*   *   *

He wrote to John Symonds at the end of August:

> I have been a pretty sick man all summer. When my doctor went away for his holiday, he said: 'Well you are in bed and you can jolly well stay there until I come back.' This I did, and am feeling very much better. I was helped immensely to recover by Frieda.[30]

But by the end of September, he was poorly again. An anxious Karl Germer sailed from New York to Antwerp. Crowley would dearly have loved to see his old friend once more. Germer was denied entry into Great Britain.

The last entry in Crowley's diary:

> Monday 3 November
>
> Sent *Olla* to Patrick Dickinson, BBC[31]

As autumn turned into freezing winter, his health declined. On 1 December 1947, in his 73rd year, Aleister Crowley died peacefully in his bed.

Pat had been present for some days, speaking to him before he slipped quietly into a coma the day before he died. At the moment of his death, she witnessed a great influx of wind that blew the curtains in, and then out again as the Beast breathed his last. She heard thunder and was convinced the gods had taken him home.

Dr W Magowan gave cause of death to John Symonds as myocardial degeneration and chronic bronchitis; he asked his name be omitted should Symonds write about the deceased.[32] Under Crowley's bed, in a cardboard box, the practically penniless mage had £450, money collected from Sascha for the publication of *Liber Aleph*; he would not touch it for personal use, though he sorely needed it. The Work always came first.[33]

On 5 December at 2.45pm, Crowley's mortal remains were cremated at Brighton public crematorium. Louis Umfraville Wilkinson, friend to the last from far-off days in Washington Square, read, with great power, the *Hymn to Pan*, selections from *The Book of the Law*, and the Collects and Anthem from Crowley's *Gnostic Mass*. There were complaints to the council that a 'Black Mass' had been held within the sacred bounds of council property.

The ashes passed into the care of Karl Germer. According to Grady McMurtry, Karl and his wife, fearing FBI observation and suffering bouts of paranoia, placed the vulnerable ashes at the foot of a tree in the grounds of their house in Hampton, New Jersey, against Crowley's wishes that they be kept by the Order. When the Germers left Hampton for California, the Beast's ashes were unrecoverable. Many years before, the poet had written: 'Bury me in a nameless grave.'

Crowley's legacy lies elsewhere.

TWENTY-EIGHT

Aleister Crowley Remembered

Where was, or is, the biographer?

(Jane Wolfe to Gerald Yorke, 26 March 1950)[1]

Nancy Cunard was abroad when Aleister Crowley died in 1947: 'I was in Mexico at that moment and revolted by the inevitable rubbish and muck and spite vented in *Time* and wanted to write and protest, and didn't, for of course they would not have printed what I would have, succinctly, sent.'[2] Nancy remembered her old friend primarily as an artist: 'He just could not stand fools and bores!' 'He certainly was an artist and had due respect, and wonder for things of the senses (and they are many!)' 'I don't know how I should sign otherwise than "Do what thou wilt" Obviously, if and when one can.'[3]

A brief notice appeared in the winter 1948 issue of the *Occult Review*:

> We regret to announce the deaths of several eminent personages in the occult and psychic world [...] Aleister Crowley, the poet whom the world has never understood, died at Hastings on December 1st, aged 72.[4]

Gerald Yorke's *Biographical Note* appeared in the *Occult Observer*, summer 1949: 'Aleister Crowley was the most colourful man of his day. Whatever Crowley was, he was not a charlatan. He believed, he worked, he suffered, he had power. He failed to put over the religion of Thelema in his lifetime, which, considering its nature, is not surprising. The

Christian world regards him as one of the Devil's Contemplatives. His few friends will not see his like again; but his still fewer disciples mourn the passing of a Magus.'[5]

Yorke added further testimony to the invaluable collection of Crowleyana he bequeathed to the Warburg Institute:

> I first met Aleister Crowley in 1928 when I joined his order, the A.'.A.'. or Silver Star. Four years later I left the order but remained friendly with Crowley until his death, for I was very fond of him.[6]
>
> Although he did his best to persuade Stalin, Hitler, and the British Government to adopt Thelema as a state religion, very few people have in fact ever heard of it, and so – at least for the time being – he should be classified as a false Messiah. As such he was fascinating to meet.

In 1949 John Symonds began to write his biography of Crowley, *The Great Beast* (1951). Andrew Green, a 22-year-old psychic investigator from Ealing, wrote: 'He was wasted in England. In Persia, or India, or Japan millions would have followed him.'[7]

Convinced Symonds' forthcoming biography would fail to do justice to Crowley's memory, Charles R Cammell wrote *Aleister Crowley, The Man, the Mage, the Poet* (1951), emphasizing Crowley's 'prodigious genius', his powerful intellect, his acute judgement. Cammell had heard Major-General JFC Fuller, 'a man famous in arms and letters, one who has known the great statesmen, warriors, dictators, of our age, declare solemnly that the greatest genius he ever knew was Crowley'.

Crowley's friend between 1936 and 1941, Cammell insisted Crowley was a world leader in many fields, from chess to philosophy, from esotericism to practical magick, from mountaineering to exploration, from religion to mysticism. But 'beyond and above all these gifts,' wrote Cammell, 'Crowley was a poet and a poet of lyric genius.'

Cammell recounted how Crowley himself urged him to take on his biography, a full-length single volume for the general reader, based on the *Confessions*. Cammell demurred; only Crowley could do his life justice. 'Can't do popular autobiography – haven't the popular touch', responded Crowley on 11 January 1937:

> Can't do any book at all, not knowing from one week to another whether I shall have a roof over my head. Utterly tired of starting things which outside disturbances won't let me finish. You could do it easily from around 800,000 words in type. But I don't know if I shall be around by publication day. My health won't stand much more. See you 8.15 Wednesday.

'This letter,' reflected Cammell, 'was the only revelation of weariness or mental depression I ever witnessed in that indomitable man.' He was aware that Crowley would be scorned in death as much as in life, but the truth would eventually out:

> Crowley living was the ideal victim for assassins of reputations. May no jackal howl around the lion's remains: no scavengers be busy around the ruins of his temple, whatever the gods he worshipped. With his gods let him be judged by the One God, who sees all, and by whom all is comprehended.

Crowley left an indelible, spiritual impression on those who got to know him. Dr Robert MacGregor-Reid left in Yorke's care a 'Memorandum' regarding Crowley.[8] He was deeply impressed by Crowley's mystical awareness. 'The Beast is Man', he asserted, '– the Lamb brought to Hermetic sacrifice'. Crowley had perceived 'the duality' in himself and in life and so 'did not confine his efforts to the spiritual alone, but delved deep into what has been described as the dark or hidden side of nature'. To Crowley, magick was 'the true wisdom, in the same sense as used by the followers of Zoroaster'. It required 'the transmuting of the Beast in man, till it becomes a true image of God'.

MacGregor-Reid believed Crowley's poetry 'into which he wove the beauty and harmony of the world' would come to be his permanent memorial. Through his writing 'he will speak to generations still unborn, and inspire many a questing soul to take up the great adventure, in search of the Holy Graal'. He recalled how quiet and impressive Crowley could be, while he could yet 'get quite enraged at the telling of near or dirty stories, or the uttering of the common words of blasphemy'.

> He did not truly understand this world, he lived in a world of his own, out of which he came, at times, filled with an old world courtesy, eager to advise, willing to help but rarely speaking of his own teachings, unless he knew to whom he was speaking.

MacGregor-Reid concluded his Memorandum with these words: 'One day the true story of his life and the things that he aimed for will be known, when the legend has been forgotten, and then we will know something of this human soul, who when all is said and done, became "Despised and rejected of men".'

*   *   *

When Yorke examined the papers of theosophist-thelemite Martha Küntzel, he found an analysis of Crowley's handwriting, which he translated. According to the anonymous German graphologist:

> Now we are here not only dealing with an eminent thinker, but also with a highly differentiated personality which certainly does not shun life. It is obvious that the life of such a differentiated 'Full-Man' cannot pass without friction [...] He will obtain insights into supersensual fields which are closed to others. Conventional moral codes cannot be accepted by this strange personality always isolated and alone. Inwardly and outwardly free he will always strive to fulfil his highest motive in life and come closer to God.[9]

This precise view of the sheer scale of Crowley's intellect, spirit and horizon of vision was shared by another German. In December 1954, Henri Birven sent his article 'Modern Occultists and Magicians' to Yorke. Birven wrote of a spirituality of Crowley's own 'reaching up to the highest regions of thought, and of a consequence and an energy hardly imaginable'. Having met Crowley in Berlin in 1930, he remarked that he could find no valid psychological approach to Aleister Crowley:

'The unique nature of this man furnishes one of the reasons for the misunderstandings he meets with.'[10]

Gerald Yorke responded to Birven on New Year's Day, 1955:

Dear Birven,

Yours 25 December 1954. Yes, the Beast 666, the 'demon Crowley' was a façade deliberately built up by A.C. as a protection from fools, to keep away undesirable disciples, but also as a battle cry – for he was very human – to satisfy his instinct for dramatic posing. It runs through all he wrote.

In his letters he constantly warned one against becoming obsessed by 'the demon Crowley'. It is surprising how many people did so become obsessed.

Yorke, a complex man, did not believe Crowley was an Ipsissimus: 'I do not believe he was. I believe he was a pseudo pseudo Messiah.' Crowley, he recalled, could use harsh methods to locate moral weaknesses, acquired or hereditary inhibitions. This was 'too much for many people', Yorke added, 'myself included'. The bigger picture, however, was very impressive:

He was, as far as I was concerned, a very good teacher. He introduced me to Hinduism and Yoga. Both simple yoga and the Western magical system as taught in the Golden Dawn and then by A.C. in his A.'.A.'. are both valid systems which work – we don't know why or how, but they are effective if you do them. As is the tantric approach through enjoyment (*bhoja*) and their *vamachara* (left hand) or *vira* approach, which A.C. taught in the O.T.O. He, and he alone, to my knowledge had practised and worked both the Eastern and Western methods.

By means of raja yoga, with a little hatha and mantra yoga thrown in, A.C. had certainly attained the lower stages of *samadhi* – perhaps the higher ones as well.

Yorke had found his own magick worked best when Crowley was there: 'He had power – as all liberated souls, all *jivanmuktas*,[11] all saints have –

of opening the spiritual world to one when one was in his presence. But one had always to take the first step.'

Yorke tried to come to a conclusion:

> I have never before or since met a man who combined all the above qualities – who taught me so much – whom I respected more.
>
> Perhaps I am blind and he was a fraud and all that most people say of him, and I am too proud to admit that I could have been deceived. But you will never get me to accept this.
>
> He was an astonishing mixture of good and apparent bad. My final judgement – which may be proved wrong – is that he was a pseudo-Messiah. He was a very complex character.
>
> Finally, what fun he was! [12]

Yorke wrote again to Birven on 28 June 1954. Birven had asked what Crowley meant by the 'Scarlet Woman'. Yorke suggested Birven think of the 'Scarlet Woman' as the 'Woman clothed with the Sun', with AC as the Sun (666). Yorke believed you get a more truthful idea of Crowley's psychology from this idea than the vulgar idea 'of a beast mounted by a woman'.

> His goal was the Brahman of the Vedantists […] the three Negative States behind *Kether* (*Ain, Ain Soph, Ain Soph Aur*). He praised the Demiurge or Creator God and the Devil equally, and worshipped both with a view first to identify with them and then to transcending both of them. He is caricatured if his Anti-Christ or the Devil side of the equation is so stressed that the other side is lost sight of.
>
> John Symonds caricatured him as he could only see the dark side. [13]

Canadian theosophist Alexander Watt corresponded with Crowley. Accepting *Liber Legis*, he was influenced by Charles Stansfeld Jones's interpretations of Crowley's teaching which emphasized man as a solar being, a source of light in a solar age. The Sun does not 'die' when it sets, it is always shining. Finding this message at odds with everything he read in Symonds' biography, he wrote to Symonds on 26 November 1951: 'You have gone to great pains to depict A.C. – as your title states – as a vile, loathsome Dugpa or Paracellian [Paracelsian] Incubi.'

> Therion tells of a 'consecrated sugar of the stars' and what else is this but Semen, the Azoth of the blood, the Candidate, that is pulled up through a hole to be present at the Royal Marriage – above?

Concerning the infamous goat incident at Cefalù, Watt maintained: 'He was of course the Goat, the Beast, the fleet-footed one.' As for Crowley's pupils, Watt asked the question: 'Were all these people dupes?' 'the Wine was GOOD! [...] Such a bottle was Crowley.'[14]

*   *   *

Keeper of Prints, Drawings and Paintings at the Victoria and Albert Museum after 1938, historian James Laver lived in Piccadilly during the war, when Crowley could be found at 93 Jermyn Street. Visiting Crowley at Hastings in June 1947, 666 enjoyed their 'delightful talks', conversations heightened by 'one hell of a storm!'. Laver left an interesting memoir with Yorke: 'Some Impressions of Aleister Crowley.' He recalled putting it to Crowley that the essence of magick was summed up in Blake's phrase: 'Push imagination to the point of vision, and the trick is done.'

'Ah!' Crowley said, 'You realise that Magick is something we do to ourselves. But it is *more convenient* to assume the objective existence of an Angel who gives us knowledge than to allege that our invocation has awakened a super-normal power in ourselves.' Crowley added, 'The Master Therion has made an Epoch in the Art of Magick by applying the Method of Science to its problems.'

Laver remembered Crowley's last words to him: 'Some can evoke and invoke; some can attain to direct communication.' Laver suggested this distinction 'was the difference between occultism and mysticism'. 'Yes,' he said, 'occultism is the longer way round, but the path is not so steep.'[15]

*   *   *

Writer and translator James Cleugh first encountered Crowley in the late 1920s when literary director of the Aquila Press:

> Like most born intellectuals he did not particularly lust after the flesh, or power over the masses of his fellow creatures. He never perpetrated cruelty or malignity for their own sake. His courage, both physical and moral, was dauntless even in old age. And he was very far from being just the silly charlatan that the more level-headed of those who never met him often took him for. It is true that he repeatedly gave himself up to orgy. But never with frenzy or in sheer helplessness. He was too good a Greek scholar for that.[16]

Crowley hated no one, Cleugh opined, 'though many, mostly simple souls, hated him'. 'Poor Aleister! He was better worth knowing than many a better man.' Cleugh did not think Crowley loved anyone or expected to be loved – a view Crowley's friends could hardly share. Cleugh had caught sight of the 'riddle' of Crowley that perplexed Cammell, as well as Nancy Cunard's observation that Crowley's makeup contained a disconcerting mix of both horrible and refined taste.

Such was Israel Regardie's experience. Encountering Crowley's writings in 1926, Regardie became Crowley's secretary in 1928, parted company in 1932, then returned to reflect on Crowley's work having established himself as a chiropractor, a doctor of Freudian, Reichian and Jungian psychoanalysis,[17] and as an authority on Kabbalah and the Golden Dawn.

Regardie's book *The Eye in the Triangle* (1970) offered a belated appraisal. He explained his delay: 'It is only within the last few years, that my admiration for him as a great mystic has triumphed over my resentment and bitterness, enabling me to put aside my contempt for the nasty, petty, vicious louse that occasionally he was on the level of practical human relations.'[18] *The Eye in the Triangle* is a moving work at a number of points. On first meeting Crowley at Paris's Gare St Lazare in 1928, Regardie 'felt confronted by authority – that was something else again. It was a quality natural to his personality, shining through even when he was most relaxed and at ease.'[19]

It is clear that he was not a man to be trifled with. Years of living by his wits as an adventurer had whittled off any useless psychological tissue – and he could play dirty.

I think his insights were superb, but his techniques for dealing with neurotic problems were woefully inadequate.[20] It is clear then that Aleister Crowley was a strange man. He embodied in himself quite overtly and unashamedly all those drives and tendencies that are concealed and latent in most of us. Credit has to be accorded him for psychological experimentation – not with laboratory animals, but with himself as the subject. As a result of this, he discovered that our current socially acceptable attitude towards man is a mass of ill-digested dogmas and irrational beliefs that have been foisted on us unthinkingly down through the centuries.

He was possessed of a wonderful sense of humour. At times it was gross and Rabelaisian; at others very warm and gentle. His humour and leg-pulling stemmed from an exuberance that would have rivalled a five-year-old. He loved playing pranks. But it always startled him, so vast was his naïvety, when people did not always realise that they were pranks.[21]

The overall impression Regardie had of Crowley was that, for all his faults, he constituted a gigantic lesson in going beyond the bounds of neurotic character armour, exploring freely beyond ego, class, society, nation, even space and time, giving us insight into what man really is, and can be. It took the *Beast 666* himself to show our untapped capacity for spiritual growth, suffocated by normalcy and fear of the world and its alleged masters. For Regardie, Crowley was 'a man, infinitely flexible, but resolute – determined to resist to the bitter end and fight to the death what he considered to be the foul symptoms of a dying and decadent culture.'[22]

Aleister Crowley was Self-realized.

*　　*　　*

Hereward Carrington (1880–1958) knew Crowley. Having joined the Society for Psychical Research before emigrating to America in 1899,[23] Carrington's introduction came through the then secretary of the SPR, Everard Feilding:

> Dear Carrington,
>
> This will introduce you to Aleister Crowley, poet, sage, mountain climber and general lunatic. I am sure you will have much in common.
>
> E. Feilding.

Carrington would participate in magical invocation ceremonies in New York with William Seabrook and remembered introducing Crowley to Leah Hirsig: 'a curious girl… and an extreme nymphomaniac. As Crowley once remarked, their relations had grown into a sort of "contest" between them.'

> Crowley's mental and moral life were as erratic as his diet. At times he lived the saintly life of a recluse, undergoing stringent spiritual exercises. Then he would suddenly disappear for a week or two, and be found in the lowest dives of underground Paris. Needless to say, his sex life was as sophisticated and as variegated as his general character. His experiences in this direction, all over the world, were amazing.

Comparing Crowley to Cagliostro, Rasputin, Cellini and Baudelaire, Carrrington was 'profoundly impressed' as well as being 'alternately amazed and amused at his incredible career':

> I never ceased to marvel at the man's versatility and many-sided genius. Nowhere could you ever meet another like him. Of all the characters I have known, he was the most bizarre and the most unforgettable.

True genius is seldom accommodated in its time; the greater the genius, the longer it takes before people wake up to what has passed among them. In the meantime, it has proved safest to condemn the interloper who has wandered into our ignorance and blindness. Most men and women in his lifetime could not see Aleister Crowley; he saw them.

We have seen Crowley's contribution to culture and history. He proposed the ends and practised the means. But how can we really assess the value of genius? Crowley's genius or 'daimon' leapt into the dangerous world and will be with us for a long time to come. Contact with that *mind* (not *image*), once made, cannot be without effect. There was a vision, and it was very great. Crowley believed that our future relies on acquiring higher intelligence coupled with the wisdom to employ it. It means saying goodbye to many a comforting fiction and leaving the four red monks carrying their black goat on their road to nowhere.

End Notes

Abbreviations:

HBC = *Biographical Notes*; *The Confessions of Aleister Crowley*; ed Hymenaeus Beta

CAC = *The Confessions of Aleister Crowley*, ed Symonds & Grant, London, RKP, 1977

ASH = Lewes Asburnham correspondence

SSA = *Secret Agent 666, Aleister Crowley, British Intelligence and the Occult*, Richard Spence, Feral, 2008

YC = Yorke Collection

HB = unpublished typescripts edited by Hymenaeus Beta

MHB = *Magick Liber Aba*, Weiser, 2004, ed Hymenaeus Beta

TSK = 'The Temple of Solomon the King' in *The Equinox* I (7,8)

Eye = *The Eye in the Triangle – an Interpretation of Aleister Crowley*, Israel Regardie, Llewellyn, 1970

Affidavit = 'Affidavit Memorandum of My Political Attitude since August 1914'. typescript, 1917, *YC*

USNA = United States National Archives, MID = Military Intelligence Division

SGM = *Magick*, ed John Symonds and Kenneth Grant, RKP, London, 1973

Chapter 2

[1] www.manicai.net/genealogy/gam_aleister.html. Family history by Cicily Mary Crowley (1905–2003)

[2] *Paupers and Pig Killers – A Diary of William Holland a Somerset Parson, 1799–1818*, Penguin, 1984. Original research on Coles by William Breeze.

[3] *The Clockmakers of Somerset, 1650–1900*, appendix: 'James Cole, James Ferguson Cole and Thomas Cole – Three Extraordinary Clockmakers from Somerset', pp380–94, AJ Moore, 1998 (with thanks to William Breeze; *HBC*)

[4] *HBC*

[5] Cited *Tom Bond Bishop of the Children's Special Service Mission*, 1923, pp20–1 in *HBC*

[6] T.B.B. of the C.S.S.M., p19, (*HBC*)

[7] 'In Memoriam A.J.B.' (*Songs of the Spirit*, 1898)

Chapter 3

1. *The Confessions of Aleister Crowley*, ed Symonds & Grant, London, RKP, 1977, *CAC*, p44
2. NL Noel, *The History of the Brethren 1826–1936*, ed William F Knapp, vol 1, Denver, WF Knapp, 1936
3. Grayson Carter, *Anglican Evangelicals: Protestant Secessions from the Via Media*, c1800–50, Oxford, OUP, 2001, p400
4. *Notes towards a Bibliography of Edward Crowley compiled by Anthony Naylor*, LHO Books, 2004
5. *PEACE AND ACCEPTANCE; LIBERTY AND SONSHIP by E.C.*, London, WH Broom and Rouse
6. *Tristram Shandy* and *Gargantua & Pantagruel* respectively
7. James Lachlan Dickson, cotton spinners agent (discovered by William Breeze)
8. Cicily Crowley
9. Edward Crowley *snr* born c1788, eldest son of Thomas and Elizabeth Crowley of Camomile Street, near Bishopsgate. Director and shareholder of the Direct London & Portsmouth Railway, the Brighton & Chichester Railway, the Dublin, Belfast & Coleraine Junction Railway and the London, Brighton & South Coast Railway. *d* 16 February 1856 (*HBC*)
10. Eldest son of Edward and Mary Crowley of Lavender Hill; civil engineer; inventor of a patented rail switching mechanism. Member of Royal Geological Society, Royal Geographical Society, Royal Institution of Great Britain, associate member of Institution of Civil Engineers; fellow of Ethnological Society. Married Agnes Hall Pope; children: Agnes, Fanny Joan and Claude Edmund (AC's cousins). Married governess, Anne Heginbottom, from Warwickshire, 1872. (*HBC*)

Chapter 4

1. *CAC*, p121
2. ASH/2903, 2904, 1876–1912: Lewes Asburnham correspondence (*ASH*) concerns the Comte de Paris, Don Alphonse de Bourbon, and other continental royals and prominent English Catholics.
3. ASH/2905 1881–1912: Don Carlos de Bourbon and his son, Don Jaime de Bourbon, Prince Louis of Bavaria, Alfonso Maria de Bourbon and other royals appear in code.
4. *CAC* chapter 45
5. *Secret Agent 666, Aleister Crowley, British Intelligence and the Occult*, Richard Spence, Feral, 2008 (hereafter *SSA*), p17; deleted extract from *CAC*
6. *CAC*, p107
7. Mina Mathers also called herself 'Moina'. She was Henri Bergson's sister
8. *The Rosicrucian Scandal*, by 'Leo Vincey' (Crowley) in *Aleister Crowley Scrapbook*, Sandy Roberston, Foulsham, 2002
9. Maria Theresa Henrietta Dorothea de Austria-Este-Modena was daughter

of the Duke of Modena, married to Ludwig, Regent – later King – Ludwig III of Bavaria.

10 William Butler Yeats (1865–1939)

11 Philip Payton (ed) *Cornish Studies* 12 (Exeter University Press, 2004); *see SSA*, p29

12 reported by the *New York Times* on 27 July 1899

13 ASH/2908 1887–91

14 Vincent John English RN; *see* 'The Carlists of Today', *Pall Mall Gazette* (10 October 1901, pp1–2; 19 October, p4; 23 October, p11)

Chapter 5

1 *The Equinox*, 'Notes of [Astral] Travel 1898–1899', *HB*

2 The second degree, Theoricus, was written as 2° = 9□ (where '9' is the ninth *sephira* called *Yesod*, or Foundation); Practicus 3° = 8□ (where '8' is *Hod* or Splendour); Philosophus 4° = 7□ (the 7th *sephira* being *Netzach* or Victory); Adeptus Minor 5° = 6□ (the 6th is *Tiphareth* or Beauty); Adeptus Major 6° = 5□ (the 5th being *Geburah* or Strength); Adeptus Exemptus 7° = 4□ (the 4th being *Chesed* or Mercy); Magister Templi 8° = 3□ (the 3rd being *Binah* or Understanding); Magus 9° = 2□ (where *Hokmah* or Wisdom is the second *sephira*); Ipsissimus 10° = 1□ (The 1st sephira is *Kether* or The Crown). In theory, on reaching the 'Crown', one has re-traced the effects of a primal 'Fall of Man' from the source of his being in God. Assumption of each grade required meditation of its meaning in relation to the whole system, including correspondences with tarot cards and astrological symbols. The Golden Dawn provided a synthesis of occult knowledge based on structures inherited from 18th-century German Rosicrucians.

3 Charles Henry Allan Bennett (1872–1923), analytical chemist and founder of the International Buddhist Society; leader of the first Buddhist mission to Great Britain.

4 *YC* EE1, vol 1, 28 October 1899

5 Undated letters, *YC* EE1, vol 1

6 Annie Horniman (1860–1937); Mathers had been her father's museum curator.

7 *YC* EE1, vol 1; letter: 3 December 1896

8 *The Golden Dawn Scrapbook*, RA Gilbert, 1997

9 *Frater Gnōthi Seauton*, William Evans Hugh Humphrys (*b*1876)

10 *A Magicall Diarie 1899*, unpublished typescript, *HB*

11 *1900 Diary*, (*HB*)

12 The woman he would help to elope – by marrying her (!) – was called Rose, and a man called Gormley would try to steal her from him.

13 *HB*

14 *You only live Twice* (United Artists, 1967) Screenplay by Roald Dahl

Chapter 6

[1] SSA
[2] *CAC*, p202
[3] I am grateful to William Breeze for information on Don Jesús
[4] published 1901
[5] In Greek το μη (*to mē*) = the NOT
[6] She was daughter to congressman and mayor of Brooklyn, Dennis Strong
[7] *CAC*, p223
[8] *HB*
[9] Advertisement for Homocea ointment: 'Homocea touches the spot and soothes the aching part.'
[10] *YC* D6

Chapter 7

[1] *YC* D6 A1a
[2] *The Sword of Song* (1904)
[3] *YC* D6
[4] *The Writings of Truth*; *YC* N20, August–October 1901
[5] Ezekiel 1.26
[6] SSA
[7] *YC* D6, 15 May 1902
[8] *Six mois dans l'Himalaya, le Karakorum et l'Hindu-Kush. Voyages et Explorations aux plus hautes montagnes du monde*, Neuchâtel, W Sandoz, 1904
[9] *YC* D6, 25 October 1902
[10] *YC* D6, February 1903. The 'Little Horses' pull a 'sulky' at a hippodrome at Cagnes-sur-Mer near Nice.
[11] Arnold Bennett, author: *Anna of the Five Towns* (1902)
[12] *Spes*: 'Hope' – motto on Crowley family crest
[13] Thanks to Ian Brooker for this information
[14] Typescripts made by GJ Yorke from notebooks (owned by Dr JP Kowal; ed Hymenaeus Beta)
[15] Trinity Fellow James George Frazer's *The Golden Bough*, used for *The Gospel according to St Bernard Shaw*
[16] See Egil Asprem's 'The Scientific Aeon: Magic, Science and Psychology in Crowley's Scientific Illuminism.' from *Twenty years of research on Aleister Crowley*, CESNUR conference, LSE, London 2008
[17] Henry Maudsley (1835–1918), founder, the Maudsley Hospital (1904)
[18] Diary 22 February 1904, *HB*
[19] *b* Rose Edith Kelly, 23 July 1874

20 *YC* D6 The reference to 'quartos' refers to cheap pamphlets or low-class magazines.

Chapter 8

1   Pub: 1905; Society for the Propagation of Religious Truth (SPRT)
2   אלהיסטהרהכרעולהי ['ALEISTEREKROWLEI'] = 666
3   February 1924, *HB*
4   *MHB*, p433
5   *YC* NS18 undated typescript
6   Diary 22 February 1904, *HB*
7   *MHB*, p433
8   Known as the 'Preliminary Invocation', pub: Charles Godwin, 1852: *Fragment of a Graeco-Egyptian Work Upon Magic*; adapted for Golden Dawn: *The Bornless Ritual for the Invocation of the Higher Genius*
9   Daily diary; *TSK*; *Equinox*, Vol I, 7, p395ff
10 *YC The Book of Results*
11 *YC* NS18 typescript, 1935; by-line: 'Strange behaviour of Ouarda.'
12 'The Temple of Solomon the King' (*TSK*); *Equinox*, Vol I, 7, p395ff
13 *Revue d'égyptologie* 20, 1968, pp149–52
14 *YC* Japanese vellum notebook: *The Invocation of Hoor* [Horus]
15 Rose's instructions for the ritual: 'To be performed before a window open to the E[ast]. Or N[orth]. Without incense. The room filled with jewels, but only diamonds to be worn. A Sword, unconsecrated. 44 pearl beads, to be told. Stand. Bright daylight at 12.30 noon. Lock doors. White robes; bare feet. Be very loud. *Die*: ♄ [*Saturday*]'
16 *MHB* p.xxxviii
17 *Book of Results*; and daily diary: *TSK*; *Equinox*, Vol I, 7, p395ff
18 *The Equinox*, vol I, 7, p395ff
19 *The Eye in the Triangle – an Interpretation of Aleister Crowley*, Israel Regardie, Llewellyn, 1970 (henceforth: *Eye*)
20 *TSK* (*Equinox* vol I, 7, p384); 'Name co-incidences of Qabalah' (Notebook No23; *YC*): 'The Beast A Ch I H A = 666 in full. (The usual spelling is ChIVA) (A = 111 ['A' standing for a word or phrase adding up to 111] Ch [standing for ChITh]= 418 I = 20 H = 6 A = 111)'
21 See 'First Knowledge Lecture', *The Golden Dawn*, Regardie, Llewelyn, p53
22 Ezekiel I.5
23 'The Secret of Wisdom': Golden Dawn euphemism for the tarot.
24 Greek ου μη (=*ou mē*): Crowley's *Adeptus Exemptus* motto means 'certainly not!'
25 Reproduced: *MHB*, p682

26 Crowley wrote *Temperance* (1939), a poem not to pious restraint but to love and intoxication.

27 *YC* 'Notebook 23'

28 *The Equinox*, vol I, 10, 1913, pp89–90

29 or 'Book Four'; (*MHB*, p433)

30 Ivor Back's father, Francis Formby Back (1852–1913), of merchant bankers *Back & Manson* bought *The Egyptian Gazette*. Francis Back was in Cairo.

31 General William Edmund Ritchie Dickson CMG (1871–1957), *b* Tehran, Persian specialist. CinC Anglo-Indian forces East Persia 1914–18; opposed British support of Reza Khan in ousting Shah of Iran 1921. Recalled, demoted Colonel, eventually re-promoted Brigadier General. Dickson was not General in 1904, but Crowley wrote in 1920s. Dickson converted to Islam; mentioned in Crowley's account.

32 Hebrew for 'angel': *Melak*, messenger or chief

33 He planned its encasement in lead against destruction.

34 *MHB*, p445

35 Chartered 1899 by the *Grande Loge de France*. Petition signed by James Lyon Bowley, British Embassy chaplain, Paris.

36 *YC* EE1; 23 July 1904, William Wynn Westcott (Supreme Magus *Societas Rosicruciana in Anglia*) to FL Gardner

37 *YC* NS18 typescript (1935)

38 'Invocation of Hoor' includes '1904 summer. Work at Bol[eskine] with Beel[zebub].'

39 *The Sword of Song – called by Christians the Book of the Beast* (Paris, 1904)

40 *YC* D6

41 SPRT published (1904) *The Argonauts, The Sword of Song, The Book of the Goetia of Solomon the King, Why Jesus Wept* (with hilarious flyer) and *In Residence*. 1905: *Oracles, Orpheus, Rosa Mundi* – and *Collected Works* vol 1.

42 *YC* NS18, undated typescript

Chapter 9

1 OTO typescript, 1905 diary, transcribed: GJ Yorke *c*1954 from Dr Kowal's notebook; *HB*

2 *see Liber HHH*

3 *Said*, May 1905: *Gargoyles* (1907)

4 *YC* NS18, undated

5 *YC* D6

6 *YC* NS18

7 Diary 19 November 1905; *HBC*

8 *SSA*

9 George Litton (1867–1906)

[10] A root cause of the Vietnam War

[11] Litton was buried by his friend George Forrest (1873–1932).

[12] *Eye*, p291

[13] *Liber Os Abysmi*; quoted in *Eye*, pp291–2

[14] *Adeptus Exemptus* 7°=4° – Inner Order GD grade

[15] *Augoeides* from Iamblichus *De Mysteriis* = concerning the Mysteries; the 'beaming' or dawning light

[16] 'Ruach' is that part of the soul centring on the body-governing ego, equating to the 'rational mind'. 'Neschamah' is spiritual intellect, receiving light 'from above'.

[17] OTO typescript by GJ Yorke from notebook original, *HB*

[18] Dr Georges Barbezieux, *b* Paris, 1860, expert on epidemiology of diseases of Indochina and Cambodia (founded with Mme Béquet de Vienne France's first refuge for unmarried mothers, 1892).

[19] French since 1884; now North Vietnam

[20] *HBC*, p222

[21] Charles Henry Brewitt-Taylor (1857–1938), scholar of Chinese. Lecturer: navigation and astronomy at Imperial Arsenal, Foochow from 1880; appointed to the Imperial Maritime Customs 1891. (*HBC*)

[22] Crowley and 18-year-old Bax (composer Arnold Bax's brother) met 23 January 1905

[23] *YC D6*

[24] The A∴A∴ established with GC Jones, 1908.

[25] *Samadhi*'s transcendence of reason must be accepted unless it is a delusion. If so, what is reason?

[26] Autumnal equinox celebrated with ritual re-written as *Liber* 671, concerning ascent of 'Mountain of Initiation'.

[27] Vera Snepp (1888–1953) became Mrs Henry Algernon Claude Graves and acted as Vera Neville. She appears as 'Lola Daydream' in Crowley's short story 'The Wake World', first published in *Konx Om Pax* (1907). Vera also inspired *Clouds without Water* (1909). Lola was the name of Crowley's second legitimate daughter.

[28] Regardie, *Eye*, p333

[29] *The Equinox*, I.6, p53ff, September 1911

Chapter 10

[1] 'The Poet' from *KONX OM PAX – Essays on Light*, Walter Scott, 1907

[2] Lt Col Joseph Andrew Gormley MD (1848–1925), head of Central Hospital, South Africa (1899–1902). Army Retired List (1903–12). Rose's first husband (1897), Surgeon-Major Frederick Thomas Skerrett MD (1858–99) lived with Rose in Diamondtown, South Africa. Gormley's

hopes raised by Skerrett's death from acute alcoholism (1899) thwarted by second marriage. (*HBC*)

3   From *Part 1 of Book 4* (yoga). *See Eye*, p331ff.

4   *The Equinox*, vol 1, 8, p38ff, September 1912

5   *HBC*, p157

6   George Montagu Bennet, 7th Earl of Tankerville, former ADC to Duke of Marlborough when Lord Lieutenant of Ireland

7   Edith Agnes Kathleen Bruce (1878–1947); sculptor (three busts in National Portrait Gallery)

8   *The Magical Dilemma of Victor Neuburg*, Jean Overton Fuller (1966)

9   'Elant' a familiar name. Maiden name: Leonora Sophie van Marter, from New York.

10 *Binah* – the coming to 'Understanding' beyond contradictions of phenomenal world, characteristic of *Magister Templi* grade.

11 *Konx Om Pax* (1908)

12 Contemporary notebook (*YC* OS37) opens: 'The Virgin Mary I desire / but arseholes set my prick on fire'.

13 *The Holy Books*, OTO/Weiser, 1988, p.xviii

14 *Eye*, p343

15 *Konx Om Pax*

Chapter 11

1   1901 census: Emily Bertha Crowley, Bedfordwell Road, Eastbourne, with companion, Elizabeth M King, 21; two servants. Died, heart attack, age 69; 8 Orchard Road, Eastbourne 14 April 1917 (*HBC*).

2   *YC* NS18

3   *Eye*, p362

4   *Magick in Theory and Practice* (1929), quoted in *Eye*, p367

5   During the 1910 *Looking Glass* trial, Ward bolted to Burma, avoiding defence subpoena. Ward's father: James Ward (1843–1925), Trinity Fellow, psychologist.

6   *HB*

7   Illustration p.xl, *MHB*

8   *MHB*

9   He had a typescript *Liber AL* in the Far East, 1906.

10 *YC* EE1

11 now Sour el Ghozlane

12 – or Zero, implying eternal orgasm.

13 Regardie, *Eye*

14 3 December 1909; budget rejected 30 November.

15 *Eye*, p407

16 *The Vision and the Voice* fills 450 pages (Weiser, 1998, ed Hymenaeus Beta).

Chapter 12

1 *YC* EE1

2 Right Reverend Ernest William Barnes (1874–1953), Royal Society, liberal Churchman

3 Horatio Bottomley (1860–1933)

4 *YC* EE1

5 *YC*, EE1, 22 March 1910

6 *YC* EE1, 29 March 1910

7 Leila Ida Nerissa Bathurst Waddell (1880–1932)

8 *See The Vision and the Voice*, ed Hymenaeus Beta, Weiser, 1998

9 *See The Magical Dilemma of Victor Neuburg*, Jean Overton Fuller.

10 *YC* EE1

11 The Wehrmacht ran with Fuller's ideas.

12 *YC* D1, Crowley to Mudd, 18 November 1923

13 Mary Desti Sturges, *b* Mary Dempsey, Quebec 1871; *d* (leukaemia), New York 1931

14 Married Turk, Veli Bey, May 1912; abandoned her in London. Mary's scarf caused Isadora Duncan's death (caught in roadster's back wheel).

15 A friend of Kenneth Mackenzie, Jennings believed the 'Rosicrucian Order' could *raise the alchemical or invisible 'fire'*: linked to phallus worship.

16 E-mail to author, January 2010

17 Correspondence destroyed by post-war UGLE librarian.

18 Martin P Starr: 'Aleister Crowley, Freemason!'; *Transactions of the Quatuor Coronati Lodge of Research* Vol. 108 (1995)

Chapter 13

1 Ernest Fittock (1882–1963), *b* Stroud, New South Wales

2 *YC* NS12; Aelfrida Tillyard's transcriptions from Yorke/Germer notebooks

3 Everard Feilding's investigation of Besant's 'Esoteric Section' informed Crowley's account of Leadbeater's purloining child Krishnamurti (*Equinox* I.10).

4 *YC* NS12

5 Headship probably to 'Papus' after Yarker. AC gave succession order as Yarker-Papus-del Villar in unpublished letter to WB Crow, 21 June 1944. *See also CAC*, p711

6 Dr Gérard-Anaclet-Vincent Encausse or 'Papus' (1865–1916). Undated letter to Reuss (1914): 'the Honorable degree of 97 of Grand Hierophant

made vacant [...] be conferred upon the most illustrious S.G.M.G. of France Dr Gérard Encausse (Papus) 33°, 90°, 96°, on account of his world wide eminence and his successful labours on behalf of the Rite.' (*YC* NS12)

7 1 September 1913 (*YC* NS12)

8 *CAC*, p692

9 *YC* NS12

10 Aelfrida Catherine Wetenhall Graham, *née* Tillyard (1883–1959), Fordfield, Cambridge, *Equinox* contributor; edited *Cambridge Poets 1900–1913* (W Heffer, 1913; including Rupert Brooke and AC).

11 *YC* NS12

12 *Ibid*

13 *CAC*, p711

14 *YC* NS12

15 *see* Stephen Graham's *Undiscovered Russia*, London, John Lane, 1914, cited in 'The Great Beast in Russia: Aleister Crowley's Theatrical Tour in 1913 and his Beastly Writings on Russia', WF Ryan, *Symbolism and After, Essays on Russian Poetry in Honour of Georgette Donchini*, p144.

16 *Memoirs of a Secret Agent* (1934), Book Two: 'The Moscow Pageant'

17 'LSE has some Feilding letters from *c*1910 where he is identified, in the online catalogue, as an intelligence officer.' (e-mail from William Breeze, July 2009).

18 *SSA*, p43ff

19 *British Agent*; New York, Putnam's, 1933, p75, cited in *SSA* n40, p48

20 Sir Robert Hamilton Bruce Lockhart KCMG 1887–1970). Lockhart 'ran' famous spy Sidney Reilly; condemned by Bolsheviks over Lenin assassination plot (released in spy-exchange).

21 *CAC*, pp715–16

22 Book Two, *Memoirs of a Secret Agent*

23 Crowley was subtly warning government of communist-socialist attempts to exploit WW2 for revolutionary purposes.

24 *YC* NS12

25 *YC* NS12

26 Austin Frederic Harrison (1873–1928), political editor *The Observer* 1904–8

27 *YC* NS12

28 Keith Richmond, *Progradior and the Beast*, Neptune Press, 2004

Chapter 14

1 'The Great War Prophesied', *YC*, NS18

2 Quinn made selections; remainder stored Detroit and lost; now mostly at University of Texas.

[3] *Affidavit*

[4] Official Secrets Act (August 1911)

[5] *YC* EE1, 1 May 1929

[6] *SSA* p54

[7] *see also* Duncan Crow, *A Man of Push and Go: The Life of George Macauley Booth*, London, Rupert Hart-Davis, 1965

[8] Clive Bayley, from New York Consulate

[9] *CAC*, p745

[10] *Affidavit* begins: 'I, Aleister Crowley, am of a Breton-Irish family, settled in England since 1500.'

[11] *b* Munich, 1884

[12] *HBC*, p749

[13] *Ibid*

[14] Concerning Russian trip summer 1913, (1942 edition, notes).

[15] Jeanne Robert Foster (*née* Oliver, 1884–1970)

[16] Belle da Costa Greene (1883–1950)

[17] *SSA*, p101

[18] 'The Gaunt-Wiseman Affair: British Intelligence in New York in 1915', *International Journal of Intelligence and Counter Intelligence*, Vol.16, #3 (2003), 448

[19] *Affidavit*, p2

[20] 'L'agent secret, fauter de paix,' Janus #2, June-September 1964, pp 49–53

[21] *Affidavit*, p2

[22] *Liber CMXXXIV The Cactus*, collection of 'trip' records. UK Customs retained *c*1924.

[23] Note diary 6 October 1931: Frau von Alvensleben, Berlin admirer

[24] Martin Starr, *The Unknown God*, p37

[25] *Liber 73, The Urn*, 1915, HB

[26] *Rex de Arte Regia* June 1915–February 1916; September 1915; thanks to William Breeze.

[27] 'Secret Service Work in the War: Sir R Nathan's Work', *The Times*, 28 June 1921, p10; *see SSA*, p111

[28] Otto Kahn (1867–1934); one of the most powerful financiers, patrons and philanthropists in the USA.

[29] *Affidavit*

[30] Frances Gregg (1885–1941)

[31] Newman, *The Tregerthen Horror*, Abraxas, p50

[32] Roger Hutchinson, *Aleister Crowley, The Beast Demystified*, Mainstream, 1998; pp145–57; appears to have accessed uncited, unadmitted, state AC files.

[33] *The Great Beast*, John Symonds, 1951

[34] USNA MID file 9140-815/1, p342; cited in *SSA*

[35] USNA MID 9140-815/1, extract of British 'Watch List', p106, entry #340, from *c*1916, concluded after US probe for German spies: 'Aleister Crowley was an employee of the British Government [...] in this country on official business of which the British Consul, New York City has full cognizance.' Cited in *SSA*.

[36] *Liber 73, The Urn*, (*HB*); 'success' means long-term plan fulfilled.

[37] Feared war secrets emerged in séances. *cf*: Superintendent Quinn's November 1916 report: AC in New York with woman of 'fortune-telling class' (Hutchinson, p149).

[38] *Ibid*

[39] *Affidavit*

[40] Emily Bertha's will, National Archives, Kew: Tom Bond Bishop sole executor. Gross value: £488-15-9. 'I give and bequeath unto my son Edward Alexander Crowley the old Devonport in my dining-room & small cabinet which belonged to the late Lady Berwick.' AC reviewed Tom Bishop's book in 1919 'Blue' *Equinox* – complained Bishop delayed money from estate sale. Emily's house might have been in AC's name, a tax dodge.

[41] *The Urn*, 14 June 1917

[42] *HBC*

[43] *SSA*, p109

[44] USNA, MID 10012-112/1 *General Summary*, 23 September, 1918, p4 British security services claim MI5 files destroyed after WW2; letters from T Denham, MI5 to Spence, 20 Jan 2003; 8 April 2005; 18 Oct 2005. *See SSA*, introduction.

[45] Hyde Park close to *Springwood*, Was, Spence asks, AC on look-out to prevent radical assault on home of Franklin D Roosevelt?

[46] *66th Congress, US Senate, Subcommittee on the Judiciary, Brewing and Liquor Interests and German and Bolshevik Propaganda, vol. 2* (Washington 1919), 2027–2028; *SSA*, p105

Chapter 15

[1] *Sunday Dispatch*, 1933

[2] *Liber 729, The Amalantrah Working* (*HB*)

[3] *Bokh*: Persian honorific, 'related to God'

[4] *Magick in Theory and Practice*

[5] OYVZ עיוז: zain=7; vau=6; yod=10; ayin=70.

[6] *Cephaloedium Working*, Villa Santa Barbara, 1920/21, 'New Commentary' *YC* K1

[7] AYVAS = איואס; samekh=60; aleph=1; vau=6; yod=10; aleph=1.

[8] OYVZ = עיוז zain=7; vau=6; yod=10; ayin=70

9 'race' probably refers to 'Indo-Aryan' or 'Aryan' civilization, alleged 'super-tribe' from the Caucasus dominating Syria, Iran and Indus Valley in second millennium BC. 'Aryans' invented by scholars. Sanskrit 'Aryan' means 'aristocratic' or 'high born', applied to Brahmin founders of 'Raja Yoga'. See *Aryan Idols – Indo-European Mythology as Ideology and Science*, Stefan Arvidsson, Chicago University Press, 2006

10 *New York Times*, 17 September 1971, kindly sent by William Breeze.

11 Knowledge of Jacobs thanks to the research of William Breeze and Martin P Starr.

12 *C.S. Jones Papers*, OTO Archives

13 *HBM*, p761

14 discovered by Martin P Starr.

15 From an essay republished in *The Revival of Magick* (OTO, 1998).

16 *HBM*, p435 and p.lxv

17 Crowley to Yorke, 3 September 1945, in *HBM*, p761

18 29 March 1948; OTO archives

19 e-mail William Breeze to author, 4 August 2005

20 Turkish view re Yezidi identity caused denial of rights as distinct people, Treaty of Lausanne (1923).

21 Drower, *Peacock Angel*, p7 Yezidis forbid saying 'Sheitan' or words like it.

22 Phillip Kreyenbroek, *Yezidism – Its Background, Observances and Textual Tradition*; Texts and Studies in Religion, Volume 62, The Edwin Mellen Press, 1995, p92

23 footnote p62 *SGM*

24 Oswald Parry's *Six Months in a Syrian Monastery*, 1895, included EG Browne's translation of *AL-Jilwah* and *Meshef Resh*. 1891: *Bibliothèque Nationale* acquired a manuscript (BN Syr. MS. 306), copied by Abdul Aziz of the Syrian Orthodox church who lived in the Yezidi village of Bashiqe. May 1904: Père Anastase made copies in the Jebel Sinjar.

25 See *SGM*, footnote p418

26 *HBM*, p277

27 *SGM*, p296 note

28 *SGM*, p172

29 Joseph, *Devil Worship: The Sacred Books and Traditions of the Yezidis*, p31

30 p31, first section, Joseph, *Devil Worship: The Sacred Books and Traditions of the Yezidis*

31 pp200–2, first section, Guest

32 p31ff, second section Joseph

33 pp200–2, third section, Guest

34 p31, first section Joseph

35 p31, first section Joseph

[36] p31ff, fourth section, Joseph
[37] pp200–2, first section, Guest
[38] pp200–2, first section, Guest
[39] p31ff, first section, Joseph
[40] pp31ff, second section, Joseph

Chapter 16

[1] *See The Vision and the Voice…and other Papers*, ed Hymenaeus Beta, pp359–60, Weiser, 1998
[2] *Rex de Arte Regia*, 21 November 1914
[3] Victor Neuburg *d* 31 May 1940, aged 57. *See* Calder-Marshall, *The Magic of my Youth* (1951) and Jean Overton Fuller's *The Magical Dilemma of Victor Neuburg* (1965). Both books resentful of Crowley.
[4] *Rex de Arte Magia*, 1915, proof, ed HB
[5] *In Search with Doris Gomez for Cocaine in New York*, reveals rare aspects of NY drug culture; *YC* EE1.
[6] When Adams published, she failed to credit AC's contribution.
[7] undated note in *YC*: Crowley bumped into Shaw in London street. AC: 'Still posing as Bernard Shaw?' Shaw: 'But I *am* Bernard Shaw!' AC: 'Exactly'.
[8] *Crowley on Christ*, CW Daniel & Co, 1973
[9] 13 September 1916
[10] Huxley spent several days with AC, Berlin 1931.
[11] Three *Sunday Dispatch* articles June–July 1933: 'The "Worst Man in the World" Tells the Astounding Story of his Life' (18 June); 'I Make Myself Invisible' (25 June) – and 'Black Magic is not a Myth' (2 July)
[12] Charles Stansfeld Jones; 2 April 1886–February 1950. *See* Martin P Starr, *The Unknown God.*
[13] 19 August 1921: Crowley explained the HGA in terms of the Unconscious to Bennett at Cefalù.
[14] *b* Trachselwald, Bern, Switzerland, 9 April 1883; *d* 22 February 1975, Meiringen, Switzerland
[15] *Liber Aleph vel CXI, The Book of Wisdom or Folly*; ed Hymenaeus Beta; Weiser, 1991
[16] Jones found Key word of *Liber L vel legis*: *AL*, Semitic for a god, or 'God'; reversed, means 'NOT' (*LA*). The gematria is 31, multiplied thrice: 93 (Thelema); *AL* has three chapters; three deities.
[17] *YC* NS29
[18] *YC* EE1 According to William Breeze's *Confessions* research, the 'stupid stories' partly refer to AC's 1919 infatuation with Helen Hollis, a black Maryland woman working in Atlantic City.

19 Carrington memoir, *see* ch 28

20 *SSA*, pp172–3

21 *The Magical Record of the Beast 666*, 26 December 1919, *HB*

22 AC's money source uncertain. No cash bequests to AC in wills of 'Annie' Crowley (*d* 23 July 1921; Emily (*d* 13 July 1917); cousin Agnes Crowley (*d* 26 May 1916); and AC's father's aunt, Isabella Crowley (*d* 2 March 1919). Annie may have helped, Christmas 1919. AC's Trust Fund? He met Trustee GC Jones 30 December 1919. Family tradition asserts Abbey was supported by Ninette and Hélène Fraux to tune of $5,000. (Source: Eric Muhler, son of Astarte Lulu Panthea, *b*1920). Antagonism between Crowley and Hélène make it likely Hélène helped Ninette, not Abbey *per se.*

23 Hodgson's Society for Psychical Research investigations into fraudulent 'Mahatma' messages received by Blavatsky in 'Hodgson Report' (1885)

24 From AC's versification of the I Ching 'Shih Yi'

25 *see* Feilding's letter to Gerald Yorke, 1 May 1929

26 10 January 1920

27 Horatio Bottomley (1860–1933), Liberal MP 1906; ejected 1912 for bankruptcy. Elected independent MP Hackney South, 1918. 1921: 'John Bull Victory Bond Club' to get people to invest in government for prizes, attacked for fraudulent conversion of shareholders' funds; convicted 1922; seven-year sentence; expelled from parliament.

Chapter 17

1 *YC* OS17

2 Jane Wolfe (1875–1958), Hollywood character actress: over 100 films 1910–20

3 *Magical Papyrus*, 46, British Museum

4 *The Magical Record of Frater Progradior*, ed Keith Richmond, Neptune, London, 2004, p47

5 *Ibid*

6 Original letters are in CSJ Papers, private collection England; typescripts in OTO Archives.

7 Crowley to Reuss, 23 November 1921, CSJ Papers, cited in *The Unknown God – W.T. Smith and the Thelemites* by Martin Starr, p112

8 27 November 1921; *YC*

9 *YC* OS D1

Chapter 18

1 London, Rupert Hart-Davis, 1951

2 *YC* OS D1

3 *YC* OS D1

4 *SSA*, pp187–90

5 *L'Archivio Centrale della Stato a Roma* (ACS, P.S., AA.G.R, 1903–49, R.G., b.1, fasciolo 20)

6 *SSA*, p189

7 Ch5: *Counter-Initiation and Conspiracy*; Equinox, 2008

8 Monseigneur Ernest Jouin (1844–1932); René Guénon (1886–1951); Julius Evola (1898–1974)

9 Joseph Ledit (1898–1986)

10 Dimitrije Mitrinović (1887–1953), Bosnian. Came to England 1914, founded English branch of International Society for Individual Psychology (Adler Society) 1927, lectures leading to The New Europe Group, aiming at European federation and cultural re-evaluation, producing (1932) New Britain Movement.

11 'M' to Ledit 28 May 1936

12 Letter from Police Commissioner of Palermo to Police Chief Arturo Bocchini, 6 June 1936, A.C.S., P.S., AA.G.R., 1903–49, R.G., b.1, fasc. 20

13 15 September 1923, from Tunisia Palace Hotel, *YC* EMH1160

14 *YC* OS 96

15 *YC* OS D1, 4 June 1923

16 *YC* OS D1

17 Edmund Hugo Saayman, *b*1897; Grey's College, Rhodes Scholar MA, BSc

18 *Magical Diaries of Aleister Crowley*, Tunisia 1923, ed Stephen Skinner, Weiser, 1996, p139

Chapter 19

1 Nietzsche appealed to nationalists, as well as individualists like Crowley.

2 *Mon curé chez les riches*, 'My priest among the rich', 1920 novel by Clément Vautel (1875–1974)

3 E-mail Eric Muhler to the author, June 2009

4 Charles John Hope-Johnstone (1883–1970), photographer. Augustus John made three plates of him in 1922 (National Gallery).

5 *SSA*, p192: John Godolphin Bennett (1897–1974) possibly a spy

6 *YC* NS18

7 Xul Solar, name of Oscar Agustín Alejandro Schulz Solari (1887–1963), Argentine artist. Paris (1924); returned Buenos Aires, joined *avant garde* 'Florida group', including close friend-to-be, Jorge Luis Borges.

8 *YC* OS11

9 *YC* OS D1

10 E-mail Eric Muhler to author, June 2009

Chapter 20

1 Heinrich Tränker (1880–1956)
2 *YC* NS12
3 Tränker's association with H Spencer Lewis, inherited from Reuss, probably behind change of mind.
4 Eugen Grosche (1888–1964)
5 Karl Johannes Germer, *b* Elberfeld, 1885, *d* California, 1962; ex-officer, served Russian Front WW1, Iron Cross (First-Class), Prussian military intelligence; entrepreneur. German rep for AP Herbert, Coventry-based arms manufacturer before WW1.
6 Berenice Abbott (1898–1991)
7 *YC* OS12
8 *Diary* 1927, *HB*

Chapter 21

1 *YC* E21
2 *SSA*, pp195–7
3 Vladislav Minaev, *Podryvnaia deiatel'nost'inostrannykh razvedok v SSR*; Moscow, 1940, p89
4 from India Office correspondence with Foreign Office, FO Library; examined by Phil Tomaselli; *SSA* p196
5 *Ibid*
6 John Yorke to author, May 2009
7 London, Hulton, 1957, p254
8 *SSA*, p209
9 Crowley refers to Sieveking's book on flying in *The Diary of a Drug Fiend* (1922).
10 Lance Sieveking (1896–1972), pioneer BBC producer, friend of Arthur Vivian Burbury (1896–1959): both men were Royal Flying Corps aces.
11 According to William Breeze: 'Special Branch Scotland Yard was all over AC in 1928 – when Yorke was first visiting. Yorke must have told them details of AC's life, as a letter from 1928 (fall I think) was sent to Hélène Fraux telling her that Astarte Lulu was in a particular school, where AC had placed her. Astarte showed me the letter. Only Yorke could have known this and passed it on. This is how she knew how to 'rescue' Astarte. AC was being manipulated – and his parental rights weren't part of someone's plans for him.' (e-mail to author, 26.2.10)
12 Aleksandr Andreev, *Okkul'tist strany sovetov*, Moscow, Eksmo, 2004
13 later OGPU, NKVD, then KGB
14 Alexander Berzin, *Russian and Japanese Involvement with pre-Communist Tibet: The Role of the Shambhala Legend*, www.berzinarchives.com/kalachakra/russian_japanese_shambhala. html

[15] OGPU: forerunner of the KGB
[16] US, Summit University Press, 1984
[17] April 1896: *The Chief Lama of Himis on the Alleged Unknown Life of Christ*
[18] *HBC*, p113
[19] Paris, 1910
[20] *Altai-Himalaya*, p148
[21] *Il Teosofismo*, vol 1, Turin, Delta Arktos, 1987, pp39–40
[22] *YC* E21, 8 January 1930 from Walter Duranty, *New York Times* correspondent, Moscow
[23] *YC* NS 20 Diary 2 April 1930

Chapter 22

[1] diary 3 May 1928: magick with Kasimira Bass; *Object*: 'Direct invocation of *Mentu*'
[2] Langston Moffett (1903–89), *New York Herald* Paris correspondent 1929–30. 'Mary Freeman' probably Mary Eleanor Wilkins Freeman (1852–1930) contributor to 1928 'American Ghost Stories' anthology.
[3] Diary, 20 November 1928: 'How shall I interest Mary Freeman financially in the Work?' Hexagram 'XLVIII *Ching* The Well Make the proposition clean and watertight.'
[4] *YC* EE2, 4 April 1928
[5] *YC* EE2
[6] Israel Regardie (1907–85)
[7] *YC* E4
[8] *Ibid. Moonchild* was originally *The Butterfly Net*. Its original draft named names.
[9] *YC* E4
[10] Letter 15 March 1929
[11] *YC* E4
[12] *Ibid* 16 December 1928
[13] *YC* E4, 28 December 1928
[14] 'The Equestrian Order of the Holy Sepulchre, M Wellhoff and the High Lodges'; Masonic section, No 6, pp156–62
[15] by Roger Duguet; Masonic section, No 9, pp217–29
[16] *Documents rapatriés*, Carton 1298, index card An Z 7633; *SSA*, p200
[17] Cover sheet to *Tsentral'nyi Gosudarstvennyi Osobyi Archiv SSSR*, Fond 7, Opis 2, Delo 5314/36457; *SSA* p203
[18] British Foreign & Commonwealth Office, Registry Index, Treaty File notes re 'Expulsion of Mr Crowley from France'
[19] E-mail from William Breeze, June 2009

[20] Original in *YC* EE2
[21] *YC* NS117
[22] *YC* E20, diary, 5 April 1929
[23] *d*1921
[24] occult section, No 5, pp133–45
[25] anonymous, Masonic section, No 20, 19 May 1929, pp497–8
[26] anonymous, occult section, No 6, 1 June 1929, pp194–6
[27] A Tarannes, occult section, No 7, 1 July 1929, pp197–214
[28] anonymous, occult section, No 12, 1 Dec 1929, pp376–9
[29] *SSA*, p210
[30] *SSA*, p211
[31] *YC* EE2
[32] *YC* EE2
[33] *YC* EE2
[34] 'Gabriel Dee', woman astrologer and psychologist, Regardie's friend in 1930s
[35] *YC* EE2
[36] *YC* EE2
[37] *SSA*, p213
[38] *Ibid*
[39] *YC* EE2
[40] *YC* NS18; 'How I was Banned at Oxford', 1935
[41] Rupert Hart Davis, 1951
[42] AC to Calder-Marshall, 9 February 1930; *YC* D5
[43] *YC* NS 20 Diary, 1 March 1930
[44] *YC* NS 20, Diary 19 February 1930
[45] *YC*; AC to Germer, February 1930
[46] *YC* EE1, vol 1

Chapter 23

[1] Diary, 1 June 1930, *HB*
[2] *YC* E19, Ninette to AC &c 1925–8
[3] E-mail to author, July 2009
[4] Diary 1926, *HB*
[5] *YC* E19
[6] in *Ovid*. A young warrior, to demonstrate loyalty to gods, plunged into a bottomless chasm which swallowed him up.
[7] *YC* E19; Ninette to AC, 27 August 1927

[8] *YC* E13; 8 September 1928

[9] *Ibid* Monday 28th unknown month 1928

[10] Information re Lulu may have come from Yorke. Sieveking's *Eye of the Beholder* describes him handing Crowley's Order list to Burbury of Foreign Office; Yorke open with authorities.

[11] *b* 2 December 1906, St Mary's Mansions, Paddington

[12] Sir Gerald Festus Kelly PRA (1879–1972). Elected Royal Academy 1930; President, 1949–54. Knighted 1945; died Exmouth 1972. The Tate holds seven of his works, including a portrait of Ivor Back.

[13] *YC* EE2. Note of GJY to letter of Lola Zaza to him: 'Lola Zaza refused to have anything to do with her father. In 1950 she was happily married, after having been employed in London as a showroom assistant.' Lola Hill died of a heart attack in Reading, 9 March 1990.

[14] *YC*, E20, diary, January 1929

[15] *YC* E13

[16] *YC* E13

[17] E-mail William Breeze, June 2009

[18] Noble Hall co-author *The Fourth Division, Its Services And Achievements In The World War; Gathered From The Records Of The Division*, with Christian A Bach, 1920, published by the [US] Fourth Division

[19] *YC* E13

[20] *YC* E13

[21] *YC* EE2

[22] *YC* EE2

[23] *YC* EE2

Chapter 24

[1] *YC* NS 20, diary 1930

[2] *YC* NS 20 diary, 3 May 1930

[3] Franz Seldte (1882–1947), founder of the Stahlhelm, *Bund der Frontsoldaten* (25 December 1918). Seldte hoped it could fill leadership gap for national conservative movement. Joined Nazi Party (1933); SA absorbed the Stahlhelm. Disliked working with Hitler; tried to get out of government (1935); Hitler refused. Arrested 1945; *d* US military hospital at Fürth, before trial.

[4] Bauer led a failed German assault on Kanchenjunga, later advising Himmler's SS-sponsored expedition to Tibet in search of ancient 'Aryan' origins.

[5] 25 February 1930

[6] Lt-Col John Fillis Carré Carter (1882–1944), born Halifax, Canada; worked with Metropolitan Police from 1919. Deputy Assistant Commissioner

(1922–38), Assistant Commissioner (1938–40): intelligence gathering. Reported by Italian writers as assisting Italian secret service OVRA over anti-Mussolini plots. *viz*: Franzinelli, Mimmo, *I tentacoli dell'Ovra*, cit, pp201–2. (The tentacles of the Ovra), subtitled: *Agenti, collaboratori e vittime della polizia politica fascista* (Agents, collaborators and victims of the fascist political police); Series: *Nuova cultura* ; 69, Torino: Bollati Boringhieri, 1999

7   *YC* EE2

8   *YC* NS 20, diary 1930

9   *see* chapter 18 on Mitrinović and 'New Britain'

10   William Horace de Vere Cole (1881–1936)

11   Fernando Pessoa (1888–1935). June 2008: Madrid controversy over planned auction of Pessoa's trunk of manuscripts/ letters including unfinished novel re AC's 'suicide', *Boca do Inferno*. Portugal's National Library threatened legal retention of 'incalculable' heritage.

12   *SSA*, p215

13   *YC* NS 117

14   *YC* EE2

15   John William Navin Sullivan (1886–1937), *Times* science correspondent; author: *The Bases of Modern Science* (1928)

16   *YC* EE2

17   Einstein File, FBI FOIA File#61-6629, 'Gibarti, Louis'; cited in *SSA* pp219, 220

18   UK National Archives, KV2/774; MI5 file on 'Wilhelm Münzenberg', note to SIS; cited in *SSA*, p217, p221

19   *YC* NS18

20   *YC* NS117

21   *YC* NS117, 29 October 1930

22   Regina Agnes Kahl (1891–1945)

23   Martin Starr, *The Unknown God, W.T. Smith and the Thelemites* (USA; Teitan Press, 2003)

24   Wolfe to Crowley, 16 January 1931, WTS Papers; Starr, *Unknown God*, p182

25   Crowley to Wolfe, 4 February 1931, OTO Archives; Starr, *Unknown God*, p183

26   =revs per minute.

27   *YC* EE2

28   *YC* D4

29   Friedrich-Werner Graf von der Schulenburg (1875–1944), German diplomat, from 1934: ambassador to USSR. Part of 1944 'Bomb Plot' to assassinate Hitler.

30   Werner von Alvensleben (1875–1947), businessman and politician,

younger brother of Gustav ('Alvo'). Imprisoned by Hitler as member of Germany's conservative opposition.

[31] YC D4

[32] Adler was staying '*bei* Dr. Guttmann 36 Düsseldorfer Str.'.

[33] 'Schiffer' was Berliner Peter Winter (1892–1932), Jewish graphic designer, painter, song lyricist – the best cabaret composer in Germany. Schiffer and Mischa Spoliansky pioneered the German musical. Fell in love with Frenchwoman Margo Lion (early 1920s). Margo joined her young girlfriend, Marlene Dietrich, in bisexual duet *When the best friend is with the best girlfriend*. Depression caused sleeping-pill overdose, 1932.

[34] *An Old Master: The Art of Aleister Crowley*, ed Hymenaeus Beta, OTO, 1998

[35] YC EE2

[36] YC D4

[37] YC D4

[38] YC EE2

[39] YC D4; 24 August 1931, Jones to Yorke: Lola now employed 'as a showroom assistant by a West End dressmaker who pays 17s a week.' Renting rooms at 21/- a week. Yorke suggested cutting Lola's share to keep AC from starvation. Jones: 'Unless he [AC] has changed radically, no small extra allowance would be any good to him.' (*YC* EE2) After Rose's death (February 11 1932), Jones wrote to Yorke (5 May) that Rose had received £230pa, so that 'if we get an S.O.S. from A.C. that he really is down and out, as you feared we might get in the near future, we shall be in the happy position of being able to provide him with the whole of the income of the Crowley Trust without leaving Lola stranded.' (*YC* EE2)

[40] Hedwig Eva Maria Kiesler (1914–2000), known to Hollywood as 'Hedy Lamarr', studied in Berlin under theatre director, Max Reinhardt; Marlene Dietrich also attended Reinhardt's acting school. Hedy starred in the film *Die Frau von Lindenau* in Berlin, 1931.

[41] On 9 January 1931, he wrote to the *British Medical Journal* concerning a pregnancy after insertion of a 'Gräfenberg ring' – Ernst 'Gräfenberg gave his name to the 'G' or 'Gräfenberg' Spot.

[42] Leslie Frewin, London, 1969, pp57ff

[43] YC D4

[44] William Ralph Inge (1874–1954), Dean of St Paul's, expert on mysticism (especially Plotinus), theology, social and philosophical issues. Crowley wrote to Inge at least twice. Inge replied to one of these letters.

[45] YC D4

[46] Isherwood wrote two novels influenced by Berlin: *Mr Norris changes Trains*, and *Goodbye to Berlin* – basis for the film *I am a Camera*, and musical, *Cabaret*. The seedy agent 'Mr Norris' is considered by Christopher McIntosh (who met Hamilton) to have been based on Hamilton.

[47] Possibly a transcription error for LIA=*League Against Imperialism*

[48] *Double Lives: Spies and Writers in the Soviet secret War of Ideas against the*

West; New York, The Free Press, 1994; pp17, 157, 341

49   *YC* EE2

50   Kurt von Schleicher appointed chancellor after von Papen failed to form a government in November 1932; the SS executed von Bredow in 1934.

51   In 1932 Leon Rosenfeld published a demonstration that Dirac's relativistic electron theory was equivalent to that of Heisenberg and Pauli. Leiden low-temperature physicist Prof Wander Johannes de Haas (1878–1960) advised the Dutch government to buy uranium oxide. Hidden, it emerged as post-war foundation for Norwegian-Dutch nuclear co-operation. Investigated for collaboration with German science he was temporarily suspended, resuming his chair in 1948.

Chapter 25

1   Aleister Crowley, *YC* NS18

2   Slocombe's MI5 'IPI-16' Personal File, (1916–49) describes a 'journalist with Daily Herald and Daily Express' (Dates: Apr 1930–May 1931; Physical description: 32p; File number: P&J/12/413; File 732/1930)

3   Article in the *Dispatch*, after the *Laughing Torso* trial verdict, 13 April 1934

4   Following the Religions of Empire Conference of 1924, Sir Denison Ross established the Society for Promoting the Study of Religions.

5   Dr W MacGregor-Reid resigned from Clapham Labour Party presidency in 1926, after attacking Socialist parties. Father George Watson Macgregor Reid (*d*1946) was a founder of the *An Druidh Uileach Braithreachas*. (ADUB), or *The Druid Circle of the Universal Bond*, appearing 1909–12.

6   Edward Arthur Donald St George Hamilton Chichester, 6th Marquess of Donegall (1903–75)

7   *Laughing Torso*, Constable & Co, 1932; Virago Press, 1984; pp174–5

8   Pearl Evelyn Driver, *b* July 1899, to stockbroker Graham Driver (w. Evelyn). Widowed December 1931 when Capt Eldred S Brooksmith, (battle honours, Jutland 1916, flagship HMS *Iron Duke*), died.

9   AC; Memo re bankruptcy, approx. March 1935; *YC* NS117

10   *YC* EE2

11   *L'Archivio Centrale della Stato a Roma*: ACS, P.S., AA.G.R, 1903–49, R.G., b.1, fasciolo 20

12   Letter *YC* E21; 12 May 1934

13   Maxwell Knight, *b* Surrey 1900, adopted right-wing views in Navy. Worked for the Economic League; joined British Fascisti (BF) 1924, countering Soviet-backed Trades Union subversion. Became BF intelligence director, attracting notice of Colonel Sir Vernon Kell, Director of Home Section of the Secret Service Bureau (MI5).

14   *YC* NS117

15 *See* Churton, *Invisibles: The True History of the Rosicrucians* (Lewis Masonic, 2009)

16 *YC* NS117

17 28 December 1936; *YC*, 117C

18 *The Cornishman*, July 1936, reproduced in Newman, *The Tregerthen Horror*, Abraxas, 2005, p131

19 Dr Wegmann (1876–1943) , co-author *Basis for the extension of the healing Art in the Light of the Knowledge gained through Spiritual Science* (1925); first director of medical section of Steiner's *Goetheanum*, Dornach, and founder of Arlesheim Clinic and Anthroposophical medical movement.

20 Pat's mother Phyllis (*b* 1882), daughter of Carrie and Thomas Cooper Gotch, the painter. Pat's father was Patrick Doherty, government mining engineer in South Africa (*d* 1918). In 1922 Phyllis married André, Marquis de Verdières, making her a countess. Phyllis married her nephew Jocelyn Bodilly. Trips to the Dornach Steiner Foundation headquarters with Thynne spawned stories of a secret group of rich occultists working against Hitler, reminiscent of a mid-60s *Avengers* adventure.

21 Reproduced: Sandy Robertson, *The Aleister Crowley Scrapbook*, Quantum, 2002

22 Vyvyan Deacon (1895–1938), spiritualist medium. 1930: moved to England from Australia; lectured to 'spiritualists'. On 9 August, Crowley records: 'Supper with the Deacons. Chinese wife charming' – Eunice, daughter of Rev Philip Lew Tong, whom Deacon met, aged 17, in Melbourne, 1912. Eunice was annoyed at Deacon's getting stoned with Crowley 1936–7, coming home late.

23 According to Gerald Yorke's son, John Yorke, (letter to author, 26 June 2009), Yorke's connections with the intelligence service in China were 'very tenuous'. It was possible that Tony Keswick, then Head of *Jardine Mathieson*, an old friend from Eton, asked him to keep his eyes open when going up country in China for anything of interest: 'a very informal arrangement'.

24 *see The Uncommon Medium*, Vivienne Browning, Skoob, 1993

25 *YC* EE2

26 *YC* EE2

27 *YC* EE2

28 Crowley tried to help Jameson; letter: 5 January 1939: 'Another point that you may or may not have missed is that the social pressure is extraordinarily strong and subtle. People are always extremely jealous of anyone in their set who starts anything on his own; people are always frightened of superiority. This is why research demands such tremendous moral courage.' (*YC* NS117)

Chapter 26

1   *The World's Tragedy*, privately printed, Paris, 1910
2   Küntzel (1857–1942) wrote 'For shame!' over this part of the letter.
3   666 to Martha Küntzel, 10 May 1939; *YC*, EE2
4   Diary, 1 June 1939; *YC* NS21. Sir Percy Alfred Harris MP, 1st Baronet Harris (1876–1952); 1939, Chief Whip, Deputy Leader of the Parliamentary Liberal Party. Appointed Privy Counsellor 1940; joined National Government. 1901, married Marguerite Frieda (*née* Bloxam, 1877–1962).
5   Diary, 2 June 1939; *YC* NS21
6   Draft 4 September 1939, from 57, Petersham Road, Richmond; E22, *YC*
7   58, 'Tui' I Ching Trigram
8   EE2, *YC*
9   dated 10 September 1939, EE2, *YC*
10 *SSA*, p248
11 *Ibid*, p248
12 *Magick without Tears*, Falcon Press, Phoenix, 1983, p93
13 'W.P.S. [Western printing Services] 31–35, Brick St, Piccadilly, W1. Poem issued by O.T.O., one penny, September 23 1939ev 10.50 p.m.'
14 Crowley to Gerald Hamilton; 1 August 1941: the landlord of the 'Masons Arms' displayed two copies of *England, stand fast!*
15 Rough draft and sketch, EE2, *YC*
16 NS22 Royal Court Diaries, *YC*; 14 February 1941
17 *Persuading the People – Government Publicity in the Second World War*, Her Majesty's Stationery Office, p33
18 Victor Auguste de Laveleye (1894–1945), Liberal Member of Parliament for Brussels (1939–45)
19 Douglas Ernest Ritchie (1905–67) joined BBC's European Service in 1939; 1941: Assistant Director BBC European Broadcasts.
20 NS22 Diary 1941, *YC*
21 *Oxford Book of Quotations*, 1941
22 'Master of the Temple' or '8°=3°' in the 'Golden Dawn' system
23 Amado Crowley, *The Secrets of Aleister Crowley*, Diamond Books, 1991
24 10 April 1941; *SSA*, p242; UKNA KV4/186
25 *Sunday Telegraph*, 5 January
26 *The Man who was M*, Blackwell, Oxford, 1984
27 Newman, *Tregerthen Horror*, p114
28 The *Aircraft Engineer & Airships* magazine 9 June 1927: OBE to Major Rupert Ernest Penny, Principal Technical Officer, Air Ministry (late of the RAF)

29 Ivan Maiskii bought *The Fun of the Fair* from Crowley 6 January 1943. Intended to promote better relations between England and the USSR, on basis that communism had not really changed the Russians; note the irony.

30 according to KGB file No 20566 'Black Bertha' analysed by Oleg Tsvarev, included in John Costello's *10 Days that saved the West*, Bantam, 1991.

31 'Memorandum', *Royal Court Diaries*, 1941, *YC* NS22

32 Collins, 1976, p112

33 *YC* Folder 117

34 'the Hess Letter above printed "to the Secret Service re Hess" Extract from the letter from Donald McCormick to GJY'.

35 *YC* EE2

36 Mainstream Publishing, Edinburgh and London 1993

37 Diary, 13 May 1941

38 Compare Cecil's statement (*The Will and the Way*) that he had no access to secret information to John Colville's *The Fringes of Power – Downing Street Diaries* 1939–1945 (Hodder & Stoughton, 1985, p97): 'Lunched at the Travellers with Robert Cecil [April 8 1940], who gave me very secret figures intended to show that the Ministry of Supply is being mismanaged and our ammunition output utterly neglected.' A footnote adds re Cecil: 'Intelligent and well-informed member of the Diplomatic Service, expert on German affairs'.

39 A draft of Crowley's (undated) letter addressed 'Dear Colonel Brittain [*sic*]' (Douglas Ritchie at the BBC) has survived: 'Plan 241=Two for one. It is the numerical value of the Greek ΑϹϴΜΑ ['Asthma'] […] This plan, written in words of one syllable, might be broadcast in German and all languages of the occupied countries as part of the V-campaign.'

40 Diary, 30, 31 July 1941, *YC* NS21

41 While the 'bloke' at the BBC was possibly de Laveleye, consider also BBC drama producer Lance Sieveking (1896–1972); Sieveking sought Crowley in Paris in 1928.

42 Probably proposed, illustrated V-sign publication. Folder 117, *YC*

43 The words appeared on the 'invitation' to Andreae's *Chemical Wedding of Christian Rosenkreuz*, Strasbourg, 1616, next to John Dee's 'hieroglyphic monad' symbol which also features a 'V' above a sun symbol. Crowley's invitation is for Germany to attend Armageddon.

44 EE2, *YC*

45 *YC* EE2

46 30 January 1942, NS22 Diary

47 *YC* EE2

48 Diary 25 June 1942

49 Robert Cecil, unpublished ms, 1993, *The Will and the Way*

50 Crowley's magical predecessor John Dee (1527–1608) gave stage advice to a

Cambridge production of Aristophanes' *The Frogs* when an undergraduate.

51 *YC* E21

52 *SSA*, p241; Oleg Tsaref and Nigel West, *The Crown Jewels: The British Secrets at the Heart of the KGB Archives*; Yale University Press, 1999, pp316–18

Chapter 27

1 *YC* D9

2 Starr, *Unknown God*, pp284–5

3 Starr, p286

4 Crowley's accounting for 1943 showed OTO monies in the past two years amounted to £830 1s.0d – more than ever received when employing sex magick regularly for funds for the Great Work. Was fiscal improvement fruit of past magical labour?

5 *YC* D9

6 *YC* D9; AC to Gerald Hamilton, 6 May 1944

7 4 April 1945, Crowley to WB Crow: 'My relations with the Gnostic Catholic Church are like the annals of the Poor – short and simple. My predecessor [Reuss] was rather keen about the Gnostics as the original founders of what, after many changes, has become the O.T.O.'

   'During my six weeks in Moscow in 1913 e.v. [*era vulgari*: the common era] I had what I can only call, almost continuous illumination, and wrote quite a number of my very best poems and essays there. Of these, the Gnostic Mass was one. It was inspired, I think, by St.Basil's.

   'It sounds rather extraordinary, but I seem to have had some premonition of the Revolution in Russia, and my idea was to write a Mass which would in one sense carry on the old Tradition, yet not come into conflict with Science. The whole thing was, as is almost invariably the case with my work, written straight off at white heat, and never underwent a revision.' (*The Unknown God*, Martin Starr, p69)

8 to WB Crow, 11 November 1944

9 *YC* NS117

10 *YC* EE2

11 *YC* E21

12 OTO Archives. Crowley also used the Latin *Fidus Achates*, trusted armour-bearer and faithful friend of Aeneas, for McMurtry's role. After Crowley's death, Germer became Outer Head of the Order (OHO). Crowley had groomed and positioned McMurtry as Germer's likely successor, giving him unique authority to be used in case of an emergency. This was prescient. Germer provoked such an emergency by failing to name his heir before he died in 1962. McMurtry activated his powers in 1969 in order to revivify the OTO internationally as Caliph and acting OHO. On McMurtry's death in 1985, he was succeeded in both offices by William

Breeze or Hymenaeus Beta (McMurtry had taken the name Hymenaeus Alpha, given him by Crowley). Hymenaeus was a god of wedding feasts and song in Greek mythology; also an opponent of St Paul at Ephesus.

13 Initiated by Germer into the OTO after Crowley's death, Germer expelled him in 1955. Kenneth Grant has since established his own Typhonian Order and has written a series of Crowley-inspired books as well as co-editing Routledge & Kegan Paul's editions of Crowley's works with John Symonds.

14 *U.S.S.R. The Story of Soviet Russia*, by Walter Duranty, Hamish Hamilton, 1944

15 Author, *Echoes of Myself, Romantic Studies of the Human Soul*, Ivan Narodny, 1909. April 1906: Narodny (1874–1953) joined Mark Twain and Maxim Gorky at 3 Fifth Avenue NY club-dinner to establish a committee to overthrow Czarism. Gorky found 'New York' meant practically the same as his home town of Nizhni Novgorod. Crowley, almost Narodny's age, visited Nizhni Novgorod in 1913 and may have spied there. Note also Narodny's *American Artists*, 1930, introduction by Nicholas Roerich, published by Roerich Museum Press. Theosophical context would hardly be lost on AC.

16 *YC* D9, 8 March 1945

17 *Remembering Aleister Crowley*, Scoob, 1991, p33

18 *YC* D9

19 *YC* NS, D9

20 *YC* D9, Letter 14 February 1946

21 *YC* D9

22 *YC* NS117

23 *YC* E21

24 Jacintha Buddicom (1901–94), poet, Oxford alumnus; childhood friend of Eric Blair (George Orwell)

25 *YC* OSD9

26 *YC* EE2

27 *YC* NS117 Letter 30 May 1947

28 *YC* E21

29 Richard David Ellman (1918–87), biographer of Oscar Wilde and James Joyce. Served in US Navy 1943–6. Goldsmith Professor of English Literature, Oxford University (1970–84); winner of Pulitzer Prize for his Wilde biography, 1989.

30 *YC* D9

31 Patrick Thomas Dickinson (1914–94), BBC poetry editor, described on jacket of autobiography *The Good Minute* as 'poet and impresario of poetry'. Home Service programme *Time for Verse* familiar to Crowley.

32 *YC* EE2

[33] *Liber Aleph* eventually published in an extremely limited edition as *The Equinox* III.6, edited by Karl Germer and Marcelo Motta. Since published by Weiser, ed Hymenaeus Beta.

Chapter 28

[1] *YC* EE1

[2] Nancy Cunard to John Symonds, 1950; *YC* Folder No 96

[3] *YC* Folder No 96

[4] *YC* NS43

[5] *YC* NS43

[6] Yorke did not leave the Order definitively. William Breeze is aware of two persons he made Probationers, one of whom was film-maker Kenneth Anger. (e-mail to author, 26.2.10)

[7] *YC* Folder No 96. Andrew Green (1927–2004), writer on the paranormal, including *Ghost Hunting: A Practical Guide*. 1952: Green formed National Federation of Psychic Research Societies.

[8] *YC* NS18 Robert MacGregor-Reid's son designed the Sex Pistols' *God Save the Queen* poster.

[9] *YC* NS18

[10] *YC* NS18

[11] *jivanmuktas*: those liberated while living.

[12] *YC* NS18

[13] *YC* NS18

[14] *YC* Letters scrapbook No 96

[15] *YC* NS18

[16] *YC* NS18 James Cleugh (1891–1969)

[17] *b* Israel Francis Regudy (1907–85), of poor orthodox Jewish parents from Zhitomir, Russia, who had settled in London. Emigrated to USA 1921.

[18] *Eye*, p10

[19] *Eye*, p6

[20] *Eye*, p17

[21] *Eye*, p19

[22] *Eye*, p21

[23] 'Haldeman-Julius pamphlet', kindly sent to me by William Breeze

Bibliography

Browning, Vivienne, *The Uncommon Medium* [Vyvyan Deacon], Skoob, 1993

Calder-Marshall, Arthur, *The Magic of my Youth*, Rupert Hart-Davis, 1951

Cammell, CR, *Aleister Crowley, The Black Magician* (publisher's title; originally, *Aleister Crowley, The Man, the Poet, the Mage*, The Richards Press, 1951), London, New English Library, 1969

Churton, Tobias, *The Invisible History of the Rosicrucians*, Rochester, Vermont, Inner Traditions, 2009

Crowley, Aleister; Wilson, Steve (Ed), *Liber TzBA Vel NIKH. Sub Figura 28 The Fountain of Hyacinth*, London, Iemanja Press (undated)

Crowley, Aleister, *Temperance, A Tract for the Times*, reprint: Neptune Press

Crowley, Aleister, *The Fun of the Fair*, reprint: London, Neptune Press

Crowley, Aleister, *The City of God, A Rhapsody*, reprint:, Neptune Press

Crowley, Aleister, *Songs for Italy*, reprint: London, Neptune Press

Crowley, Aleister, with Victor B Neuburg and Mary Desti, *The Vision and the Voice, with Commentary and other Papers*, NY, Weiser, 1998

Crowley, Aleister, *Thelema, The Holy Books of Thelema*, NY, 93 Publishing, Weiser, 1989

Crowley, Aleister, and contributors, *The Equinox, The Review of Scientific Illuminism*, Vol I, Nos I–X (1908–12)

Crowley, Aleister, *The Book of Lies*, NY, Weiser, 1991

Crowley, Aleister; Skinner, Stephen (Ed), *Magical Diaries of Aleister Crowley, Tunisia 1923*, NY, Weiser, 1996

Crowley, Aleister (The Master Therion), *Liber Aleph vel CXI, The Book of Wisdom or Folly*, NY, Weiser, 1991

Crowley, Aleister (The Master Therion), *The Book of Thoth, Egyptian Tarot, Equinox Vol. III, No.V*, US Games Systems Inc 1974

Crowley, Aleister, *The Drug and other Stories*, Wordsworth Editions, 2010

Crowley, Aleister, *The Works of Aleister Crowley, with Portraits*, 3 vols, Foyers, SPRT; reprint: Des Plaines, Illinois, Yogi Publication Society (undated)

Crowley, Aleister; Louis Wilkinson & Hymenaeus Beta (Ed), *The Law is for All*, Tempe, Az, New Falcon Publications, 2002

Crowley, Aleister, with Mary Desti and Leila Waddell; Hymenaeus Beta (Ed), *Magick Liber ABA, Book Four, Parts I-IV*, NY, Weiser, 2004

Crowley, Aleister; John Symonds & Kenneth Grant (Ed), *The Confessions of Aleister Crowley*, London, Routledge & Kegan Paul, 1979

Crowley, Aleister; John Symonds & Kenneth Grant (Ed), *Magick*, London, Routledge & Kegan Paul, 1973

Crowley, Aleister; John Symonds & Kenneth Grant (Ed), *The Magical Record of the Beast 666*, London, Duckworth, 1972

Crowley, Aleister; Francis King (Ed), *Crowley on Christ*, London, CW Daniel Co Ltd, 1974

Crowley, Aleister; Hymenaeus Beta & Richard Kaczynski (Ed), *The Revival of Magick and other Essays, Oriflamme 2*, Tempe, Az, New Falcon/OTO International, 1998

Crowley, Aleister, *Clouds without Water, Edited from a Private MS. by the Rev. C. Verey*, reprint: Des Plaines, Illinois, Yogi Publication Society (undated)

Crowley, Aleister, *Eight Lectures on Yoga*, reprint: Phoenix, Az, Falcon Press, 1987

Crowley, Aleister; Regardie, Israel (introduction), *Magick without Tears*, Phoenix, Az, Falcon Press, 1983

Crowley, Aleister; Starr, Martin P (Ed), *The Scrutinies of Simon Iff*, Chicago, Teitan Press, 1987

Crowley, Aleister; John Symonds & Kenneth Grant (Ed), *The Complete Astrological Writings*, London, Duckworth, 1988

Crowley, Aleister, *Ambergris – A Selection from the Poems of Aleister Crowley*, London, Elkin Matthews, 1910

Crowley, Aleister, *Moonchild, A Prologue*, reprint: NY, Weiser, 1991

Crowley, Aleister, *The Diary of a Drug Fiend*, reprint: NY, Weiser, 1978

Crowley, Amado, *The Secrets of Aleister Crowley*, Diamond Books, 1991

D'Arch Smith, Timothy, *The Books of the Beast*, Mandrake, 1991

De Salvo, John, *The Lost Art of Enochian Magic*, Vermont, Destiny Books, 2010

Fuller, Jean Overton, *The Magical Dilemma of Victor Neuburg*, Oxford, Mandrake, 1990

Grant, Kenneth, *Remembering Aleister Crowley*, Skoob, 1991

Gunn, Joshua, *Modern Occult Rhetoric, Mass Media and the Drama of Secrecy in the 20th Century*, University of Alabama Press, 2005

Hamnett, Nina, *Laughing Torso*, Virago (orig 1931), 1984

Hutchinson, Roger, *Aleister Crowley, The Beast Demystified*, Mainstream Publishing, 1998

Hymenaeus Beta (Ed), *An Old Master, The Art of Aleister Crowley*, OTO International, 1998

Iamblichus; Taylor, Thomas (trans), *On the Mysteries*, reprint: Miami, Fl, Cruzian Mystic Books, 2006

Khan, Khaled (Aleister Crowley), *The Heart of the Master*, London, OTO, 1938ev [era vulgaris = common era]

King, Francis, *The Magical World of Aleister Crowley*, London, Arrow Books, 1977

King, Francis, *Magic, The Western Tradition*, BCA, 1975

Lévi, Eliphas; Crowley, Aleister (translator), *The Key of the Mysteries*, London, Rider, 1977

McMillin, Arnold (Ed); Ryan, WF, *Symbolism and After, Essays on Russian Poetry in Honour of Georgette Donchin*, 'The Great Beast in Russia', Bristol Classical Press (undated)

Naylor, Anthony, R, *Notes towards a Bibliography of Edward Crowley*, Thame, I-H-O Books, 2004

Newman, Paul, *The Tregerthen Horror*, Abraxas Editions, 2005

Newman, Paul, *Ancestral Voices Prophesying War, A Tale of Two Suicides*, St Austell, Abraxas Editions (undated)

Rabelais, François, *The Heroic Deeds of Gargantua and Pantagruel, Vol. I.*, London, JM Dent & Son

Regardie, Israel, *The Eye in the Triangle, An Interpretation of Aleister Crowley*, Phoenix, Az, Falcon Press, 1986

Richmond, Keith; Crowley, Aleister, *Progradior and the Beast*, London, Neptune Press, 2004

Richmond, Keith; Crowley, Aleister; Bennett, Frank, *The Magical Record of Frater Progradior*, London, Neptune Press, 2004

Roberston, Sandy, *The Aleister Crowley Scrapbook*, Quantum, 2002

Sieveking, Lance, *The Eye of the Beholder*, Hulton Press, 1957

Spence, Richard B, *Secret Agent 666, Aleister Crowley, British Intelligence and the Occult*, Feral House, 2008

Starr, Martin P, *Aleister Crowley: Freemason!* London, AQC, Vol 108, 1995

Starr, Martin P, *The Unknown God, W.T. Smith and the Thelemites*, Bolingbrook, Teitan Press, 2003

Stephensen, PR; Regardie, Israel, *The Legend of Aleister Crowley*, St Paul, Minnesota, Lewellyn Publications, 1970

Symonds, John, *The Great Beast, The Life and Magick of Aleister Crowley*, Mayflower, 1973

Tompkins, Peter, *The Magic of Obelisks*, New York, Harper & Row, 1981

Index